FICTI

12. MAY 1987

23. MAY 1987   -4. NOV. 1988

-2. JUL. 1987

27. AUG. 1987   12. DEC. 1988

-1. OCT 1987
15. DEC. 1987   12. JAN. 1989

24. MAR. 1988
-5. APR. 1988

-7. MAY 1988

D1587453

Born of Woman

Also by Wendy Perriam

Absinthe for Elevenses
Cuckoo
After Purple

WENDY PERRIAM

Born of Woman

Michael Joseph
London

First published in Great Britain by Michael Joseph Ltd
44 Bedford Square, London WC1
1983

© Wendy Perriam 1983

ISBN 0 7181 2262 3

Photo-set by Colset Ltd, Singapore
Printed and bound in Great Britain
by Billing & Sons, Worcester

For L. W.
rarest and most precious of lilies.

I

'Stand by, everybody. Total quiet now, please. Thirty seconds, twenty-five . . .'

Help! This is it. I'm on. Cameras surrounding me, zooming in with their prying spy eyes. Lights huge and hot, melting me away.

Twenty, fifteen, ten . . .

Relief to melt away. To be only a grease-pool on the studio floor, instead of a celebrity with two hundred people watching me out there and another ten million due to switch on in two hours' time. I *can't* be a celebrity. Celebrities are always Other People. People with cast-iron nerves and proper talents. People like Vita Sampson. She's a household name, yet she's sitting there, just opposite, in her chrome and vinyl chair. She's the latest goddess on BBC's 'In Town' and 'In Town' has reached the Top Ten and Matthew said you're made if you appear on it.

Ten, nine, eight . . .

There must be some mistake. I'm only Jennifer Winterton — somebody else's name, somebody else's creation. I'm only good at small things — planning herbaceous borders, messing about in the kitchen. Only a housewife, really; not even a wife — not now — well, not in *bed*. Pray they don't find that out, start asking questions about . . .

Seven, six, five . . .

Stop! They're counting too fast. Set the clock again. No — must get a grip on myself. Matthew's watching me. Remember what he said. Relax, deep breathe, be gracious. You are the natural woman, sweet and unaggressive, the quiet, chaste, old-fashioned country girl. No, I'm not, I'm . . .

Four, three, two . . .

Oh, help me, God! Smile. Matthew says always smile. One second left. Can't escape — I'm *ON*!

'Hold it!'

What's happened? Floor manager tense and sweating, dashing on to the set. Technicians appearing from nowhere. Frantic consultations. My own mouth won't work at all. It's stiff and stuck together, tongue thick and dry like blotting-paper. I try to force it open. 'What's wrong?' I mouth to Vita.

'Minor technical hitch,' she smiles. 'Just sit tight.'

I couldn't get up if I wanted. My spine has turned to string. The lights are so hot, I'm scared wet patches will show beneath my underarms. Why did Matthew make me wear this dress? It's hot, confining, claustrophobic

1

— like the studio itself. We're shut in like a space capsule, black ceiling starred with lights, only a frightening void beyond. Void is a word Lyn taught me. He sees voids everywhere. If only he were with me now, instead of moping back at home. Oh, Lyn, I want you — you know that. I promise you it'll be better once . . .

Careful! People are still watching. Not tonight's ten million, but the two hundred flesh-and-blood ones staring from that darkness, suspended in that void. Live audience, they call it. 'Live' sounds dangerous like sharks. I've got to please them somehow, got to swell the ratings. TV time is the most precious thing on earth. What did Matthew say it cost? Fifty thousand pounds to make a thirty-second commercial, up to three hundred thousand for an hour of TV drama.

Money like that set all the terrors off again. Jennifer Winterton drowning and choking in figures. Thousands of bank notes fluttering through her stomach, bags of coins dumped heavy in her gut. Ten million viewers had marched into her body and were tramping round and round it. And she wasn't even *on*, yet! Sound-man still baffled and huddled, struggling with yards of cable and a microphone. Floor manager with tie askew and jacket off, communicating (via headphones) with distant and disembodied gods. Jennifer swallowed. Tried to stop her hands shaking, fix her attention on something. The book, of course, the book.

She glanced down at the heavy, glossy volume preening on the coffee table — the only reason she was here at all. On the cover, Mrs Winterton Senior almost-smiled above her prim white collar. Hester Winterton. The public loved the name — old-fashioned, biblical, dignified. The photo wasn't right, though. They had made Hester too insipid. Her husband's mother was as powerful as the countryside she came from. That was on the back — the Cheviot Hills, the stern Northumbrian landscape soaring into a steel and granite heaven. Hester was trapped between those covers — the entries in her diaries, the entries in her life — soldiers in trenches, scullery maids in kitchens, babies in cradles, farm and home in crisis.

The smile was counterfeit. Hester wasn't pleased. She had been publicised and packaged, thrown to the modern world like a bag of sweets in pretty coloured wrappings; a world she had hated and shut out, a life she had kept as secret as her diaries — those crabbed and weeping notebooks she had coffined in a wooden chest and buried in the cellar.

Jennifer closed her eyes, saw the photo still, but darkened with a frown now. 'Hester, I'm sorry, I never knew they'd . . .'

'Right. Here we go then. Take two. Everybody quiet, please.'

Someone set the clock again. Every eye fixed on that slow, jerking finger, pouncing on the seconds. Sixty, fifty, forty, thirty . . . Quick. Practise your first sentence. SMILE!

Her jaw ached, her lips burned, her eyes were puckering at the corners. Cameras closing in like kidnappers on soft, treacherous feet — so close now, there was nothing left but smile. She could feel her heart thump-thumping like a . . .

'Cut! Sorry, everybody. There's a jinx on us this evening.' Floor manager dashing on set again, audience growing restive in the darkness. Matthew was out there somewhere, fretting at the delay, ready to check and judge her every word — like God. Jennifer couldn't see him. Only a blur of faces, a choppy sea of heads. She was in a separate world, bounded by the cameras, blinded by the lights. It was Matthew who had decided her husband couldn't come. 'He'll only make you nervous.' She was nervous, anyway. These last few weeks had worn her out, almost changed her character. She'd never been like this before — panicky and hollow, fixated on herself — *her* fears, *her* face, her . . . All the publicity had ground her down. Fourteen days rushing up and down the country. Strange beds, snatched meals, photographers lurking, interviewers pouncing; everything she did or said turned into a headline. She had become a legend in a fortnight, the reincarnated Hester Winterton with her message of wholesome country living, now shut up in a cage, trapped in a grid of headlines. She was still pale and shaking (underneath the greasepaint); had only just returned, thrust on television before she had barely caught her breath.

She opened her eyes. Vita was speaking, trying to reassure her. 'All right, Jennifer? I don't think they'll be long now.'

She mumbled some reply. Ought to call her Vita. Celebrities were always Christian names. It had been like that on radio. Phil, Dave, Tony, Rosie, darling. Instant intimacy in twenty different towns.

'Right, that's really it now. Silence on the floor, please. Take three. One minute countdown.'

Vita Sampson's long silk legs uncrossed. She snapped on her own slick professional smile.

'Good evening — and welcome to "In Town".'

Ten million people smiling back at Vita from John o' Groats to Land's End, goggling at her outfit, staring at her legs. Jennifer didn't exist yet. The cameras still had to create her. They were the gods — the cameras — giving life, withholding it, cutting off limbs, words, gestures, shutting out whole scenes. It was still Vita they were ogling now.

'My first guest tonight needs no introduction. The book which has made her famous has sold twenty thousand copies in a fortnight and is well on its way to becoming a household name. *Born With The Century* is the story of a remarkable woman who began her long and busy life in 1900, endured two World Wars and many personal hardships, yet who found purpose and fulfilment by living close to nature and achieving self-sufficiency. She has left us an enthralling record of her life in the diaries she kept from the age of fourteen until 1948 when her son Lyn was born — diaries packed with vivid and touching details of public and private events. These diaries have now been published with a mass of

3

other records and a fascinating preface by her daughter-in-law, who pays tribute to the older woman's skills, not only in this book, but in her own simple natural life-style . . . .' Vita's pause was like a fanfare before the triumphant name which followed. 'Jennifer Winterton.'

Creation. Cameras swooping now on her fair, plumpish, unfashionable, almost pretty face, eyes dilated with fear. What in God's name was that roaring noise exploding through the studio? She glanced around in panic, wincing at the din. ('Never look at the cameras, *never* at the audience. Keep your attention fixed always on the interviewer.' Matthew's Ten Commandments — a hundred thousand commandments.) Jennifer dared to break one of them, tried to focus on the abyss beyond the lights. Pale bun-faces ghostly in the gloom, eyes and spectacles glinting through the shadows. Hands on hands. Applause, *Applause*! That's all it was, the roar — people clapping Jennifer Winterton. Stop! she almost shouted. She didn't deserve applause. She was only a tiny photo on the inside flap of a book jacket. You couldn't coop Lyn's mother in a couple of hundred pages or a clutch of pretty pictures.

Applause dying down now. Silence still more frightening than the roar. Vita Sampson leaning threateningly towards her, cameras creeping up behind.

'Jennifer, hallo and welcome.'

'H . . . hallo.' Voice skidding across her throat, words disintegrating. Vita Sampson rushing ahead too fast. Sales, statistics, figures, facts. The Book cradled in Vita's arms. Red-taloned finger pointing to the text.

Her own mouth muttering things she didn't know it knew. Her mind cut off from its moorings, zooming in and out of cul-de-sacs while her lips stuck and stumbled and fell over their own smile. Lights glaring, cameras swarming. Impossible to think, plan, speak, stop, STOP.

'Jennifer, I think you said . . .'

'Jennifer, I know you feel . . .'

'Jennifer, how can you justify . . .?'

'Jennifer, what makes you assume . . .?'

I don't, I didn't, I can't, I'm not. Wait . . . What did Matthew say? If you're flummoxed, gain time by repeating the question. What *was* the question? Do I believe in ghosts? Matthew told me not to mention ghosts — not as such — just keep on stressing Hester's continuing presence. They'll never understand, though. They'll label me a crack-pot, say I'm inventing things.

Vita speaking again. Must have read my thoughts. 'You say you're aware of Hester's influence, even after her death. I wonder, Jennifer, do you sense her as a type of *spirit*, then?'

No, no. Hester is rock and bone and vigour, not a spirit. Yet Matthew keeps on urging me to bring in the supernatural. How can I, when there aren't the words for it and people think I'm . . .?

Questions flying faster now. Can't speak. Can't think. Stop! Cut! Let

4

me out! Face cracking up like crazy-paving, traitorous things happening to my voice. Haven't got a face or voice, only a mask which is breaking into bits. It's not me under there. I'm at home with Lyn, planting out begonias. Smile at the begonias, hold Lyn's hand, pull yourself together. Smile. SMILE. I'm *crying*. Impossible! Blink the tears away. Quick — cough, sneeze, clear your throat — anything but tears. Vita's as worried as I am. Asking easy questions. Treating me like a child.

No. The sobbing's louder now. The cameras can't resist it. No one's cried on 'In Town' — not a real good howl. There have been tears before, but only stifled ones, and from people with a reason for them — saints and zealots weeping for man's messes, choked and dazzled footballers, defeated presidents, Miss Worlds paying back their crowns.

Cameras cock-a-hoop now, highlighting the tears, presenting them in full colour close-up to tonight's ten million viewers, trying every angle, cutting between Jennifer's streaming eyes and all the saddest pictures on the caption-stand — lance corporal shot in the stomach, dole queues shivering on Tyneside, rotting harvests, starving lambs. Vita solicitous and skilful, trying to weave the crisis into the interview, explain it to the viewers.

'Perhaps you could try and tell us, Jennifer, what aspect of Hester's life upsets you most?'

No answer.

'You're obviously very distressed by certain memories. Hester's life was certainly a hard one and her book has maybe touched some nerve . . .'

'I . . . I . . .' More sobs.

'This was, of course, a harsh and terrible century. So many young and talented men cut down in their prime, so many private tragedies in two massive global wars. Hester's own three brothers were all killed in the trenches. It seems to me that you identify with Hester. I mean, does your awareness of her . . . her presence mean you share her actual grief?'

Jennifer gulped. 'Yes, that's . . . r . . . right. That's . . .' Words almost indecipherable. Untruthful words, in any case. She is crying for herself, not for Hester's brothers — for her exhaustion and her problems, her stupidity and fear. Crying because she can't smile and doesn't know the answers. Because she's a stupid stuttering pathetic waste of money — waste of *Matthew*'s money. She's failed him, let him down. Crying because her husband doesn't desire her and she lies awake at night wondering if he ever will again. Crying because she's tired and tense and . . .

'CUT!'

'Fantastic, Jennifer! That really was a scoop. Genuine emotion always makes the news. The Press Office are on to it already. They want a few shots to splash around tomorrow's dailies. This way, please. They're waiting in the Green Room — panting to see you, in fact!'

Different cameras in the Green Room. Smaller bolder ones, jumping out at her before she has arranged her face or forced a smile. They don't *want* a smile — not any longer. Tears are far more profitable. Tears sell newspapers and newspapers sell books. Tears swell ratings, tears mean cash.

Cry, cry, cry.

II

'Don't cry.'

Lyn Winterton watched his wife's tears glaze the cold, buttered surface of her toast. He hated her to cry. He had eaten nothing, just mangled his hot cross bun into shreds and pickings. 'You can't cry for someone you've never even met, Jennifer.' It sounded harsh, when he had intended it as loving.

'But she's your *mother*, Lyn.'

Which meant he should be crying. He couldn't cry. His mother had taught him not to. Even with his stupid fancy girl's name, he wasn't allowed to blab.

'Anyway, I feel . . . as if I know . . . her.' Jennifer's voice was frayed and pulled apart. 'I mean, you t . . . talk about her so much.'

Lyn made a pellet from a scrap of bun. So she noticed, did she, the way Hester seeped and trickled into everything? Even with three hundred miles between them and a wife who loved him more than his mother did. He forced the pellet down. Jennifer had saved him the last, staling, home-baked hot cross bun, left over from their breakfast. He had never really cared for hot cross buns, but they were precious like the love. She made them every year with such devotion, chopping peel and kneading dough, the whole kitchen warm and spiced. He leaned across and touched her hand, hand that had shaped the buns. 'It's *you* who are obsessed with her.'

'Only because you've never let me meet her.'

'It's not that . . . simple.' He picked up Jennifer's toast and bit into it, hard. What was wrong with it? Had she made the jam with salt instead of sugar? No, it wasn't salt, but tears. He was swallowing Jennifer's tears. He liked that. To be part of her, made of her. She was special, blessed, serene. That's why he'd married her. Shouldn't have married her. Hester wouldn't be ill now, if he hadn't. He swamped the tears with jam — Jennifer's strawberry in a Branston Pickle jar. He'd grown the straw-

6

berries himself — large, fat, shouting scarlet ones. Now they were only shrunk and faded pulp. That's what cooking did — took living, breathing things and turned them into corpses. All good cooks were murderers. Jennifer had won prizes for her cooking. He glanced at her small, strong, sticky, lethal hands. 'My mother's always preferred to keep herself to herself.'

'But she's *dying*, darling. It's different if she's dying. I can't bear the thought of never having seen her.'

Lyn split a currant with a fingernail. Hester wasn't dying — couldn't be. She had always told him that she lived for him. Thirty years she'd done that, kept him for herself. More than thirty, actually. Other men got married at eighteen. 'Look, all she needs is a day or two in bed. Some decent food, someone to . . .'

'But I could *cook* the food. Look after her. I'd like to. Please. If anything . . . happens, then I'll feel we . . .'

'It won't.' Can't.

'But she's eighty-two.'

'Her mother lived till *ninety*-two. And her mother's mother till two days off a hundred.' That's why he'd had to marry. Couldn't wait until Hester was gone and he was middle-aged and past it. She had had him far too late. Other mothers didn't have babies in their late forties. There had been kids at his school with grandmas younger than his mother was. 'You don't understand, she's *always* been old. It makes no difference what her birthday says.'

'Don't be silly, darling — of course it does. Hester can't defy all natural laws, just because she's your mother.'

Why was his wife so literal? He meant old like the hills were old, or like himself. He had lived twelve years longer than Jennifer, which hardly counted when it was a matter of birth certificates or candles on his cake. But in terms of drought and rusting, winters, terrors, cold, he was a hundred thousand years older. She was a child still — child bride — pink and eager and easy. He loved her for it, married her because she had all the things his mother never had. Long, soft, messy hair which sprawled on her shoulders instead of being coiled in contours with a barbed-wire fence of hairpins; legs which opened and closed where his mother was only a clothes peg beneath a starched apron. Breasts. He suddenly longed to hold the breasts, anchor himself to her body.

'You haven't touched your tea,' he said, instead.

'No.' She was stabbing at stray crumbs spilt on the tablecloth in the same nervous, distracted way she kept picking at his mother. 'Look, she *must* be bad, or Mrs Bertram wouldn't have got in touch with you. Didn't you say she went out specially?'

'Mm. Her own phone was out of order.'

'Well, then . . . And today's a public holiday and . . .'

Lyn shrugged. Good Friday. Christ on a cross and traffic jams on all the roads. The nearest public phone box to the Bertram farm was three whole miles away. Molly Bertram's mother had been only a few years younger than his own and had known him as a baby, as a boy. He hated that. He had cancelled his whole boyhood by moving south to Jennifer, by marrying. He wiped strawberry from his mouth.

'All right, she's ill, but it's probably nothing much. The Bertrams love to stir things up. The whole village thrives on drama. Why d'you think I left there?' A thousand reasons, and Jennifer the main one, although it had been Matthew's money and Matthew's influence which brought him down to London in the first place. Matthew had even found him Jennifer. He sometimes felt he had never done a thing except through his brother (*half*-brother). Matthew had introduced him to Jennifer in the same smug, efficient, all-controlling way he'd offered help, cash, art-school, housing, job. Jennifer meant more than all of them. She had blushed when he first asked her out. Girls didn't blush in the hard-boiled 1980s. She had cooked for him the second time he saw her — not hot cross buns, but chicken breasts in wine. He had hardly touched a mouthful — he was looking at her own breasts. Soft blue angora following him round the room, bending over the oven, wobbling when she laughed.

After dinner, they sat on two stiff chairs and talked about safe permitted things like television (which he hardly ever watched) and Art which she awarded a capital A, then kept respectfully away from. He knew he would have to choose between her and Hester, her and Hernhope. He no longer needed that cold creaking house footprinted with his fear, blabbing tales of his lonely barbed-wire boyhood. He wanted to shake free of it, move south of it. Jennifer *was* south. She came from a small, good-tempered Sussex townlet where the hills were only swellings and the wind ruffled rather than uprooted. She had south in her face and figure. A gentle, temperate girl who wasn't exactly beautiful, but had something of summer in her — something warm, ripe, plumpish, mellow, ready, when he and Hester were rough, bitter, bowed. Her hair was the faded, sun-streaked colour of shredded wheat, too long to be tidy and too wavy to be chic; her eyes a frail, fragile blue which in some lights paled to woodsmoke and were barely defined by her fine fair brows. All her lines were soft — breasts, profile, features — nothing sharp or angular. A girl you could sink into.

They had married in a dark church on a pale grey morning with a few frail spokes of sunshine nudging the narcissi on the altar. Three years ago. Three hundred years ago. His mother hadn't attended. Hester had treated the wedding as if it were somebody else's letter delivered to the wrong address. He sent her photos, money, endless reparation. He couldn't phone. Hester didn't believe in easy, instant communication. She preferred struggle and crossed lines.

Since the wedding, he had never returned to see her. Every week he planned to; every month he pencilled it in his diary, underneath the guilt.

8

Jennifer coaxed him, urged him, suggested dates, made plans. He always agreed until the date came round. He hardly understood his own reluctance. Perhaps he feared to return in case he became Hester's child again. There should never have been a Mrs Winterton Junior in the first place. He cleared his throat, tried to sound decisive.

'You'll only make her worse if you try to interfere, Jennifer. She'll say you're . . . spying on her. My mother never cared for company and now she's almost a . . . recluse.' He shut his eyes. Their tiny rickety table was lengthening into twelve foot of Spanish oak — the overweening table which had stood stern and massive in his childhood home, solid as a ship. It *had* been a ship, hammered from the decking of an eighteenth-century frigate wrecked off the north-east coast. He and Hester had sat marooned at one small corner of it, dwarfed by its proportions, the row of empty chairs mocking their aloneness. Often, as a boy, he had filled those chairs with instant family — sisters with bare arms, all beautiful, all saving him the best bits, cushioned grandmas, cuddly aunts. Later he invited guests, figures from his school-books, Mohammed and Copernicus, artists — especially artists — people he could confide in, show his drawings to. Leonardo da Vinci, El Greco, Pieter Brueghel. Nice to have a name like Leonardo, instead of sissy Lyn. ('Lyn's a *girl*!' they had chanted at his school.)

He opened his eyes, stared down at the tablecloth. He and Hester had eaten off bare wood. Jennifer had made an 'H' out of the crumbs, his mother's initial facing them both ways, legs firmly planted, arms folded tight across her middle.

'Are you all right, darling?' Jennifer had got up from her chair and was hovering there beside him.

'Y . . . yes. Yes, of course I am.' He tugged at the cloth. The 'H' shivered and collapsed. Jennifer's hand was stroking down his neck. He seized it, trapped it between his own, pulled her down to him. He had all her hair spread out across his lap when the phone shrilled. He pushed her off, as if his mother had come in. He knew it was Northumberland before he even answered — let her answer.

'Hallo? Oh, Mrs Bertram. Yes, Lyn did explain. You won't know me. I'm his wife, Jennifer. I . . .'

Of course Molly Bertram knew her. Everyone knew everyone up there, gossiped about him and the wife he had never presented for their inspection. (Probably thought she was odd or cracked or crippled because he had hidden her.) How he had run away and left his mother to rot; how he was arty, selfish, never really fitted, couldn't farm, fence, marry, couple, sow . . .

'How *is* my mother-in-law?'

He winced. Jennifer mustn't call her that. Mother-in-law meant marriage and Hester hadn't sanctioned any marriage.

'What, the doctor? Oh, I see.' She didn't see. She had never lived there.

9

Hernhope for her was merely a quaint and pretty name on an Ordnance Survey map, not a house which had lost its farm, its fields, its sons, abandoned in one of the remotest parts of England. England stopped at Newcastle for most people. It was easy to forget the country north of it, which butted against the Border and lost itself in the lonely Cheviots where your nearest neighbour (bar the sheep and crows) could be several miles away. He remembered looking at the map when he was just a boy at school and seeing his home in the scrawniest bit of England, as if someone had grabbed it by the neck and squeezed and squeezed until all the life and flesh and flowers had bulged above it or below it, leaving it bare and bruised, the hills still marked with purple-swollen thumb-prints. Northumberland had always been a strange uneasy county. Even at the time of the *Domesday Book*, it hadn't been included — too lawless and remote.

Jennifer was frowning as she replaced the receiver. 'I'm afraid your mother's . . . worse, Lyn. Mrs Bertram says she shouldn't be left alone. She's been sitting with her herself, but they're so busy with the lambing, she can't tear herself in two. And her eldest daughter's gone to Glasgow for the week so she can't help. Hester's refused the doctor *and* the hospital. Mrs Bertram says she'd never forgive herself if anything happened when she wasn't there. We'll *have* to go up now. In fact, we ought to leave immediately.'

'We . . . c . . . can't. I've got things to finish, w . . . work to . . .'

'But you said you wouldn't work. You said we'd go to Matthew's all day tomorrow. Can't we cancel that and go up North instead?'

Christ! His family both sides of him. One threatening from Northumberland, one holding court in Putney, both insisting on his presence. Yet he would have liked to please them all — be son, brother, husband, not just self. Self was always bullying, though — bullying and scared.

'We can't let Matthew down, Jennifer. You know what he's like. He'll have killed the fatted calf by now.'

'Matthew ought to go himself. I mean, considering Hester brought him up, surely he . . .'

'Oh, don't start that again.' Lyn hated 'oughts'. There were enough sticking in his own flesh. 'Matthew's done a lot for me. That's his way of squaring things.'

'Sunday, then. Let's go first thing Sunday morning.'

'That's Easter. We can't travel Easter Sunday.'

'Why not?'

'Well . . . traffic, holiday   ryone on the roads.'

'They'll all be gone by then. Ɪt's a very good day to travel, actually. The crush will be today and Monday. OK? If that's all right, I'll go and sort the cases out.'

*   *   *

'Look, you'd better let me drive now, Jennifer.' Lyn laid his hand on the

10

steering wheel, next to his wife's. Their hands looked strange together, as if they were two unrelated species — his lean, sallow, bony; hers plump and pink and warm.

'Oh no, Lyn, I'm enjoying it.'

'But we're getting nearer.' He couldn't arrive at Hester's being driven by a wife. 'You won't be able to manage. The roads get really rough soon.'

'You said that half an hour ago.'

He could see she didn't believe him any longer. The sun had dogged and dazzled the hedgerows all the way from London when he had promised cold. The countryside was gentle, when he had shaped it cruel. A hundred times she had slowed and gazed, exclaiming. 'But, Lyn, it's *beautiful*' — almost accusing him of fraud. 'It's not remotely bleak at all.'

She had no real right to judge, yet. These were still the lowlands — lush, green, self-indulgent meadows loping towards the smudged and hazy brush-stroke of the horizon. But the Cheviots were waiting just beyond, drawn up in battle-lines, ready to jump out on him, each phalanx higher than the lowering one below it.

He tried to see the country through her eyes. Rooks flapped idly over new-combed fields; gaunt and gappy hawthorn hedges were breaking into leaf so fiercely green it hurt. Lambs, skippy white against their stained and stolid mothers, piston-shot away from the rumble of the wheels. The sky — blue, serene, unbounded — admired itself in the bright mirror of a burn. Things had let him down. Daffodils in full deceitful flower, blowing garish yellow trumpets in front of squat grey houses.

'They won't even have had a spring yet,' he had told her late last night, tugging a dead daffodil from the arrangement on the dressing-table. 'Look, ours are almost over, while theirs won't be in bud. Everything's much later than down south.'

'Nice,' she'd said, tissuing a blouse. 'We'll get two springs that way. Ours we've had, and theirs to come. Anyway, it can't be that cold. A woman on the radio said she'd heard a cuckoo in Morpeth.'

Child again. Romanticising. She had never been further north than Birmingham. Sussex was fat flowery toytown land (thatch and honeysuckle), its feet dangling in the warm piddling waters of the Channel. *He* had grown up in battle country where the scarred hills bled towards the borders. Hills frowning with castles, raided by the Scots. Some years, they didn't hear the cuckoo till early Ju

He jumped as the car lurched over a rabbit already flattened on the tarmac. A cortege of little corpses left behind them on the road — a decapitated pigeon, a hedgehog with its front paws clasped together as if praying for revival. There was blood even on the windscreen, tiny orangey splodges splattered on the glass where hordes of little insects had suicided into it. In the country, death stared you in the face. A row of shrivelled

11

moles strung by their lips on the spikes of a barbed-wire fence. The knell of gunfire echoing from corpses. It was death he had run away from in the first place. The men up here all shot and trapped and murdered, won status with their guns. Mick Bertram's rough-cut father had called him chicken-livered because he preferred a pencil to a rifle, or chose to sketch the muscles of a fox rather than paralyse them.

'Look, I said I wanted to drive, darling.' His voice sounded rougher than he had meant it to. He rarely called her darling. That was Jennifer's word, one which had embarrassed him at first. He wasn't used to darlings — Hester never used them — almost feared his wife was mocking him. But soon he had accepted them, grown fat on them.

'Aren't you too tired to drive?'

'No,' he lied. He had hardly slept last night. They'd had lamb for lunch at Matthew's, followed by sherry syllabub and acid indigestion which lasted through the highest of high teas and on through Jennifer's over-rich and quite superfluous supper. He had gulped down Alka Seltzer and gone to bed — spent three hours steering their low-slung double bed through a tangled motorway of blankets. At 3 am there'd been a pile-up in the overtaking lane. He had burrowed through the wreckage for his wife.

'It's all right, Lyn. I'm here. It was only a nightmare.'

Only. The headlamps faded into their beaming bedside lights. His heart was still thumping like a ten-ton lorry hurtling over shale. He lay restless till the dawn, listening to Jennifer's relaxed and heavy breathing. Almost resented her sometimes because she could return to sleep so easily. He glanced at her now, humming to herself, some cheerful schmaltzy tune he didn't know. A pilgrimage to Hernhope was just a drive to her, a spree.

She drew into a lay-by, got out and stretched her legs. 'It's hot, Lyn. Beautiful. Just look at that sun! It's almost like July.'

He narrowed his eyes against it — 'Freakish' — slipped into her seat. It was warm beneath his bottom. His wife was always warm. She was clambering in beside him, the curve of her breast blocking out the sky. He kept his hands firmly on the wheel. Mustn't think about the breasts. His mother could probably see him now. Hester could scan the whole of England, just lying on her bed. He pressed his foot down, swerved to avoid a pheasant dazzling across the road.

'Oh, Lyn, it's *gorgeous*. See those colours on its neck?'

'They're two a penny up here. They fatten them up deliberately, so there's more of them to shoot.'

'You mean they're only bred to be killed?'

'Yes. Like the lambs. That nice little joint we had at Matthew's yesterday probably hailed from here.' He wanted her to see it how it was. Lambs were only cuddly toys in London, or plastic packages in Sainsbury's Fresh Meat section. You could avoid death in the town.

12

He tried to picture Hester pale and silent. Almost worse than her re-proaches. He turned a groan into a yawn. He *was* tired. Not just from the drive, the miles, the constant fear and fretting about his mother, but from all the painful memories that lengthened with the road. Jennifer couldn't feel them. Even now, she was fairy-taling the map, squeezing romance and fantasy into the place-names which had hemmed him in from childhood, turning them into poetry, when for him they were obituaries or bad school reports, etched deep into his soul.

' "Lord's Seat". Isn't that nice? And "Nagshead Knowe". And "Angryhaugh" and "Bleakhope". There's a tremendous lot of "hopes" around — "Milkhope", "Wholehope", "Nettlehope", "Hernhope". What does "hope" *mean* exactly?'

'Not what you think it does.' Hope had been in short supply up here.

'Well, what then?'

'It means a sort of valley.' A blind valley. Hernhope had seemed blind — windows dark and shuttered, light filched by the forest, cloud-banks closing in.

'But I thought you said your house was in the *hills?*'

He nodded. Jennifer unwrapped two fruit drops, passed him the red one. 'Is the "Hern" bit short for heron?'

'Mmm.' He hated all her questions. For three sweet years he had let this landscape dwindle, shut out all the memories, built new ones with his wife. He slipped the sweet into his pocket, frowned against the sun.

'*Are* there heron there?'

'Oh yes.' He had watched them as a boy, one-footed in the water, heads hunched between their shoulders, their amber eyes half closed, but missing nothing. Skilled and lethal killers. Stab, stab, stab — spearing a squirming fish and tearing the flesh from white and screaming bones, wolfing the small ones whole in a single gulp. Damned aggressive birds. Even their mating displays were like a wrestling match.

Jennifer's fruit-drop sucked and scrunched at the silence. She folded the map into more manageable size. 'Mepperton's your village, isn't it? I've found it now. It looks quite a way from Hernhope, though.'

'Everything's quite a way from Hernhope.'

'Yes — there's your house — just a little dot among the contour lines, sitting on its own. I can't imagine living somewhere that remote.'

'It was even worse in the old days. The road was only a track, then. It had thirteen fords across it and seven gates to open and shut. There's a story about a shepherd's wife who lived a mile or so from us when my father was a boy. The place is just a ruin now. Hester said that once that woman was installed there, she never went out again — not once in her whole life.'

'I don't believe it. She must have needed shopping or . . .'

'No, her husband brought supplies back when he went to the mart. We were cut off ourselves when the snow was bad. I've been a prisoner there for weeks.'

He shivered. It was colder suddenly. The sun had gone behind a cloud, fields rearing up on end, the horizon creeping closer as suddenly the Cheviots marched over it, curve after curve closing in on them, ringing them round. Not green, these hills, but brown, bare, grazed and bruised as if someone had laid violent hands on them. Greyish smudges underneath their eyes. Deep puckers on their foreheads.

He stopped the car so suddenly, she fell against the dashboard.

'What's wrong, Lyn?'

They had been following the river. It had grown wider, steeper, gorging itself on tiny tributaries rushing from the hills. Lyn stumbled out, hearing the water suckle at the stones, sun breaking ripples into razzle-dazzle reflections, like a kaleidoscope. He stood trembling on the bank, legs unsteady, as if the whole force of the landscape had gathered itself together and punched him in the gut, the vast rolling sky crammed inside his head and splitting it apart. He had felt that force before, when he had learnt at school how ancient these rocks were and was dwarfed by such a time-scale, humbled by the *enormity* of things, the endless spaces stretching back and out. A puny lad who hadn't made a decade yet, was only a sneeze or a pinprick in a world which counted in millennia. Was that the reason he had started drawing — to make himself more permanent? He could see those sketches, reprinted on the landscape, distorted copies, but still witness to his power. There were more as he got older, sent secretly to Matthew, or slipped between his floorboards, or hidden in the cellar. They would be faded rubbish now.

Jennifer had followed him and was plucking at his sleeve. 'What *is* it?' she repeated.

Couldn't she *see* what he was seeing, the power and passion of this land-scape which had moulded his whole vision, stunned and overwhelmed him? He longed to share it with her, swap her eyes for his. He was a child again, standing on the topmost rung of England, head in the sky, feet planted on a million million years of rock, watching the hills collide with the horizon, the clouds hurtle on to God. He had tried to explain before to her, cursed himself because the things he felt didn't fit the language, sounded simply fatuous. Safer to keep quiet — lock away the feelings as he had done as a child, bury them with his art. Jennifer hadn't seen that either — or very little of it. He'd had to renounce it before she came along. Matthew had produced her as the consolation prize.

He forced his gaze away from the grandeur of the hills, stared down at the river.

'See that.'

'What?' She looked where he was pointing. A dead lamb was floating in the water, jammed against the bank, its fleece still white and woolly, but bloated, waterlogged — its tiny ears twitching with the pull and motion of the current as if it were still alive, its eyes only empty sockets.

'The crows always peck their eyes out. They do it sometimes when the lambs are still alive but stuck in snowdrifts. The farmers have to kill them. That's Matthew's prime roast lamb.' Cruel again, sadistic. Why point out carrion when he had meant to paint her splendour? Yet the two were always linked. One spring he had gone out with the ranger in the forest — a boy of nine awe-struck by the trees — stumbled upon a rotting pile of corpses, eleven roe deer perished from starvation after a fighting winter, their flesh half-gnawed by desperate crows and foxes. The ranger had been his only friend, taught him to sleuth shy and secret creatures, like shrews and slow-worms, otters and goosanders, pointed out badgers and birds' eggs. But after that time, he refused to go out with him again. The ranger dealt in death, carried a gun, shot the deer the snow had spared. He preferred to stay inside and draw.

Except drawing was disapproved of — especially as he grew older. All those brawny foresters and farmers regarded art as child's play or as a harmless little hobby for their womenfolk once they'd finished all the chores. *Real* men worked the land with sweat and tractor, turned stone and soil into flock or food or cash. Only poufs and sissies played with paints.

Lyn stared at his reflection in the rippling distorting stream. Did he look a pansy? He had always been too slight. Tallish, yes, but not broad or tough enough. Jennifer said nice things about his looks, but that might be love, or even pity. At least he had good features — full mouth, straight nose. He flung a stone in the water, shattered nose and mouth. Jennifer's reflection approached his in the water.

'We really ought to hurry, darling. Hester may be worse.'

He followed her back to the car. Not worse, he prayed, not angry, not reproachful. 'Don't worry, we're not far now.' He knew, because his palms were sweaty on the steering-wheel, his throat gritty and bad-tempered like the road. He drove doggedly round the twisting narrowing bends. Everything was harsher, the hills so steep, the stunted thorn trees clung to their sides almost horizontally. Bare rock grinned through scrubby yellowed grass. Even the sheep were different — Cheviot and Blackface — hardier breeds which could cope with months of snow, but whose bleating sounded thinner and more desolate. The light was fading, colour draining out of everything, as if the whole land had suffered a shock. Hills, car, earth, road, sky — all cut from the same coarse and fading fabric. It was a struggle to steer the car straight. Shale and boulders had fallen from the hillside and were littered on the track. He stopped in a sneeze of stones.

'Are we there?' Jennifer eager, trusting, too pink and bland for this pinched and pitiless landscape.

'Not quite.'

'So why have we stopped? Is the road too rough?'

'Oh, no. It's often worse than this.'

'Why, then?'

'I . . . think we ought to go . . . back.' The hills closed around his words

15

like ripples, pebbles sucked into a pond.

'*Back*?'

He nodded.

'But we've been driving all *day*, darling. Your mother'll be expecting us. Mrs Bertram told her we were coming.'

The gentle, rational arguing again. If only she'd curse him, *force* him on.

'Look, I, I . . . don't want to disturb her. She may have gone to bed.'

'But it's only just past seven. Anway, we don't have to wake her up. We can wait a while, if you like, until she's rested.'

'No — I'd . . . rather turn round.' Once the engine died, he could hear the silence moving in on them, seeping from the hills, stuffing all the gaps between them like the crumpled tissue paper she had folded between her dresses in the case. He didn't *want* any gaps. He longed to be fused with Jennifer, be one with her, have her strength, her easy, blinkered power. He pulled her over to him, joined them with her hair.

'Snookie . . .' Silly secret name he used in bed. His mother must never hear it. If only they were in bed now, three hundred miles down south . . . She kissed him, more as child than man, got out of the car and coaxed him into her seat.

'Let *me* drive, darling. You're tired, that's all. You should never have taken over in the first place.'

He didn't argue, though the road tried every trick on her. Looped, twisted, doubled back, rumbled her with cattle grids, defied her with five-bar gates. She survived them all. Three gates more and they turned on to a cart track. The Morris groaned and juddered. He shut his eyes. At least he wouldn't see when they turned the corner and the hills turned into forest. He felt the last wooden bridge sway and mutter as the car bumped over it.

Jennifer was slowing now. 'Oh, Lyn,' she cried. 'Just look!'

He didn't look. He feared to. That forest had killed the farmlands, as the farm had killed his father. There would never have been a forest without his father's bankruptcy. His father was only a photo on the mantelpiece, a five by ten sepia-tinted half-plate who had married his housekeeper when he had nothing else left, then doubled his shame by dying on her. The funeral baked meats were barely cold when the Forestry Commission came to woo the widow. Hester had succumbed. She was tired of labour and they were short of land. He had been just a hump beneath a pram-rug. Those trees had lived nearly as long as he had, feeding off his father, off his fields.

He opened his eyes and glimpsed the dark stain on the landscape, grim and straight-spined conifers gobbling up the light. They were mainly sitka spruce, one of the hardiest trees in the world which had evolved in the age of the reptiles and still kept the thin scaly bark which proved they were cold-blooded. They had been wrenched from the snows of northern Canada to withstand stony soils and slapping winds, where other, sissier trees would droop or die.

His wife was rhapsodising. He watched her watch the trees. The marriage service talked about one flesh, but he knew it was

16

different forests they were seeing.

There had been sheep there once, his father's sheep, the flock and father he had never seen. His first memories were sullen steel-jawed tractors, dragging vicious ploughs behind them, tearing up the pastureland, preparing it for trees. Five farms had gone in all. The other families which had sold out to the Forestry had all four moved away, their houses ruined now, their lands merged with the Wintertons' to make a cage for conifers. Only he and Hester had remained inside the cage.

They turned the corner and Hernhope leapt towards him, a grim grey house dwarfed by the larger sky. Fold upon fold of hill curved and crisscrossed behind it, shreds of cloud caught on its roof like rags. He held his breath as Jennifer jammed the brakes on, dared not speak or move. He had to worship a moment, give thanks that the place still stood, as proud, as powerful as he had remembered it — grey stone, grey slate, merging into the pearlier grey beyond, until it lost itself in purple. The moment swelled into a lifetime — baby in the blanket, boy in the hayloft, man hiding from his mother. However tall he grew, the house was always taller. Now he lived in a doll's house down in Cobham, playing at farming on a cabbage patch.

Jennifer switched the engine off and silence plunged between them. He hardly dared to look at her. Why had she stopped her chattering and exclaiming? Did she *fear* the house? See it as scowling, peevish, hostile — legs buckled, face cracked — no creepers round its neck to hide the damp-stains, no easy pretty garden to soften the stone; no smile, no open arms? He squinted through his eyelids and saw her hands twisted together on the steering wheel. The stillness was so utter, he could hear the trees holding their breath around him, the clouds rolling into void. He let his gaze inch up towards her face. Her eyes were shining, her lips parted as if he had just made love to her.

'Oh, Lyn,' she breathed. 'It's *wonderful*! So lonely, it's like the last house in the world.'

III

Jennifer entered first. The door was stiff, heavy, but unlocked. She jumped as something scurried away from her. Only two or three brown leaves from another season, bellying in the draught. Lyn heard a curlew rip the silence as he shut out cloud and conifer.

The dark passage hemmed them in as they tiptoed towards the kitchen. Strange to feel claustrophobic when there was no other house for miles and the horizon touched the floor of heaven. Three years had made no difference to the place. The same cold and echoing flagstones softened with Hester's rag-mats; the same low, uneven ceilings, beams blackened with age and wood-smoke. Walls built two feet thick to withstand Scot and storm; windows small and suspicious with drawn-down brows to conserve every ounce of heat.

It wasn't as cold as he'd remembered it. Someone had lit the range. That bad-tempered black-iron monster had watched him as a boy — a braggart growing fiercer as it gobbled peat and logs. He turned his back on it. Jennifer cooked on an all-electric Creda Circulaire, a wedding gift from Matthew. The room was barely breathing. The clock had stopped at half-past one (a.m.? p.m.?) There was no fruit, flower, light, air. A bunch of shrivelled onions hung above the sink. The sink tap dripped and plopped. Had it always been stained like that? Cracked so badly? Or did he only notice because his wife was there? She was marvelling at the table, swamping it with modern, mocking things — bright enamel cake-tins, hollow Easter eggs in glittering coloured foil. They had filled the car with presents — mostly peace-offerings, recompense for the time he had been away. The shopping looked too garish — tins with gaudy labels, packets screaming promises, food which grew in the glare and cackle of supermarkets rather than the silence of the soil. He removed her jacket from his father's chair — a chair for corpses, ghosts.

Jennifer seemed tired now. The hills peering in at the windows had snatched the colour from her face. 'Look,' she said, 'there's a note from Mrs Bertram.'

His fingers trembled as he picked it up. Pain? Reproaches? Crisis? *'Hester seems a little better now. I have given her milk and soup and left her dozing.'*

The relief was so great, he shouted. 'Look, I'll go up and see her. You stay here and make some tea.'

'Hush,' she warned. 'She's probably still asleep.'

*   *   *

She wasn't. He was glad she wasn't sleeping. He might have run away if he'd found her with her eyes closed. He wanted to get it over, make her understand why he hadn't come before, how it hadn't been neglect, but . . . Reassure her that Jennifer wouldn't stay long, wouldn't interfere. But his mouth was a broken hinge and he couldn't get the words out. All he could do was stare. The room was deep in shadow, the curtains semi-closed, but even so, he could see how she had aged. It was as if every second of every day he had been away had worn her down like water dripping on a stone. Her face was less flesh than bone now, her slack veiny hands smudged with age spots, her hair so thin, he could see her scalp staring through the grey straggly wisps. He touched her fingers a moment, as if that way he could speak to her. They were chilly. The hot and bossy blood which had once surged around her body had turned into

18

a trickle of icy water.

She lay in the high, hard bed, shrunken and exhausted, but smiling slightly as if any other greeting was too much effort. He could hardly bear to look at her. Even her usual harshness was better than this impotence, her frown less cruel than that dumb and ashen smile. He wanted to kick and savage the years which had done such damage. Once she had kept the whole world in her pocket like a thimble or a coin. He closed his eyes, saw her towering over his boyhood, keeping the terrors out, slapping his shirts with soap and vehemence as if they had no right to be dirty, turning milk into butter, wood into fire. Everything obeyed her then — hills, house, weather, soil — yet now she was too frail to move a finger.

'Hester,' he mouthed. He never called her mother. He supposed once he must have done, but he couldn't remember when. The name had never fitted. He wanted to *make* it fit, force it on her while she was still alive to hear it, but he couldn't get it out — couldn't speak at all.

'Matthew sends his love,' he muttered, at last. Even a mumble sounded blasphemously loud in the silence of the sickroom. He knew she wouldn't believe him, anyway. Matthew sent money, provisions, presents — never love. 'We were with him yesterday,' he added lamely. He longed to seize her, hug her, not sit there muttering bread-and-butter inanities.

She had hardly moved at all. He realised she was so old and tired, every tiny gesture cost. Her skin was stretched too taut across her face, as if some grudging tailor-God had cut her out of a remnant or an off-cut, and then sewn her up so tightly that all the fabric had puckered into creases.

He could feel tears pricking against his eyelids. Impossible to snivel. He fumbled in his pocket for a handkerchief, felt the still uneaten fruit-drop sticky at the bottom. He had always hoarded sweets. Cash had been tight in his boyhood. Hester had trounced bankruptcy by selling off the farm, but the proceeds had to last. He had copied her economies. A roll of Polos or a twist of sherbet might be saved up for a month or more. She had almost spun herself out, refusing to die or retire because there was always too much to be done. She had made everything herself — sheets, quilts, cheeses, soaps, soups, herbal remedies, even his shirts and trousers. He had loathed it at the time — caged and chafed in prickly serge and fly buttons when other boys had Terylene and zips; or swallowing murky potions with brown bits at the bottom instead of pretty coloured pills. He had been born to death and bankruptcy, but Hester had turned them sides to middle like her thinning sheets and made life and service out of them. She had never added trimmings. Never fun or flowers or laughter. They were Jennifer's. Even now, Hester was smiling only with her mouth, a smile he couldn't remember and didn't like. His mother's frown had crumbled the stars like biscuits, made the world hang loose upon its hinge. Smiles were as rare as Polos. Or had he remembered her wrongly? She was so feeble now, he could have blown her out like a candle.

He stared at the eyes he shared with her. People had always marvelled at their eyes, so exactly reproduced it was as if Hester had ordered two identical pairs from the same mail-order catalogue and then sewn his on as a sort of tag or name-tape, so that he could never stray too far or deny her as his mother. Other times, when he looked into the mirror, he had the strange sensation that Hester had climbed into his skull and was staring out from his empty eye-sockets. No one else in the world had eyes that shade — eyes which mixed blue and grey and black in equal parts, then set light to all three and conjured a different colour from their ashes.

He only wished they didn't look so changed — not only dimmed and paled, but now defeated. Always before, they had chided and chivvied the world, flashed and frowned it into dumb submission. Perhaps Jennifer would make them flash again, the wife he shouldn't have.

He went to the door and called her. 'Look, leave the tea,' he shouted. 'Come and say hallo.'

A minute passed. Another. He tried to tame the silence by telling Hester about his Cobham garden, filling the room with fancy southern flowers. Only the hardier breeds survived at Hernhope, the braver birds.

Jennifer had reached the top of the stairs. He heard the staircase creak and grouse a little as she hesitated on the landing. There were five doors leading off, all half closed.

'In here,' he called. 'Last door on the right.' Hester was still smiling. She wouldn't when she saw his wife. Jennifer's sweater was too clingy and she hadn't combed her hair.

He could see the door was grudging, reluctant to admit her. A shaft of light from the passage fell across the lino. His wife was trapped in it — golden, shining, mockingly young and healthy. He wished he could tone her down a bit, shade Hester from her glare.

'This is . . . Jennifer,' he told her.

Neither of them spoke. He felt angry, suddenly. Couldn't they make it easy for him, help him out, even shout or quarrel? Anything was better than this cold and gaping silence.

'Can't you say "hallo", Jennifer?'

'H . . . hallo?'

'Yes, of course, what's the matter? Introduce yourself.'

'Lyn, *don't*, she's . . . I think she's . . .'

'Could you manage the range?'

'Well, yes . . . I . . .'

'Good. Shall we have that tea, then? She likes it strong. No sugar. Give her the cup with roses on. That's her special one. You'll find it on the dresser. Well, don't just stand there. What's wrong, for heaven's sake?'

Jennifer clutched his arm so tight, her fingers hurt. 'She's . . . y . . . your mother's . . . *dead*, Lyn.'

Dead? Hester couldn't die until he had explained things to her, paid his debts, made her understand.

'D . . . don't be silly. She's just dozed off, that's all. She was awake a moment ago. I was telling her about . . .'

'No, Lyn, she couldn't have been. She's . . .'

'Ssh,' he said. 'You'll wake her.' He smoothed the counterpane, picked up a crumpled Kleenex from the floor.

Jennifer was still fussing. 'Look, go and lie down, my darling. I'll stay with your mother.'

She *mustn't* call him 'darling', not in front of Hester. And Hester wouldn't want her — only him. He should never have gone away from her, then she would still be well. Perhaps she had died the very day he married and had lain here three whole years, coldly smiling while he rutted with a wife. Maybe those crabbed and grieving Christmas letters had been written by a corpse, a corpse with open eyes.

He tried to fill the eyes with words. 'Do you want *me* to make the tea? I could do with a cup myself. And how about a biscuit? Hester's probably hungry. We brought some with us, didn't we?'

'Y . . . yes, but . . .'

'Good, pick her out a plain one.' It was always plain biscuits with Hester, hunks of doorstep bread. Only in his dreams did mothers feed him fancy sugared sweetmeats, tiny crustless sandwiches, comfits in his satchel, kisses in his bed. He fumbled in his pocket and felt the fruit-drop hard and reassuring. He was glad it was a red one. Red. Dead. Funny when things rhymed. 'Dead', Jennifer had told him. She wasn't often wrong.

'Dead,' he muttered. He had to try the word out. It meant nothing much at all. Just a sound, four letters — two vowels, two consonants. He stared at his mother and saw the letters had spread all over her. Strange he hadn't noticed.

He prised the fruit-drop out, picked it clean of fluff, and put it in his mouth.

'Dead,' he said again, and listened to the crunching in his head.

IV

'*I am the resurrection and I am the life; he who believes in me, though he die, yet shall he live . . .*'

The words sounded wrong. Lyn had rarely been to church, but when he had, there had been fire and poetry in the prayers, not this new, flat, grating prose. He remembered now. The vicar had called (after the doctor and the undertaker) and discussed the funeral with them.

21

Something about the Alternative Service Book and keeping up to date with modern trends. He had barely listened. He'd been choking on his mother, lying dead upstairs. Jennifer had entertained the Reverend, shown him the body, cut him walnut cake, chosen flowers and date and hymns. The vicar was using some new-fangled translation of the Bible which was an insult to Hester, who had probably never heard of it. He wasn't a vicar at all. His body was a footballer's, his voice a referee's. Funerals should slink and whisper, not boom and jar like this.

The church was still dressed for Easter. Narcissi and blue iris, the young, slim, still-closed buds of pointed beech leaves, flowering redcurrant, blossom sprays, fat and pricey white chrysanthemums. Easter flowers still blooming and triumphant, out-scenting the forced, cribbed, formal wreaths, which almost hid the coffin. Who had sent all those wreaths? The tiny church was packed as if for a wedding, the wedding he had never had up here, neighbours jostling and whispering in the pews, people he didn't know and didn't want, inviting themselves to share his grief, his wife. He glanced at Jennifer looking strange and strained in black. He hated her in black. His mother had worn it since his father died, which meant she had always worn it. His birth was a sort of mourning for that death. He couldn't think of death. Every time he tried, his mind glazed over or filled with stupid things like hot cross buns or wedding cakes. What was he doing here — dressed in someone else's suit at some empty social gathering arranged by Jennifer?

When he'd grown up in Mepperton, God had been out-of-bounds like so much else. Church was what other people did on Sunday mornings, in order to be first with the gossip in the pub. Pub and church stood almost cheek by jowl, so the faithful moved from chalice to tankard, unbuttoning coats and throats as fug and babble took over from cold stone. Hester had kept him strictly away from both. He had always felt that sense of not belonging. Church was part of the village, part of life. You knelt in your pew on Sundays to prove you still existed. Which meant he and Hester didn't.

He glanced uneasily around. People might be criticising him for having ignored church all his life and only now exploiting it when he had a body to dispose of. He hadn't had much choice. The nearest crematorium was Newcastle, and you couldn't burn a mother anyway. Hester loomed too large in life and death to end as a pinch of ashes on a mantelpiece. Besides, all his ancestors were buried in this churchyard.

He shut his eyes, tried to block Hester out. She, too, might be criticising. She had always been so solitary, she would hardly approve of all these nosy neighbours mumbling prayers and murdering hymns around her, before she was crammed into an over-crowded boneyard.

The congregation shuffled to its feet, cracked and wavering voices upsetting Hester's peace as *The Lord's My Shepherd* rasped from sixty throats. There were shepherds just behind him, gnarled and ruddy men looking stiff and strange in jackets and black ties. Two o'clock on a weekday they should have been in their work-clothes on the hills, tugging new-born lambs from ewes. Why should they risk their flock and waste their time putting Hester in the earth? Was it respect, curiosity, or the hope of a free meal? Jennifer had cooked the meal. He had tried to tell her not to. Custom and tradition ruled up here. Whisky and ham sandwiches was the usual simple fare. Jennifer had been fiddling about with vol-au-vents and trifles, pastries and meringues. He didn't want his mother swamped in mushroom sauce and egg whites, her kitchen taken over, her body embalmed in cooking smells.

He tried to join in the singing, stumbled on the words. '*Though I walk through the valley of the shadow of death . . .*'

Death. His mother cold and bloodless in a box. Jennifer had ordered a coffin as casually as she might have bought a coat. He stared at it squatting brashly in the aisle — a mean and ugly thing knocked together by some Philistine who saw coffins as his bread-and-butter. It couldn't be his mother's — she had never been that small. She had towered above his childhood, her head had touched the sky. There had been only Hester in the whole of England (him always in parentheses — safer in parentheses — safe and overlooked). He wished they'd stop the singing. It was such a sluggish, doleful sound. The colours from the stained glass windows leapt across the altar and fell like petals on the grey stone floor of the nave, shimmering in the sunlight. The sun hadn't been invited, yet it gate-crashed, interrupted, couldn't even sit still. The vicar bowed and strutted in the glare.

'*Hear my prayer O Lord . . . for I am but a stranger with you, a passing guest as all my fathers were.*' That was more like it. A stranger, yes, and he had never had a father. Never a brother, either. Only Matthew who boasted a different (dead) younger, tragic mother. Everything came through Matthew, even Hester. Hester arrived at Hernhope to replace the mother Matthew had killed in being born. Hester had been the housekeeper. (Impressive heritage — his mother a servant and his father a bankrupt.) Only years later had she married his father and become Mrs Thomas Winterton instead of Hester Ainsley. She was punished for the marriage because Thomas died within the year, before he, Lyn, was even born.

He and Matthew had both killed off a parent — he a father and Matthew a mother — the young and beautiful Susannah, Thomas's first wife who had died at just eighteen. Their headstones stood together in the churchyard, leaning towards each other as if hungry to embrace. Susannah's was the larger and more elaborate, since all the widower's love and loss and passion (and a large chunk of his cash) had gone into the stone, whereas when Hester buried Thomas, love and money were both more strictly rationed. Time and weather had lashed against the sandstone, leaving it storm-shocked, moss-encrusted, streaked with tears of rain.

23

As a boy, he had often sat beside the grave, mourning not so much his father, as Matthew's romantic mother who had become a fairy-tale. He would trace the crumbling inscription with a finger. *Susannah Jane, adored and beloved wife of . . .* The adored and beloved roused him, as if he had come across Susannah with her clothes off. His own mother had never been adored, never naked, never even young. Hester was gaunt, lined, buttoned-to-the-neck, and regarded love as an insubstantial extravagance like sherbet. He had never had a sister. Susannah became sister, beloved, adored and — soon — obsession. He had heard she was fair, so he made her lily-white; he knew she was young, so he turned her into a child-bride who was somehow also his mother (which was irrational and impossible since she had died fourteen years before his own conception). But Susannah stood for youth and hope and beauty, allowed him to do the things Hester considered wicked or disgusting, embroidered multi-coloured mystery and romance on the drab worsted of his life. Other times, he *feared* her as a mother, guessed she would be too flighty or too dangerous, neglect him for her lovers. Then he craved for Hester — the moat and drawbridge of her scratchy skirts and enveloping overalls, the way she could pluck a chicken, lance a boil, lance his terrors and squeeze the pus from them, put boundaries round things. In the end he fused them, joining Matthew's shimmering mirage of a mother to his own stern and solid one, so that although he had only the one parent, there were always two of her — a wild girl gowned in scarlet and a warden garbed in black.

'*We brought nothing into the world*,' intoned the vicar, '*And we take nothing out.*' Birth and death again. Birth always sprang from death. He had seen it in the churchyard. New spring flowers twining round the almost eroded 'S' of Susannah Jane. New born lambs huddled behind the larger older graves. Daffodils in flower along a path made of old uprooted tombstones. He had trodden on a skull and crossbones carved in stone. '*Sacred to the memory of . . .*' Except it wasn't sacred. Someone had pulled it down to make a path. Would Hester be a path? People trampling on her? Impossible.

Jennifer was nudging him, coaxing him from his knees on to his seat. What was happening now? The vicar loomed ten foot taller, braying from the pulpit about our dear departed sister going to her rest.

Hester was nobody's sister — too closed and private for that — and of course she would never rest. Always too much to do — range to be stoked, bread to be baked, cheese to be made and sold to buy his shoes. Even in heaven, she'd be up at five, laundering whole skies, polishing angels.

The vicar's voice echoed and crescendoed. Empty churchy words resounding with stained-glass nothing. Lyn stared at the coloured window which showed Adam and Eve driven out of Eden, Adam guilty and abashed, hiding his thing with a limp and furtive hand. His mother had made him feel like that, as if his body were a sin and he were permanently

24

naked, even with his clothes on. Eve was a Susannah — young, full-bodied, frivolous — golden ringlets serpenting down her breasts. He had read in an art book once that lilies were the flowers which sprang from Eve's tears as she stumbled out of Paradise. The name Susannah came from the Hebrew word for lily, so it all tied up. Lilies for purity and innocence, yet linked to that first flush female whose name was sin and shame. Matthew had sent lilies only yesterday. He had flung them in the dustbin. Susannah belonged to *him* now.

The vicar had glided down to ground level and everyone was standing. The organ added sobs to its mournful drone. Four local farmers were parading down the aisle with a coffin on their shoulders, their coarse quaffing mouths set in pious Sunday smirks. Lyn had somehow made his feet work and was blundering along behind them, glued to Jennifer's arm, all the congregation pouring out of their pews and trailing after him.

The sun winked and sniggered as the cortege snailed into the churchyard. Ever since he'd arrived here the sun had kept on shining, turning winter into summer, death into carnival, gilding things when he wanted them in black.

Most of the graves were tangled and neglected, weeds choking mothers, creepers strangling sons. Some of the older tombstones had sagged or shifted as if they no longer had the heart to stand up straight. Moss and lichen blanked out loving inscriptions as their owners crumbled from pain and loss to memory, to void.

Jennifer was leading him like a child. He hardly knew what was happening, except he was stumbling over tussocks, following a rag and tag of people who were gathering round a hole. The Winterton plot had been full for more than thirty years. They had opened it for Thomas, but he had been the last. Hester's grave was two down from her husband's and shaded by the relics of a diseased and dying elm. The first and younger wife had pride of place.

Lyn stared at the raw scarred earth, bleeding against the tangled undergrowth. All the ground around him was writhing with dead bodies, vanished Wintertons pointing bony fingers at his shame and folly in leaving the family home. He dared not look in the hole in case it plunged him into nothingness. That hollow heartless coffin was bad enough.

The vicar had blown his whistle for the second half. Lyn jumped as words spattered on the coffin.

'*I heard a voice from heaven saying, "Write this: Happy are the dead . . ."* '

Peculiar word, happy — especially at a funeral. Lyn sucked it like a fruit-drop. A word like hope which meant something different from what it should. Nobody looked happy. Molly Bertram was weeping and the shepherd's wife from Nettleburn emitting little sobs and gasps which collided with the psalms.

Even Jennifer was crying — mourning a woman she had never known and who had forbidden her to exist. Jennifer had washed the body, closed

25

the eyes. Lyn shivered. When she had finished she even smelt of Hester, his mother's droppings and dribblings staining his wife's clothes. She had picked flowers and filled his mother's room with them — more for a wedding than a funeral. Was Hester's death Jennifer's decree absolute? Were they solemnising their marriage because only now was he divorced and parted from his mother?

Shouldn't *he* be crying? His eyes did ache, but it was only from the sun. Crying was so ugly. He longed for some nobler, cleaner, keener, fiercer grief. How could you shroud Hester in a snivel, splutter her away in sodden scraps of Kleenex? The vicar kept on booming.

'Man born of a woman has but a short time to live. Like a flower he blossoms, then withers; like a shadow he flees and never stays.'

Born of woman. Even in the Alternative Service Book, it sounded strange. How else could you be born? Was that what frightened him in women? To be shut up in them, coffined in them, gulping down their food supplies, squawling out between their legs?

They were lowering in the coffin, straining against the straps. Was Hester fighting them, refusing to go down? Lyn glimpsed the neat squared-off edges of the hole. They had tried to soften it with wreaths — 'floral tributes' the undertaker had called them, a puffed-up little man with laquered hair, who looked as if he had tried to embalm himself. The wreaths were mostly hideous — decapitated flowerheads squashed into solid cushions, blooms snared and scalped and pinioned, as if they were crying out in pain, satin ribbons lassooing plastic foliage.

The vicar flung his handful of dust, *'Ashes to ashes'* punched out like a rugby song. Lyn stared at the oblong box lying so snugly in its oblong hole. Never before had Hester been so submissive, fitted the space she was given, done what she was told. He felt he ought to haul her out again, rip the wood apart and let her holler. He stepped towards the edge. The ground came rushing towards him, Hester's mouth a black and screaming hole. The vicar grabbed his elbow, led him away. Jennifer was already standing by the porch and he was pushed into position beside her. Death was still muddled up with weddings — a long reception-line snaking towards him, queuing up to pump him by the hand. Jennifer was sniffing and smiling at once, as she had done three years ago, except she had been white and radiant then, instead of black.

All the locals' names were crumbling into dust. Three short years he had been away, and they all looked much the same as when he'd left, but the last few days had warped time like elastic, mouldered all his brain cells. He was blanking out on people he had known for thirty years or more. Thank God for Jennifer who was collecting names and inviting them back for tea. Half of them declined, cold-shouldering her fairy cakes and trifles, preferring a double whisky in the Rose and Crown. Special licence for a funeral. The publican already counting up his profits. Molly Bertram was shepherding the rest. 'Over here, Mrs Walters. Jack can

26

take one more. No, you go with Peggy, Mr Bryant.'

Revving of engines, slamming of car doors. He was the host and he couldn't even drive. His legs were made of sunlight, his hands were lumps of wood. He climbed into a Land Rover. His own car was packed with strangers, the vicar's full of hats. People chatted to him as they laboured up the hill, scraps and shreds of Hester passed between them.

'Marvellous for her age . . .'

'Of course, she *was* so independent . . .'

'At least it was over quickly . . .'

'Mustn't blame yourself . . .'

Blame . . . *Blame*? How had they found him out? If he had gone up earlier, done what his wife advised, hadn't wasted a whole Saturday with Matthew, then Hester wouldn't have died. He'd have had time to call the doctor, phone the ambulance, found her still alive.

He had killed her, then — or he and Matthew had. Matthew had sent messages and money (always money with Matthew) and sensible advice. Drive in daylight, try and keep her cheerful, phone if you need us, always ready to help.

More time wasted fondling Jennifer. Caressing her breasts while Hester gasped for water. Stopping for picnic kisses when his mother was a corpse. They were probably filling in that hole now, earth falling on her face.

'Mind the step,' said the driver. Somehow they had reached the house while he was still fighting off the grave-diggers, scrabbling at the soil. How could he have missed road and hills and forest; bumped across seven cattle-grids and not even felt them rumble?

He staggered up the path into his house — *Hester*'s house — except, for the first time in his life, she wasn't there. His wife was Mrs Winterton now, already pouring tea. She was using the best gold-rimmed Dresden china which Hester had packed away when Thomas died, the damask cloths, the silver apostle spoons. All those fine fancy things belonged to Matthew's era. He and Hester had made do with earthenware — thick brown clumsy stuff laid on the bare boards. He feared his mother might march back and demand less fuss.

'Have a cup of tea, Lyn. You look frozen stiff.' Molly Bertram mothering him, passing him Jennifer's ham-and-mushroom patties. 'Try one of these. You ought to eat, you know.' Eating herself, mouth full, a mushroom fragment caught in one side tooth; dressed in some skittish mauvey thing instead of seemly black.

People thronging all around him, invading Hester's privacy. Half of them had shunned his invitation, yet the house still bulged with bodies. He crept towards the hearth. Despite the sun, he felt chilled and corpse-like from the inside out. However many fires they lit, the house refused to thaw. Jennifer had tried to tame it, but it still shrugged off her overtures. It was an uneasy mixture now of her and Hester — Jennifer's blaze and

27

polish on the ground floor, and the barer, greyer death-knell of the bedrooms.

Someone joined him by the hearth. 'How's Matthew?'

Lyn jumped. 'Er . . . fine.'

'Couldn't he come up?'

'Well, no, he . . .'

'Are his boys doing well?'

'Yes. Very.'

'Any sons yourself yet, Lyn?'

'N . . . no.' He turned away, grabbed a sausage roll to stop his mouth. You had to breed up here. Sons meant extra pairs of hands to help with the harvest or the lambing, to carry on the line. They'd be wondering what was wrong with him. A strong young wife like Jennifer should be swelling out by now. He pushed through the crowd to find her. She was surrounded by a group of older women, all mobbing her with questions.

'Such a pleasure to meet you, Mrs Winterton. We always wondered why you'd never . . .'

'How did you come to meet your husband, dear?'

'Reckon you'd like to stay up here — make the house more modern? Remember what I told you. If there's anything you want, even if it's only a chat or a . . .'

'I understand no one's found a Will?'

Lyn winced, tried to catch Jennifer's eye. She had created a sort of *party* all around her — fancy clothes, fancy food, hum of conversation. Hester would have hated it. Hester kept her doors shut, her parlour blinds drawn down. Even the vicar had swapped his tea for Scotch and was stuffing himself with cake.

'Delicious chocolate gâteau, Mrs Winterton. You're a very good cook, I see.'

'It's my job, Mr Arnold. I was trained in domestic science.'

'Oh, you cook for a living, do you?' Little flakes of chocolate spraying from his lip.

'No, nothing as grand as that. I do a few dinner parties for people, or things like weddings, sometimes. And I sell my stuff — you know, jams, chutneys, pâtés, to the local delicatessen.'

Lyn slipped into the circle. 'She does it for *fun*,' he muttered. 'Just a hobby.' Didn't want them saying he couldn't keep her, that his own job was underpaid and tied to Matthew's whim, that Matthew paid the bills but kept the purse-strings.

The vicar stroked his chin, left a smear of chocolate icing. 'Pity you didn't meet your mother-in-law. She was a very inventive cook, you know. Found ingredients in the fields and hedgerows and concocted all sorts of things, even her own medicines. And she was the only one up here who still made cheeses.'

'*Cheeses*?'

28

'Oh yes, you've probably seen the moulds. They're . . .'

Lyn tried to manoeuvre his wife into a corner, get her on her own. 'Ask them to *leave*,' he whispered. 'I don't feel well.'

'Hush, darling — they'll hear you. Go and lie down for a minute. They'll understand. They'll be leaving soon, in any case.'

'No, they won't, they'll . . .' He was talking to the wall. His wife had been swallowed up again.

'Mr Winterton?'

He jumped. Another face ballooning from his childhood — grizzled perm, scatty hat, eyes lost in their wrinkles. Mrs Wise from Alwinton smiling with her off-white china teeth. He tried to make his mouth work, use solemn straitjacketed words to fit a death. A blob of trifle was quivering on her spoon.

'Yes, it . . . er . . . *was* a shock, Mrs Wise.' Yellow custard plopping onto her lilac Crimplene bodice, sliding down her cleavage. 'No, the doctor wasn't there. I'm afraid he . . .'

He lurched away, collided with someone else, a tall tweedy woman who smelt of dogs. She grabbed his arm, bony fingers digging in his flesh. 'We're all so *very* sorry, Mr Winterton.' Face thrust close to his. Purple gauze of thread-veins, mole with a coarse black hair in it sprouting from her cheek. 'I understand it happened very suddenly?'

He nodded, pulled his arm free. Impossible to escape. People all around him — mouths, mouths, mouths. Everybody guzzling — swilling tea, gorging cakes, gulping down his mother. He was bleeding like those cherries in the trifle, red stain into white. His head was a meringue — hollow, full of air. The smallest guest could have crunched him up to nothing, crumbled him away. Clack-clack-clacking. Empty words.

'No, thanks, Mrs Dixon, I've still got half a cup left. No, we weren't there when it . . .' He picked up a cupcake, put it down again. Pink sugared petals sprinkled on white icing. Flowers on a winding-sheet. 'We couldn't leave before, you see. We didn't realise quite how bad she . . . b . . . bad . . . she . . .'

Go *away*!

They didn't go till evening. Lyn lay on the high, narrow bed — Susannah's bed — the one she had died in. Both his mothers dead now. He tried to make some sense of it — poke a finger in his grief and feel it smart and bleed. It didn't. Death was still a party dragging on downstairs.

He pressed his aching head against the pillow. Susannah must have lain here, exhausted from such company. How had she ever borne it — so young and dazzling a creature amongst all these country bumpkins with their coarse complexions and their baggy clothes? Susannah's skin was Dresden, her body cut from silk. He knew because he had seen her. Just a glimpse of her, hidden in a locket, one curl of her hair. He had found the locket when he was still a stripling in short pants, rifling through the huge mahogany roll-top which belonged to his dead father. The desk was locked and the room was out-of-bounds, but Hester had gone shopping and a boy at school had taught him to pick locks.

He had held the booty in his hands — a heavy heart-shaped locket on a golden chain. He'd forced it with his dirty fingernails. One side opened to reveal a lock of hair, faded but still fair, curling gently like a smile. The other side was jammed. He put a penknife to it, sliced his finger, bled through two large handkerchiefs before he won. The prize was worth the blood. The young girl gazing at him was a different species from the rugged village women who creaked and clacked in Mepperton or the spindly schoolgirls he avoided at his school. Her face was prouder, finer, with high, preening cheekbones contradicted by the wanton tumble of hair which cascaded to her shoulders, one daring curl falling across the cleavage which the locket-frame cut off. Her eyes were huge, wooing, shameless; long lashes almost fluttering him towards her; moist lips slightly parted as if to proposition him.

'*Susannah*,' he whispered. He knew who she was, because he had already drawn her in his dreams. Now he made his sketches fit the truth, until Susannah rose huge and three-dimensional in every surface of his life. For eleven days he owned and worshipped her (*adored, beloved*), sleeping with her locket every night, staring at it, touching it cool against his heated body — touching himself.

When he came, Susannah held him stiff, reassured him afterwards when he felt shamed and sticky; kissed his lips apart when he had bitten them to stop himself from crying out.

The eleventh night he was lying awake with her, pyjama cord undone, locket against his groin. They were making noise together, forgetting the other, second, older mother whose bedroom door was opposite and who didn't have a groin. Suddenly Hester was looming up above them, white shadow shaming the darkness, frown stretching to the ceiling.

He dragged his pyjamas back again, hauled the blankets over him. There was a tiny thud as the locket fell off the bed and glinted on the floorboards. Hester pounced.

He never saw the golden heart again. Nothing was ever said. The night was locked away, the desk was sold, and Hester kept her bedroom door ajar. For a month he slept with his hands outside the blankets.

His mind was less obedient. When he tried again, he found Susannah as unabashed and eager as before. He no longer had her photograph, but he had transferred the negative deep inside his soul and printed and reprinted it so that her features smiled from each room and shelf and mantel, as they had done once when Thomas was alive. It was only Hester who had removed her rival's likeness from the house, after she'd married the widower. Matthew had told him that, much later on — one of the reasons Matthew had left for London. Lyn often wondered where those photos were — burnt or smashed or . . .

He leapt off the bed. He could hear voices in the hallway, the front door slamming, opening, slamming. The guests must be leaving now. He had gone upstairs to rest and be alone, not tangle with Susannah. If he was well enough for her, then he should be down there with the others, dragging out his duty, sharing the farewells. He stared in the small scratched mirror on the dressing table. His eyes looked like singe-holes in a sheet, too dark and fierce for his pallid washed-out face.

He smoothed his crumpled jacket, stood listening at the door. Goodbyes and thank-yous echoing up the staircase, offers of help, bounty, comfort, patronage; Jennifer netted down in Village Aid; sucked into coffee mornings, shopping rotas, sewing circles, church bazaars. Nothing of her left.

The door closed on the last of them. Silence tiptoed out from corners and stretched itself like a cat which had been shooed away by too much noise. Lyn walked warily downstairs, glanced into the sitting-room. Yes — everyone had gone now, but the place was littered with their droppings. Ashtrays belching on to tables, cake crumbs trodden into rugs. They had even left their *smell* behind — the faint and lingering odour of feet and sweat and bodies, cigarettes and scent. He shut the door on it, went through into the kitchen. Jennifer was swaddling pies in greaseproof, packing cakes away, all the surfaces around her piled high with dirty dishes. She came towards him.

'I hoped you'd be asleep, darling. Do you feel a little better? Is there anything you want?'

'No,' he said to both. 'Look, let me help with that.'

She shook her head. 'You go back to bed. You look quite washed out.'

He rubbed at a lipstick stain on a gold-rimmed Dresden cup, smeared it, made it worse. 'I'd have thought *Molly* might have . . .'

'She offered — more than once — but I wouldn't let her help. She's done enough already. Anyway, I'm quite enjoying it. It went so well today, I . . .'

'*Well?*'

'Yes. Everyone was so wonderfully kind and helpful and really interested in us. I'm amazed so many came, Lyn. There must have been over sixty at the service. They just turned up, some of them from miles away. I think that's . . . marvellous. I mean in Cobham you only go to a funeral if you're a close friend or relation with your own private invitation. The church was full today without *any* invitations. Do you know what Molly said . . .'

'Quite a lot, I imagine.'

'Oh, Lyn, don't. She's been such a comfort. She said it's like a *family* up here. That's why all those people were at the service. It's a sort of loyalty. You see, even if your mother was . . . well . . . a bit of a private

31

person, she was still one of the family. *You* are, too, she said.'

Lyn slooshed tea-leaves down the sink, dregs clammy and still warm. So Molly Bertram was his mother now — sister, cousin, keeper. Jennifer was forging all those friendly pressed-steel handcuffs his mother had spent a lifetime snapping out of.

'Molly told me how talented you were. She said her mother knew you as a boy and even then . . .'

'*No* one knew us, Jennifer. We hardly went anywhere. We were never like the rest. We stayed shut up like . . .' He hated the self-pity in his voice. People with unhappy childhoods should be banned.

'Darling . . .' She kissed him. 'It's over now. Things will be better — you'll see. I mean, there's nothing to . . . keep you here now. You could even sell the house if you . . .'

'Don't be stupid.' He pounced on the wreckage of a cheese-and-onion quiche. If Hernhope went, he wouldn't exist at all. Matthew had taken over his head and hands, and Jennifer owned the body in between. He might snuff out his boyhood, but he didn't want the whole place razed, Hernhope Tipp-Exed off the map like some gigantic error. Hernhope was like God. You might not believe in Him, but you couldn't do without Him. Even if you yawned through services or shivered in the cold vaults of the church, you still preferred to keep the temple standing.

'Look, I'm sorry I shouted. I . . .'

'Don't worry, darling. Look, why don't you go back upstairs and try and sleep?'

He couldn't sleep, but he trailed upstairs again, simply because it was tidier and his wife wasn't there to make him feel a brute. He stopped outside Susannah's bedroom door. He and Jennifer were sleeping in that room, not only because his own was dark and cramped, but because he had always longed to infiltrate it. In his boyhood it had been permanently shut up, as if the doomed young hussy were a dangerous presence still. He had often tried the door, peered in through the keyhole, imagined Susannah, flushed and voluptuous, lying on the bed. All he had seen was a tiny patch of floorboard.

He had been stunned to find the room so *ordinary*. The bare essentials — bare. Bed and wardrobe, washstand, hard cane chair. The whole of Hester's house was sparsely furnished. She had sold the larger and more expensive items, and disapproved of frilly and frivolous extras like cushions, pictures, pets. In Jennifer's home they'd had velvet rocking chairs, cocker spaniels, silken tassels on the curtains, and little embroidered tray cloths under plates of langues de chat. He envied Jennifer's fat upholstered childhood with its plumped-up bolsters and its solemn photographs in silver frames. (Susannah had silver frames and velvet fingers. Susannah had a lap-dog.)

He dragged his clothes off, shivering in the cold. The sun had stayed behind in the churchyard. Even when it shone, it never really warmed you. Just a bright veneer of enamel over the iron core of the countryside, dazzle without heart. He touched his face. The skin felt dry and smooth. He hadn't cried yet. People must have noticed. Unnatural, they'd be saying — callous and hard-hearted. He could feel the tears dammed somewhere in his gut, underneath that one small sausage roll which was all he had eaten since the day before, but which had swollen like a boulder. When *Jennifer*'s mother had died just eighteen months ago, she had sobbed for three whole days. Real tears which soaked the sheets. He kicked the skirting. Self-pitying again. He had a wife, for heaven's sake — a bloody saint, in fact, who put up with his moods — a job, a house, a . . .

He lingered by the window, dusk floundering into darkness, hills keeping endless watch around the house. The sheep grazed further down now, banished by the forest which overshadowed them. He could hear the bleating of the lambs. The place was like a labour ward in April. He remembered a schoolfriend's father who had built extensive lambing sheds to increase his yield. He had often stood there as a lad, watching scores of panting ewes jammed together in the pens, their straw sour and stained with dung, bloody mucous trails or bulging sacs of waters hanging from their backsides. He had breathed in the stench, the mess, the clamour, seen lambs born wet and slimy, some not born at all. Shepherds tugging malformed limbs from wombs, deaths mourned only as loss of cash.

He drew the curtains, turned his back. Birth and death were both so cruel up here, so casual. Nature simply shrugged. He wished Jennifer would hurry. He'd feel better with her there. He could hear her closing cupboards, locking doors, then coming up the stairs, fiddling in the bathroom, flushing toilet, running taps.

'Snookie,' he shouted. No — mustn't call her Snookie. She might think that he wanted it.

She stood at the door, too plump and flushed to be in mourning, hair falling round her shoulders. She was dressed in white now, not in black, wearing some long, trailing thing he didn't recognise. He could see her nipples pushing through the stuff. Wrong to notice nipples when his mother was a headstone.

'Hurry up and get undressed. I'm whacked.'

'I *am* undressed. This is my nightie.'

Nightie? It looked more like a shroud. 'I've never seen it before. It's not Hester's, is it? You're not wearing her clothes?'

'Lyn, you're crazy. I've had it months. Your mother wouldn't wear a thing like this. I've seen her nightgowns — real old-fashioned flannel with ruffles round the sleeves.'

He tried to imagine Hester wearing ruffles. Impossible. She had always snipped the frills off things, wrapped life in plain brown paper.

Jennifer turned the covers back.

'Come to bed, darling, and let's try and get some sleep. Gosh! You're freezing. Snuggle close and I'll warm you up a bit.'

She flopped towards him, warm and heavy. He had already switched the light off, so he could no longer see the shadow of her nipples, the faint bloom of down above her upper lip. Lips were the most dangerous things of all. Unzip a mouth and it unlatched things lower down. She was so close now, he could feel her almost breathing for him, the edges of her body unravelling into his. He pulled away, rolled over to face the wall. You didn't grab your wife when the flowers on your mother's grave were still alive.

'Turn round, Linnet. Just let me hold you a moment.'

Linnet. Baby name he had never had with Hester. Name his wife was forbidden ever (*ever*) to say in public. Stupid, sissy, girly, beloved name. He turned.

She kissed him. He was stiff in seconds. How could he not be, when this was Susannah's bed and he still had that locket cold against his heat? Now he was older, Susannah could do more for him — deep-throat him, swallow him, have him forbidden ways. He kicked the blankets off. Hester was barely cold. Trouble was, he hadn't had it for six days. Not since the death, of course — only brutes did that — but even *before*, the news of Hester's illness had put him off his stroke. They had tried it on the Easter Saturday night, but Matthew had somehow ruined it. It was *Matthew's* face he'd seen frowning up from the pillow, nagging about his job. His thing had curled up and died. Now it was rampant when it was blasphemy to own a cock at all. Trust him to stiffen when his duty was to sob. It had been the other way round on his wedding night — lying limp and almost blabbing with a real live woman panting there beside him, naked with her legs open. He had almost botched that night. Hester had taught him it must be forced and furtive, that women didn't fancy it. Jennifer did. She was too loving and assiduous, the bed too damned co-operative. He had often dreamed of *forcing* girls — sometimes forced Susannah in his fantasies, flung her on her front and rammed in the forbidden way. He never dared with Jennifer — wanted to, but feared to. A wife might be offended.

He couldn't screw her, anyway — not even conventional fashion. It wasn't just the funeral — he had no Durex with him. He had never entered Jennifer in a whole three years of marriage without that rubber skin between them. He hated Durex — damn-fool fiddly things. But Jennifer refused the Pill, rejected every contraceptive. Jennifer wanted babies. Well, so did he — not just *yet*, that's all. It was a matter of time, money, jobs, convenience. You had to plan these things. Anyway, even without the babies, he preferred to put a layer between himself and any woman, including his own wife. It was safer, somehow, cleaner. Made the thing less crucial. Stopped him touching her most private places. It meant he could keep a shell around himself, one last barrier — enter her

34

and yet still be separate. Hester would have approved of Durex if she had permitted sex at all.

He had never once had sex in his mother's house. The rare times he had brought a girlfriend back, they had sat in the front parlour and Hester had fed them rock cakes and stony glances until the hussy left at ten. He had done it in ditches, sometimes, to escape her, lying on dirty sacking or dead leaves, crouching under hedgerows when his mother had five spare beds, all virgin, all unslept in. Yet in some ways he admired her. It was sluttish to sleep around, wallow in it, couple like a dog with some bitch on heat he had sniffed out in an alleyway, then slip in late with a weight on his conscience, bits of bracken in his hair.

That's why he had married Jennifer. She made it decent, gave the dog a pedigree. He sat up on his elbow, stared down at her breasts. They looked larger the way she was lying, cupped and squeezed together until they overflowed. One hand was bent towards them, her fingers curving just below the nipple. The same fingers which had closed his mother's eyes. Were they really closed, or was Hester spying on him still? No, he *did*n't want babies. Wanted to want them, at least for Jennifer's sake, but he knew he'd make a hash of it. He'd seen what sons had done to Matthew — sucked him dry. They had to have the best of everything — clothes, food, schools, holidays. Matthew had turned into a sort of manic money machine, working eight days out of seven, cracking his whip at the world, putting his wife to work, his half-brother, conjuring jobs out of scraps of paper, profit out of stones.

He couldn't work like that to keep a son. Sons grew taller than you did, took everything you had, including your wife. If you had a mother, you couldn't have a wife. For years he'd had two mothers, Hester and Susannah, conflicting and fighting in his head, tearing him apart. One beckoning, one warning; one wise and withered and sacred, one wet, hot, sluttish, eager, open. He couldn't endure it any longer. He wanted only Jennifer — simple, powerful, strong. She had gone to sleep already.

He leant across and kissed the back of her neck, ran his fingers slowly down her spine from nape to coccyx, leaving his hand cupped beneath her buttocks. He prayed she would wake and want it. Then he could tell himself she had knocked him off his guard. Her breathing hardly wavered. He turned away, touched himself instead. He rarely masturbated now — less need to with a wife. He could feel the locket hard against his thighs, Susannah opening everything towards him.

Why in God's name was Susannah still alive? Because he had *kept* her alive, not only in his mind, but in his drawings — sketched her a thousand times in pencil, charcoal, ink; ripped off her clothes and made her the model in his own private life-class. Later, in his art books, he'd seen public paintings of her — 'Susannah Bathing', 'Susannah and the Elders' — huge fleshy women with thighs you could get lost in. Laboriously he had copied Rembrandt, Rubens, Tintoretto — using coloured

35

pencils this time, or — daringly — a tiny box of watercolours which cost him five weeks' pocket money. He always waited till Hester was out or asleep, adding embellishments, erotica, making himself a handmaid attending at her bath, or a slavering elder spying from a bush, admiring those lewd curves and creases dimpled across her flesh. He longed to paint in oils, to give Susannah's haunches that ripe and rippling texture he had fingered in the books, but how could he hide a canvas or disperse the smell of turps, even if he'd had the money to afford them? At least with watercolours, he could keep his paintings small and secret, hide or destroy each scrap of paper. Only his model survived. *Still* survived, when she would be well into her sixties now. Impossible! Susannah was always seventeen, caught forever in her youth and bath as she was in those Old Masters. Even now she was lying there beside him, still wet and tousled from bathing, her taunting teenage body whispering into his, her fingers tight around him. Susannah had more fingers than any woman he had ever known. One up his arse, two around his balls, three stroking him bigger, one touching up herself.

He grabbed the minx awake, turned her into Jennifer. 'Lie on your front,' he whispered.

Jennifer slumped over, still half asleep. She had told him he could wake her if he felt bad, but she'd meant sobbing over Hester, not slavering over Susannah. She would gladly kiss his tears away, but not a bloody great erection. It wasn't fair to rouse her, anyway. She was exhausted from the day — all that cooking, coping, hostessing. He'd just lie against her, hold her, feel her body soft and calming under his. He envied her that calmness. The way she could sleep the minute she was tired, fit sex into a schedule, sob when it was time to, smile when it was not. With him, everything was scrambled screaming up together — grief, guilt, lust, fever — all revving between his legs. The more he tried to still himself, the more his body urged. He had cramp in his leg, pain in his chest, anger blasting through his bloodstream. Anger with that stubborn, shameless part of him which still cocked up when everything decent begged it to lie down.

He wasn't even comfortable. He was lying half on top of a sprawled and supine body, one leg slumped across it, chin against a spine. Warm fleshy buttocks pressed against his balls, keeping him excited, while Jennifer's deep, shuddering breathing warned him off. Maybe he could do it while she slept — sneak in very gently and be out again before she was fully awake. At least it would be less blatant. But it wouldn't solve the baby thing. She might swell up in revenge, produce a kid to shame him. A kid could *kill* a wife — had already killed Susannah. Jennifer mustn't die. He didn't want her split apart in childbirth, slimy and heaving like those blood-stained sheep.

Why enter her at all? If he touched himself again, he could come just lying close to her, spill out on her thighs. He hated that. Made him feel a boy again, furtive and humiliated. He didn't *want* it passive, forced to

36

stifle his cries as he had done all his boyhood, having to leak and creep and dissemble when he ached to ram and shout. It wasn't simply lust. He could make it sacred if Jennifer joined in. Coming would be like crying, a release and a relief.

He sat up in bed, switched the bedside light on. Jennifer stirred and mumbled something, turned her head away. Slowly he peeled the covers back, eased her nightie up until he could see the long slope of her back, curving out into full fleshy buttocks dappled in the light. He slipped his hands beneath her belly and coaxed her up and back until she was crouched on all fours with her bottom humped towards him. He sniffed her faint female odour of mingled scent and sweat. She was trying to slump down again, burrow back into the blankets.

'Tired, darling. Want to sleep.' Her voice was slurred, husky, unbearably exciting.

'Ssshh,' he whispered, ran a finger slowly across her buttocks, down into the crease, found the forbidden hole, stroked around it. It was resisting him — tight, unwilling, locked. Hadn't he learned to break locks? He eased the finger in, felt it give a little. Coiled spring around his finger. Rat-trap. Wedding-ring. She shocked awake, trying to push him off and tensing all her muscles. The trap closed tighter.

'*Don't*. You're hurting, Linnet.'

Stupid name. He wanted to gag her, force her. Sick of all the restraint, the rules, the should-nots, the gentle solemn loving, the pretty passive names. Right, he'd *be* a dog — a cocking, snuffling mongrel without his pedigree, a dog who had slipped his lead.

He jerked the finger out and held her open while he eased the other in. It went only a grudging straining centimetre, then stopped. She was virgin there as she had been when he met her — everywhere — zipped up to the neck. He tried to force the zip down — two centimetres — three. It felt tight and fierce like handcuffs round a wrist. Jennifer was whimpering, making little gasping noises of pain or fear or shock. At least she wouldn't swell. You couldn't conceive in an arse-hole. He *liked* it in her arse-hole. It was tighter, safer, and she didn't have a face — just that huge heaving arse rearing up in front of him, imprisoning him inside her. He had snapped the handcuffs now and found space and shaft beyond. Every tight, tighter thrust was tying them together, cancelling out his separateness. The bed creaked hoarsely underneath them. For a sudden anguished moment he heard Hester braying out her fury in the bed-springs. He closed his ears, thrust harder. He wouldn't let her in.

'Jennifer!' he shouted. If he had her loud enough, Hester would be drowned. His wife was noisy, too, now, little noises spitting out from under her as if she were an animal.

'*Darling*,' she was crying in a sort of muffled breathless gasp. Darling could mean anything — pain or bliss or anger. She was butting her head against the pillow, arching up her back, twisting her buttocks so that he almost lost his grip. Was she trying to shake him off or goad him on? Couldn't stop now, anyway. Not a mind or body any more, just a ramming thrusting piston. All his grief, fear, fury, force, centred on one point.

His nails were digging into her back, his breathing laboured and distorted. She and the bed were both rocking underneath him, the squeaking of the springs cutting through her cries. She wasn't fighting any longer but moving with him, thrusting with him, making her pace and rhythm one with his. Shameless, brazen woman who purred in the drawing-room and buggered in the kitchen, blotting out the funeral, bringing passion out of pain. As tight and wild as Susannah. Sluttish marvellous woman debauching all his boyhood, branding all his paintings, coming when he came. He was schoolboy, lover, husband, coming, *COMING* . . .

His cry cut the room in half. He collapsed on top of Jennifer, sheet tangled round their limbs, blankets tumbled to the floor. He could feel her shuddering into stillness underneath him.

'Darling,' she was sobbing. 'Oh, my darling.'

V

'Ah, Jennifer! We were just wondering where you'd got to. Do come in.' Molly Bertram opened the door on a barking tangle of dogs. 'We started dinner without you. Hope you don't mind, but the men have to get back to the lambing. Where's Lyn?'

Jennifer returned the overtures of two small but boisterous border terriers. 'He's . . . er . . . not too well. That's why I'm late, in fact. I'm sorry.'

'Don't worry, love. Better for him to rest. He's probably still shocked by the funeral. He always took things hard, did Lyn. *Down*, Ben! He's really wild, that one. Thinks he's still a pup when he's coming up to ten.'

'I don't mind. I love dogs.' Jennifer followed Molly into the hall — walked into warmth, noise, colour, cooking smells. Outside, the Bertram farmhouse was the same slate-roofed stone as Hester's — grey, solid, stern. Inside it was still old-fashioned and well-worn, but alive where Hester's was dead. All the rooms glowed with chintzy cushions and brightly coloured rugs. Every shelf and surface was crowded with ornaments and photographs, cats napped on window-seats, logs purred in the great open fireplace in the hall. Molly paused a moment, kicking back a log which was smouldering in the grate.

'Look, before we face the troops, tell me how things are. Apart from Lyn, I mean.'

Jennifer hesitated. 'Er . . . fine.' How could you say 'apart from Lyn', when her life was woven into his like a two-colour knitting pattern? And how could she explain to Molly about his moods? Everything about Molly was comfortable and solid — her stocky figure which had neither bust, nor waist, nor hips, but ran them all together in a well-upholstered mass; her coarse springy hair which looked much the same whether she had come straight from the hairdresser or just tumbled out of bed; her ruddy, wind-burnt face. Cheeks like apples, people said. Apples varied, though. Molly's were red like a Worcester, roughened like a Russet, slightly shrivelled and blemished as if the fruit had been in store too long. Her eyes were the colour of the apple pips, a dark glossy brown which made her whole face come alive; hands broad, almost clumsy, with chapped skin and broken nails — hands which held the household together, coped with children, crises, animals.

'Come through, love. You don't mind the kitchen, do you? I'm afraid we don't go in for fancy living here.'

'No, I *love* your kitchen.' The first time she'd seen it, Jennifer had felt a sense of total welcome, as if the room itself had leapt forward to embrace her, and then relaxed and put its feet up, so that she could only do the same. She had arrived one afternoon from Hester's house, with the corpse still lying cold and stiff upstairs, and found Molly baking, hot loaves steaming on the table, warm eggs piled in a china bowl, little shreds of feather still clinging to their shells, haunches of bacon hanging from the ceiling, the smells of yeast, spice, polish, and old dog all mingled up together. Crumpled newspapers and ancient *Farmers' Weeklies* were scattered on the huge lumpy sofa which lolled beneath the window. A sofa in a kitchen! It was really more a living-room — truly living — full of children, bustle, stir. Modern kitchens were often more like morgues or museums, all chilly stainless steel and dead Formica, but in the Bertram kitchen, everything spilled out and tumbled over in an exuberant cornucopia, each work-top hatching its crop of food or fruit or clutter; the floor-space busy with toys, boots, dog baskets, bulging sacks of dog-meal and potatoes; even the cups and saucers not stacked away in cupboards, but making a blue dazzle on the dresser.

Today, it was *more* a mess, more crowded. As Molly opened the door, ten pairs of eyes looked up from the loaded table, ten knives and forks paused in mid-eating, and silence rushed in like a draught from the door. Jennifer wasn't used to facing such a tableful, not only brawny Mick and his fierce five-foot-nothing mother, but all five Bertram children and three total strangers — two young men and one older, sitting in their socks, muddy boots left outside the door. Everyone looked shabby, dressed in working gear — stained and baggy sweaters, skirts and grubby

39

jeans. Jennifer wished she hadn't changed. Her skirt was too neat, her blouse too pale and prissy. These were all working people, without time to spare for fripperies like clothes. Lambing time was the busiest month of the year, a time when every pair of hands was needed on the farm. Molly was up at five each morning and still working late at night. She had more mouths to feed than usual, more clothes to dry, orphan lambs to warm and bottle-feed, her day stretched out in all directions.

Even now she was doing several things at once — serving up an extra lunch, keeping an eye on the stock-pot still simmering on the hob, hushing children, quietening dogs, making introductions.

'Mick you know, of course, and Nan, his mother. This is Chris, my eldest. She was up in Glasgow when you came before. That's Josh, our shepherd, Paddy and Colin next to him, and . . .'

Jennifer tried to remember all the names. The children she had sorted out already. The three girls came first — Ruth and Helen after Chris — Tim and Rory last. Paddy and Colin were students from the local agricultural college who were staying just a month or so, using their Easter holidays to help out with the lambing. Paddy was the shy gingery lad blushing as much as she was. Colin, fair and skinny, looked strange among the big-boned, brown-eyed Bertrams. Josh was permanent and older, so brown and gnarled, he looked as if he had been cut out of the hills on which he worked. He just mumbled something indecipherable and went on with his lunch. The others smiled and nodded.

'Sit next to Mick, Jenny. You don't mind Jenny, do you? Jennifer's such a mouthful.'

'No, of course not.' Nobody called her Jenny. It felt strange, like wearing someone else's shoes. Molly had piled her plate with chicken casserole, potatoes, parsnips, peas.

'We're half-way through ours, I'm afraid, but take your time.'

'Where's Lyn?' barked Mick's mother, laying down her fork. Her stiff grey curls were caged in a hair-net. Her bosom was a shelf on which she stored not just antique brooches whose silver claws held jagged lumps of stone or staring bright glass eyes, but also stray safety-pins and needles, jabbing dangerous things which warned you off.

'He's . . . er . . . not too well, Mrs Bertram.'

'None of that "Mrs" for me, dear. No one calls me Mrs. I'm Nana to my grandchildren and Nan to everyone else. I told you that before. What's wrong with him?'

'I'm . . . not quite sure. He's sleeping badly and he's lost his appetite and . . .'

'Thinks too much, that's *his* trouble — always was. How a sensible lass like yourself ever managed to . . .'

'Where d'you live?' asked Chris. All the Bertram children interrupted, barged in and out of any conversation as they pleased. Matthew would have muzzled them.

40

'Cobham,' Jennifer said, glad of the interruption. Nan and Lyn had little patience with each other.

'Where's that? Town or country?'

'Sort of fake country. It likes to call itself a village, but it's really commuter land with cows. There *are* fields and farms and things, but with a great bypass running through them. We live in a tiny terraced house which the estate agents describe as a workman's cottage, but Lyn goes up to London every day and works in a cramped and noisy office in the city.'

'I can't imagine *that*,' said Molly. 'You could never cage Lyn up.'

'He works for Matthew, actually. In fact, the house is Matthew's, too. He bought it very cheap and doesn't intend to sell until the market improves. He let us live there in return for doing it up for him — you know, painting and plastering and . . .'

'Well, you'll hardly need a workman's cottage *now*,' Mick cut in. 'When you've got a place like Hernhope. I presume it goes to Lyn as Hester's only son? Thomas left her everything, you know. Did you ever find the Will?'

'No.' Jennifer put her fork down. The whole subject of whether they stayed or whether they left was fraught with problems. All the Bertrams naturally assumed that they would stay, if for no other reason than the fact that Wintertons had lived up here for centuries and people hated change. Yet Lyn had been ailing and uneasy since the funeral. She kept suggesting they return to Cobham, where at least they would be removed from all those shadowy lives and memories which clogged the house like cobwebs, three hundred miles away from the grave he refused to visit and yet kept digging up in nightmares. But every time she tried to fix a date for their return, he just went silent, and if she changed her tack and made tentative plans for renovating Hernhope or centring their life there, then he snapped at her as a dreamer and a fool.

'Perhaps Hester didn't *make* a Will,' said Chris.

'She did. Lyn's sure of that.' Jennifer forked in a mouthful of chicken. He had told her about the Will before their marriage, yet now he disliked her even mentioning it. Strange how little he seemed to care about his property, whereas Matthew would have engaged a team of bloodhounds if a legacy were at stake.

'Have *you* got a cow?' asked Rory, bored with Wills. 'One of those ones in Cobham, on the bypass?'

Everybody laughed.

'No, I'm afraid we haven't,' said Jennifer. 'I don't know where we'd keep it. We've only got a tiny garden and that's crammed full of bulbs. We do have an allotment, though, which is the nearest we get to farming, I suppose. We grow all our own vegetables and soft fruit in the summer and . . .'

'You don't mean to tell me Lyn Winterton turns his hand to *gardening*?' Nan again, voice jabbing like the pins.

41

'He's very good at it.' Jennifer tried to defend her husband. 'Things grow for him when they sulk or wilt for me.' She saw Lyn's lean strong hands, grubby from the soil, bedding out begonias, then stopping a moment to grope her thigh or touch her nipples through her tee-shirt. She sometimes feared that was all they had in common — hoeing onion beds, debudding blackcurrants, groping. There was so much else she couldn't share with him. Lyn had visions, nightmares, spiritual crises, revelations, crippling stomach pains, when she had only minor domestic problems like meringues which flopped or frayed stair carpet. She had married Lyn because he was all the things she wasn't — clever, angry, artistic, anguished, gaunt. Even at her Church of England day school she had always admired the geniuses and rebels, those Higher Souls who dazzled or defied when she could only plod. She had carried their books for them, offered to clean their bikes or do their shopping. That way, some of their glory and their *angst* had rubbed against her own soul. It was much the same with Lyn. Except sometimes she felt exhausted by trying to cope with him or even understand him. Easier, really, to have married a stolid and un-complicated Mick, a man who needed only simple things like clean socks and hot meals, and confined his talk to forage costs or stock improvement. Even now, Mick was deep in discussion with his shepherd about the morning's work, Colin and Paddy chipping in to mention tricky births or feeding problems. She ought to show some interest. There were other things in life besides missing Wills and moody husbands. She waited for Josh to finish, his slow halting voice stumbling on the longer words as if they were boulders in a field.

'Er . . . how many lambs are born each year?' she asked. She knew almost nothing about sheep. They all looked much the same to her. The men had turned to stare at her. She still felt shy of them. Her own father had been a minor civil servant who commuted to the City from their gentrified Sussex village and always wore dark suits. He had never mixed with farm-ing people, never grown so much as a Brussels sprout. Their garden had been mainly crazy-paving with little clumps of lobelia and alyssum alter-nated with scarlet salvias.

'Well, close on fifteen million are born in Britain as a whole,' said Mick, shovelling in the last of his potatoes. 'On this farm, it's more like seven or eight hundred. You don't get so many twins up here as in the valley, and almost no triplets. It's a tougher life in the hills and the ewes have their work cut out to feed *one* lamb, let alone three. One or two of them can't feed at all. Or won't. Josh had a problem-mum this morning. Refused to have any-thing to do with her lamb at all.'

'What d'you do then?'

'You can pen them up together and try to bond them. But sheep can be stubborn creatures, and if they still refuse, then it's best to set the lamb on to another ewe — one that's lost its own lamb or has plenty of milk for two.' Mick wiped his mouth on his hand and pushed his empty plate away.

42

Jennifer still had half a chicken left. 'But don't they know it's not their own?'

'There are ways of fooling them. It's the smell that counts, you see. The ewe knows her lamb by its smell, so if she's just given birth, you can rub the mucous from her new-born lamb all over the motherless one. Or tie the two lambs in a sack together before presenting them both to the mother. That seems to do the trick. If her own lamb's dead, it's best to skin the little blighter and drape its fleece on the new one. I've even known a shepherd rub ewe and lamb with best Scotch whisky until they fairly reek of it, then pen them up together. Frankly, I wouldn't waste it! Once the lamb has suckled the ewe and then excreted her milk, it seems to smell OK to her and she'll accept it as her own. Mind you, there's always the . . .'

'Have *you* got any children, Jenny?' Ruth asked, interrupting her father and rocking on her chair.

Jennifer torpedoed the tidy pile of peas she had heaped in the centre of her plate. 'Er . . . no,' she said. 'Not *yet*,' she added, and then regretted it as she saw Chris glancing at her stomach. She had made it sound as if she were expecting. Not much hope, with Lyn the way he was. Ever since their wedding she had been gently nudging him towards the idea of a family, but he went on buying Durex Extra-Safe in dozen packets. Even now he'd dispensed with them, he still contrived to have his sex without the risk of babies. The first time, it had intrigued her — that violent hurting back way, where pain and force were all mixed up with some new forbidden excitement, but now she was beginning to dislike it. He was doing it too often — seemed to have forgotten there was any other way of making love. Was it love at all, or some pent-up lust or anger released by Hester's death? How could he love her when she wanted a child so much and he wouldn't even consider one? She was twenty-four already — young, maybe — but she sometimes felt much older. Her father had died when she was just thirteen, and she had gone straight from child to black. She was still Chief Mourner and Mother's Supporter when Lyn was introduced to her, and she had moved from her mother's tissue-papered home to Matthew's tutelage. There had never been a time between for discos, giggles, rave-ups, sharing flats or trying jobs, experimenting with life and liberty. Children would be life. She had never seen them as constraint and inconvenience, as some other women did, but as a challenge and fulfilment. She sometimes feared it was Matthew who kept them barren. It wasn't that she didn't like Lyn's brother — admire and respect him even — but he somehow took them over, prevented them from flowering except as forced and grafted budlets in his nursery. She felt desperate on occasion, especially in the spring, when every other creature seemed to be broody and breeding, only she sterile and frustrated.

'You don't mind if we start on the pudding, do you?' Molly was already stacking plates. 'The men can't stop too long, you see. This weather's so grand, they like to take advantage of it. It could be snow tomorrow.'

'Surely not?' Jennifer took a sip of cider. It was stifling inside, sun blazing through the windows, heat blasting from the range.

'Oh, yeah,' said Mick. 'This sun's unusual. Last year we were lambing in six feet of snow and howling blizzards. We lost a third of all our lambs. That's rare, of course, but you have to be prepared for almost anything.'

Jennifer laid her fork down. How precarious life was up here. Her father's job had been utterly predictable. The steady increment each year, the four-square pension plan, the plodding progress towards a slightly larger office or marginally longer leave. Snow and blizzard might do their worst, but all they affected was the 8.02 to Charing Cross, or the journey home from the annual office party. Up here, they could demolish a farm, ruin a family, bankrupt a man like Thomas Winterton. Jennifer stacked her plate with the rest. She hadn't finished yet, but Nan was already serving out the gooseberry pie, crust stained with burnt-on juices and blackened round the edge.

Ruth grabbed her helping and submerged it under half a pound of sugar. No one told her to stop, or pass the sugar to others first, or not start eating until everyone else was served. It was so different from Matthew's house. Nan believed in discipline, but she was more or less ignored. The children still grabbed and jostled and shouted. They were such happy, easy kids, not stiff and submerged in rules as Matthew's were.

If she and Lyn could somehow stay up here, then Matthew's power would fade. There were other kinds of power — Molly's, for example. Molly rarely raised her voice, yet she ruled the house and kept the farm together. She was its centre, heart and pivot. Although she was always busy, she still managed to enjoy her work, never thought in terms of women's rights or oppression, nor counted her hours or begrudged her lack of pay.

Jennifer envied her. Back in Cobham, many of the women were bored and discontented, their husbands out of the house from eight till eight, their sparse and well-spaced children absent at boarding schools. Apart from one or two small farms, and their own shabby little backstreet which Matthew hoped would soon be redeveloped, Cobham was an expensive, exclusive suburb where coffee mornings or bridge parties were the norm. Jennifer had never felt she quite belonged there. She wasn't plush enough. Matthew's street was shunned by most of the 'village' where bay trees and burglar alarms stood guard outside double garages and neo-Tudor beams. Their do-it-yourself interior and junk-shop furnishings had never been accepted. She and Lyn would fit in better here, where Molly's rooms bore battle-scars from claws and paws and children.

The dogs were rampant again, barking and circling as the men got up from the table and prepared to return to the fields. Molly was filling Thermoses, fetching anoraks. She finally closed the door on them and poured coffee for the rest.

'I'm sorry it's a bit stewed,' she said 'I can't turn that damn range low enough. That's why I burnt the pie.'

Jennifer turned to glance at the highly-polished range with its two separate ovens and little fiddly knobs and handles, all meticulously black-leaded. 'I'd *love* a stove like that at home — all hot and bright and crackling, instead of my stiff white dead electric one which looks more like a fridge.'

'You're just a romantic, love. That thing's more bother than it's worth. I'd swap with you tomorrow! There's no mains electricity at all up here, and we didn't even get our generator until 1959. It was a real red-letter day when they installed it, I can tell you. Though I must admit I was scared stiff of the stuff at first — wouldn't even turn a switch on, in case it blew the place up. I'd stand trembling over the toaster, ready to run a mile!'

1959 — Jennifer had been only one year old then — an all-electric baby. Molly already had two babies of her own, lighting them to bed with oil-lamps, wringing out their nappies on an ancient wooden mangle, pressing cot-sheets and nightdresses with flat irons heated on the range. And Hester in the next house up, sitting in the gloom with Lyn . . .

'I suppose you all . . . knew Hester?'

'As far as you could *ever* know her,' Nan rejoined, scooping pastry fragments from the table. 'She kept herself to herself, you see. When Thomas was alive, I was in and out of that house like one of the family, but once she took over, I might as well have been a total stranger. All wrong, it was. You Wintertons have always been our nearest neighbours. The two farms shared boundaries once. Thomas and my husband often worked together, helped each other out. That's the way up here. Everyone depends on everybody else. You couldn't survive otherwise.'

Molly pulled her chair back, stretched her legs. 'Nan used to help Susannah — you know, Matthew's poor young mother.'

'Well, someone had to, didn't they? She was a fancy little minx, and frail with it. Never run a farm in her life. I was only six or seven years older, but I had farming in my blood. Her father was a financier — something grand like that. She needed someone practical around. When she died I had a bairn myself, only two months older. I fed them both, you know, until the housekeeper arrived.'

Jennifer took a sip of coffee. 'You mean . . . Hester?' Strange to hear Lyn's all-powerful mother referred to as a housekeeper. Stranger still to think that Nan had suckled Matthew. Hester had stayed nearly fifty years. Changed housekeeper to wife. Swapped Matthew for her own son.

Molly was already on her feet again, clearing the table. 'It can't have been easy for Hester, taking the place of a young and pretty teenager everyone adored. Forgive me, Jenny, but your mother-in-law was rather . . . plain herself and a bit severe. And people always saw her as an alien.'

'But I thought Lyn said she was born up here.'

'Well, Fernfield. That's still Northumberland, but it's a good way south, you know. ''Local'' up here means not much more than a ten-mile radius. Anything more is ''foreign'', especially in the thirties when transport was less good. Anyway, Hester had been working down in London, so they regarded her as a "townie". And she never spoke about herself or had visits from her family or . . .'

'Look, let me help with those.' Jennifer picked up a sodden tea-towel and joined Nan at the sink where she was pummelling plates and dishes. 'What was Matthew like as a baby, Nan?'

'Small and noisy. No, don't use that. There's a clean one in the drawer. He was that puny, he looked like a skinned rabbit. My bairn weighed almost double at the same age.'

'Matthew — *small*?'

'Oh yes, and sickly. Couldn't keep his feeds down. I'll say this for your mother-in-law. She had a picky child on her hands. He didn't even sleep through the night until he was almost eighteen months.'

Jennifer stared at Nan's gnarled and bony hands. Could Matthew ever have been sickly, ever have been a bairn at all — all six-foot-steel of him with his computer-brain and that everlasting sceptre in his hands?

Molly was chopping onions for a home-made soup. '*I* remember Matthew. He was fourteen when he left here and I was eight or nine. He wasn't small then. I was secretly in love with him. He was very tall and lanky with dark hair.'

'What made him leave?'

'What had he to stay for?' Nan was tackling the saucepans now — six or seven of them. 'He'd lost both his parents. Hester had married his father just before he died. I doubt if Matthew approved of that. He was quite a little snob, you know. She hadn't much time for him, anyway, once the new bairn was born. And the farm was a write-off, more or less. Money was short, the house was dark and cold. I'd have had him here, but Hester wouldn't hear of it. In the end, one of Thomas's fancy relatives turned up from London and took Matthew off her hands. Offered to pay his fees at boarding school — even kept him in the holidays. No one saw him up here after that.'

'Did Hester . . . mind? I mean, if she'd looked after him since he was a baby — fourteen years or so, then surely she must have . . .'

Nan rested her dish-mop for a moment. 'I doubt if she'd *time* to mind, she was that busy. She had debts, you see, and it was quite a struggle to pay them off and run the house and . . . She made extra cheese and butter and sold them in the village. And you should have seen her eiderdowns! Real hand-quilted jobs stuffed with feathers from her own ducks. She never asked enough for them, considering how many hours of work they took her. No one saw her much, to tell the truth. She was always stuck at home, sewing or scrimping or cooking. We tried to help, of course, but she cut herself off more or less completely. My husband even offered to buy the farm — combine it with ours and offer her security. She wouldn't even discuss it, so when she went ahead and sold the place to the Forestry, my John lost patience. After that she fobbed everybody off and lived like a recluse. We worried about the lad — your Lyn. We hoped he'd stay and make a go of it up here. But he went Matthew's way.'

Molly was crying from the onions. She mopped her eyes on her pinafore. 'He had to, Nan. There was nothing for him here. No job, no future — not for someone arty.'

Nan sniffed. 'Arty's not what I'd call it.'

'Is it hard to get jobs up here?' Jennifer steered the conversation away from Lyn again. 'I mean, suppose I wanted a job. Do many women work?'

'We never stop,' grinned Molly, straining scum off the stockpot, then turning back to peel and chop some carrots.

'No, I mean jobs outside the home.'

'There aren't any,' snapped Nan. 'And just as well. A woman's got enough to do without . . .'

'It's funny, though,' Molly cut in. 'We may seem far less liberated than you London lot, but in a way, we rule the roost up here. The men can't manage without us — well, not the farmers, anyway. A woman can almost make or break a farm. That's why Hester was so important. Thomas would have more or less gone under without her to support him. She helped with everything — lambing, calving, milking, gardening, making bread and jams and butter, even cheeses. I don't know anyone else who makes their own cheese now. It's too damned fiddly. The skill must have died with her. And then there was all the paperwork. The women often took that on as well. My mother worked every bit as hard. *And* Nan. All the women did.'

'I had six bairns,' said Nan. 'And we didn't even have running water until 1945. Wash-day meant what it said — a whole day put aside for the laundry — not just a quick whirl in a machine. We had to collect rain-water in a butt, heat it on the range, then scrub away by hand with a bar of soap. You have to be dedicated if you farm up here. It isn't just a job, it's a way of life. And now, if you'll excuse me, I'm going to have my forty winks. There wasn't time for naps in my younger days, but now I'm over seventy I reckon I deserve one. Goodbye, my dear. And tell that man of yours it's only the guilty who can't sleep at night.'

She banged the door behind her. Molly grinned. 'She's quite fond of Lyn underneath,' she said. 'Often talks about him. Look, leave all that. Ruth'll do it. Go and put your feet up.'

Jennifer stretched herself out on the sofa. The old Jack Russell, lame and almost blind, padded over and flopped down at her feet. There was more room in the kitchen now. Four of the children had disappeared upstairs. Only Ruth remained, humming as she put the plates away. There was a general hum of satisfaction — cats purring, the chunter of the hens outside, stockpot burbling to itself beside the gently sizzling onions, the rasping snore of the terriers, replete after their lunch.

'Molly . . .' Jennifer said.

'What, love?'

'Could an outsider make a go of it?'

'How d'you mean?'

'Well, live up here. Be accepted. Even if she was one of those . . . aliens from the south?'

Molly laughed. 'Oh, yes. The shepherd's wife at Nettleburn used to live in London. She worked as a check-out girl in Tesco's and the only sheep she ever saw were those in the advertisements for New Zealand lamb stuck over the frozen meats section. She was terrified when she first came up here — said she'd never imagined anywhere so lonely. Yet now she admits she's got more friends than she ever had in a city of seven million.'

Molly had turned the onions off and was heating milk for her shedful of orphan lambs. 'Nan tends to sneer at people like that. Calls them foreigners and says they don't fit in. But one or two of them have made a real success of it, gone back to all the old traditional crafts — quilting, smocking, patchwork, curing bacon, making their own sausages. There's another girl who married the farmer at Biddlehope. She only came up here two years ago, yet she took half the prizes at our local show.'

Jennifer longed to do the same, leave her Cobham neighbours with their gleaming labour-saving homes and start again up here. She already had the skills. She was trained in domestic science, good at sewing, knitting, homemaking. Even Lyn had a feel and flair for gardening. Only one step further to set up a smallholding or market-garden and try to make a living from it. He might well be more contented self-employed and self-sufficient, instead of slaving in the city with Matthew as his task-master. All right, he'd never want six children, but even *one* would be a start. And they could maybe take a lodger in, or let out part of Hernhope to holiday guests. Nice to have more to cook for, a family around her, people dependent on her skills. She had never had sisters or brothers, grandparents or aunts. Just her and her parents becalmed in a small, quiet, cosy home on the commuter-line to London, and — after her father's death — she and her mother cowering in a bungalow with a couple of ageing cocker spaniels. It had been too sheltered, too restrictive. Lyn was as bad — almost a recluse. They must expand, develop, become part of a larger whole, part of a community. Lyn already had a long tradition behind him. He was a native, born and bred here, not an outsider like the girl who worked at Tesco's or the wife at Biddlehope. And she herself would soon fit in. Molly would help — not only as friend and nearest neighbour, but someone she could model her own life on.

She needn't take things too far. Lyn wouldn't want her fat and dowdy, dressed in men's corduroys with cats on every chair. She glanced across at Molly — flour in her hair, rent in her sleeve — splashing milk on to her shoes as she filled five baby bottles for the lambs.

'Want to help me feed them?' Molly asked, heaving her shoulder against the heavy kitchen door. 'Gosh, this sun's amazing! You must have brought it with you.'

Jennifer smiled. Nice that, like an omen. Bringing the sun from London to warm and nurture Hernhope, nurse it back to life. Molly tugged back the bolts on the shed. Four lambs rushed towards her, butting their heads against her legs, reaching for the bottles. The fifth and smallest one lay shivering in the straw.

'That's Sooty. Sweet, isn't he? Black lambs are rare up here, you know. He was only born this morning. Quite a tricky birth, I'm afraid. Mick couldn't save his mother. Want to give him his bottle? Right, go and sit on that bale. You'll be more comfortable there. Now try and coax him to his feet, then hold him firm between your knees. Don't be frightened of him. He's tougher than he looks. No, tilt the bottle more. Good — you've got the hang of it. He's sucking well now.'

Jennifer stroked the tiny furry head, watched the black throat gulping and straining as the white milk dribbled down it. She had never fed a baby. It gave her almost a sense of power — the lamb trusting her, dependent on her, its whole effort and attention focused on her as wet-nurse and provider.

'OK there, Mum?' grinned Molly, who with two bottles in each hand was managing to feed all four remaining lambs at once. Jennifer glanced up at the window set high in the shed, a square of sky with a curve of hill trapped in it. Such space up here, such possibilities. Long hours and hard labour hardly mattered, so long as you had purpose.

'Yes,' she murmured, snuggling the lamb towards her, so that it was almost in her lap. 'Just perfect.'

VI

Snow.

Not falling any longer, just lying dumb and treacherous, the hills like flanks of huge white animals, stunned and shivering where they had collapsed. The forest dark and spiky against the white blinding softness heaped around it. Every window etched with ice. Snow in April, almost May. Snow baffling new-born lambs, muffling new-sown barley, blocking paths, confusing birds, blanking out all landmarks. Jennifer pushed the curtain aside, added her doodle to the etching on the glass, stared out at the blinkered trees, the huddled sheep further down the valley, tiny whitish dots against the whiter hills.

'It's beautiful,' she said.

'*Cold*,' Lyn shivered.

'Look, you go back to bed, darling. You shouldn't be up at all with a temperature. It's higher than it was last night. I wish you'd let me fetch the doctor.'

49

'He'd never get out in this. Nor would you. We're more or less cut off.'

'Cut *off?*' Crazy to be excited when lambs were dying, farmers frantic. It could be hazardous even for Lyn. Supposing he got worse and needed medicines? Supposing their food ran out? She *was* excited. She had never seen snow so all-enveloping — the world changed overnight from green to white, snow with the sun on it, making every smallest crystal flash and shine, dark-winged birds soaring against the whiteness, lending their shadows briefly to the hills. She was concerned for the Bertrams, worried for the farmers, but, secretly, she saw the snow as a bonus, since it would keep Lyn at Hernhope a little longer, stop him running south.

She let the curtain fall, joined him at the fire. The sturdy pine-logs which Mick had cut for them with his chain-saw were a glowing rubble of ash and embers now. Jennifer threw on another log, watched it spit and spark.

'Go easy!' said Lyn. 'We ought to save that fuel. We don't know how long this cold spell's going to last.' Lyn sneezed, coughed, blew. He didn't have a cold. The cold had him — had laid its hands on every part of him — nose, ears, larynx, temples, chest.

'You mean we could be snowed up for *days*?'

'Easily. And if it was January or February, it could even be *weeks*. I remember one winter, the snow was so high we had foxes walking on the roof. And the icicles at the windows got longer and longer, until they hung there like a second pair of curtains, and another year, one of the forestry workers stapled his finger to the fence when he was working in thirty degrees of frost. He was so numb, he didn't even feel it. Actually, I liked it as a boy, because I missed a lot of school. We had to *prepare* for winter, so we didn't starve. Hester bought flour and sugar in hundredweight sacks at the beginning of November, but I remember sometimes dreaming of bananas or treacle toffees or some treat in the shops which might have been on the moon for all we could reach them.' He laughed, which triggered off a protracted fit of coughing. 'Damn! This cold's got worse. D'you realise, Jennifer, they're still basking in spring sunshine in the south? The minute it thaws, I want to get back home.'

Jennifer frowned. *This* was home, now, wasn't it? She had done everything she could to make it so — scrubbed the scum and stain off wood and stone, opened all the windows (some stiff in the joints and grumbling as she heaved), replaced the smell of damp with the tang of polish, lit all the rooms with daffodils. At first it had been suspicious — sulked, creaked, fobbed her off. But she went on quietly cleaning and slowly the house tiptoed up towards her and ate out of her hand. She still felt Hester's presence — her footsteps in the passage, her breath trapped in the joists, her fingerprints blurring walls and furniture even after she'd scrubbed. She was the one who had washed the corpse and laid the body out, yet even while she was brushing the hair and coaxing the stiffening limbs into a clean nightgown, she had somehow been aware of Hester watching her. She had feared to close those eyes — *Lyn*'s eyes. It would be like extinguishing both son and mother, mother-in-law

50

and husband. Yet, once she had plucked up courage enough to do it, she realised that Hester was inextinguishable. She walked the house, watched the hills, sat down to meals with them — not as a ghost or restless spirit, but as someone who simply belonged there — always would.

She tried to propitiate her, bow to her taste and judgement, transform the house only slowly and with tact. Even if they remained up here, she would never replace the huge old-fashioned bath with its four enamelled feet, or the ancient cast-iron cisterns and polished wooden seats in both the lavatories. Hester would hate fibreglass or plastic, modern low-flush toilets, prissy pastel baths.

Lyn was also aware of Hester, but more distressingly. His mother barged into his dreams, blamed him for her death, kept him continually cold and small and shivering. He was constantly making plans to leave, fretting about the Cobham house or allotment, worrying about the work he had promised Matthew. Yet, for all his fears, he still hadn't run away. In fact, he had started making a garden — removing stones, turning the soil, marking out a border. It was covered up with snow now, but things were growing underneath (flowers, hope, a future?). He had been waiting for the swallows, even *drawing* swallows — tangled lines against the blur of hill. Jennifer had pinned his sketches on the wall. He ripped them down again, looked almost scared.

'Don't *do* that, Jennifer.'

'Why not?'

'They're . . . not good enough. I'm out of practice.'

She glanced at him now, huddled on the sofa, rough grey coat buttoned over blue pyjamas. He had refused to let her pack his dressing-gown. 'It's not worth it, Jennifer. We won't be staying long.'

Longer than they'd planned, though; longer still if the snow was on their side.

Lyn blew his nose, mopped his eyes, ripped open a second box of Kleenex. 'We must get back. We're just messing around up here. If the roads are clear, we'd better leave on Saturday.'

He had said that last weekend. She had even started packing. He unpacked the cases himself, not systematically, just bits and pieces, as he needed them. By Wednesday they were almost empty again.

'But you might still be feverish, darling. Why don't we wait and see.'

'I can't talk any more, I'm sorry. My throat feels like splintered glass.'

'Can I get you something — a gargle or a . . .?'

'No thanks.'

'I saw one of those inhaler things when I was in the cellar. Why don't I go and . . .'

'Jennifer, I asked you not to poke around the cellar.'

'I didn't. I only went to see if I could find another lamp. There's loads of stuff down there. Someone ought to sort it out.'

'No.'

51

'D'you remember those inhalers, Lyn? Or were they called vaporisers? You know, metal things with a nightlight under them and a little hole in the top. My mother lit one in my bedroom every time I had a cold. There was some antiseptic stuff inside, which puffed out of the hole and made the room all smelly. You must have seen them, surely.'

'No. Never heard of them.'

'Well, there's one downstairs. I saw it. It's an old one, but it probably still works. Why don't I fetch it for you?'

'No.'

It was an irritable, impatient 'no' which could have meant 'yes'. She always had to interpret all Lyn's 'no's'. Had Hester done the same? Found it equally exasperating? She sometimes felt a bond with Hester, the two of them united through the foibles of her son.

'I think I'll go back to bed. You coming, Jennifer? We can put the fire out then. Save some fuel.'

'It's only eight o'clock, darling. I'll stay a while if you don't mind. I feel restless, anyway. I'll only keep you awake.'

He would keep *her* awake. Had done all week. It wasn't just the coughing — he was restless, feverish, shouting in his sleep. She should feel sorry for him. The trouble was, the sorrow was tinged with anger. Unfair irrational anger that he wasn't a Mick Bertram who could run a farm, or sire a family. Resentment at their constant sterile sex. She had been strange herself after her mother's death, bursting into tears in shops and streets, hoarding her mother's shabby useless things like her hairbrush and her limp unfinished knitting. She had cried so much, her eyes had puffed and swollen for a week. Lyn hadn't cried at all, yet. Perhaps that was the trouble. His grief was still inside him, corked like a sour fermenting liquid in a bottle. He needed cleansing and release. He couldn't plan for the future because the black-banded weight of the past was pressing down on top of him.

She was glad he had gone upstairs. The place felt more relaxed now. Molly had lent her a lamp and a pile of cushions, and although the room was still sombre and dark-toned, it no longer looked forbidding. The newly polished brass gleamed and rippled in the pouncing light of the fire. She threw another log on — almost *wanted* to waste them — to be a squanderer for a change. She had filled the bowls with nuts and apples, arranged beech twigs in a vase, their brave green burst of leaf contradicting the wintry snow outside. Lyn had closed the curtains to keep the weather out, but it wasn't even dark yet. She drew them back again and let the hills surge into the sitting-room. The sun was setting — fire on ice, blood on bandages. Its raw red disc blazed so fiercely against the white and grey around it, it looked as if it had dropped from another stranger planet where everything was hotter and more violent. The sky was flaming with it — gold and scarlet streaked across the clouds, paling to pink and topaz in its reflection on the snow.

Jennifer pulled on her coat and boots and went outside. She yearned to be part of all that radiance, lose her pale quiet self in scarlet flame. She sometimes felt so *ordinary*. Other people could write odes to snow or set sunsets to music. All she could do was gawp at them. She hardly felt the cold. She was watching a last ray of light kindle every fold of hills until their gilded peaks leapt into the sky. She had never seen a sky as huge as that. There were no buildings to shut it off, no tower-blocks to diminish it. Hernhope was the last man-made thing before infinity. The house was set high, nearly a thousand feet, Molly had told her, but it wasn't just a matter of feet and inches. They were higher in some more vital way. Words kept forming in her head, dusty biblical words with cobwebs in their corners. '*Lord, it is well that we are here.*'

Except for her wedding, she hadn't been to church since childhood, but Hester's funeral had set up echoes in her head, words from half-forgotten services, bits of gospels, fragments of old hymns. What was it called, that time when Christ took His disciples up on to a high mountain, His face shining like the sun and His garments dazzling as if they were made of snow? The Transfiguration, wasn't it? Something about Moses and Elijah, though she wasn't sure how they came into it. But all the rest was there — the sun, the snow, the mountain, even the shining. Everything was shining. And she was part of it. She might be ordinary, but she still groped towards those strange sacred feelings she imagined Lyn must burn with. She had always been praised as sensible and practical, the sort of person who could cope in a crisis and kept her feet planted firmly on the ground. Yet there was another secret part of her which no one ever saw. Even as a child, she had yearned to be someone different — a princess or a snowbird who could soar beyond her Sussex cul-de-sac.

'*And a voice spoke to them as if from a cloud.*' The words were coming back now, the scene surging up from some long-forgotten Sunday school. '*This is my beloved son in whom I am well pleased.*' She could almost hear the voice herself. The cloud was there, hanging gold and huge and scarlet with the sun trapped hot inside it. Yet no one could have spoken. There was only the sky, the snow, the dumb and muffled trees. Was it *Hester*'s voice she was hearing on the hills? Had she ever said 'beloved son'? She craved a son of her own. Children were less moody and closed than husbands, less grey and formal than fathers. Perhaps it was the only relationship where you were really one with someone, flesh of their flesh. What could she do if Lyn went on refusing?

'*And Peter said, "Lord, it is well that we are here."*' It *was* well. She had some deep instinctive feeling that they were meant to stay. She had only to keep still, not to doubt or run. Everything was planned — the sun at first to warm and lull, and then the snow to wall them up and hold them, give her time to turn Lyn into a father, the house into a home. However much Lyn jibbed, this was where his roots were. Only here could he be calmed and healed, linked with his ancestors, certain of his future.

Hester had conceived him when she was almost past the age for child-bearing, and only months before her husband died. He was thus a special child — twice special. Had Hester waited just a year or two, or Thomas's

53

death come sooner, then he would simply not have existed. She had never thought like that before. It was as if Hester were giving her some insight, pointing out that Lyn's birth was not simply a mistake or an embarrassment, but something intended and important. It was partly a question of carrying on the line. Matthew had done that already — four times over — but Matthew had moved to London, wrenched the Winterton name and heritage away from its roots, set it up in a city where it would only shrink and wither. If Hernhope was to survive, then she and Lyn must stay. True, Lyn had run away himself, but he hadn't had a wife then, hadn't been accepted. She could help him now, support him, pioneer some different way of life which would bring them both peace and purpose. Hester herself was showing them the way. She had survived debt and bereavement, hostility and hazard. They could do the same.

The light was fading now. The scarlet shriek of the sun had left only an echo behind, a last whisper of pink and silver before night closed all around it. Towards the east, the hills were grey and shadowed, the sky swooping down to kidnap them with cloud. Colour seeped out and cold crept in, jabbing its icy fingers through her clothes. There were long streaked furrows on the snow, more grey in them than gold now. Tiny noises stained and blurred the silence, so faint they were only shadows of shadows themselves.

She turned to face the house which was fading into the fading hills around it, save for the sheen of snow and one dim lamp glowing through the window. The bedroom was in darkness. She hoped Lyn was asleep, not lying waiting for her, too hoarse and cold to sleep. She crept back in, tugged off her boots, switched off the light in the sitting-room. The fire still lit up the room, as if all the red and gold of the vanished sun had been thrown into the grate. She damped it down, then went upstairs to Lyn. He was lying diagonally across the bed with half the covers tangled on the floor, breathing hoarsely and irregularly with little shuddering gasps puncturing the in-breaths. He had drawn the curtains, but the moon had slunk between them and was playing chequers on his face.

He looked sickly with his eyes shut. His eyes were the feature that made him come alive. They were large, dark and angry in a face quiet and plain without them. She could never have described their shade — that burnt, blackish, brackish lava colour — assumed it was unique in all the world until she saw his mother's. His brows were fine, but often kept drawn down as if he were warding off the world or shutting out the sun. His eyelashes were lavish like a child's — a sort of luxury in a face otherwise ascetic — a pale, almost sallow face, with too many hollows in it. He had straight soft hair — child's hair — the same uncertain brown as Matthew's sons. Matthew's hair was darker, yet both men had some slightly foreign look about them, as if they were two black lambs in a field and flock of white.

Jennifer longed to take Lyn in her arms and reassure him. He looked feverish, uncomfortable — younger than he was, as if all that he had felt and suffered had gone inwards to his soul and left his face untouched by it. His

54

hands were long and thin, the fingers fidgety and nervous. Even now, they were twitching in his sleep. Although he was a light-boned man, lean and almost gaunt, when he was up he seemed to tower above her, be living on a different plane. She could never own him, never understand him, was frightened sometimes that she had even married him.

When she had first met him, he had been wary and unpredictable. Men in books courted you with flowers and compliments. Lyn had wooed her with his strangeness, his unexpected passions about things, his endearing combination of shyness and intensity. He never kissed her, never asked her questions. The nevers grew into a need. A need to stop him brooding, make him happy, make him kiss. She loved him for the things he wouldn't do, but once they were married, the nevers grew more menacing. He kissed her now (incomparably), but supposing he never wished to own a house or sire a child or break free of brother Matthew? The first year hadn't mattered. It was an escapade, a joyride, an escape from both their mothers. Now, ironically, both those mothers were dead and it was Lyn himself who seemed to tie her down. She had to admit a certain streak of restlessness — resentment even, a longing for a proper home and children.

He was breathing painfully, a hoarse rasping sound which almost hurt her own throat. She would go and fetch the vaporiser. Despite his refusals, he probably wished he had tried it, but was too proud to change his mind. She crept downstairs again, stood at the cellar door. The light from the window opposite sent splintered shadows down the steep stone steps. She shivered, glad she had kept her coat on. It was damp in the cellar, a different and more dishonest cold from the bracing one outside, one which lured you down and then slowly squeezed in after you and stripped all the warmth and comfort from your limbs. There was a smell of must and age, as if all the centuries had crumbled into a pot pourri, made not of petals but of time.

She loved cellars, attics, glory-holes — anywhere where history crouched in corners and cobwebs wreathed old lives. Hester's house had history stamped right into it, like letters in a stick of rock. The Scots had burned and pillaged it when they had skirmished from the border. The Wintertons (more Wintertons) had shored it up again. There had been a fire in 1780, a major rebuilding in 1822. Bits and pieces had been added or subtracted until, when Thomas took it over, it was a sturdy, self-opinionated house with farm buildings and outhouses clinging to its skirts. Hester had pared it down again, allowing barns and stables to fall into disrepair or be annexed by the Forestry. But the cellar remained inviolate, safe beneath the staircase in the very centre and foundation of the house. Any passing history had dripped and dribbled into it, left stains and footprints there.

Cellars were unusual in the hills. Even when it was possible to dig them out of the shallow rocky soil, the need was seldom felt for them. The weather was too raw to justify cold storage. Yet this dark and secret cellar was somehow in keeping with Hester and her house.

There was no electric light down there, so Jennifer fetched a paraffin lamp

55

and watched its pale sickly beam turn humped and shadowy shapes into living objects. A dark blur became a baby's cradle, hand-carved and set on rockers. She touched one end and set it rocking. Huge shadows lurched across the wall. Beside it stood a wooden butter-churn, shaped like a beer barrel and mounted on a stand, its handle wreathed in cobwebs. There were more exotic cobwebs all along one wall, little specks of flaking plaster trapped in them like snowflakes and glistening in the lamplight. She had only been in the cellar once before, and then Lyn had called her back. It was as if he wanted everything to fossilise at the time of Hester's death, nothing to be touched or salvaged.

Surely an old tin vaporiser couldn't hurt? It was there, where she had left it, in a crate of books and jumble. It wasn't even as dusty as the other things around it, and there was a box of matches ready in the carton. Had Hester used it for a recent cold? Hester suddenly loomed nearer — coughing, shivering, left alone to die. They should have insisted that she came down south to live with them, but you couldn't insist with Hester, any more than with Lyn.

Jennifer set the vaporiser on an upturned box, checked the wick, poured old and sticky fluid into the container. The first match didn't strike. She tried a third, a fourth, a fifth, went on striking automatically. The tenth match took her by surprise. She jumped as its fierce and tiny flame cut a halo through the gloom. She lit the nightlight, placed the metal cover over. In only minutes, the powerful antiseptic smell was seeping through the cellar, nervous shadows from the nightlight entangled with the softer ones which fluttered round the lamp.

Strange that Lyn had never seen a vaporiser. She had always assumed they were an essential part of childhood like Sunday School or jellies. He had never had those either. She had made him a jelly in a rabbit mould on their first wedding anniversary. He had been so enchanted, he'd refused to put a spoon into it, and it sat there on the sideboard slowly shrinking. In the end, it had sprouted greyish mould. Her childhood had fairly *glowed* with jellies, fat Victoria sponges with little silver balls on, warm and sticky gingerbread men.

As children, they'd been far apart, both in age and geography, yet they had both been only children; both had old, careful mothers who kept the rest of the world away, as being too hazardous in her case and too invasive in his. He had never seen his father; and even before hers had died, he had been distant and unapproachable. Neither of them had had anyone *young* around, no one carefree or impetuous. Was that why they had married — to reassure each other, to carry on that same silent suspicious way of life? It was time they changed it for a noisy, normal family — pets, children, friends — challenge, even risk.

She ought to go up to him now, take the vaporiser, settle down to sleep. Yet she was reluctant to leave the cellar, to lie quiet and rigid in a narrow bed beside a restless husband when there was so much to explore. She glanced around her. Trunks and boxes veiled with dust, abandoned furniture, piles of newspapers. Stone shelves with cobwebby bottles stacked across them — perhaps old and priceless claret; a hat-stand made of antlers, a wooden milking-stool. She could spend hours down here, prying and probing, rescuing things, restoring them. There was a tattered patchwork bedspread she perhaps could mend and clean, a stone hot-water bottle — that would do for Lyn; a set of wooden butter moulds. Even solid everyday objects looked exotic in the shadows.

She picked up the lamp and moved a little further in, where the ceiling crouched down lower and the shadows were double-layered. Two leggy spiders scuttled across the floor. At the very end of the cellar was the largest chest of all, battered but still handsome, a wooden one, maroon with metal edges. On top of it stood a cardboard box full of broken coat-hangers. She lugged it off, revealing a brighter patch of colour underneath where it had protected the chest from grime. She tried the lid. It was locked. She shouldn't really force it. She felt guilty suddenly, snooping around the bowels of Hester's house. Except it was *their* house now. Even without the Will, it would go to Lyn as Hester's only son and heir, and if it were his, then it must be partly hers as well. It wasn't that she was greedy or acquisitive, just craved for continuity, something with roots, history, solidity, something which Matthew hadn't bought and parcelled out to them.

She fiddled with the clasps, which remained firmly shut. She remembered seeing an old wire coat-hanger flung on one of the tea-chests. She went to fetch it, wrenching it out of shape so she could use it as a tool to force the lock. It wasn't easy, but it gave at last. The lid creaked open and she smelt the fusty mouldering smell which gets trapped in old school halls or lingers in the folds of ancient velvet curtains or is sold at auctions or pressed between the pages of old books. The chest was packed with books, old and faded ones with leather covers. She picked up the very top one, blew the dust from it. *Annals of the Ancient County of Northumbria* by the Reverend Matthew Winterton. (Winterton again. And even a Matthew. *Reverend* Matthew — he'd love them all to call him that!) A bulky vellum-covered book with yellowing engravings of churches and castles, pele towers and sheep stells. She sat on the floor, clutched her coat more tightly round her, opened the book and read. 'The Northumbrian character is a proud and lawless one — a product of his history. His shire has long been a scarred and bloody battle-ground where it was not just a wasteland. He is more often a raider or a rebel than a settled church-goer.' Jennifer smiled. Her husband matched his shire.

She leafed through the pages, looking at the pictures. Except for the forests, the landscape had hardly changed. She stopped. There was a drawing of Hernhope, spreading in all its glory as a farm. She hardly recognised it. It was not only so much larger, then, but more important and alive. Animals were grazing all around it, children playing on the steps, men with buckets in the yard — all frozen in immobility and yet still busy, still involved. She longed to put it back like that, colour it in as she had done as a child with the black and white engravings in her Bible. Flesh out the children and the animals, add Lyn himself sketching in the fields.

She was glad Lyn had started drawing. It wasn't just the swallows he had sketched — he had made studies of the landscape, hurling it on to paper, distorting all its lines. She didn't understand why he had made it look so threatening, the hills rearing up to crush him, the sky darker than the trees. Yet she felt excited by his work, the swift nervous way the charcoal streaked across the paper, sometimes snapping, so that he swore and used the stub. The results were nothing like these gentle tranquil pictures in the *Annals of Northumbria*, with their smiling skies and quiet and well-tamed fields.

She snapped the book shut and picked up the next one, a leather-bound journal with *Game Book* tooled on the front in gold italic. Inside were handwritten records of all the local shoots arranged in columns, each signed underneath in wavering copperplate. She tried to make the name out — R.B. Winterton. Was that Lyn's father? No, he was a 'T', and later. This was dated 1896. There were little spaces for all the different game birds — grouse, partridge, teal, pigeon, pheasant. She remembered the pheasants dazzling across the road the day they travelled up here; Lyn telling her they were bred only for the shoot. It no longer seemed so cruel. R.B.'s gentle, kindly, sometimes humorous comments made it just an innocent diversion.

She could see the damp burnished mornings, mist on the hills and the trees beginning to turn, Mr Winterton striding out with his guns and gamebags, then returning home for a nap and partridge pie. September shivered into Christmas. Chilblains, blizzards, warm corpses steaming in the frozen air, Mrs Winterton ready with hot punch and plucking knife.

She leafed towards the later entries — pages scanning decades — nineties, nineteen hundreds, twenties, thirties. Now it was 1934 and 'R.B.' had changed to 'T'. The writing was smaller, almost spiteful. '*A very poor season for everything,*' he had written. '*The weather wet and inclement for weeks on end. Hardly worth going out at all.*'

That was the year his wife Susannah had died, Matthew just a bundle in a shawl. Thomas's bereavement had affected everything, even the game birds and the weather. Had he come in from the shooting and found only Hester scowling and aloof? No welcome from a young and pretty wife. After that bitter scribble there were no more entries. Grief had silenced Thomas Winterton's guns. Nor had his children taken them up again. Both sons had slipped away.

Strange how little Lyn ever mentioned his father. True, he had never known him, but didn't he ever *think* about him, speculate, wonder how things might have been had Thomas lived? It was as if Hester had loomed so large in his life, there wasn't room for a father, not even thoughts of him.

Jennifer rummaged in the trunk again, picked out a *Letter Book*, copies of correspondence in staid and careful copperplate, all of them relating to the farm. Records of rents and tenancies, interest rates and wages. As she read, Hernhope surged and expanded, prospered, shivered, fell.

She was suddenly greedy to be part of all this history, to keep it going, further it. She *was* already part of it — a Winterton, the same name which had marched through all those letters, collected all those monies, shot and stalked and hunted, given birth and died. It was as if these books and records were underlining what she had felt already, out in the sunset and the snow. Almost like a calling — something urging her to stay here, add their story to the house, carry on its history and tradition, make Hernhope live again. Why should the name and house become a ruin? She had seen other ruins dotted on the hills, once cherished houses left to crumble, weeds choking them, snow spitting in their faces. Hernhope was too ancient and too precious to end as a heap of stones.

All the history of the house was there beneath her hands — ledgers and account books, annals and anthologies, catalogues from shops and sales, manuals for machinery — endless records joining her to all Lyn's ancestors, linking her with Hester. Her hands were grimed and gritty, a soft dust had settled on her clothes. The insistent reek of antiseptic fumes had filled the whole cellar now like some vital elixir, fusing her childhood with her future. She was cold, cramped, uncomfortable, yet she hardly cared. It was as if she had entered some strange, soundless other century.

She dug deeper into the chest. At the very bottom, jammed beneath a Bible so large she could barely lift it, was a bulky package wrapped in newspaper. She dragged it out, feeling excitement mixed with guilt. It had obviously been hidden there. She fumbled with the wrappings, revealed a large brown envelope sealed with sticky tape and a cache of notebooks strung together, some with stiff-backed mottled covers, others cheap and scraggy like school jotters. She opened the one on top. Every page was covered with close-packed script in a bold and vigorous hand. She recognised that hand. It was younger, firmer, but still the distinctive writing she had seen on Hester's Christmas letters. Only Hester gave her l's those strange bulging loops, crossed her t's with that over-emphatic stroke as if she were angry with them.

The only gaps in the writing were those between one day's date and the next. The dates were written out in full, and underlined. The thing must be a diary — Hester's diary — books and books of it. She shouldn't pry. Diaries were always private and Hester sounded the most strictly private person ever born. She must return the books to their wrappings and go upstairs to Lyn. She had been so deep in his past, she had almost forgotten he was a living person with a streaming cold.

Her eye trespassed down the page, took in a date or two. 1914. So this was a *child*'s diary — well, still half and half a child. Hester was as old as the century, so she had been fourteen when she wrote it. That made it different, surely. It was probably only some school thing anyway, some trifling teenage outpouring. It couldn't hurt to read a bit.

'*31st October 1914. A telegram arrived this morning. My brother has been killed in Ypres. I cried all day. My mother appeared at dinner, but could not speak. I had already*

59

bought his birthday present. He would have been nineteen in a fortnight.'

Jennifer stared in horror at the page. An eighteen-year-old stripling snuffed out in the mud and carnage of the trenches, and before war had hardly started. She tried to read no further, but the words sobbed and stumbled on, written by a schoolgirl already dressed in mourning. Simple misspelt sentences mopping up world wars, riversful of carnage flowing between a quiet, sedate account of a country childhood. Yellowed photographs of battle scenes, torn raggedly from newspapers, slipped between pages describing boating trips or strawberry parties. Anguished letters from her eldest brother, nicknamed Tubby, still alive, but fighting at the Marne.

'My dearest sister . . .' Fancy loops and arabesques describing bullet wounds and sieges. The vellum was expensive, the writing was an officer's. Hester's family was clearly rich, respected. She wrote about ponies, servants, her mother's social round. So how had she become a humble housekeeper? What had happened to her? Why had she been driven into service when her family was high-born and superior, with servants of its own?

Jennifer turned page after page, then moved to the second notebook. The same padded leather cover and heavy expensive paper recording war, losses, death — Tubby blown to bits by a grenade; then only six weeks later, her last remaining brother shot down at Messines. Hester's father collapsing with a stroke brought on by grief and shock. The widow bravely struggling on, staunching her tears for the sake of her two daughters — the only children left now.

Hester rarely mentioned her sister, despite the fact the girls seemed close in age. Had they been jealous of each other, Ellen prettier than Hester, or favoured by the parents? Jennifer went on reading, found Ellen featured again — both girls staying with their grandmother in a summer by the sea Hester recorded all the details — swimming, shrimping, rainstorms, a fall off a cousin's bicycle, ices on the pier. There were even a few photographs leafed between the pages, their backgrounds brown and faded, their subjects speckled with mould — a moustachioed man in a one-piece bathing-suit, a woman with a parasol strolling on the sea-front, a shot of crashing waves.

But after that visit to the grandmother, dated July 1918, the entries suddenly stopped. The rest of the notebook was blank, its pages empty and unused. What had happened to the diarist? There had been gaps before, sometimes of several months, but the writing had always started up again. Was she ill, busy, mourning, or had she simply wearied of scribbling all those words?

No, the diaries continued in a score of other notebooks, going right up to the forties. Jennifer rubbed her eyes, eased her aching legs. She would need days and days to read them all. She ought to pack them away now and start again in the morning, with Lyn to share her find. Yet she had reached such a crucial point, it was impossible to stop. 1918 was the most momentous year of the war and July its turning-point. November would bring the Armistice, the end of the war to end all wars. She burned to know what Hester had written about it, her feelings of relief, what victory celebrations she had witnessed.

She opened the next notebook in the pile — the war must be continued there. No. That was headed 1920 and the next one a year later. So where were the months between? She could find nothing until February 1919 which was the date on the thinnest, cheapest notebook, tucked away at the bottom of the pile. No stiff cover this time or heavy expensive paper. Even the writing seemed to have fallen off in quality and was now so cramped and squashed together, Jennifer could hardly make it out. It was as if Hester had made it deliberately illegible.

'22/2', she deciphered. So Hester had jumped ahead from the summer, ignoring all the drama and upheavals of the last lap of the war and the first sweet months of peace. Perhaps she was too shocked and overcome by her bereavements to share in the general rejoicing, and had only picked up her pen again after a spell of private mourning.

Jennifer held the page closer to the lamp, which was dimming now and flickering. Slowly, she made the words out. *'St Saviour's Hostel, Southwark. Today my son was born after twenty hours in labour. I was mostly left alone. He is nine pounds and bald.'*

Jennifer stared. *What* son? Hester had borne no child until her forties. Even Matthew, who was only her charge and not her child, had not arrived till 1934. This was 1919. And why was she in Southwark? Molly had told her Hester's family came from Fernfield. She was a native there, a country girl. She had just been reading about that country life in Hester's own words. The snug Northumbrian mansion with its gardens and its stables, the local ties and friendships, the secure and solid family. Where were they all when Hester had her baby? Why was she left alone and in a hostel?

Jennifer stared at the page again. She had stumbled on a scandal, some secret buried for over sixty years. Hester's baby must surely have been illegitimate. That would explain her sudden flight to London. There was no record of a marriage, no reference to a husband. Molly had mentioned neither. Hester for her was just the housekeeper, and one who had never had a child till Lyn was born, twenty long years later.

Lyn! This would be an utter shock to him. She was almost certain he knew nothing of Hester's past. He had often said how reticent she was, how little she had told him. All he knew was that she had led a hard and blinkered life with stern and modest parents long since dead. But now this puritanical mother appeared to have flouted all her own rules, fallen pregnant at eighteen with no husband on the scene, and been forced to flee from a grand and gracious home. How would Lyn feel to know he was no longer her first-born, had never been her unique and only son? He had never had to share her before, not even with a husband or a father. There had been always just the two of them, almost oppressively exclusive, Hester's rigid moral standards

61

shutting out the world. A bastard brother would break all that apart, make Lyn doubt his own identity, sow new resentment and confusion in his mind.

Other men might take the whole thing lightly, treat a deceased mother's teenage pregnancy as little more than a long-forgotten escapade with no bearing on their lives. But Lyn was so unpredictable, there was no knowing what he'd do. He was in mourning already for an old and respected mother who had led a chaste and blameless life. It would be a double death to kill her off and replace her with this lax and reckless girl.

A thousand questions were whirling through Jennifer's head. What had happened to the child? Who had fathered it and why had he disappeared? Where had Hester gone from Southwark? Yet she hardly dared read on. She had already trespassed too far, unravelled a past kept locked and barricaded for a lifetime. Supposing she discovered some still more damaging secret? A baby abandoned somewhere, cruelly treated . . .

Fearfully, she turned the page — found only a list of prices on the next one — random jottings, doodlings, blots. The diary started up again in March and still with a Southwark heading. Jennifer raced through the entries, seeking some reference to the child. Had it been adopted, left behind at the hostel, or kept secretly by Hester down in London? There was nothing, nothing. Not the slightest mention of a baby, no record of its growth (or even death), no correspondence with children's home or foster-parent. There were very few personal details at all, until Hester applied for a job in a large hotel and moved her lodgings. Even then, she presented herself as single, a modest young girl with only herself to support.

If Lyn found out that his strict and sinless mother had not only had a bastard child, but had turned her back on it, perhaps even left it to die of cold or exposure . . . Jennifer shuddered. She mustn't dramatise. There was no proof of that at all. Yet why had Hester lived so closed and strange a life? Why did people seem so hostile to her? Perhaps her secret had seeped out and harmed her reputation.

She turned to the later notebooks, the ones written in the 'thirties, when Hester had come to Hernhope. Was there some clue there, perhaps? No. Again, she had come single and childless — a simple spinster housekeeper to Thomas Winterton and Matthew Thomas Charles, his baby son. The entries were briefer now, mostly recording her work. Hester hadn't time for ponies, parties, long indulgent ramblings, only household chores and farm-work or attending to the child. Matthew featured often. '*The child was awake five hours last night with croup. Mr Winterton was not disturbed.*' '*Matthew refused to eat again this morning.*' '*My charge continues sick and undersized*'. Nan had already mentioned Matthew's puniness, but how much more vivid it was in Hester's words, and with all the problems of the farm erupting in the background. '*A third of our lambs were lost in the recent snowstorm*'. '*The vet came again but could do nothing for the cow. It seems that we shall lose her*'.

The squallings of the 'thirties burst into the shriek of a second bloody war. Thomas Winterton, as farmer, was excused from active service. Bombs were rarely heard in Mepperton. Evacuees from Newcastle stared at cows and wept for trolley-buses. The war dragged on through yet another note-book. D-day wasn't recorded. There were more omissions now. Was Hester just too busy, or had she lost her will to write about a broken world?

A few thin pages covered eight long years. Jennifer turned to 1948, the year that Lyn was born. The diary stopped long before his birthday. There was one last entry, the writing wobbly, stumbling, bursting into tears of blots.

'*I am writing this the day my husband died. If you can call him husband. We were married a few short months and he will never see his child.*'

Tears were pricking at Jennifer's eyes. Hester seemed to have been built for tragedy. Her father and three brothers dead before she was twenty — her youth and home and status lost as well. Pregnant and presumably disowned for it, she had fled to the shame and loneliness of London, swapping her party flounces for a cap and apron. The baby she had suffered for had died or disappeared. When, at last, she returned to her native Northumberland, it was not to her family, but as a servant and a stranger, and with no one she could really call her own. A second war added hardships, shock and struggle. Then, at Molly Bertram's age, the husband she had lacked for half a lifetime died after a few months' marriage, leaving her pregnant, bankrupt and alone.

Was it any wonder she had turned strange and sour, kept away from people, tried to protect her second son from the malicious gossip centered on the first? Jennifer felt like a defendant in the dock, championing Hester, excusing her, trying to make the court see the confused and suffering girl beneath the older, harsher woman. She felt strangely close to Hester, living in her house, married to her son, and now reading her own words. Surely Lyn, too, would feel greater tolerance once he understood the hardships of her life. She longed to rush upstairs and pile the notebooks on his bed, so that he could substitute this sympathetic figure for the stern and judging pres-ence in his head. Yet how could she do that without also dumping an unwelcome bastard brother on him? She couldn't risk his anger, years of new resentment which might make him even more unwilling to have a child himself.

She sat back on her heels, shivering in the dim uncertain light. Even the vaporiser had spluttered out, a dead black wick in a pool of spastic wax. There were so many complications. How could she hide Lyn's own mother from him, live with all this knowledge of her, when it was closed and barred to him? There was nowhere safe to conceal the diaries, anyway. Lyn had promised the solicitor that he would scour the house to find the missing Will. That would include the cellar. Worse for Lyn to find these diaries himself, come face to face with the shock of Hester's pregnancy without her to pre-pare him. He was sure to search these chests. They were an obvious place to hide a Will. She might even find it herself, tucked away with all these other treasures. That would solve some problems. Not only would it stop Lyn coming down here, so that at least she could suppress the diaries until she had decided what to do; it would also save further expense with lawyers and give them both the comfort of a settled home and secure inheritance.

There was still the large brown envelope which she hadn't even opened yet. Could it be in there? It was perhaps too bulky for a Will, yet it was so securely sealed, it looked important. She coaxed it open, peered inside. Only a faded sketchbook and a package tied with ribbon. She opened the sketch-book first. Even the wavering light could not disguise the skill and delicacy of the lively drawings which tumbled across the pages — mostly birds and animals, sketched with a wealth of detail and quite uncommon talent — a field mouse with its tail wrapped round a corn-stalk, a choir of comic frogs croaking round a pond, a double spread of seagulls, their swift soaring bodies criss-crossing against a choppy sea of clouds.

These must be *Hester*'s drawings — not the bowed and workworn house-keeper, but a younger freer Hester with leisure-time for hobbies. There was compassion in these sketches, insight, sensitivity. Lyn had never mentioned that his mother had such talents, yet what could be more natural when he had inherited them himself? She had always thought it strange that Lyn should have sprung from such a family — his father a farmer and his mother a simple housekeeper with only domestic skills. Yet here was a different Hester, one he had probably never known.

Jennifer leafed through the sketchbook, admiring flocks of starlings, sprays of blackthorn blossom, the taut and darting body of a ferret. On the very last page was a drawing of a young and pretty girl with untidy curls and a high pale forehead. That must be Hester herself, a self-portrait done before she left for London. She looked about eighteen. It was nothing like the corpse she had washed, but that corpse had been worn down by eighty unrelenting years. This drawing showed a simple, pretty, indulged and gentle child. How different from the portrait Lyn had always painted — the grim, plain woman somewhere between a martyr and a monster, a jailer and a saint. Yet wasn't everything Lyn told her somehow harsher and more intractable than she had found it in reality?

True, Lyn had never known the girl, not even the young woman. Hester was worn and widowed before he was even born. But wouldn't it be better if he knew her, help to resolve his bitterness, show him a mother who was more approachable, more lovable, and who, above all, shared his skills?

Why hide all these redeeming features for the sake of just two lines on one small page of one small notebook? As far as she could see, there was no other reference to Hester's pregnancy, nothing more at all. If she simply removed that page, the whole episode would vanish. Perhaps it was wrong to deface a diary or falsify a record, but wasn't it equally irresponsible to allow distrust and bitterness to sour her husband's life, and at a time when they had planned to start afresh? She could always keep the page, replace it later, break the news to Lyn when he was calmer and more confident. Meanwhile, they could read the rest of the diaries together, get to know the girl who had done the drawings. Those alone could banish the myth of the grey and granite Hester who still terrorised his dreams.

She reached across for the thin and faded notebook dated 1919, stared at the first page. Surely it couldn't matter if she tore it out? Hester had guarded her secret all her life. All she was doing was helping her hush it up a little longer. Very carefully she eased back the covers of the notebook. The binding was slack, in any case. Bit by bit, she worked the page free, making sure there were no ragged edges, nothing to incriminate her. She folded the page into nothing, concealed it in the pocket of her coat. She would hide it later in her Tampax box — one place Lyn would never look. He was almost prissily fastidious about anything to do with menstruation, preferred to believe it didn't occur at all.

She shut the notebook. The baby didn't exist now. Hester had gone to London simply to get a job, her family dispersed and ruined by the war. In all the turmoil and upheaval which followed in its wake, hundreds of girls must have left their homes or changed their way of life. When Lyn got round to reading the London entries, she would explain them in that light. She picked up the sketchbook again. Best to show him the drawings first, in any case. Lyn could relate to line and shadow, animal and bird.

She stumbled suddenly as the lamp gave a final flicker before drowning in the blackness all around it. It was as if her tampering with the diary had brought instant retribution. She rubbed her eyes. Her body felt stiff and stupid with exhaustion as if she had lived through all those decades of the diaries, endured every raid and battle of two world wars, groaned through twenty hours of labour. Her clothes were covered in a shroud of dust, little flakes of plaster confettied her hair. She started to pack the books back, floundering in the dark like a blind person, groping around the floor, scared of the spooky fingers of darkness catching at her hair. A sudden rustle made her start. A rat? A bat? She shuddered, wanted only to get out now.

She blundered towards the door, tripping over boxes, imagining faces in the gloom. A cobweb brushed against her cheek; she stubbed her toe on a loose uneven floorboard. She had reached the steps now, started fumbling up them, clutching at the wall.

She stopped in horror. The door was opening before she had even touched the handle. She screamed, fell back, as a shaft of hurting light dazzled her eyes.

'Jennifer! What in God's name are you doing? I thought I heard you down here.' Lyn was standing in the doorway in his crumpled blue pyjamas, flashing a torch as if to flush her out. 'Are you all right?'

'Y . . . yes. I think so. I was just . . . er . . . fetching that inhaler thing.' Jennifer's hand flew instinctively to her pocket, checked the torn-out page, remained palm across it like a shield.

'I told you I didn't want it. I wondered where on earth you were. I've been searching the whole house for you. I woke up in a sweat and . . .'

65

'I'm sorry. Let's g . . . go back to bed now. You'll catch your death down here.'

'Where is it, then?'

'What?'

'The inhaler. I may as well use it, now you've dug it out.' He wrinkled up his nose. 'Ugh! The whole place reeks of menthol. Whatever were you doing lighting it down here?' He flashed his torch again. 'Can't see it. That's a book you're holding, isn't it?'

Jennifer didn't answer. She had taken the sketchbook with her to show Lyn in the morning. She was too weary now for all the explanations. They would get no more sleep tonight if she embarked on the whole saga of Hester's life. Lyn sounded irritable, in any case.

'I told you not to prowl around in here. What *is* the book?'

'Oh . . . nothing.'

'What d'you mean, nothing?' Lyn ventured down two steps, reached across and grabbed it. He opened it at random, shining his torch on the page, stared down at the drawings, then back at her. 'Where did you find this, Jennifer?' He had collapsed on to the steps, leafing through the pages with an almost wild excitement, hand trembling on the cover.

'You shouldn't sit there, Lyn. That stone's damp and cold and you've got almost nothing on. You'll . . .'

'Jennifer, I must know where you found this.' Lyn had stopped at one of the drawings and was gazing at it intently, nose almost on the page. She peered over his shoulder. It was a river scene she had admired herself — preening mallard and nesting moorhen fringed by water-lilies.

'It was in a sort of . . . chest thing, right at the back down here.' She paused. No point lying when he would be searching the cellar himself in a matter of days. Crazy, really, ever to have imagined she could conceal his mother's life and history from him. She had never believed in deception in a marriage, and if she was forced to suppress a single page for the sake of Lyn's own sanity, then at least she should open up the rest.

She crouched down beside him, laid her hand on his. 'Listen, darling, there's a lot of . . . important stuff down here. I think we ought to look at it together — as soon as you're better, I mean. All your family records and Hester's things as well — her diaries and these drawings. You never told me she could draw.'

'She couldn't.' Lyn had turned another page now, found the comic frogs. He wasn't smiling, though. His brows were drawn right down and a tiny muscle was twitching in his face.

'My mother couldn't draw to save her life. She not only couldn't, she disapproved of drawing. Wasting time, she called it.'

'But that was only *later*, darling, when she was busy and tired and . . . She did these as a girl. I've found out a lot about her life already. Her family were well-to-do, so she probably had governesses and proper drawing lessons. These are mostly nature studies, but there's a sketch of her at the

66

back. At least, I *think* it must be her — a self-portrait, I suppose. Gosh! I'm frozen stiff, aren't you? It's like a morgue down here. Let's go upstairs before . . .'

'Where? Where is it — that portrait of her? Show me.'

Jennifer took the book from him, turned to the last page. The girl looked changed now in the torchlight, harsher and less gentle, with an almost blowsy beauty, the smile curling on her lips. 'There she is. It's funny, really, but I never imagined your mother quite like that. I know she's only young there, but she looks so . . . Lyn, what are you *doing*?'

'Going to search that chest.' He pushed past her on the steps, hurtled down them.

'Not now, Lyn. You've got a temperature. Wait until you're better, or at least until the morning, then we can . . .'

He didn't stop to answer. She heard him trip on something, swear.

'Be careful!' She was groping after him, following the torch-beam. He had already reached the chest. A few books were still strewn around it, along with the second package from the sealed brown envelope which she had missed in her haste and fear.

Lyn fell on his knees, ripped the package open, stared at the sheaf of photos in his hands — their old, brown, faded paper contradicted by the young and radiant female printed on them. There were ten or eleven photographs, all of the same woman — that tousled girl of the sketchbook, except the camera had somehow made her flesh and blood. The hair was fairer, the eyes larger and more provocative, the plunging cleavages certainly more daring. Most of the photos were cut off at the waist, but all displayed the dazzling neck and shoulders draped in silk, muslin, velvet, or adorned with scarves and flowers. Lyn had grabbed the torch and was shining it on each photograph in turn, laying them out on the dusty cellar floor. He placed the portrait underneath them, tracing the full lips with his finger. '*Susannah*',' he whispered.

'What did you say?' Jennifer took off her coat and draped it round his shoulders. It was madness for him to be down here with a streaming cold, clad only in thin pyjamas on one of the coldest nights of the year.

Lyn picked up the largest of the photos and thrust it in her hands. 'That's *her* — Susannah — Matthew's mother. Don't you understand? She did those drawings and these are her photographs. Matthew told me the house was full of them once. When he was a boy, he couldn't walk into a single room without his dead mother . . . watching him from the mantelpiece. But *I* never saw them. They'd all disappeared by the time I was born. I've looked for them before, searched for years, in fact. Given up long ago. Do you realise, Jennifer, how strange this is — that you should . . . well — lead me to them, after all this time? It's extraordinary, uncanny . . .'

'But, I don't quite . . . I mean, why Susannah, Lyn, when she died years before you were even . . .?'

'It doesn't matter why. Doesn't matter. Doesn't . . . Oh, Snookie, oh . . .'

He clung to her, almost crushing her. She couldn't hear what he was saying, only feel him sobbing into her, as she lay twisted and uncomfortable beneath him. He couldn't cry, not even at the funeral. Days and days had passed and he had shown no outward sign of grief. Even when he had sat staring at Hester's death certificate or found a letter written to him in her now frail and feeble writing — unfinished, broken off — he had still stayed stony-faced. She had longed for him to cry, to mourn his mother in some more natural, open fashion. Yet now he was mourning *Matthew's* mother, crying before he had even read the diaries, before Hester's life had thawed and melted his — weeping over a burst of blackthorn blossom, a page of frozen birds.

'Lyn,' she whispered. 'Darling . . .' She hardly knew what to say to him. Her usual words of comfort seemed too pat and feeble for this storm of grief. Tears were sliding down her own face, trickling slow and salty into the corners of her mouth. She couldn't bear to see him so distraught. She tried to mop her eyes, but one hand was twisted back behind her and Lyn's whole weight pressing down on top, his body heaving against hers. She longed to find a handkerchief, a more comfortable position, but she dared not push him off. He needed to cry, to break the grip of that black and heavy grief which had held him prisoner since the funeral.

The torch had fallen from his hand and shone feebly in the wrong direction, an eye of light staring in the darkness. The floor pressed hard cold hands along her spine. Time seemed to have injured itself and slowed to a limp, so that every slow-coach second hobbled through the whole length of the cellar before stumbling on the next. She lay there, sniffing, aching, trying to mumble comfort through her rough tweed coat which covered both of them. At least Lyn had calmed a little, the sobs faltering into hoarse and laboured breaths.

'All right now, darling?'

Silence. It was as if he had almost forgotten where he was and was drifting back to sleep again. Best to let him rest until he was quite recovered. She shifted a little, easing her aching hand, tried to relax as well. But every time she closed her eyes Hester's life kept rushing into the cold black space behind them — snippets from the diaries, phrases she remembered, wars, deaths, casualties — the bald, abandoned baby, the three young brothers shell-shocked in the trenches, bloodying the mud. She shuddered. Lyn looked dead himself, his body slumped on hers, cold and motionless like a casualty from some other, recent war.

She pushed him with her knee. He had to move, breathe, live. 'Get up!' she shouted, surprised at how fiercely her voice had cut across the silence.

Slowly he struggled to his knees, pulled her to him, stared into her face. Suddenly he was kissing her, so roughly, so intensely, her mouth stung and throbbed with the pressure of his tongue. His breath smelt of cough-sweets, his face felt stubbly where he hadn't shaved, yet hot and wet from crying.

She tried to pull away, but he held her shoulders, traced a finger along her lips as he had done with the portrait. 'I love you, Snookie. I love you, I *love* you. You know that, don't you, darling? I love you more than I've ever . . . Oh, don't die. Don't ever die.'

He had thrown off the coat and was unbuttoning his pyjamas. 'Put your arms around me, *tight*. I want to feel your body close to mine.'

'Lyn, no.' She shrank away. 'You're out of your mind! It's far too cold to . . .'

'Please, darling. There must be nothing between us. Nothing. Not even our clothes. I can't explain, but . . .' He was pulling up her sweater, trying to slide his hands beneath her breasts.

She removed the hands, almost slapped them off. Why should she feel so hostile when he was telling her he loved her? She tried to calm herself, lay back on the floor. She must remember he was ill, try and make allowances. She fumbled for the coat, dragged it half across him.

'No, leave it, Snookie. It's right like this. I know it is. I must be . . . close to you, feel we're joined and . . .'

He sounded so intense, she dared not push him off again. She stared up, past his shoulder, at the dark lowering ceiling with its shadowy beams. She felt like wood herself, dead and rigid.

He kissed her again, less roughly now, but pressing down so close, it was as if he wished to lose his mouth and self inside her. She tried to respond, ashamed of her hostility. He needed her so fiercely, seemed so strange and vulnerable. Her lips relaxed a little. He only wanted comfort, her body to block the darkness out, to cling to like a child.

No, not a child. She could feel him stiffening lower down, stirring against her thighs. She tensed. Surely he couldn't actually want to . . . not in the dark and damp with swollen glands and a temperature? It was ridiculous, perverse. She closed her legs, pulled her mouth away.

'*Please*, my darling.' He was fumbling with her tights now, dragging them down and almost off. She shivered as the cold pounced on her thighs.

'No, Lyn. I . . .'

Her hands were fighting his, refusing to let him remove her skirt. He took the hands, covered them with kisses, then placed them on the floor above her head as if they were some piece of lumber he had found and didn't need. He left the skirt on, but pushed her sweater up, unhooked the bra beneath it, kissed her nipples, then pressed his own bare chest against them. His body felt chilled and sweaty against her own, forehead burning on her cheek, clammy hands trembling down her back. She was crushed not just by his weight, but by the fear of her own anger. She rarely felt such anger, and never when he was making love to her. That was the trouble, though — it wasn't love. He was forcing her again, tricking her with kisses and caresses, so that he could knock her off her guard, then enter her that

69

violent fruitless back way. She'd had enough of it, didn't want it even in the warmth of her own bed, let alone on a dusty cellar floor. The dust had got into his throat and started off his cough again — a hoarse desperate cough which echoed through the cellar. It was crazy for them to lie there any longer, and she for one was going back upstairs. She tried to struggle up, but a further spasm of coughing pinioned his body closer to her own.

'Lyn, *move*. I want to . . .'

He could hardly speak. His eyes were streaming, his chest racked. She felt a stab of pain between her thighs. She was too dry and tense to take him, but he was forcing in between the coughs. She still had her skirt on, but it was rucked up round her middle, uncomfortable where he was pushing down on top of her.

Anger exploded into shock. He had entered her without a Durex, not the back way, but the normal, fertile dangerous way. He had never done that before, not in all three years of their marriage, not even when it was comparatively safe, just before or after her period. This was the most dangerous time of all, the middle of her cycle, the prime time for conceiving. She was so astonished, she just lay there like a sack. He was thrusting very slowly. He must be keeping it slow on purpose, so he wouldn't lose control. He would come out again in a moment — surely. Lyn would never risk a child.

'L . . . Lyn, hadn't you better . . .?'

'I love you,' he whispered, in answer. 'I *love* you, Snookie. You don't understand, but . . .'

She lay back, silent now. She didn't understand. Why was he so ardent when she herself felt distanced from him, her resentment barring him off from her as if it were a Durex stretched taut across her soul? She had longed for him to enter her like this, but now it was actually happening, all she was aware of was the turmoil in her head. Her body seemed to have shrivelled or cut off. Yet she had to admit there was something changed about him. Although he had forced her in the first place, he seemed a different person now from the one who had pushed her to her knees those last few days.

The words of the marriage service chimed a moment in her head. '*With my body, I thee worship.*' Lyn was worshipping, hands hymning down her breasts, lips whispering across her eyelids like the feathers on Susannah's birds. Those shy, swift birds had somehow tamed and softened him, made this moment sacred. Anger seeped away like dirty water. Lyn was still inside her. She understood it now. It wasn't just a mistake or aberration, some reckless impulse he would all too soon regret; it was a deliberate gift to her, offered tenderly and freely, some lasting transformation in himself.

She lay completely still. If, by some miracle, this was to be their child, then he must never say that she had forced it on him. There was no need for her own pleasure. It was enough that it was happening, slow and

70

solemn like a sacrament. She had been fretting about the cold, the dust, the hard, unyielding floor, but all around her were dead and watching Wintertons murmuring from the Game Books, imploring from the letters, waiting for their heir. The torch had gone out, so she had lost her own outlines now, her edges blurring with Lyn's and all his ancestors'. Somewhere in the shadows, she heard Hester confiding to her diary, 'Today my son was born'.

Lyn was breathing faster now. She could feel the long, slow, urgent piston-shots gathering pace and speed. He was coming . . . coming slowly, very slowly, but unmistakably. Coming right inside her. *No*. Impossible. Prohibited. It couldn't happen. Wouldn't. She had been romanticising, dreaming — kidding herself he wanted a child instead of just excitement. Any second now, he would wrench away and out of her, realise the risk he was taking and withdraw before that final clinching moment which could change their lives.

He went on thrusting. She recognised that rhythm, that force he couldn't stop. He wasn't going to withdraw. Suddenly she rocked and twisted underneath him, arched her whole body, drew up her knees, held him so tightly, they were one blurred shape, one body in the darkness. She must be part of this moment, this climax, this night, this child — this *child*. She heard him gasp with pleasure as she circled with her thighs. He was panting now, stabbing out 'I love you' between his wilder fiercer thrusts.

Shock and love and thrill were all mixed up now. Her body had come clamouring back, demanding to join in. In those few astounding seconds, she was responding more wildly than she had done in three whole years of marriage. She shut her eyes to concentrate, fused her mouth with Lyn's, as he flooded in, in, into her, and four hundred million spermatozoa leapt towards her womb.

VII

'Matthew, you're not even facing the problems. If Lyn doesn't want to publish, then . . .'

'He's *got* to want to. For heaven's sake, Anne, this is the most exciting collection of material I've seen in years. It's got everything — two world wars, nostalgia, heartbreak, below-stairs romances, letters from the Front, country high-life, London low-life . . . We could really make something of it. The drawings alone merit a whole book to themselves.

Thank God you prised it from them before they messed it up.'

'They're hardly likely to do that.' Anne unlocked her own small office in Matthew's building and pulled the blinds up. The July sun streamed in, dazzling her a moment. She turned back to her husband, who had already commandeered her desk and was sitting at it, sorting through the mail. 'Jennifer treats that stuff like Holy Writ. She only let you borrow it on condition you returned it to her this evening. You won't forget that, will you, Matthew? I'll take it down myself, if you like. I ought to see how she is.'

Matthew frowned. 'Can't you leave it for a day or two? I've only had half a weekend to look through a pile of stuff that would take a trained historian half a lifetime.'

'No, I promised, darling. Lyn was annoyed enough about my taking it at all, and Jennifer wants to go on copying out the recipes.'

'I thought you said she was ill.'

'She is. But she's been doing it in bed.'

Matthew flung a wad of circulars into the waste-bin. 'I can't understand why she didn't tell us earlier. *Weeks* ago, I mean, when she first discovered it. Some of that stuff could be really valuable.'

'How could she, when they were so many miles away and without a phone? Anyway, I expect Lyn told her not to. You know what he's like about his mother — anything connected with her and he just clams up. That's why I don't think you ought to publish.'

'Look here, Anne, a lot of that material is connected with my own family. I'm the elder son, remember. All right, I admit that Hester's diaries are the star attraction as far as publication's concerned, but Hester married my father, for heaven's sake. If I've agreed to open up my family to the public, I can't see why Lyn should object. In fact, you could say it's much more delicate for me — as publisher. Winterton promoting Winterton. It could make for very unpleasant gossip. At least Lyn can stay out of the limelight.'

Anne had joined Matthew at her desk, standing beside him and checking those letters which needed her attention. 'But this whole thing's almost remote for you. You only lived at Hernhope as a boy and you've never been back since. You haven't even seen the place for thirty years — more than thirty. Lyn spent most of his life there.'

'Yes, but Hester's dead now. That makes a difference, surely. The house is empty, the whole tradition finished. We're talking about a way of life that's nothing to do with me or Lyn any longer.'

'You're wrong, Matthew. Jennifer told me they wouldn't have come back to Cobham at all, if she hadn't been unwell. She's absolutely obsessed with Hernhope — talked about nothing else — all the friends she's made up there, what she's done to the house, how she's joined the Mepperton Young Wives and even been asked to . . .'

'Yes, and who was *paying* for them to kick their heels in the country? Do you realise, Anne, they were away almost eleven weeks? I wrote to Lyn at least four times — told him there wouldn't *be* a job if he didn't show up soon.'

'Well, I wouldn't bank on him returning. From what I could gather from Jennifer, she's hoping to persuade him to go up north again — as soon as she's better, that is.'

'Out of the question! The idea's total moonshine. What's wrong with her, in any case?'

'I'm not quite sure. I tried to probe, but they both seemed very vague about it. Apparently, Lyn insisted she see her own doctor down in Cobham, but she was obviously bitterly disappointed at being back at all.'

'She probably caught a chill camping out like that in the back of beyond. Hernhope was always perishing cold and it's probably half derelict by now.'

'No, it's basically quite sound, so Jennifer said, and they've made a lot of improvements already. She told me even Lyn got quite enthusiastic, once he'd recovered from the shock of the funeral. I must admit he certainly seems better for the break.'

Matthew opened his last letter, perused it briefly, scribbled something on the back and left it on Anne's typewriter. 'I'm glad to hear it. He can put his new energies to work for me. I'll need a really good designer for this Hernhope thing. Lyn's the obvious choice. It will be an extra selling-point to say that Hester's own son helped to put the book together.'

'Except Hester's own son doesn't want a book.'

'He'll come round — he'll have to. The firm's losing money at the moment. We need something big to put it on its feet again. This latest find is perfect. Nostalgia's still big business. So is back-to-the-land. Sob stuff from the First World War never fails to sell. And if we build the whole thing round Hester herself, we've got the perfect peg to hang it on.'

'Lyn doesn't see his mother as a peg, darling.'

'Look, Anne, Lyn's costing me a lot of money at the moment. I've paid his salary in full for the last eleven weeks when he hasn't done a stroke. And what about the Cobham house? He shouldn't have left it empty all that time. It could have been vandalised or burgled or . . . He just takes the place for granted. Doesn't pay a penny for it, not even rent or rates. In fact, I'm running into problems on that property. I never said they could entrench themselves for ever. There's less than twenty years left on the lease and if I don't sell it soon I won't get a sale at all. People won't touch short leases. I really ought to put it on the market right away. Summer's the best time.'

'You could always buy the freehold. Then you'd sell it for more, and you could leave the sale till . . .'

'I can't afford that, Anne. I need some ready cash.'

'Well, Lyn and Jennifer have got to live somewhere. Wouldn't it be better if they went back to Hernhope and made that their permanent home?'

'No — totally impractical. Only farmers and shepherds can scrape a living in that wilderness. Hernhope's got no land left at all, and even if it had, Lyn couldn't cope with it. I want him living near me, so that I can keep an eye on him. He needs me to keep his feet on the ground, keep him in employment. The sooner that house is sold, the better. The trouble is, Lyn's using the missing Will as an excuse to twiddle his thumbs. What he *ought* to do is get off his back and see a solicitor. There's a perfectly simple procedure when a Will is lost. He can be appointed as administrator which gives him the power to act and sell the place.'

'But he doesn't want to sell it, Matthew — and I can sympathise. In fact, I'm surprised you should even suggest it. It's a family house — *your* family. Wintertons have lived there for generations. Just because your father left it to Hester when he died, so now it's Lyn's property instead of yours. I don't see why . . .'

'That's nothing to do with it. And, anyway, you're appealing to empty sentimentalism. The earlier Wintertons were farmers, so it suited them to live in a . . . barn. I'm a businessman . . . and it galls me that Lyn should be behaving in so unbusiness-like a fashion over what could be a useful and valuable asset.' Matthew was pacing up and down now.

Anne reclaimed her chair and started sorting through the in-tray. 'And where are Lyn and Jennifer supposed to live in the meantime? You can't turf them out in the street.'

'Don't be absurd, Anne.' Matthew straightened a picture on the wall. 'If Lyn agrees to let me publish, he can live in a palace if he likes. There's money in that stuff. I'm absolutely convinced of it. We could make enough to build palaces all round.'

'Matthew, that's . . . almost blackmail.'

'Not at all. It's simply time Lyn faced up to facts. He's been *playing* recently. Even before Hester's death, he was doing work I could have put a school-leaver on at half the salary.'

'Darling, that isn't fair. Lyn's got enormous talent. You wouldn't find a school-leaver turning out designs like the ones he did for *Europe's Last Great Kings*.'

'Yes, and America turned it down. And *The Medieval Bestiary*. I've got to make some money — and make it fast. Anyway, it's more than just a matter of cash. We have almost a duty to publish, in a way — for educational reasons. If Lyn just sits on unique historical records, then we're depriving the nation of . . .'

'Oh, Matthew, *really* . . . If you couldn't see a profit in it, you'd have shoved the stuff in a drawer and forgotten all about it.'

'There's nothing wrong with profit, Anne. I've told you that before. If my firm makes money out of what could prove to be a valuable national archive of historical importance, then the nation gains twice over. Profit is simply a measure of success. And if I don't get down to work soon, there won't be any success. I've wasted quite enough time talking, as it is. I want to tie up as many ends as possible this week, so I can clear the decks for Hernhope. It's going to be big, that book — great, I might even venture. Bring me a coffee, would you, please, and try to make it strong. We had dishwater all last week.'

Matthew walked slowly up the stairs to his own office which took up most of the top floor and was cut off from the rest of the staff, who were crammed into smaller quarters with inter-connecting doors. He stopped several times on the way, peering into offices, spot-checking desks and drawers, rifling through waste-paper baskets. The cleaners' negligence in emptying them had often proved to his advantage. He didn't pay expensive staff to waste their time on noughts and crosses, or freelance work for other firms, or puerile attempts at love letters. Matthew strove to maintain an everlasting vigilance. It was not just a question of value for his money, but a vital matter of principle. He had deliberately installed his wife on the ground floor at the front so that she could check on everybody's movements, including unnecessarily protracted lunch breaks, late arrivals, or furtive getaways at ten past five.

He opened the door of his office, frowned at the cleaner's efforts. There was still dust on the filing cabinet, a dirty cup and saucer on his desk. The room had been decorated in a more astringent and expensive style than any other in the building. Everything was brown. A daunting expanse of thick-pile nigger carpet stretched from door to desk. The walls were hessian, the colour of burnt toast. The desk itself he kept uncluttered. No personal weaknesses such as family photographs distracted his attention from the job in hand, no tycoon trinkery, no overflowing in-trays. Just six-foot-four of Victorian mahogany frowning between him and any underling. His was the only chair. Colleagues were waved to a Regency chaise longue of excruciating hardness. Not only did its obvious style add cachet to the furnishings, it also proved invaluable in maintaining his advantage, especially at a meeting. By throwing his staff together on a sofa, depriving them of the status, security and territorial rights of their own individual chair, Matthew found it easier to subdue them. With knees touching and backs aching, their arguments lost force.

Despite the summer morning, the heavy velvet curtains were still drawn close. Matthew left them so, sat at his desk in the gloom, staring at his expensive stationery with its tasteful heading (in sombre brown again) 'Winterton and Allenby, Publishers'. It would have looked better, of course, without the Allenby. Jim Allenby was a crude, conceited man, too young to be trusted and too bright to be ignored, with an appalling taste in ties and wines, and whose one advantage was that he had offered a hundred thousand pounds in cash to a Matthew rich in ambition, but low in funds. A sum like that could hardly be turned down, even at the cost of diluting and polluting the name of Winterton. Matthew had moved from minor public school, paid for by his uncle, to minor university (having tried and failed Oxbridge), with a feared and hated National Service smarting in between. He had then squeezed his way into the editorial department of a minor publishing house by taking a summer filing job and proving indispensable. He worked long and punishing hours, devouring information and manuscripts — always eager, early, charming, willing, wily — then going on to evening classes in printing and computer studies. He mugged up reports, contracts, sales figures, libel laws and editorial minutes, making himself familiar with every branch of the business and courting every member of staff, from tea-boy to directors.

By dint of changing firms three times, he finally became an editor, with his name on the door of a small and windowless office, and even half a secretary. He realised, though, that he was still less skilful in recognising a masterpiece or commissioning a runaway best-seller than the younger, smarter men who put in half his hours. He *used* these men — picked their brains, read their memos, expropriated their successes while disclaiming any involvement in their failures.

After eleven years, he had mastered all their skills, but lost his youth in the process. Middle age was not recognised in publishing which preferred unflagging brain-cells. Matthew found youth, brain and capital most conveniently combined in James Spencer Allenby whom he wooed away from Weidenfeld's to his own less illustrious premises, then allocated the gloomiest office next to the lavatory and the oldest (married) secretary. Neither quenched Jim's spirit. He it was who had suggested that they set up as what was called a packaging firm, rather than yet another small-scale publisher. Packagers were a fairly recent development which had first appeared in the early 1960s as book production companies concentrating chiefly on design and editorial, turning out lavish illustrated books which they then sold to publishers around the world. They produced only a small number of titles, but gave each of them more specialised attention than the average hard-pressed publishing house had time for.

Matthew disliked the term packager. Some of them had already won respect, but the word suggested low-grade manufacturers churning out detergent cartons, rather than editorial specialists creating works of high quality and educational worth. He glanced around at the books which lined the walls of his office, shelves and shelves of books — his own creations — reached above his desk to caress their glossy spines. On the far wall hung the framed design awards his firm had won, a few outstanding pieces of artwork, and the most brilliant of their book jackets, also framed. The wall was like a miniature art gallery, proof of his firm's prowess. He had Lyn to thank for most of it, but it was his own scrupulous attention to detail which had gained Winterton and Allenby its solid reputation. Even in the fat years, he had refused to relax his grip. Profit had never made him lazy or extravagant, only spurred him on. The last two years, however, had proved a bitter disappointment. The same exacting labours and painstaking involvement had brought only low returns, and his two most recent ventures had completely fizzled out. It was vital now for the firm to recoup its losses and save its name. The Hernhope find could make that possible.

Of course, there were risks in publication — and not only financial ones. Matthew understood his brother's fears. The journals had been as much a shock to himself as they were for Hester's own son. Matthew had built his whole boyhood on contempt for Hester. As soon as he was old enough to know she was not, in fact, his mother, he had blamed her for the deception and confusion, even held her responsible for his own mother's death, since she had arrived so promptly after it. His father had never, in fact, allowed Susannah to die, but had kept her alive in constant reminiscences, in sad, smiling photographs which haunted all the rooms, in endless visits to the cemetery. Matthew tagged along with him, gazing up at the sky for a glimpse of that Perfect Mother who now lived with the angels, and then returning back to earth, damp, cramped and disappointed, to Hester and cold supper.

Fourteen years later, his father married Hester. Matthew was confused. The woman whose chief failing was that she could never replace Susannah, now appeared to have done so. The photos disappeared, weeds grew around the gravestone, as the former drudge and housekeeper now lorded it as mistress. Matthew could only believe that Hester herself had engineered the marriage, taking advantage of his father's declining health and increasing money worries to entrench her own position and at least inherit the house. More confusion followed, as his father wasted and Hester and the rumours swelled. Within the year his father died, Hester gave birth and Matthew fled.

Yet, reading her diaries had revealed to him a very different woman. Gone was the drudge, the skivvy, the scheming interloper who had in some way killed off both his parents. In her place was a stoical, hardworking woman as well-born as Susannah herself. The servant he had scorned and patronised had been born in a mansion, the daughter of a gentleman, and seemed to have lost her standing only through the death of that same father and the horrors of the war. He blushed to think that he had even been ashamed of her, not at Hernhope, but later, at his boarding school, where the other boys had gracious leisured mothers who wore hats and nylon stockings and did nothing more exacting than embroidery. It was not smart to be an orphan — almost contemptible to have an eccentric frowsty stepmother who doctored cows and mucked out pigsties and had further embarrassed him by giving birth when she already had wrinkles and grey hair. In the end, he cut Hester and Hernhope off. His uncle was more acceptable. He was his father's brother to start with, and ran a Humber Super Snipe instead of a pony cart.

Now he knew not only that Hester's family had been as substantial as his uncle's, but also that Hester herself had held both house and farm together when his father was too bitter and crazed with grief to cope with either. He himself had been an added burden, a sickly fractious child she had nursed through infant gripes and adolescent tantrums until he finally ran off and left her — the only time she might have needed him.

Reading through those records had been like stripping a piece of Band-Aid off his soul. Griefs, shames and longings which he had refused to acknowledge at the time, came gushing out to confuse and overwhelm him; facts turned on their heads, resentments seen as lies. His first thought, like his brother's, was to hide the evidence. Who wanted all those reproachful, unexpected facts, Hester's role re-written, his own shown up as meaner and less martyred than he remembered it himself? It had been easy to label Hester as a sour and loveless drudge until he actually read her words, saw how often she had worried about his health and happiness, how many hours she had sat by his bed with cold flannels or hot drinks. There was even a postcard with a Humpty Dumpty doodled on the front, and a verse in her bold black writing on the back:

'*Poor little Matthew sat on the wall,*
Poor little Matthew had a great fall.
Out rushed big Hester with two brawny men
And put little Matthew together again.'

He had forgotten that event till now — a bad fall on his head off a high stone wall. Now the whole scene flooded back. The sting of iodine, the smell of disinfectant, Hester's stern but careful hands patching him up, putting him to bed. When he couldn't sleep that night, she had sat up with him till morning, sung him the rhyme, then wrote it on a postcard for him and left it on his breakfast tray. He couldn't have treasured it, since it was back in her possession, but now it seemed ridiculously precious.

The diaries were full of such embarrassments — soulless chores Hester had done without complaining, tendernesses he had forgotten or denied. He sat in his study trying to decide whether to leave them as private record of his vanished childhood, or turn them into profit. In the end, business sense prevailed. When he emerged at midnight, his eyes and mind were clear. No one had any right to bury history. All it needed — like his life — was clever editing. Put together with the letters and the drawings and all the records of the house itself, Hester's diaries could make a package of such profit and potential, only a fool would turn his back on it.

Lyn was a fool, of course, but he himself as entrepreneur and father of four could not afford to be. Indeed, without his patronage, Lyn might be on the dole by now, or living as some down-and-out eccentric in a North-umbrian wilderness. Whatever the merits of the Hester of the diaries, the widow who survived them had become a strange, embittered woman, who had made her son both cranky and dependent, cut him off from

78

normal social intercourse and could well have blighted all his prospects. It was Matthew who had bailed him out, coaxed him down to London, and encouraged talents already gone to waste. His half-brother had always been artistic, and the firm could use a promising young designer who was more interested in fulfilment than in cash. He had arranged a vocational course in graphics at the sort of commercially orientated art school where Lyn would not be distracted by romantic notions of Fine Art or *ars gratia artis* and had negotiated a full grant, despite Lyn's lack of qualifications and the fact that he was well past student age.

Lyn never completed the course. One of Matthew's designers demanded a higher salary and waved an offer from a rival firm as proof that he should get it. Matthew let him go and offered the job to Lyn who was still a year away from his final diploma. Not only could he pay Lyn less on the grounds of his being technically unqualified, he could also prevent him touting around for other jobs, most of which required that vital piece of paper.

He hadn't done his brother down. Lyn was lucky to land such a responsible position at all. Matthew had also secured him a house, a future and a wife. The least Lyn could do in return was relinquish his rights to the diaries and help the firm present them as tastefully and as profitably as possible.

Matthew opened his briefcase and drew out one or two of the notebooks which he had brought from his study at home. He still had to decide how best to present this precious cache of diaries, letters, rent books, game books, cookbooks. His first thought had been to centre it on Hernhope, the story of the house itself. But that would omit the record of Hester's youth at Fernfield, followed by her struggles down in London. Hester's diaries were so full, so vivid, so intensely personal, she herself should be the star and centre of any publication. It was an added bonus that she had been born in 1900, so her story was that of the century itself. He had even thought of a title — *Born With The Century*. It was catchy, apt and memorable. No doubt it had been used before, but one of his skills was to cash in on other men's ideas and turn them to his own advantage. This project couldn't fail. There was enough material for several books, in fact, though he might well weave it all together to make a compendium of dazzling range and interest. The recipes alone were remarkably original. Jennifer had stumbled on those in a separate chest, the morning after her main discovery. She had then tried them out at Hernhope, working through soups and savouries, pies and puddings, pickles and preserves.

One of Hester's charms was the quirky way she muddled things together — shopping lists and local superstitions jostling with accounts of national events or international wars; the grim statistics of a local influenza epidemic immediately followed by a recipe for boot varnish. Matthew stopped at that.

'Mix six ounces of best gum arabic, three ounces of sugar-candy, a good measure of brown sherry and a pint of ink, and set it to boil in a saucepan . . .'

He smiled. Utterly delightful. 'When cold, add a quarter of a pint of spirits of wine and shake well. If too thick, dilute with a teaspoonful of claret.' The boots would be *alcoholic*!

There was a knock on the door. He had assumed that none of his staff was in yet. He and Anne often arrived an hour or so before the rest, not only to set an example of commitment and hard work, but also to take advantage of the lull before the squall of phones and typewriters which began at half-past nine.

'Who is it?' he called.

'Only me, darling. I've brought your coffee up.' He had trained even Anne to knock. Colleagues were all too ready to accuse him of favouritism, even nepotism. That was one of the reasons he was always strict with Lyn.

'Thanks. Put it down there, would you.' Matthew moved the notebook. 'Here, take a look at Hester's boozy boot varnish. It sounds like something out of the Arabian Nights.'

Anne laughed. 'Yes, I've seen it. Jennifer showed it to me — along with the boots she'd treated with it. They were shining like black glass.'

'You mean, she actually tried it out? It sounds totally fantastical.'

'No, it really works. She was quite surprised herself, I think. When she was at Hernhope, she made up most of Hester's potions — everything from silver cleaner to hair tonic. Oh — and a lot of the herbal medicines as well.'

Matthew poured his coffee. 'Pity she didn't try those on herself. Then perhaps she wouldn't be lying around in bed.'

'She did. And on Lyn. He had quite a nasty cough which lingered on for weeks, so she treated him with a mixture of — what did she say it was? Sage and coltsfoot, I think — something strange like that. Anyway, it seemed to work. Then he had trouble sleeping, so she tackled that with hops and camomile. She was so impressed, she's thinking of growing herbs herself now.'

Matthew rose slowly from his chair and walked towards the window. He drew the curtains back, blinked against the glare. 'Do you realise, Anne, we could use all this.'

'All what, darling.'

'Well, *Jennifer*. All these brews and potions. Modern woman carrying on the old traditions, reviving ancient skills. Don't you see, we can give the book a whole new contemporary relevance. Not just a vanished way of life, but something which still has value and importance even today. Perhaps especially today, when people are so worried about ecology and unemployment and the side effects of modern drugs and junk food. Jennifer herself can be the link. Become a second Hester, if you like. They've even got the same name. Mrs living Winterton paying homage

80

to the dead one, vouching for her wisdom, finding comfort and fulfilment in the old ways. The answer to machine-age woman's general lack of purpose. Back to the stock pot and the herb garden.'

'But women don't want that, Matthew. We've spent the last fifty years trying to escape it. Look at me, for instance. I've only just squeezed into your office, after . . .'

'You're not typical. Anyway, there's bound to be a backlash. There always is. Women's lib has created a lot of anxiety and turmoil — and not only among males. I can see Jennifer as a sort of spearhead of a passive revolution — women in their nurturing role, fighting back on their own home ground with the weapons of contentment and creativity, finding power in healing, not in strife. Jennifer would be perfect for it. She's . . .'

'But she doesn't want you to publish, Matthew. Or even if she does, she'd never say so. She always sides with Lyn.'

'And, so, it seems, do you, Anne. You're all so blinkered. Publishers have power, you know. Power to change ideas. It may sound grandiose, but some of the greatest upheavals in history came through books. Now, if you'll excuse me, I'm going to jot down some of these selling-points while they're still fresh in my head.'

He winced as she let the door bang. It annoyed him, really, the way she always stuck up for Lyn. Why did he have such power? He himself had been a slave to it. He could have easily ignored the boy, cut off all contact with him from the day he left Hernhope for his boarding school, as he had done with Hester herself. Lyn was just an infant then and it would have been easy to have blanked him out. Yet, despite the gulf between them — in age, in miles, in education — Matthew had felt still haunted by his half-brother. It was partly his talent, of course. He had always respected talent and Lyn had been precocious, as a child. Matthew had written to him as soon as he could read, and went on writing until the lad was in his twenties. In reply he received short and scrappy letters with drawings on the back, amazing drawings with a charge behind them and a depth and strangeness of vision he could only wonder at.

He had sent money, presents, encouragement, received further drawings in return — each year more skilled and startling, until finally he lured Lyn down to London and the child-stranger turned into a brother and a man. Was that what he had craved for all along, a real flesh-and-blood sibling who could keep his father alive by sharing his genes with him, some last surviving link with Hernhope? Or was it more than that — some recompense to Hester, so that in supporting her son he absolved himself from the guilt of abandoning her? It had never been an easy task. Despite his skills Lyn was too proud, aloof and spiky to make good career material.

Matthew frowned into his coffee. Lyn now had the power to thwart him in one of the most important and ambitious projects he had ever contemplated. He had better go down to Cobham himself this evening and use some really forceful tactics. It wasn't just a question of Lyn handing over the diaries — though he seemed reluctant enough to agree even to that. He wanted the thing done properly, officially, with a valid legal agreement which would safeguard his own position when he came to draw up a contract with his publishers. It was actually quite simple. All Lyn had to do, in the absence of a Will, was get himself appointed as administrator of Hester's estate. Then, any arrangement he made concerning his mother's property (which included all her writings) would be sound and incontestable. It would also give Lyn the right to sell the house, and whatever Anne might say, Hernhope was better sold. It would realise some ready cash (desperately needed by them all) and prevent his brother running off to live in some outlandish fashion in the back of beyond when he, Matthew, required his services in London.

It wasn't mere self-interest. Lyn would gain as well, all along the line. Not only would he raise a tidy sum from the sale of the property and be free of its expenses and demands, he would also be paid a royalty on the published book. He might even offer an extra and immediate sum in cash, to tide his brother over until the house was sold and Hester's diaries published.

Matthew jabbed his pen against the blotter. Perhaps it wouldn't be that simple. Lyn could still refuse — had always been strangely proof against what he saw as bribes. Well — he shrugged — if reasonable persuasion didn't work, he would have to resort to threats. His brother must be forced to see his own advantage. Meanwhile, he would lock Lyn away with the notebooks and get down to a little planning on the book itself.

He took a piece of paper and jotted some figures on it — royalties, percentages, production budget, printing costs. There were endless decisions to be made, not just the financial ones, but the whole style and format of the book, the way he should present it, the type of market he was aiming for, its length, scope, size and content, the ratio of text to illustration, the whole production schedule. The actual marketing of the book would not be in his hands. Packaging firms like his had no sales or publicity departments of their own, but sold their books to big-name publishers who, with their greater financial resources and professional sales forces, were then responsible for promotion and distribution.

He had to choose his publisher, woo him with an attractive presentation. He already had a favourite one in mind. Hartley Davies were the obvious choice for this style and type of book and he had worked with them successfully before. They were a bright young firm in Bedford Square, large and well-established enough to support the book to the tune of some forty thousand copies, yet with unstuffy and flexible directors who would allow him his own head.

An American publisher was even more important, since a sale to the States would allow him to print a far greater number of copies and so improve his costings. In fact, a book like this could sell right across the world. He must put feelers out in every direction, bring in as many foreign contracts as he could, negotiate translation rights, a major Book Club deal, a television series, serialisation in one of the quality papers. Even with his publisher's help and backing, it would take months of planning and hard work, and he hadn't even secured his basic material.

He sat drumming his fingers on the desk. Better not wait till the evening to talk Lyn round. He'd clear his desk this morning, work through lunch, and be down in Cobham by early afternoon.

There was a tap on the door. It was James Spencer Allenby looking too relaxed in green and navy chequered golfing trews.

'What are you up to, Matthew? I've just been on the blower to Old Cognet and he says you've found our answer to *The Country Diary*.'

Matthew smiled. He had deliberately made one or two important phonecalls late last night. It wasn't too early to start a few rumours circulating, build up excitement and speculation. He had no intention of handing the thing to Hartley Davies on a plate. He wanted competition, rival bids to push the price up, maybe a cliff-hanging auction with all the top publishers outgunning each other, before he finally clinched the deal of his career.

'Come and sit down, Jim,' he said. 'Yes, I *have* got something to show you. Have you any interest at all in boot varnish?'

VIII

Matthew lowered his aching body on to the narrow iron bedstead spread with its two white towels, each stamped 'City of Westminster'. He still had his pin-striped suit on, even his shoes. Undressing came later, with shower, steam-baths, hot-rooms, cold plunge, and finally the body-scrub. First, he had to think.

Other men used clubs or libraries to do their thinking. Matthew preferred the old-fashioned gloom and splendour of the Porchester Baths, one of the last remaining Turkish Baths in London. The building was impressive, the location sufficiently out of the way to prevent him rubbing shoulders with other publishers. Indeed, the baths were relatively empty in the summer, when heat and humidity were high enough outside without doubling them in steam rooms. Matthew ignored the weather. He had been a regular client at Porchester Hall through almost thirty summers. He was respected there, known by name, assured of a gratifying combination of privacy and service.

All the heat and bustle of the baths themselves were sited conveniently downstairs. Here, on the ground floor, were only rows of little cubicles, each with its individual bed and chair, each curtained off by dark and heavy curtains, turning it into a monastic cell or sanctuary. Matthew always requested the far bed in the corner, the furthest removed from the muffled sounds of dressing or undressing, or the chatter of other clients. One of the attractions of the place was that it reminded him of his boarding school. There, too, he had had a cell with the same hard and narrow bed, the same confining curtains to prevent intimacy between boys. School had been a safe and solid place where emotions were cropped as short as hair and the outside world labelled strictly out of bounds. There could be no more abrupt unsettling changes — marriage, death, birth, bankruptcy. Unvarying rules and time-tabling kept life mercifully predictable. He didn't even need to mourn his parents because no one else had parents — at least not until the holidays — and most of those he spent at school as well. Ashdown Park was echoing and empty in vacations, but there was still a timetable, things you could depend on — hot roasts on Sundays, cold cuts Mondays, study in the mornings, a walk with Matron in the afternoons. Matron had aluminium fingers and a chalk-on-blackboard voice. Grey skin, grey hair, and the same stiff-white apron that Hester wore for baking.

Matthew lay back on the one thin City of Westminster pillow, closed his eyes. Hester's apron flared into a maternity-smock, her tight-coiled bun into swinging schoolgirl pigtails. Hester young, shameless, pregnant at eighteen. Impossible! He had come here partly to recover from the shock. He drew his wallet from his pocket, unfolded the torn-out diary page, read it for the tenth time. '*22/2, 1919. St Saviour's Hostel, Southwark. Today my son was born . . .*' That one short line had thrown him into confusion, sent his mind and emotions spinning again, when he had spent all last night imposing tight controls. He had done his best to conceal his shock from Jennifer. She had seemed upset enough herself and had only shown him the page with extreme misgivings.

He had driven down to Cobham that afternoon, stood puzzled in the overgrown front garden. Why had no one let him in, when he could hear a radio caterwauling? He tried the door. It wasn't locked. It was his house, anyway, so why not just walk in? He found Jennifer alone upstairs in the small and poky bedroom, lying in bed looking pale until she blushed. She was trying to cover her thin transparent nightie with the sheet.

'I'm sorry, my dear, I should have brought you grapes or flowers. I didn't realise you were so ill you couldn't even answer the door.'

She blushed still harder. 'It's . . . er . . . not that, Matthew. It's just that I've . . . Look, do sit down.'

There was nowhere much to sit except the bed. He had avoided that, perched himself on the window-sill between two wilting potted plants.

The window was open, but it was still stifling in the room, a sultry summer's day with no stir of breeze. He ran a finger along his constricting collar, envying Jennifer her naked neck and shoulders.

'Take your tie off, Matthew, if you're hot. Lyn's at the launderette. He'll make us a pot of tea when he gets back.'

It was more than tea he wanted. He used Lyn's absence to start on his campaign. He had rehearsed his arguments all the way down in the car — the importance of the diaries to history and posterity, and Lyn's selfishness in trying to keep their discovery to himself; his 'tribute to Hester' theme — a book of exceptional quality and beauty to be published as a memorial to Lyn's mother and a living monument to Hernhope; Jennifer's own contribution and fulfilment as a second Hester carrying on the traditions of the first. So far so good. He had thus established the solemnity and challenge of the project, its intellectual calibre, its historical importance. Only then had he moved on to matters of hard cash, hinting at insolvency if they impeded publication. A few hard allusions to the rising cost of living, the soaring cost of properties, the unfortunate necessity of selling the Cobham house, his firm's new money problems and urgent need for a really big success, its uncertain future without one, *Lyn*'s uncertain future . . .

Jennifer was looking more and more upset. He had slipped down from his window-seat, perched on the very edge of the bed. 'Look, my dear, I don't want to worry you, but there's simply not enough work for my designers at the moment, not without the Hernhope book. That would solve everything, of course, but if Lyn refuses to let me publish, then . . . You see, he's just not earning his salary at the moment. First he disappears for three months and now he's playing nursemaid here and . . .'

Jennifer struggled up from the pillows. He tried not to notice the way her nipples showed through the thin blue nylon nightie. She had nicer breasts than Anne. Anne had worn hers out by suckling four sons in succession.

'Matthew, listen — I know you think I'm just . . . what's that word? — malingering. But I'm *not*, I promise you. If I had 'flu or something, of course Lyn would go to work, but you see, I'm . . . not allowed up at all, not even to the bathroom.' She stared down, embarrassed, at her hands, then suddenly blurted out. 'I'm . . . pregnant, Matthew, and I've started to haemorrhage, and the doctor says if I want to save the baby, then I've got to lie absolutely still. *Now* do you understand?'

He had muttered a jumbled mixture of congratulations and condolences. His mind was reeling. He felt pleased for Jennifer, worried for her, but how would this latest news affect his project? He had been planning to use her to help sell and publicise the book. By the time it was published, her baby would be born, so long as all went well. A baby could be an extra selling-point. Babies had been used successfully to market everything from life insurance to face-cream. Jennifer would fit her nurturing role still better with an enchanting little infant in her arms, and radiant with new contented motherhood. He could even use the child, plug it as Hester's first grandchild and the new heir to Hernhope.

He took her hand. 'I'm thrilled, my dear. And so will Anne be when she hears. You should have told her yourself, you know. You're getting as secretive as Lyn is.'

She bit her lip. 'I'm sorry. Lyn's a bit . . . well . . . worried about it all and he . . . thought it best to . . .' Her voice had petered out. He noticed the nervous way her hands were picking at the fringes of the bedspread. There had been problems, obviously. He was well aware that Lyn had never showed much enthusiasm for the ties and responsibility of a family. Maybe he could exploit that when he tackled Lyn himself. The expense of babies, their need for a solid future and a settled home, how a family man could never afford to turn down any chance to improve his circumstances or benefit his child.

It hadn't worked like that. Lyn hadn't even listened. When he returned with the laundry and the shopping he had been brusque and unco-operative, annoyed that Matthew was there at all, resentful that Jennifer had told him she was pregnant. He finally slammed out again, leaving Jennifer in tears and all the groceries littered round her bed.

It was then she mentioned the diary page. She had been almost incoherent, sobbing about Lyn's moodiness and how he mustn't receive another shock since he was upset enough about her own condition, and if she showed it to him, would Matthew make a solemn promise that he would never, ever pass it on to Lyn nor include it in the published work, and if he was aware of what the page contained already, then please, oh please, would he . . .

Matthew rubbed his eyes. He felt drained by all the uproar. She had even asked him to unearth the page himself, extract it from a Tampax box, of all things! She wasn't allowed to move, not even as far as her own chest of drawers, where she had concealed the box by wrapping it in a pair of Aertex knickers, then stuffing it at the very bottom of the bottom drawer and piling clothes on top. It was all so cloak-and-dagger, so unnecessarily dramatic. That was why he had come here — driven straight to the Turkish Baths from Cobham, bypassing home and dinner. He needed time to recover, time to think.

He switched off the light in his tiny cell, lay in gloom except for the thin ribbon of light which crept between the curtains. Outside, two raucous clients were laughing and joking as they got undressed. Matthew frowned. The notices said SILENCE, yet were all too often ignored. He longed to close his eyes and just shut off. The diaries had taken their toll.

'Mr Winterton, your tea, sir.'

Matthew jumped. The attendant had slipped between the curtains with the tea-tray, placed it on the bedside table. He glanced at the thick white china (school china), the strong stewed tea-bag tea, the two uneven scoops of pink icecream, the cellophane-wrapped biscuits (McVitie's digestive sweetmeal). All comfortingly familiar. He never touched sweet things at home, drank only weak Earl Grey, but here in his secret hide-away he could become a child again. They had had pink icecream at school every Monday evening. It was Monday evening now. There was still some order in the world.

Or was there? Hester had dropped a bombshell through it. He had problems enough in deciding how to present the book at all, without this new perplexing issue of the baby. Should he include the mysterious pregnancy, or ignore it? It would certainly make a dramatic story, pro-vide a whiff of scandal for the prurient, a tale of loss and heartbreak for the sentimental, plus an almost Dickensian element of mystery and drama in the unknown parentage of a missing child. All things which would push his sales. Yet it was the mystery which worried him. If he introduced the baby, his readers would expect to see its picture, know its fate, and that fate might besmirch the Hester he had decided to present as a blameless model of old-fashioned womanhood.

Somehow, he wished to see her that way himself. It was a slur on his own family to think that Hester had come to Hernhope with some dubi-ous past behind her which she had concealed from her employer, and then to have married that employer under what were strictly false pretences, since she had led him to believe that she had neither man nor past nor child. All those stern morals had been covering something else. The woman who had slapped him down if he ever touched himself, had lain trembling and panting under a rutting man, maybe even encouraged her seducer. Matthew let the last spoonful of icecream slide slowly down his throat. He had to admit there was something intriguing about that seduc-tion, even provocative. He could see Hester rolling down her stockings, pushing up her skirts . . .

He snapped the light back on, forced his mind back to the issue of the baby. Probably best to kill it off, abort it before it ever saw the light of day on the printed page. He would reach a wider market if his book received a 'U' certificate, as wholesome all-round family entertainment with noth-ing to slur its country-fresh appeal or his own upstanding family. There was also his promise to Jennifer. Promises could be broken, of course, if a Higher Good demanded it, but he needed Jennifer's goodwill and co-operation if he were to use her in the project. She was right about her husband — Lyn *would* be shocked and confounded by the news of Hester's past. And he was relying on Lyn to do all the main design work on the book. No one else could touch him for skill and originality, no one else provide that all-important selling-point of being Hernhope's heir and Hester's son. It would be madness to upset him once he'd been persuaded to embark on the project and relinquish his rights to the material — and that was proving hard enough, for God's sake. Not only was he jibbing at the whole idea of publication, he also flatly refused to get himself appointed as administrator. Maybe that was just as well, since the whole situation was now dangerously complicated. They would have to swear in front of lawyers that Lyn was Hester's only child, and though Lyn himself might escape the charge of perjury since he knew nothing of an elder son, what about his own case? Was he obliged to inform his brother of the changed situation before making any deal with him, and if he failed to do so, was he then guilty by default?

Yet how *could* he break the news — risk upsetting Lyn so gravely that the downgraded second son might refuse to make a deal with him at all? Anyway, he was as wary now of lawyers as Lyn himself. They could waste months of precious time searching for an heir he was almost sure had died in infancy. There had never been the slightest hint or rumour in his boyhood of Hester having any living son — no mention of it in the diaries beyond those two brief lines. Until Lyn was born, years later, Hester's only child and interest had been himself.

He would check of course — double, triple check — search the records at Somerset House, snoop around that Southwark hostel, make a few discreet enquiries both at Mepperton and Fernfield. But he was almost sure he would draw a blank. So why allow solicitors to poke their expensive noses into private family matters he could settle on his own in quarter the time?

Best to bar the lawyers altogether. Nothing should go wrong if he were to make a private agreement with his brother, without letters of administration, once he had satisfied himself that the elder son was dead and Lyn still the only living offspring. All right, it wouldn't be quite as watertight as a formal legal contract drawn up with Lyn as administrator, but there were advantages, nonetheless. He might get a better deal that way, fob Lyn off with less, and it would certainly be less risky than raising the spectre of a rival heir. That mysterious nine-pound baby must return to the darkness where it had lain for sixty years, and neither his readers nor his brother must ever know it had seen the light at all.

Matthew eased himself off the bed, unbuckled his belt, untied his shoes. He had made his main decisions, and though Lyn still had to be persuaded to make any deal at all, he was confident he could change his brother's mind. He'd return to Cobham, intensify the pressures — but that could wait till morning. It was getting late now, and he'd better go down to the baths, before they closed. He removed his shirt and trousers, leaving his clothes folded neatly on the chair, remembering wryly that it was Hester who had taught him his neatness and efficiency. Strange how much he owed her, really. Gratitude was still mixed with resentment, excitement with distaste. He *would* make his book a tribute to her.

He walked down the steps into the hot and steamy basement, glanced at his body as he stood under the shower. Thank God he hadn't run to fat. He loathed obesity, worked at his figure with the same vigour and single-mindedness he brought to his business or his tax affairs. Endless self-control and a master plan. If he indulged in strawberry ice–cream once or twice a month, then he had it instead of dinner, not as well as. A small slice of toast for breakfast — nothing else — sugarless tea and coffee, using his legs instead of lazy elevators.

The water was gushing warm across his shoulders. He turned the dial to cold. It was a school shower now with its old-fashioned metal taps, its complaining whine and gurgle, its ice-cold water punishing the flesh. He cocooned himself in his towels and walked briskly to the steam-room, recoiling from the naked bodies all around him, with their slack distended stomachs, their flaccid folds of flesh. He closed his eyes, tried to plan his overseas campaign. . . .

All the different countries were running into each other, melting in the heat. He could feel his mind shutting off, his limbs relaxing, as heat engulfed him like a woman's body. Water was running down the walls, dripping off the pipes, plopping in warm droplets from the ceiling, mixing with his own sweat. Normally, he never perspired. He was a cold man, a controlled one, always buttoned up. It was a relief to be naked now, to feel his own dampness seeping into the towel, to taste biscuit crumbs still sweet and forbidden in his mouth.

The eighteen-year-old Hester was suddenly on the bench beside him, her shameful flaunting belly pressed against his own, her breasts leaking strawberry flavoured milk as he tongued and muzzled them. He tried to push her off. She herself had taught him to fear and discipline the flesh. Now he understood why. It was all too easy to sin, to fall. He had never allowed his own sons to indulge in 'dirty talk' or bring dubious comics home. Sex with Anne was quick and clinical. He had always preferred it when he was trying to make her pregnant, transforming that flat chest and girlish waist into the fruitful curves he craved. There was some god-like power in creating living sons from sperm and slime. Some men disliked the idea of sex with lumberingly pregnant wives, but the more Anne swelled, the more he had desired her. She had been working for him then, not just in his office but in some more basic and important way, carrying on his genes, his looks, his line, proving his fertility and his manhood. *He* had made her swell like that, changed her shape, endowed her with that seductive combination of hallowedness and vulnerability. He could see her now, nine months gone with Charles, her small face and narrow frame contradicted by that awesome bulge.

He groped out his hand towards her, touched only hard wet wood, forced his mind back to plans and timetable. He must produce his book as soon as possible, before any further crises could affect it — aim for a summery publication date such as middle May or June. If he started design in mid-August and production in October, he would have more or less nine months. That would be his *own* pregnancy — nine month' labour before he delivered his fine and bouncing offspring to the world, his profits running over, his coffers swollen with cash.

The problem was, could he deliver it on time? He really needed the gestation period of an elephant or a giraffe — but he couldn't wait that long to make some money. It was already early July and he hadn't won Lyn round yet, nor confirmed the death or disappearance of that irksome elder son. He would then need a breathing-space to study all the materials, decide on his plan and presentation, produce a dummy and sell it to a publisher. Even without wasting time on lawyers, it would still be an infernal rush. Yet he had to keep his cool, especially with all the worry of his tax affairs. One false step and . . .

He mopped his streaming forehead with his towel. It was difficult to concentrate. Someone had turned the dials up and the whole room was writhing with clouds of steam, swirling in his eyes, his mind. He groped through the warm wet fog to the hottest of the hot rooms — dry heat there — no vapour. He could almost *see* the heat, stretched like a shimmering gauze across the room, scalding the delicate membranes of his nose and throat. He could hardly breathe. The bench scorched his buttocks, the floor was too hot to step on. He lay back, smelling heat, tasting it on his dry and burning lips. It was too extreme for any woman, yet they had followed him even here. Anne gloriously pregnant with Hugh now, the teenage Hester still sprawling on her back, pigtails unplaited and tumbling round her shoulders. Now Jennifer had joined them, in her thin blue nylon nightdress, pulling down the ruching, letting her breasts spill over in his hands. Pregnant breasts again, full and firm. The room was packed with females — all young, pregnant, taunting. He stretched out a dozen mouths, a score of hands . . .

'Mr Winterton, sir, I believe you booked a body scrub. I'm ready for you now.'

Matthew opened his eyes. A brawny attendant dressed in gym shoes and a rubber apron was standing over him.

'Er . . . yes, Len. I . . . hadn't forgotten.'

He followed the attendant to the shower-room, stretched himself out on the cold white marble slab, wincing as it shocked his still hot and sluggish body. Len filled a metal bowl with icy water, flung it over Matthew's lower half. Thoughts of Hester drained away. A second bowlful, aimed at his chest and shoulders, sent Anne and Jennifer gasping down the sluice.

'Late for you, sir, isn't it?'

'I've had a busy day, Len.'

'You'll have the glove, sir, will you?'

'Please.'

The last of the pregnant schoolgirls crept away as Len picked up the scratchy loofah glove and scoured it across Matthew's thighs and stomach. He lay helpless on his back, a child again, being punished for his idleness, his forbidden feast of biscuits, his shameful private orgy in the hot room. Nanny Len flipped him on his front, drubbed him with a vicious bristled brush.

'Family all well, sir?'

'Fine, thanks.' They would have cleared away the dinner by now, the boys settled down to their homework, Anne preparing for the morning rush. He hadn't finished his own homework, got too distracted and aroused, but he would start again first thing in the morning.

Len rinsed him off with three sluicings of cold water, then slapped and pummelled his flesh as a final service. 'Right, that's it, Mr Winterton. Have a good evening, sir. It's still hot outside, they tell me. And lovely weather forecast again tomorrow.'

Tomorrow. Matthew climbed off the slab, purged, restored, refreshed. Tomorrow he must work on Lyn again, invite Hartley Davies's chairman for a drink and start a few rumours going, persuade his staff to curtail their summer holidays, think about a printer. Tomorrow . . .

'Business going better, sir?' Len was still hovering for his tip.

'Yes, Len, thanks. I think I can truly say that things are looking up.'

IX

Jennifer lay alone in her squalid bedroom, tried to ignore the dust, the mess, the overflowing waste-bin. A few short hours and she could be up again, make a start on the house. The haemorrhaging had stopped, the doctor was hopeful, she had saved her baby. She should feel more triumphant, but her early elation had withered like a rose attacked by blackfly. There were roses in the room, huge scarlet ones from Matthew's garden, brought on his second visit as a bribe and a reward. They needed water. They were drooping in the vase, petals already falling, splashed like pools of blood on her cheap white dressing-table.

Thank God she had stopped bleeding. Every drop had seemed like a cell or pore of her precious baby flushed down the lavatory or seeping into a sanitary towel. Even now, she feared it might be born minus vital bits and pieces, as if what had leaked away could never be replaced. 'Complete rest and relaxation', Dr Groves had urged, and as if in mockery, there had been constant turmoil and upheaval. Everything had got muddled up together — her baby, their return to Cobham, Lyn's fury, Hester's diaries, Matthew's pleadings and all their jobs and futures.

She closed her eyes and saw Matthew sitting there, his tall grey form shaming and over-awing the shabby little room, his voice booming and wheedling on, confusing her, enticing her, taking things away. She had been torn between him and Lyn, Lyn and the baby, even Lyn and herself. Now she felt only drained and exhausted.

She slumped back against the pillows, stared through the window at the jumbled roofs and chimneys jigsawed against the tiny square of sky. Cobham felt so confining after the splendour of the Cheviots. She missed Hester's house already. Eleven weeks had made her joint mistress of it, and even Lyn had seemed content to stay there, once he had recovered from his cold.

Spring had come and helped them renovate the house. Bare branches trembled into leaf, grass changed from grudging scrub to cocksure green, birds coupled, hatched and flew. Lyn had been a different person, then. They had laughed together, talked together, made love inside, outside, on walks, in woods, in bed. Proper love — the front way — but always with a Durex now. She'd had a strange instinctive feeling that it was too late for Durex, that she was already pregnant from their one encounter in the cellar, but dared not say in case words could somehow puncture it, make it just a dream. It *was* a dream in some ways — living in the country, working in the sunshine, watching Lyn grow healthy and contented as she cooked Hester's dishes, tried out Hester's herbs, and felt Hester's grandchild build from cell to cell inside her.

Only when her period was two weeks overdue did she feel she had to tell him. He might well have noticed himself, except he was always vague and ostrich-like about things like periods. She tried to choose her moment. It wasn't easy. They seemed always to be busy — eating, working, sleeping, discussing something else, even making love. It was worse when they made love — seemed a double deception to let him go on fumbling with those futile rubbers, taking all that trouble to prevent a baby who was there. Or was it? Could she be that sure? She had seen no doctor, had no test. Perhaps she was so eager to be pregnant, she was holding off her period by the sheer force of her will. Better see if she missed a second one.

She did. By then she was feeling sick as well, and her breasts were taut and swollen, which was harder to conceal. She couldn't bear to deceive Lyn any longer, but every time she tried to broach the subject, the words aborted on her lips. All the ordinary words like baby, expectant, pregnant, were somehow too worn and faded for the wild scared excitement leaping in her belly. It was more than just a baby — part of a whole tradition and a lineage. She had conceived this child the night she found the diaries, so it was special, sacred, meant. How could she present it to its father in stale, insipid clichés, while they were munching toast and marmalade or plastering a wall?

In the end, she made an occasion of it, cooked Hester's Celebration Pie and packed it in a basket with a chocolate cherry cake and a bottle of home-made wine. It was a shimmering summer evening in the first week of July, and they were lying on the grass at Windy Gyle, the hills crouched all around them, the sky so close it was almost touching their heads. They had picnicked there, alone except for the curlews and the sheep. She packed away the wrappers, scattered crumbs for birds, then stuttered out her news, voice weak and tiny like an embryo itself.

Lyn had said nothing, absolutely nothing. She wasn't sure if he had even heard. The steady munching of the sheep seemed to move closer and closer until it was roaring in her ears.

'Lyn, did you hear what I said?'

'Yes.' There was less blue in the sky, more cloud now.

'Did you know already? Had you guessed?'

'No.'

'Well, aren't you going to say something?'

'I . . . I don't know what to say.'

'You're pleased. Or worried. Or even angry. You must feel something about a child. *Our* child.'

'It's n . . . *not* a child. You . . . you probably missed your period because of the shock of Hester's death. Or being in a strange environment or . . .' Lyn was torturing a piece of grass, slitting it with his thumbnail into smaller and smaller shreds. 'Look, we'd better go back. It's getting cold.'

When they got in, Lyn went straight upstairs. She could hear him opening cupboards, slamming drawers, went up after him. Their suitcases were lying on the bed, already overflowing — not her careful tissued packing, but muddy shoes on top of shirts, books creasing up her clothes.

'What are you doing, Lyn?'

'We've got to leave. Now.'

'Leave? Why? Whatever for? I thought we'd planned to . . .'

They had argued for an hour or more, Lyn insisting that the idyll was over now and he must return to work and Matthew's office before they were destitute; she begging that they stay and suggesting ways of survival. They could become almost self-sufficient with a few hens and ducks, a vegetable plot, an animal or two . . .

'And what are we going to use to buy our animals?' Lyn made them sound ridiculous, impossible like dinosaurs.

'Well, we could both get jobs to start with — to tide us over the bad patch. *Any* jobs — casual ones, just to save enough to set us up. And I could work at home, as well. Make things and sell them, like Hester did herself.'

He had gone silent then, pacing up and down the bedroom, hands clenched, head down. She sat and watched him, struggling with her own rage and disappointment.

'How *can* we go? Just waltz off and leave the house to fall apart? We haven't even finished the repairs. And all those things we planted in the garden — they'll be ruined if we go. And what about my friends? Molly was coming round for lunch tomorrow, and I'd promised to help with . . .' Her voice was rising, losing its control.

'We can phone Molly — now. Ask her to keep an eye on things. Tell her you're not well.'

'That's not true, and anyway she'd think we're mad rushing off like this. It *is* mad, Lyn, you know it is. Totally unreasonable.'

He had suddenly swung round, heaved the suitcase to the floor, pulled her on to the bed instead, clung to her, almost hurt her with the fierceness of his grip. 'OK, it *is* unreasonable — unfair, insane — I admit all that, but what else can I do? Don't you see, I'll lose my job if we stay up here? You know what Matthew's like. How can I keep a . . . a family if I'm out of work or on the dole or something? Anyway, it's not just a question of money. It's . . . it's . . . I can't explain, but it would be lousy for a child if its father didn't . . . Anyway, it's not a child — of course it's not. You're probably just unwell. We must get back to Cobham. You can see Dr Groves there and he'll give you a proper check-up and . . . Oh, please don't cry, don't *cry* . . .'

*   *   *

They had motored back to Cobham in under nine hours. Lyn drove so fast, she had felt jolted, sick and terrified, not the glorious morning sickness of early pregnancy, but a sour and desperate nausea as their protesting Morris gasped along the motorway.

The Cobham house smelt fusty when they entered it at dawn, seemed small and makeshift after the solid walls of Hernhope. The garden was a wilderness. Morning sulked through the windows with drizzle and grey skies. Lyn had put the kettle on. It seemed strange to turn a switch instead of stoke a range.

'Cup of tea? You look pale, Snookie.' He had used her love-name only in relief because they were home and she had already started bleeding. Just a spot or two of blood, but enough to threaten a pregnancy. She turned day into night and went to bed at seven in the morning. The bleeding got slowly worse. The next day the doctor came — not the cheery, swarthy Mepperton hack, but the suave and Old-Spiced Cobham thoroughbred who expected sherry on his house-calls.

He confirmed the pregnancy. 'But you'll have to rest, my dear. Go to bed and don't get up at all until the bleeding's stopped completely. That long drive probably shook things up a bit, gave your babe a fright, but if you stay put now, you can save it.'

She had sunk back against the pillows and felt her fear and nausea turn slowly into triumph. The baby she had craved and willed and prayed for was now a concrete medical fact. She hadn't dreamed it, hadn't just imagined it, and she would lie in bed for nine whole months, if necessary, so long as she could save it. Lyn had snatched his coat and slammed the door. It was the first and only time she had been totally at odds with him.

94

It was as if the baby had cut her off from being a faithful reflection of his moods. Instead of fretting with him, she had felt like a firework — sparking, fizzing, glittering — a shower of Golden Rain lighting up the whole of greater London.

When Matthew came on Monday, the firework had burnt out. The bleeding hadn't stopped yet, sleep had proved impossible, and Lyn who needed nannying himself, was having to act as char and nurse. He couldn't cook, so he brought up little messes, sloppy scrambled egg with baked beans floating in it, burst and blackened sausages, even a jelly which refused to set. There were worse messes under her bed. She found it unbearably embarrassing that he had to empty all her chamber-pots — cope with smells, excretions, urine mixed with blood. She was totally dependent on him, for her food, her potties, even a clean nightie. It frightened both of them.

She had been almost relieved when Matthew walked upstairs. The house was so tense, she was glad of any distraction. Lyn had urged her to keep quiet about the baby, yet she longed to share her news, make it a triumph again, instead of the crime and tribulation Lyn had turned it into. But there were only further problems, so it seemed. All the things they had returned to Cobham for — the house itself, Lyn's job, his security and steady salary — were now threatened and at risk. 'Unless you agree to publish,' Matthew smiled.

That only set up fresh fears. He had alarmed her with his talk of unique historical documents, his insistence on employing experts and research-ers to fill in all the background to the diaries and create a living slice of history. What if one of his experts discovered she had tampered with the record, by tearing out a page, accused her of falsifying history, defacing important documents? Or supposing Matthew simply guessed that some-thing had happened to Hester, to account for the gap in the diaries and her puzzling change in life-style? Even Lyn had thought it strange when he read his mother's jottings as a servant down in London and the sudden break with her gracious Fernfield childhood. She had had to keep reiterating how war disrupted *every*one, and how the death of Hester's father (like his own) had obviously resulted in a total change of fortune.

With Lyn, it had been a private matter only, but Matthew was planning to open up the diaries to the world. In the end, she was so scared, confused, exhausted, so upset by Lyn's latest bout of anger, that she confessed about the page she had removed, blushing crimson as she rummaged in her Tampax box. She'd felt relief as well as shame. At least she wasn't the only one who knew now. She had also done her best to protect her husband, save him further shock. Yet Lyn still refused to agree to publication. She herself had reluctantly acceded, as the only way to save them all from a bleak uncertain future. She tried to talk him into it, in return for Matthew's help.

'*No*,' he'd said, banging down a bowl of tinned rice pudding and a spoon. She couldn't eat it, not when he had garnished it with anger. It was still congealing there when Matthew and the doctor arrived almost simultaneously the following afternoon, Matthew with his roses, the doctor in his riding mac. The fine spell had broken now and it was drenching down with rain. But there hadn't been a drop of blood since midnight.

Matthew had prowled around the kitchen while Lyn took the dripping coat and showed Dr Groves upstairs. He felt her tummy, examined her breasts. Lyn was staring at the floor, one foot tapping nervously.

'Fine, Mrs Winterton. Things have obviously settled down now, but I'd like you to stay there another forty-eight hours, just to be absolutely safe. If there's no more bleeding at all, you can get up and carry on as usual, but nothing strenuous please. I won't call round again. Just make an appointment to see me in my surgery and we'll book you a bed for your confinement.'

Lyn had showed him out again. She'd watched them from the window, the doctor's Cambridge-blue Rover 3500 gliding round the corner, Lyn drooping by the gate, rain darkening his shirt-sleeves, beating on his head. He had started to walk away from her, down the narrow street, shoulders hunched, hands stuck in his pockets.

'Lyn,' she'd called. 'Come back!'

He returned an hour later, shoes squelching, trousers waterlogged, and clutching a bedraggled bunch of anemones in a soggy twist of paper. 'For the baby,' he had murmured and tossed them on the bed. Matthew's Crimson Glories were already smirking in a cut-glass vase, Matthew himself sitting on the bed, pouring tea from an expensive china teapot they used only as an ornament.

'Tea for you, Lyn?'

'No, thanks.'

She had poured him one herself. 'Look, have a cup. You're soaked. There's a dry shirt in that drawer there. And you ought to change your shoes. You'll . . .'

He hadn't moved, hadn't touched the tea, just slumped by the wall, hair dripping on to his shirt. She was damp herself, the wet stems of the anemones seeping through the sheet. She picked them up and smelt them. The blooms looked bruised and feverish, smelt of nothing.

No one spoke. Matthew checked the teapot, cleared his throat. An aeroplane droned over, and in the next-door garden a child began to cry — a shrill and fractious wail which got slowly louder. Lyn suddenly sprang up, lurched towards the door.

'All right,' he said. 'You win, Matthew. You always win.' His voice was very low and controlled as if he feared to let it off the leash. 'Publish your bloody book and be done with it. There's no way out if I've got another mouth to feed.'

The very next day, he returned to Matthew's office and started work on the layout of the book. Matthew didn't believe in wasting time. The arguments continued. Matthew was planning to use the flower and wild-life drawings in the sketchbook as another aspect of Hester's charm and skill. Lyn insisted they were Susannah's work and had no place in the book.

'You can't *prove* they're Hester's,' he muttered.

'And you can't prove they're Susannah's.'

Lyn flung his pencil down. 'Look, I know this isn't Hester's work. You're just hoodwinking the public, spoiling the book by packing it full of lies.'

'I'm *pleasing* my public, Lyn, and enhancing the book with some delightful illustrations. There's no proof who did them either way, in fact, so let's not argue, shall we?'

Jennifer turned on her side, tried to get more comfortable. At least the quarrels were confined to the office now. She was glad Lyn was back at work. She needed peace to recover, adjust to her new role. She was to be not just a mother — that was promotion and wonder enough — but a vital part of Matthew's whole new project. He had explored their Cobham kitchen, marvelling at booty brought from Hernhope, recognising almost forgotten objects from his boyhood — Hester's wooden gingerbread moulds with their carved design of rose and thistle, the handsome ham-stand with its central spike, the smoked glass spice jars still mostly full and fragrant, the cream and butter coolers. Even in the rush of leaving Hernhope, she had insisted on collecting up these treasures so that she could take some part of Hester back with her.

'Do you realise, Jennifer, we're both working for the same end — to glorify and resurrect Lyn's mother? You see that, don't you? We have a personal responsibility to her, a family pride and loyalty to safeguard and perpetuate everything she wrote.'

He made it sound solemn and exalted, close to the sense of mission she had experienced herself. She tried to explain to Matthew what Hernhope meant to her, how she longed to return there and make it live again. Couldn't they use their own share of the money to turn dream into reality?

Matthew hesitated. It wasn't quite as simple as that, he explained. He was working out a scheme whereby she and Lyn would receive a royalty, but royalties took time to dribble in, and even when they did, it would be wiser to invest the cash rather than blue it straight away. Money should be used to make more money. Once the book was doing well and had been sold around the world, then they could discuss properties. For the moment, though, he preferred them both to live close by, so they could all pull together on his project.

She had to admit she liked the idea of unity and harmony, an end to all the bickering, the constant divided aims. While she was pregnant, she was content to live at Cobham anyway — especially since the bleeding. She had seen it as a warning, decided to take things quieter now, avoid all risks. A smaller house would be easier to manage. Besides, her baby was due in the very worst of winter, when snow could cut her off in a remote and hilly spot like Hernhope. Safer to have it here in the milder south, with help and hospitals more accessible. Matthew had even promised to pay her a mini-salary if she stayed at Cobham and continued her work on Hester's recipes. That was money for fun. She could transform the place into a tiny southern Hernhope, a shrine to Hester herself.

What worried her more were Matthew's plans for using her to help publicise the project. He had mentioned a trade launch and sales conference, to be held as early as November, and then a mass of interviews in publication month. Her baby would be four months old when the book was launched in May, but Matthew said they could hire a nanny for a while. It all sounded rather grand and very frightening. She had found it hard enough to address the Mepperton Young Wives, let alone a throng of important publishing men.

Yet she had promised to co-operate. Matthew had already paid them a small lump sum for relinquishing the diaries, plus the prospect of Big Money once the book had proved itself. All Lyn's grouses about the financial impossibility of living up at Hernhope could then be overruled. For once, she was grateful to Matthew, glad he was around. Now that she was pregnant, she needed someone strong and solid to lean against, a shrewd businessman to take care of all the problems.

Slowly, she eased herself out of bed. She was allowed to go to the bathroom now — thank God — and by six o'clock this evening, she could get up altogether. She glanced at herself in the mirror — cheeks pink again, as if all the relief of Lyn's surrender and the thrill of the doctor's reference to her confinement had blossomed on her face. Lyn was none too happy yet about the baby, but he would come round in time. Even Matthew, who was stern and strange enough in many ways, still delighted in his children, and had even once admitted he would have gladly welcomed more.

She picked up one of the pillows, cradled it in her arms. It was May now, not July — May ten months away — and she was a mother and a media-person. She wasn't quite sure what she was meant to say, or where. Press conferences and sales conferences were all muddled up together in her mind. She imagined somewhere grand like the Albert Hall, with delegates and journalists jostling in the aisles.

'Ladies and gentleman, I'm not much good at speeches, but . . .'

A sudden cramping pain zig-zagged across her belly. She lurched into the bathroom, leaned against the wall, tried to steady herself. A second spasm collapsed her on the toilet seat. She bent double, face in her lap, half sobbing, half imploring.

'Help!' she called. 'Lyn . . .'

Lyn was in Matthew's office, turning Susannah's drawings into Hester's, setting Hester's words.

The pains were stabbing now, continuously. She needed a doctor or an ambulance, but how could she get downstairs to phone one? No, mustn't panic. Better stay where she was and just let herself go limp, concentrate on breathing. She tried to inhale slowly and rhythmically while counting up to ten. That would calm her down. One, two, three . . . She shouldn't have got up at all. As soon as the pain had eased a bit, she would struggle back to bed — on her hands and knees, if necessary — and stay there until Lyn returned, insist he called for help.

Wait . . . things were calming now. She would count on up to twenty, then try to creep downstairs. Safer to phone immediately, not waste any time. Eleven, twelve, thirteen . . . A pain ripped through the fourteen, turned it into a gasp. She felt a violent urge to empty her bladder, void her bowels. She hardly knew which, because pain and urge and panic were now all mixed up and jabbing.

Groaning, she bore down, stared between her legs as the shining scarlet clots and lumps she had been nursing as her baby, plopped and slithered into the toilet-bowl.

X

November 21st.

London fumes and sleet outside, but green fields and country vistas within the glowing confines of the hotel room. The publicity department at Hartley Davies had never before lavished so much time and effort on a sales conference. Huge blown-up photographs of the Cheviot Hills rolled across the walls. Jennifer's home-made cheeses were piled like a golden harvest on the tables. Bowls of flowers stood all around the room — country flowers forced out of season in a London incubator.

Hartley Davies had booked this second, larger salon to hold the lunch. The conference room upstairs where the morning's less illustrious books were still being discussed over orangeade and biscuits, was hardly equal to the Publishing Sensation of the Year. Matthew sat waiting for the session to finish and for Hartley Davies's sales team, gathered there from every part of the British Isles, to troop downstairs for the most important item on the agenda.

Allenby was with him and his most trusted editor, Kenneth Ruth-erford, a man who could set him off without eclipsing him, and who combined good appearance with a sympathetic manner and articulate sincerity. All three of them sported large white daisies in their buttonholes — bogus, Matthew felt, but a gimmick suggested by Publicity to attract attention and create a country mood. Gimmicks *worked* in publishing. The whole business was a gimmick, in a sense, and yet with a book like theirs, the thing retained its dignity and style. Matthew Winterton could be seen to be furthering the cause of education, upholding art and style, raising publishing standards right across the board. He had always refused to work with trashy books. Profit didn't have to mean the gutter.

Christ, though, he needed profit at the moment. The boys' school fees had just gone up for the second time that year; his tax affairs might suddenly backfire; two of his younger editors were pressing for a rise; and the firm still had to recoup its losses from both *The Medieval Bestiary* and *Europe's Last Great Kings*. If cockatrice and crowns couldn't fill his coffers, then Hester Ainsley must.

Privately, he still thought of her as Ainsley. After the first raw shock of discovering the true facts of Hester's life and parentage, Matthew preferred to regard her as he always had — as housekeeper and nursemaid. It made it easier. Now that her diaries had become a job of work for him, the main hope and promise of his firm, he found it essential to drown all personal feelings as distracting and undignified, to forget pity or remorse and see Hester purely as a source of profit. On the other hand, the fact that she had become a Winterton could only help his own share in the monies. Thus she remained Ainsley in his memory, while signing her name as Mrs Thomas Winterton across his bank account.

That name had been tattooed into his soul, branded across the foreheads of his staff, scrawled up and down his office walls, written in the sky. He had worked so hard on Hester Winterton that he found, even in his sleep, the letters of her name would hover huge above his pillow and shrill till they had woken him. He had got the price he wanted in the auction, but then followed weeks of unrelenting slog. He had far too short a time to produce the materials needed for this conference and for the Frankfurt Book Fair in October, where he aimed to clinch his US deal. Allenby advised postponing publication till autumn the following year, instead of May, but Matthew was obsessed now and refused to brook delay. He bribed his staff to cut down on holidays, extend their working day, and fit in all the extra overtime they could.

Matthew had learnt, only late in life, that it paid to be munificent. That way he kept tighter discipline, yet still retained his staff. One man, highly paid but working well, still cost less than two middle-range salaries for virtual layabouts. He also believed in his own brand of incentive scheme, whereby extra work was handsomely rewarded. He had observed that his staff's absorption in a project increased in direct ratio to the size of the carrot dangled in front of them. He had been dangling giant-sized carrots these last few months. Even so, he was impressed by their loyalty and sheer hard labour. It was as if the book itself had brought out the best in them.

He glanced at Kenneth sitting on his right. He looked pale, drawn, short of sleep. He suddenly longed to grip his hand, embrace him, blab out an ardent thank you for his efforts. He had thanked his colleagues formally, of course, in a brief typewritten memo. Emotions were always safer when channelled through the barrier of dictaphones or secretaries. All the same, it would be nice to risk a word or two in person. He cleared his throat. 'I've . . . er . . . been meaning to say . . .'

'They're coming!' Kenneth rose to his feet, brushing down his already immaculate suit. The doors were opening and the tide of representatives shambling in, with the Hartley Davies team snapping at their heels like sheepdogs. Matthew glimpsed receding foreheads, flabby stomachs, inferior dental work in ill-shaped mouths. The human race resembled a badly executed book put together by an idle or even malevolent production team. If *he* had been its managing director, he would have made a better job of it. His own dark hair might be silvering at the edges, but had neither receded nor thinned. He weighed less now than when he was a youth. His teeth were all his own and had never been allowed to glut themselves on sweets. He had never smoked, drank only as a social duty and made a principle of refusing second helpings.

The Hartley Davies chairman, Sir Basil Brooks, wore his second helpings like a padded lining to his suit, and would have failed a medical on girth alone. His fat cigar was a permanent eleventh finger, the other ten jaundiced with nicotine.

'Ah — Matthew — good to see you.'

'You're looking well, Sir Basil.' Matthew shook the stained hand, tangled a moment with the mingled waft of Havanas, sweat and Aramis, and was swept into the circle of salesmen, several of whom he recognised from a previous Hartley Davies sales conference. Packagers rarely attended sales conferences, in fact. It was more common for the publishers themselves to present the books to their representatives. But Matthew had always insisted on full involvement. Like a mother with her baby, he trusted no one else. It was also helpful to get to know the reps in person, make sure they understood the full value and importance of his projects.

Sales had never been so vital. *Born With The Century* had cost him more, so far, than any book he had ever handled before. He had to recoup that cash. Hartley Davies had committed themselves to a substantial order, of course, but they were so large and successful a company, failure could only graze or ruffle them, not kick them in the gutter. *He* needed success, not only for his status, but for survival.

He glanced swiftly around to make sure his staff were earning their inflated salaries. They were. Kenneth was thawing the notoriously moody Scottish representative, and Jim had taken on the clown who covered Derby and South Yorkshire who had two wives, six children and a fund of dirty jokes. The Hartley Davies mob were equally hard-working. Their publicity manager was filling glasses — mixing sherry with sales promotion puffs — while the marketing director rounded up the stragglers and swept them towards the loaded tables.

It was almost time for lunch, not just a stop-gap sandwich, but a campaign and celebration in itself, planned as a vital part of the whole promotion. Rustic serving wenches in low-cut gowns had been hired from Party Promotions Limited and were carrying in home-cured hams and duck terrine, pigeon breasts and turkey galantine. Many of the dishes had been prepared from Hester's own rural recipes, but enlivened by additional ingredients which she herself could never have afforded, and washed down with country wines in a quantity she would have strictly disapproved of. Each table had its centre-piece of a huge pheasant pâté — moulded in the shape of the bird itself, with real feathers stream-ing from its tail, legs and claws fashioned out of asparagus spears, and glistening black olive eyes. Everyone was crowding round the tables exclaiming and admiring. Hester Winterton had transformed the stand-ard conference fare of tasteless chicken and tinned fruit salad into this lavish country spread.

Sir Basil Brooks waved his cigar for silence. Babble and brouhaha were replaced by a sudden shrill from the Northumbrian pipes, as Jennifer swept in. Her entrance had been staged, like every other detail of the promotion. She was dressed demurely in a becomingly old-fashioned skirt and high-necked blouse, with her hair piled up on top and make-up as artlessly natural as art could make it. Round her neck gleamed a cameo of Mrs Winterton senior, scaled down from one of the photographs. She carried a wicker basket piled high with fruit and flowers, and fragrant with sprigs of lavender and thyme. Matthew felt this was taking things too far and cheapened Jennifer as some latter-day Nell Gwyn. But Hartley Davies's new publicity girl had spent three years in New York, where even full-grown authors prancing around as bunny-girls or spacemen were not considered vulgar, so long as they helped sales.

Certainly Jennifer was the centre of attention as she was led blushing to her seat beside Brendan Holdsworth (London North) who had won the award for Top Salesman of the Year. Matthew prayed she wouldn't let them down. Jim Allenby had been strictly opposed to involving her at all. He claimed the book was Hester's and needed no one else. He also feared that Jennifer had not the force and personality ('oomph' he called it, vulgarly) to launch so vast a project. But Hartley Davies had backed Jennifer from the start. They felt she gave the book a contemporary relevance, linked it to the present, provided an appeal to the younger, modern woman for whom nostalgia meant little. Not that Jennifer was modern. That was the charm of it. She was inherently so home-spun and domesticated, it was simply natural casting to turn her into Hester's mouthpiece, the female who ran an empire from her cottage, could cope with anything from chickens to chicken-pox, and who fused nature and nurture in a new appealing package.

Matthew glanced across at her, smiled encouragingly from his own adjoining table. Hartley Davies's staff and his had been deliberately seated among the salesmen to prime and rally them. The serving girls presented each representative with a pewter goblet of home-brewed country wine. Goblets, wine and wenches had all come from the same promotions firm. It was that fine attention to detail which had won Hartley Davies respect; the way they could turn a book into a fanfare or a conference into a carnival. The representatives would not forget this lunch. Hester Winterton would sit in their stomachs all through the winter months, and gently remind them she deserved their support and sales until her Second Coming in the spring.

Matthew himself was toying with half a slice of ham and a glass of Evian water. Let the rest upset their stomachs while he retained his control and confidence. There could still be tricky questions. London Central's Larry Barker was already on the attack.

'Isn't it a little strange promoting a book that's based on your own family?'

Matthew smiled at the sallow face and heavy spectacles. He had feared that question from the start. The whole Hester Winterton project could be seen all too easily as vulgar profiteering, marketing his own family house and history in return for hard cash.

'Well, not strictly *my* family.' Matthew filled Barker's glass. The country elderflower was a strong and tactful wine, ideally suited to covering awkward pauses. 'Only part of the book deals with my father and his farm at all and even then it's really Hester's story. I did have qualms, of course, about publishing the material. In fact, I wondered once or twice if I shouldn't hand the whole lot over to someone else — someone completely detached from it. But then I feared we might lose that very emotional involvement which gives the thing its charm. Besides, I wanted to ensure a really high standard for the book. Another firm might have trivialised it or tried to cut corners or save on costs. We decided on the highest quality for every single aspect of it — paper, printing, production, photographs. And we've designed a whole country range of . . . Ah, but I'm giving away my secrets, aren't I? Those must wait till after lunch.' Matthew's smile ached. These junketings could be more of a strain than the presentation itself. The noise was roaring round him like a tide. Wherever he looked, mouths were rudely masticating, laughs exploding like wine-corks, wine flushing faces, food swelling girths. Pheasant pâtés were now empty plates of feathers, pigeon breasts pathetic piles of bones. The crisp white tablecloths were stained with wine and strawberries, crumbs and olives trampled into the floor. He had often wished the human race had been programmed differently, so that it required not these slavering blow-outs, but merely a pill or two washed down with a glass of water between one meeting and the next. But at least this lunch had proved successful. Hester Winterton was no longer simply Item Twenty on a tedious agenda, but a woman who had wined and dined them, made them feel important, left them happy sated suitors.

Coffee was served with tiny almond sweetmeats and a concealed cassette of birdsong, which was all but drowned in the general hum and chatter. Matthew slipped out for a moment. He owed himself ten minutes in the Gents' to run through his breathing exercises and check on the notes for his speech. He emerged steeled and spruce, almost bumping into Jennifer who was slinking out of the adjoining Ladies' room.

'All right, my dear?'

'Y . . . yes — well — maybe a bit . . . nervous about my speech. I still wish Lyn was . . .'

'Lyn's better off at home. He'd only distract you, anyway. Don't worry, you'll do absolutely fine.' Matthew took her arm. He was relieved that Lyn had refused to attend the conference. That way, he could sell his brother's elegant design-work without risking the problems of his presence. Lyn was still moody and unpredictable, apparently furious with himself that he had ever agreed to support the book at all.

'Right, up we go, my dear. Mustn't keep them waiting. Only two-and-a-half minutes to kick-off.'

*   *   *

The smaller conference room had also been transformed. A huge retouched and tinted photograph of Hester Winterton stared down from the main wall, flanked by smaller portraits of the actors in her drama and stirring pictures of peace and war, disaster and romance. Lyn's own exquisite hand-lettered map of Northumberland had been mounted on a screen, showing Hernhope with its crown of hills, Fernfield with its river. More flowers now graced the tables, and bowls of fragrant pot-pourri outscented the cigar smoke. Every representative had his special Hester Winterton presentation pack including samples and illustrations of all the spin-off merchandise (country cookbooks and facsimile greetings cards, herb pillows and pomanders, floral scents and soaps), together with photographs and family trees, a copy of Lyn's map, and a fully illustrated calendar of the Shepherd's Year.

The dummy itself was mainly blank beneath its attractive cover, but a few sample spreads gave a foretaste of its range and splendour. It was a big book, a weighty book, enlivened with charming drawings and old-world photographs, and combining diary, history, and farm and kitchen management with wildlife, folklore and a wealth of town and country detail. It would be a prize, a triumph, a collector's item, the perfect gift for a wedding or a birthday, the one bright star in Winterton and Allenby's firmament.

Matthew took his seat between Sir Basil and Jim Allenby. His own men and the Hartley Davies team were drawn up on one side of the table facing the reps on the opposite side, as if they were poised for battle. It *was* a battle. The reps could make or break a book. However much time and trouble a publisher might lavish on a project, if the salesmen didn't back it, it was doomed.

The Hartley Davies chairman rose slowly to his feet. The hum of conversation stuttered into silence as forty pairs of eyes fixed on the wavering point of his cigar.

'Ladies and Gentlemen, I think I can safely say without any fear of contradiction, that we have reached the high point of this conference. We now present a venture which can only be the envy of every other publisher in England.' A pause, as growing expectation rippled round the room. 'We have, as you know, worked with Winterton and Allenby before, so we are well aware of the exacting standards and meticulous attention to detail they lavish on every book they produce. This time, Matthew Winterton's own family provides the background to the most important and exciting project he has ever launched' — longer pause before a clarion call — '*Born With The Century* — the story of a house, an age, and a most amazing woman.'

Matthew rose. Every eye had shifted to him now. Long, lean frame, narrow shoulders, everything sculpted to its sternest outlines. Pale, pinched face he liked to regard as sensitive, though some had called it cadaverous. Thin lips, sharp nose, no spare flesh to bulge or compromise. Well-defined eyebrows darker than the hair. Eyes of a daunting brown which could stare you into silence. Hands as restless as his brother's, but better trained.

'Good afternoon.' The slightest curving of the lips — broad smiles were Jennifer's department. 'Ladies and gentlemen, I neither like nor trust superlatives. In fact, as my colleagues know, I very rarely use them, but this is a book which deserves all the superlatives already heaped upon it and which is perfectly suited to the mood of the country at this moment. We have all seen the strong current interest in nostalgia, the fascination with "Upstairs, Downstairs", the continuing curiosity and compassion aroused by both world wars. *Born With The Century* satisfies *all* those interests. It also contains some of the most delightful nature paintings ever done by an amateur. Hartley Davies have already proved the popularity and profitability of back-to-nature books. This book is set against the background of one of the most remote and beautiful of England's landscapes, but it is more than just a nature book. It tells the story of a country woman's courage in a world twice torn by war. It does not neglect the seamier side of life. Hester Winterton's family was ruined by the First World War, so she was forced to come to London to take a humble job, moving from gracious living in a country mansion to the pains and perils of a servant's life in the below-stairs quarters of a large hotel. After the drama of these tough but fascinating years, we return to Northumberland again — this time to a remote hill-farm in the Cheviots, my own father's home, in fact, where Hester came as housekeeper and nanny. We follow the toils and triumphs of the farming year, a way of life still almost medieval in its simplicity and peace. War and unemployment hardly touch these hardy hill farmers, yet we, the readers, are not denied the political and military dramas of the 'thirties and 'forties. Letters to Hester from her former friends in London, reports from her cousin who was fighting with the Eighth Army, cuttings from the Newcastle newspapers on riots and rationing, bombs and blackshirts — all these are preserved in this truly amazing record of our century.'

Matthew took a sip of water. It gave him a chance to assess the mood of the conference. No one was doodling, fidgeting or slumped; all eyes were still turned towards him, faces rapt. He carried on.

'This book is fundamentally different from any I have been involved in, not only on account of its scale and quality, but because it is a personal book, a family one, built on my own name. I did, of course, have many worries on that score. My brother, Lyn, Hester's own son and the exceptionally gifted designer of the project was, in fact, extremely reluctant to publish the material at all. I shared his doubts. But the more I studied it and came to realise just how unique and valuable it was, the more I felt we had a duty to the public. Some of these records have a genuine historical importance or add to our understanding of country life or social customs. It seemed wrong and small-minded to keep them to ourselves. Events have proved me right. An enormous interest and excitement has already been aroused by this book. Those who have seen the original documents and diaries share my own feeling that we are making not only publishing history, but history itself. The book was a triumph at Frankfurt where we attracted an enormous amount of interest from foreign publishers and opened negotiations with five of them. Cindy Scott will tell you more about her extensive publicity plans and impressive advertising schedule in just a moment, but before that, I would like to present a brief videotape based on the material of the book itself, to show you something of its charm and range.'

Lights down. Bitter-sweet music to create the mood. Hester Winterton's sad, solemn face staring from the screen, then fading into the Northumbrian hills. Matthew felt memory and longing tug a moment at his soul, as the grey-browed farmhouse loomed out of the mist, trembled into focus and seemed almost to accuse him. Ridiculous. No one could live in a wilderness like that, let alone make money or reputation. He was lucky to have escaped it. These images had been carefully selected to work on the sentiments of the sales reps — not his own. He glanced around. The watching faces revealed not just the bored obedience of men paying back their lunch, but genuine interest and emotion. The film had been skilfully directed. Photographs of Hester and her family were fused with live footage of public and political highlights of the period. The scene swept from seething London life to lonely curlews calling on the hills.

106

Kings, coffins, babies, bullets, lambs — all the things which aroused shock, outrage, tenderness or pride — clustered round the central figure of Hester, as if she herself had set life and death in motion.

Matthew kept his eyes on the audience rather than the screen. The film had touched them, moved them, taken them beyond the level of mere sales and statistics and shown them a life they could personally respond to. He let the silence linger for a while as the last image faded on the screen, and the music, sadder now, sobbed slowly to its close. This was the moment to punch home the media schedule, to switch from soft sentiments to hard sell. The one had been fostered only to effect the other.

The publicity girl from Hartley Davies was already on her feet, an over-painted blonde with a geometric haircut and a loud clinching voice she used like a hammer in an auction room.

'Hi there! I'm Cindy Scott, Publicity. Nice to see you all, and I can certainly promise you some really ritzy spending on this book. We're pushing it harder than all our other spring books put together — with big press coverage, including full-page ads in all the Sunday colour supplements, plus features in two nationals and several women's magazines. Radio 4 have already been wooing us about the possibility of a half-hour programme based on the book, and we're also angling for some television time — an interview on BBC's "In Town", perhaps, or one of the classier chat-shows. We've also planned . . .'

Matthew was smiling as he listened, relishing the details. He glanced across at Jennifer. She was staring down at the table, face flushed, chewing on a pencil. A tendril of her hair had slipped from the hairpins and was trailing down her collar. She looked vulnerable, bewildered, and totally out of place, as if she had strayed in from another century. He tried to catch her eye, to reassure her, but she was communing only with the table-top. The boom and clang of Cindy's voice seemed hardly to affect her, even when it spoke her name.

'And then of course there's Jennifer — who will be the vital link in this campaign, the living breathing Mrs Winterton, almost an advertisement for the book herself. Jennifer has been modelling her life and larder on her mother-in-law's and has made some very exciting discoveries already. I'll leave her to tell you about them in just a moment. Let me add that we intend to exploit this angle, to cash in on current fads and crazes. The whole natural foods, natural-living thing, for instance, is getting really strong right across all age groups. It used to be a middle-class minority interest. Not any more. It's a universal passion — anti-drugs, anti-doctors, back-to-nature, back-to-the land. You can't open a paper nowadays without some mention of bran or honey or wholemeal bread, or alternative medicine or throw-away-your-junk-foods. Well, Hester Winterton is our perfect prophet, the guru of this whole country movement. She lived like that all her life, more or less, grew her own vegetables, baked her own bread, cured her own bacon; managed without all our modern aids. Even when she lived in London, she still made her own cosmetics out of homely things like lemon juice and oatmeal, and dosed the other servants with her home-made herbal mixtures. In the 'thirties, when she was back again in Northumberland, she kept her own house-cow and made cheese and butter — both by hand. Jennifer hasn't got room for a cow yet,' (laughter) 'but she's working on it. She's carrying on all the old traditions. She must be one of the few girls in England who actually makes her own cheese, single-handed, using Hester's own equipment, and milk from a local farm. You've sampled the cheese already — *and* her home-made bread. In fact, most of the delicious dishes we've just enjoyed at lunch were adapted by Jennifer from Hester's recipes. She's tested them all and brought them up to date. She's also proved that Hester's herbal medicines are not only effective but a lot less dangerous than our modern drugs. This is the message of the book. It's not just empty nostalgia. Nostalgia alone has been worked to death. We're offering a dramatic slice of history, but tied firmly to the present, Hester's life made even more exciting and important by Jennifer's involvement in it.'

Matthew made a quick check along the line of reps. He could see they were still intrigued. But it was essential now that Jennifer should raise her head and make some contact with them. The whole conference was discussing her, centred on her, yet she was still slumped in her seat, eyes cast down. Cindy was sitting on the table now, one long leg crossed high above the other. At least the reps had something to distract them.

'Jennifer will, of course, help to launch the book. She's a winner, as I see it. It's not every girl who's turned a tiny workman's cottage into a full-scale farmhouse and a cabbage patch into a pharmacy. That's news itself. We're going to send her out to sell this book for us, and I don't think she can fail.'

Fail. Cindy banged the word down so vehemently it seemed to shatter on the table. Matthew shrank away from its broken fragments. What if Jennifer *did* fail? Could she really bear the burden of this whole campaign; or had he been foolish to ignore Jim's warnings? Even now, when everyone was waiting for her to get up and introduce herself, she was still just a bowed fair head without a face. Cindy had to act as puppet master, pull her by her strings. As she trembled up, another strand of hair tumbled from her top-knot. She tried to fix it, lost a shower of hairpins, glanced desperately at Matthew.

'Er . . . good afternoon.' Her cheeks were so flushed, the words came out pale and sickly in comparison.

'Louder', he mouthed.

'G . . . Good *afternoon*.' Her voice tailed off again. 'I . . . er . . . don't quite know what to say.'

Christ — she ought to know. He had been coaching her for weeks. He tried to prompt her, cue her in, but she was still dithering there without a tongue. Perhaps he should get up and speak again, himself. There was still time to change the media plans. Jennifer wasn't a hundred per cent essential. They could phase her out, present the book another way, work on a new publicity angle. Yet they couldn't save this conference. If Jennifer dried up now, or proved herself an impossible figurehead for so vital and prestigious a campaign, then all their preparatory work, all that expense and trouble on the lunch, would be so much mockery. The reps would return to their regions at best confused, at worst contemptuous.

The room was so tautly silent that noises from the street outside were trespassing in and taking over — the nervous stops and starts of London traffic, the scream of an electric drill. Up till now, there hadn't been a world outside, only the sob and smile of Hester's century. Jennifer shifted from one foot to the other. Matthew was *willing* her to speak, reciting her words over and over again in his own head, as if he could somehow squeeze them out of his brain into hers. Ah — he tensed. At least she had opened her mouth and was saying *something*.

He held his breath. It was not the speech he had written for her. She was venturing out on some new tack of her own. And wasn't she slurring her words a bit, swaying very slightly on her feet? Good Christ! The girl was tipsy. Why on earth hadn't he realised before? He remembered, now, watching her at lunch. She had eaten almost nothing, but had been clutching on to her wine glass as a prop. Brendan Holdsworth must have filled it once too often. That would explain the flush, the sway, the fluster, the lapse of memory. Supposing she went further — belched, hic-coughed, disgraced herself and him? He hardly dared to listen as she stuttered on.

'Actually, I . . . never knew my mother-in-law. She always sounded . . . frightening. I mean, when people talked about her, she seemed . . . well . . . almost like a . . . witch.'

Matthew shut his eyes. Words like 'witch' were utterly forbidden. She must have found them in the wine. What was Jennifer saying? She could ruin everything by being too outspoken, departing from her brief, the deftly crafted paean he had so carefully prepared for her. Hester was to be presented as a dignified and towering figure — aloof, perhaps, but never eccentric.

'To tell the truth, the only time I saw her, she was . . . *dead*.' (Matthew winced). 'So I thought I'd be . . . doubly frightened. The undertaker couldn't come till the next day. My husband was naturally . . . dis-traught, so I did . . . everything myself. I'd never touched a corpse before. When my own mother died they took the body away, and I was so upset, I was useless anyway. But with Hester, I felt . . .'

Matthew's hands were normally cool and dry, but now he could feel traitorous sweat slinking across his palms. You didn't bring death to sales conferences — or at least, only boastful death on battlefields or tragic epitaphs softened by stirring text or skilful photographs — not these sordid and tasteless references to corpses. The reps had only just finished their lunch and hardly wished to be transported to a sick room with a dead and stinking body upsetting their digestions.

'I *was* scared, in fact, but when I plucked up courage and went to close her eyes, she was . . . sort of . . . *watching* me. Oh, I know this sounds quite crazy. I don't even have the words to explain it properly, but it was as if she *had*n't died — well — not completely.'

Matthew cleared his throat in warning. If Jennifer went any further with this ghost-and-spirit lark, this airy-fairy supernatural rubbish, they would label her as cracked, dismiss her out of hand. She must be stopped immediately. The trouble was, she had her back to him now. He had told her a hundred times to face the reps when she was speaking to them, and that bit she had remembered, while forgetting all the rest. He coughed again, tried to warn her off, but she was in the middle of her story and seemed determined to continue, talking louder, with fewer 'ums' and pauses.

'The next day, various neighbours called, including a very old woman who used to work as a midwife and often helped at deaths, as well. She told me, in the old days, the room where a person had died was always draped in white, and sometimes a sprig of yew was tucked in the folds of the shroud before the coffin was nailed down. She said yew was a symbol of immortality, you see, and the white meant resurrection and prepared you for the after-life.'

Matthew's nails were digging into his palms. Shrouds and coffins were hardly selling-points. Jennifer had been instructed to laud the *living* Hester, not a body in a winding sheet. Yet there she was, still loitering by the death-bed.

'Actually, I don't believe in . . . heaven and things myself, but I did feel then that perhaps some people — special people or wise ones or just very strong and determined characters like Hester — could perhaps live on down . . . here, in some . . . strange way we can't yet understand. Anyway, I draped everything in white. I found some beautiful white damask in the linen chest which I used for the shroud itself. I wanted everything to be . . . right. I had to go miles to find a yew tree. All the trees around the house seemed to be spruce or fir or pine. I broke a bit off and laid it between her hands. That way, I knew I could . . . preserve her. Oh, I know it sounds . . . peculiar, but . . .'

Downright crazy, Matthew thought. If Jennifer went on like this, his whole project would be doomed. Wine had clouded her powers of judgement, wrecked his careful plans. She had never been used to alcohol, so even a little could push her over the top. Mind you, at least she had stopped swaying and seemed reasonably in control. It could have been *worse*, he supposed. She might have broken down in giggles or . . . He shuddered. The most important thing now was to shut her up. If she maundered on much longer, his book and reputation would both be ruined. Even now, she had only reached the funeral.

'It was rather strange, you see, because at the service the Vicar was

110

wearing white vestments. That's unusual for a funeral. I mean, white is for joy and celebration, not death and mourning. I suppose it was because it was still so close to Easter, but all the same, I took it as a sign that . . . Oh I don't know — it all sounds so far-fetched when I try and tell you, but I just felt Hester's . . . presence all around me, not dead, but watching still. Then, when I found her diaries, I had this weird feeling it was — well — *meant*, that Hester and I were somehow . . . *linked*, brought together by some . . . outside power.'

Matthew's cheeks were flaming with embarrassment, hands clutching at the table-edge, gaze fixed on the carpet. He dared not catch the representatives' eyes. He would have to interrupt this hocus-pocus, this rambling gibberish before Jennifer was catcalled out of the room. Slowly he looked up. Every eye was turned to her, not scoffing or ridiculing, but fascinated, rapt.

He stared. Surely he was mistaken. Perhaps that total pin-drop silence was due to boredom, not attentiveness. But no. Even Basil Brooks himself was utterly absorbed. Matthew could hardly understand it. It couldn't be her charm or sex appeal. Jennifer had never been a beauty, and frankly looked a mess now. The whole elaborate hair-do had tumbled into anarchy, the country flowers were fading, the careful make-up streaked. It was her words which had caught their interest, those very words he had blushed and cringed at himself. He had judged too swiftly, reacted too unfairly. There was a lot of current interest in the supernatural and Jennifer had somehow harnessed it, hit on a brand new selling-point, without any formal briefing. Her scrag-end of a speech was working far more effectively than the professional polished piece he had so laboriously prepared for her. She was even selling the diaries now, in her own strange and fumbling fashion.

'I just wanted you all to know how . . . *real* those diaries were for me. Once I'd found them, I was almost . . . taken over. I never imagined for a moment they'd be published. In fact, I even opposed the scheme at first, but now I'm glad everyone else can share them. I've really got to know Hester these last few months. She's taught me such a lot, you know, about plants and birds and animals. And a mass of household hints, and new skills like lace-making. More important things as well — things I can hardly . . .'

Matthew stared at the radiant girl, transformed by her own enthusiasm. She was half-turned towards him now, and he could see her eager open face, completely free from guile or affectation. These men were so accustomed to the slick patter of the sales drive, the polished posturing performances laid on for them like false and heartless television commercials, that Jennifer's integrity had a shining power and truth. She spoke so feelingly, so naturally, she made girls like Cindy Scott seem bogus and rehearsed. And she was even gaining confidence — describing Hernhope now, with fewer hesitations.

111

'It's *Hester*'s house, of course. It always will be. You probably think I'm making too much of Hester. I did wonder that myself, in fact — whether the shock of her death was making me just imagine things. But it *wasn't* imagination. You see even after the funeral, when I felt perfectly calm and rested, I was . . . still aware of her. One afternoon, I was walking along the valley, collecting dandelions. I was trying out one of her recipes for home-made wine. She said it was most important to gather the dandelions before the twelfth of May, because the flowers are larger and brighter then, and they make the wine smile. It was May the ninth, I remember, a rather wet and blustery day with lots of fat white clouds tearing along the sky. I couldn't have felt more normal. I'd spent the morning scrubbing out drawers and cupboards and making leek and potato soup. I wasn't tired or hungry or drugged or shocked or anything. And it wasn't even spooky dusk or twilight, just a plain, quiet, ordinary afternoon. And yet I heard her voice. *Hester*'s . . . Speaking to me.'

Jennifer paused, rubbed her eyes, smudging the mascara. The silence was electric. It was because she looked so ordinary, the sort of fairish, prettyish, untidy girl-next-door whom everyone felt at ease with, that her words were so convincing. She was not marketing a gimmick or selling a commodity for someone else's profit. She was telling her own truth. He could have paid a hundred thousand pounds to try and create such drama and excitement, and still not brought it off. Jennifer had achieved it by her own ingenuousness. She was still speaking in that excited, artless fashion.

'And that wasn't the first time. I'd heard her voice before — the day I found the diaries. That's partly why I felt . . . Oh, gosh!' She suddenly broke off, turned round to face her brother-in-law, stared at him in horror. 'Matthew, I'm *sorry*. I'm meant to be making a speech, and I've been rambling on so long, I haven't even started it.'

Everybody laughed. It was the relief they had been waiting for. The supernatural had worked its subtle magic, but now they needed a break. Again, Jennifer provided it. She had sunk back in her seat, blushing and apologising, all the reps craning towards her, asking questions, genuinely fascinated. It was as if the conference had slipped out of its straitjacket and was now sprawling in its shirt-sleeves.

Treat the sales reps as your friends, he had advised her, and she had taken him at his word. She was chatting to them as freely and unaffectedly as she might have done to Anne, promising them favours, cheeses, herbal remedies; doing more for his book than he had ever planned on paper.

His mind was working furiously. He must exploit these new factors in his publicity campaign. He could weave the supernatural into interviews and press reports, get Jennifer to repeat her performance up and down the land. He wouldn't sweat so much, now, about careful formal speeches. Jennifer's own impulsive spontaneity had profit gushing out of it. He would have to coach her still, of course — all those falterings would never work on television, but she needed rehearsing in her own fresh and artless style.

He could hear her now, babbling on about some tonic which Hester had concocted for Thomas Winterton for vigour in old age. She didn't even realise its sexual implications. Innocence — that was the word he wanted. It was rare enough these days, yet Jennifer had brought it to this conference and won them over with it. She wasn't the slick professional Allenby had wanted, but it was because of that she had made her points so well. He could see it working right across the media. Jennifer would stun them as a novelty, someone honest and refreshing after a string of jaded veterans.

Matthew picked up the dummy, turned to the inside back cover where Jennifer's photo smiled uncertainly, still shy, endearing, modest. She would bring it off. It was Hester he was selling, but in six months' time, her daughter-in-law would be bewitching her way into every home in England.

XI

T V TEARS SENSATION!
VITA SAYS 'I DIDN'T MAKE HER CRY.'
BEST SELLER BOO-HOO!
TOP SHOW ENDS IN TEARS
SOB STORY!

Jennifer stared at the rack of morning papers shouting out her shame to the whole of Waterloo Station in the rush hour — to *all* the stations, all the newsagents, in all the towns and hamlets of the British Isles. She could hardly believe how she had been rocketed from obscurity to fame — or notoriety — in the space of just a fortnight. The six long months before that, she had stayed mercifully out of the limelight while Matthew produced his book and began to sell it round the world. Then came publication day in England, and she had been launched on her glittering trajectory up and down the country in a fallout of promotion.

Even so, she had never made the headlines. There had been interviews on radio, signing sessions in book shops, quiet and flattering profiles on the inside pages of magazines and newspapers — not these vulgar slurs hogging the front pages, tasteless photos of her distorted features and streaming eyes upsetting people's day. The trouble was, there was so little other vital major news. No one had tried to assassinate a president or kidnap a tycoon. No Paisleyite had knifed a Papist, nor pig's heart been transplanted into man. All that was left was Jennifer Winterton's tears, hallowed and increased in value because she had shed them over Vita Sampson. Vita was always News. Men found themselves bewitched by her, women jealous, hostile, or slavishly in thrall to her, copying every detail of her hair, her dress, her glare. If Jennifer had the temerity to upstage her on her own programme, then it could only add a frisson to the nation's breakfast.

Jennifer hadn't wanted breakfast. She was still slumped sleepless in their Cobham sitting-room when Matthew phoned at seven o'clock that morning, and invited (ordered) her to meet him at the Ritz for a breakfast interview with Rowan Childs. Her stomach heaved at both the breakfast and the name. She had never met Ms Childs, but had been belaboured in her column. Ms Childs disliked the book and had attacked what she saw as its sentimental sham, with her characteristic mixture of parody and poison. Jennifer had been worsted in the first round and would be trounced in the second.

She hadn't slept at all. She had arrived home late and trembling from the television studio, and found Lyn already in pyjamas, angry and embarrassed that his wife's emotions should be served up to the nation like so much pap. She had sat with him in their denuded sitting-room, surrounded by wooden crates and packing-cases, and tried to calm him down.

It wasn't easy. She was so exhausted and disoriented from her whistle-stop tour of Britain, she needed calming down herself. As the pressure and publicity increased, so also did the problems. The most recent one was the sale of the Cobham house. Matthew had assured them that the offer was too generous to be refused, and since they would soon be looking for their own bigger, better place, the sale had come at a most convenient time.

'Convenient for who?' stormed Lyn. 'We've hardly received a penny from Matthew yet, let alone enough to buy a property.'

'We will,' said Jennifer. 'Just be patient, darling. Anyway, there's still Hernhope. I don't see why we shouldn't live there, despite what Matthew . . .'

'Oh, don't start that again, for God's sake.'

'I'm sorry.' Jennifer kicked her shoes off. Her own patience was stretched like old elastic. She was annoyed with Matthew herself. Cobham had never been perfect, never even been their own, but at least it had proved a refuge from the glare and roar of the publicity campaign, and she had spent precious time and trouble transforming it into a tiny model Hernhope.

The irony was that the real and larger Hernhope was standing empty while they were doubly homeless. Matthew kept reiterating that they shouldn't presume to live there without proper legal sanction. Molly disagreed. She missed Molly, longed to be her neighbour again, instead of just a distant voice at the other end of a phone.

'Of *course* you can take the house on,' Molly had boomed down the line, the last time she had rung. 'Who could stop you anyway? If you ask me, Jenny, Matthew's pulling the wool over your eyes, so he can keep you where he wants you. It suits him, doesn't it, to invent reasons why you mustn't move up here?'

'Yes, but . . .' Jennifer's voice tailed off. She had suspected that herself. Matthew had taken a trip to Mepperton nearly a year ago now — the first visit since his boyhood — checking on that mysterious bastard baby. He had also prowled round Hernhope, come back reporting problems. There was trouble with the generator, the water supply was dodgy. Yet when she and Lyn were living there, both power and water were fine, and anyway, things could always be repaired. Lyn was working a ten-hour day in Matthew's office and could hardly commute from a northern wilderness — wasn't *that* the crux? How could she argue, though, when Lyn himself refused to return, hated her to mention Hernhope at all? So she had done her best to compromise, created Hester's empire down at Cobham, on a smaller, humbler scale. But now it would be taken over by careless urban strangers while she and Lyn lived out of packing-cases.

Lyn was swatting his leg with his dressing-gown cord. 'You're never here, in any case. What's the point of having a home at all, if you spend half your time in television studios and the other half dashing up and down the country?'

'It was only for a fortnight, Lyn. And it's nearly over now. Things will be back to normal in a week or two.'

'I'll believe that when I see it. The phone's been ringing non-stop since that wretched programme. Every Vita fan in the country seemed to want to speak to you or dry your tears or send you a box of Kleenex. It'd still be ringing now if I hadn't taken it off the hook.'

'You shouldn't do that, Lyn. Matthew may be trying to get hold of me or Hartley Davies or even . . .'

'See? You're as bad as they are. Can't bear to miss a chance to hog the limelight. Try the "News At Ten", next. It gets even higher viewing figures than Vita Sampson, some nights.'

'Lyn. That's . . . mean. Horrid.'

'Forgive me.' He came across and held her, hugged her so hard she could hardly breathe. 'I *love* you, Jennifer, but I'm not too keen to share you. Can't you understand that? I've hardly seen you these last few weeks and everything's such a mess and . . .'

In the end, she soothed him off to bed and sat alone downstairs, collapsed on the sofa with a cup of instant soup. Things *were* a mess, all round. She glanced around the room. Even here, she couldn't avoid the book. Copies of it were littered on the sofa, looming on the shelves; press

115

cuttings scattered on every surface, letters from readers, agents, publishers. This was the publication which was meant to have brought them peace and happiness, a new life in the country, an end to money wrangles. Instead, it had set off a tide of disagreements, even with her husband. And now, a whole year on from those first fruitful days at Hernhope, here they were, still tied to Matthew's apron strings — homeless, childless, sleepless.

She had stretched out on the sofa — tried to switch her mind off — only half succeeded when dawn tapped at the window with its squall of birds. At least she was bathed and dressed when Matthew rang with his summons to the Ritz. She had to re-do her face and hair, of course. A quick comb and a dab of lipstick weren't enough for London's leading female journalist. She patted her head to make sure the elaborate coiffure wasn't tumbling from its pins after the shove and jostle of the crowded commuter train.

She was still dithering in the station, trapped in the tide of impatient office workers pushing and pressing past her as she stood staring at the newspaper-rack. She longed to swap with them, to face only an in-tray or a typewriter instead of Rowan Childs. The station seethed and swirled around her, sun shut out of it, air stale and over-breathed. Someone tapped her on the shoulder. She swung round.

'Excuse me, Miss. You're Jennifer Winterton, aren't you — the girl who cried on the Vita Show last night? You really had her worried.'

'No, I'm . . . sorry. You've . . . er . . . made a mistake.'

'Who you kidding? Look, there's your photo in the *Mirror*. Trying to tell me you're her twin or something?'

Jennifer dodged away. Crazy to stand in front of all those newspapers, reflecting her face and pointing their fingers at her. Behind them, in the station Smith's, copies of the book itself were piled high in the bestseller section, shouting out her name. That name had always been a small and private thing before, signed neat on cheques or sitting unobtrusively on birthday cards or letters. Now it had introduced itself to every reader in the land, forced itself on strangers. The book was *part* of her, its ink and pages fashioned from her flesh and blood. Every time she glimpsed it in a book shop, she felt as if a lump of her own dismembered body had been left on the counter for crowds to poke and peer at. She and Hester had swelled and multiplied until they filled the British Isles. More than twenty thousand copies sold already. Twenty thousand people gouging pieces out of her, snapping off her limbs for souvenirs.

Now she'd appeared on television, her pursuers came in *millions*. Ten million viewers panting for her autograph, stopping her in stations. She wasn't worthy of it. Someone else had cut and styled and coiffed the book, doctored and distorted it, woven all the threads together, then thrown it to the masses in a champagne froth of bubbles. She was just the figurehead, mouthing Matthew's opinions, signing her name to a preface she hadn't even written, shining up her smile.

She had assumed that it was over, that now at last she could return to peace and Lyn and anonymity, but one stupid, shameful breakdown had thrust her into another round of being a primped and public person. Lyn *loathed* that public person. The book had forced itself between them like one of those huge bolsters placed between courting couples in medieval times to prevent them having contact. It was as if Hester were alive again — not the gentle, human Hester she had discovered in the diaries, but Lyn's all-powerful Mother, spying, forbidding, terrorising. Hester was angry about the invasion of her privacy, the way her private diaries had been thrown as sob-stuff to the world. The loyal and gentle tribute originally intended, had grown less reverent and more vulgarly commercialised.

Jennifer glanced at the Smith's display stand, where twenty Hesters stared her accusingly in the eye. Matthew had found an old and faded photograph and instructed his art department to retouch and refine it. Yet, for all their pains, it had somehow come out wrong. Hester was strength, force, monument — the guardian spirit of Hernhope, yet they had watered down her vigour, removed her grit and toughness, turned her into a sweet and simple rustic. Hester was iron with a streak of gold trapped in it, not buttercups and muslin.

Her own photo was equally misleading, although smaller and less prominent, tucked away on the back flap of the cover. The hair was false, the smile bogus; eyes and mouth retouched to make them larger, the whole thing posturing and painted. They had been obliged to make her glamorous to match all those glamorous people — journalists and disc jockeys, interviewers and publicity agents, photographers and columnists, all skilled in the art of sham.

Lyn was jealous of the lot of them, especially as he had stayed at home while she swanned about on tour. She had gone instead with Jonathan, Cindy Scott's assistant at Hartley Davies. Jonathan was blond, spruce, smooth and safely homosexual. Lyn distrusted and despised him. Queers made him uneasy. He had been accused too often of being one himself.

At least Jonathan wasn't accompanying her today. Matthew had decided to take on Rowan Childs himself. She had already accused him (in her column) of distorting history and romanticising war. He would be smiling at her now, pouring her tea and sugaring it with charm. She mustn't keep them waiting. She hurried to the exit and joined the queue for taxis, eyes fixed firmly on the pavement. That queue was composed of readers, viewers, listeners, all eager to cross-question her, denounce her as a cry-baby. She had always hated London as an uncaring, anonymous city, but now it was the overtures she dreaded, the tapping on the shoulder, the shaking by her hand.

A taxi swooped mercifully to a halt. She climbed in, slammed the door.

'Where to?' asked the driver, turning round and staring at her. 'Ah — the Ritz, is it? Yeah — thought I recognised you. I knocked off early for a change last night and just caught the end of Vita Sampson. She really got you, didn't she? Not that I blame you, love. She's that tough she'd make *me* cry.'

Jennifer mumbled some reply. She didn't want to think about Vita Sampson when it was Rowan Childs she was about to battle with. She peered at her reflection in the taxi window, tugged at the hairpins in her coiled and uneasy bun. She hated it swept up like that, but Matthew insisted that she dress in the spirit of the book. The week before publication, Hartley Davies Publicity had packaged her like another of their products. Television was cruel to curves, they told her, so she had been forced on a rigid diet and squeezed into stern black skirts and throttling high-necked blouses. Once the tour began, she lost half a stone through nerves. Meals became not sustenance, but Sales. Up at six in strange hotels, swotting up her speeches at the breakfast table or spouting them at lunches, lashes stiff and sticky with mascara, excess lipstick bleeding on to coffee cups, five-course dinners hiccoughing into midnight over expansive port and brandy when all she wanted was Horlicks and her bed. Today, it was back to the arena — her real self left at Cobham and only a hollow mask to face the world. She felt her fear heavy like the make-up, sticky like the hair lacquer, holding all that falseness in its place.

Trafalgar Square was choked with rush-hour traffic. It seemed extravagant to dawdle in the snarl-up with the meter ticking over, but if she got out and walked, she was bound to be accosted.

'Didn't I see you on . . .?'

'Wasn't it you who . . .?'

She wasn't *any*body. She would only disappoint them. They'd expect a historian, an expert, a sparkling girl who could juggle words about, not a tired, jaded bungler who could neither speak nor write. Even the taxi driver was pestering her with questions as he turned into Arlington Street and pulled up outside the Ritz, where a supercilious doorman helped her out. She over-tipped them both. (At least Jonathan had spared her the intricacies of tipping.) She paused a moment at the daunting hotel entrance with its banked flowers and frock-coated lackey standing just inside. A woman in a nylon overall and yellow rubber gloves was scrubbing down the steps. Sixty years ago, she could have been a Hester. Hester had worked in a grand hotel like this, where the rich still battened on a thousand menials who rose at five to lay fires and empty slops, then crawled to bed in their cramped and chilly attic rooms, while the guests were still carousing in the ballrooms. Those were some of the saddest entries in the diaries, the ones Hester had written from her lonely garret as she stared out at the rude and unfamiliar London streets and was stunned by the city's cackle after the velvet-fingered quiet and dark of Fernfield.

Jennifer stopped. How could she swan into a hotel built of gold-dust where a single night could set you back a hundred pounds? That was more than a whole year's wages for a Hester in the 'twenties. She trailed down the steps again, stood on the pavement surrounded by a pile of dustbin bags overflowing with rubbish. Those were the Ritz's faeces, its excrement and phlegm — rotting strawberries grey with cigarette ash, broken bottles bleeding into mouldy bread.

She stood dithering on the kerb, watching the flies buzzing round a fishbone. Matthew would be waiting for her, frowning at his watch, Rowan Childs glaring there beside him. She turned again towards the lights and flowers.

'May I help you, Madam?' The doorman looked suspicious. Visitors to the Ritz didn't paddle in the rubbish.

'I'm . . . er . . . meeting someone.'

'In the foyer, Madam, or out here?'

'I'm not sure. We're . . . er . . . having breakfast.'

'Ah, you'll want the restaurant, then. Go right along the corridor and you'll see it straight in front of you.'

'Thank you.' Did she tip him again? If only Matthew had arranged to meet her here, instead of leaving her to face those sneering lackeys with their gold braid and their tailcoats, those miles of hostile corridor.

She walked through the revolving doors and was assaulted by the glare of lights, the gleam of gold and marble, the echoing dazzle of gilded mirrors repeating and repeating her. A priceless Chinese carpet stifled her footsteps, towering ceilings reduced her to pygmy scale. The scent of hot-house roses made her own cheap perfume seem vulgar and oppressive. Everyone else was grander, glossier, gift-wrapped — tourists with calf-skin cases and cashmere cardigans, businessmen in Cardin suits. The corridor seemed endless. Chandeliers beamed at themselves against the mirrored backdrops, marble pillars framed a shell-niche fountain where a goddess garbed only in gold-leaf stared at two cherub mermaids. The restaurant itself looked more like a salon in a French Renaissance palace. It seemed almost blasphemous to eat eggs and bacon amidst all that swagged and gilded decoration. The painted beauty of the cloud-swept ceiling echoed the real white clouds beyond the ruched and tasselled curtains with their froth of nets. Pink tablecloths and napkins matched the chic rococo chairs. Jennifer thought of Lyn perched on a packing-case in their Cobham kitchen, drinking cut-price instant coffee and trying to scramble eggs.

'Good morning, Madam. Are you taking breakfast? Mr Winterton? Ah yes, he's waiting for you.'

She stumbled after the waiter. The restaurant was already busy, tycoons and tourists propped behind their newspapers. Someone was sure to recognise her. She should have worn dark glasses, except they made you still more conspicuous. Only pop stars or major alcoholics took breakfast in dark glasses. The waiter was still striding across the redmedallioned carpet. She could feel a hundred eyes stalking after her.

'Ah, Jennifer. At last.'

She jumped. It was Matthew rising from his table in the corner, immaculate in thunder-grey.

'Am I late? I'm sorry. The traffic was really awful. Oh *gosh* — you've brought the papers.' There they were, piled beside his table, screaming headlines, sobbing photographs, invading this pretty-pretty, never-never world where no one talked above a whisper, let alone burst into vulgar tears.

'Well done, my dear. This is the best coup we've had yet and just when our publicity needed a final boost. I've been swamped with calls already.'

'Where's . . . er . . . you know . . .?'

'Rowan? She phoned to say she's been delayed in traffic and she'll be a little late. That's all to the good. It gives us time to prepare. I won't order breakfast until she comes, of course. But how about a cup of tea? There's plenty in the pot.'

'No thanks.'

'Cheer up. We're all thrilled with you. It's not quite what we planned, of course, but things often work out better when they're — well — spontaneous. You've always had that gift, Jennifer, to be entirely natural.'

'Matthew, you don't understand. I feel an utter fool. All those people watching me break down like that. And losing control and . . .'

'It was delightful, Jennifer, a proof of your genuine involvement and integrity. People warmed to you. They felt you were human, someone like themselves. It was exciting for them, in a way, to see real emotion on the screen, instead of the prefabricated kind, or poker-faced reactions.'

'But everybody's looking at me. I mean, even on the station, total strangers came up and . . .'

'That's good — the sort of publicity publishers dream about. It can only help the book.'

Book, book, book. Sometimes it felt so large and omnipresent, it was as if it were pressing her down like a gigantic metal clamp, squeezing all the life and joy out of everything she touched. Take breakfast at the Ritz. In any other circumstances, she would have enjoyed it as a treat — munched her way through the menu, marvelled at the marble walls, the glittering golden carvings on the ceiling. Instead, she felt sick with dread.

'Matthew, *please* put those papers down. I don't want people staring. Look at that waiter over there. He can hardly tear his eyes away.'

'Don't be absurd, my dear. They're far too well trained to stare. Famous people are two a penny here. Now how about a glass of orange juice?'

'No, really, I'm . . .'

'Well at least have a look at the menu and decide what you want to eat. Once Rowan arrives, we don't want to waste precious time on nonessentials. Her paper's got a circulation of three-and-a-quarter million, which means an actual readership some three or four times that. You see, if you take the average newspaper, it's read by . . .'

'Yes, Matthew, I know. You explained all that before.'

Jennifer stared at the people eating and drinking all around her, American tourists with three fried eggs apiece, Japanese businessmen tackling melons filled with strawberries. Hester had fed on broth and scraps when she had been working as a maid. One unplanned pregnancy had tipped her from a teeming white-clothed table to a quick crust in the scullery. Babies had such *power*. Even in her own case, one unformed embryo had endless repercussions. If she hadn't fallen pregnant, they might never have left Hernhope, never got involved in publication, never . . . She closed the menu.

'I'm sorry, I'm not hungry.'

'Well, just have a slice of toast, then. You'll need something to keep you going. I've arranged an on-the-line interview with BBC Radio Ulster as soon as this one's finished.'

'Oh *no*, Matthew. I thought you said I'd . . .'

'Jennifer, please be sensible. It's better than flying to Belfast, isn't it? The whole thing will be over in less than half an hour. Jonathan will drive you to Portland Place, so you haven't even got to hail a taxi. We want to make the very most we can out of last night's . . . episode. You're Big News now, and it would be unforgivable not to take advantage of it. Now, have you got it straight? You cried because of the grief of Hester's life, the horrors of the war. You *identify* with her — so much so, that you are aware of her as a living presence still. Don't forget that aspect, please. It always rouses interest. Whatever Rowan asks, return to the point of how strongly Hester's life affects you, how you feel involved with her, linked with her. All right? Remember what I told you, Jennifer. Your aim is to *control* the interview. A skilful interviewee can always choose her own subjects.'

'Not with Rowan Childs, she can't. She's such a cynic, Matthew. She's already called me a traitor and a prig.'

'It doesn't matter what she calls you, so long as it sells the book. Do you realise you could . . . Ah, she's coming now.'

Matthew arranged his features somewhere between dignity and welcome. Rowan Childs was loping towards them in a magenta boiler suit which made the pink chairs blanch, her fringed silver ankle boots matching the streak of silver in her hair. Jennifer's beige polyester dress lay down and died against the competition.

'Hi, Matthew! Nice to see you again. Sorry I'm late. I got stuck behind an agoraphobic learner driver on his first day out. Jennifer — hallo. So glad to meet you at last. Congratulations on the book! You seem to be making quite a stir with it. Those tears were *most* original.'

Matthew unfolded his napkin and swathed it on his lap. 'Rowan, I'd like to try and explain to you how . . .'

'Haven't you started breakfast yet? You should have gone ahead without me. I'm on this *fearful* diet — black coffee and fresh air, with the odd raw mushroom thrown in as a treat. You've probably read about it — the Dr Schreiber Shrink-Plan. I was at the party for his book last night and I promised to give it a whirl and then write up the results.'

Matthew frowned. He had planned to weaken Rowan through her stomach. 'What are *you* eating, Jennifer?'

'Er — just a slice of toast, please.'

The gleaming array of cutlery looked suddenly superfluous — porridge spoons and grapefruit spoons, heavy silver fish forks, steak knives and butter knives, salt and pepper shakers. Jennifer's stomach was already full with apprehension.

Rowan was fumbling in her handbag, which had been torn from some rare animal, then muzzled with silver clasps. 'You don't mind if I smoke, do you? Matthew, I know you don't indulge, and I suppose you can't, Jennifer, with your healthy living line.' Rowan drew out a cream and scarlet cigarette carton with Cartier emblazoned on the front. 'Actually, I quit myself last week — went two full days without a single puff — but then I was invited to a Cartier launch and they sent me a whole crateful. I didn't even know they made the things. I must admit I'd rather have had the odd diamond-studded watch.' Her own watch was a man's one — big and blatant — dwarfing her wrist to sparrow's leg proportions.

Matthew passed the ashtray. 'Perhaps you'd allow me to fill in some of the background to last night's . . .'

Rowan ripped the cellophane with purple-varnished fingernails ringed with nicotine. 'I'd rather have Jennifer's *own* words. It's more spontaneous, isn't it? And shall we have our coffee first? I'm never quite *compos mentis* until I've had at least two cups. I was most intrigued, Jennifer, to read about Hester's home-made brew. What was it now — dandelion and daisies?'

'D . . . dandelion root and chicory.'

'Ah, yes — delightful! You must give me the full instructions. In fact, our Women's Page Editor is very chuffed with Hester's recipes. She thought there might be some mileage in the economy angle — you know, finding free ingredients in the hedgerows instead of . . . Ah! Here's our own coffee — hardly free, I fear.'

Jennifer spooned sugar into her cup. Rowan wasn't as alarming as she had feared. She was obviously the chatty type — even seemed quite human. Any woman on a diet roused her instant sympathy, especially one as Twiggy-thin as Rowan. Her own cottage cheese and grapefruit fortnight had been gruelling enough.

'Look, er . . . Rowan.' She tried to toss the name off casually. Christian names were still a hurdle for her when the person was a virtual stranger, but in the media world a surname was regarded as a strait-

122

jacket. 'I don't know whether you're interested, but there is another coffee substitute — a milder one — which really tastes quite nice. It's a sort of fruit and grain mixture which Hester invented herself. It might be better for you, because it doesn't have the caffeine. I could make you up a pound or two if you think it would help your diet.'

'Jennifer, how *kind*! I'd be absolutely thrilled. I must admit though, I didn't know you still had time for that sort of domestic detail. From all I've heard, your life is rather different now from the one you recommend in *Born With The Century*.'

Matthew put his cup down. 'Not at all, Rowan. Of course, there has been the distraction of the publicity campaign, but apart from that . . .'

'Do let Jennifer speak. She speaks so well.' Rowan flashed a purple-lip-sticked smile. Lips and nails looked as if they had come from the same high-gloss paint-pot. 'Jennifer, I know you say you model your life on Hester's, but I must confess, I can also see some differences. I mean, take something very basic like where you live. Your book's essentially a back-to-nature thing, so I took it you'd be a country girl yourself, living in the wilds, yet I understand you have a small town-house in a built-up street of a rather fancy suburb.'

'It's a . . . cottage, actually.'

'On a commuter line to London?' Rowan drew out a notebook from the bottom of her bag, whose contents were now spilling on the table — a passport in a snakeskin case, an impressive clutch of credit cards, a tiny bijou pill-box carved in jade.

Jennifer stowed her own British Home Stores leather-look safely out of sight.

'Well, yes, but . . .'

'You see, after reading your very persuasive preface, I assumed you'd have taken over Hernhope. Yet I gather Hester's home is lying empty — even in danger of becoming derelict. Why's that?' Rowan had her notebook poised.

Matthew cut in again, frowning into his dry toast and sugarless tea. 'Of course it's not derelict. There was a . . . er . . .' He faltered. 'A . . . bit of trouble with the generator — that's all. It needed some attention, so . . .'

'I see. And when it's fixed, Jennifer will move there, will she? Make it the sort of place your book suggests?'

Matthew paused a moment, drained his cup. 'Her plans are very . . . fluid at the moment. They have to be. The book is already proving so successful, that alone may affect where and how she lives.'

Rowan smoked and scribbled. 'Another difference from Hester. That's what interests me, you see — how your lives have somehow diverged, despite the book — or perhaps because of it. I mean, Hester was very poor for much of her adult life and worked extremely hard for all of it, first as a servant, then as a housekeeper cum farmer. *Your* life, Jennifer, appears — if you'll forgive me — fairly cushy in comparison. You have a small and compact house, no money worries, no real need to work, no ties . . .'

Jennifer stared down at the tablecloth. She couldn't deny the charges. She had always felt a fraud presenting herself as another, younger Hester, when she had suffered none of the older woman's grief and toil, and was living within twenty miles of London in a house with all mod cons.

'There's something else I'd like to ask. You encourage woman to return to their natural nurturing role, to exchange the office and the briefcase for the kitchen and the cradle, to become biological creatures giving birth to babies and home-made bread. That's wonderful — delightful! But I understand you have no family yourself? I'm right about that, aren't I, Jennifer? You haven't any children?'

'Er . . . no. Not yet.' Jennifer shifted on her chair. One of the Japanese tycoons had mashed his strawberries to a scarlet pulp. Scarlet foetus flushed down the lavatory; three days in Epsom District Hospital, scraping out the last lost traces of it; hobbling down the ward and seeing other, luckier women with babies in their arms. The smoke from Rowan's cigarette made her feel suddenly nauseous.

Rowan flicked ash into her saucer. 'I know you told the *Mail* last month that you intend to carry on the Winterton line, so presumably you plan a child?'

'Oh yes. Of . . . course.' Jennifer bit hard into her toast. The crust was so thin and crisp, it cut her gums. What right had any stranger to ask these intimate personal questions, to gouge out every secret from private lives? How could she plan a child when Lyn refused to sleep with her? Thank God the papers couldn't pounce on *that*. No one knew in the world how frustratingly long it had been since she and Lyn had last made love. He still kissed her, touched her, still seemed to scorch and smoulder, but as soon as they were near it, he would suddenly leap away, or turn his back, or mumble vague excuses. She glanced at the next table where a young and tousled girl was feeding an older man with morsels of her croissant. They had probably shared a room last night as well as sharing breakfast. Could Lyn have a mistress? Would that explain why he no longer desired his wife?

Mustn't think about it. Must try and concentrate, block out the rest of the restaurant — the glide and hover of waiters, chink of cups on saucers, stab of knives and forks — listen only to Rowan's questions, the rapid purr of her pencil across the page.

She tried to keep her answers short and simple, remember Matthew's pointers. Yes, she identified with Hester, felt her presence still, did intend to model her life on hers. Yes, she was studying herbal medicine, had tried quilting, tatting, lace-making and many of the ancient crafts and skills. Only give her time and she'd make Hernhope live again. Yes, she *did* believe that Hester had special powers. . . .

Rowan seemed impressed, yet there was still a trace of vitriol in all the honeyed phrases, catches in the casual smiling questions.

'It's fascinating, isn't it, how Hester has grown so *large*? I mean, the thing's more than just a book, now. In fact, it has been suggested that some of the publicity was deliberately presented as a thinly disguised attack on Women's Lib. How d'you feel about that, Jennifer?'

'Well, I . . .' A waiter drowned her reply in coffee — just as well. This was tricky ground and it was dangerous to answer too spontaneously when every word could be twisted or distorted. She had learnt from previous interviews that what you said was rarely what they said you said. Tomorrow, she could be sitting stripped and plucked in twenty column inches, served up like a titbit to those mocking millions who would pounce on the words she hadn't used or didn't mean, until they flung her in the waste-bin or used her to wrap their weekend fish and chips.

Rowan was still probing. 'I believe the *Guardian* commented that your book could be seen as part of a general conspiracy to coax women out of scarce and valuable jobs and back into the kitchen, so leaving the market free for males. Do you think women *want* that, Jennifer — or can even afford it? I know they made the point that you don't need a job, now that you're making so much money from the book, but that not all your hard-pressed sisters had country seats or ancient families to turn into a gold-mine. I'm sure the report exaggerated, but — tell me — how much money do you stand to make, in fact?'

Jennifer flushed. The *Guardian* line had been not only harsh, but highly ironical. The so-called gold mine seemed very low on ingots, and those produced were Matthew's property. As for the ancient family, it was barred from its country seat, and now living out of packing-cases. She glanced across at Matthew, relieved to see him taking up the cudgels.

'Rowan, *please* — if the book has aroused strong feelings, then . . .'

Jennifer slumped back in her chair, listened to them spar, watching their smiles disguising unsheathed claws. They had moved from Women's Lib to last night's tears on television, which Rowan saw as deliberately planned and skilfully exploited. Matthew steered the conversation back to Hester, then on to books in general, and soon he and Rowan were scorching through the Literary World, flinging names about. Jennifer tried to squint at her watch without either of them noticing. Surely they could leave soon?

'Rowan, *darling!*'

Jennifer swung round. A small thin-faced man had come up to their table and was standing just behind her. He was dressed in a three-piece suit of standard grey and an unobtrusive tie. His eyes were also grey, behind the spectacles, his complexion pale and smoothly shaven.

'Jasper!' Rowan leapt to her feet and hugged him. 'Wonderful to see you! I thought you were in Tashkent.'

'No, that's next week — and don't remind me! I loathe Russian cuisine. We had cold pickled eggs and sugar buns for breakfast last time — served together!'

'Sounds superb! Jennifer — let me introduce you. This is Jasper Prince. Or perhaps you've already met?'

'Er . . . no.' Jennifer half got up, then subsided again as Matthew caught her eye and frowned. Everyone knew Jasper Prince — at least by name — London's most feared and feted gossip columnist who attracted dirt and scandal like a magnet. She was astonished he should look so . . . so *ordinary*. A man of his power and influence should surely be tall, impressive — at least imperious. Jasper was five-foot eight, with mousy hair already thinning at the sides and forehead.

'Thrilled to meet you, Jennifer. I *adored* the book! So utterly refreshing to put a toe into the simple life.'

'Th . . . thank you.'

'And this is Matthew Winterton, the publisher. Matthew — Jasper Prince.'

Jasper flashed more tooth, expensively capped by a Wimpole Street dentist he had since ruined in his column. 'I think we've met before, Matthew. Ah yes — I remember — that river boat rave-up last July to celebrate Beacon Books' centenary. What an evening! There was more Bollinger on board than water underneath us.'

'How do you do.' Matthew's voice was cool.

Jasper pumped Matthew's hand, then turned again to Jennifer. 'I understand we're neighbours. I've got a little hideaway in Northumberland myself — not quite as remote as Hernhope, though. It's nearer Wansbeck, actually.'

Matthew's frown cut deeper between his brows. 'Wansbeck? That's very close to Fernfield, isn't it?'

'Yes. Superb shooting country. Rowan's kind enough to call my place a shooting lodge. Barn's the word *I*'d use. Mind you, she's a marvellous guest. Always supplies the cabaret. There was no real shooting in May, of course, but we let her have the odd pot at a rabbit and you should have seen her with a gun! Even the dogs were scared.'

Matthew didn't laugh. 'You mean you've been staying up near Fernfield, Rowan?'

'Oh — just for the odd day or two.' Rowan had eased back into her chair.

'You didn't say.'

'Why should I? One gets about so much, one can't fill in every last weekend.'

Jasper was nodding at an obese Jewish gentleman seated in the corner. He appeared to be on nodding acquaintance with half the Ritz, continually darting glances over his shoulder as if he were worried he were missing Bigger Game while wasting words on them.

'Must leave you, I'm afraid. I'm breakfasting with . . .' He lowered his voice as he laid the Name on their table like a jewel. 'She *loathes* unpunctuality and I'm expected in her suite in exactly two seconds. Such a pleasure to meet you, though, and best of luck with the book.'

126

He backed away, still bowing and smiling. Jennifer swivelled round to stare. The star he had mentioned was one of the brightest in London's galaxy.

'Extraordinary coincidence.' Rowan was exclaiming. 'Jasper and I actually work in the same office — would you believe — yet the only time we ever seem to see each other is in public bars and restaurants. Last time I bumped into him, we . . .'

'And how did you both enjoy Northumberland?' Matthew cut in.

'Jasper had a ball — he always does. But to be honest with you, I'm not a country girl myself. All that mud and empty space is very lowering. After forty-eight hours or so, I began to develop withdrawal symptoms and had to dash back to London for an injection of Real Life.'

'You surprise me.' Matthew gave an icy smile. 'With Fernfield so close, I'd have thought there was a lot to interest you. I mean, *Hester* lived in Fernfield as a girl — you can't have forgotten that. Didn't you visit the house? It's a ruin now, of course, but the grounds are still magnificent — very overgrown, but . . .'

'Yes, I did pop over, actually, Jasper dropped me off there on his way to some sheep show or beagle sale or something. Sad to see a house like that demolished.'

'There's one staff cottage left — almost hidden in all that jungled garden. Did you notice it?'

'Yes, delightful little place. Genuine eighteenth-century and enough roses for a chocolate box.'

Matthew folded his napkin into a perfect square, 'A Mrs Croft lives there. I expect she tried to collar you. Old Annie loves a gossip.'

'Oh, you know her, do you, Matthew?'

'I have made her acquaintance — yes. She used to work for Hester's mother.'

'How fascinating.'

'Surely she mentioned it? She tells everyone she meets. She's very proud of herself now that her mistress's daughter has become something of a celebrity. I'd have thought you might have chatted with her.'

Rowan flipped a saccharin into her second cup of coffee. 'We did exchange a few words. She was in her garden when I passed. I assumed she was slightly dotty, actually.'

'Doddery, rather than dotty. She's nearly ninety, after all. Her memory's still quite good, though.'

'Really? You've talked to her a lot, then?'

Matthew brushed a non-existent crumb from his lapel. 'Oh, no.'

'When were you last up there?'

'Quite some time ago now. I've been far too busy recently for any time away.'

Jennifer was listening in apprehensive silence. Matthew was up to something — obviously — though she wasn't sure whether he was on the attack or the defensive. Both he and Rowan seemed to be circling round each other, as if testing out how much the other knew.

Rowan took a sip of coffee, then dabbed her mouth with her napkin, leaving a purple smile behind. 'I met her a second time, in fact — quite by chance. I was in the village store when she came in for some eggs. The old dear who runs the shop is almost as old as she is, and the two of them started tattling about the old days. I hadn't much choice but to listen, since no one was being served until they'd finished. Actually, I was quite surprised to hear that the Ainsley house was still a solid prosperous home right up to the forties. I presumed it had been demolished *years* before. I mean, in your book, you suggest that Hester only moved away because her family were dispersed and ruined in the war. Yet Annie was saying that Hester's mother and sister and most of the servants stayed on there long after Hester herself had left.'

Matthew tensed. 'The . . . er . . . book was quite tricky to put together. I mean, some parts of the material were obviously more detailed than the rest. Other times, we simply had to . . . guess. Editing is a highly sensitive job, of course — deciding what to leave out and what to . . .'

'Well, I certainly should have welcomed a little more explanation as to why Hester left her family home at all. I mean, it's a little odd, isn't it? Why should she have moved to one of the noisiest and busiest parts of London when she was basically a country girl born and bred in the wilds?'

Matthew was fiddling with the salt-cellar, spilling salt on the cloth. Whatever advantage he'd had, he now had lost. 'We . . . er . . . hadn't room for everything. The book's long enough as it is. We wanted to start it with the period of the diaries, not go right back to Hester's childhood.'

'Yes, but there's a break in the diaries, isn't there? In fact, now we're on the subject, perhaps you could help me out. I must admit I've never quite grasped why Hester took that London job in the first place. It seems so out of character. I mean, her family were wealthy, weren't they, and rooted in the rural north with a passionate love of the countryside and yet . . .'

Jennifer clutched at her chair arm as if it were a life-raft. What was Rowan implying? Had she guessed Hester's secret, or been told some spicy gossip by Old Annie? Surely not. Matthew had grilled the old crone himself and got nothing out of her. He had talked to *all* the locals, followed up every other possible source of information, and had satisfied himself that nobody in Fernfield had heard even a hint or rumour of Hester's pregnancy. He had also been to Somerset House and found no birth certificate, scoured the baptismal registers in a score of London churches. Nothing. He had thus assumed the baby dead. The infant mortality rate was exceptionally high in the war years, so he told her. Food was scarce, disease was rife, and many babies died from natural causes in the first few weeks of life. Yet Jennifer had always felt a tiny twinge of suspicion, a stirring of unease. She couldn't forget the article she had once read about unmarried mothers *destroying* their own babies, leaving them to starve. Supposing Rowan had picked up a rumour of that kind? After all, the baby's death was every bit as mysterious as his birth. There was no death certificate, no record of a funeral, no two secret lines in the diary: 'Today my son was buried.' The child had simply disappeared. Reporters *thrived* on mystery — it left them free to speculate, hatch their ugly rumours. A few random hints and guesses and Hester could become a suspect, even an infanticide — all the innocent charm of the diaries blighted and destroyed.

Rowan was on to *something* — that was obvious. Why else should she be prowling round the site of Hester's girlhood home, interviewing servants? She hadn't mentioned the visit until Jasper let it out. That was odd itself. And how many of her suspicions had she already shared with Jasper who had driven her there in the first place? They were not only colleagues, but obviously good friends — maybe even lovers. Murdered bastard babies were just in Jasper's line. His favourite pastime was toppling the smug and shining from their pedestals. Even now, he was simpering upstairs with a star whose name had lit up Shaftesbury Avenue but whose latest role off-stage in a smutty divorce case would soon fuse all those lights. He could do the same with Hester. Her story would have a strong personal appeal for him, since he owned a house in the area and had easy access to any local gossip.

Jennifer picked up her cup and put it down again. Even the coffee tasted tainted now. She had partly brought this crisis on herself. It was she who had persuaded Lyn into accepting Matthew's deal, and so made Hester public. True, she had insisted that the birth of the bastard child should be totally suppressed out of love for Lyn and loyalty to Hester. But if she had been truly loving, truly loyal, she should have joined her husband in his refusal to publish at all. Instead, she had swallowed Matthew's high-sounding adjectives — historical, educational, memorial — his stirring talk of tributes and tradition, and used them for her own ends. She had never wanted a gold mine, never presumed to oppose the feminists or tell women how to live, but she had to admit she had allowed her pregnancy to influence her judgement. She had been blind to everything but the welfare of her baby, fixed only on the need for its security. Matthew had been offering them security — or so it seemed at the time. If she hadn't been expecting, she might well have risked a poor and uncertain future, but how could she inflict it on a child? The irony was, that child had been coffined in an S-bend before the ink on the contract was dry.

A waiter removed her almost untouched toast. The restaurant was emptying now, people drifting off. She longed to escape herself, but Rowan was feeding a long new lead into her gold propelling pencil. She smiled across at them.

'Actually, my Editor did suggest me doing a separate piece on Fernfield — a sort of general picture of the place with a bit of local tittle-tattle — you know — the odd murder or juicy scandal — the saintly postmistress who knocks her husband off and buries him in the cabbage-patch . . .'

Jennifer choked on the word murder. Was Rowan simply joking, or making an oblique and sinister reference to the fact that she did have certain suspicions and intended to follow them up? Matthew hadn't blanched. Was she over-reacting or imagining crimes where there were none? Rowan was still speaking, discussing the format of her article.

'I might do a potted history of the old house itself, and everyone who lived there. I thought I could trace what happened to them all and . . .'

'The sons were killed — all three of them.' Matthew was giving nothing away. *That* was in the book.

Rowan nodded. 'What about the other daughter, though — Hester's sister Ellen?'

'She . . . moved away — abroad.'

'Didn't she return, though?'

'Return?'

'Yes, I heard a rumour fairly recently. It was probably total moonshine. One hears so many rumours in this job and most of them are way off-beam.'

Matthew jerked forward in his seat. 'Who was it who told you?'

'I can't remember now, to tell the truth. I meet scores of different people every week and . . .'

'Not people who know Ellen, though. It wasn't Annie, was it — Mrs Croft?'

'Good heavens, no! She hardly talked coherently at all. That's why I was so intrigued to hear of your little session with her. Did she mention Ellen then?'

Matthew paused. 'Only in passing.' He pushed his chair back, gestured for the bill. 'I'm sorry, Rowan, but I'll have to call a halt now. Jennifer's expected at Portland Place in less than fifteen minutes.'

'Another round of radio? How *nice*! It's a pity to have to stop, though. I was so enjoying our chat.'

'We could always meet again — just the two of us. Perhaps you'd allow me to buy you lunch next week? There's one or two things I'd like to touch on . . .'

Rowan snapped her handbag shut. 'Next week's a stinker, I'm afraid. I'll give you a tinkle, though.' She swivelled back to Jennifer. 'Thrilled to have met the Country Girl! I'm recommending the book to *all* my friends.' The smile was blinding. 'Best of luck with your interviews. It'll be hard to top those tears!'

Jennifer could still smell Chanel and Cartier as Rowan whirled through the revolving doors and out into the sunshine. She and Matthew were standing in the foyer, awaiting Jonathan's Porsche.

'Matthew, what's she *up* to? I don't like the sound of it. I mean, if she's been pumping all the locals, they might well have . . .'

'She's simply bluffing, I suspect.' Matthew ran a finger beneath his collar. There were beads of perspiration on his neck. 'I've told you already, no one up in Fernfield knows anything at all.'

'Yes, but Annie worked for Mrs Ainsley, lived in the same house. She can't have missed much, surely? Anyway, what if Rowan's simply guessed — put two and two together, or followed a hunch or something? And how about the sister? I mean, she's bound to know about the baby, and if she has come back to England, then . . .'

'Impossible! Ellen's almost eighty now and when I made my own enquiries, I was told she had some chronic ailment and rarely went out at all. She's hardly likely to travel five thousand miles when she can't even make it to her nearest village shop. Anyway, why should she return after all these years? She made her home in India, permanently.'

'Then how d'you explain the rumour?'

'There'll always be rumours, Jennifer — as long as there's human beings. Rowan admitted herself that most of them are groundless. The trouble is with journalists, they have so few hard facts to go on, they often resort to the flimsiest sort of hearsay. Rowan herself was pumping me, in fact — trying to see what I knew. She's obviously in the dark herself, just groping about for any straw she can.'

'Yes, but she must be suspicious, Matthew, or why should she bother at all? And it's worse in a way to have no facts because it gives her an excuse to start spreading rumours herself. It's not just Hester I'm worried about — it's Lyn as well. If he picks up some sordid story after all we've done to . . .'

'Look, my dear, you concentrate on your interviews and leave Rowan Childs to me. I'll follow the matter up, of course — invite her to my Club and try and pump her. But I doubt if she's heard anything at all beyond the harmless local chit-chat she's collecting for her article.'

'Well, what about that business of Hester leaving home? You could *see* she smelt a rat there! I mean, she actually said . . .'

'*Leave* it, I said.' Matthew sounded sharp. 'Journalists are a law unto themselves, Jennifer. Asking awkward questions is simply part of their job. Now, let's go over my Golden Rules for Radio. The voice is all-important, don't forget, so . . . Ah! Here's Jonathan. I've asked him to drive you back to Putney when the interviews are over. Anne has planned a celebration dinner.'

'Celebration?' The single mouthful of toast Jennifer had swallowed seemed to have swollen in her stomach and set solid like cement. 'What are we . . . celebrating?'

'How can you ask? The book has sold twenty thousand copies already and looks set to beat all records. We've just negotiated a sale of another fifty thousand copies to the Book Club. And you and Lyn are coming to stay with us at Putney.'

'Oh, I . . . see. That's . . . er . . . settled then?'

'Yes, my dear. There's too many problems at Hernhope, and you've enough on your plate at the moment without rushing into property negotiations somewhere else. You want to take your time, find a place you really like. You'll be better off at Putney, anyway — at least for a while. It's closer in to London, so you won't have so much travelling to your interviews.'

'But they're finished, Matthew. You said only a week or so, and I've done double that already.'

'That's marvellous, Jennifer. It shows how much interest you've aroused. It's only a matter of days now, anyway. Every book reaches saturation point and then one *has* to stop, but it would be very foolish not to see it through. Now hurry up, my dear. Jonathan's being hooted by at least a dozen taxis. Best of luck and remember to relax. I've arranged Radio Merseyside after Radio Ireland. Jonathan's got the details. He can phone me at the office when they're over and let me know how you got on. I'll see you later this evening, back at Putney. Anne's bought a *splendid* turkey.'

XII

'I don't *like* turkey.'

'You hogged enough at Christmas.'

'That was different. I'm a vegetarian now.'

'You can't be a vegetarian. You're always eating sausages.'

'Sausages aren't meat.'

'Yes they are.'

'They're not.'

'They are, aren't they, Auntie Jennifer?'

Jennifer laid her fork down. Matthew's two elder boys were both appealing to her, often used her as a referee. It was hard to be fair, when Charles was her favourite, a second, smaller Lyn. 'Well, you can get meatless ones.'

'Oliver's weren't meatless. They were prime pork. It said so on the packet.'

'What's prime pork?'

Anne tapped a serving spoon sharply on the table. 'Be quiet, boys. Your father will be back soon and he won't want all this noise.'

'It's not fair. Daddy almost kills us if we turn up late for meals, yet he's always late himself.'

'That's different, Hugh. He's working. Eat nicely, please. We don't spend all that money on your school fees just to watch you pig yourself like that.'

132

Jennifer looked anxiously at Lyn. He had hardly said a word. The boys distrusted him because he couldn't joke or chatter or relax. Too much like their father, in that respect. Lyn hated family gatherings, the strain of being surrounded, the effort of smiles and small talk. She wished she could reassure him, catch his eye or squeeze his hand, but they had a mile of mahogany table looming between them. Disconcerting for him to move from a Cobham doll's house into a London mansion, to swap his peace and privacy for a table set for nine. It was easier for her. She *wanted* a family and Anne's was at least a substitute — the only family she had ever really had.

She glanced around the table at the four dark heads. Outwardly, they were grave and solemn children like their father, sitting straight in their neat school uniforms with their short-cropped hair and earnest, formal names. Yet it amused her, somehow, that Anne and Matthew, with all their seriousness, all the drive and effort of their combined and forceful genes, could still produce children who muffed exams or squandered their allowances on horror comics or made silly, flagging jokes.

'Auntie Jennifer, what's another name for a vegetarian cannibal?'

'I've no idea, but I expect he'd soon be hungry.'

'Susie's boyfriend's a vegetarian. He told me so.'

'That's *not* her boyfriend, stupid. She hasn't got a boyfriend.'

'Who is it, then?'

'Some man who brought her home.'

'If he brought her home, where is she now?'

'She went for a ride on his motorbike. He's got a Kawasaki Z 400.'

'Cor! I wish he'd give *me* a ride.'

'You're not allowed to say "cor". Daddy says it's vulgar.'

'Susie says it all the time.'

'Well, Susie's vulgar, then.'

'She's not.'

'Is.'

'That's enough now, boys.' Anne frowned them into silence. 'You haven't met Susie, have you, Jennifer? She's helping me out in the house. I can usually manage on my own, but I seem to be working later and later at the moment and with the school holidays approaching, I'll need someone to look after the boys. She should be here, in fact. I like her to be in for meals, but I'm afraid she's not the most punctual of people. She needs a little . . . training, I suppose. More turkey for you, by the way?'

'No thanks.' Jennifer mopped her forehead with her napkin. It was far too hot to eat. Although it was evening, the close muggy stupor of the afternoon still hung like a tarpaulin over the house, the smell of turkey fat entangled with the scent of roses. Matthew's Crimson Glories were shadowed by the dark swarthy trees which patrolled the garden — dense and ancient yews with distorted trunks, scraggy conifers shutting out the sun. Even in the summer, the place was sombre. Every window had its blinds

133

and shutters, its heavy velvet curtains, double-barred with nets. The furniture was Victorian mahogany, formal and oppressive, the floors and walls panelled in dark oak. You could enter the house in August from a light sun-dappled street and feel gloom and winter close around you. It was worse with Matthew there. When he came in, the whole house stood up straighter; jokes and chatter faded into silence.

Jennifer could see Anne listening for him now, like a dog trained to greet its master. She had never got to know Anne, or only her exterior. That seemed pleasant enough — always welcoming, polite, subservient to Matthew, but sometimes she suspected hidden depths in her sister-in-law, hidden resentments, even, towards the man she lived her life round

'Ah, there he is.' Anne got up to greet him, take his briefcase, pour his glass of Perrier.

All four boys stopped talking as Matthew took his seat at the head of the table — the only chair with arms — smiled across at Jennifer, nodded at his sons.

'Enjoying your turkey?'

'Yes,' said Robert, taking care to finish his mouthful before he spoke, and not to make it just an Mm.

'Yes, *thank* you,' corrected Matthew.

There was silence for a moment.

'Finished the drawings, Lyn?' Matthew tried again.

'Not quite. I spent half my time packing up and getting here.'

'Settled in now, I hope? How was your maths test, Charles?'

'OK.'

'What do you mean, "OK"?'

'Well — OK — all right. Hey, Dad, did you remember my stapler?'

'I'm sorry, Charles, I didn't have time to look it out today.'

'You said that yesterday.'

'We're very busy at the moment, aren't we, Jennifer?'

Jennifer mumbled something indecipherable. She disliked siding with Matthew against the boys.

'Jonathan told me your interviews went well, especially Radio Ireland.'

'Yes . . . er . . . thanks.' She wished she could answer 'OK' and grin at Charles. He and his brothers seemed to have dwindled and diminished in their father's presence, yet their names were never shortened. Each of them had three Christian names apiece, all grave, dignified or regal, to match their grave regal father and his dark earnest house.

'Robert, I've told you before, I will not have you picking up your bones.'

'Susie's boyfriend does.'

'Don't answer me back, please.' Matthew carved himself a turkey wing, while Anne brought hot broccoli and potatoes from the kitchen. 'Anne, what's this about a boyfriend?'

134

'I don't know much about it, I'm afraid. The boys appear to have met him here.'

Oliver put his fork down. 'He's called Sparrow and he's got tattoos all over his arms. Snakes and dragons and things.'

'*Sparrow*? What a crummy name.'

'Be quiet, Hugh.' Matthew frowned. 'I don't encourage boyfriends, Anne.'

'I'm sorry, but if I'm working in your office, I can't really oversee what's happening at home as well.'

Oliver wriggled on his chair. 'I thought this was meant to be a celebration. Everyone's so gloomy, it's more like a funeral.'

'It *is* a celebration. In fact, I thought we'd open a decent bottle of claret, if it's not too late. Lyn, some wine for you?'

'No thanks.'

'*I*'ll have Uncle Lyn's.'

'No you won't, Robert. Eight-year-olds should stick to water. A little claret for you, Jennifer?'

'Yes, please.' Jennifer sipped. The wine looked dark and heavy in her glass — dark like blood. Her period had just begun. Every period was a wasted baby now. She couldn't even hope that she was pregnant, unless you could conceive a child without a man — what Anne had done, perhaps. It seemed almost less miraculous than the fact that Matthew had taken off his clothes and thrust in and out on top of her. Anne and Matthew had had their children late. The first six years of their marriage they had concentrated on building up a business rather than a family. She should take heart from that. Anne had had all four sons in her thirties. Still time for her and Lyn. Perhaps they ought to . . .

'Hi, folks! Sorry I'm late. Met a friend.'

Suddenly there was light and colour in the room. The door had heaved open and a beam of sunlight flickered through it, flinging its yellow arm across the face and shoulders of a young tousled girl in scarlet dungarees.

'Ah, Susie, you're back. We do like to eat at half-past seven, you know. That's quite late enough for the boys.'

'Sorry, boys! Gosh. I'm starving. Any turkey left? Hey!' She swivelled round. 'You must be Jennifer — the famous one! Great to meet you! I'm Susie.'

Jennifer mumbled hallo. Anne was making more formal introductions. Names like Susie didn't belong in Matthew's house. They were too lightweight, too informal, Susie herself too dazzling. Her sneakers were peacock-blue with tartan laces. An African violet tee-shirt shouted at the scarlet. Every nail was varnished a different colour, her lashes spiky with navy blue mascara.

She was staring at Jennifer as openly and directly as a child. 'Cor! You're completely different from what you were on telly. I thought you'd be more — well — you know . . .'

Jennifer *did* know — more talented, more beautiful, more artistic, more impressive. Susie would have done better in her place. She was like a commercial for shampoo — one of those young, healthy, bouncy girls who manage to look appealing even dressed in sackcloth or overalls, or with their hair soaking wet and clinging to them. Susie's hair was long and thick. You couldn't truthfully call it blond, but it had streaks and highlights in it which glittered in the light. The sun moved across the room with her, so that she was alive and golden when everyone else was drab. Her features seemed to leap out of her face and fling themselves towards you — huge grey eyes, large mobile mouth — open, laughing, gabbling — eyebrows lifted astonished or delighted, hands like little darting animals. Anne looked like a portrait beside her, a rigid composition darkened by age and varnish, which had hung on the same spot of wall for nearly half a century. Susie was an impressionistic sketch, lines dashing off the page, colours splashed at random and clashing with each other. She had thin gold chains around her wrists and neck, a row of metal badges on her tee-shirt — 'Consenting Adult', 'Teachers' Pet', 'Dominate me', 'Get 'em down'. If Matthew's sons had worn them, they would have been told to leave the table.

Jennifer glanced at Matthew. He looked sombre and inscrutable like a piece of his own furniture. Anne was trying to smile, but she was stiff and rigid where Susie sparked and sparkled. Her hair was coiled up smoothly round her head with no stray curls or disobedient wisps. Her face and figure had no spare flesh on them, as if she had given all her curves away to build her sons. She wasn't unattractive. She had a dark earnest stillness, which made you turn round and look at her again. She was like a Spanish ballet dancer who had never danced — taut, lean, steely, her body trained and disciplined, but never letting go. But Susie made her plain. Susie made them all plain. The table had gone dead, the dinner cold, while all the light, life and heat poured into Susie. She was a sweetmeat, a soufflé, something frothier and lighter than the grave substantial Wintertons.

Jennifer had never met a girl with such a presence. Susie was a magnet, pulling you towards her, keeping you in orbit. The sunbeam had shifted a little, so that now it fell across the table, trapping them both inside it, yoking them together, the only two fair heads in a room of dark ones.

Susie pulled out a chair and shattered the sun into fragments, disunited them. She was sitting in Lyn's shadow now — turned to face him. 'At least *you* haven't finished yet. I hate eating on my tod. You must be Lyn. I've heard a lot about you.'

Lyn picked up his fork and put it down again.

'Aren't you going to ask me what I've heard?'

'Well, I . . .'

'You *are* the artist, aren't you?'

'Hardly.'

'Shame! I was hoping you'd paint my portrait.'

'I don't do portraits, I'm afraid.'

136

'Only a joke. I'm learning to paint myself, in fact — at night school. It's a hoot! The teacher's very old and shrivelled and . . . Hey, can I have a leg, Anne? I hate breast.'

Jennifer glanced at Susie's own breasts. They were full and firm, emphasised still further by the packet of Woodbines stuffed in the top pocket of her dungarees and bulging over them.

'Mm — super bird!' Susie was talking with her mouth full. 'Wish I could cook. All I can manage is sausages.'

'You're telling me!' Hugh turned to Jennifer. 'D'you know, we've had sausages every single morning since Susie arrived?'

'*Burnt* sausages!' Oliver chipped in. 'The next-door cat almost broke its teeth on them.'

Lyn was struggling to his feet, food untouched, frown cutting between his eyebrows. 'I'm sorry, Matthew . . . it's stifling in here. If you'll excuse me, I'll go outside and get some air.'

'But we haven't finished dinner yet.' Matthew never allowed the boys to get up before the meal was over. 'I was going to open some port as you didn't fancy claret. I wanted to drink a toast to you and the Book, and to your most impressive work on it. We're *celebrating*, Lyn.'

'*I'm* not.'

Jennifer willed him to sit down again. Susie was staring at him. Stupid to care what a teenage mother's help thought, but somehow she wanted Susie to see him as intelligent and sensitive, not bad-mannered and unsociable.

Matthew moved his fork a fraction, so that it was lying exactly parallel with the knife beside it. 'Well, stay for just a moment. Anne and I have got some news for you all. Very exciting news.'

Lyn jabbed his foot against the chair-leg. 'You've sold thirty thousand copies instead of twenty thousand.'

'Well, it is to do with sales, in fact. As you know, I'd planned a trip to Japan this summer. We've had a lot of interest from a Tokyo publisher, and I also want to oversee some colour printing. So I thought I'd combine the two — clinch my contract in Japan, then stop off in Hong Kong to talk to the printers . . .'

Hugh speared a piece of broccoli. 'That's not news, Daddy. You told us that at Easter. All it means is that you won't take *us* away.'

'Quiet, Hugh, I haven't finished yet. The exciting bit is that I'm going to include Australia as well, and your mother's coming with me.'

'Mummy? But she never goes. She's . . .'

'Lucky Mum! Can we come?'

' 'Fraid not, old chap. It's a business trip, not a joyride.'

Lyn sat down again, but pushed his chair right back, so that he was no longer part of the group around the table. 'I only hope you're not including Jennifer. Her British tour was bad enough, but I draw the line at the out-back.'

'Well, there was some talk of her appearing on Australian television, but they've invited me, instead. That's partly what made up my mind about the trip. There's already enormous interest in the book and very impressive sales there, and this can only clinch it. I'll be taking my next year's books, of course, and seeing as many publishers as possible. It's the sort of chance which might never come again, so I've got to take advantage of it.'

Charles retrieved his napkin from the floor. 'Why are you going, Mum? You never have before.'

Matthew answered for her. 'Your mother needs a break — and I need her. There'll be a lot of work, you realise.'

Robert's face was crumpling up. 'Who'll look after *us*, though?'

'Well, Susie will be here. That's partly what she's come for. Mrs Briggs will help her with the cleaning so she'll have more time for you boys. And I'm sure your Auntie Jennifer won't abandon you.'

Lyn flung his chair back. 'Look here, Matthew, I was reluctant enough to camp here in the first place, but if you're now expecting us to babysit while you . . .'

'For heaven's sake, Lyn, no one's expecting anything. You can take some leave if you like — make the most of being close to London. It's less than half an hour if you take the car, and that's right to the West End. You can visit all the galleries, book some theatre tickets, catch up on the films. Or if you want a rest, well, just stay home and sun yourselves in the garden. You'll have more room in the house with myself and Anne away, and Mrs Briggs to wait on you and . . .'

'I don't want anyone to wait on me. Just my own place and a bit of peace and quiet.'

'If you want peace, Lyn, then I suggest you stop the shouting. Come on, now — be a good chap and sit down. Let's all drink to the trip.'

'*You* drink to what you like. I'm getting out.'

He didn't slam the door, but it felt as if he had done. Even the boys were cowed. Matthew was trying to woo them, pouring them each half an inch of port in his Waterford crystal glasses. Charles drained his at a gulp. 'When are you planning to leave, Dad?'

'About the middle of July.'

'That's when we break up. We never seem to see you.'

'I'll bring you back a present, to make up. Something really different.'

Jennifer was half standing, half sitting. She knew she ought to follow Lyn, reason with him, calm him down. Yet she was reluctant to disrupt the meal. Anne had rushed home early to prepare it and even Matthew was trying to be genial. Anyway, she was keen to hear Anne and Matthew's plans. She felt a strange excitement that both of them would be absent, leaving her and Susie to play parents to the boys. Susie was only a name as yet, but this was the perfect chance to get to know her. Lyn was a problem, of course, but he would be a problem anywhere. Almost a relief to dilute his gloomy presence with Susie's glowing one. She drained her wine, then started on the port.

'Matthew, I'm sorry to bring it up now, but I presume this means my interviews are over?' If she could turn her back on the media, the summer would be fun.

'Not quite, my dear. There's a couple of things on radio and the chance of another television appearance which might come up in July — Tyne Tees in Newcastle. Don't worry, you can leave it all to Jonathan. He'll look after you. If you do go North, he'll blow it up a bit — canvass the local papers and the bookshops, play on the regional aspect.'

'Oh Matthew, no. You promised no more tours.'

'Hardly a tour, my dear — just a little back-up to the television. If that comes off, it's a real feather in your cap. The chap who hosts the show has enormous influence. You can hardly turn it down when Big-Name stars are falling over themselves to appear on his programme.'

'Yes, but . . .'

'Forgive me interrupting, but we must finish dinner.' Anne had hardly said a word since Matthew entered. 'There's still some fruit and cheese.'

Matthew folded his napkin into a perfect square. 'I'm sorry, Anne, we haven't time for anything more. We're expected at the Spencers' for a drink. David Spencer toured Australia last year and met a lot of influential people. He could be *very* useful.'

Once she heard the front door close, and the boys disperse, apples in their pockets to eat upstairs, Susie sprang to her feet and moved to Matthew's chair. She took a sip of his mineral water, shook out his napkin, frowned and tapped the table.

'Leave the room, Hugh.'

Jennifer didn't laugh. She had to be careful not to be disloyal. Susie might even be an Enemy. She didn't look like one, but Matthew saw Enemies everywhere. Agents were Enemies, other publishers, neighbours (except the Spencers), socialists, bureaucrats, the Inland Revenue — even Lyn, at times. Lyn had still not reappeared. Jennifer had made a quick search of the house for him while Anne was fetching her jacket. He had probably gone out to clear his head. Best to leave him — let him walk his anger off. Anyway, it would give her a chance to talk to Susie alone. They would have to get to know each other if they were spending the summer together. She piled the glasses on a tray, tipped Lyn's almost untouched turkey onto the pile of scraps.

Susie lit a Woodbine. 'Look, leave those. That's *my* job. You're far too grand to be a waitress.'

'Grand?'

'Well, I mean, on telly and everything. You're a real live star now, aren't you?'

'Hardly. I made such a fool of myself last night, I go hot all over when I think of it.'

'I liked it. It was smashing — especially when you cried.'

'Don't remind me!' Jennifer moved into the kitchen, tried to distract herself by starting on the washing-up. The tears were bad enough, but they had led on to Rowan, and Rowan on to Jasper, and Jasper on to scandal and bastard babies — even murdered bastard babies. How on earth would Lyn react if he . . .?' She'd been trying to block it out, trying not to worry, refused to bring breakfast down to dinner.

Susie had followed her out to the kitchen and was sitting on the work-top, blowing smoke over the turkey carcass. 'Do you really believe it, though — all that stuff you spouted about back-to-the-land and natural living? I can't see the point myself, when we've got machines and convenience foods and things, to have to go grubbing around with yeast and manure and . . . All you're doing is putting the clock back — plonking women back in the kitchen or the farmyard when they've spent the last twenty years trying to get out. I'm all for women's lib myself.'

Jennifer said nothing. The subject was too fraught. Until the book, feminism had been one of those vague, prickly topics she rarely thought about. She knew she was old-fashioned, but she preferred to live that way. Anyway, she couldn't be a libber because that would mean attacking Lyn and he was too battle-scarred already to endure another skirmish. Her role was to heal and soothe him, not open up the wounds. She scrubbed harshly at the plates. The water had turned grey and greasy now, little scraps of debris murky at the bottom.

Susie had found a tea-towel and had semi-dried two plates. 'That's where I go in the evenings — a Women's Group. Don't tell Anne, though. She's sure to disapprove. *She* prefers the painting classes. They finished months ago, in fact. The course closed down for lack of funds.'

'What d'you do at Women's Groups?'

'Talk, drink, smoke. Hold debates on all the issues. Support our suffering sisters. Plot Death to the Male.'

Jennifer ran clean water into the sink. The heavy silver cutlery deserved reverential treatment. 'But I thought you . . . I mean, the boys were saying they'd seen you with a male.'

'Yeah — Sparrow.' Susie was using the meat tin as an ashtray. 'His mates call him that because he's six-foot-three with shoulders like an ox. He's been here once or twice. Charles fell in love with his bike.'

'What's he like?'

'Great! Won't be seeing him much more, though.' Susie turned away, ground her fag-end into pulp. 'Let's change the subject, shall we? Is Lyn really Matthew's brother? They don't look much alike.'

'Mmm. More or less.'

'You're as mysterious as Anne. It's a crummy house, this. No one tells me a thing. I mean Matthew didn't even make it clear he was careering round the world like that. When I first arrived here, he said he'd be away and could I cope, but I thought he meant a week or two, not half the bloody summer. Lyn seemed pretty sore about it, too. Did *you* know they were going?'

'Well, Matthew always travels quite a lot, and to tell the truth, I'm just thoroughly relieved it's not *me* that's involved as well. I almost died when he mentioned Australian television. Look, if you're worried about the boys, I'll help. I'd like to. I'm very fond of them.'

'They're all right, I s'pose. I'm just off kids in general at the moment. What I really want to do is act — you know — on the stage. This job's only a stop-gap, until I land a part, or sleep with some film director or something. Cor! I really envy you. You've got all the things I'd give my right arm for — fame, money, freedom . . .'

'But I haven't, Susie. You're wrong. I . . .'

'I'd love to have my photo in all the papers. And people like Parky and Russell Farty begging me to spare them half an hour. And that Tyne Tees thing you're complaining about — wow! The only time *I* ever went to Newcastle, all I saw was the bloody coach-station and some flea-pit Chinese restaurant. I bet you live it up!'

Jennifer found a second tea-towel and started on the drying. 'I've been already — just two weeks ago and I hated every minute of it. I had to stand for hours in stupid poses with everybody staring and . . .'

'Who's that Jonathan bloke Matthew mentioned? I s'pose he drives a red Ferrari and buys you exotic cocktails in American bars.'

Jennifer laughed. 'Oh Susie, we really ought to swap. Jonathan did buy me cocktails — enormous ones with half a fruit salad floating in them and little flags on top, and all the time I was dying to be back home in my nice warm bed with a Mars bar and a magazine. He's the publicity man from Hartley Davies. Very sort of . . . smooth. We never say anything *real*.'

'Christ! I would. Do you fancy him?'

'How d'you mean?'

'Oh come on, Jen. Don't be coy.'

'Well . . . he's . . . you know — doesn't go for women.'

'Gay, you mean.'

'I . . . think so.'

'All the best men *are* these days. And half the women, judging by our Women's Group.'

Jennifer mumbled something indecipherable. She was embarrassed by the subject. Best to change it, start a safer one. She had learnt that trick from Matthew. 'Er . . . where d'you come from, Susie? You're not a Londoner, are you?'

Susie's accent was difficult to place. There was a trace of London in it, but overlaying something more provincial. The result sounded mixed and mongrel, but Susie's voice was like the rest of her. It never droned or faltered, but jumped straight out at you, loud and clear and cocky.

'I was born in Nottingham, moved five times in seven years, up and down the country, until my parents finally settled in Great Yarmouth, having produced a child in every town. I'm the eldest.'

'How old *are* you?' Jennifer polished up a glass. 'You don't mind me asking, do you?'

'No. Seventeen and a quarter. How about you?'

'Twenty-five.' It sounded settled, almost senile. Seventeen was light years away. She hadn't met Lyn then, didn't have a book, a public, hadn't learnt to lie. And when she was that age, she had never looked like Susie, never been so carefree and outspoken, or worn gold and silver eyeshadow, one above the other, or bought scarlet dungarees. She glanced down at her own boring summer frock, a limp brown thing patterned like the lino. Everything Susie did was somehow colourful and stylish, even eating cold potatoes with her fingers or lighting up another of her crushed and scraggy Woodbines. She felt strangely drawn by her, as if Susie were a flame herself, and she a drab brown moth.

Susie blew the match out. 'Your husband's older, isn't he?'

'Well, yes. A bit.'

'D'you mind?'

'No, of course not.' Lies were almost easy now. Would a younger man go off you, renounce sex, live like a monk without a monk's serenity?

'Bit ratty, isn't he?'

'He's . . . er . . . not too well at the moment.'

'What's wrong with him?'

'Oh . . . headaches.'

'Nerves, I bet. Did you see that thing in *Cosmo*? They said men were getting headaches now, like women used to do — because they didn't want it.'

'Want . . . what?'

'Sex, of course. They're frightened of our orgasms, so they pretend they're feeling rough, and then they don't have to compete. D'you read *Cosmo*?'

'N . . . no.'

'I'll lend you mine. There's a quiz this month. "Is Your Guy A Romeo?" You have to answer questions and award your partner stars for things like foreplay. How many stars would Lyn get?'

Jennifer banged the last fork on the tray. 'That's *nothing* to do with you.'

Susie laughed. 'You sound just like Matthew. No stars at all, then, I bet.'

'Look here, Susie, I only met you an hour or so ago and I've no intention of . . .'

'Keep your hair on. Why all the aggro? Screwing's only like eating — bit cheaper, that's all. I had five different blokes in a week, once. I'm off it now, though. Wouldn't mind if I never saw a guy again.' Susie flung her still-dry tea-towel on the table. 'Cor! You're a whizz at washing-up. It takes me hours when I do it on my own. I notice all the boys have disappeared. They always do when there's work around. Fancy a cup of coffee?'

142

'No thanks. I'm going out.'

'Oh, still offended, are we?'

'No, I ought to look for Lyn.'

'Leave him. If he wants to sulk, that's his hard cheese.'

Jennifer hesitated. Stupid to take notice of a seventeen-year-old's remarks, and a sluttish one at that. How could anyone have five men in a week and then boast about it afterwards? She stared at Susie's fag-ends, lipstick-stained and shredded — felt like one herself, stale, snuffed, spent. All the exhaustion of the last few weeks seemed to have settled on her body like a dirty film of ash — the publicity tour itself, the fret and glare of the television studio, the horror of her tears, the gruelling breakfast interview with its spin-off of new terrors, the wrench and chore of packing up from Cobham — and now Lyn's disappearance. She dithered at the door, not knowing what to do. If she went chasing after Lyn, Susie would despise her for it. It was probably pointless, anyway. She would never find him in the maze of Putney streets. Best to go upstairs. She had a griping period pain and it would be a relief to lie and rest.

She said a brief goodnight to Susie, then walked into the hall and up the dark curving staircase with its heavy bannister and sombre carpet. She could hear Hugh's radio punching out pop music, he and Robert giggling. It seemed sad they had to grow grey and stern like Matthew, put away their comics and their cowboy hats and do earnest blinkered things like Growing Up and Getting On. She walked into their den, a strange, hybrid room where Anne's elegant taste and furnishings had been overlaid and pock-marked. The huge mahogany tallboy had almost disappeared beneath its frieze of posters, the expensive rug converted into an air-strip and a motorway.

Robert was lying on his bed in crimson Y-fronts. 'Done your teeth?' she asked him.

'Did them yesterday. If you brush them too much, you wear them down to stumps. A boy at school warned me just in time.'

Jennifer smiled, tucked them up in turn. Hugh smelt of toothpaste, Robert of bubblegum and hot pennies. Robert kissed her greedily, arms flung around her neck, pulling her down into the pillow. Hugh was more wary. When she got to Charles's room, there was no kiss at all. Charles was in his teens, already half grown-up and thus inhibited. He was too like Lyn — thin, intense and moody, with the same long lashes, the same angry troubled eyes. He was standing up, politely, but she could see he was wait-ing for her to leave. She longed to hug him, make him laugh, tear him away from that frowning pile of books.

'Goodnight, then, darling.'

' 'Night.'

She trailed into her own room, a large and gloomy one with a high wooden bed and two Victorian wardrobes blocking out the light. There were no frills, no fripperies. The walls were solemn brown, the windows gagged and blinkered with heavy curtains. She pushed them back, tried to coax the late evening fragrance of the garden up into the room. The sky was dark and troubled now, bloodied with scarlet clouds. She lay on the bed feeling her own blood seep into the Tampax.

In three weeks' time, it would be exactly a year since she had lost the baby. Lyn had never called it a baby, never now referred to it at all. She almost wished she could be a different sort of woman, one who didn't need marriage and a man or crave old-fashioned things like children. If she were a feminist like Susie claimed to be, then she'd be cock-a-hoop with all that she had achieved — not just a job, but recognition, fame.

But fame had threatened her more important job — that of wife to Lyn. It wasn't simply virtue which made her want it back. There was safety in it and a sort of power. Lyn completed her, gave her a role and purpose. He needed her, relied on her, clung to her as a bulwark or a beacon. His weakness was her strength. She knew he could be touchy, that other people criticised the way she pandered to him, but they only saw the outside. Underneath was talent, passion, anguish — a depth of feeling which both jolted and excited her, expanded her own small and shallow world. Recently, however, the anguish had been more obvious than the passion. That made it harder to put up with his moods. Always before, he had used sex as restitution, apologising with his mouth, his hands, his body. Now he used his hands still, but little else.

Had Susie *really* had five blokes in a week? The phrase kept exploding in her ears, contrasting with and mocking at her own total lack of sex. She wouldn't want five men — not in a hundred years, but five Lyns a week — oh, yes. That's how it used to be, before the book, the baby.

With any other man, she might have made an issue of it, stood up to him and demanded her marital rights — or at least an explanation — threatened to find fulfilment somewhere else. But there wasn't anyone else. She was tied to Lyn in a way she could hardly explain to friends who disapproved of him. Besides, it wasn't just rejection on his part. There was fear in it as well — fear of babies, fear of sharing her, more complicated fears she could only feel as vague and threatening shadows. That was partly why she was so alarmed by Rowan's snooping. Ordinary life was ordeal enough for Lyn, without added shock and scandal. Even now, he was probably inflating his outburst at the dinner-table into some cosmic crisis. Perhaps she should have followed him, tried to coax him back.

'Jennifer? You there?'

She jumped. It wasn't Lyn, only a muffled whisper outside the door.

'Who's that?' She was still confused, half dozing.

'Me. Susie. May I come in?' Susie didn't wait for an answer, just burst through the door and stood with her back to it, one foot twisted round the other. She was wearing a sort of smock thing, a cross between a nightie and a mini-dress, feet bare, hair in two fat pigtails. 'Just came to say goodnight. You're not still mad at me, are you?'

'N . . . no. Of course not. Sorry I snapped. I was just a bit on edge. Lyn may seem . . . ratty, as you call it, but . . .'

'Hasn't he come back yet?'

'No. He will, though. He often goes for evening prowls. It helps to calm him down.'

Susie walked over to the bed, flopped down on the end of it. 'Do you *like* being married?'

If she paused, it was only for a second. 'Oh, yes.'

'I'd loathe it. Being tied to someone all the time — all their moods and fuss-pottings. And having to fit in with them — eating when they wanted to, or going to bed at ten just 'cause they were pooped, or wasting your weekends cleaning cars and mowing lawns and . . .'

'We never clean the car.'

'Oh, you know what I mean, Jen.'

'Yes, I suppose I do. But I've always wanted those things. Surely it's worse to eat alone or go to bed with only a teddy bear or have no one to care about you or . . .'

'Does Lyn care?'

'Course.'

'I mean, I can see you slaving your guts out over him, but not the other way round.'

'Susie, you only met him this evening. How can you be so . . . hostile?'

'Oh, I dunno. I'm off all men at the moment. To tell the truth, I'm not too happy here. Anne and Matthew make everything so heavy. It's all gloom and doom with them. The whole damned household gets on my wick a bit. Not *you* — you're different. I like you, Jen. In fact, I wondered if we could be . . . mates?' Susie was squatting on the end of the bed, knees hunched up to chest, nightie barely covering them. She was plumper than she looked in dungarees, breasts pushing against the ruched and ribboned top and spilling over it. Her feet were grubby and there was a dirty Band-Aid on her leg. She was half child, half hussy — still with that magnet pull and charm. Jennifer tossed her one of the pillows. She liked the term 'mates' — it was easy and informal. Making friends took ages normally — observing all those slow and stiff conventions, groping only warily from bread-and-butter clichés to real and lasting bonds. All right — Susie was outspoken, even coarse, but at least she was someone young and easy-going, someone she could laugh with when Matthew was growling, or her husband agonising.

Susie yawned hugely. 'Well, I'd better trot off and get my beauty sleep. I have to be up at the crack of dawn to help Anne with the boys. Will you be around that early?'

'Oh yes.'

'See you at breakfast, then. Goodnight.'

'Goodnight.'

145

Susie leant across the bed. 'Give us a kiss, then, love.'

Jennifer flushed. Susie was so close, she could smell her scent of hot body and cheap talc. The breasts hung almost free now, only inches from her own. Susie kissed her full on the mouth — a damp childish kiss, eager, unembarrassed.

'Sweet dreams — and mind the bugs don't bite!'

The door slammed shut behind her. Jennifer wiped her mouth. Susie was so direct. She acted like a child, but her body was a woman's and it was somehow disconcerting. She couldn't understand how Anne and Matthew had ever employed her in the first place. She would have expected someone older and more serious to be the Winterton help and nanny — a dedicated spinster who was addressed by her surname and taught the boys deportment. She was glad they had chosen Susie. If she hadn't been there this evening, she would have spent far longer fretting over Lyn, or worrying about Vita, Rowan, Jasper.

How did Lyn see Susie? He could hardly have failed to notice those bra-less breasts jutting through her tee-shirt. She had glimpsed those breasts in close-up, just a moment ago. They were fuller than her own, with larger darker circles ringing squat pink nipples. Breasts varied as much as faces, she supposed. Not that she had seen many. She undressed and lay naked on the bed. It was far too hot for covers or even for a nightie. She glanced down at her own breasts. They weren't as boastful as Susie's, but Lyn had always cherished them — sometimes spending half an hour or more simply kissing and caressing them before he entered her. Rubbing his chin across the nipples so that his scratchy stubble kindled them erect, teasing, almost hurting them with his lips and teeth and tongue, sucking them like a baby laying his thing between them, then squeezing them round it until it was like a sausage in a roll.

Not any more. He touched them sometimes, but only warily, defensively, and if she murmured or responded, he immediately turned over, backed away. Would he do the same with Susie? Or was it only his dull and prudish wife who turned him off? She wasn't prudish. Her hand strayed to her nipple. She could feel it tautening, sending messages down between her legs. If Lyn came in, perhaps she could simply stretch out her arms and hold him, coax him down on top of her, pretend all those sexless days and weeks and months had never been. For a long time now, she had tried to stifle her feelings of frustration, pretend she didn't care about the lack of sex. It made it easier, blocked off her resentment. But now her body was insisting and demanding. It was as if Susie had somehow stirred her up, produced some new strange candle-flame excitement.

She lay flat on her back, trailed her hand down across her stomach, left it on her thigh. She rarely touched herself. She had been too innocent as a teenager and once she married Lyn, there was rarely any need. Now the need was like an ache, a fever. She had been patient far too long and her body was crying out for some release. She slipped a finger between her legs.

146

It was messy with a period, but she felt a slut tonight — wanted some wild sweaty man to sprawl on top of her and have her, curse and all. *Screw* her, Susie would say. There wasn't any man, but her Tampax made a tiny substitute. She jabbed it deeper and deeper inside her, scratching her nails up and down her labia.

She used her free hand on her breasts, circling them slowly, slowly, with the very tips of her fingers, until the nipples were stiff and standing up. She shut her eyes. They were Susie's breasts now, fuller, greedier. Susie's five blokes were panting round the bed — a whole week's worth in an evening — five tongues plumping out the nipples, ten hands teasing further down. She could feel the pressure of their fingers rough against her smooth and slippery body. She was sweating in the stifling summer night. Everything was slimy — blood on her hand, perspiration trickling down her belly. Disgusting. *Marvellous*. Her thighs were shuddering, her whole body joining in. She grabbed the bedhead, tautened herself against it, jerking and rubbing until she could feel the ripples reach even to her feet.

She tried to stop. Someone was creeping along the passage. It could be Lyn, Matthew, even a truant boy come to ask for a drink. They mustn't find her. Must stop. *Must.* She let go of the bedhead, but the other hand continued. Couldn't stop. She had reached that point where there was only go on, go on, go *on*. Her mouth was open, her eyes shut, fingers circling, jabbing. Footsteps getting nearer. Door creaking open. It must be Lyn. Anyone else would knock. She stifled her cries, wrenched her hand away, dragged the covers over her, tried to hide her flushed and burning face.

'Hey, Jen? Are you awake?' Footsteps thudding across the carpet, blankets hauled back, Susie's icy fingers shocking her bare shoulders.

'Can I get in? I'm cold.'

'*No.*' Jennifer was trembling. 'You shouldn't barge in here, Susie. The least you could do is knock. I might have been asleep.'

Susie grinned. 'You weren't though, were you?' She eased into bed beside her. 'Phew! You're boiling! You can warm me up a bit. My room's like an ice-box. Even in the summer, the sun never seems to reach it.'

'Get *out*, Susie.' Jennifer inched to the far edge of the bed until she was almost falling off it. She longed to dart out to the bathroom, escape altogether, but she didn't have her clothes. She was trapped, humiliated. Had Susie realised what she'd been doing? Her body was betraying her, throbbing and revving still, wild and overheated, probably even smelly. She pressed her legs together, tried to calm her breathing. 'I said "GET out." '

Susie groped a hand towards her. 'Cool it, Jen. We're mates, aren't we?'

'Leave me alone.' Mates shared beers and pizzas, not a bed. Why in God's name had she ever encouraged Susie in the first place? She would be pestered now continually, lose every scrap of privacy. She had never met a girl so blatant.

Even now, Susie was hogging the bed, sprawling right across it, talking through a yawn. 'I only came to say I'd stay and chat with you till Lyn turned up. I thought you might be moping and it would take your mind off things. We could play Scrabble, if you like, or go down and make some milk-shakes.'

'I'd rather *sleep*, if you don't mind. And I'd like my bed to myself.'

'You're very grouchy, aren't you? Almost as bad as Lyn. Must be catching.'

Jennifer said nothing. Was she grouchy? Had Lyn made her so, tainted her with his own fears and squeamishness?

'It's cosy like this.' Susie grinned and stretched. 'Reminds me of home. I used to share a bed with both my sisters and half their toys as well. Sometimes I'd wake up with a bloody great fire-engine sticking in my bottom or a doll's leg in my eye.'

Jennifer shifted a fraction. Sisters *did* share beds, especially younger ones. Hadn't she always longed to have a sister — someone really close like the sort of chum you read about in school stories to share everything, including confidences?

Susie was kneeing her in the spine. 'Do you have to turn your back like that? I haven't got the plague, you know. Hold on — I'll shove over and give you a bit more room. That better?'

'Mmm.'

'Do you always sleep without a nightie? I suppose Lyn likes it, does he? Sparrow used to . . .'

'Look, Susie, I think we ought to try and get some sleep now. It's getting late.'

'Can I sleep down here, then? I get lonesome on my own. My room's miles from anyone else's, up a horrid spooky staircase.'

'Yes, but Lyn . . .'

'Don't worry, I'll piss off as soon as he shows up. You won't catch *me* playing gooseberry. Mind you, he's quite good-looking, isn't he, your bloke? I like those skinny types. Matthew's almost *too* thin. He'd have to run around in a rain-storm for half an hour, just to get wet.'

Jennifer laughed. The laugh surprised her. Laughs were rare these days. 'Oh, Susie . . .'

'What?'

'Nothing. I . . . like you, that's all.'

'Like you, too, mate.'

They lay together, in silence, for a moment. Jennifer had moved towards the middle of the bed and felt Susie's body soft and solid like a pillow. The bed was warm and messy. She supposed she ought to be worrying over Lyn, but Susie made it more difficult to worry.

She turned on her back, stared up at the ceiling. She wished she had her nightdress on. It felt strange to be lying there stark naked, next to another woman. Susie's presence was disturbing. She tried to ignore her, settle down to sleep, but sleep played hard to get. Her body was too awake and too demanding. She had been only seconds away from coming when Susie first barged in. Those seconds seemed to be throbbing through her thighs now, churning her up.

148

'Nice boobs you got,' Susie murmured, through a yawn.

Jennifer froze. Did Susie *know* what she was feeling? She edged away a little, covered her chest with her arms.

'One of my mates is almost completely flat. Nothing there at all. She doesn't need a bra — just a couple of corn plasters.'

Jennifer smiled. Mustn't think of breasts. Her own felt taut and pushy. She was still wet between the legs. She longed to touch herself, carry on where she had been forced to leave off earlier. She shut her eyes, inched her thighs apart. Susie wouldn't notice. She was too busy rattling on. She crept a finger down the inside of her thigh, inching it nearer, nearer. *She* was the slut, not Susie — wanted a hundred blokes, not five. The finger stopped — *had* to stop. She couldn't touch herself, not with Susie there.

'Tell you what, Jen — why don't we go and see her — one evening when I'm off? Debbie would love to meet you, now you're famous. She's ever such a . . . What's that noise?'

'What noise?' The finger was almost there now — frantic, begging, deaf.

'I thought I heard the front door close, and footsteps. Yeah — some-one's coming up the stairs.'

Jennifer shot up in bed. 'It's Lyn — it must be. Get out, Susie, quick.'

'What's the panic? I'm not a bloke, for heaven's sake. He's not going to beat me up, is he?'

'Look, Susie, if you don't get out, I'll . . .'

'OK, keep your hair on.' Susie heaved out of bed, skipped towards the door and collided with Lyn head-on. 'Sorry, mate. Just saying goodnight to your wife. She couldn't sleep for worrying about you, so you'd better make it up to her. At least I've kept the bed warm.' Susie grinned before she slammed the door. 'Goodnight, lovebirds.'

XIII

'Right, darling, tip your head a little. No, the other way. Bit more, bit more. Whoa! That's it. Good. Now look at the camera. Don't frown like that, my love. Nice big smile. S-u-per!'

Jennifer blinked in the flash, tried to keep the pose through the next flash and the next and the . . . She was perched high up on the roof of the multi-storey car park in Gateshead, overlooking the jumbled haze of Newcastle, its rackety streets and sullen concrete tower-blocks, its railway and its brown, sluggish river. It was the photographer's idea to provide a panoramic view of the city in the drizzle as background to his shots of Jennifer Winterton. More conventional photographers had headed straight for parks and gardens and posed the Country Woman in a country setting. Oz Steadman wanted something more dramatic.

Jennifer stared far into the distance while Oz changed a lens and fiddled with his light meter. To the north lay Hernhope and the Cheviot Hills, beyond the roofs, spires, towers, which were all that she could see. Tantalising to be but two hours' drive away, and yet unable to move an inch beyond her schedule. She was still trapped in the world of radio stations and newspaper offices, smart hotels and cocktail bars. She had survived her television appearance on Tyne Tees' 'Arts Night Special', had crammed in ten more interviews with press and radio and had one last dinner left before flying back to Putney in the morning.

It would be nice to get back home. It wasn't really home, but Susie made it seem so. The Putney house unbent a bit with Susie there as new kid sister. She could see her now, standing on her head in the shocked and stuffy drawing-room, all four boys upside down beside her in a row of waving legs. She grinned.

'Fantastic smile, Jennifer — the first one I've really believed in. Try and hold it, will you?' Oz was shouting against the brutal interruption of a Boeing. 'OK — relax now. I want to move to the other side of the roof and get those tower-blocks in as background.'

Jennifer picked up her skirt, hop-scotched the puddles, tried to protect her hair from the sudden gusts of wind which blew grit and litter across the wasteland of the car park — thirteen storeys, most of them half-empty. Here, on the roof, there were no cars at all, save Jonathan's hired Mercedes shouting scarlet against sallow concrete stained with bird-shit. Jonathan himself kept bravely smiling as he helped to lug Oz's equipment and Jennifer's props across the roof until they were all three staring out, not at Tyne and city, but at cranes and factories, wharves and sheds, with a raw new housing development cutting across the bleak industrial landscape. Oz was aiming for a photographic contrast between the old and quaint and rural, and the new urban brutish. He made sure the jutting rectangles of the high-rise flats cut behind the flounces of Jennifer's skirt and frilly parasol. The light was perfect. Clouds lifting, sun shining on the puddles, atmospheric haze shrouding squat and ugly factories, tangled motorways.

Jennifer shivered. She was still damp from the shots he had taken earlier. It amazed her how they got through so much film. One or two quick snaps were surely quite sufficient, but every photographer she had met so far went on flashing, flashing, flashing — changing films, changing lenses, even changing cameras — jumping on to benches, crawling on their stomachs, rearranging props and towns and scenery to achieve some subtle or sensational effect.

'Look, I think I'll *use* that puddle. Get some reflection and some light

150

effects. Can you move nearer to it, darling. That's good — almost in it, please. Now bend over a little. More. Put a hand up to your hair. No, don't hide your face like that. Just rest the fingers along the chin. That's great, Jennifer! Terrific! Jonathan, the skirt please. It's dragging in the puddle — BLAST!'

The rain was suddenly cascading from the sky, as if God had let out the plug from the floor of heaven. They all three rushed for cover, Oz gathering up his gear, while Jonathan held an umbrella over Jennifer as she struggled with skirt, flowers and flounces.

They stood listening to the rain nag and spit against the concrete struts. All they could see now were the tallest buildings — multi-storey supermarkets, factory chimneys, grimy steeples of half forgotten churches. Roads and river, shops and people, all had fallen away. Jennifer stared down through haze and smoke. She felt strangely out of touch, as if she had soared up to some exalted yet bleak and empty plane, where there was nothing man-sized, nothing human-scale. Even the rain seemed colder, greyer here. Oz frowned into his light meter.

'I suggest we make a get-away. Find somewhere less exposed. I know — how about the railway station? I can get some sensational shots in there, with that marvellous cast-iron roof and all the sidings.'

'But won't it be terribly crowded?' Jennifer objected.

'All the better. It'll help publicity.' Jonathan was already stuffing props into his capacious leather holdall. 'I'll drive us, shall I?'

Jonathan only existed to be helpful. He was so endlessly attentive, he made Jennifer uneasy. He soothed, oiled, balmed, smiled; fetched and carried, scraped and bowed. He picked up bills before they could embarrass her, waved away bad weather or bad taste, assured her she was fantastic when she had hashed or stuttered her way through a chat-show or an interview, eased in and out of traffic jams, checked timetables, booked planes. He always had aspirins in his pocket and Kleenex in his car, a smile to charm a journalist, a joke to calm her nerves. He acted as nanny and alarm clock, chauffeur, guide and God. With Jonathan, she was never late or lost, rushed or fazed or mobbed. Neither was she happy. His presence stultified her. Her face ached with the strain of endless small-talk. Even with this photographer, she would rather have been alone. Jonathan inhibited her, made it less easy to take up the easy natural poses Oz demanded.

Oz himself was continually in motion, bending back, swooping sideways, crouching on his haunches. Part of his job, presumably, to find exciting camera angles, but she found herself disturbed by it, kept glancing at his body as it rippled through his clothes. He was wearing skin-tight jeans with tiny brass studs outlining the back pockets, which clung against a narrow bottom and made Jonathan's porridge-coloured flannels look effete and middle-aged. His hair was long, thick, dark and artfully untidy, his face pale beneath the tinted sunglasses. She hadn't seen his eyes. He called her (and everybody) darling. She tried to call him nothing. Names like Oz stuck in her throat like gristle. Perhaps it was short for Oscar, Oswald, Osbert — all of which sounded both idiotic and intimidating. Names had been a nightmare in the last few weeks. She had met so many people who immediately called her Jen or Jenny (or darling) while she was still struggling to remember who they were or what they did.

Jonathan took her arm and, braving the rain, dashed from their shelter to the car. He held the door while she climbed into the back, followed by Oz and both his cameras.

'Know the way, do you, Jon? It's only a matter of minutes.'

Jonathan wound round and round, down and down, until thirteen storeys steadied into floor level, pin-men swelled into human size again, and the clouds soared back to their position overhead. Jonathan paid (and charmed) the attendant and whisked them northwards across the High Level Bridge. Jennifer stared down at the water, dilapidated warehouses throwing grotesque and jagged shadows across oil slicks and driftwood. So this was the famous Tyne. She inched towards the window. Oz's thigh kept jiggling against her own.

'Oz. . .' She dared his name. 'I'd like a few shots with the book in them, if possible.' Matthew had told her always to insist. The book must appear every time that she did. She was only its servant and ambassador.

'Sorry, darling. That's been done to death. I'm trying to present you in a different way — to point the contrast, if you like. We live in an age of planes and high-speed trains, tower-blocks and microchips, yet you've chosen to bask in a country cottage, making cheeses and lavender bags, and dressing like an Edwardian recluse.'

Jennifer swallowed. The only place she was living at the moment was a room in Matthew's house. Their Cobham place was sold and both allotments had been given up as well — the original plot for vegetables, and the second plot they had rented after coming back from Hernhope and made into a herb garden modelled on Hester's own. She no longer grew her saxifrage and comfrey, her carrots and her beans. Her cheese-making equipment was piled in cardboard boxes in Matthew's garage. Now she bought her cheese plastic-wrapped, on shopping trips with Susie to Waitrose or Fine Fare. As for dressing like an Edwardian recluse, the last garment she had purchased — under Susie's tutelage — was a pair of scarlet jeans two sizes smaller than her usual safe and roomy skirts.

In fact, the greater the fanfare for the book, the more she was abandoning the very things it stood for. Take this trip. She was staying in a sprawling industrial city in a glass and concrete hotel, dashing about in cars and planes, stuffing herself with junk foods, swallowing pills to help her sleep, then washing them out with stimulants and coffee to wake her up again. All the natural herbal homely things which she and Hester had been preaching to the world had no place in her schedule. She was the Natural Woman leading an ersatz unnatural life; raving to reporters about basic homecrafts when she had neither home nor craft nor garden, hailing nature and nurture without sex or seed or child.

Oz's denimed thigh was still nudging against her skirt. She hoped it was only the motion of the car throwing them together. 'You must miss that place in the country,' he was saying. 'What's it called — Hernhope? I've read the book, you know — well, most of it. Incredible house it looks. You'll be going back there, will you, after this?'

'Er . . . no. Not *quite* yet.' She hadn't even seen the place for over a year. Molly continued to keep an eye on it, while Matthew still made problems about the missing Will. Maybe he was right about all the legal and financial complications, but all the same, it suited him to keep her and Lyn at Putney, especially now he was absent in Australia, and she and Susie were sharing duties as Cook and Nanny. She had to admit, though, she was quite enjoying it. Susie made things fun, persuaded her into instant foods or take-away, crazy picnics, sudden impulsive sprees. She wished Susie was with her now. She missed her constantly, as if she had known her half a lifetime, instead of a few short weeks. Susie had sneaked into her life like a keepsake in her handbag, a photo by her bed. Susie was so *easy*. She didn't brood like Lyn did, or need asbestos gloves and armour before she dared get close, or add all the world's anguish to a headache or a tiff. Even now, when they were parted, she found herself using Susie-phrases — chuffed, knackered, chatted-up — choosing Susie-food. Last night at dinner, she had ordered cocktails instead of her usual boring grapefruit juice — gaudy concoctions piled with fruit and froth, scoffed them all for Susie. (Scoffed was another Susie word.) She had even . . .

'Right, here we are.' Jonathan drew up in front of the imposing stone façade of Newcastle's Central Station.

'Thanks, Jon.' Oz jumped out after Jennifer. 'We'll see you on the platform. The car park's just a few yards on. Could you be a sport and buy some vegetables? You know, leeks, carrots, sweetcorn — things with shape and texture. Try and get carrots with those feathery bits on top. They make a more interesting picture.'

Oz took Jennifer's arm and steered her through cars and crowds into the station, stopping a moment beneath the soaring stone arches of its entrance.

'You're quite a girl, you know,' he murmured, turning her to face him. 'Fancy a drink this evening? I'd like to get to know you better.'

Jennifer blushed. She wasn't the sort of person photographers chatted up. She was too pale and dull and homely, trapped and barred by Lyn, Matthew, Jonathan, who towered like a palisade around her. It was probably only the make-up which had fooled him. She had larded it on to woo and please the cameras. He would be cruelly disillusioned if he saw her naked-faced and boring, without her fancy dress.

'N . . . no, I'm sorry. I'm afraid I'm having dinner with a man from the *Newcastle Journal*.'

'Can't you escape? Just for an hour or so?'

'Not . . . really. It's a formal interview. And, anyway, Jonathan will be there and he's my . . . chaperon.' She tried to laugh, make it sound the joke it wasn't.

'*I*'ll be your chaperon instead. I'd like that.'

Jennifer smiled. 'I'm sorry, but it really isn't possible. Those dinners last for hours, you see, and then I've got to pack and . . .'

'OK. No hassle. If you're free, call me. If not, forget it. There's my card. I'm always up late.'

Jennifer took the card and slipped it in her handbag. She would give it to Susie as a souvenir. She had been collecting things for Susie all through the trip — silly gifts, stolen menus, after-dinner mints. On her first and longer tour, it was Lyn she had bought presents for, Lyn she had phoned and fretted over. Now he had faded to a vague and gloomy presence. She had seen very little of him in these last few weeks. He had refused to take any leave, but had been working as hard and conscientiously as if he were a Matthew, roughing out designs for the firm's next two books. So she had embarked instead on a sort of holiday with Susie — Susie and the boys. They had gone to zoos and fairgrounds, stately homes and cricket matches, booked day-trips to the sea or just messed about making fudge or playing tag or hopscotch under the garden hose. If Lyn was sulking, she wasn't there to notice, and at night she simply went to sleep, since he offered nothing better. She had confessed to an incredulous Susie about the non-existent sex.

'You're *kidding*! No one goes that long without it. There must be something wrong with him.'

'There isn't, Susie. Well, nothing physical. It's just that . . .' Her voice had petered out. All the sympathy she had felt for Lyn, the forgiving explanations, the endless kind excuses, seemed merely fatuous now. Susie's own contempt and irritation were disturbingly infectious.

'If I was you, I wouldn't waste your time on him. There's plenty of other blokes around.'

Susie was right, it seemed. She had already received two eager propositions from men at the hotel and now a famous photographer had asked her out for a drink. Susie would approve of Oz. She was opposed to men in general, but she liked them in particular — especially when they had Hasselblads dangling round their necks, Equity admission cards weighing down their pockets. Perhaps she ought to go out with him just for Susie's sake. Or the sake of those brass studs. She could see them now — the perfect frame they made for his taut provoking bottom as he bent to change the film.

He stood up, strode ahead, barged his way through the barrier without a platform ticket, then started pacing up and down, checking angles and

154

locations. She followed nervously.

'Right, Jennifer, I want to pose you in the centre of that footbridge. There's some fantastic textural detail with the criss-cross pattern of the bridge leading the eye to the girders of the roof, and those railway lines echoing the curve and . . .'

Jennifer tried to appreciate his fantastic textural detail. All she could see were crowds of impatient passengers struggling to cross the footbridge with their luggage and their pushchairs while she and Jonathan blocked their way or delayed important journeys. Other people stopped to stare, creating more obstruction.

'*Fantastic*!' Oz was murmuring, as she arranged her arm against a complex intersection of metal curves and struts. Fantastic was like darling — a word which had lost its heart. Yet she clung to it like some addict to his fix. If they said just 'good' or even 'excellent', she felt a nonentity, a failure. The trouble was, the book had made her vain and introspective, fretting about her looks or her performance, her speeches or her image. She felt like a pop-star with her attendant gaggle of groupies, tried to ignore them, smile only for the camera. Matthew had told her to treat the camera as a friend. Oz had added, 'Flirt with it. Woo it like a lover.' She saw it rather as a snooper and a spy, sleuthing her up and down the city, in and out of cul-de-sacs, jumping out from corners, breathing down her neck. Susie would adore it, pose and pout and swank for it, respond to its advances.

'Now, I'd like you to look mysterious — stare into the distance, raise your head a bit.' Oz had stopped being the Romeo and become the professional again. She could hardly hear him against the clank and roar of trains, the cackle of loudspeakers.

'This is a platform alteration. The 15.50 to London King's Cross, will now depart from Platform 9. Will all passengers for London King's Cross kindly proceed to . . .'

She longed just to drop everything and run. King's Cross was only forty minutes' drive from Putney. It might be dry there — dry and bright, Susie in the garden with the boys. A week ago, she had daubed them all with body paint — Hugh and Robert red with spots, even the solemn Charles a zizzy green. They had used an ice-cold garden hose to yell and gasp it off. No one said 'Be quiet' or 'Don't be puerile'. Matthew couldn't see them from Australia, and Lyn was in his office in the City. After that, they had a barbeque. With Susie there, things which had loomed and threatened seemed somehow less important — Hernhope, house sales, even sex and babies — all took second place to charcoal-burnt chipolatas, ten-pin bowling, boat trips on the Thames.

'Jennifer, you're flagging, darling. Just one more shot and then we'll stop, I promise.' Oz was changing lenses again. 'Lean forward a little, will you, and then I can get that . . . Ah, Jonathan, you're back.'

'Am I too late? I'm sorry.' Jonathan's cream suede shoes were

155

squelching, his hair darkened and flattened by the rain. 'The sweetcorn wasn't easy. I got the other things, but then I had to . . .'

Oz waved away the split and sodden paper bags of vegetables. 'Don't worry — I managed without them. Thanks all the same, but we'll have to finish now. Perhaps you could drop me off on the way to your hotel?'

'Of course.'

Jonathan drove them back through traffic-jams and rainstorm, left Jennifer in her room to bath and change. Jennifer stripped off her clothes and stretched naked on the bed. Strange to think of Jonathan being homosexual. He didn't seem sexual at all. She couldn't imagine a panting, thrusting body beneath that immaculate façade. She was obsessed with bodies at the moment. The longer she was deprived of sex, the more she felt constantly on edge, on heat, spinning fantasies from damp and steaming denim, from gleaming teasing studs. Or perhaps it was simply Susie talking about bodies in a way she kept recalling: 'A screw's only like a meal', 'Love's a mixture of hormones and hot air.'

Susie brought up subjects she had avoided all her life, took the blush and censure out of sex and discussed it as freely as books or records. She somehow found it threatening and disturbing, torn between Susie's easy-going sluttishness and her own more stolid views. Susie was still a child in some respects, yet sexually she was so much more experienced. She had slept with a score of different men, even with a woman. Susie had poured out all the details, seemed to have relished the affair.

Jennifer had listened, shocked and yet excited. When Susie tried to kiss her, she always pulled away. Women shouldn't kiss. Yet she found herself dwelling on the kisses, thinking about them when Susie wasn't there—childish kisses too fervent for a child's, tasting of chewing-gum and cheap scented lipstick, overlaid with nicotine. Susie had even touched her breasts one evening — sort of casually as if it hardly mattered. When she pushed her off, Susie had pouted and called her a prude, explained that in her Women's Group they learnt to give pleasure to their own and each other's bodies, instead of always waiting for *men* to dish it out.

Jennifer trailed a hand across her breasts, remembering Susie's hand — a hot, sticky hand which knew exactly where to linger. Shouldn't do it, not even on her own. This was Newcastle's most decorous hotel. Touching yourself was bound to be forbidden, like a lot of other things — the regulations on the door were almost longer than the Bible by the bed. It would be nice to talk to Susie, giggle over Oz. She ought to phone, in any case, check on the boys, make sure Mrs Briggs was coping, have a word with Lyn. She turned on her tummy, dialled the Putney number.

'Wormwood Scrubs.' That was Hugh's giggle, not Susie's.

'Police Sergeant Bloggs here. I've just apprehended Jack the Ripper. Want me to bring him in?'

'Auntie Jennifer! Where are you?'

'Newcastle.'

'What, *still*? I thought you were going to Scotland.'

156

'We've been and gone — in less than half a day.'

'Crikey! You must have gone on Concorde. Did you buy me some Edinburgh rock?'

'Sorry, darling, I was so rushed, I didn't even see a shop. How are you?'

'Fine.'

'Everyone else all right?'

'Yup. We don't like Susie's cooking though. She tried to make a curry and it looked like sort of dog's mess.'

'Is Susie there?'

'No. She went out.'

'OK, I'll have a word with Lyn, then.'

'He's out, too.'

'You mean, he's not back from the office yet?'

'Well, yes . . . but then he went out again. Pushed off with Susie. In the car.'

'With *Susie*?'

'Yeah, they took a picnic. Meanies. Wouldn't let us come.'

'When, Hugh? When did they go?'

'Oh, hours ago.'

'Who's looking after you, then?'

'No one. We don't need looking after. Susie left us some supper — tins and things.'

'When did they say they'd be back, then?'

'They didn't. Not till late, I imagine. They were out till one last night.'

'*One*?'

'Yup. Susie woke me up when she came in. She tripped on the mat and started giggling.'

'But surely Lyn wasn't . . .? I mean, Susie was probably at her Women's Group. She's often late back from that.'

'Yeah. Maybe. I thought I heard Lyn come in with her, but it may have been some other bloke. Hey, want to speak to Oliver? He's dying to tell you about his . . .'

'Er . . . not now, darling. I'll phone again later. I . . . I've got to get ready for dinner now. L . . . love to everyone.'

Jennifer rolled over on the bed. The receiver felt damp and heavy in her hand. She let it fall, stared up at the ceiling. All she could see was Susie — Susie sprawling on the picnic rug, walking the streets with Lyn till one in the morning, kissing in some doorway . . . No, of course they hadn't kissed. Lyn had always steered clear of Susie, treated her like a schoolgirl.

So what were they doing out together — alone, without the boys? Picnics and sprees were her-and-Susie things, not Lyn's. Susie was betraying her, betraying her own views, criticising men and all they stood for, then grabbing her husband the minute she was gone. Yet Susie could hardly help herself. It was almost second nature for her to flirt and taunt

157

and charm — part of her attraction.

The picnic rug had spread right across the ceiling. Jennifer shut her eyes, but she could still see Susie lolling on her back, feeding Lyn with little bits of sausage, giggling through her cider. The rug changed to a counterpane, afternoon to night. Lyn was creeping upstairs in dogged pursuit of Susie, wheedling outside her door, then slipping in and turning the key behind him. Ridiculous. He had never once set foot inside her room. It was an attic room up a little narrow staircase which Lyn studiously avoided. He was usually fast asleep by one. Susie had probably come in with some casual local pick-up, some twenty-year-old with acne and tattoos.

Jennifer swung off the bed, dragged on her dressing-gown, paced up and down between bed and window, bed and chair. That only left the picnic. Was it really so unthinkable that Lyn should go out for some fresh air and a sandwich on a summer afternoon with a girl who shared the house? Except it was no longer afternoon. So why were they still out? And why had they barred the boys?

She could see Susie's hand again, reaching out to Lyn, this time, fondling him instead. Could she be jealous of a woman? She was jealous of them both — angry with Lyn for taking her place as Susie's mate and confidant, bitter with Susie for sneaking off with a man she denounced as a chauvinist and pretended to despise.

Yet who was *she* to censure? Hadn't she echoed all the criticisms, let her own resentment feed on Susie's? More than that — she had even started borrowing Susie's fantasies, allowing herself to be tempted by strangers in hotels or flattered by photographers, casual chat-ups, vulgar overtures. Susie was too young and irresponsible to understand the complex bonds of marriage. She was a temporary, a fly-by-night, who would have vanished in a month or so, off to be an actress, or a mistress, charming someone else. Whereas Lyn was hers for ever, marriage was for ever, and she had simply shrugged it off, risking lasting sacred things for the sake of a few cheap thrills.

She trailed into the bathroom, ran the taps. She had to admit she would *miss* the thrills. She had enjoyed her break at Putney, yet she had enjoyed it at a cost. Lyn had always been excluded, the one outsider in a family of seven. She felt a sudden rush of pity as she saw him sitting on his own at nights, tired and supperless, while she and her new-found siblings shared chopsticks and chop suey in the Yang Tse Kiang or stuffed themselves with popcorn at the Putney ABC.

She stepped into the bath, rubbed her body harshly with the flannel, soaped the make-up off, the sham, the shame. She had only one last dinner left, then she would return and be his wife again, not Matthew's creature or Hartley Davies's star — not even Susie's playmate. Susie was a danger. They must escape her influence before things went too far. She tried not to guess how far they had gone already. Lyn was off sex at the moment, but a younger girl might be just the cure he needed — some flighty little teenager with no hang-ups at all. Susie probably liked the back way, was probably on the Pill, and for all her gripes she had admitted Lyn attracted her. It would be milder in the south, a balmy evening full of scents and stars — the whole of Putney Heath as their double bed . . .

Jennifer jerked out the plug, drubbed herself dry, returned to the bedroom cocooned in two large towels. Lyn and Susie simply wouldn't work. She might flirt with him, try to add him to her list of pick-ups, but she would never understand him. He was too sensitive, too complex. That was *her* role and no one else would snatch it from her. They would have to get away, leave Susie safely behind. Why risk rows and jealousies, ugly complications? Lyn hated it at Putney, anyway, complained about the continual noise — the five competing radios, the stampedings on the stairs, the lack of a free bathroom, the long-drawn-out formal meals. It surprised her, really, he had put up with it so long, especially with their neglect of him added on as well. No wonder he had responded when . . .

Better not to think about it. She walked to the window, double-netted, double-glazed, pushed the nets aside, looked out at only grey — the sky a traffic-jam of weeping roofs and gutters, rain drumming on the pane.

'*I stayed a night in Newcastle before continuing my journey. I could not sleep for nerves. It rained and rained.*' Jennifer suddenly remembered that entry in the diaries, scribbled in the scrawny green-backed notebook which Hester had brought with her from London to Northumberland, returning there after fifteen years away, to be housekeeper to Thomas Winterton. She had stayed not in a tower-block, but in a humble guesthouse where they burnt the rissoles and rain splattered on the floorboards from a leaky roof.

Next day, the sky had cleared and Hester's nerves sparked into excitement as she caught the country bus and rumbled away from the city to the hills. Hester had been writing on her knee — wildly lurching scribbles as they swung round corners or jolted over pot-holes — glimpse of a hare sitting motionless in a field of freckled clover; gleam of a wagtail as it flashed across a burn; grease on the page where she had paused to eat her cheese and pickle sandwiches.

The passage was so vivid, Jennifer could almost taste the pickle on her tongue, see the green and purple hills peering in at the windows of the bus. She pressed her nose to her own pane, the smirch of rain now blurring with a belch of smoke from a distant factory chimney. No tree, no hint of green here, yet less than fifty miles away, the wild and lonely Cheviots reared huge against a wide and free horizon.

She let the curtain fall. *They* could follow Hester, drive to Hernhope, swap the city for the hills. She was almost there, for heaven's sake. Why return to Putney at all, when Lyn could come up North instead, meet her here in Newcastle and then drive on to Mepperton, now — immediately — or at least tomorrow morning? The idea was so bold and yet so simple, it took her breath away. She sank down on the bed. Always before, she had let Matthew overrule her when she tried to mention Hernhope and her longing to return there. Matthew fussed and quibbled, warned of legal tangles, but they could cut through complications simply by ignoring them. All they had to do was slip away and take over Hester's house without arguments or lawyers or any more delay. It had been impossible before. She had been tied to the book and Matthew's apron strings. But now Matthew was half a world away and all the publicity finished save one last evening. The book would sell without her, buoyed by its own momentum. If she flew tamely back in the morning, Putney would close around her like a cage again. A gilded cage, maybe. She had to admit she was still tempted by Susie and the boys, the affection and attraction of a family, but if her new kid sister had designs on Lyn, then it was safer for them to leave.

True, Lyn himself was a problem. He had been strangely guarded about his mother's house, seemed almost to ignore its existence and his rights there — but then Lyn was strange about a lot of things, especially recently. Living at Putney had only made him worse. It was time *she* took command for once, stopped listening to his fears or Matthew's fusspottings, and returned where they belonged. A move to Hernhope would solve several problems at once — give Lyn the peace and privacy he needed, remove him from the threat of Susie, remove herself from the grab and glare of London, make a final break with Matthew.

She shifted on the bed, secured the slipping towels. Was that fair on Matthew — to take advantage of his absence, when he was slaving to earn the cash which would make them free of him? Was it fair on the boys to turn her back on them, with their parents both away? Was it even fair on Susie? Could she really leave one scatty teenager to cope with all four children? And how would Anne regard it? Supposing Lyn refused to leave at all or . . .

Her head was aching with all the complications. She tried to distract herself, picked up the hotel Bible lying on top of the local phone directory, thumbed idly through its pages. It was a new modern translation to match the new modern room. She shut her eyes, opened the book at random, jabbed her finger down. They had played that game at Sunday School when she was still in single figures. You opened your eyes, and whichever verse your finger pointed at, was your personal message from God. Half the time, the passage was irrelevant or they couldn't understand the King James purple prose, but it had passed the time while they waited for the vicar, or dozed their way through prayers.

She sat there for a moment, Bible on her lap, finger pointing, eyes still closed. She should be getting dressed, choosing her most appealing outfit for her final interview, rehearsing her opinions. Yet she couldn't settle, couldn't concentrate. Until she had spoken to Lyn, she was tugged in two.

Slowly, she opened her eyes, stared at the verses underneath her finger. It was Jeremiah — not a Book she knew — chapter thirty-three. She peered at the tiny print on the cheap and grainy paper.

'*The Lord Almighty said, "In this land that is like a desert and where no people or animals live, there will once again be pastures where shepherds can take their sheep."*'

The words leapt and dazzled on the page. Despite the flat and casual language, they were so strikingly appropriate, it was as if God indeed had spoken. Hernhope was a desert, the farm sold, the house abandoned. Matthew himself had dismissed it as a wilderness. Yet here was a pledge and promise that it would revive again, the sheep return, the life return. Her eye strayed to the verse above.

'*In these places, you will hear again the shouts of gladness and joy and the happy sounds of wedding feasts . . . I will make this land as prosperous as it was before.*'

Wasn't that a prophecy — that she and Lyn would return to Hernhope as bride and bridegroom, man and wife, and that joy and wealth would follow them? It could be just coincidence, but even so, it was still extraordinary when there were more than a thousand pages in the Bible, more than thirty thousand verses, and when she had just been struggling with her own decision. She didn't believe in a formal churchy God who spoke through Bibles or thundered out of pulpits, but she did believe in powers and presences shaping people's lives. It was as if Hester had returned, after months of anger and estrangement to be the guide and spirit she had seemed at Hernhope.

'*Although still queasy from the bus, I took a glass of punch with Mr Winterton on arriving at his house, which is more remote than any I have seen. Some would call it bleak, but I find a peace already here. The view is wonderful.*'

The view is . . . Jennifer stared across at stained and puking chimneys, the sprawl of ugly roofs — the spew and dross of Newcastle's bird's eye view. Was it any wonder that Hester had kept her distance, when she had cut herself off from all that she had stood for, left her house to rot? If she had harboured any doubts, they were now completely stifled. The finger which had pointed to the verses was somehow Hester's finger, the prophecy her gift. She and Lyn must return to hill and forest, find Hernhope's peace again. She would phone Lyn after dinner, share her plan with him, coax him up to Newcastle in the morning. All the reporters assumed Hernhope was her home, even if they attacked her for turning her back on it. Well, this time, they'd have no reason for attack. She would complete her last interview, then drive back home to Mepperton to be the Country Woman they had hailed and publicised.

She lay back against the pillows, closed her eyes. She could already see lights beaconing from the windows, cheeses in the larder, flowers softening the stone . . .

'Jennifer?'

She started, clutched the towels around her. Jonathan was knocking at the door. He would never presume to enter, but she recognised

161

his purr, his unobtrusive tap.

'Sorry to rush you, but remember we're meeting early for a drink. So if you could be down in just five minutes . . .'

Jennifer dashed to the wardrobe, took out the soft blue shirtwaister which had always been Lyn's favourite. She would dress for him tonight, not for the book or Newcastle's leading newspaper. Her face looked nude without its make-up, but she refused to hide behind it. It was only false and she was herself again — and Lyn's. Her cheeks were glowing, anyway, with the excitement of her plan.

This time tomorrow they would be back in Hester's house.

XIV

'Absolutely fantastic!' Jonathan thrilled. 'That was the best interview I've ever heard you give. I could almost *see* Hernhope, the way you described it. That chap was totally captivated. What luck he was a Borders man himself. I hardly had to say a word this time, with you two bubbling over. You sounded so elated.'

'Yes. I am.'

'At going home, I suppose?'

'Yes.' Jonathan meant Putney. She meant home, real home.

'How about another drink, then? To celebrate a really sparkling interview and a most successful tour. We could go on somewhere different, if you like. I know a nice little bar just across the . . .'

'If you don't mind, Jonathan, I'd rather call it a day now. We've got to be up early for the plane and . . .' She hadn't told him yet that she didn't intend to catch it. No point worrying him. Matthew had instructed him to shepherd her safely back to Putney, so how could he allow her to drive the other way? Better to talk to Lyn first, make her plans with him, then simply inform Jonathan in the morning.

She floated up the stairs, drunk not only with her last after-dinner cocktail, but with the relief of her decision, the success of her interview. Naked-faced and ordinary, she had somehow become the star she had never managed in all her paint and plumes. It hadn't been an effort. She had simply poured out her excitement, the strange dazzling promise of the Jeremiah verses, her faith and joy in Hernhope, in Hester's return.

The bedroom seemed confining after the sweep and swank downstairs. She kicked off her shoes, removed her watch and bracelet. The paper bags of vegetables were still lying on the chest of drawers where Jonathan had

162

left them. She drew out a carrot, a swollen head of corn. Lyn had grown corn and carrots up at Hernhope, tiny seedlings fighting bare and stony soil. When they left, they had been a flare and boast of green above the stones. It was too late to plant a second crop, but they could prepare the ground for autumn, plan a bumper harvest, make up for all those months of negligence.

She lay on the bed to make her call. Her legs were made of cocktails. The phone seemed to ring for ever until its shrill changed to a grunt.

'Who is it?' Grudging male voice not deep enough for Lyn's.

'Auntie Jennifer here. That you, Charles?'

'Mm. You woke me up.'

'I'm sorry, love. How are you?'

'Tired.'

'Well, you can go straight back to sleep. Just get Lyn for me, would you darling?'

'Lyn's not here.'

'Not there?' So the picnic *had* gone on. 'Where is he, then?' Copses, bushes, double beds, flashed across her mind like crude and out-of-focus snapshots.

'Well, he did come back and then pissed off again.'

'Charles!'

'I'm only using Susie's word. That's what she said. She had a row with him. They came screaming in about nine o'clock and started fighting with each other. We were pretty scared. They were even throwing things. In the end, Uncle Lyn slammed out.'

Relief and horror curdled in her head. 'L . . . look, I'd better speak to Susie. Could you get her?'

'She won't come. She's locked herself in the loo and refuses to open the door.'

'She'll come for me, Charles. Tell her it's urgent, will you.'

'Hell! I'll never get to sleep with all this uproar. *Okay*, I'll go. Hang on a minute.'

The minute seemed to grow like a beanstalk, shooting up, up, up, sending out shoots and branches until it was tapping against the ceiling, choking her in its tendrils. What in heaven's name had happened?

The phone suddenly came alive and was screaming in her ear. She winced and held it from her.

'Listen, Jennifer, I've had more than I can take of that bloke of yours. He's the most uncouth, neurotic, unreasonable, impossible, self-centred . . . pig I've ever had to deal with. And I told him so. Don't think I'm going to . . .'

'What happened, Susie? What . . .'

'I'm bloody *glad* he pissed off. I told him not to come back — ever. We don't want him here. No one does. Not even you. I told him what you said about his being such a bloody pain and . . .'

163

'Susie, how could you? Look, I only meant . . .'

'No, you didn't. You're fed up to the teeth with him as well. It's obvious. You only ever relax when he's out of the way. He's ruining your life. Can't you see that? Well, I won't have him ruining mine as well. I've got enough problems as it is. You don't know half of it. Now let me get to bed, Jen. I'm shattered.'

'No — wait, Susie, *please*. Don't go yet. I must know where he is. I've got to speak to him and . . .'

'I don't know and I don't care. All I know is he can't get back in here. I've bolted all the doors.'

'Susie, please unbolt them. You can't leave him out all night. It's pouring down with rain. At least, it is up here. He'll catch a chill and . . .'

'Balls! He's as strong as an ox. You just fuss him all the time which makes him pretend he's feeble. Anyway, he's got his bloody car. He can sit in that and shiver, then perhaps he'll have come to his senses by the morning.'

The phone was amplifying Susie's voice until it sounded like a howl of pain. Jennifer tried to stop her own voice crumpling up. 'Yes, but what about the morning? I mean, the boys and everything? If Lyn comes back, please don't start a row again. It's not good for them to hear all that fighting and quarrelling, not with their parents away and . . .'

'Christ, Jen! My parents threw things at each other almost every mealtime. You're all so bloody sheltered in this house.'

'That's not true, Susie. Lyn had a difficult start himself and . . .'

'Yeah, and what about *your* life? Aren't *you* entitled to a bit of fun? God! He treats you like a nun and you sit there and accept it. If it was me, I'd screw everything in sight just to pay him out. He's not the only man in the universe, you know. In fact, I doubt if he's even a proper man at all.'

'Susie, be quiet. I won't have you running him down like that. He happens to be my husband and I love him.'

'Love? Balls! What d'you mean by love? Habit, safety, handcuffs, clinging on to someone because you're too bloody scared to face life on your own. Right — I've said enough. I'm going to bed. And if I was you, I'd go out on the town and pick up the first randy bloke you can find, and maybe you'll actually enjoy yourself for once, instead of pining and rusting with your own — ha ha! — man.'

The phone slammed down the other end. Jennifer was trembling. She still had no idea what had happened, why Lyn and Susie had quarrelled in the first place. She hardly knew whose side to take. It had been easy to plan her get-away with Lyn, when Susie seemed remote, but as soon as she heard her voice again, she was thrown into confusion. Susie hollered out the criticisms she had spent three years hushing up. She could hear her taunts still snarling round the room.

I doubt if he's a man at all . . .

Neurotic impossible self-centred pig . . .

164

Bloody glad he's pissed off — didn't want him here . . .
Treats you like a nun . . .

Furious with Susie for saying things like that — rude, unfair, untrue, uncaring things. No, not unfair. Rude, maybe, but not untrue. Angry with Lyn, not Susie. *Furious* with Lyn. Impossible, self-centred Lyn, keeping her in handcuffs, trampling on her confidence, denying her a normal married life.

. . . screw everything in sight . . .

Ridiculous. Only sluts behaved like that. She was Jennifer Winterton, calm, famous, charming, chaste. *Sometimes, I wish to God I'd never married him.* No, she hadn't said that. Someone else was speaking, someone cruel and selfish. Turn the muzak on. Nice quiet schmaltzy melody from South Pacific. '*Some enchanted evening . . .*' She undid her dress — Lyn's favourite dress. She should have worn her scarlet jeans for Susie. Scarlet jeans with studs. '*. . . you will see a stranger.*'

A stranger. *If I was you, I'd go out on the town and pick up the first randy bloke . . .* That was just Susie being childish. She stripped off tights and bra and pants. If Jennifer Winterton went out on the town, she had to have an escort and a chaperon, a reporter and a photographer.

Photographer. She was already in her nightie. Turn the music off and get into bed. A pill if she was overwrought, a nice quiet read to calm her down. She picked up her magazine. She was in the middle of a story, had reached the bit where the foreign diplomat was fondling his new interpreter, fingers fumbling through the housecoat for her breasts. She touched her own nipples, surprised to find them hard. Hard like studs. Must disown them, go to bed — alone. She paused a moment before switching off the radio. She liked the man who was singing. He had a deep, throaty voice which reminded her of Oz's, a voice which lapped against her body.

'*Who can explain it, who can tell you why?*
Fools give you . . .'

She turned up the volume, so that the 'fools' shouted through the room. She was a fool, a fool — crazy, wild, resentful, furious. It was *sex* she wanted. That word she was never allowed to say because she was the contented Country Woman who got all her satisfactions from her happy solid marriage and her fulfilling country crafts; because she was delightfully old-fashioned and made love and cheeses with the same retiring modesty.

Rubbish! She hadn't made a cheese since the Sales Conference and she hadn't made love for so long, she had probably rusted up. Anyway, it *wasn't* love. Love was habit, safety, handcuffs, clinging on to someone because . . .

She flung the magazine down, dragged on her clothes again. She didn't bother with bra or tights, just dress and pants and sandals. She reached for her handbag, scrabbled at the bottom, drew out the crumpled card.

Oz Steadman, Photographer.
40 Elm Gardens, Jesmond.

He wasn't a stranger, he was a photographer. Perhaps he'd like another session, fit in some night shots, try a different angle. All she wanted, really, was to talk to someone.

Oz had *invited* her to call him, told her he stayed up late. She picked up the receiver, dialled his number, put it down again. Mustn't act impulsively. Better wait till morning, phone Putney again, coax Susie to unlock the doors and drag Lyn to the phone. He really ought to leave, still — both of them escape from Susie's pull.

She started unbuttoning her dress. Stopped at the second button. Would Oz still have those jeans on, or would he have changed into pyjamas? Maybe he slept naked in silk sheets or . . .

He wouldn't be up at all if she didn't phone him soon. But she wasn't going to phone. She was going to wait for Lyn and morning — romantic tryst at dawn before striking north for Hernhope — the house which was a wilderness, the husband who was an impossible neurotic gloomy selfish pig and who'd see in the dawn slumped in his car outside Susie's bolted doors.

The number sounded sleepy when it rang.

'Steadman.' If only he'd said hallo. Surnames were so hostile on their own.

'It's . . . er . . . Jennifer here.'

'Who?'

'Jennifer Winterton. You . . . um . . . took some photographs of me this afternoon.'

'Oh yeah — course. Sorry, darling. Bit late for calls, isn't it?'

'I'm sorry. I've . . . only just got back from dinner. Thought you might like that . . . drink you mentioned.'

'What, now?'

Jennifer shut the Bible, stuffed it in the drawer. 'W . . . Why not?'

'OK. Want me to come round?'

'Oh, no, no. Not here. I mean . . .' Jonathan's room was just along the corridor. He was trained to respond to her every murmur, meet her every need. If he heard her stir, he might come fussing along with aspirins or Alka Seltzer.

'My place, then?'

'Well, I thought we might — you know — go to a bar or something.' What would *Susie* suggest? 'Or how about a disco?'

'I'm flaked, darling. I've been working since five am. Grab a taxi and come over here, if you like. Jesmond's only a mile or so from the centre. I'll fix you a nightcap, shall I?'

'Oh . . . right. Thanks.'

Slut. Flirt. Fool. *I'd screw every bloody man I could lay my hands on . . . There will once again be pastures. . . . Jennifer Winterton continues the serene pastoral tradition of her mother-in-law, returning to a life where fulfil-*

166

ment lies in . . . Screwing's only like eating. . . . Five blokes in a night . . . Impossible, neurotic pig . . . She has deliberately chosen the rural backwater and high ideals which belong strictly to a . . . I don't know how you stand it. Go and pick up the first randy bloke . . .

'Silence!' she almost shouted. One footling nightcap couldn't be worth this conflict and upheaval. She would go simply to escape herself, her multitude of selves. Go for a breath of air, a glass of wine, a snatch or two of normal conversation.

She closed her bedroom door as softly as she could, crept down the stairs, dodged the receptionist. It was all so easy. The doorman hailed her a taxi within ten seconds, and the driver had whisked her to Elm Gardens before she had finished first-aiding her face. The street looked reassuringly suburban, even in the dark. Three weren't any elms, but neat front gardens with pink geraniums glowing in the porch lights and even the odd gnome grinning among the salvias and stocks. It seemed a hundred miles from the grimy, noisy centre of the town. Oz couldn't be too dangerous if he lived in a pebble-dash and stucco semi with a crazy-paving path.

She walked up the path and knocked. They could always chat about gardening. His buddleia needed trimming and that holly bush was hogging all the light.

Oz came to the door still in his dark glasses and the jeans. He had changed his purple shirt, though, and now wore a black one, straining against a heavy leather belt. He had flung a sweater round his shoulders, which emphasised their width and contrasted with the narrow denimed hips. His clothes seemed not so much to cover him as display the structure underneath.

'H . . . hallo.' Stupid to be blushing when she was meant to be a Name.

'Hi there! Come on in.'

'I . . . like your garden.'

'It's poison! The woman next door complained about the weeds, so I went all helpless male, until she offered to look after it. She was busy enough with three kids and four cats. Now she's got two gardens and six gnomes. Mind you, I'm not so sure that gnomes are any advance on dandelions. I loathe the outdoor life myself. Sit down.'

Somehow Jennifer had reached his living-room and was standing staring at a sort of picture gallery. The whole downstairs of the house had been knocked into one large room, its walls almost entirely covered with blown-up photographs. The subjects were mostly women and mostly naked. Jennifer averted her eyes from nipples and buttocks and looked for something to sit on. There were no safe or solid chairs, only a vast upholstered couch with neither back nor arms, and a pile of purple cushions. She chose a cushion, tried to yank her skirt down over her knees. There were naked knees interspersed among the nipples on the wall.

Oz was searching through a trayful of glasses, trying to find two clean ones. 'What'll you have to drink? Damn! There's only whisky or an inch or two of rum.'

167

'Er . . . whisky, then.' She hated whisky, but at least it might help her to relax. A lean and scraggy mongrel was growling in a corner, white teeth bared in a savage-looking jaw.

'Good boy,' she said, holding out her hand.

'He's not good. A pain in the arse, in fact. Thank God he's not permanent. A fashion model friend of mine asked me to look after him. When she said ''pooch'', I somehow pictured something tiny like a chihuahua, or endearing like a spaniel, or at least a pedigree. She found him shivering in the gutter and took him in. I suspect he calms her social conscience. She can't be criticised for earning ten times more than a nurse or social worker when she's relieving the pressure on the Battersea Dogs' Home. No, I wouldn't touch him, if I were you. He's not too keen on strangers.'

Stranger. *Some enchanted evening*. Nothing very enchanted about it yet. She could hear the rain still slapping against the windows. Her back ached from perching on the cushion, trying to tuck her bare legs out of sight. The whisky tasted bitter, the glass had a chip in it. Wherever she looked, Oz's work embarrassed or depressed her. Between the nudes were full-frontal studies of bleeding butchered casualties from some indeterminate war. Oz himself was hacking ice out of a tray, cursing when a cube slipped from his fingers and skidded to the floor.

'You want ice, do you?'

'Er . . . please.'

He lounged across, plopped two cubes in her glass. She tugged at her dress again, clamped her knees together. Oz was crouching right in front of her, jeans straining across his groin, face very close to hers.

'Cheers,' he said.

'Ch . . . cheers.' She could smell newly applied after-shave, mixed with all-day sweat.

'Enjoying your tour?'

'Yes. It's . . . er . . . finished now, though. I'm flying back tomorrow.'

'Shame.' Oz stretched, yawned, returned to the whisky bottle, poured himself a double. She wished she could see his eyes. The dark glasses made her nervous. She couldn't tell where he was looking or judge the expression on his face. She felt somehow in the way. He had probably been about to go to bed, and she was keeping him up, forcing him into small talk. She didn't even have the talk. He would be used to witty repartee from model girls and jet-setters, and she had hardly said a word, yet. She glanced around the room for inspiration, stared at a colour shot of six out-of-focus Pepsi Cola cans towering above a napalm victim.

'Are these your . . . *own* photographs?'

'Yeah, most of them.'

'Do you do much advertising work?'

'Work's finished, sweet.'

Silence. He sounded bored now, even irritable, totally different from Oz the Photographer who had dazzled her and Newcastle only hours ago.

Then, he'd been all sinewy grace and charm, all interest and encouragement. Now, he was standing tense and rigid by the mantelpiece, fiddling
with an ornament. He was probably shocked by her appearance, the change
from full regalia to her present slovenly dress. Susie's *Cosmopolitan* said if you
weren't a natural beauty, then try Sympathetic Seductress. Ask him about
his hobbies, listen, draw him out. Oz's hobby was music — that was
obvious.

'I . . . er . . . like your stereo.'

'So you should! That's more than a thousand quid's worth. I've just
bought bigger speakers with the most fantastic bass. Want to hear?'

'Mmm. That would be nice.' Music would fill the silence, make things
more relaxed.

'Anything you fancy?' Oz waved at half a wall of records and cassettes.

'Y . . . you choose.'

'I'm a Westbrook fan myself.' Oz was kneeling in front of his record
collection like a worshipper at a shrine. 'Know the latest album?'

'N . . . no. Not . . . *well*.'

'It really breaks new ground. I'll play it for you, shall I?'

'Yes, please.' She tried to sound eager, prayed he would leave the record-
sleeve on show, so that at least she could discover whether Westbrook was
male or female, pop or rock.

'Why don't you sit on the couch? The acoustics are better there. You'll be
bang between the speakers.'

'Oh . . . right.' Jennifer eased up from her cushion. The dog had sleuthed
her and was standing guard like a gaoler with his prisoner, hackles raised,
jaw still menacing. She shifted her legs from the radius of his teeth. 'Good
fellow. Sit then, *sit*.'

Oz swivelled round. 'The only word he understands is kill. Down, Bruce!
Get away.'

Bruce sprang. Jennifer dodged, backed, capsized her glass of whisky with
her foot. 'Gosh, I'm sorry. I've spoilt your carpet and . . .' She watched the
amber liquid soak into the pile, fumbled for the Kleenex she knew she hadn't
got.

'Don't worry. It's had worse than that spilt on it. It's that bloody hound's
fault. Get *out*, Bruce! Are you OK? He hasn't hurt you, has he? Here, let me
get you a fill-up.'

Jennifer passed her glass across. Matthew would have fussed around with
floorcloths, made her feel a clumsy bungling child. Oz sounded quite solicitous — more concerned for her than for his carpet. She had probably misjudged him. He was just tired, perhaps, or even shy without the panoply of
his cameras to hide behind. She sympathised with shyness. They needed
Susie there, to help them change the mood. Susie was never at a loss. She
would be on her feet by now, kicking off her shoes, gulping down Oz's
whisky, whirling him round the room with her, enjoying what she called a
bit of fun.

Jennifer took a cautious sip from her newly refilled glass. 'Shall we have that . . . music now?'

'Yes, of course.' Oz still had his back to her. Nice to be the sort of girl no man could take his eyes off. He was obviously more interested in Westbrook — cleaning the disc, offering it to the turntable like a precious sacrifice. Now Lyn no longer fancied her, she felt less and less desirable, like a piece of marked-down merchandise labelled 'seconds'.

He swivelled round, still crouching on the carpet, one hand fondling the polished wood of the cabinet. 'Right, listen to this track. It's mind-blowing.'

A sudden hail of drums shattered the quiet suburban cul-de-sac of Jesmond, followed by bumptious bragging brass. She might have called it jazz, had it sounded less distorted. The rhythm was there, but continually warped and broken. Shrill complaining noises cut across the beat, as if the disc had been recorded on a busy city street with drills and sirens contributing their sound, horns and hooters blaring, brakes wincing on the tarmac. She felt extinguished by the sound, unable to think or speak or block it out. And yet it wasn't simply noise like Susie's groups were noise. This was clever frightening music, the sort of sound intellectuals wrote about in the superior Sunday arts columns. She only hoped he wouldn't discuss it with her afterwards, expect her to have sharp informed opinions on things she didn't understand.

The tiny pause between the tracks was like soothing ointment on a burn, but then the smart and stab surged back again, with a rising rhythmic bellow. Bruce's growls were completely swallowed up now. The dog seemed cowered and frightened by the noise — in that way, they were allies. His gaze never faltered from her face. She longed to stroke his ears, make some overture, but his eyes had a snarl in them — dark pleading eyes, sad and dangerous both at once. She realised suddenly why he made her feel uneasy — he reminded her of Lyn — both lean, suspicious strays who had been hurt and kicked around. The music wept for both of them. It was softer now, but sadder. A plaintive sobbing from the saxophones was echoed by an anguished oboe wail.

'God, this sound's fantastic! Listen to that flugelhorn.'

She tried to concentrate. The trumpets had taken over now, whoopee-ing out a crazy wedding march. Mustn't think of weddings. *Wilt thou have this man to* . . .? Lyn had been sick the night before their wedding — sick with nerves, not from any stag party. *Wilt thou love, honour and keep him, forsaking all other*? Lyn had made the same vow. Had he broken it, forsaken her for . . .?

'Ba-ba ba-ba ba-baaaa . . .' Oz trumpeted. The room echoed and repeated him. He sank on to the couch, sprawled his length beside her. She edged away. Didn't want him there, now. Something strange was happening to her face and she mustn't let him see it.

'Used to play the skins myself. Bloody marvellous group that was. Do you play any instrument?'

'N . . . no.' She sniffed, swallowed, tried desperately to gain control. 'Well, as a child, I . . .' A sob broke up the sentence.

'What's up, sweet?'

'I don't know. It's . . . it's Br . . . Bruce. He's so, so . . .'

'Bruce? No one could cry over that flea-bitten hunk of hell-hound. God Almighty! He's just tried to make you mincemeat. Here. Take my hankie. It looks as if you need it. And how about another . . .?'

She could hardly hear him. The music was howling louder now than she was. She had ruined the record for him, ruined the whole evening. 'Look, I'm sorry. I'm so sorry . . .'

'It's OK. Go ahead. Often best to cry and get it over.'

He was so kind, he made it worse. She had slumped against his chest and he had an arm around her shoulders. It felt solid, comforting. Why not confide in him? He might be sympathetic, understand what she hardly grasped herself. 'Look, I know it sounds . . . stupid, but there's this g . . . girl called Susie, and I think I . . . *love* her. Oh, not like that, but . . . It's all rather complicated. You see, my husband refuses to . . . Well, I suppose I shouldn't say ''refuses'' — it's not that simple, but I'm frightened now that he and Susie may . . .'

'Look, sweet, I think you need a drink — a stiff one. You've hardly touched your whisky. Get that down inside you and you'll feel more human. Here, grab your glass.'

She struggled up, stared at him in shock. He had taken his glasses off and the eyes behind them were weak, uncertain, blinking in the light. The huge tinted spectacles had added mystery and glamour to his face. Without them, he was ordinary — a myopic, not a sun-worshipper, his whole face vulnerable. Tears threatened her again. 'Oh, g . . . gosh, I'm sorry. I just don't know what's . . .' A trumpet screamed in mockery. She was weeping now for his pale and peering eyes, his stained and grubby carpet, his chipped tumblers and lack of furniture, his lack of a wife to clean and care for him, his bleeding napalm victims. The handkerchief was sodden.

Oz had moved away. He was obviously getting impatient as well as damp. She hardly blamed him. He had been expecting a quiet drink with a celebrity, not hysterics with a nut-case. She gulped her whisky down. Right — they'd had their drink — now she'd better leave. 'Look, I'm . . . OK now. Honestly. I'm s . . . sorry I've been such . . . such rotten company. I ought to go now — really. I'll be better for some sleep and I know I'm keeping you up. Thanks for the drink and being so nice and everything. Perhaps you'd get me a t . . . taxi?'

'Yes, of course. Dry your eyes, though, or they'll think I've been beating you up.'

She tried to smile, but she knew what he was getting at. She must look quite appalling — eyes puffy, nose red, skin all marked and blotchy. 'You couldn't lend me a c . . . comb, could you? I seem to have come without my . . .'

'Without your bra,' he murmured. He had returned to sit beside her on the couch.

'What?' Perhaps she hadn't heard right.

'It's nice. I noticed it as soon as you walked in.' Oz's hand was creeping down her neck. The top button of her shirtwaister was already half undone. He was undoing the second one, very matter-of-factly, as if he were undressing a hurt and fractious child. He slipped his hand between the buttonholes, stroked across her nipples. She lay rigid and astonished.

'You've got fantastic tits, you know.'

She could feel her blush seep right across her chest. Ought to remove the hand, but how could she do it without offending him? She could hardly slap him down in return for all his kindness. The record was still shrilling on. She shut her eyes, tried to concentrate on drums and saxophones. At least they might distract her from the tremor in her nipples. Her breasts were tautening, reaching out to him. Surely she couldn't want him? She was upset, distracted, married, for God's sake. '*With my body, I thee worship* . . .' She didn't trust her body. It alarmed her more than his did. The strange tingly feelings were creeping lower, lower down. Must be something to do with the drink. She wasn't used to whisky. It had joined the cocktails and stirred them up again, done strange things to her head.

'Look, Oz, I think I ought to . . .' Her words were crushed against his lips. He was kissing her, not a kiss-it-better peck, but a wild wet hurting lunge, passionate and hungry. He used his tongue to prise her lips apart, found her own tongue, hooked it into his. He tasted of Polos, overlaid with whisky. They were joined now, mouth to mouth. She could feel his teeth grazing against her lips, sending sharp glorious shivers down her spine. One dangerous hand was creeping slowly across her belly, slowly towards her . . .

Must stop the hand, stop the kiss. Susie wouldn't stop it. It was only fun, for heaven's sake. She deserved a bit of fun, after all the tears and upset. At least she was relaxing now. Sounds and colours were clashing on the ceiling, bits of her body floating off and drifting round the room. Another drink would probably detach her mind, blot the vicar's voice out. '*To have and to hold, to love and to* . . .' She eased her mouth from his, struggled up, fumbled for her glass.

'Look, could I have a . . . fill-up?' That was Oz's word.

'Try a sip of mine.'

Oz dipped his fingers in his tumbler, slipped them between her lips. 'Suck,' he whispered.

She sucked. His fingers tasted sweet and bitter at once, disgustingly exciting.

'Bite them,' he said.

She bit — gently at first, then harder. She was so distracted by the

172

sensations in her mouth, she hardly noticed what he was doing to her dress. It had slipped off her shoulders and was creeping past her belly. He kissed the belly, tongue busy in the nável. She could feel her breasts jealous of his mouth, begging for it, betraying her with blatant stiff-tipped nipples. She heard her voice, still tremulous, making lewd animal sounds it shouldn't know, as Oz's hands went wilder, deeper, lower.

He paused a moment, face damp and squashed from her stomach. 'You're much more beautiful undressed, you know. It's the other way round with model girls. They're just skin and bone — no curves at all.' His hands were outlining the curves, easing the dress gently over her hips, caressing down her thighs . . .

She stared at the bulge between his jeans. She had never seen any man but Lyn. Oz looked bigger than Lyn, more swollen. Shouldn't look. She groped towards his shoulders, hid her face against his neck, blocked his body out. The music mocked her, egged her on, brass climaxing already.

Slowly, her hands fumbled down his back, found the studs, pressed against them, traced the outline of his buttocks. Oz took her hands and guided them to the front, cupped them round the bulge. It was hot, throbbing, straining through the denim, sending shivers through her body like the loudest and most imploring of the instruments.

'Undo me.'

It made it easier when he gave commands. He was the photographer, again, the cool, assured professional, and this was simply an extension of the session. She owed him something, didn't she? Had to pay him back. The zip was so distended, it was difficult to budge, especially with her clumsy virgin fingers. Her heart was pounding with the music in a wild distorted rhythm.

'That's it. You've got it now.' His voice was jagged with excitement. He had no pants on. The bragging trombone pushed almost in her face.

'Kiss it.' Another order.

Whisky and fanfares were whooping in her head. She bent down, inched her lips towards the mouthpiece, gagged, choked, pulled away, rolled over, tipped onto the floor. Oz followed, pinioned her on her back, dragged her pants off. He straddled her body, crushed against it, ground her into the carpet.

Wilt thou have this man to . . .? He was stabbing into her, splitting her apart. He was huge, he was hurting, he was . . .

Yes, I will, I will, I *will*. It's bloody wonderful. *With my body I thee worship* . . . You're worshipping me with yours. No — screwing me, fucking me. Mustn't say those words. Susie words. Wicked traitor words. Fucking, fucking, fucking. Go *on* fucking — go on. I'm howling, I'm barking. No, someone else is barking, but it's all mixed up with my own noise. I never make a noise. I'm a quiet, chaste, old-fashioned country woman. Old-fashioned country slut. Don't stop — oh please don't stop! Five blokes in a night. Trombones tearing into me, shrieking in and out. Thought I

173

couldn't do it any more. Haven't done it for a year. Scared I'd be all rusty, but I'm not. I'm wet and oiled instead. Wet and hot, hot, hot . . . We should have used the couch. The floor's hard. *You're* hard. Love you hard. Love the floor. Some enchanted evening. Some enchanted music. Don't *STOP*. I'm coming, I'm really coming. God! It's . . . *yes* . . . harder, harder. Yes, use your nails. That's it. Oh yes, oh, *yes*, oh . . .

XV

Jane Susan Grant. Susannah Jane Grant. Jane Susannah Grant. Susannah Susie Grant. Susie Jane Grant. Susannah Susie Susie . . .

STOP!

The lights screamed red, but Lyn hadn't even seen them. The Ford behind him blared its horn in warning. Two oncoming cars swerved to a screeching halt.

'Bloody fool!'

Lyn accelerated past them, swung into a side road and jammed on the brake. His hands were trembling on the steering wheel, his heart had stopped pumping blood. All it could do was thump out Susie's name — Susie, Susie, Susie. The rain panting on the windscreen contradicted it — Sus-ann-ah, Sus-ann-ah, Sus-ann-ah. He stuffed his fingers in his ears. Now he could see her mouth — open, laughing, scarlet like a stop-light he had disobeyed, grinning from the road. He switched his head-lights off and the smile dissolved in darkness, but he could still feel her hands creeping round his waist, pushing up his sweater, hot and sticky on his naked chest. No, she was the one who was naked. He had seen her nude when she didn't know it. Peered at her through binoculars when she was sunbathing at the furthest end of the high-walled Putney garden. A white flower opening on a dark lawn. Open. He closed his eyes, but she was still there, a plucked staring flowerhead, with no leaves to muzzle it. He had glimpsed her in the bathroom when she left the door ajar. She did things like that on purpose, taunting him continually, following him, unravelling him, flaunting her mouth, her breasts, her name.

He never used her name. It was too informal and provocative. Only in his head did he whisper it and whisper it.

'My first name's Jane,' she had told him, when he was sitting in Matthew's study trying to do some work. She was enticing him even then — wearing some flimsy nightdress thing in the middle of the day. All right — it was hot, but that didn't mean she could walk around half naked.

'Is it?' He'd learnt to speak in monosyllables, pretend he was hardly listening. Her breasts were larger than Jennifer's, nearer to him, somehow, always pushing themselves towards him, through rooms, through high brick walls.

'Yeah. Crummy name, isn't it? Plain Jane. Priggish Jane. Quiet little sit-in-a-corner Jane. My mother knew she'd made a mistake as soon as she heard me open my fat red mouth and bawl. So then she switched to Susie.'

Fat red mouth. He laid his brushes down. He'd been working on some lettering, but she would keep interrupting, barging into the study — something Jennifer never did. He had been using quiet Madonna colours — gold and azure — but now scarlet had intruded, bleeding from her mouth on to the page. 'Why Susie?'

'That was my second name. Jane Susan Grant. Boring, isn't it? I'd like to have been called something exotic like Camilla or Ariadne.'

'Grant?' he had repeated. He must have known her surname. Someone must have told him, introduced her in the first place, asked for her on the phone. But somehow he never remembered hearing it. She had never been more than Susie — the sort of girl who didn't own a surname, didn't need a background. She was like a dog, a pet, a child — Flossy, Topsy, Susie.

'Grant?' he checked again. Impossible. Susannah's name had been Grant before she married — Susannah Jane Grant. Jane. Another Jane. Doubly impossible. Jane Susannah Grant. Susie Susannah Grant. How could they be so different, yet the same? Both fair, young, flaunting, *wanting* it, yet Susannah so refined — never chewing gum or swearing or doing handstands on the carpet. Christ! That had turned him on, though, seeing Susie's skirt fall around her face and her skimpy see-through briefs outlining her crotch with its shock of pubic hair.

'Go away!' he'd shouted. 'I'm working. Can't you see I'm working?' She had slammed the door and he picked up his brush and dipped it in the scarlet. He was trembling so much, fat red droplets spattered on the page. He smeared them with his finger, drew an 'S', then sat and stared at it. Of all the letters in the alphabet, S was the most provocative — a taunting serpent letter, curving out above and below, facing both ways at once, half a labyrinth, a plump, young, unsagging, swaggering letter. H was different. H was older, upright, towering, like his mother, standing with two firm legs upon the ground instead of wobbling and giggling back and forth. H was all straight lines, not entrapping coils and curves. J was somewhere in between them. Started off straight and honourable, then curved away at the base where it should have been most steady. That was Jennifer.

He opened his eyes. There was half a J in front of him — the top part — lying on its side. A road-sign. He was meant to be driving as fast as he could make it, and he and his car were slumped shivering in a cul-de-sac.

175

He glanced at his watch. It wasn't there. Susie had removed it on the picnic, giggling as she snatched it off and hid it in her handbag.

'Now we've got forever,' she had whispered. 'There isn't any time. And if we stay out here till dark, we can . . .'

He had left her and the house *before* dark and had been driving through the night. It must be the early hours now, but the blackness seemed to be deepening rather than fraying into dawn. He wound down the window, listened to the night — drippings, rustlings, the sudden start of a screech-owl ripping through the muffled rumble of the road. The traffic was thinning, anyway. The only cars still out were isolates and fugitives, plunging into darkness. He, too, was escaping — running away from Susie, from Susannah Jane Grant who had just screamed at him and bolted all the doors. Before that, she had kissed him — just his hand at first, a *joke* at first — tickling between the fingers, teasing her lips against the pale bracelet of flesh where she had taken off his watch-strap. Her mouth moved up to his arm, lingered across his shoulders, then up, up, until it met his own lips . . .

He switched the engine on, swung out into the road. The Morris rattled and protested, spat against the rain, headlights dazzling puddles, tinselling black trees. All the weeks and months he hadn't screwed were screaming between his legs, but sex was dangerous, far too close to violence. A kiss could explode to rape, a caress create a kid. Sex always led on to kids — that terrible bloody mess Jennifer had aborted and then christened as their child. He had sold the diaries for the sake of that non-existent child, sold Hester's life like a pound of butter or a can of beans, seen his mother advertised on television, mixed up with dogfood and detergents, her cold glittering principles reduced to cash and sales. He had only done it because he feared that speck of a cell in Jennifer, growing every minute until it split her open and burst out like an angry, greedy fledgling — beak gaping and insatiable — sending him back and forth, back and forth, to hunt for worms, grubs, insects, cash, cash. He didn't have the cash. Alone with Jennifer, he could manage with a battered car and a room or two in someone else's house. But a child would jeer at him, expect a rich, successful father who could toss him the whole world like a beach-ball.

'*No*,' he had said to Matthew, when Jennifer started bleeding and his brother came wheedling for the diaries. He was furious she had told him about the pregnancy. Matthew had exploited it, listed all the expenses of being a father, the worries and the ties, hinted that he would never cope with them. According to Matthew, he had never coped with anything without his elder brother's help. Matthew undermined him, made him doubt his powers. Perhaps he hadn't any powers.

'*No*,' he said again, when Jennifer went on bleeding and he brought her tea and towels, sat on her bed feeling his terror clammy on his hands. He peered into her chamber-pots before he emptied them. Little clots of blood.

The fledgling didn't budge. 'If she rests, she'll save it,' said the doctor.

He almost killed the doctor. The chamber-pots were clear now.

'The lambs are born so easily,' Jennifer had said when they were still at Hernhope and had just returned from Molly's. 'They seem to slither out with almost no fuss at all, and they're up and suckling within a matter of minutes.'

He had been less than five when he watched a local shepherd tug two decomposing lambs from their heaving mother. The festering limbs had crumbled in the shepherd's hands. The ewe had had twin-lamb disease. They had saved her life, but both her lambs had putrified inside her. All that day, he had carried the smell around with him. He had been punished for leaving his dinner, but mince and semolina had turned into fetid flesh. He remembered another ewe which had died in labour, collapsing in the snow with half a lamb protruding from her hindquarters, its bulging tongue lolling from the stuck and swollen head. The huntsman's van had carted her away, tossed her bloated carcass on a pile of bloodstained new-borns with their dead and stinking mothers — the casualties of birth. As a boy, he had often seen that van, doing its round of the local farms and villages — peered inside with fascinated horror — calves with glassy eyes and twisted limbs flung like rubbish on top of rotting lambs. The huntsman would be whistling as he made room for one last ewe, swollen sac of waters ballooning from her rear. The corpses would all be skinned and fleeced, then hacked into pieces and stewed up in a saucepan, or dumped in a deep-freeze as dinner for the hounds.

Once, he had had a nightmare — saw Susannah, dead in childbirth, tossed into that van — blood on her belly, unformed foetus trailing from her thighs. The image stayed around, curdling all his dinners, laying fear down in his body instead of fat or flesh. If Jennifer died in childbirth, then he would be the murderer, since he had made her pregnant. He didn't trust that slick and smarmy doctor. He ought to get a specialist, the finest obstetrician in the county. Except specialists cost money — the sort of money only Matthew had.

'All *right*,' he stormed at Matthew. 'Publish your bloody book.'

Everything was bloody — the bed, the carpet, the bathroom. Jennifer had phoned him at the office before she phoned the ambulance. When he reached the house, she wasn't there — only the traces of the baby he had sold his pride and mother for. He found her note, followed her to the hospital. Everything was white there. White wife on a white sheet with a foaming wake of white and sodden Kleenex scattered all around her on the bedspread. He had tried to comfort her, but the words came out still-born. He knew she knew he had never wanted a baby. Perhaps it wasn't a baby at all, but a nightmare or a haemorrhage — even a plot engineered by Matthew. After all, he had never seen the money Matthew promised — or only a fraction of it. ('There are more efficient ways of paying you than straight money on the table.' Who were *they* to argue?)

After a week in hospital, where they scraped out any remnant of a child, the doctor called again and while admiring the campanulas, advised no sex for a month. Lyn spun it into two. Didn't want to hurt his wife, make her bleed again. The campanulas began to fade and shrivel.

'It's all right, now, darling, really it is.' Jennifer was wearing her most transparent nightie, leaning over him so that he could see the plunge between her breasts. 'There's nothing wrong with me.'

Something wrong with him, though. He escaped into the bathroom. He wasn't impotent — not physically — but all the fears had blown up in his head like dead and bloated lambs. *New* fears, now, about the book they were preparing, the book which kept reminding him of babies and defeat, which was a betrayal of his mother, a distortion of her life.

Soon, his wife was trapped in the book as well, fused with his mother, when they were completely unalike. Both had been distorted and the resultant dual female was a danger and a sham — a woman far too powerful, yet who somehow wasn't there. In publication month, his wife literally wasn't there. She was too busy becoming famous, leaving him behind — every male in England gawping at her, while the only one who loved her sat alone at home without her. He was simply Jennifer Winterton's husband, Hester Winterton's son, the little lad at Hernhope, cowering in the shadows.

There were shadows across the road, flickering lights and signals, lorries roaring past him, wheels spinning in his head. He was really making speed now, the car gulping down the miles, its staring yellow eyes never wavering from the tarmac. He was amazed his ancient Morris could go so well. He rarely drove it over forty for fear it would stall or sulk. But now it seemed to understand his urgency, be as keen as he was to reach Northumberland. It was only the row with Susie which had forced him to act at all. Mustn't think of Susie. Shouldn't have touched her breasts. He had craved those breasts for months. Lain in bed saying 'no' to Jennifer and 'yes' to Susie, fondling Susie's nipples, screaming out in nightmares, waking up and finding Jennifer there, waking her, wanting her, refusing her again. Dared not risk it — not even through a Durex. Stupid comic things. No man used a Durex. Only fumbling schoolboys or henpecked timid husbands. He wasn't timid — wasn't impotent. Better if he were. If only he could stop thinking about it, feeling it rise hard and gross between his legs, nudging him in the morning, reproaching him at night, urging 'grab her, make her, force her'.

He didn't know which her. Susie and his wife had become fused in all his fantasies, Susie and Susannah. It was Susie who had tempted him — truly, not in fantasy — pressing against his body with those shameless breasts of hers, bringing back all his childish lusts and longings, choosing a day when it was so stifling hot and muggy he was almost off his guard, damp shirt sticking to his chest, her shirt with a button off and a gap between the . . .

'PISS OFF!'

He swerved, almost hit a lorry, winced as the driver opened fire with a fusillade of curses on his horn. Susie had cursed him, too. 'Piss off' was just the start of it. She was furious because he couldn't (wouldn't?) help her. She should never have confided in him. He'd wanted kisses, not a crisis. All that agonising had ruined everything.

He stared at the compass needle. Whichever way it pointed, some woman was looming up in front of him. South was Jennifer and her cosy Sussex background showing up his own; north was Hester, filling the whole horizon; east was Susie whose family had settled in Great Yarmouth, a huge, messy, feckless family who were all the things he dreaded — violent, squalid, stupid and in trouble; west was Somerset, where Susannah's ancestors had come from before they moved up north in 1850. Should he turn off west? No, he had no choice. He had to go to Hernhope and had to get there swiftly, before light and morning spied on him. He didn't want snooping Molly Bertrams bidding him good-day, or crafty solicitors lying there in wait for him.

He pressed his foot down hard, envying that needle its total lack of doubt. Jennifer would be flying south from Newcastle as he raced north to Hernhope. Or was she travelling in the morning? He didn't even know. It was Susie she told her plans to now, Susie she confided in. Jennifer had soaked up her crass women's lib ideas like a piece of pink spongy blotting-paper. They were printed on his wife now, but all the letters were the wrong way round. They didn't suit her and she didn't understand them. All they did was confuse and cheapen her, make her Susie's chattel and her mouth-piece. That's why he had to leave. Susie was polluting all of them. Too many problems at Putney, anyway. He didn't belong in a family, with its squalls and taunts and babble, its three phones shrilling — one on every floor, breaking apart his meals, his sleep, his work. Too many hands grabbing at the table, too many eyes staring at his untouched food. Even if he escaped to the office, he still had all the grime and grind of London. He didn't fit in with the men he had to work with — jokes and nudges and coarse talk with the secretaries, beer and fake bravado in the pub. Then back to a wife divided into six, he left only with the scraps and gristle of her, the fat and flesh already gone to Susie. Even when he dragged her away from Susie and lay next to her in bed, he still couldn't make her his. It wasn't just the old fears. How could he relax with four inquisitive and sharp-eared boys sleeping just across the corridor? It had been even worse with Matthew there — he and Anne lying one thin wall away, judging him, sneering at his efforts, listening to how short or long or ludicrous it was. He had rarely heard a sound from their side. A cough, perhaps, a muttered word, a shuffle. They must have done it at least four times to produce those four huge sons. How could Matthew be increased by four? Or did he mean diminished? Sons grew taller than you did, cleverer. They giggled at you in corners, whispered behind their hands, asked you riddles which didn't have an answer, demanded money all the time. He didn't begrudge the money, if only he could be certain they weren't jeering at him the minute he had parted with it, mouthing 'Stupid isn't he? Sissy Uncle Lyn.'

The 'sissy' swelled into a roar, the roar of four wheels and an engine fighting with the miles. The road was galloping now, towns and houses left behind, city lights and dazzle long ago extinguished. Nothing existed except the yard or two of tarmac created by his headlights. There was no horizon, no kindly guiding star, only the prison bars of hedgerows with darkness closing in behind them. *He* could go to prison. It was a crime he had committed. He had looked it up in a lawbook in the library. To hide a Will was an indictable offence which could be punished with imprisonment. But since he was the rightful heir, it was only himself he was defrauding, concealing his own rights because he feared them. He had always feared them, but especially since November 1969, when Hester had made her Will. It was the day of his twenty-first birthday, and the two events were linked. The house was his birthday present — something more substantial than the two small books she had stuffed in a paper bag for him or the meagre cake she had burnt on her moody range. It was as if she were saying, 'Wait until I'm dead, son, and I'll leave you everything. When I'm gone, you'll have a present worthy of you.'

He didn't want her dead, didn't want everything. Property brought worries, duties, involvement in a wilderness, obedience, ties, hard work. He was already planning to leave her and, there she was, tying the knot between them still more tightly by bequeathing him her house. It had been her property for over twenty years. His father's Will had been revoked on the second marriage and when he died, Matthew inherited nothing but his debts. Those were settled by selling the land to the Forestry. The house and Lyn survived.

He remembered the day she had bought the Will-form, journeying all the way to Newcastle in the stern black coat she had worn only once before, for someone else's funeral. She refused to employ a solicitor, wrote it herself in secret and had it witnessed by two odd-job men who were all but illiterate and weren't allowed to read it anyway. He had never read it himself. He simply knew that Hernhope would belong to him. He tried to forget the fact, to dodge the labour and responsibility she was laying on him like a burden. She mentioned it only rarely. 'You'll remember what I told you, Lyn, about my Will. You know where it's hidden, don't you? You'll do what I ask?'

He had always nodded, changed the subject. A Will meant death and Hester couldn't die. Death would only shroud him in guilt and terror, and he had guilt enough from marrying Jennifer. The last time Hester reminded him, he had already run away, shackled himself to Jennifer and the South, tied his work to Matthew's.

After her death, he found the Will in the locked drawer in her bureau, exactly as she had said. More than a Will, a package tied in ribbons. He had left it there, scared even to touch it. The funeral roared past him. Everyone was buzzing about a Will, the Bertrams interfering, the vicar cross-questioning him, the whole village speculating, even Jennifer probing.

'It's not where she said', he told her. I can't understand it. It isn't any-where.'

When she searched, he searched along with her. He had already hidden it, still unopened and unread. That couldn't be a crime. Crimes were cool, deliberated things, plotted for one's gain, whereas he had acted in a frenzy — sweating, shivering, dithering — and only for his loss. It was partly all the tittle-tattle which had confused and frightened him. The village was encroaching, using Hester's funeral as an excuse to suck them in. Jennifer was oblivious. 'So friendly,' she kept saying, as greedy hands stretched out to grab her time, her mind.

Now, he saw things differently. A buzz of country cackle was nothing compared with the whole of England shouting out his name. His wife was not just Queen of Mepperton, but Toast of the British Isles. She had become a piece of public property, gabbling on the radio, sobbing on the television, barging her way into all the newspapers. They had even tried to hassle *him*, grill him about his childhood, pry into his marriage. He had to get away. Putney wasn't safe, not with Susie-Susannah prowling through every chink and crack of it, but Hernhope could be a sanctuary, too far away for most of the fans to follow, and too dead-and-alive for Susie. Susie would never settle somewhere without a disco or a take-away. If he put all these miles between them, she would shrivel and diminish, fade into a caged and muzzled photograph, no bigger than Susannah's. He could make the house his stronghold and escape-tower, fence and fortify it, shut out not only Susie, Matthew, and the whole of London, but his own lusts and crimes and fears.

The roar of the road was like a blessing now. Only twenty short miles left. The Morris slowed and laboured as the hedgerows narrowed and the road began its tricks. A faint white mist clung like sheep's wool to the blue-black blur of fields and hills. Dawn always broke so stealthily, tiny shreds and glints of light seeping over the horizon, the stars still faint grey pinpricks on the slowly unfurling blackout of the sky. An owl flapped white against the gallows of two blasted elms, its screech disturbing the burble of the river. Shapes and textures began to free themselves from the clogging darkness which had made them all one mass. Lyn could distinguish colours now — blue from black, grey from blue, could see the fuzzed dividing-lines between field and sky, grass and corn. The wheat was high, soon ready for the scythe. '*In the morning it is green and groweth up, but in the evening . . .*'

A startled flock of sheep shambled away from the snort of his wheels. The lambs were no longer skittish, but grubby plodders munching like their mothers. In a few short weeks, they would be bleating through the mint sauce on someone's carving dish. Nothing could stay young up here for long. Calves were veal, kittens drowned, pups must be trained for their serious work as sheepdogs, fledglings learn to fly before hawks or foxes scrunched them, children learn to fear.

The village was deserted as he rumbled through it. A dog barked threat-

181

eningly, a woman tugged a curtain back, let it fall again. The sky was now a dull watery grey, thick with birdcalls. The road began to climb. Astounding, really, that the car had ever made it. Even now, it was rattling like a rickshaw on tracks that were meant for sheep. Five more miles to go. Lyn dared not pass the Bertrams' house. The shepherds would be stirring, the dogs set up a racket as he passed. A mile from their farm, he drove off the road and concealed the car in one of the straggling offshoots of the forest. He sat there a moment, dwarfed by the giant's-back of hills which had loomed out of the shadows, changed from black to grey to olive, and were now tinged pink from the first wavering radiance of the sun. Their beauty almost hurt. He wanted to wrench it from them, fling it on to paper, pin it down in brush-strokes. If he had been born to different parents, he might now be a painter, a proper landscape artist. Hundreds of artists starved, of course, if they refused to compromise or didn't have the talent or the luck. But at least he would have tried — gone to decent art school instead of that crass commercial course where slickness counted more than vision.

He licked his finger, drew a second range of Cheviots on the window of the car which his breath had misted up. He longed to hold a brush again, swap his London office lay-out pad and Letraset for oils and canvas in this heady landscape. He still had vision, even skill. All he needed was time, peace, money, independence. The sun sparkled on the window. It had broken through at last, the whole eastern flank of hills blazing scarlet while the west still slumbered grey. The sky was like a palette with all the golds and reds he would ever need. He sprang out of the car. He would do the rest on foot now, climb the back way up to Hernhope, avoiding the main track.

The ground was steep and rocky. He used his hands to heave him up, slipping on patches of damp and tussocky grass, stubbing his toes on stones. Despite the sun, the moon still hung pale and glassy like a lemon fruit-drop sucked to its last sliver in the sky. He watched it fade to nothing, caught his breath as he breasted the hill and glimpsed the solid walls of Hernhope frowning in the distance. How could a simple house set off such fear? Or was it fear? Everything was peaceful — plash of the burn, lovesick morning wooing of the wood pigeons.

He tiptoed towards the house, as if scared he might startle or offend it. It looked tidy and well-groomed. The garden they had planted was neither choked with weeds nor had reverted back to wasteland. He glanced around. Who had been working on it? Had Hester jumped up from her coffin and come with spade and trowel to carry on his labour? She had never idled all her life, so how could she lie dead and disabled now, when weeds were choking cabbages or debris blocking drains? He fumbled in his pocket. Thank God he had kept the keys. However much he feared its obligations, this house was his inheritance and he wanted entry to it. He made straight for the kitchen — Hester's chief domain. Last time he had seen it, Jennifer's handiwork had brightened all the surfaces — buttercups in jamjars, bread and cakes and cheeses in the larder, jellies glistening in the fridge. The shelves were empty now, but not as damp or dusty as he had

182

feared. Molly must have come from time to time, kept her promise to guard and tend the house. He hadn't time to linger. Molly might appear this very morning, with garden fork or duster, or a solicitor with a warrant. It surprised him really that Matthew had choked off all the lawyers, stopped pressing for him to be administrator. Christ! That was a relief. It would have been a second crime to swear on oath that there was no Will when he himself had hidden it. Why the hell should he *want* to be administrator, when he'd gone to so much trouble avoiding all official ties?

He picked up the torch he had brought from the car, unlocked the cellar door. It was night again in the cellar, a second night, arriving prematurely, blotting out the hour or two of dawn. The chests and trunks were stacked as neatly as Jennifer had left them thirteen months ago. Only the shadows were ragged and untidy. Lyn groped his way to the very end of the cellar. Three suitcases were piled against the wall, concealing a low flush door which led into a second smaller cellar. Jennifer had never found that door, knew nothing of this secret hidey-hole. You had to crawl to get into it at all, and the door was still stiff despite the fact he had eased and oiled it last time. He had chosen a day when his wife was safe at Molly's, crept in like a criminal, quaking and sweaty-palmed. Stupid to feel so guilty. All he had done was hidden a Will he hadn't even glanced at. Deliberately, he had never opened it, never so much as slit the envelope, so that he could say more honestly, 'I've never seen it — *never*.' If you were bequeathed a house, you had either to live in it or sell it — and both had seemed impossible. Gossip and accusation would babble forth again, 'Lyn Winterton refused his mother's gift. She left him her house and he doesn't even bother with it . . . denying his wife a proper home, letting down his ancestors . . .'

Once it was hidden, he had felt smaller — like a child again — lighter with relief. He and Jennifer had simply lingered on at Hernhope, without the onus of ownership, the tie of heirs — no long-term plans, no binding obligations, until Jennifer told him she was . . .

He crashed the cases out of the way, heaved himself against the tiny secret door until he had rammed it open, then crawled on his hands and knees beneath the low confining ceiling. He sneezed in the dust, wishing now he had never hidden the Will in so dark and grimy a dungeon. Yet Jennifer would have found it otherwise. She had explored every chink and cranny of the house as she might have explored a lover's body. At least he could make her happy if he brought her back to Hernhope. All he had done so far was reject and deny her, turn his back in bed. He hated himself for his coldness to her, even cruelty. He had become prickly like those hawthorns which only survived on their bleak and wind-torn hillsides by growing stunted and distorted. In the book, the hawthorns glowed with berries, their thorns disguised by whorls of new spring leaves. That was what he disliked about the book — its dishonesty, its gloss — the way it romanticised his mother and the landscape, played down all their quirks and cruelties.

183

Damn the book. He must drag his wife away from it, kidnap her here before the media world devoured her. He need never admit he had hidden the Will at all — just pretend he'd found it on this second visit when he was searching for some childhood toy or keepsake.

He glanced around the dingy shivering space. A pre-war sewing machine lay half dismantled on the floor, a carton of old newspapers latticed with grey cobwebs. Nice to have recognised some loyal old friend like a sturdy rocking horse, a box of bricks. He couldn't remember childhood toys at all, not ones that came from toyshops. He had played mostly with his mother's buttons, which shone and rattled in a huge square biscuit tin with a picture of a thatched and rose-blown cottage on the lid, the sort of cottage Jennifer had sprung from. He had sat for hours under the dark oak table, sorting the yellows from the reds, creating pictures with them, shading the blues into greys and the greys into browns; making stepping-stones or mazes, banquets or flower-beds, or just holding a button in his palm and feeling it cold, hard, knobbly, smooth or rounded.

Hester had always saved her buttons, even if the garments themselves were shrunken or outgrown. Those buttons spelt the scenes of her past — tiny mother-of-pearl ones from Matthew's baby clothes, swanky brass from his father's hunting coat; drab, battered things from a house-keeper's overalls; triumphant blue from her wedding outfit. The younger buttons were as old as he was. Some of them had fallen from his mother's underclothes, had touched her breasts, sat against her skin. He would pick them up and sniff them, but all he could smell were his own grimy sticky hands.

Why did he keep stopping, wasting time? He crawled along again, nose down like a dog. There was work to be done, a Will to be read, a whole new life and property to grapple with. He dragged himself towards the smallest case which he had double-locked and draped in a tarpaulin. He almost hoped the lock might stick, but it opened eagerly. He rifled through the pile of magazines he had laid on top as a decoy and disguise. The Will might not be there. Despite all his precautions, someone might have stolen it — Hester, even, come from her grave to snatch the thing away.

No. His fingers had already touched the edges of the stiff white envelope. It was tied with emerald ribbon to a larger package — other papers, probably — official matters relating to the house. He drew the bundle out. The first time he had seen it, he had felt a sort of curdled shock, leavened with excitement. Now he felt only weary. He was lying full length on the floor, stomach downwards, as if he were a child again. He shut his eyes. If he stayed there, night would come again (real night) and let him sleep for ever, swallow him. He switched off the torch and the papers disappeared. There was no Will now, nothing left but darkness.

Through the darkness shrilled the bright, reckless sound of Susie's laugh, her squeals of fury as she rammed the bolts. If he gave up now, they would only smell him out, drag him back to Putney. He would lose his soul to Susie, his wife to Susie, his life and strength to Matthew.

Better to live here, make the house a fortress, summon Jennifer and shut the others out. He switched on the torch again, untied the ribbons, slit the long white envelope. Inside was the Will-form, folded round a smaller, flimsy envelope which fluttered to the floor. He smoothed out the parchment, bordered in red as if it heralded a celebration rather than a death. 'THIS IS THE LAST WILL AND TESTAMENT OF' was printed in scarlet LETTERS across the top. Hester had added in black ink, 'Hester Margaret Winterton of Hernhope, Mepperton, in Northumberland'. He had almost forgotten her second name was Margaret. It didn't suit her, somehow. Margaret was too placid and soft-centred.

'*I hereby revoke all former Wills heretofore made by me* . . .' The language was high-flown, highfalutin, almost biblical. Hester must have copied it from some other Will or document. She could never invent a stilted prose like that. The lines were so straight, she must have ruled them first; her writing so neat it seemed to wear a straitjacket. It was all part of her gift to him — the care, the trouble, the handsome emerald ribbon. A scribble and a paper-bag had done him in her lifetime.

'*I give, devise and bequeath the whole of my estate of whatsoever nature to* . . .' The torch was flickering. He shook it, turned it upside down, fiddled with the switch. The beam steadied.

'. . . *to my first and elder son* . . .' Lyn sneezed. Shaking the torch had disturbed another layer of dust.

'. . . *Edward Arthur James Ainsley.*'

Wait a moment, he wasn't seeing right. The dust had affected his eyes. He was imagining names, inventing them, not reading what was written in the Will.

He shone the torch-beam directly on the name. '*Edward Arthur Ja* . . .'

Could a Will tell lies, play tricks on him, like Matthew's boys at Putney? He closed his eyes a moment. They were tired from the long drive. When he opened them again, the letters would be changed: 'I bequeath the whole of my estate to my only son Lyn Winterton.'

He wished he could sit up straight. Reading a Will half sprawling on a damp stone floor, in the more or less pitch dark, was uncomfortable, even dangerous — could lead to misinterpretations and mistakes.

'*I bequeath the whole of my estate to my first and elder* . . .' He stopped. First and elder son was wrong to start with. Hester had wed so late, it was a miracle she had had a son at all. She had married Thomas as a middle-aged spinster whose only previous child had been the infant Matthew, her charge and now her stepson. *He* was her only son, born in the last shudder of her reproductive life. So who the hell was Edward Arthur?

Lyn hardly dared to ask. A hundred fingers were pointing in accusation, a hundred rumours whispering through his head. If Edward's name was Ainsley, that could mean one thing only — he was *spinster* Ainsley's son, born *before* she married Thomas, and with no proper legal father to give him a name and respectability.

Impossible! His mother's rigorous moral principles were as much a part of her as her frowning brow and determined jaw. He had often kicked against those principles, but to imagine Hester now without them was to throw morality itself into the gutter. Hester would *never* have risked a pregnancy, rollicked with some fancy man, tarnished her family name. In any case, how could she have concealed a child for all those years? Edward would be a full-grown man by now, older than he himself was. So where in God's name was he hiding?

Lyn flung the Will away from him. He didn't want to know, didn't want to meet some upstart interloper who had cut his own certainties from under him, grabbed his rights and property, been favoured by a mother he no longer recognised. *He* was Hester's son, her unique and only son, the one who had shared her life and home for thirty years and more; he her rightful heir — not this preening bastard.

But perhaps he was maligning her, jumping to conclusions. Edward needn't be a bastard. There were other ways of explaining it. Hester might have contracted a first and earlier marriage to a cousin of the same name — that would explain the Ainsley — hushed it up because the degree of kinship was too close, or her parents disapproved of him, or . . .

Lyn rubbed his eyes, tried to get more comfortable in the cold confining space. Even a legitimate son was hardly any better — still a rival, an intruder, a jolting sickening shock. He had to know, had to find some evidence. He grabbed the small brown envelope which had fallen to the floor. The Will had been folded round it, so it must afford some clue. He ripped it open, drew out a yellowed piece of paper, folded into four. 'Certificate of Baptism', he read. Instinctively, he covered it with his hands. He had already seen those bragging names sitting on the top, shouting out their claim — Edward Arthur James. He shifted his hand a centimetre, glimpsed the next printed heading on the form — 'Name of Parents'. He made himself look down, fingers trembling on the paper. There wasn't any cousin, any father — only one accusing name — Hester Margaret Ainsley. The letters writhed and floundered on the page, as if grovelling in shame. So his mother *was* a sham, a slut — a woman without scruple or even sense. She should have *invented* a father, filled in a name — any name — so long as it redeemed and hid her fall.

The torch was fainting now, in shock. Lyn held it only an inch or two from the paper, peered at the date on the certificate. The ink had run into a blot there and was difficult to decipher. '9th March', he made out. '1919'.

1919? But that was another world ago! He must have read it wrong. No, there it was again, on the top of the paper, following the name of the church — Christchurch, Blackfriars. Lyn crouched back on his heels, stared at name and date. A teenage Hester and a London church. Suddenly, all the pieces of the jigsaw snapped together in his head, and he winced in horror at the picture on the puzzle-box. Now, at last, he understood that sudden break and change in Hester's life, that gap in the diaries no one could explain. Why should a girl from a close and prosperous family suddenly take to her heels and bury herself in a sordid job in London? Wasn't it obvious, once you thought about it? How had they not suspected it before? Even Matthew had been stupidly naïve. They had all been blinded by the notebooks, assumed Hester had no secrets from her diary, recorded everything. God alone knew what else she had left out, what other frauds and secrets he might stumble on.

Even this baptism was something of a fraud. Hester had always refused to play the Christian or kowtow to any vicar. He had never been baptised himself, an omission he resented since the church had been so central in village life. It had cut him off from other normal children, made him feel an alien. Yet here was a genuine alien, some whipper-snapper bastard revelling in those sacred Christian rituals which had been denied and barred to him. And a bastard with three names! Three manly regal names as arrogant as Matthew's three, while he made do with one short sissy girl's name. The names were a fraud as well — just swanky padding to disguise the lack of a father's name, or to hide his lowly origins. Edward Arthur James could well be just a cowherd's son. All that hole-and-corner secrecy, the subterfuge, the poverty, all pointed to a low and base seduction, some vulgar grope and fumble by a jumped-up servant or a sozzled lance corporal on a fortnight's leave. Perhaps Hester hadn't even known the ruffian's name, or had been pawed by more than one of them. The whole thing had a grubby feel about it. Any decent man would have married her, sought the forgiveness and understanding of her parents, saved her all those years of shame and skivvying.

He stuffed the certificate back into its envelope. He should feel sorry for his mother, pity her youth, her snatched and shattered virtue, yet all he could feel was anger. Why had Hester always botched her life, even as a girl, found lust instead of love, toil and exploitation instead of status and contentment? That's what she had bequeathed to him — not her house and property — but her ill fortune and her joylessness. They had passed into his bloodstream and tainted his own life.

That life was pulled apart now, tangled up with lies. He had lost not just his inheritance, but his strong and scrupulous mother, his place as only son. If only she could have warned him, prepared him for this blow, confessed her past in person instead of throwing him the evidence when she was safely past reproach. She must have known how it would hurt him, confuse and anger him. And what a fool she had made him look — worrying about a property which wasn't even his, refusing a gift nobody had left him.

But if he had refused it so wholeheartedly, why should he want it now, why covet something he had feared and run away from? He had hidden the Will, declined the role of heir. It was *relief* he should be feeling, a sense of lightness and escape that he had avoided all those burdens, those ties and responsibilities. He was no longed saddled with a house too big and grim for him, or the guilt of trying to sell it with his ancestors' bones accusing all around. Those were *Edward*'s problems now, Edward's obligations.

It was that he couldn't bear. To be kicked aside, by some braggart charlatan who had never shown his face up here. Or had he? Perhaps Edward had been his neighbour all along, spying on him, feeding off his mother, laughing up his sleeve. Hester could have brought him north with her when she took the job with Thomas, left him in the care of a local cottager, stolen out to visit him in secret. No! Secrets were never safe in Mepperton. The whole village would have buzzed with it fifty years ago.

Lyn groped for the Will, shone the torch again, saw his *own* name staring from the middle paragraph.

'*I appoint my second son, Lyn Winterton, to be the sole executor of this my Will, and to inform the beneficiary Edward Arthur J . . .*'

Lyn rammed his fist against the floor. *Second* son, executor — so that was his role — to bow and scrape to Edward Arthur James. Thirteen years ago, his mother had asked him if he would be executor. How could he refuse when all he was doing, he presumed, was handling the transfer of his own property? But she had deceived him, tricked him, left him with nothing but the dirty work, the job of messenger. Frowning, he read on. There was some letter he must post, informing the new heir of his rights. He would find it, Hester wrote, in the second, larger package.

He snatched up all the documents, crawled with them through the door into the main part of the cellar. He would no longer crouch like an animal, prostrating himself to Edward. He leant against a packing-case, easing his aching limbs before he ripped the package open. It was full of letters, tied together in that mocking emerald ribbon — with one separate envelope addressed in Hester's handwriting — not her usual scrawl, but the pruned and formal script she had used on the Will-form. He stared at the address.

Edward Ainsley Esquire, (Could a *bastard* be Esquire?)

Woodlawns,

River Road,

Warkworth,

New Zealand.

New Zealand! Thirteen thousand miles between them. Lyn felt a flicker of relief. At least his rival wasn't squatting on these hills, waiting to move in. The envelope was sealed, then stuck across with Sellotape. He dared not tamper with it — turned instead to the other letters, slipped them from their ribbon. Some were airmail envelopes with fancy New Zealand stamps, others postmarked London — all dated between 1919 and 1921 and all addressed to Hester. It would be impossible to read them in the grudging light of the torch. He groped towards the door, climbed the stairs to daylight — light so vigorous it was like a searchlight blinding him.

Almost automatically, he turned his steps to the kitchen — sat at the table, hands trembling on the envelopes, sorting them into ordinary and airmail. The New Zealand ones had the sender's name and address printed on the back — a Mrs Alice Fraser from Woodlawns, Warkworth again.

Fraser? He had seen that name before. An Alice and Edward Fraser had appeared on the Certificate of Baptism in the section headed 'God parents'. Another Edward — that feared and fateful name. Lyn skimmed through the letters, tried to get the gist of them. Yes — the infant Edward had been taken to New Zealand by his godparents, except they seemed more like foster-parents, with total charge of the child. The letters were mainly progress reports for Hester — clever little Edward had learnt to crawl, swollen little Edward had cut his first tooth, lisped his first word . . .

There were even a couple of photographs and a lock of hair cocooned in tissue paper — fine baby hair with a natural curl to it, faded, but still golden. Edward was hairless in his first photo, but plump and smug and smiling. In the second, the golden curls haloed a face so sweet and simpering, Lyn almost expected wings.

He flipped the photos over, so that both smiles hit the dust. To hell with their little angel! What he really burned to know was who these Frasers were, and how they got the baby in the first place. He turned to the letters postmarked London, opened the earliest one, dated first of March, 1919.

As he read, horror poured between the lines. Hester appeared to have sold her son for cash. Lyn raced through the other London letters, tried to piece the story together from Alice Fraser's ramblings. She had obviously had time and leisure enough to pour out all her hopes and fears, writing to Hester almost every day in those two tense weeks in March, often confirming conversations the two had had in person. Lyn had only her side of the story, but he could read between the lines, pad the details out.

Edward and Alice Fraser appeared to be a wealthy childless couple, connected with the Colonial Office, who were stationed in London during the hostilities, and planned to return to Warkworth once the war was over and the ships resumed their sailings. Hester had met Alice in some Southwark hostel where the *grande dame* played at Good Works on Wednesday afternoons. Her other days she passed more salubriously in a Georgian house in Knightsbridge, surrounded by her poodles. The dogs were simply a substitute. Alice Fraser was desperate for a child. Hester had a child and was desperate generally. Thus they made a deal. The Frasers got their baby, Hester got her cash. She also resumed her former virgin status. A child could be negated, once safely despatched to the other side of the globe. Only Alice seemed to fear the distance.

'We should like the child baptised', she wrote, 'before we take him on so long a voyage.' Perhaps the ships were old and creaking from the war, or Alice was keen to ensure that if she lost her son at sea, at least they would meet again in heaven. Hence the Christian rituals. Hester appeared to have agreed to them only with some reluctance and after a fairly heated argument over names. First-born Fraser sons were always christened Edward Arthur James, so Alice wrote. There had been Edward Arthur James Frasers going back more than a hundred years, and she was loath to break so strong and established a tradition. Yes, but this wasn't their first-

189

born son, Hester must have objected, because Alice's next letter picked up on this point and was obviously distressed by it.

Time was getting short and tempers slightly frayed, judging by the tone of Alice's next two letters. Hester had at last agreed to the Christian names, but produced her own trump card. The child must retain her own surname and be Edward Arthur James *Ainsley*. Was this merely tit-for-tat, Lyn wondered, or genuine concern that the Ainsley name would otherwise die out, since both Hester's father and grandfather had been only children, and all her brothers killed? Or just a simple wish that something of herself should remain with a child she was about to lose for ever? Whatever the reason, Alice was disquieted. *No*, she begged in copperplate, a different surname from their own would only confuse the child and prove a burden and embarrassment. That was the last letter on the subject. It was Edward Arthur James Ainsley whom Mrs E.A.J. Fraser carried from the font.

Lyn laid the letters down. Even at nineteen, Hester had displayed that obstinacy and independence which had typified her later. She had also resisted any formal adoption procedures and refused to register the baby's birth. As for the baptism itself, it was clearly a major concession on her part, and she must have expressed her fears about its official and public nature, since one of the letters assured her of total secrecy. 'Leave it in our hands,' wrote Alice. 'My husband has much influence with churchmen, and if you insist on the utmost privacy and confidentiality — which of course I understand — he will see that the child exists in the eyes of God alone.'

Edward Arthur James had suddenly diminished — become a secret and a subterfuge, a bundle in a shawl with no official identity, a piece of extra luggage smuggled on a boat, a burden to his mother. But if such a burden, then why had she left him all her property and a letter to go with it, why revived a correspondence which had been allowed to lapse since 1921? As far as letters went, precious little Edward had remained stunted at age two. Yet here was Hester making him her heir.

Lyn glanced around the kitchen — the blackened beams, the solid walls. This grim entrapping house was no longer his to resent and run away from; no longer his to refuse to Jennifer, to curse and criticise. Yet now he craved it. It had never belonged to anyone but him. His whole life was chiselled into it, even his height recorded on that kitchen wall, where, every six months, Hester had made a pencil mark level with the top of his head. The marks seemed to rise so grudgingly, until suddenly, at seventeen, the pencil had surprised them all and the last swaggering mark was higher than the mantelshelf. He went and stood against it. He was even taller now, but, for all it meant, he might be baby Edward's size, a child so paltry, he had been simply overlooked.

He stared out through the window, glimpsed a speck of a dog, circling in the distance. A dog could mean an owner. He must get out before he was found. Anyone could come there — forestry official, shepherd, hiker, Mick or Molly Bertram. He no longer had any right to be in the house at all.

He was a trespasser, a thief — a true criminal, now, who had defrauded a man of his rightful property for fifteen months or more. The papers seemed to scorch and blister his hands. He rummaged in the drawer, found a plastic bag, bundled them inside his shirt, then sprinted through the hall and locked the front door behind him.

He stumbled across the mocking tidy garden. Molly had cleared the weeds for Edward's sake, nannied the house for Edward, and before that, his wife had scrubbed and laboured for that bastard. He himself had lived there thirty years, ministering to his mother, shoring up the house, protecting it from wind and time and weather, so that an alien, a peasant-born and rapist-fathered trickster could take it over with the minimum of work.

Lyn was running up the hill, panting towards the dark and sullen forest. He feared those trees. They had only grown as tall because they were feeding off his father. The farm had been lost and now the house was lost. He stared at the ruin of another, smaller house — one which had been sold to the Forestry the same year as their land, and had been allowed to fall apart. Its windows were gaping wounds now, nettles choked its blackened boarded door. Hernhope had survived, despite bankruptcy and hardship, had stood for three proud centuries, outsmarting man and nature. And now a stranger could simply tear it down, lift his little finger and turn it into scrap.

He faced towards the east, the whole flaunt and grandeur of the Cheviots swaggering around him, still white with morning mist as if they had been wrapped in tissue paper like a precious gift. A flap of rooks cawed towards the sun, dipped their wings in gold, then wheeled down and back again. The sky dazzled with the ardour of the sunrise. It was Edward's now — Edward's sun and sky.

'No!' he whispered, and turned his back on it, slunk towards the prison of the trees.

*   *   *

No sun, now. Only shreds and freckles of light piercing the tangled canopy of branches. Lyn threaded his way between the serried rows of trunks, twigs catching in his hair, sudden flutters and rustlings startling the dark green pool of silence. He had never cared for conifers. They weren't England's native trees like oak or beech, but intruders from an alien continent, as Edward Ainsley was. He remembered as a lad, one burly labourer boasting that he had planted forty-eight thousand sitka spruce by hand in five short weeks. They'd been spindly then, little more than thin and ragged urchins, but had soon grown faster than he had, darkening the whole sky. Now they were so dense, they had squeezed out all the flowers and vegetation. Only creeping things like shrews and snakes had room to live there, only birds which thrived in darkness.

Even those had made themselves invisible. Everything seemed lifeless — the dry brown ruff of branches which fringed the trunks before they soared to green, the dusty ground without a blade of grass, the shrouding silence. As a boy, he had seen squirrels in the forest, roe deer, sparrowhawks. He had picked fern and heather, even foxgloves. The Book was

191

crammed with all that bounty.

The *book*! Lyn grabbed at a trunk to steady him. How in God's name would this news of Edward square with it? Hester had been depicted as a virtuous woman of high old-fashioned principle, not an unmarried mother auctioning off her baby. The media would go mad about it, pounce on Edward in triumph and derision. Jennifer would be hunted down as well, dragged back into the limelight. And Matthew? He hardly knew whether Matthew would be furious and fretful, or thrilled by the floodtide of publicity, but in either case, he would start bossing and dictating once again, barking out his orders for this new contingency.

Lyn flung himself on the ground, pine needles prickling against his neck, fir cones thrown like tiny bombs waiting to blow his life apart. He had *two* half-brothers now — both elder, wealthier brothers, expecting service and salaams. Lyn hurled a stone against a scaly trunk. He could see the whole world throwing stones — contemptuous of him and Hester, angry with him for hiding the Will at all.

Why not hide it again — leave it hidden this time? It might be fairer on them all, in fact, even the legatee. What would Edward want with a grim old pile in the middle of a wilderness? He already had a house — Woodlawns. How elegant it sounded. Edward would have no wish to tear himself away from it, involve himself in journeys and decisions for the sake of some dilapidated property he didn't even need. The Frasers must have died by now, left him their own inheritance. First and elder son again — first and only. He could well have sons himself, or grandsons — more Edward Arthurs carrying on the line. Why scare them all with skeletons in cupboards, dig up a past which might embarrass them? That past had hardly happened. Nine months blushing in a womb, a few days howling in a hostel, were nothing compared with sixty settled years in a kinder, milder clime.

Edward might even be *dead*, for heaven's sake, or have moved away, or changed his name to Fraser, in deference to his foster parents and that hundred years' tradition. Hester's letter might never find him, be returned to England marked 'unknown at this address'. When she wrote it, she was already old and failing, had hardly known what . . .

No. Hester had never failed — or only hours before her death. The day she wrote the Will, her mind and pen had been as sharp as ever. So how could he disobey her, refuse to be executor? Except things were different now. There was a book to take account of, a whole greedy pointing world to keep at bay. Hester had entrusted her secret to him alone, not to every media man in Britain. Yet if he protected Hester, then he defrauded her elder son, could even risk a jail sentence.

His head ached with all the 'ifs', his stomach kicked with hunger. He had eaten nothing since the picnic with Susie yesterday. He thought he had problems then, but Susie was simply a shrug and a parenthesis compared with this tumult of new fears. He almost longed for her, for Jennifer, for someone with soft hands who could wipe his eyes and take it all away.

Sissy! He was the executor, the one who must act and organise, read documents, post letters. He rifled through the plastic bag, snatched the letter out. Why had Hester sealed it so securely? Didn't she trust him? It could only be some dry official thing, couched in formal legal language like the Will, some second footling contract. She couldn't have much of consequence to say to a son she had sold like a piece of furniture. He scratched at the Sellotape with his thumb-nail, trying to coax the letter open as carefully as possible, so that no one would suspect he had ever tampered with it. The paper wasn't white and formal like the Will, but Hester's own cheap and flimsy airmail folded into three. There was no address, no date. The letter plunged straight in.

'My beloved son', it said.

Lyn had thought the wood was silent, but the noise had turned almost to a roar — rustlings in the undergrowth, twitterings in the trees, branches sighing and shifting against each other, flutterings of trapped and frightened birds.

He had rarely had a letter from his mother, but when he did, it always began 'Dear Lyn'. Never 'dearest', never even 'darling' — those words were not in her vocabulary. 'Beloved' was almost criminal. There was passion in it, idolatry. It was a dangerous word, especially in a forest. It could set the trees alight, run wildfire through the undergrowth. He could feel it burning already against his eyes. He must quench it, prevent a conflagration.

He slung the letter back into its envelope, stuffed it at the bottom of the plastic bag, stowed all the other documents on top. '*Fresh Foods From Sainsbury*' said the bag. Wrong. It wasn't food, wasn't even fresh. There was a corpse in there, the body of a baby. The child had perished — not in the Southwark hostel, or in a storm at sea, as Alice Fraser had feared, but just now, just here, in this dark funereal forest. There were no Frasers, no letters, no Woodlawns, River Road. Just a tiny corpse it was his duty to dispose of, before it could taint his mother or his brother. His only brother, Matthew.

He knew how to plan a funeral — had seen Jennifer do it a year or so ago. She had been solemn and meticulous, made death a thing of dignity. He would do the same. His mother trusted him, had only made him executor so that he could deal with things like this.

He stood up, pushed his way through the crowded hampering trees, paused a moment to listen to a skylark singing matins on the hillside. He could barely see the hills, only a tease and snatch of green beyond the darker green of forest. Perfect spot for a grave — secret and secluded, yet so high up, it was only a hand's span from the floor of heaven. The golden glint of morning was knifing through the spaces between the trunks. Edward would be safe here. No one would ever disturb him. The trees would grow taller and taller year by year, hemming in the coffin, rooting down the grave.

Lyn struggled on, plunging into the thickest part of the forest, kicking out

193

at branches in his way, trampling through the undergrowth. The light grew dimmer, colder. He could smell the scented needles of a Douglas fir — a smell like incense, fitting for a funeral. He stopped, knelt. The tree was so huge, it would mark the spot, provide a monument. He fell on his knees in front of it, scrabbled with his hands, tried to break the soil up, snapped off a branch and jabbed and thrust with it. The hole was still too small. He dragged off his shoe and used it as a scraper, burrowed like a dog, broke his nails, chafed his hands. Still not deep enough. Sweat was seeping down his back, despite the chill and dankness of the trees. He used the other shoe with the foot still in it — kicked with the toe, pounded with the heel. The hole was getting deeper. More like a proper grave now. He shaped it with his hands, smoothed the earth, collected the softest pine needles he could find and made a bed of them. He searched around for moss, scraped soft green fuzz from stones and laid it in the grave like treasure. Must observe the decencies, make things beautiful. This was a brilliant babe, a prodigy, who deserved the proper rites.

He lowered the infant in, covered him with earth, tucked the soil around him like a blanket. The child would be warm and cosy there, sheltered from the wind. He removed all traces of his digging, sprinkled mulch on top and pine needles, tried to make the ground look virgin.

Everything was safe now, Hester a virgin when she married, he her only child. He wished he had some white and maiden flowers to celebrate his mother — snowdrops, lilies — fusing death and innocence. There were no flowers nor wreaths at all, no mourners, save himself. He bowed his head, felt his tears fall stupid through his hands.

'Beloved son,' he whispered. 'Beloved son.'

XVI

'Smooth landing,' smiled Jonathan, as the BAC 111 touched down at Heathrow Airport.

Jennifer's nails were digging into the armrest. How could anything be smooth? She had slept with a man she hardly even knew, enjoyed it, relished it, spent half the night repeating it — standing, lying, kneeling, adding variations — in the bath, in the shower, on the floor, in front of the silvered mirrors in Oz's studio. Two of her, three of her in the mirrors, all sluts, all faithless adulterous wives. She had always thought a first affair would be something of a failure, a fumbling furtive thing riddled with embarrassment and nerves. Not at all. She had behaved

194

like a professional whore.

The sixty-minute plane journey had seemed to last for days, Oz still throbbing under her as they hit a patch of turbulence or dived out of an air pocket. She was sore between her legs. She had been like a starving woman who had suddenly seen food again and crammed everything in sight into her mouth, her throat, her . . . She and Oz had hardly paused till dawn came like a spoilsport chaperon and dragged her back to her cold unslept-in bed. She had crept past Jonathan's room, heard him already awake and running taps.

She dared not glance at the crowded Heathrow news-stands in case the whole affair had reached London before she had and was already polluting all the papers. Oz was a photographer, a newsman. It might all have been a trap — some hidden camera recording her adultery.

Jonathan was hovering with the cases. 'Right, I'll just get the car. We should be back in Putney in well under an hour.'

Putney. She wasn't ready yet. Hadn't washed the sex off. Yet somehow, she wanted to keep it there, wet and hot and smarting. Oz had reminded her that her body still existed. Why should Lyn keep snuffing it out again, leaving her cold and unkindled like a summer fire?

The house looked grave, inscrutable. No boy or bike in the garden, no angry Lyn sulking outside a still locked and bolted door.

'Won't you come in for a coffee?' she asked, as Jonathan helped her out of the car.

'No, really, Jennifer. It's sweet of you, but I must get up to the office. Thank you for the trip. I enjoyed it thoroughly.'

'Thank *you*.'

Twin smiles. They had spent hours and hours together in the last few weeks, but never got beneath the smiles. Jonathan was her chaperon, yet did he even guess she'd been screwing with a stranger half the night? Were there teeth-marks on her neck, pock-marks on her soul?

Her own smile faded as she turned to face the house, walked through the unlocked door — moving from sunshine into gloom, smelling the faint musty odour of the pot-pourri which Anne bought from Liberty's every Christmas.

'Lyn?' she called. Must find him first, reassure him, reassure herself. She could bury last night, then, make it just a fantasy. And yet she was almost scared to see her husband, scared of his suspicion which for the first time had some grounds, impatient of his moods and his demands. For the last few months, the media world had knelt to her. It wasn't easy to return to a man who, instead of homage, laid grudges at her feet.

'Lyn!' she called again.

No answer. Couldn't he at least come down to greet her, help her with her luggage? And where were the boys — and Susie? They must have heard the car. Susie should have rocketed in by now, crushed her in a bear-hug. Unless she was hugging Lyn, instead — cocooned on a couch with him, making up their quarrel.

'Lyn? Susie? I'm back. Is no one in?'

No one. She picked up a handful of pot-pourri and let it trickle through her fingers — dry and faded dust which had once been full-blown roses, glowing gold and scarlet among glossy leaves and thorns. She could hardly be jealous of Susie, when she had traces of Oz still clinging to her body like dirty underwear.

She was jealous. *And* resentful. On her publicity tours, people mobbed and feted her as soon as she opened a door. She had longed for peace and privacy, yet somehow, now she had it, she missed the roar of approbation. Jennifer Winterton was used to welcoming committees, not silent empty halls. She walked upstairs, to try the upper floors. Three boys' bedrooms ownerless, her and Lyn's room chillingly bare and tidy, the bed unslept in, Lyn's shoes gaping like two slack and empty mouths. She went on up to the tiny attic room where Susie slept, the only part of the house which shared Susie's bright and wild disorder.

'Susie?' She could hear a muffled noise.

'Go away.'

'Susie, it's Jen.'

No answer. Jennifer opened the door an inch or two. Susie was lying sobbing on her tangled bed — still not dressed — dishevelled head pillowed in the duvet.

'What is it, Susie? What's the matter?'

A sniff. A mumble. 'Nothing.'

'Are the boys all right? Where are they?'

'Out.'

'Nothing's happened to them?'

'Bloody hell!' More sobbing. 'That's all you think about.'

'I'm sorry, I was just a bit . . . worried when the house seemed so deserted.'

'They're at the . . . b . . . baths.' Susie rolled over, rubbed her sore and swollen eyes. Her face was puffed and blotchy, all her bounce and sparkle drained away.

Jennifer knelt and put her arms around her, tried to dry her tears. She had cried like that herself and Oz had kissed her better. Must erase those kisses, rip them off with her luggage labels, discard them like the disposable plastic titbits they had served up on the plane. It wasn't safe to bring Oz back with her.

She stroked back Susie's hair — a new punk style which was sticking up in front, but still long and wild and tangled at the back.

'Look, let me get you something — a cup of tea or . . .'

'No.'

'Aren't you going to tell me what's the matter?'

'It's . . . nothing really. I'm just a bit . . . Oh — forget it. I'm glad you're back.' Susie sat up and scrubbed her face with a tissue. Last night's mascara had run and streaked beneath her eyes, leaving panda circles. Her breasts were half-escaping from her nightdress. She had tied it round the middle with a long black shoelace from one of Oliver's rugger boots.

Jennifer was shredding a Kleenex into tiny mangled wisps. She had misjudged her husband. He wasn't wooing Susie, but had been out all night, cramped and camping in his car or pacing the streets in gloom. She ought to go and find him, make things right between them. She squeezed Susie's hand.

'Well, I'm not going away any more, I promise you. I'll be here all summer. We can have some fun.'

'No, we can't. We can't.' Susie was crying again, tears running into her mouth, stabbing on the sheets.

'Why not?'

'You d . . . don't understand.'

'How can I understand if you won't tell me anything?' Jennifer stared at the plump body, the almost naked breasts. 'It's not . . . Lyn, is it? I mean, you're not upset about that . . . row you had?'

'No fear!'

'What happened, Susie? You still haven't explained yet.' She'd have to know. If Susie didn't tell her, Lyn would.

'Oh, leave it, Jen. It'll only make me mad again. I don't know how you stick that man.' Susie snatched up her packet of Woodbines, lit a match with an angry trembling hand.

'He *is* my husband.'

'Worse luck! You'd be better off without him.'

'Where is he, Susie? Look, I want to know.' Jennifer tried to keep the impatience from her voice. She had missed Susie, longed for her, yet now she felt annoyed with her. It was Susie's fault she was back at Putney at all. If she hadn't locked Lyn out, she might be safe with him at Hernhope now, instead of paying for adultery with terror and remorse. Susie might be moping, but at least her life was her own. She could sob or screw or slop around in nighties without the entire media world pouncing on her crimes. She wasn't married, with vows and rules and loyalties like a fence around her freedom.

'I dunno where he is.' Susie was sniffing and smoking at the same time, dropping ash on to the duvet. 'I unbolted the doors at eight o'clock this morning. If he wants to go on sulking, that's his hard cheese.'

'But why did he go in the first place? You must have upset him, Susie. He wouldn't leave for nothing.'

'Oh, it's my fault, is it? He wasn't a moody neurotic pig until *I* came on the scene. God! You told me yourself he was a crackpot and a cry-baby and more or less a bloody nun.'

'I didn't, Susie. I've never used words like that.'

'Fuck the words! It's what you meant that counts. If a guy hasn't screwed his wife for over a year, there must be something wrong with him.'

'I wish I'd never mentioned it. It was disloyal of me to . . .'

'I don't blame you. You're right — he *is* a nun. Frankly, I didn't believe it when you told me. I've never met a bloke who's gone that long without it. So I thought I'd try him out. I wanted to see if he'd . . . change his mind — you know, with a different bird.'

'Wh . . . What d'you mean?'

'Oh, it was only a giggle, really. I . . . took all my clothes off and walked into his room. Just to see what he'd do.'

'Susie! You . . .' Jennifer sprang towards her, almost hitting out. Was this the girl she loved, for heaven's sake?

She stared at the dishevelled bed, the creased and grubby sheet. Had Lyn been lying there, helping to make those creases? She could see Oz's bed again, semen stains accusing on his fuzzy dark blue blankets, pillows humped beneath her as they tried some new position.

'Don't look so huffy, Jen.' Susie was fiddling with the match-box. 'Nothing bloody happened — well, *almost* nothing.'

'How could you, Susie? Lyn's married. You can't just . . . go for him like one of your casual . . . pick-ups.'

'I told you, Jen, it was stalemate.'

'Well, you shouldn't have even tried. Supposing he hadn't refused you? Then what?'

'Look, I don't want your bloody husband — not if he came begging. He's worse than useless — in bed and out of it.'

'That's a lie!'

'Is it? So why did you tell me all that sob stuff? How every day he refused you made it worse, and you were getting so frustrated, you were beginning to understand how people had affairs and you'd even started . . .'

'I . . . didn't.' Jennifer turned away. She was lying now herself. She had always avoided lies before, not simply on principle, but because lying was a skill she hadn't mastered. She was doing a crash-course in it now, cutting up truth into little bits like patchwork and making patterns with them, hemming all the edges, so nothing would fray or fall apart. Since the book her whole life had been a lie — false face, false words, false . . .

'In fact, you even said it would serve Lyn right if you did have someone on the side. I remember it distinctly. You were sitting on my bed and you . . .'

'Look, get out, Susie, before I . . .'

'*You* get out,' Susie's voice was splintering into sobs again. 'I never asked you up here. I felt bad enough already without you barging in and . . .'

'And what d'you think I feel? I've been up all night and travelling half the morning and . . .'

'Big deal! Flying first class with everybody fawning on you and lolling about in swanky hotels with half a dozen bell-boys at your . . .'

'It's *not* like that. You know it's not. I'm sick of the whole thing, any-way — careering around the country, smarming and smiling all the time, when . . .'

'That's hardly my fault, is it?'

'Maybe not, but at least your life's your own.'

'No, it's not, it's not. You don't understand.' Susie had sprung off the bed and was blocking the doorway. 'My life's *not* my own — not any more, it isn't.' She grabbed Jennifer by the elbow, clung to her, tears streaming down her cheeks. 'Please don't go. Don't leave me. I'm sorry about Lyn. It wasn't just a grope, honest it wasn't. I wanted him to h . . . help me, Jen. You see . . . Oh God! I don't know how to tell you this, but . . . but — I'm going to have a . . . baby.'

Jennifer stopped, hand on the door knob, words spinning in her ears. Her legs had turned from flesh and bone to pulp. '*What?*'

'Yeah, I'm bloody pregnant. And I don't even know who the f . . . father is.'

'Susie!'

'Oh, you're shocked, I suppose. Like Lyn. Yeah, your precious hus-band was horrified. That's why we had the row.'

'You t . . . *told* him?' Lyn who hated babies, feared them; who tried to pretend they didn't grow in women, but sprung unmessy and unseeded from some supermarket shelf.

'There was no one else to tell, Jen. Look, I've been trying and trying to pretend it wasn't happening, that I've been missing periods through nerves or chance or something. Yesterday, I went to the doctor. Forced myself. His hands were freezing cold and he had this stupid little laugh. About fourteen weeks, he said.'

'Fourteen *weeks*!'

'Yeah. Five-and-a-half months to go and I'll be pushing the pram.'

'But why didn't you go to someone earlier?'

'I didn't dare. Oh, I know it sounds crazy, but I thought if I don't admit to it, it'll go away. I just told myself I couldn't be pregnant, that it simply wasn't happening — not to me. When I felt sick, I put it down to a hangover, or something I'd eaten which didn't agree with me. Does that sound mad to you?'

'N . . . No.' Not mad. She had done the same herself, but the other way round. Believed she was pregnant when Lyn hadn't even slept with her. Revelled in morning sickness when it was a case of simple indigestion. Felt her breasts filling up with milk when they were merely bloated and pre-menstrual. The only child she had was a big and bouncing bestseller, a press-cuttings folder in place of a baby-book. She sagged down on a chair. Susie's rag-doll was lying on the floor. She picked it up, stared into its sight-less button eyes. 'You should have told me, Susie — before.'

'How could I? I know you're dying for a child yourself. I couldn't just blurt out that it was *me* who was expecting, when I don't even want a fucking kid.'

'You don't . . . *want* it?'

'Of course I bloody don't. Are you mad or something?'

'You mean you're going to get rid of . . .? Have an . . .?'

'No, it's too late for that. I thought about it — course I did — but I was scared of that, as well. It's not that I'm against abortion. All that stuff about the right to life is only bullshit broadcast by the Pope, but somehow, I . . .'

Jennifer gagged the rag-doll with her hands. There *was* a right to life. A right which Lyn denied her. She glanced at Susie's stomach — it looked flatter than her own. 'Are you sure you're pregnant? Absolutely certain? I mean, even doctors are mistaken sometimes.' She remembered her own GP a year ago. 'You'll save it if you rest.' She'd rested. 'I mean, you don't look any different.'

'Balls! You're all so blind.' Susie pulled her nightie up. 'Look, see that little bulge? And my breasts have blown up like melons. I've just been sitting round the place waiting for someone to notice and throw me out. That's why I told Lyn. I caught him staring at my breasts. I thought he'd guessed.'

Jennifer was staring at them, too — useful fruitful breasts swelling for a baby. Her own had been like that for a few sweet deceitful weeks, and Lyn had refused even to look at them.

'Lyn went quite berserk, shot away from me as if I had the pox. Accused me of being a slut and a tramp and a whole lot worse. I was trying to get a bit of help and comfort and he reacted like the Pope himself.'

Shot away from her? What did Susie mean? What had they been doing when she confided in him? She wouldn't have confided at all unless they were close. How close?

'What am I going to *do*, Jen? I mean, I can't stay here much longer. Anne and Matthew are hardly likely to approve of an unmarried child-minder with her own built-in child.'

Jennifer tried to think straight. Petty and selfish to be jealous when Susie was in trouble. 'But surely you knew that when you came here? I mean, wouldn't it have been better to have taken a different job where . . .'

'What sort of job? I'm not qualified. No one wants an unmarried teen-age mother without a CSE to her name.'

Unmarried teenage mother. Hester. The whole, hopeless, helpless saga all over again. Except this was the 1980s, not 1919.

'What about your parents? Won't they help?'

'You must be joking! They'd have a fit. It's not that they're narrow-minded. My ma had lovers all her life, but she's too bogged down in her own hassles to be any help with mine. I couldn't even tell them. My Dad would probably beat me and Mum would go hysterical and then slam out and get blotto in the pub, and blame me when she fell downstairs and broke her teeth again.'

'Oh, Susie . . .' Jennifer took her hand a moment, squeezed it. Her own mother's life had been velveteen and roses — her only lover her pipe-and-slippers husband, her only tipple one small Sunday sherry after church with hat and gloves.

'Look, *I'll* keep you, darling, until you've had the baby.'

Susie lit a second cigarette. '*How*, for heaven's sake? You haven't even got a home yourself.'

'We'll find a place — rent a room or something. You can't stay here, that's obvious. Matthew would go berserk.'

'Bugger Matthew!'

'No, don't — we need him. He's got all the cash.'

'What d'you mean? I thought you were a bloody millionairess.'

'That's what everybody thinks. Actually, I've hardly seen a penny yet.'

'But didn't Matthew pay you for handing over the diaries in the first place?'

'Well, yes — we did get a small lump sum, but it wasn't very much, and by the time we'd paid off all our debts and bought the plants for the herb garden, there was nothing left of it.'

'But surely you get something else as well? I mean, the book's going like a bomb.'

'The money's is rather complicated. Lyn gets what's called a royalty, but Matthew's been investing it for us, so we get a bit of interest. It's decent of him, actually. Lyn knows nothing about money and he'd probably just blue it all if it was handed to him on a plate, whereas Matthew finds the best returns and minimises our tax and . . . You see, when we're ready to buy something major like a house, the money will be there.' Jennifer made a pattern out of hairpins on the dressing-table. Why should they buy a house. Hernhope was already waiting for them. Except she couldn't go there now. Susie needed her — and Susie's baby.

'It sounds nuts to me. What's the point of cash if you can't actually splash out with it on something?'

'Oh, Susie, do be sensible. The money comes in very slowly, in dribs and drabs. And, even then, there's a lot of other people who have to take their share.'

'Like Matthew. I suppose?'

'Not just him — his colleagues. He's got all the salaries to pay, and rents and rates and things, and a large whack of the profits goes to Hartley Davies, anyway, and then there's . . .'

'And the mug who found the diaries in the first place has to grovel to Uncle Matthew every time she needs a piddling 10p pocket money.'

'It's not like that, Susie. It just takes time, that's all.'

'I haven't *got* time.'

'Yes, you have. Matthew's still away for a while. He's going on to Japan when he's finished in Australia.'

'So how do you plan to get the cash from him when he's whizzing between Tokyo and . . .'

'Oh God! I hadn't thought of that. What about the . . . er . . . father?'

Susie grinned. 'Which one? I told you, I don't know who he is.'

'Yes, but surely you . . .'

'Well, there's three possibles. One of them is seventeen and still at school. Actually, it couldn't be him. He didn't even come and I had my period, anyway. That was what put him off, I think.'

Jennifer stared into the mirror where Susie sprawled behind her — legs open even now — too slack, too easy-going. Was there *any* man she hadn't risked a baby with? Yet who was she to criticise? Oz had been a blur behind a camera before she went grovelling to him on heat.

'What about the others?'

'I think Sparrow's the real father.'

'Sparrow?'

'You know, the big one with the motorbike. He used to be my steady. He came here once or twice — showed the boys his tattoos.'

'But I thought you said you'd . . . given him up?'

'Yeah. Had to, didn't I? He doesn't fancy birds with babies. He'd go spare if he heard about the kid. He couldn't help me, anyway. He's broke — continually. Either on the dole or blueing what he's got by rushing off abroad or buying bigger bikes. I had to give him the push before *he* deserted me, so I said I was going to Dublin to live with some Irish bloke I'd met at a party. He was quite upset, I think.'

Jennifer jabbed at her thumb with a hairpin. 'He made the bulge, for heaven's sake. It's just as much his responsibility as yours. I mean, what about all that women's lib stuff? Why should he go scot free, when you're left with all the hassle and expense?'

'Because I can't prove he's the father.'

'Who's the third, then? Can't he help?'

'No.'

'Why not?'

'He can't, that's all.' Susie rolled off the bed, picked up a comb and tore it through her hair with an ugly ripping sound.

'Look, *tell* me, Susie. If I'm going to help you, I've got to know the facts.'

'He's . . . foreign. Lives abroad. He was only in London for a month or two — sort of passing through. He's gone home now and I don't have his address. Even if I did, I couldn't write. It wouldn't be fair. He's got a . . . wife . . . and kids of his own and . . .'

'Well, he should have thought of them before. These men are so damned casual. I mean, why should they . . .?'

'Cool it, Jen. I'm on my own in this.'

'No, you're not. I'm here and I intend to see you through it.'

'Why should you?'

'No reason.' Hester was a reason. And her own lost baby. Babies must survive. Jennifer started tidying up the room, plumping cushions, folding clothes. Must keep busy, mustn't think.

Susie took a step towards her, hugged her suddenly. 'Thanks, love, you're an angel.'

Jennifer stood a moment, Susie's body merging into hers, smelling her hair, her lily-of-the-valley chain-store scent; feeling her breasts swollen as she'd said; her own body hollow and unfruitful. She pulled away. 'Look, I'd . . . er . . . better get the lunch.'

'Who for?' Susie was drooling ash into her make-up drawer. 'I packed the boys off to the swimming baths and gave them money for some fish and chips. Told them not to come back here on pain of death till tea-time at the earliest — and if they could make it midnight, all the better.'

'Susie, I don't think Anne would . . .'

'Anne's not here. It'll do 'em good. Make 'em independent. They'll grow up rotten selfish bastards, the way she waits on them.'

Jennifer sank down on the bed. She felt pulled in all directions at once. She ought to go and search for Lyn, stay and comfort Susie, had a duty to Anne and Matthew to make sure the boys were safe. 'Look, I'll get *us* lunch.' Cooking a meal would be a simple solid chore, anchor her mind to something.

'Not hungry, thanks.'

'You *ought* to eat, you know, now you're pregnant.'

'Oh, stuff it, Jen. I had enough of that from the doctor. You eat if you want.'

Jennifer wasn't hungry either, but she walked down to the kitchen, counting on her fingers. Fourteen weeks, Susie's GP had said. That meant Susie had conceived at the end of April — the same month *she* had conceived, a year ago. She stood at the kitchen door, stared in horror at the mess. Every surface was cluttered with dirty dishes, the floor a maze of footmarks, sink clogged with soggy teabags and old potato peelings. She felt a sudden pang of guilt. She had been planning to escape with Lyn, leave Susie in sole charge. This was the shambles Anne and Matthew would have found on their return.

She scraped back her hair in a rubber band, tied on a dirty apron. She was glad no one could see her. The girl who had gilded Newcastle was now a Cinderella. Half the North had flocked to worship her, yet back in London, her own husband hadn't bothered to say hallo. And when he did show up, she would have to face his shock over Susie's baby. If he found it so upsetting that a girl who meant nothing to him should be pregnant and unmarried, then how would he react to the news of his mother's bastard? She hoped to God he would never hear about it. Rowan Childs had been mercifully quiet, using her column to attack Irish Catholics and anti-vivisectionists rather than describe further forays to Hernhope. Yet she could still be secretly ferreting out the facts, Jasper Prince sharpening up his pen.

Jennifer sank on to a stool. The sun was streaming through the window, rainbowing the dust — a tranquil summer morning, too bright for all these problems. She screwed up her eyes against it. Everything was so confused — remorse over Oz tinged with triumph that he had desired her at all; concern and pity for Susie all mixed up with envy of her pregnancy and anger at her carelessness; a longing for Lyn contradicted by worry and resentment.

She picked up the dishcloth, swatted at the work-top, put it down again — felt too weary to tackle such disorder. Best to springclean herself first, scour off all the traces of last night.

She trailed upstairs again, ran a bath. There was a tidemark all around the tub and one grubby towel flung into a corner. She took off her clothes, stared at her naked body in the mirror. Shouldn't it look different after . . .?

'Fancy a drink, love?' Susie was standing in the doorway, clutching a bottle of gin.

Jennifer grabbed the towel to cover herself. 'You shouldn't drink, Susie. It's bad for the baby.'

'Look, this kid's a hundred per cent shockproof. I tried everything to budge it. Bottlesful of vodka after boiling hot baths, roasting myself on the top shelf of a sauna, riding pillion on a 1000 cc Kawasaki — even some herbal stuff I got from an Indian girl who swore it would bring on my period in an hour. All it brought on was diarrhoea and a blinding headache. So if you think one mingy little gin's going to upset it . . .'

Jennifer turned away. She had done everything she could to save her own child — stayed in bed, hardly moving even there, swallowed every vitamin, called on Hester's powers, prayed to a God she didn't quite believe in. And there was Susie gulping gin and lighting a cigarette.

'Smoking's bad, as well. It affects the . . .'

'Do lay off, Jen. Have a gin yourself. You sound as if you need one. Let's drink to the little bastard.'

Jennifer turned the taps off. She did need a drink, to calm all the confusions, lull her constant dread and hope of Lyn's return. She was worried by his absence, yet almost relieved to have an hour or two without him. She couldn't face his fears on top of all the other turmoil. Susie was slopping gin into a tooth-mug.

'Isn't there any wine, Susie?'

'No — I drank it all last week. Had to steel myself to make that appointment with the doc. There's some very classy whisky, though.'

Jennifer shuddered. Not whisky again. She could taste Oz's Haig-flavoured kisses, tongue searching out her . . .

'Tell you what —' Susie sprang up from the bathroom stool, hair flicking in Jennifer's face. 'Let's make cocktails — you know — those ones you had with Jonathan.'

'We can't. They're made with liqueurs and grenadine and things. Matthew hasn't got those.'

'Yes, he has. Well, not grenadine, maybe, but lots of other stuff. His sideboard's bulging with it. Anne told me to help myself to what I needed.'

'She meant . . . food, though.'

'What's the difference? We'll have a liquid lunch instead of . . . Oh, go on, Jen — don't be such a meanie. You've been knocking back cocktails all week. Can't we have just one?'

*　　*　　*

'Susie, I love you.'

'Love you, too, mate. Love Micky Mouse. Love Mohammed Ali. Love . . .'

'Hey, stop splashing, will you? The water's tipping over the side. This bath wasn't built for two.'

Jennifer shifted her bottom, unhooked her feet from Susie's, displacing still more water, and peered over the edge of the bath. The floor was soaked, their clothes a sodden jumble. She giggled.

'Want another Brain Buster?' Susie grabbed one of the liquor bottles ranged along the side of the bath next to the pine-foam and shampoos.

'No, thanks.' Jennifer clutched the taps for support. The whole room was shimmying. 'I prefer the Double Devils. D'you think we should have mixed them, though? I feel a bit . . . well . . . floaty.'

'Shouldn't worry. They're all the same basically. Have some brandy straight. It works like medicine. Here, swig it from the bottle.'

Jennifer swigged. The bottle felt cold against her pink-flushed breasts. She lay back in the water. Susie had poured in at least a pint of Crazy Foam. The bubbles seemed to be seeping inside her skull, shimmering and popping in her head. She wasn't exactly sure how she and Susie had landed up in the tub together. They had been sitting on the bathmat, mixing cocktails, she wrapped only in her towel still. Susie had brought up half of Matthew's sideboard, turned bathroom into bar. The bath was ready run and cooling. At some point, Susie had started slooshing gin into the water.

'In Hollywood they bath in booze, Jen.'

'Champagne, though, not Gordon's. And don't waste it.'

After that, things were more a blur — still were. She opened her eyes. Steam was billowing round the ceiling, drops of water sweating down the tiles. The room had lost its square and solid walls and was bulging out of shape.

'D'you ever bath with Lyn?' Susie was popping bubbles with her finger.

'N . . . no.'

'Sparrow's got this thing about doing it in water. I suppose it's because

205

he's Pisces. His great ambition was to do it under Niagara Falls in one of those plastic raincoat things they give you. Hey, Jen . . .'

'What?'

'Did you really not notice my bulge? I imagine everyone's sort of . . . gawping at me.'

Jennifer was still cradling the brandy bottle. She took another gulp. '*I* felt that when I was pregnant. Thought the whole world was admiring.' She glanced at Susie's stomach, another blur beneath the bubbles. Her child had never made it to fourteen weeks.

'Jen?'

'Mmm?'

'You know you said you loved me. Did you mean it?'

'Mm.'

'No one's ever loved me. Not really. I mean, lots of blokes have said it, but only because I've sucked them off or something. It's just lust with them, I reckon. Sometimes I wish I'd never slept with anyone.'

'Why? Oh — you mean the baby.'

'No, I don't. It's just that . . . well — it hasn't ever really meant much. I mean, for you it all seems sort of . . . holy. I used to think you were just a prude, refusing to sleep with anyone but Lyn — and not even with him — but now I almost envy you.'

'I shouldn't.' Jennifer lurched forward to replace the brandy, picked up another bottle. 'Have a gin.'

'No. I'm trying to be serious. Anyway, that's beer shampoo, not gin. Listen, Jen, d'you think someone like me could change — be more like you? D'you realise, I started when I was twelve and didn't really care who the hell I had it off with. Yet you were still a virgin at nineteen — and you've stuck to the same one guy every single day since then.'

Jennifer shut her eyes. Peacock coloured water was still frothing beneath her lids. 'Not . . . quite.'

'What d'you mean? I thought you said . . .'

'I'm getting out now. My skin has gone all wrinkly. It must be that foam. It's full of chemicals.' Jennifer stood up. The bathroom walls were made of steam, writhing in and out.

'No, tell me, Jen. If Lyn wasn't your first, then who the hell . . .?'

'He was.'

'You mean you had an affair *after* you were married?'

'No. Well . . . not an *affair*.'

'But you told me you'd never even . . .'

Jennifer was shivering on the bathmat, little bubbles still pricking on her skin. 'Where are all the towels? There's only this grubby thing and it's soaking wet already.'

'There's about half a hundred in the laundry basket. The boys went swimming every day and I never got round to doing a wash. Look, come upstairs to my room and you can borrow my towelling dressing-gown. That'll mop you up. It's even semi-clean. Hold on — I'll get it for you.' Susie heaved herself out of the water. 'Seems a shame to waste these bubbles. Still . . .' She shrugged, followed Jennifer up the attic stairs, both girls dripping wet and naked. They dried each other with a combination of Susie's towelling dressing-gown and a couple of Aertex shirts.

'My feet are still wet.'

'I'll dry them.'

'Don't! It tickles.'

'You've got funny feet, you know.'

'I haven't.'

'Nice and funny. Stop wriggling! You can't be all that ticklish.'

'I am. Ow! Don't! Susie stop!' Jennifer yanked her feet away. Susie lunged, grabbed them, tipped her off the chair. She sprawled on the carpet, still laughing, the scratchy cord rough against her breasts. She had lain like that with Oz, naked again, laughing again . . . She reached out her hand for Susie's drunken golliwog propped against the skirting, its stuffing leaking, its limbs splayed out, as slack and pie-eyed as she was.

'Listen, Susie . . .'

'What?'

'If you really want to know . . .' She was addressing the golly — he was too stupid to be shocked. 'I hadn't slept with anyone — not until last night, that is.'

Susie rocketed up. 'Last night? You mean . . .?'

'Yes. In Newcastle. Oh, Susie. I hardly knew the guy.'

'And you had it away, you mean?'

'Mm.' The golliwog's cheeks were two burning scarlet blobs. 'I feel an utter slut.'

'Come off it, mate! What's one little screw when you've gone more than a year without it? I'd have been humping the whole of Newcastle.'

'It wasn't one. We did it at least five times — no, six.'

'Christ! Who the hell was he? Son of James Bond?'

'Well, he was introduced as Oz Steadman. But halfway through the night, he admitted he'd been christened Brian.' Jennifer tried to laugh, but it came out like a sob. 'Brian . . . B . . . Blenkins.'

'Blenkins?' Susie giggled. 'I don't believe it. Where did you pick him up? In the lift?'

'No, he's a . . . photographer.'

'Cor! you lucky dog! Did he take your picture?'

'Not . . . then, silly.'

'Well, he might have had a Polaroid. I can just see you on Page 3, Jen!'

Jennifer shuddered. 'Don't.'

'Cor! I've never had a guy come more than twice. Beginner's luck, I s'pose. If it was *me* who'd gone to bed with him, he'd have been a premature ejaculator or into S.M. or something. Tell me what he did. I want a blow-by-blow account.'

'No, Susie. It's . . . embarrassing. I don't want to talk about it.'

'Why not? In our Women's Group, sex is the favourite subject.'

'Yes, but only sexual rights and things. Not all the actual . . . details.'

'You'd be surprised! Our leader's a bit kinky, I suspect. She's always on about sex and bodies and things. Jo, she's called — probably short for Joseph. She's so butch herself, I doubt if she'd want a bloke, but she laps up all our stories as if she's dying for it. Then she turns round and says we don't need men at all — we've got to love our own bodies. We're meant to admire ourselves in the mirror and buy flowers for our own birthdays and give ourselves massages and . . . Tell you what, I'll give you a massage.'

'N . . . no, Susie. We ought to get dressed.'

'What for?'

'Well, we can't just sit here naked all afternoon.'

'Why not? Jo's always telling us to strip off and walk around in the altogether. She says we've got to feel at ease with our bodies and tell ourselves we're beautiful, even if we're twenty stone or got leprosy or something. Want some of this?'

'What is it?'

'‘Boots' Dry Skin gunge. My skin's all grotty since that bath. It's a wonder Robert hasn't got leprosy himself if he always baths in Crazy Foam.'

'He doesn't use the whole bottle, though. Mmm — smells nice.'

'It shouldn't. It's only shark's oil or axle-grease or something. Hold on — I'll rub some in for you. Lie on the bed. This carpet's like a hair-shirt.'

Jennifer eased up from the floor, flopped on to the bed. Her body still felt limp, limbs floppy like a rag-doll's. Susie was a second doll sprawling there beside her, a doll with working hands. The Women's Group was right — there was nothing wrong with bodies. It was only Lyn who had made her doubt her own. Susie was admiring it. So had Oz, last night.

She closed her eyes. Thinking of Oz had stirred up strange sensations. Or was it Susie's hands? They were stroking low along her back now, had already reached her buttocks. She could feel Susie's own excitement feeding on Oz as well. She kept sipping at him like a new exotic cocktail.

'Did he . . . kiss you? You know, lower down?'

'Y . . . yes.'

'A lot of men won't, I find. They expect you to almost choke on them, but it's all a one-way business. Was it good?'

'Mmmm.' It was good now, the soft lulling pressure of Susie's hands, her tickly hair teasing across her shoulders.

Susie dolloped out more lotion. 'Turn round again.'

She turned. Oz had given commands. She could feel his hands busy on her breasts, rubbing in the lotion. Hands too soft and gentle for a man's.

208

Yet how could a woman's hands arouse her, stir up such deep feelings?

'Susie, don't . . . I . . .'

'Have you ever used a paint-brush? One of those very soft ones made of squirrel hair? They're fantastic on the nipples. Sparrow tried it on mine when I was doing art at night-school and had all the different brushes. He even painted my nipples once, but the brush feels better dry. Hold on a sec — I'll show you. This is only a lip-brush, but there's not much difference. Nice?'

'Mm.'

'Do it on mine. Bit harder. That's great! Now the other one. You've stirred them up. Go on — rub some lotion in. It'll stop me getting stretch marks.'

'You don't get stretch marks on . . . boobs.'

'Yes, you do. The doctor told me. Don't just dab — rub hard.'

Strange to touch another woman's breasts. Pregnant breasts, taut and swollen as if they were already full of milk. Jennifer traced the tiny bluish veins throbbing under Susie's skin. The nipples were hard and stiffening like her own. She was only excited because of Susie's baby — the fact and closeness of it, the thought of the man who had put it there. One of three — that made it more exciting. She could see the three, throwing off their clothes — the schoolboy with his small shy hands, Sparrow under Niagara Falls shouting in the spray, the foreigner just passing through Susie's body on his way back to his wife's. She wanted all of them — Oz and Lyn as well — all shooting sperm inside her, giving *her* a baby.

'Don't stop, Jen. It's fantastic.'

She had to stop. Susie's face was moving down towards her, trapping her in a tent of still damp hair. Susie's lips were reaching for her own lips. Women didn't kiss.

The kiss felt strangely soft. No bristly chin like Oz's, no two-day stubble like Lyn's on a Sunday night. Jennifer sank back. She could smell strawberry-scented hair conditioner instead of after-shave, taste chewing-gum and brandy. Her mouth was opening as it had with Oz. Not so different, really. The same wet, seeking strangeness, tongues twined and probing. Minutes passed before she pulled away.

'What's wrong?'

'N . . . nothing.'

'You're a great kisser, you know. Thought you said you'd never kissed a bird.'

'I . . . haven't.'

'Don't believe it. Kiss my breasts.'

'N . . . no.'

'Why not? What's wrong with 'em?'

'Nothing. It's . . . me. I keep thinking we shouldn't really be . . .'

'Don't think. Jo says you have to kick your mind out of the bedroom to

209

stop it lousing up your body. Hey — look at your nipples! You've got one stiff and standing up and the other sort of squashed. That means half of you fancies it, and the other half doesn't. Why don't you relax, Jen? They were both stiff before. That's how I knew you wanted it.'

'I didn't, Susie. I've never . . .'

'Just lie back and enjoy it, can't you?'

Jennifer lay back. Simpler to obey. Susie was using the brush again, painting soft and shivery circles on her stomach, her other hand stroking across her breasts. She smoothed back Susie's hair. Susie grinned. She traced the outline of the smile, touched the soft open lips with just one finger.

The second kiss was longer. Susie's lips moved from mouth to throat to breast. Jennifer felt her bloodstream change to brandy as Susie's tongue flicked across her nipples. Oz had done the same last night, suckled her like a baby. They might have *made* a baby, if he hadn't been so careful. She groped a hand out, touched the slight swollen curve of Susie's stomach. That curve excited her. She longed to lay her cheek against it, feel the growing child.

Susie's hands were groping lower now, dawdling down Jennifer's thighs — and up. She tensed. Dangerous ground again. Yet the stroking was so soothing, so hard to fight against. Her whole body was warm and sinking down, merging into Susie's. The fingers kept pausing on the inside of her thigh, whispering and teasing. Jennifer tried to close her legs, but Susie's finger had already slipped between them, coaxed them open again.

'No, Susie. I've already said not there.'

Susie's hand was deaf. The tip of just one finger was probing in, in . . .

'N . . . no,' Jennifer said again, but it was almost indecipherable. Her body was contradicting her.

Two fingers now, both pressing on that one tiny flashpoint her whole body was wired up to. It was like a switch which turned the shock-waves on.

Susie was using her whole hand now, pummelling her, hurting her. 'I'm not hurting, am I, Jen?'

'Yes. No. Go *on*.'

She was sore from Oz, wild from Oz, but she wanted to be *more* sore. She wasn't a torpid rag-doll any more, but a living thrusting body. She had forgotten where Susie ended and she began. She was part of Susie, fused with her, joined by a clutch of fingers. Nothing left but fingers — fingers up to the hilt.

'Susie, where are you? Susie!' Someone calling, fainter than her own cries, doors slamming downstairs, feet pounding across the hall.

She closed her ears, opened her legs still wider. 'Go *on*, Susie, go on. It's wonderful, it's absolutely . . .'

'Be *quiet*, you nut! The boys are back.' Susie shocked and sitting up, fingers snatched away.

Jennifer grabbed the hand, clamped it back between her legs again. 'Don't stop — please don't stop. Oh, that's *fantastic*, Susie. God! It's . . .'

Susie had suddenly swivelled round and was kneeling with her feet by Jennifer's head. Her mouth had replaced the hand. Jennifer felt uneasy — but only for a second. It was impossible to think. The feelings were too total, Susie's tongue too swift and skilful. It was pushing up, up, inside her, circling and insisting. Nothing else existed except that long, wild, clever, flicking tongue. Jennifer's back was arched, legs tensed against the mattress. There *weren't* any legs or back. Only the hot wet fevered bit between them. Susie's mouth was trapped inside her — part of her — her own mouth shouting in response. 'Oh, God! Oh, stop! That's it. Oh, wonderful . . .' She flopped back on the bed, silent now except for her gasping breaths. She could still hear shouting somewhere way beyond her — someone else's yells.

'Susie! Why can't you answer? Robert's grazed his knee again and he wants a . . .'

Susie sprang up and off. 'Quick! Hide yourself. They're coming up and there's no lock on this door.'

'Oh, Susie, that was wonderful! I just can't tell you. It felt absolutely . . .'

'Shut up, you crazy woman! They'll hear you.' Susie was dragging on her dressing-gown, damp and creased since they had used it as a towel. 'Quick! Get under the bed or something. They're here.' Voices right outside the door now, feet crashing up the last short flight of stairs.

Jennifer struggled up. Too late. Susie shoved her down again, flung the duvet over her, squashed her face beneath a pile of pillows as Oliver bombarded through the door, the younger two behind him.

'Why didn't you answer, Susie? We've been yelling for you for hours and . . .'

Jennifer was smothering. Susie had sprawled across the duvet to conceal her from the boys, pressing on her stomach, legs across her face.

'There's a terrible mess in the bathroom. And who's nicked my Crazy Foam? And a brandy bottle's broken and . . .'

Jennifer tried to breathe. What in God's name was she up to, lying naked and on heat beneath a heavy stifling Susie, when she should be looking after the boys? Anne and Matthew trusted her, had left her in charge.

Susie's foot was jabbing in her eye. She dared not shift it, dared not stir at all until the boys had gone. She lay and listened to Susie fob them off.

'No, I didn't nick it, Oliver. It was Auntie Jen. She was all grotty after her flight so . . .'

'Auntie Jennifer wouldn't make a mess like that.'

'You mean she's *back*?' Hugh was cock-a-hoop and shouting.

'Yeah.'

'Great! Where is she?'

'In the . . . garden.'

211

Six legs went crashing off again. Susie knelt up gingerly. 'Hope I haven't pulped you, but there was nothing else to do. You can come out now, but hurry.'

Jennifer didn't move. It was not just Susie who was crushing her. All the problems had returned and were pressing down like a second stone-filled duvet — Susie pregnant with no cash, Lyn moody and resentful, herself adulterous — and worse. She'd had whisky and sperm for supper, Susie cocktails for lunch — was still panting like a steam-engine, leaking between the legs.

Suddenly, she laughed. 'Oh, Susie,' she said. 'I think I'm going to need another Double Devil if I've got to face the boys.'

'Stuff the boys!' said Susie. 'Shove over and shut up. It's *my* turn now!'

XVII

Lyn stared at his drawing, the most complete he had done yet, and the most assured. The charcoal had streaked across the paper as if all the pent-up power within him had surged into his fingers, guided his hand. The drawing was good, damned good. There was depth in it, intensity, a firm structure and coherence beneath the bold and sweeping lines. He frowned critically at the bottom right-hand corner, smudged the outlines a little with a finger, re-drew the curve of a tree root so that its serpenting line repeated the curve of the hill itself.

All the curves were linked, all caught and held by bold slashed lines of rough cross-hatching. He had made a cage and pattern out of landscape. He had seen the forest as a cage when he was locked in it two days ago — the steely strength of the bars and infinite space beyond them. He had transferred it all to paper, trapped its terror. He reached out and touched the page, felt like a god who had lifted his finger and added something to the world. Creator.

He eased up from the ground, brushing his trousers free of leaves and twigs. This sweep of hill was his studio, the car his gallery. He opened the boot and laid the drawing with the rest — drawings done on scraps of waste-paper, broken-up cardboard boxes, paper bags, brown wrapping-paper — anything he could scrounge or steal. Two days ago, he had been too shocked and stupid even to hold a pencil. He had lain in the forest beside the grave, his mind slapping and rocking with problems. How could he return to Jennifer and tell her Hernhope was no longer theirs, accept that he was second son, disinherited son; Hester a mother he could no longer recognise?

He spent all day in the forest, and all night, neither eating nor sleeping, lapping water out of puddles like an animal. Dawn came sullenly, the huge dark conifers holding up their arms to block out the light which only trickled through in mean and grudging driblets. He tried his legs. They were still leaden and unwilling, but he would have to leave. He pushed through scaly trunks, fought with rough and tangled undergrowth. Overhanging branches grabbed at his face and snagged it. At last, he reached the fence, squeezed through the wire, stood on the bare brow of the hill. The whole world was wrapped in grey, dense cloud rolling in from the horizon like a sea-swell drowning fern and heather. He used the cloud as his disguise, slinking back to the car in cloak and shroud.

It felt strange to drive again. The gears seemed stiff, the steering wheel too large. Every loop and twist of the road exhausted him. He took it slowly, like an invalid, creeping along the hedges until, slowly, cloud cleared and knife-sharp swallows cut and re-cut the sky into jigsaw patterns gilded by the sun. He avoided the motorways, drove south along narrow empty roads half swamped in unscythed hedgerow, watching the countryside grow softer and less bleak. He hardly noticed the signposts, kept his map-book closed. When he stopped, it was only because he was too weary to go on. He sat slouched in the seat, trying to make plans. He must phone Jennifer to stop her worrying, tell her he was safe. *Safe?* He needed food and petrol. Money was short. He must decide what to do tomorrow and the next day and the . . .

He did nothing. Just slumped there with his eyes closed. His mind was overshadowed by a tree, a Douglas fir marking out a grave. He could see its grainy bark, its thin tough trunk, the swags of foliage shutting out the sky. He fumbled in his pocket, found a worn-down length of pencil, sharpened it with his pocket-knife. No paper. He picked up his map-book, turned to the one blank page facing the list of contents, made a mark on it. He extended the mark into a line, two lines. Two lines became a trunk. He wasn't really drawing, just distracting himself from the pain of elder brothers. The trunk grew branches, the branches twigs. The foliage on the twigs began to push against the margins. The page was too small for a two hundred-foot conifer. He started again on the inside back cover, drew across two pages. The tree became more detailed. He could see its structure, the whole shape and hang of it, the precise dovetailing where twig joined twig and trunk soared into branch.

It startled him — the way the tree was somehow *there* on paper — its power, its hugeness. It wasn't the Douglas fir which had marked out Edward's grave, but a still taller tree from some prehistoric forest, older, far, than the one which shadowed Hernhope. It had seen death and death and death, and gone on living. It was living on his page now, in the bold sweep of the trunk, the rough corky bark with its creviced whorls and gashes, the sense of age, of menace. He hardly knew how he had done it. He was tired, confused. He should have been blabbing over Edward, not creating giants with an inch or two of pencil.

He must try again, make sure it was not just a fluke, a one-off stroke of luck which could never be repeated. He drew a second fir — a lightning-blasted one he remembered from his boyhoood — limbs twisted, trunk split apart and gaping. It was harder to bring off. He stopped, re-started, stopped again, used his finger as an eraser, rubbed out half of what he had done. He sat staring at his messy page, scared to re-draw the lines, his hand refusing to respond to his eye, the bond between them broken. He abandoned the tree, drew a fir-cone instead — something smaller, more precise. The cone came quickly and in such minute and careful detail, it was as if he had simply picked one up from the forest and laid it on his page. He was surprised he could remember the exact and complex struc-ture of a Douglas fir-cone — the triple-pointed bracts protruding from every scale, their pale and feathery tridents contrasting with the broader darker scales and breaking the smooth outlines of the oval.

Reassured, he went back to his tree. He could see now how to tackle it. The perfect cone had seeded a perfect trunk. Once he had the outlines down, he struck with lightning, split the wood apart, distorted his careful structure. He was winning now. The tree was real and suffering. The wounds in the bark seemed to bleed and leer. The broken-off branches were both menacing and pitiful.

He switched to pines — Lodgepole, Scots pine, Western White. There were no more blank pages in the map-book, so he drew across the maps themselves, afforesting new areas of England, conifers sprouting in Liverpool and Bournemouth, cones tumbling on the jammed and tar-mac roads of central London. His fingers were cramped from the blunt and scratchy pencil, worn down to a stub, now, and almost too small to hold. He found a felt-tip in the glove-compartment. Still no paper. He started up the engine, drove back on to a main road until he reached a layby and a litter bin. He poked among the rubbish, extracted a Kentucky chicken carton, a battered cardboard box. It was like being a small boy again, with no money for artists' materials, and not allowed them anyway, scribbling on scraps of greaseproof paper hoarded from Hester's baking sessions, or on the backs of old envelopes and bills. He had even stolen paper — filched it from school or shops when nobody was looking. His drawings had a punch then — the strange distorting power of childhood. He could see it repeated in these sketches, but now chan-nelled and controlled. He felt the same intense excitement as he had done as a ten-year-old, when his rough spontaneous daubings turned into forms and structures with a new life of their own. They had come from him, were part of him, yet were separate, stronger — made *him* stronger for having produced them in the first place. He thought he had lost those skills. His art had grown slick and flabby, commercial art, always tied to Matthew, drawings to sell books and keep four boys in shoes.

He slit the paper bag to make it larger, smoothed it out and rested it on the cover of the map-book. He drew more boldly now, using the same swift catapulting lines he had dared as a boy when he was less tense and self-conscious about making marks on paper. He kept the sketches small. He had to — even the cardboard box was only one foot square — but they were soaring in his mind. He craved oils, canvas, a proper stool and easel. He stared at the latest sketches — still trees, still bloody good. Gaunt and dogged Lodgepole pines, ramrod sitka spruce. All the gnarled stoicism of conifers caught in his strong black lines. He got out and stretched his legs. He had used up all his materials. Even the chicken carton had sprouted a vast cedar. The felt-tip had run dry.

He drove to the nearest village, found only an ironmonger's and a general store. They would have to do. He bought ten large sheets of plain brown wrapping-paper, a piece of hardboard to pin them to, a reel of masking-tape, a box of children's chalks. He went into the food shop, picked up a crusty loaf — insisted they double-wrap it. Two extra sheets of drawing-paper. 'Good day,' he said. It *was* good.

He drove even slower now, crawling along the roads, staring through gaps in the hedgerows. He knew what he was looking for, the right bones beneath the flesh of grass and soil, some unique configuration of cloud and contour. He stopped in a valley where a huge sky crouched over cornfields and one orphaned tree dissected the horizon. The land was made of patchwork — a golden square of high and burnished barley stitched beside a duller stubble square, then blocks of green, mustard, olive, ochre, green again.

His chalks were pale things in comparison, but he would make them work for him. He roughed out the main lines in black, rubbed in yellow to get his ochre, scribbled in a green field beyond it, then swept in the broad curve of the sky with its choppy clouds. There was no noise, no tractor, no distracting voices or vulgar picnickers. Rooks spiralled up and down from trees, midges flitted round his head. He brushed them off. He needed all his concentration. He was drawing on a larger scale than he had done for years. The work he did for Matthew was always finicky and footling. Now he was trying to cram a chunk and slice of the world on to a single sheet of paper and not break it in the process.

He stopped only to stretch his legs and rest his back, or tear hunks out of the loaf when he was hungry. The drawing wasn't easy. It had some-how become too complex, the first spontaneous urgent lines swamped in shackling detail. He returned to his black chalk, switched from cloud to field, reworked the patchwork squares and made them simpler. The thing took off from there. Shapes gelled and soared, the whole structure

215

stabilised. He knew he was drawing better than he had ever done before. Some new skill and virtuosity had been released in him. He dared not question it, dared not turn his mind to Wills again, to Hester. He must simply go on drawing while that extraordinary charge was there.

At dusk, he stopped — fingers aching, back stiff. He rolled up his paper, stowed it in the boot. He drove back to the village, ordered a pint in the Rose and Crown as an excuse to use their phone. People stared. He hadn't changed his clothes for forty-eight hours. They were stained and dirty from lying on the ground. He had torn his shirt on brambles, his chin was a stubble-field.

He dialled the Putney number. Jennifer answered in a sob and rush of words.

'Oh darling. Thank God! I've been so worried about you. I thought you might have had a . . .'

'I love you,' he said, in answer. People could hear, but now he didn't care.

'What happened? What are you doing? I've been worried sick.'

'I'm drawing. I mean *really* drawing. Listen, darling, I think this is important. I've . . .'

'Drawing? But where? Why? I thought you'd be . . . Susie said you were absolutely . . .'

He tried to remember Susie. Susie Susannah Jane. Bloody lambs, half-formed foetuses. Undoing his pyjama cord a hundred years ago. Undoing Susie's buttons on a picnic, just three days before. Susie, pregnant, panicking. He felt her panic clammy on his palms. Mustn't think. Fear could stop him drawing. He shifted the phone to the other hand, leaned against the oak-beamed wall. He needed something strong and solid behind him. 'That's over,' he said. 'Finished.'

'Over? What d'you mean, Lyn. What's going on, for heaven's sake? Where *are* you? Susie still hasn't said why you left, you know — not really. I mean, she told me about the . . . pregnancy, but . . .'

Why did his wife keep harking back to Susie when he longed to swamp her with his love, impress her with his work? 'I'm sorry I didn't phone before. Forgive me. I hate you to worry, Snookie. I . . . I didn't feel too good. But I'm OK now. This drawing I'm doing — it's good, it's really good. You must see it. I want you to know what I can . . .'

'Look here, Lyn, you can't just disappear like that and then phone up and say you're . . . *drawing*, as if nothing's happened at all and you're simply on a sketching trip or something. I've been in a terrible state about you. When are you coming back?'

'Soon, I promise. Just give me a few more days. I daren't stop working now. I might never be able to . . .'

'But where are you? And how are you living? You've got none of your things with you. Your toothbrush's still here and all your clothes and . . .'

216

'I don't need toothbrushes. I'm living rough, sleeping in the car or in the fields.'

'You'll get ill, Lyn. It poured last night. The ground must be very damp.'

'It didn't rain here.'

'Where's "here"?'

'Northamptonshire. I'm phoning from Cheetham. It's a tiny village with just a pub and a couple of shops.'

'Why on earth Northamptonshire?'

'I don't know. I just drove here. The landscape's wonderful. It's very flat, but the skies are huge. There's such a sense of . . . space. I don't want hills at the moment, hemming me in. I've been working on something new for me today. Mostly skies — and how they sort of . . . press down on the fields. There's this . . . this terrific sense of tension where they meet and . . . Oh, Snookie, please try and understand. It's for *you*, the drawing — partly. I want to give you something. I want you to see me as a . . .'

'I'd prefer it if you gave me some thought, Lyn. Didn't it even occur to you I might be worried? I almost rang the police, except Susie said it was stupid to make such a fuss and if you wanted to piss off, then . . .'

The receiver dropped from Lyn's hands, dangled on its lead. He could hear the anger in Jennifer's voice. Susie's anger, Susie's words. Susie dragging his wife away from him. He would lose her, as he had just lost his mother. For thirty years and more, Hester had put him first. However stern she was, she had lived for him alone; everything she had and was was his. Until two days ago, until the Will. Then, he saw it had all been a delusion. He had never had his mother to himself at all. Edward had been always there, a third invisible presence — taller than he was, older — with first claim on Hester's love and property. Only claim. In that Will, she had cut him off, snuffed him out completely. Supposing Jennifer did the same? He had been first with her as well, taken her love for granted. It was only now he realised how desperately he needed her. But Susie was threatenng that love, pushing a rival claim.

'Lyn? *Lyn*? Are you still there? What's happened? The phone's gone dead.' Jennifer's voice, faint and half-distorted, talking to the wall.

He grabbed the receiver. 'No, it hasn't. I'm here. Look, Snookie, I'm sorry. I'm desperately sorry. I don't want to hurt you. You're right — I should have phoned before, but . . .' The pips shrilled against his voice. 'Wait! Please don't go. Hang on.' He fumbled for another 10p piece, found only a handful of pennies. 'I *love* you,' he blurted out. 'I love you more than . . .'

His love was swamped in a high-pitched whine. He had already been cut off.

He slumped on the bench beside the phone. Why did he always muff things? He had wanted to make her happy, explain his work to her. He had

217

hardly thought at all whilst he was drawing — needed all his concentration to get it right. But the thoughts had been jamming up inside his head, ready to flood over when he laid his chalks and paper down. Thoughts about love, loss, Hester, Jennifer. 'Beloved son', Hester had written, but not to him. He would never be beloved now, except by Jennifer. He had heard her love on the phone just now, underneath the anger. Fussing about his safety, worrying in case the ground was damp. She cared enough to worry, the only one who did. He longed to recompense her, shower her with gifts and flowers, make up for the months and months of misery he had dumped on her instead. He always got it wrong. Even now, he had left her anxious and resentful, when he had rung to reassure her.

He drained his beer, slunk out of the pub. No one had spoken a word to him. He was used to that. People always shunned him, kept their distance. It was probably his own fault. He hardly knew how to be charming and approachable as Jennifer was so naturally. She would have smiled at people, got into conversation with some local farmer's wife, instead of freezing any overture with a scowl. It was something to do with their backgrounds. Jennifer's loving sheltered childhood had *made* her loving, made her trust the world. She loved him, despite the scowls. That love was intensely precious, all he had.

He crossed the road, unlocked the car, drove off into darkness. He longed for Jennifer to be sitting there beside him, ached to touch her body. He couldn't do that yet, couldn't even return yet. He saw now he had never been what she wanted. She had loved an artist and married a hack. He could still change, be worthy of her, prove himself. Tomorrow, he would find a town with a decent art-shop — buy the few basic materials he could afford — and paint her a new dowry.

*   *   *

Lyn stopped the car on the last fringes of the countryside before the road plunged into the sprawl and fret of London. He got out and opened the boot — took one last look at the dowry. It was a rich one, despite his limited resources. Landscapes in chalk, charcoal, children's paints; broad sweeping compositons on sheets of wrapping-paper; miniatures on matchboxes or beer-mats. Never before had he produced such impressive work so quickly. He had felt a wild exhilaration as the landscape sprang on to his paper, still alive. The triumph was still there, buzzing in his head like the throb of grasshoppers in the tangled grass behind him.

He stripped off his shirt. The day was hot and close. Swifts with scythe-shaped wings soared above the wasteground. Wild forget-me-nots pushed through patchy weeds and dregs of picnic litter. Nice name, that — forget-me-not. He picked a spray or two, stared at the tiny golden eye in each blue star of petals. He would bring them back for Jennifer, fill his arms with flowers for her. Only sissy men picked flowers, but he had spent his last

218

penny on paints and petrol, so he couldn't buy her any. He would choose only blue ones, blue to match her eyes and match the sky. He found a few frail harebells, pushed through the hedge into a copse and searched for viper's bugloss, its long pink stamens protruding from the deep blue mouths of bell-shaped flowers. He snapped off rough and hairy borage stems, scalped a clump of speedwell. He tied his bouquet with grass, laid it in the boot beside the drawings, then flopped back in the car.

Putney, twenty miles.

It seemed strange to be in a house again, to have roof and ceiling above him instead of boundless sky, walls hemming him in, where there had been only trees and hills for eight whole days. Lyn paced in and out of all the downstairs rooms — Matthew's rooms — with their sombre colours and heavy furniture. The house even smelt of Matthew — a smell of polish and success. Anne and Matthew were still in Tokyo, everyone else was out. Susie and Jennifer must have taken the boys on one of their expeditions — a boat on the Thames, a picnic by the sea. He felt excluded, as he had been all the summer. Yet why should they want him with them — a gloomy silent man who didn't know any jokes and had never gone ten-pin bowling or watched 'Top of the Pops'? He had tried to phone, warn them he was coming, but got no answer. All the way back across the long stifling traffic-jam of London, he had fantasised his welcome — Jennifer alone, watching for him, ready to spring up and embrace him as soon as she heard the car wheels in the drive. No one had sprung out except the next-door cat, which spat at him, then ran the other way.

He grinned, picked up a small bronze statue of a naked warrior — one of Matthew's trophies — put it down again. The whole house was a monument to Matthew. All his achievements only underlined the younger brother's failures, his sense of nothingness. Even his drawings seemed less assured now, his triumph empty posturing. In Matthew's house he was nothing — not an artist, hardly even a man. Couldn't paint, couldn't fuck. Matthew had castrated him.

He walked to the window, stared out at the sullen yew trees closing off the garden. He had to get away, save his skills before they shrivelled up again. Hester had left him nothing, not even a fiver, but Matthew owed him money from the book. He must demand it as soon as his brother returned, use it to buy their own place. Never mind dividends or interest — other things were most important now. Jennifer, for instance. He must get her out of Putney before Susie took her over, before Matthew stormed the media again and pushed her into another round of simpering and strutting. He would have to work for Matthew — other jobs were scarce and insecure — but he would work only freelance and for only half the week. Matthew valued him more now, since he had proved his worth on *Born With The Century* and the two books after it, so he could afford to make a stand. He had to give Jennifer something, find her the place in the country she had wanted all along. It couldn't be Northumberland or a house as grand as Hernhope — only a room or two, perhaps, with a scrap of garden, but at least it would be their own. *His* paintings on the walls, not these stuffy portraits and boring landscapes in their fancy gilded frames.

He walked upstairs, stopped outside the room which Anne called his and Jennifer's. Anne was wrong. The house was Matthew's — every inch of it — Matthew's finger-prints on every piece of furniture, Matthew's eyes peering through the slats of every blind. The door was half ajar, but Lyn still stood motionless outside it. He didn't want to see that double bed, the one he had used only for sleeping, and fitful sleep at that. It seemed cruel now, incredible, that he could have turned his back on Jennifer, gone so long without it. Tonight, he would change all that. Except Susie would still be there. Susie angry and taunting still, calling him a nun. Susie pregnant . . .

He walked back along the passage, paused at the foot of the narrow attic staircase which led to Susie's room; suddenly ran up. He knew she wouldn't be there. Nobody was in. Front and back doors had both been locked when he arrived, five bottles of milk curdling on the step. He opened Susie's door, stared in shock. The room was bare. No Susie mess and clutter, no clothes in the wardrobe nor make-up on the dressing-table. No dolls or teddies on the bed. Susie had decamped.

Shock turned to pain — a sudden smarting sense of loss. Stupid and irrational, when he had just been wishing Susie gone. Of course she couldn't stay. Anne and Matthew would hardly allow an unmarried teenage mother on their premises. Relief slowly flooded in, confusing him still further. He sank down on the window-seat, tried to numb the shock, swell out the relief. No more taunts or temptations. No more Susannah Jane running pale fingers up and down his groin. His wife would be his own now. Susie had always been a rival, demanding Jennifer's attention and her company, changing her views, even her style of dress. He didn't want a wife in jeans and sneakers. One of the joys of Jennifer was her clothes — soft fuzzy fabrics he could fondle, old-fashioned frilly things which lay against her skin and were perfumed from it when she took them off.

He sprang to his feet. Supposing Jennifer had left as well, paid him back for pushing off himself. She might have gone with Susie, taken her to her parents' or a friend's. He dashed down to their bedroom, laughed out loud in relief. The room was full of Jennifer — her blue shirtwaister and white lace bra draped across the bed, her absurdly fluffy slippers moulting under the dressing-table, the silver-backed hairbrush tangled with her fine fair hairs. He spread out the dress and lay on top of it, buried his face in the bodice, sniffed her scent of talc and honeysuckle. He picked up her bra. The cups were bellying slightly, as if still moulded round her breasts. He

220

kissed each cup, closed his eyes. She didn't always wear her bra — not now. That was Susie's influence. It drove him wild, the blur of her nipples beneath a blouse, the bounce and lurch of her bosom when she laughed. For weeks and weeks he'd had to look away, restrain himself, think of something else. Dared not touch her breasts. Lusted and slavered, but kept his bloody hands off. Hardly knew why, except it seemed so dangerous. Now, it was all changed. Couldn't explain that, either. Just knew he had to have her, knew it would be all right. He was stiff already. He would make love to her for hours — love her with every part of him — mind, body, soul, prick, art. Susie was gone — that would make it safer. And he could always bribe the boys to stay out late — give them money for a film or meal or something. He hadn't any money, but Jennifer would have some, even if it were only Anne's housekeeping. This was just what he had longed for — the house to himself and his wife in his arms again.

He turned his fists into breasts inside the bra-cups, swelled them out more fully. He longed to touch himself, spill out across the dress, but he must save it up for later. He stripped off his clothes, ignoring his erection. He was sweaty and grimy from eight days in the wilds. He had bathed in streams and ponds, but now he needed a good hot bath with soap and scrubbing brush.

He stepped into the steaming water, wincing as it stung his calves. His prick was still half stiff, still twitching for his wife. Jennifer was everywhere — in his head, across his body, running down the walls in tiny droplets, teasing in the fug and heat and steam. He stepped out again — he had heard a noise — car wheels in the drive, the scrunch of pebbles. He grabbed a towel, strode along the passage to the landing window. There *was* a car — Anne's car with Jennifer at the wheel. Jennifer alone.

He rushed downstairs, towel flapping, cold air on his thighs. 'Snookie!' he shouted. 'Darling.'

She jumped, said nothing, simply stared.

'I'm back! I tried to phone, but . . . Aren't you glad to see me?'

'Yes, of . . . course I am. H . . how *are* you? Is . . . everything all right?'

'Yes. wonderful,' She hadn't kissed him yet, seemed more dazed than delighted. Perhaps he had taken her by surprise, startled her a bit. He clasped her in his arms, tried to hug her close.

She pulled away.

'I'm sorry. Do I stink? That's living like a nomad for you! I was just stepping into the bath when I heard the car. Why not come upstairs with me while I scrub the grime off? Oh, Snookie, I've so much to tell you! I've only just got back and . . .' He broke off. She seemed tense and fidgety, was hardly even listening. 'What's wrong? What's the matter? I suppose you're . . . angry still. Look, I know I shouldn't have disappeared like that, but once I'd phoned you and told you where I was, I thought . . .'

'I'm not cross, Lyn — not now. I must admit I *was*, but . . .' She kissed

221

him. The kiss was brief and skimped. 'It is good to see you, especially looking so well and tanned and everything. It's just that . . .'

'You look marvellous, too. I love the freckles! You've got at least a hundred new ones.' Her eyes were a bolder blue against her sun-tanned face and arms — the blue of borage, bugloss. She was minus her bra again. The breasts would not be freckled. Pale and full like moons. He could see the shaft of white swooping down between them, contrasting with the flushed brown of her neck. 'I've brought you all sorts of things. Surprises. I've left them in the car. I didn't want the boys to see.'

'The boys aren't here.'

'So I gathered. Where are they?'

'At Mrs Briggs's. They're . . . staying the night with her.'

'What, all of them?'

'Yes.'

'That's wonderful! We'll have the whole house to ourselves. Oh, darling, I want to make it up to you. I've been a bloody misery. I didn't even *see* it — not till I was away. But now I'm going to . . .'

'Look, I'm . . . sorry, Lyn, it's marvellous to have you back — honestly it is, but I'm afraid I've got to . . . go.'

'Go? Go where?'

'I'll be back as soon as possible, I promise, but it may not be till . . .'

'But where are you going?'

'S . . . Southwark.'

'Whatever for? You don't know anyone at Southwark.'

'It's Susie. She's . . . Oh, Lyn — it's all such a muddle.' Jennifer sank down on the stairs, kicked off her sandals. Lyn took her in his arms, slipped a hand inside her tee-shirt.

'Lyn, don't — not now. I'm in such a state. Matthew phoned yesterday to say he and Anne are catching the overnight flight tomorrow and will be here first thing Sunday morning.'

'They can't be. They've got at least another week in Japan. Even two. I remember Matthew telling me he had to . . .'

'No. He's decided to cut it short. The Australian trip was a great success, apparently, but the man he wanted to see in Japan was rushed into hospital the day before he arrived there. Then Anne got ill and he's worried about some trouble in the office, so he's decided to cut his losses and come back.'

'Oh, I see. I'm . . . sorry,' Lyn tried to concentrate. The stir of his naked prick beneath the towel kept distracting him, Jennifer's long freckled legs barely covered by her flimsy skirt. 'But that still doesn't explain why you're rushing off to Southwark.'

'No. Well, yes, it does. We've got to get Susie out, you see, before they return. Matthew mustn't see she's pregnant. You know how puritanical he is. The baby hardly shows at all yet, but it will do soon. So we made up this story about Susie's mother having had a stroke or something — all very sudden — and Susie as eldest child has to go back and hold the fort. Of course, she can't go home really. Her father would be even more shocked than Matthew, and her mother's no use at all, and she's no other relations and hardly any money and . . . Oh, Lyn, I've been so *frantic*. You see, we thought we had nearly a whole fortnight to sort things out, find her a room, or a friend who'd let her stay or . . . But then Matthew phoned, and we had just a couple of days to get her off the premises. I asked Mrs Briggs to take the boys — told her Susie's mother was seriously ill and she had to go back and nurse her. The boys all believe it, of course, and *they*'re upset and . . . I loathe all this lying, but what else could I do, Lyn? Anyway, we spent all day yesterday searching for a bed-sit. They're all so expensive and slummy and . . . We didn't find a thing until this morning. It's a horrid gloomy basement in one of the grottiest parts of Southwark, but we were so desperate, we had to take it. At least the woman said Susie could move in straight away. The trouble is, she hates it. She's in a dreadful state. That's why I've got to go. I left her there, you see — in tears. She said she refused to stop without me. So I agreed to stay the first night with her, just to get her settled in — or till we thought of something else. I came back to get my night things and . . .'

The flood of words had suddenly petered out. Lyn tried to make his own voice calm and reasonable. 'So you're spending the night with Susie in a Southwark bed-sit?'

'Well, yes. No . . I mean, I didn't know you'd be *here*, Lyn. You hadn't phoned or . . . I'm sorry, but it's all been such a panic and . . .'

Her voice ran dry again. Lyn didn't answer, just gripped her hand, interlaced their fingers. 'I love you,' he said, at last. He had to fill the silence.

'Oh, Lyn, I'm so glad you understand. I mean, if Susie wasn't pregnant, it would be different, but it's bad for the baby for her to get in such a state and . . .'

'Come . . . upstairs. Just for a moment, Snookie.'

'Darling, I can't. Susie's almost hysterical. I promised I'd come straight here and straight back. In fact, I don't know how I'm going to manage. I ought to clean the house and get some food in and . . . The place looks like a pigsty, and if Anne's unwell, she'll hardly want to . . .' Jennifer was buckling back her sandals, starting towards the kitchen.

Lyn pulled her down again. 'Listen, Jennifer, we've got to get out of here. Not just Susie — all of us. I don't *want* you cleaning Matthew's house, as if you're his . . . galley-slave or something. I'm going to take a stand — demand that money he owes us, and get the hell out. While I was away, I suddenly realised how . . . wrongly we're both living. That book has ruined everything and we've got to put a stop to it.'

'Oh, Lyn.' She was hugging him now. 'I never thought you'd say that. I feel just the same myself. When I was up in Newcastle, I had a chance to

223

think a bit, and it just seemed so . . . ridiculous to be living on top of Matthew when we could have Hernhope to ourselves and a life of our own and . . . I tried to phone you and discuss it. I wanted just to run away, there and then, like you do now. Look, let me just get Susie over this crisis, and then we'll leave. Oh, darling — I can't wait to see that house again. It'll be elbow-deep in dust, of course, but once we've . . .'

'Look, I . . . didn't mean . . . *there*. Not Hernhope.'

'Why not? What *did* you mean? I don't understand. I . . .'

'Somewhere . . . else. Somewhere smaller.'

'But why, Lyn? Why bother with another place when Hernhope's there and waiting?'

'It's . . . not.'

'What are you talking about?'

'Nothing. There's . . . er . . . just a bit of a . . . legal problem still.'

'There can't be! Anyway, does it really matter? Can't we just ignore it? Molly says . . .'

'No, we can't ignore it, Jennifer'

'Well, let's get some proper advice, then. Hire a lawyer or a . . .? I mean, surely someone can settle it after all this time?'

'Well . . . maybe soon. But not soon enough for me. I've got to act immediately, while I've got the courage. I feel changed now, stronger. I've been steeling myself all week, working myself up to it. If I don't stand up to Matthew now, I never shall. Don't you see that, Jennifer? The minute he comes back, I'm going to put it to him, ask him for that money. I won't take "no" this time.'

'Oh, Lyn, I'm so relieved. I've been worried sick about the money side myself. I mean, I didn't mind until this Susie thing cropped up, but I can't pay rent out of air. As it was, I had to borrow from Anne's emergency fund and I've been lying awake at night worrying about how on earth I'd find the money every week. But if Matthew pays our royalties, then . . . You won't let him talk you out of it. You will be strong and . . .?'

'I've said that, haven't I?'

'You're marvellous, darling. I love you. When d'you think we can leave?'

'As soon as you like. As soon as we've found a pad.'

'We can have a garden, can't we? Just a little one.'

'Course.'

'We'll plant bulbs and things. A whole lawnful of daffodils.'

'No, crocuses.'

'Daffodils *and* crocuses.'

'How about a rock garden?'

'Oh, yes. All those lovely Alpine plants . . .'

'Gentians . .'

'Dianthus . .'

224

'Yes and lots more crocuses. Those Cloth of Gold ones with the tiny browny stripes.'

'Yes.'

'Kiss me.'

'Yes.'

It was a long, slow, careful, probing kiss. Jennifer pulled away, reluctantly. 'I'm sorry, darling, but I must go back to Susie. She'll be wondering where on earth I am. I won't stay long, I promise — not all night. Not now. I'm sure she'll understand. I'll just go and explain what's happened and calm her down and then come back and . . .' Jennifer scooped the car keys off the floor, retrieved her handbag, made towards the door — paused — edged back again.

'Lyn . .'

'What?'

'Could . . . Susie come?'

'Come where?'

'Well, with us. To our new place. Oh, I know I shouldn't ask you, but it *would* be a solution. I mean, not for long. Just until she's had the baby. That's only five months now — less than half a year. We could get rid of that dreadful hole in Southwark, then. Or just keep it for a month or two, until we've got our own place. Susie wouldn't mind so much if she knew it was only temporary. We could move her in with us as soon as possible and keep her sort of . . in hiding until . . . Oh, I know it's a bit of a cheek, darling, when you've quarrelled with her and . . . everything. I wouldn't even suggest it, if I wasn't so worried about her. But what else can we do? I mean it would be different if she had money or a decent stable family. Even her boyfriend's left her, or she's left him, and she doesn't seem to have a . . .'

Lyn grabbed the bannister. There wasn't room for Susie. It would be only a tiny house — all three crammed together — hot dangerous bodies touching. Four including the baby. More than four. The hall was filling now with writhing shadowy figures. Susannah Jane screaming and bloody in childbirth. Edward Arthur James snatching Hernhope like a toy and tossing it across the globe until it hit New Zealand. A two-year-old with ringlets and a smile. Susie with a smile. Susie's mouth opening wider wider wider, splitting like a cunt. He might split her even further if she lived with them — harm the baby, smash Susannah . . .

'Lyn, what d'you think, darling? I mean, if I went and told Susie now, it would cheer her up no end. Give her something to hang on to.'

'Y . . yes,' Lyn said. 'All right.' He couldn't shout or scream. He had returned to be a loving giving husband. He could feel himself shrivelling everywhere. Susie would make him a nun again. If he seized her, she would only laugh. Watch his grab turning limp and weak and stupid. She and Jennifer giggling at his impotence, whispering in corners, sharing confidences, shutting him out, betraying him.

225

'I'd . . . er . . . better have my bath.'

'Yes, you do that. I'll be as quick as I can, I promise. You *are* a darling, to be so understanding. Give me a kiss before I go.'

'No. I . . .'

'All right, keep it for me. I'll be back to claim it. 'Bye, sweetheart.'

Sweetheart. She hadn't called him that for months. Only said it now because she was thrilled about the thought of Susie living with them. She laughed with Susie — never laughed with him. Susie had giggled when he kissed her. Supposing he kissed her again? Threw her on the bed, made her a Susannah? He couldn't live with Susie. Too dangerous, too confusing. Susie swollen with another Edward, pushing him out of the nest, snatching his wife away when he had already lost his mother. All his fears returning. Jennifer returning. Dashing across the hall again. What did she want now? Come to ask if Susie could share their bed? He heaved up from the stairs.

'Lyn, Lyn! It's Matthew. He's back. He's *here* — just outside with Anne. They're paying off the taxi. What shall we do?

'Matthew?' Lyn clawed at the wall to steady himself. 'But . . . but you said he was flying back tomorrow — overnight.'

'Yes, that's right. He wasn't due to arrive till first thing Sunday morning. I was going to meet their plane. — 6.05. Terminal 3. It was all arranged.'

'Quick! Let's get out, then. Slip out of the back while they come in the front. I can't face Matthew now.'

'But you're not dressed, Lyn. You can't go out in a towel. Look, grab a mac or something, to . . .'

'No, don't. They're coming. Hide!'

'Jennifer! Hallo, my dear. Where *are* you dashing off to? Sorry to surprise you like this, but Anne took a turn for the worse, so we managed to change our tickets and come home earlier.' Matthew swept through the door, a suitcase in each hand, Anne pale and stooping behind him. 'Though I don't know why we bothered, there were so many delays. We should have been in hours ago, but these airlines are totally inefficient.' He put the cases down, kissed Jennifer on the cheek. 'You look extremely well yourself, I'm glad to say. It *is* nice to be back. Everything all right?'

'Er . . . yes. Fine. Welcome back. H . . . how was the . . . trip?'

'Good and bad. Australia was wonderful. A triumph, you might say. They were eating out of my hand by the time we left. Japan less so. We ran into a few problems there, unfortunately. Ah, Lyn — hallo. Been hiding, have you? I'm not sure I approve of the South Seas style of dress.'

'Sorry. Just had a . . . bath.' Lyn clutched the towel around him, bolted upstairs.

Jennifer longed to dash after him, smiled at Anne instead. 'Look, let me take those bags from you. You don't look well at all. How are you feeling?'

'Rotten, I'm afraid. I've had some stupid bug for the last three weeks. It

226

spoilt more than half of the trip, and even now, I can't seem to shake it off.'

'What a shame. I'm sorry. Why don't you go straight upstairs to bed? I'll sort out the cases.'

'Good idea, Anne.' Matthew removed his jacket. 'You go up and rest.'

'No, I'd rather see the boys first. I've missed them terribly. Where are they? Out with Susie?'

'They . . . er . . . won't be long. Let me make you a cup of tea or something. You must be exhausted after the journey.'

'That would be nice. I've been longing for some proper English tea. How is Susie, by the way? I hope she's been some use.' Anne had followed Jennifer into the kitchen and was glancing around at the pile of dirty dishes, the cooker splashed with grease.

'Oh, yes. A great help.'

'Where's she taken the boys?'

'She . . . er . . . hasn't.'

'Where is she, then?'

'I'm afraid she's . . . Well, she . . . I mean, she had to . . . leave. This morning.'

'Leave?' Matthew had swooped into the kitchen. 'What do you mean?'

'It's her . . . mother. She was taken ill. A stroke. It was all quite unexpected. The . . . er . . . father phoned and said Susie had to return immediately.'

'Oh dear, I am sorry.' Anne sat down, her face ashen beside Matthew's sallow one.

'Look, you ought to go to bed, Anne. You look awfully pale, you know. I'll bring your tea up.'

'No, really, thanks. I'd rather have it here. I want to know what's going on. When did all this happen?'

'Just this morning. About . . . ten o'clock Susie had the call, and she was on the train by lunchtime.'

'Poor girl. What a shock for her. Did she have enough money for the fare? It's quite a distance, isn't it, Great Yarmouth?'

'Yes. We . . er . . took it from your emergency fund. I hope you don't mind. It was all such a rush, you see, and . . .'

'No, that's quite all right. That's what it's there for. Is her mother expected to . . .? I mean, d'you think there's any chance of Susie coming back here?'

'Well, not for a . . . while, I shouldn't think. I mean, there's all the other children to look after, all younger, and . . .'

Matthew was pacing up and down in front of the window, blocking out the light. 'Well, it is *most* unfortunate. I mean, to lose er at this time — with Anne unwell and the boys needing all their school things sorting out. Where are they, did you say?'

'At . . . er . . . Mrs Briggs.'

227

'Mrs Briggs? We *never* let them go there! Charlie Briggs's language leaves a lot to be desired, and Mrs Briggs may *call* herself a cleaner, but her own house doesn't show much sign of it. She doesn't appear to have done much here, in fact.'

'No. Well — I . . . let her have some time off. She kept complaining that . . .'

'*I* decide her holidays, Jennifer, if you don't mind. She's a born complainer. What you should have done was . . .'

Lyn had slipped into the kitchen, now dressed in corduroys and a shirt. 'Look here, Matthew, Jennifer's worked bloody hard all summer. Taken the boys out, mended and cooked and cleaned for them, done the garden, dealt with Mrs Briggs, and all you can do is start . . .'

Anne got up. 'We're *very* grateful, Lyn. Of course, we are. We couldn't have managed without you both.' She reeled, clutched the table. 'Oh dear, I do feel dizzy. I think I'd better go and rest.'

She closed the door. Matthew frowned. 'I'm going to phone the doctor in the morning. Make sure she has a really thorough check-up. We only saw some . . . quack out there, who seems to have made her worse. She's missed the boys, of course. She's never left them so long before and I think it's been upsetting her. They're all well, I hope?'

'Oh, yes. Thriving. Look, I'll go and fetch them shall I? It might cheer her up to see them.'

'That *is* kind, Jennifer. Thank you.'

Lyn saw her to the car. 'Listen,' she whispered to him. 'I only said I'd go so I'd have an excuse to call on Susie. I'll race to Southwark first and warn her what's happened, then go and fetch the boys. You keep Matthew happy. If he wonders why I'm gone so long, make up some excuse. All right?'

Lyn nodded, walked slowly back to the kitchen. Matthew had gone upstairs to Anne. He picked up Jennifer's cup, sipped her tea. He must imbibe her strength, her resourcefulness. This could be their last month in Matthew's house, the end of Matthew's tutelage, if only he didn't weaken.

Matthew was standing at the door. 'Anne's half asleep already. I'm afraid this trip's exhausted her. I like to keep up the pace, but she's less used to it, especially in the heat. *You* look well, Lyn. You've caught the sun, I see.'

'Yes.'

'Everything all right in the office?'

'More or less, I think. I . . . er . . . haven't been there for a week or so. I took some . . . leave, as you suggested.'

'Good, good. You'll be nicely rested for our next project. I've got some very exciting plans. *Born With The Century* has really taken off in Australia and they're talking about a sequel. Something built round Jennifer, this time, rather than Hester. A sort of self-sufficiency book for the modern woman. There's a lot of interest in Jennifer, you know. In fact, I'm hoping to take her with me on another foreign tour. I had a long talk with the publicity man at . . .'

'*No.*' Lyn said. Jennifer's tea was only dregs now. He could see half a face in the tea-leaves. A battered face.

'Now, be a good chap, Lyn. You mustn't stand in Jennifer's way, you know.'

'She doesn't want it herself — never did.'

'This is completely different. A chance to see the world, broaden her horizons. We can keep her schedule very undemanding, if that's what you . . .'

'I said "no".'

'Surely that's for Jennifer to say.'

'We've already discussed it. We've just been talking, in fact, half an hour ago. We've both had more than enough of the book. We want to get away, buy our own place.'

'Of course you do. I know that. It's all part of my plan. I'm investing your money with that in mind. But you ought to wait a while. Summer's never a good time for buying property. Leave it till Christmas and you'll get a better buy, and there'll be more money in the kitty anyway. You should be able to afford something with some character — even a bit of ground. And meanwhile you can stay on here, and if I need Jennifer for any more publicity, then she's right on the spot and . . .'

'I'm sorry, Matthew, she's not doing any more. We've made up our minds. I want that money you owe me — *now*, not Christmas time — and I want it in cash, not promises or investments or useless bits of paper.'

'Lyn, I've only just walked in, for heaven's sake. I've been travelling for more than eighteen hours, plus all those long delays. It's a little unreasonable to make demands like this before I've even had a . . . wash.'

'I wouldn't need to make them if you'd paid me my share of the royalties all along.'

'That's hardly fair, Lyn. We agreed that I'd invest your . . .'

'*You* agreed. I didn't.'

'Look, let's have a sherry, shall we? Calm down a bit.'

'I'm calm, thanks. And I'd better warn you, Matthew, whatever you say, Jennifer and I are leaving the minute we've found another place to live. We've agreed on that. We must be on our own. I've hardly seen my wife all summer, she's been so busy with the boys and the house and . . . But now you're back, there's no reason for us to stay here. In fact, it's probably best we leave immediately. Decide on the area we want to live and rent a room there while we do our house-hunting. There'll be far less travelling, that way. We can even treat it as a sort of . . . holiday.'

'It sounds most impractical to me, and hardly fair at the moment with Anne unwell. She can't cope from her sick-bed, not with Susie gone. She

229

needs looking after herself.'

'Well, Jennifer's not the one who's going to do it. She's done enough. You'll have to hire some help, Matthew. You can easily afford it — a nanny *and* a nurse — and a decent cleaner as well, if you're so browned off with your present one. Mrs Briggs has got her grievances, too, you know. I heard her telling Jennifer she's very rarely paid on time. Perhaps you're investing *her* money.'

'That's not funny. I feel quite upset, Lyn, to hear you talking like this after all the trouble I've taken with your affairs. Jennifer particularly asked me to look after the financial side.'

'I wasn't aware of that.'

'Maybe not. There are quite a lot of things you're not aware of. Which perhaps is why your wife prefers to trust *me* on money matters.'

'Are you suggesting that . . .'

'I'm not suggesting anything. I merely feel that my superior knowledge and experience of the . . . Good God! Must the boys slam the front door like that? I've told them a hundred times. They'll break the . . .'

'Jen . . . Jen! Where the bloody hell are you? You *said* you'd come. You said you wouldn't leave me. I've spent all my fucking money on a taxi and now I've . . . Jennifer!'

Susie burst into the kitchen, tears streaming down her cheeks, a long and grubby raincoat billowing over bare legs and gym shoes. She stopped dead, stared at Lyn and Matthew. 'Oh, Christ!' she said and began to back away.

Matthew lunged towards her. 'Susie! What are you doing here? I understood you were on the train to Great Yarmouth.'

'Yeah . . . yeah, I was.' Susie spoke in little gasping sobs. 'I . . . er . . . got off again . . . came back.'

'Came back? But I thought your mother was ill. Gravely ill.'

'She is. Yeah . . . that's right.' Susie wiped her nose on her sleeve, sniffed, gulped, tried to get control of her voice. 'I got . . . scared, though. You know, thinking about it — death and stuff. Jennifer said she'd come with me — on the . . . train, I mean. Just as . . . company. I . . . er . . . told her not to bother, but then I changed my mind and . . . Where *is* she? I *want* her to come now.'

'I'm sorry, Susie, but I'm afraid that won't be possible. Jennifer's needed here — at least until we've arranged some alternative help. Anne's very unwell, you see. Now come along, my dear, don't cry. I'll drive you to the station. You can travel first-class, if you like. You'll be quite all right once you're settled in a nice comfortable carriage with a book and a cup of coffee and . . .'

'No, I won't. I can't. I . . .'

Lyn got up himself. He had to *do* something. Susie and Jennifer had obviously missed each other, Jennifer tearing off to Southwark just as Susie was hailing a taxi to come and find her. Jennifer would never forgive him if

230

he left Susie and Matthew together and Susie blurted something out. 'Look, I'll drive her, Matthew. You've only just got in. I've got to go out anyway and . . .'

Susie tossed her hair back. 'I don't w . . want either of you to take me anywhere. I've got to speak to Jennifer.'

'She's not here, Susie.'

'Of course she is. You're lying. She's upstairs, I bet, fussing over your precious Anne. I'm going to find her.'

'No, you're not!' Matthew started after her, grabbed her by the raincoat tail. 'Anne's asleep and I don't want her disturbed.'

Susie tried to shake him off. Matthew was left with a limp and empty raincoat in his hands, while Susie darted free towards the stairs. Both men stared at her in shock. She had nothing on beneath the mac save a blue gingham nightdress which barely covered her thighs. One of the shoulder straps was sagging, the other fastened with a safety-pin. Lyn felt a sudden shudder of excitement. He had glimpsed her breasts, bare almost to the nipples. He wanted to undo that pin, wrench down the other strap. He turned away. The fear was there again. They were *pregnant* breasts. If Susie came to live with them, her huge bloated belly would swell to fill the house, trap him against the walls, flatten him to nothing.

He slunk back into the kitchen. Matthew followed. He had Susie by the arm, and was draping the raincoat over her. 'Susie, make yourself decent at once. What *are* you doing in your night attire? I can hardly believe you were travelling in public like that, half . . . naked. And what about your luggage? All right, there's no need to start crying again. You've had a shock — I realise that. You probably got confused. Now, listen, my dear, we're all here to help you. It's distressing news about your mother, but you must calm down. You'll be no use to her at all in this state. Now why don't you wash your face and put on something sensible and . . .'

'I've packed all my clothes. They're . . .'

Lyn tried to drag his gaze from Susie's thighs, still uncovered by the mac. He must get Susie away from Matthew, tell her where Jennifer was and what had happened. On the other hand, he shouldn't be alone with her. Supposing she tried to . . . 'Look, Susie, why don't you . . . borrow a dress of . . . Jennifer's? She won't mind. C . . . come upstairs with me and I'll dig you something out.'

Matthew frowned. 'Well, don't wake Anne. She's hardly slept at all the last two nights.'

'It's all right. I'm awake.' Anne's voice echoed plaintive from the hall. 'I heard the noise. What's up?' Anne was also in her nightdress, a long white Victorian one which made her look still paler. 'Susie! What *are* you doing back? And half undressed! What's happened, dear?'

Susie was bent over the table, shoulders shaking, hair trailing across the teacups.

231

'Don't cry.' Anne smoothed her hair back. 'Is your mother worse? Look, try and quieten down a bit and tell me what's the matter.'

'No, I can't, I can't. You'll . . . never understand.' Susie rubbed her eyes, blew her nose. 'Where's J . . . Jennifer? Please tell me where she is.'

Lyn was hovering by Susie's chair. 'She won't be long. She's only gone to . . .'

'Well, she shouldn't have gone anywhere. I'm bloody pissed off with her. She promised she'd . . .'

'Susie, please. Pull yourself together.' Matthew was taking over now. 'Anne's very unwell herself. She needs some peace and quiet, not all this uproar.'

Susie sprang up from the table. 'Stuff Anne! She's just had six whole weeks lolling about in the sunshine, and then you have the cheek to say she's ill. *I*'m ill. I feel sick and dizzy and faint and . . . If you really want to know, I'm . . .'

Lyn was almost shouting. 'Shut up, Susie.'

'Yes, *you* join in. That's all I need. You don't give a shit about me — any of you — you least of all, Lyn. I asked you to help me, didn't I — and what did you do — run off like a cry-baby. I'm sick of the lot of you. No, leave me, Anne. You're ill. You've got to rest after all that hard grind in a five-star hotel with nothing to do but lie about and sip champagne and . . .'

'That's not fair, Susie. It's not. I *have* been working hard. And I d . . . do feel rotten. I've g . . . got a . . .' Anne's voice was cracking up, tears stabbing down her cheeks. She lurched from the room, collided with Hugh and Oliver who were stampeding towards the kitchen.

'Mum! What's wrong? What's happened? You're crying.'

'N . . . nothing.' Anne hugged them, tried to hide her face. 'How are you, darlings? I've missed you.' She was kissing all four boys at once.

Hugh suddenly pulled free. 'Hey, look! There's Susie. Susie's back. She's crying too. Her mother must have died. Is that why you're upset, Mum? Charles, Robert, listen! Susie's mother's dead, I think. Everybody's crying.'

Robert burst into tears himself. 'Oh, no! I don't *want* her to die. I prayed she wouldn't die. I asked God not to l . . . let her . . .'

Matthew grabbed him by the sleeve. 'Robert! Control yourself. Nobody's dead at all. Charles, will you please come here and . . .'

Jennifer stepped into the hall, loaded down with all the boys' bags, her forehead creased with worry. 'Lyn, I must see Lyn. *Susie!* You're here. Thank God! I've . . . What's the matter, Anne? What on earth is going on? Why is everybody crying? Susie, you haven't . . .'

'Her mother's dead.'

'She's *not* dead.'

'Mrs Briggs said . . .'

'Fuck Mrs Briggs! I've got this lousy pain and . . .'

'Susie, I will not have you using language like that in front of . . .'

'Why is Mummy in her nightie?'

'Where in fuck's name have you been, Jen? You promised you'd come back and . . .'

'Susie, I've warned you once already. Would you . . .'

'Susie's in her nightie, too.'

'Shall we get in pyjamas?'

'Don't be stupid. It's only teatime.'

'What's for tea?'

'You can't eat tea when people are dead.'

'They're *not* dead.'

'Listen, Jen, if you change your mind now, when . . .'

Lyn leapt up from his chair, rocketed into the hall. 'Shut *up*!' he yelled. 'The lot of you! I can't stand a minute more of this. Get to your rooms, boys — all of you. Go on, get out, before I . . .'

There was a sudden deafening silence. Everybody stared. Lyn had never taken charge before, never given orders, least of all in Matthew's presence in Matthew's house. The boys slunk away, scared and disbelieving. The silence tautened, broken only by a muffled wail from Susie, a gasping breath from Anne.

Lyn was trembling. He fled up the stairs, stopped, paused, turned to face them, slowly stumbled down again. 'Listen. I want you to h . . . hear this — all of you — so that you can't pretend you didn't understand or . . . Jennifer and I are . . . *going*. Not this minute. We'll stay and help you unpack this evening and clear up the house and . . . I'll phone a few agencies, if you like, and try and get you a nurse or a . . . housekeeper or something. But after that, we're leaving — first thing in the morning. Is that clear?'

Jennifer ran up to him. 'Lyn, *no*,' she whispered. 'Not now — not with Anne ill and . . .'

'You *can't* leave,' Susie yelled. 'You can't! Jennifer promised she wouldn't . . .'

'Now look, old chap, do be reasonable. I quite understand that you want to be on your . . .'

'Is that clear, Matthew?'

Lyn pushed Susie out of the way, seized the two heaviest suitcases and staggered upstairs with them. No one moved. The phone rang suddenly, shrilling through the hall. Nobody answered it. They were like carved and rigid figures on a frieze. Matthew broke out of the picture, marched to his study, closed the door. The ringing stopped.

Susie clutched her stomach. 'Jen, please help! I've got such a lousy pain, I think I'm going to throw up.'

'Go to the downstairs cloakroom then.' Jennifer's voice was very quiet. 'I'll be with you in a minute.' She picked up the last of the luggage and took it up to Matthew's room.

She found Lyn with his back to her, standing in their own room by the window, staring out.

'You shouldn't have said that, Lyn — not with everybody so upset and . . .'

He didn't turn round. 'You told me to say it. You begged me to be strong.'

'Yes, strong, but not . . . callous. We can't just walk out on Anne when she's . . .'

'If she's really ill, then Matthew can hire a nurse for her. I'm not c . . . callous, Jennifer, but if we stay on now, there'll never be an end to it. We'll be tied down here for ever.'

'Yes, but Susie . . . She's in a dreadful state. She'll never stay at Southwark now. And what about Anne and Matthew? They're expecting me to put her on a train and pack her off to her mother's.'

'It would be better if you did.'

'Oh, Lyn, you know she can't go there. They'll turn her out the minute they find she's . . . pregnant.'

Lyn's hands were trembling on the window-frame. 'There are hostels, aren't there? And social workers and special grants and . . . We've got a welfare state, Jennifer.'

'Susie doesn't want all that.'

'She doesn't have much choice. Either that, or stand on her own two feet.'

'Lyn, she's still in her teens, for heaven's sake. You can't expect her to manage on her own when she's not even married or . . .'

Lyn rammed his fist against the window-frame. 'Hester bloody did.'

Jennifer backed away. The sun was streaming through the window, unconcerned. An aeroplane roared overhead. She waited for its vibration to die away. Lyn's three last words were still throbbing underneath it. 'W . . . *what* did you say, Lyn?'

'Nothing. I d . . . don't know what I'm saying. You're confusing me. This whole day's been a . . . nightmare. It's all the more proof we can't stay here. The place is like a madhouse. We'll never have a moment's peace if we . . .'

'You said "Hester managed".'

'No, I didn't. I . . .'

'You did, Lyn. What d'you mean? Y . . . you don't know about . . .'

'About what?'

'Oh, forget it.'

'No, tell me what you were going to say.'

'It doesn't matter.'

'Yes, it does.'

234

The silence was thick, like gum. Lyn walked slowly to the bed, sank down on it. 'Snookie,' he said. 'Come here.' He took her hand, pulled her down beside him. 'You mean, y . . . *you* know, too?' He wanted her to know, to share it with him. Was that why he had let it out?

Jennifer swallowed. 'I'm n . . . not quite sure if we're talking about the . . . same thing.'

'Hester?'

'Yes.'

'Hester's . . . *baby*?'

'Yes.'

'Her . . . first baby?'

'Yes.' Jennifer sprang up. 'Oh, God! You mean, Matthew *told* you? How could he? He promised faithfully he wouldn't breathe a . . .'

'What you talking about?'

'Lyn, I'm horrified. I mean, I know Matthew's overbearing, even a bit of a . . . bully, sometimes, but I never thought he'd break his word, not after I'd . . .'

'What is all this? Matthew hasn't said a thing . . .'

'Oh, I see. I'm . . . sorry. I thought . . . But how did you know, then?'

'I found . . . a letter.'

'What sort of letter? Where? When? Who from?'

'Never mind. What's far more important is how you and Matthew knew.' Lyn had got up himself now, and was pacing up and down in front of the window.'

'It was . . . in the diaries.'

'It wasn't! There's not a single word about it, not in all that stack of notebooks. My mother wasn't like that. She didn't blab or . . .'

Jennifer shut her eyes, leant against the chest of drawers. 'There was just . . . one page, Lyn.'

'Which page? I never saw it.'

'N . . . no.'

'Where is it, then?'

'M . . . Matthew's got it.'

'*Matthew*?'

'Yes, I . . . gave it to him.'

'You *gave* it to him? To Matthew?'

'Yes.' Jennifer went up to him — had to stop him pacing — took his hand, gripped his fingers. 'You see, when I first found the diaries . . . in the cellar, I was reading through them all, and I came across this . . . page — just a line or two, that's all it was, recording the baby's birth. It was a . . . shock, Lyn — even for me. You'd had shocks enough — the funeral and . . . everything. I didn't want to upset you any more, so I . . . tore it out and . . .'

'Tore it out?' He felt like a parrot repeating all her words, a dumb, stupid parrot with its claws clipped, chained up on a perch.

'I'm sorry. It was . . . wrong, I know, but you were in such a . . . state already, darling, and then when Matthew wanted to publish, I was scared he might find out, or might even know himself, or . . .'

'So you . . . "confessed" to Matthew?'

'Y . . . yes.'

'And told him not to tell me?'

'Well, yes, Lyn, . . . but only because I didn't want to hurt you. I wasn't aware you knew, you see. You'd never said or . . .'

'I see. You assumed I knew nothing about such a vital event in my mother's life — in my *own* life, for God's sake — and yet instead of telling me, putting me right about it, trying to help me understand and accept and cope and come to terms with it, you shared the news with . . . Matthew.'

'It wasn't like that, Lyn. I was simply trying to . . . I mean, I never thought you'd . . . Look, let's not discuss it now. I ought to go down to Susie. I promised her I'd . . .'

'*Damn* Susie! Look, I want to know exactly what . . .' He broke off. He was gripping the bedhead so hard, his hand was marked with little ridges. Didn't want to hurt him, she had said — then gone on to kick him into the gutter. Ganged up with Matthew against him. Joined the enemy. His head was reeling. A pneumatic drill was braying from some roadworks down the street. It seemed to move in closer now, boring into his skull. All his certainties crumbling into rubble. Jennifer — his wife, his ally, the one person he had trusted, had turned to Matthew instead of him, had deliberately concealed from him such a crucial personal matter. And not just for a day or two, while she recovered from the shock herself, or decided what to do, but for a whole year — more than a year. All that time, she and Matthew had been sharing secrets, drawing closer, discussing a bastard baby which he had only stumbled on a week or so ago. He remembered all the occasions they had been closeted alone together — ostensibly discussing publicity for the Book. God alone knew what they had really been discussing, what other vital issues they had kept strictly between the two of them.

He remembered Matthew's words now, spoken less than half an hour ago, and with such apparent artlessness. 'There are a *lot* of things you're not aware of . . .' 'Perhaps your wife prefers to trust *me* on . . .' He had hardly listened, shrugged them off. How had he been so blind? His wife and his half-brother were obviously more intimate than he had ever realised. What else had Matthew said? 'Jennifer particularly asked me to look after the financial side . . .'

Oh, she had, had she? So she didn't trust *him* on money matters. He was just a child, a fool. 'Trying to protect you,' she had said. 'Don't want to upset you.' Matthew had always patronised him, but for his wife to join in as well . . . They despised him — that was obvious — and they had protected him from nothing. In fact, by keeping him in ignorance, they had increased his shock, his stunned sense of betrayal, when he finally

236

discovered Edward in the Will. He had tried to bury that baby, hide it from the world, yet all the time it had been bawling in Matthew and Jennifer's arms? Did they know about the Will, as well, know he was disinherited?

Jennifer came up to him, put her arms around him. 'Lyn — darling, please don't be upset. I didn't realise you'd . . .'

He shook her off. He should have known he couldn't trust her. She had already blabbed to Susie, told her things which were strictly fiercely private, split about their non-existent sex life. Susie had called him a nun, used disloyal insulting words which she could only have heard from Jennifer. He had tried to blot them out, even blame himself because he was the one who was denying her in bed, but now he realised she had betrayed him all along. Run him down to Susie while pretending that she loved him.

The sun had disappeared, the sky looked pale and swollen. There was a cold lumpy silence in the room. Jennifer made another move towards him. 'Linnet . . .'

'Don't call me that.'

'Please try and understand. I . . . love you, darling.'

'I'm sure you do. It's very loving, isn't it, to give Susie a full detailed record of all my . . . failures. I believe you also discussed with her what . . . positions I liked best and how I hurt you when I . . . buggered you — that was the word she used.'

Jennifer was scarlet, floundering. He longed for her to deny it — knew she wouldn't, couldn't. 'I wasn't . . . aware I'd hurt you that way, and I'm . . . sorry if it's true. But I'd rather you told . . . me about it, not shared our intimate life with Susie or Matthew or . . .' He turned away. The pneumatic drill had stopped now, but had left ugly gaping holes. His straight and honest wife had betrayed his trust twice over, his stern and upright mother been proved a hypocrite. Nothing was pure or straightforward any more. Even Susannah was polluted — tangled up with Susie — Susie Jane. There was no one he could trust. He had always admired his wife as totally honourable — the sort of person who would never snoop or gossip or read other people's letters or betray a confidence. But now . . .

Was he over-reacting? Damning her too harshly? He could hardly think straight. He tried to review the arid months which had passed since Hester's death and Jennifer's miscarriage. Wasn't it obvious that his wife had been withdrawing from him? He had lost her first to Matthew, now to Susie. He had blamed it on the book, at first, but it was more than that, he realised now. Jennifer didn't take him seriously, scarcely needed him. All the crucial issues she reserved for Matthew's judgement, all the lighter ones she preferred to discuss with Susie. Even the book itself was more of a sham than it appeared. He had always known that Matthew had doctored the diaries ('editing', he called it) and had passed Susannah's drawings off as Hester's, but it was a new shock to realise that both Jennifer and Matthew had been willing to present Hester as a pure and virtuous woman

237

when they knew full well about her secret past. He had been right to oppose the very idea of publication, but, even there, his wife had sided with Matthew against him.

'Lyn, listen, my darling — *please.*'

Lyn swung round, stared. Jennifer had been towering in his thoughts like an Amazon, but she now looked small and vulnerable, one foot twisted round the other, hands trembling, her whole face contorted with concern. He almost weakened. He could smell her scent, see the tiny mole on the left side of her neck. *His* mole. He had kissed it so often, he had made it his. He touched her fingers, just for a second. 'Snookie . . .'

'Yes, I'm here, darling. I love you. You mustn't think I'm . . .' Her voice was blitzed by a pounding on the door.

'Jen! Where are you? You promised you'd come down. I've sicked almost my whole guts up.' Susie burst in, her nightdress flecked with vomit, her face totally drained of colour. 'And I still feel lousy and Robert's in floods of tears and Anne says she thinks she's going to . . .'

Lyn elbowed his wife aside, strode to the door himself. 'I'm sorry, Susie. I really am. I know you're not well and I wish we could help, but we're leaving — now — this minute.'

Jennifer grabbed his arm. 'Lyn — no! I can't walk out on Susie. I . . .'

'So you'd prefer to walk out on me?'

'Of course not, darling. But . . .'

'Well, I'm not staying here — not in all this uproar. I think we ought to cut our losses and . . .'

'All right — we'll go if you insist — but all of us. Susie as well.'

Lyn turned on his heel, walked slowly back to the window. 'No.' he said. His voice was very quiet.

Susie flung herself on the bed. 'Forget it! I don't care. I'm not going where I'm not wanted. I'd rather die. I'd rather . . .'

Jennifer hovered between the two of them. 'Susie, don't say that. You *are* wanted. Of course you are. It's just that Lyn feels . . .'

There was a sudden shriek outside the door. 'Auntie Jen, please come.' Hugh was panting on the landing, socks around his ankles. 'Mummy's fainted. She's gone all white and sort of . . . numb. Daddy's phoning the doctor but I'm scared she might . . .'

Jennifer squeezed Lyn's hand, then dashed out after Hugh. 'Wait, Lyn, darling, please. I'll be back in just a moment.'

She had already disappeared, Susie loping after her, groping along the passage, clutching her stomach. Lyn watched her go, softly shut the door.

He picked up Jennifer's dress — silky perfumed dress, the same blue as her eyes — buried his face in it, pressed it against his lips. He stood totally still for a moment — eyes closed, barely breathing — then unclasped his hands, let it fall. It billowed out a moment, sank limply to the ground. He walked round it, opened the wardrobe, took out his jacket with the cheque-book in the pocket, a shirt or two, a sweater — stuffed them in a bag.

The staircase was deserted. All the drama was in Anne and Matthew's room. He could hear the voices floating up and back behind him — Matthew hectoring, the boys panicking and squabbling, only Jennifer calm. They *needed* her.

He slipped out the back way, crept round to his car. The lawn looked more brown than green. There were dead heads on the roses. The golden-rod had tarnished, tall fronds bent and sagging. Summer was over. The first yellow leaves were blemishing the beech hedge. He opened the boot, picked up Jennifer's flowers. He sniffed them. They smelt of petrol and decay. All the blues had faded, leaves wilting, petals falling. They were summer flowers, so had perished with the summer. He tossed the whole bouquet into a holly bush, turned to his stack of drawings, sorted through the pile — trees, fields, landscapes, skies. They seemed pointless now, pathetic. Rubbish drawn on rubbish. He stared at the flattened chicken carton, the grubby paper bags. Only a dumb-fool amateur would have wasted his time on trash like that.

He picked up his whole week's work, crushed it between his hands, wrenched and pummelled it until it was a less overweening size. He carried the wreckage to Matthew's dustbin, lifted up the lid. The bin was almost full. Empty cans, broken bottles, eggshells, tea-leaves, rotting vegetables. He stuffed the paintings in, ramming the rubbish down with them, wrinkling his nose against the smell of garbage. Mouldy beetroot bled across his skyscapes, coffee grounds made black bogs in his fields.

As he drove away, he glanced in his mirror to see if anyone had seen him. Jennifer's face at a window, Jennifer's cry, 'Come back!'

No one. Nothing. Only the next-door cat sneaking behind a clump of crippled lupins and one brown beech leaf fluttering to the ground.

XVIII

'All men are guilty of rape . . .'

Jennifer jumped. Her mind had been elsewhere — on Lyn, as always. It was traitorous for her to be longing for a man when the leader of the Women's Group was denouncing them so vehemently. Jo relished the word rape. She had never had a man herself, condemned the entire male sex without personal experience, denouncing it as brutal and oppressive.

Jennifer glanced across at her — grey hair, putty face, long bony feet with yellowed toenails. Jo was wearing open sandals in late October and a grubby dirndl skirt — no tights, no scrap of make-up. Her hair was teased

239

into a coarse and frizzy Afro-cut like a grizzled ball of wool let loose among a colony of wildcats. She had been a radical feminist before feminism was fashionable or radicalism accepted, had trained as a librarian, switched to social work, and now styled herself a sex therapist. Probably a compensation for a life without *any* sex, thought Jennifer unkindly.

Jo was reading now from a revolutionary statement by a group of radical lesbians.

'*Heterosexual intercourse is an act of vital symbolical significance by which the oppressor enters the body of the oppressed . . .*'

Jennifer tried to concentrate. She could see *Lyn*'s body — lean, pale, hard, worshipping. The only opression was that it hadn't entered her, not for months, months, months, and was even less likely to do so now, when they were no longer under the same roof and hadn't even seen each other for nearly seven weeks. It still seemed unbelievable that the two of them had separated — not formally, not even by deliberate choice or inclination, but simply through a series of crises.

When she realised that he had gone, packed his things and simply driven off that crazy confusing Friday in the first week of September, with Anne lying white and still upstairs and Matthew working off his jet-lag on the boys, she had felt shock, resentment, relief and misery, all mixed up and churning. He had phoned her the next morning from a call-box. He had already driven a hundred miles or so, sounded strange, disorientated, still bitter and distrustful. Yet he begged her to join him, cut her links with Matthew. He made it like a test case. If she loved him, she'd obey — honour her marriage vows, put her husband first. If not . . .

Yet it wasn't quite that simple. Anne was ill. She was acting nurse. She had been rallying round the bedside when the phone rang.

'Of *course* I love you, Lyn, but it's difficult to talk just now. Dr Cooper's here, you see. No, Matthew's gone to the office. Yes, I know it's Saturday, but he had to see a . . . Yes, I realise that, but there's no one else to hold the fort here. All right. I will. I promise. Look, I'll have to go. I'm sorry, darling, but the doctor's coming down now.'

Lyn had phoned again the next day and the next. Anne was making progress. The drugs had worked dramatically, and she was already sitting up and taking food. Susie had been coaxed into her Southwark hideaway by a combination of threats and blandishments, Mrs Briggs was back on form, the boys preparing for school. She could leave now, could join him — so long as she squared it first with Susie, made sure she understood.

She took the bus to Southwark, found Susie pale and irritable, hunched in a corner, smoking.

'Look what the cat's brought in! I never thought you'd tear yourself away from all the family.'

Jennifer tried to ignore the taunts, cheer Susie with the news that at least they were in funds. Matthew had obviously been shocked by Lyn's outburst and departure, and had responded with a surprising open-handedness. He had given her an immediate sum in cash and then gone on to deposit money in Lyn's bank account, with a promise of more to come. The three of them could share it, Jennifer said. She was committed now to buying a house with Lyn, but that didn't mean she wouldn't have time to help Susie find a better flat in a nicer part of the country, perhaps not too far from them. Susie might even find a flatmate, a girl in the same position, maybe, who could pay half the rent and provide some company and . . .

Susie hadn't answered, just heaved her suitcase down from the top of the wardrobe.

'What are you doing?'

'Nothing. Don't worry about *me*. You save yourself for your precious Lyn.' Susie wrenched the top drawer from the dressing-table, staggered with it to the bed and tipped all its contents out onto the counterpane.

Jennifer jumped up. 'Careful! You mustn't lift heavy weights like that. You'll harm the baby.'

'Good!'

'Don't say things like that, Susie. It's wrong. I read somewhere that even foetuses have feelings and can sort of . . . pick up atmospheres and . . .'

'I shouldn't worry, if I was you. Even if it's heard every fucking word I've said — which, frankly, I think is piffle — it won't have much longer to brood about it.'

'W . . . what d'you mean?'

'Well, if you really want to know, I've decided to get rid of the kid.'

'You've . . . *what*?'

'Pull the plug on the little blighter. Flush it out. It's not that difficult. Someone gave me an address the other day. You know, one of those backstreet hags in Soho.'

Jennifer clutched at the wall for support. She felt faint, sick. 'Susie, you can't, you *must*n't. It's far too late for that. It's . . . murder. It's . . .'

'OK, so I'm a murderer. You get off to Lyn before he wastes his precious money on another phonecall. And how about dear Anne? Isn't it time for her supper or her pills? She'll be ringing that little bell of hers and . . .'

Jennifer burst into tears. Susie followed suit. They wept and stormed for half an hour. In the end, Jennifer did return to Putney, but only for one night, spent an anguished evening packing up her things. She prayed that Lyn would phone so that she could try and make him understand, beg him to be an alibi. Anne and Matthew must think she was leaving to join him, not sneaking back to Susie. They were out for the evening, with the boys, had invited her to join them, but she had pleaded a bad headache. By ten o'clock, her head was truly pounding. Lyn still hadn't phoned. How could she leave in the morning without explaining her plans to him, or giving him her Southwark address? And what about her alibi? She couldn't leave at all unless he agreed to support her story.

At ten past ten, the phone rang. Her mouth was so dry, she could hardly say hallo. It was a friend of Charles checking up on a school project which they were meant to have completed in the summer break. At twenty past, it rang again. This time she didn't hurry.

'Yes, hallo. I'm sorry, I can't hear you. Could you speak up, please. *Lyn*! Thank God. Where *are* you?' All his calls were from different parts of the country. He was driving north, south, east, west, in aimless frenzied circles. The pips went twice before she had even begun to explain.

'I don't know what to *do*, darling. I would come if I could — please believe me. But it's Susie, you see. She's . . .'

Blackmail. That's what Susie had tried. Tried and got away with it. Jennifer dared not call her bluff. She could still get rid of the baby. She hardly knew why Susie's child was so precious. Except it felt almost like her own child.

*   *   *

The next day she left for Southwark — more for the baby's sake than Susie's — crept out of Putney like a criminal. Fortunately, the boys had returned to school that morning and all the rush and bustle of a new school term helped divert attention from her own tense and restless state. She waited till everyone had gone — Anne and Matthew safely in the office, even Mrs Briggs departed after her morning's cleaning. The official story was that Lyn was picking her up in the car at half-past one, and they were driving up to Bedfordshire to the tiny flat he had rented until they found a permanent home. At half-past one, she staggered down the basement steps at Southwark with a suitcase and three bulging plastic bags.

Susie was waiting with a litre of Oddbin's Beaujolais and three cream doughnuts still in their paper bag.

'One each and one for the baby, and you're a bloody angel, Jen, and I love *love* you and I promise I'll be good and do the washing-up and drink my rotten milk, but right now, let's open the plonk.'

They got high that evening. It was the only thing to do, when Jennifer's head was whirling from all the lies and deceptions she had strewn like weeds at Putney, and which could grow tall and rank and choke her in their tangles. Supposing Matthew decided to visit the Bedfordshire flat? Fortunately, he was always too busy for visits and Anne had been told to rest and so was limiting her activities to a shorter day at the office and no extra travel or upheaval. But either of them might spot her still in London, or — horrors — still with Susie. There was also the danger of Lyn. Would he support her story, as she had begged him to during that last traumatic phonecall, (which had been interrupted by the whole family returning) or become so jealous and resentful that he would blow the thing apart? Had she made the right decision in the first place? She felt guilty towards everyone, tried to drown the guilts in Beaujolais and Susie's spaghetti Southwarkese.

They were still high in the morning — on Sugar Puffs and Nescafé — larked about like schoolgirls, laughed at nothing. There was some huge airy feeling of relief, as if Matthew's three-storey mansion had been a prison or a dungeon, while their cramped and dingy basement was open to the stars. They dawdled down to Tesco's, bought the crazy childish junk-foods Jennifer normally abhorred — Instant Whips and Kit-Kats, Alphabetti Spaghetti, endless tins of beans. Jennifer sewed, scrubbed, painted, renovated, almost like a game. They were playing at mothers and fathers, with a real live baby to make it all worthwhile.

They had been there almost two whole months now. Every day of every week Jennifer had watched the baby grow, studied its development. She knew exactly how it was lying in the womb, what limbs it had, what organs, how much it weighed, the tiny vital refinements cell by cell. She looked after it by looking after Susie, took it to the antenatal clinic by forcing Susie to go along with her, assured its peace by making Susie rest.

She was father as well as mother. She paid for it, supported it. Matthew's money helped, but she had taken a job as well — a part-time job as a cost clerk in a local insurance office — the sort of dead-end, low-paid work the Women's Group deplored. It felt strange to be an office-girl, especially in contrast with her glamorous life of just five months ago. Instead of dashing round the country in a froth of fame and fans, she was chained to a desk by a pile of paperwork — checking premiums and commissions, sending advice notes out to agents, distracted by the squall of phones and clatter of typewriters. Yet at least it meant that Susie didn't have to stand or slave all day, and the baby wasn't harmed. It wasn't kindness or self-sacrifice. In fact, it was almost selfish. It was *her* child she was working for — and Hester's. The more she did for it, the more it became her own.

Half of the girls in the Women's Group had never had a child and never wanted one. The other half resented their kids and complained about their pregnancies. Jo encouraged them. If they had to bear children at all, she hoped at least they would bypass normal intercourse. That was a favourite theme of the meetings. Jo was hammering it home now.

'The latest developments in AID and test-tube babies mean we're less dependent now on men or marriage, or all the oppressive conventions of . . .'

Jennifer eased her aching legs, tried to get more comfortable on the bare and scratchy floorboards. Jo made her feel a renegade for craving the things the Group denounced. She was a traitor to them all because she *wanted* to serve a man, yearned to conceive and bear his child the old-fashioned oppressive way, was happy to feed his stomach and his ego. Instead, she was feeding Susie. It was ironical, in fact. She was still a slave in women's liberation terms — devoting her life to someone else, accepting a job well below her capabilities, returning home from it to cook and clean.

The girls had attacked her at first, not only for her way of life, but for her subversive role as Mrs Winterton Junior, luring women back to home and kitchen, submerging them in curds and whey, sentimentalising slavery. Now they were more friendly. In fact, after seven weeks of attending all their meetings, Jennifer saw the Group as something like a family — a haven and support now she and Susie were hiding from the world. Jo herself had helped them from the start — turned her hand to painting, lent them furniture, dug out crockery and bed linen she vowed she didn't need. She almost welcomed Susie's pregnancy as a useful teaching aid, a flagrant example of man's perfidy and selfishness. Nonetheless, Jennifer still remained uneasy. Even now, Jo's shrill litany of statistics about women's pay and job conditions was making her uncomfortable. She had been relieved to get a job at all, glad of *any* pay.

She shifted position on the floor again, glanced around the room — girls sprawling, smoking, chewing gum — all concerned with winning rights and freedoms she knew she ought to value, but which seemed vastly less important than having Lyn back in her life and bed, his baby in her womb. Most of the girls wore faded jeans and baggy tops and looked as shabby as their surroundings. The meetings were held in a bleak church hall in Clapham, with Jesus posters on the walls and shelves of battered hymn-books. They even met on Sundays, the 'service' followed by coffee as in many modern congregations.

It was time for coffee now. Jo had finished speaking, at last, and two of the girls were boiling kettles and clattering cups, while the rest broke into little groups, chatting and relaxing.

'How you doing, Susie?'

'OK, I s'pose.'

'I only hope it's not a boy — after all Jo said against them.'

'I bet it is! I felt it kick like crazy every time she called man the enemy.'

Everybody laughed. Jennifer kept her fingers crossed. She hoped it would be a girl. Female babies were easier and stronger, had fewer ills and infections than boys. She had wanted a girl herself when she was pregnant. Lyn might have accepted a girl more easily — less rivalry, less threat. Despite his moods and touchiness, she still longed to have a child made in his image — a dark, artistic, moody, brilliant child. But how would she ever achieve it when she hardly had a husband any longer?

'Thought of a name yet?' A small, pale, breastless girl in a studded leather jacket was passing Susie her coffee.

'No, I haven't bothered, really. I shan't keep the kid, you see — it's going to be adopted and the new parents choose the name.'

'Not necessarily.' Jennifer banged her cup down. She hated the thought of adoption. Even the social worker had tried to talk Susie out of it, impressed upon her that more and more single girls now chose to keep their babies, and that help and money were both available, even sheltered accommodation and special jobs. Susie refused to listen; she didn't want a baby — only freedom and her figure back.

What other solution was there? Jennifer couldn't help beyond the birth. She was committed to Susie for the next few months, perhaps, not another twenty years on top of that. The rest of her life was Lyn's. Susie's baby was a once-in-a-lifetime labour like the book had been. Once it was safely delivered and Susie free to work, she must return to Lyn again, build some life and future of their own, fade all the scars of pain and separation. She could still love Susie, but only at a distance, as a friend, not with such intensity and risk.

All the same, the word adoption hurt. She tried to blank it out, pretend it wouldn't happen. The baby was hers at least a little longer. If Susie wouldn't choose a name, then she had thought of scores — bought three separate books of babies' names, one with detailed glosses on their meanings. The meanings were mostly wrong. Matthew meant Gift of God, Susie meant a lily. She glanced across at Susie, sprawling with her legs apart, the six-month bulge pushing out her scarlet smock which was already splashed with coffee. Her hair was tousled, her purple nail varnish chipped and flaking off. Some lily!

Hester meant a star. That was closer. She *had* been a guiding star. Jennifer was still aware of her presence, especially since the move to Southwark where Hester herself had lived as an unmarried pregnant girl. Jennifer had deliberately chosen Southwark when she first went to find a room for Susie — not simply because it was an inexpensive area, but because of the parallels. She only hoped Rowan Childs was not still digging up the corpse of Hester's baby. She, too, might have an interest in those parallels.

Jennifer was always scared that the media would somehow track her down, find the Country Woman living in a London slum. She hated being in hiding, not only from Anne and Matthew, but also from the book. Now that the first elation had seeped away, she felt less like a carefree schoolgirl, more like a criminal lying low. She had become so fraught and anxious that Anne and Matthew would find her out, she had started phoning them each week, even visiting them occasionally on a fictitious day-return from Bedfordshire, to try and lull their suspicions, or at least prevent them writing to that mythical address.

'How's *Lyn*?' Anne always asked. 'Do bring him with you next time.'

She had explained away his absence with a score of different stories. He was finishing a painting, checking on a house, recovering from colds, coughs, flu, or lack of sleep. She hated the deception, blushed as she wove the lies. Her own mounting worry made every fable worse. How would Anne and Matthew react if they knew the actual truth — that she hadn't heard a word from Lyn since his last phonecall to Putney, way back at the beginning of September? She tried to discuss it with Susie, share and dilute her fears.

245

'Of *course* he's OK, Jen. Just sulking, I expect. You did your nut before, and he rolled up fit and well.'

'That was only a week, though.'

'Makes no difference. He's just bloody unreliable — or artistic, or whatever you call it. He's probably working on his masterpiece and the oils need time to dry. Keep away from Putney. It's only Matthew who makes you sweat.'

Susie didn't understand. There was almost a compulsion to maintain her ties with Putney, despite all the deception. She could hardly explain it herself, except that it kept her still a Winterton, joined her to a family. Anyway, she had to collect her letters, check on any phonecalls, keep up to date with the progress of the book.

It was selling without her now — spectacularly in England, solidly abroad — always top of the charts, always in the news. Matthew was cock-a-hoop, wooed by jealous publishers, feted at literary parties. He had taken over the publicity himself, with the loyal support of Jonathan and a second-stage campaign by Hartley Davies. She had longed for it all to end, but once she was out of the spotlight, the stage seemed dim and cramped. She had gone too far the other way, perhaps. Instead of chauffeured Mercedes, there were long wet waits in bus queues, a one-room basement in place of four-star hotels. Yet neither role was real. She felt more and more confused, more torn between extreme and contradictory views.

'Ta-ta, you girls!' Jo had finished her coffee and was gathering up her things. 'Must get off sharp today. I've got a woman coming to supper who's very big in the EOC. See you next week.'

Jennifer and Susie left soon after, walking arm in arm towards the Common where they caught a bus to Southwark, then walked north towards the river. The area was a hotch-potch of building styles — once proud Victorian mansions collapsing into glass and concrete tower-blocks, tiny fly-blown caffs dwarfed by huge abandoned factories with half their windows boarded up. Scaffolding was everywhere — old streets half destroyed, new projects semi-finished but already vandalised. It was only five o'clock, but the light was fading and a grey drizzle dirtying the air. The streets were deserted. Only the scrawled graffiti defacing walls and posters proved people still existed.

In this nothern stretch of Southwark, there were very few houses left. Most of the ordinary homes which Hester would have known, had been demolished to build banks and offices, warehouses or pubs. People were too puny and unprofitable to be allowed space to simply live. Jennifer thought of Lyn's ancestors pacing their spread of hills. There was no green here but the blight of a weed pushing through a paving-stone or the rash of mould on a damp and cracking wall.

They turned into their own street — one of the few still saved from the bulldozers — a dingy row of ancient terraced houses with flaked and peeling paint. Jennifer walked down the steps to the basement, fumbled for the

246

key, winced as she opened the door. She had done her best on a low budget and with everything against her. The room itself was oddly shaped and facing north. The furniture was a mish-mash — half Jo's, half junk-shop. A tatty brocaded sofa faced two armchairs, one maroon leatherette with a rent in the seat, one poppied chintz with broken springs and all its poppies fading. The sofa was Jennifer's bed. Susie's bed was grander — an old-fashioned brass affair, embellished by an embroidered tasselled counterpane which had belonged to Jo's great-aunt. The 'kitchen' was a double gas-ring, a moody electric kettle and a shelf of groceries. The bathroom was up two flights, the nearest lavatory a dark and smelly closet in the back yard.

Jennifer lit the gas fire, drew the curtains close, so they could forget the drizzle outside. She had made the curtains herself, added matching cushions, painted the chest of drawers and the battered wardrobe. The place certainly looked more cheerful, but it wasn't home, didn't have a garden, didn't have a Lyn. Lyn's name was like a pain still — the jagged pain of longing, made fiercer by resentment. She dragged her mind away from him, turned to Susie, who was kicking off her shoes.

'What's for tea? I'm starving.'

'What d'you fancy?'

'Fillet steak and strawberries.'

'Coming up. I'll call the chef.'

Susie giggled. 'Oh, Jen . . .'

'What?'

'I am . . . you know . . . grateful and everything. I mean, it can't be much fun for you, cooped up here, waiting for me to pod.'

'That's all right. How about a nice cheap nutritious egg Mornay, instead of steak?'

'How about a kiss?' Susie came up behind her, put her arms around her. 'It's the cook's night off, OK?'

'OK.'

'Relax, then. You're all tensed up. You never come near me now. I suppose you don't fancy me with this great lump stuck out front.'

'Oh Susie, I do. I love your little lump! It's just that . . .'

'What?'

'Well, I feel it's . . . bad for the baby. Not physically, but . . . you know — as if we're sort of . . . perverting it.'

'Perverting? You do use funny words.'

'I can't explain, but last time we . . . er . . ., I was worried that . . . Oh, I don't know — forget it.' Jennifer edged away. It was only *later* that she had worried, and even then she could hardly put it rationally. It was as if the baby had been watching their every movement, staring from its cradle in Susie's belly, feeling strange sensations shock against its frame as their three bodies heaved and intertwined. She was concerned about the child. It had already had an unequal start in life, daily doses of gin and nicotine, no father, no real home or family. It had sat and listened to militant feminists denouncing the male sex. It would probably grow up neurotic and confused.

She was confused herself about the whole awkward business of what she did with Susie. She accepted now, in theory, that sex between two females was neither wicked nor disgusting, yet part of her was still profoundly shocked that one of those females should actually have been herself. Their first amazing session together had never been repeated. She hardly knew how it had ever even happened, except it was all tied up with Oz, and with the guilt, thrill and terror of her first and only adultery which she had shared and heightened with Susie in a semi-tipsy state.

'Nothing wrong,' said Susie. 'Just a bit of fun.'

'Comfort,' corrected Jennifer. That was all they wanted really — comfort and affection — another body to cuddle up against, block out the anxieties. Better to lie with Susie than fret alone. She glanced across at Susie now. She was sprawling in the chintz armchair, struggling with the nappy-pin which held her jeans together.

'Christ! I must get out of these. I think I'll put my nightie on. At least it's loose.'

Jennifer yawned, stood up. Perhaps they'd both get into their dressing-gowns, have an early night. She was tired herself, tired of her constant brooding over Lyn, tried of the boring office job which would claim her again in the morning — the crowded in-tray, the endless rows of figures. 'Good idea. I'll get it for you, shall I?'

'Thanks. It's under the pillow.'

It wasn't. Jennifer eventually tracked it down in the upstairs bathroom, flung into a corner. When she returned, Susie was lying stretched out on the sofa with her eyes shut, naked except for a skimpy pair of pants. Jennifer stood at the door a moment, awed by her pregnant body — the deep curve of the belly, the majestic swelling breasts. She crept across, placed a hand on the bulge.

Susie jumped. 'Gosh. You scared me — *and* the baby. Feel it kicking?'

'Yes — sorry. Here's your nightie.'

'Ta. It's nice with nothing on, though. The sofa sort of . . . prickles. Why not take your clothes off too and we'll have a little cuddle.'

'No. I . . .'

'You've gone off me, haven't you, Jen?'

'I haven't.'

'Kiss me, then.'

They kissed — a brief and nervous kiss. Jennifer pulled away. It was uncomfortable on the sofa. The upholstery scratched rather than prickled and the cushions smelt of cat's pee.

'You are a fidget, Jen. You've still got your shoes on, for heaven's sake. No wonder you can't relax.'

Jennifer kicked her sandals off, curled up her bare toes.

248

Susie grinned. 'Funny feet!'

'You're always saying that. What's wrong with them?'

'I dunno. Just funny. Hey, have you ever had your big toe kissed?'

'My *what*?'

'Big toe. I know it sounds a laugh, but it's actually quite fantastic. Here, give me your foot up.'

'Susie, don't. I . . .'

'No, wait. Hang on. You'll love it!' Susie knelt up, placed her lips round Jennifer's big toe and drew it slowly into her mouth, tightened her grip on it. She flicked her tongue over and under and around it, grazed it with her teeth, used her lips to chafe and knead and nip. Her teeth scratched across the toenail, sank into the skin. The tongue followed, soothing and swaddling, cancelling out the pain.

Jennifer shut her eyes. It *was* fantastic. It was as if her toe were a tiny phallus erect in Susie's mouth, sending strange wild sensations along her legs and right up through her body to her own mouth. She tried to stop the feelings, or at least to blank them out. They weren't allowed — besides the fact she must look quite ridiculous, gasping and jiggling with one leg cocked up and her toe in Susie's mouth. 'Susie, please, you mustn't . . .'

Susie was gagged — couldn't speak, didn't appear to have heard. The long sweep of her hair hung down each side of Jennifer's leg, tickling and caressing it as her tongue was doing higher up. She had sucked the toe deep inside her mouth. That was how a *man* must feel when a woman tongued him — swallowed his prick right up to the hilt — the hot wet wild barbed softness, the padlock of teeth tightening and closing around him.

'*Wonderful*!' Jennifer was shouting under her breath. 'Incredible. Fantastic.' 'That's enough' she said aloud. 'We really shouldn't . . .'

'Hush up and take your clothes off. *I*'ll do it if you won't. That's better — kick 'em off. Christ, Jen!' Susie froze. 'What's that?'

They jumped apart — sat up. The door-bell had shrilled like a siren. No one called at Southwark. They had gone underground with no public address.

'Quick! Get up. It's Matthew.' Jennifer was already on her feet.

Susie pulled her back again. 'Don't be stupid. Matthew doesn't even know we're here. I'm in Great Yarmouth and you're living up with . . .'

'*No* one knows we're here. Well, only Jo, and she's busy cooking supper for her Queen Bee.'

'Don't go, then. It's probably only someone selling flags, or a boy scout or . . .'

Jennifer lay flat. 'Sshh. If we both stay quiet, they'll probably go away.'

The bell pealed again, and longer.

'Are you sure it's our bell and not the one upstairs?'

'Oh, yes. We'd never hear that down here.'

Susie swore, hid her face in the cushions.

'Susie, listen — I've just had a thought. Supposing it's Lyn. It could be. *He* knows our address. I must go and check. If it is him and he goes away, I'll never forgive myself.'

Jennifer grabbed her skirt and draped it round her like a towel. She peered up through the window bars. 'I can't see a thing. This window's set too low.'

'Come back to bed, then. They've probably gone away now.'

The door-bell contradicted her. Boy scouts and flag-sellers were never that insistent.

'I'm sure it's Lyn. I'll have to go and see.' Jennifer was dragging on the skirt now, zipping it up. She dashed along the passage. 'Let it be Lyn,' she prayed. 'Let him have found a house and . . .' He could have changed his mind, come to tell her that they could all move in together, Susie too. They could pack their cases and leave that very evening, start a new existence. 'Let it be all right,' she whispered. 'Let there be no rows or . . .'

She opened the door. It wasn't Lyn. It wasn't a boy scout. It was a tall brawny man she had never seen before, with dark short-cropped curly hair and eyes too baby-blue to match the rest of him. He had an opera singer's chest, a weight-lifter's muscles, the build and bearing of an ox. He wore no coat or jacket despite the rain. His shirt was open almost to the waist, revealing little whorls of tangled body hair. His forearms were tattooed with electric-blue snakes writhing between scarlet hearts and flowers. He placed one foot on the step, wedged one massive shoulder in the door.

'Susie Grant live here?'

'Er . . . no. She's . . . er . . .'

'She told me 32B. B for basement. That's here, innit?'

'Y . . . yes, it is, but . . . May I ask who *you* are?'

'The name's Bartlett. Sam Bartlett.'

Bartlett? Susie had never mentioned a Sam Bartlett in her life. Supposing Matthew had sent him? Or he was someone from the social services, an official come to snoop or spy. No. Social workers didn't sport tattoos. The man looked dangerous. She shouldn't have opened the door to him at all. Supposing he pulled a knife on her or . . .

'Just tell her it's Sparrow, will yer?'

'*Sparrow*. Oh, I see.' She noticed the Kawasaki now, gleaming on the kerb. 'I'm . . . sorry. I didn't realise who . . .'

'Told yer about me, has she?'

'Er . . . yes. She . . . did mention . . .'

'She wrote to me — gave me her address. That's why I called. Out at the moment, is she?'

'Well, n . . . no, she's . . . er . . . Look, you'd better come in.'

'Ta.'

He followed her down the passage. His footsteps echoed through the house like hammer-blows. He seemed to fill and swamp their room. He had already noticed Susie's clothes, lying dishevelled on the floor. Jennifer picked them up, stuffed them in a drawer. Susie had disappeared.

'D . . . do sit down.' Even the broad-shouldered chintz armchair looked too small and frail to hold him. 'I'll just go and find her for you.'

Jennifer raced along the passage in the opposite direction now, out into the back yard. She hammered on the lavatory door. Susie pushed it open. She was sitting on the toilet seat, swaddled in the counterpane.

'It's . . . it's Sparrow, Susie.'

'*Sparrow*! You're joking.'

'No. I'm not. He's here. He says you wrote to him. You never told me, Susie, you . . .'

'Sparrow! I can't believe it. Hey, he is *waiting*, isn't he? You didn't send him away or . . .?'

'No. He's in our room. He's . . .'

Susie charged across the yard into the house, trailing her counterpane. Jennifer could hear her pounding feet, her shouts of welcome. She stood leaning against the lavatory door, rain soaking into her blouse. Surely she wasn't jealous? How could she be, when she had just been hoping and praying it was Lyn? She forced herself to smile. She and Susie were both desperate for their men, denouncing them in theory in the Women's Group, yet wooing them in private. Susie had actually written to her man, kept the letter secret. She felt betrayed by that. She had never liked the sound of Sparrow, anyway. Even without the Women's Group, she disapproved of men who made their girlfriends pregnant, yet refused to take any responsibility. Sparrow had offered neither money nor support. How dare he just show up like this, expect a quick pint, or even a quick screw, and then piss off again — as Susie would have put it — leaving *her* to work and worry for the baby. Yet if he stayed with Susie, that would be worse still. She had to admit there *was* a twinge of jealousy. Lyn and her and Susie was fine, but not her and Susie and Sparrow.

She walked slowly back to the basement, coughed outside the door. They were probably in a clinch by now. She knocked, walked in. Susie was half dressed — the bottom half — dragging on a pair of voluminous dungarees. She could see Sparrow gawping at her breasts, lewdly, not paternally. Both of them were smoking Sparrow's Marlboroughs.

'We're just going out — OK?' Susie rooted round for her high-heeled scarlet sandals, found them under the bed. 'Want to come with us? You don't mind, do you, Sparrow?' Susie was leaning against him while she buckled up her sandal.

He frowned, clamped her arm with his own huge hairy hand. 'Well . . . er . . . I did want to talk to you private like. Anyway, I'm on my bike and there's not room for three.'

'Susie, you're not to go on a motorbike! Not now. It's absolutely crazy. Supposing . . .'

'OK, OK, we'll walk. Keep your hair on.' Susie grinned. 'Tell you

251

what, we'll bring you back a pizza — a jumbo one with half the shop on it. All right?'

'All right, Jennifer forced herself to smile. Mustn't be unfair. Susie needed a change of scene. If she felt confined and irritable herself, that only proved how selfish she had become. She had kidded herself if she thought she could find contentment cowering in a basement, her only company the embattled Women's Group who opposed all the things she cherished.

Susie was struggling into a jacket, trying to make the buttons meet. She kissed Jennifer briefly, almost in apology, then teetered through the door arm in arm with Sparrow. Jennifer peered up through the window bars, watched their two pairs of legs pass along the pavement, side by side.

When they had disappeared, the silence seemed to choke her. It was still thirteen weeks till the baby was due. How could she stay in Southwark for another thirteen weeks, living this rootless Lyn-less life, lying to Anne and Matthew, losing touch with everyone she knew? The baby grew so slowly, dawdling into life, cell by cell, pore by pore, while her husband roamed the country in impatience and despair. She realised now how desperately she missed him. She had always tried to deny it, forced herself to block him out, put the baby first. But now all her fears and longings had flooded through the dam. It was Sparrow who had breached it. She had seen how avidly Susie had leapt on him, how much she craved her man. *She* would have been the same. She and Susie had been using each other simply as substitutes. It was Lyn she truly wanted — in bed and out of it.

Susie had written to Sparrow, but she couldn't write to Lyn. She had no address. He should have written to her. She had told him where she was living, begged him to keep in touch. When he didn't, she hadn't been that concerned — not at first. His strange and frenzied calls to Putney had been something of a strain, and it had been almost a relief to be without a phone at Southwark. She needed a breathing space to adjust to her new surroundings, book Susie into a hospital, arrange her antenatal care, begin to prepare for the baby.

It was only when the first two weeks had passed that she began to fret again. She tried not to look for the postman — tried not to count the days. Lyn was busy — that was all — would contact her as soon as he had some news. The fortnight limped into a month, September darkened to October. Lyn had always loved the autumn. Other years, she had found coloured leaves pressed between the pages of his books, misshapen conkers shrivelling on his desk. He always saved the distorted ones, the runts with growths and lumps. He had made her a necklace once of spastic conkers. It was *stupid* things she kept remembering — the way he ate his fruit cake, crumbling the slice to pieces with his fingers, picking out the cherries and saving them till last. The careful ritual of his shaving, soaping his face, not once, but twice, screwing up his eyes in concentration, making strange shapes with his mouth, jutting out his chin, refusing to speak at all until the job was finished and the razor cleaned and put away. He never used an

252

electric one. She saw him in the house, eyes closed, shoulders hunched, sitting totally still as if he were listening to some strange silent music inside his head, then suddenly charging out, as if he could bear the sound no longer, and flinging himself into some frenzied task like chopping wood. She could even smell his duffel coat — a smell of wood smoke and wet string.

All her efforts to shut him out had been so much autumn mist. She realised she had been thinking of him constantly — expecting him each day for fifty-two whole days now — listening for his footsteps, rushing to the post, hoping, praying, longing, but suppressing all her feelings, so that she hardly knew their force. The ring on the door had released them like a tidal wave, swamped her in disappointment and despair.

She glanced around the room. There was nothing of Lyn there — not even his photograph. She had deliberately excluded him in deference to Susie. Now he was lost to her and she hadn't even realised it. She picked up Susie's sneakers, flung them in the wardrobe. What in God's name was she doing — shacking up with a girl who might trade her in for Sparrow after the second gin, staking everything on a baby who would be swallowed up in adoption forms the minute it was born? She had always reassured herself that the arrangement was only temporary, somehow imagined that Lyn would change his mind, accept Susie and her pregnancy, so that they could all move in together and muddle along as best they could until Susie was delivered and they were free to lead their own life. But that was simply moonshine. Lyn had cut his ties, turned his back — might even have disappeared abroad, found another woman. He was her sacred wedded husband and she had no more notion where he was than if he had been a nomad wandering the dark side of the world.

She glanced at the tattered calendar pinned beside the wardrobe — the rows and rows of days and dates printed in red. Bleeding days because Lyn had been moving further and further away from her with every one that passed. Almost November now. The nights were getting colder, winter creeping up. Just last night, the clocks had gone back to mark the end of British Summer Time. Darkness was winning — dark and death.

She grabbed her keys and a raincoat. She had to get out, stop herself from panicking. It was raining harder, pavements wet and glassy in the sickly light of the lampposts. She plodded down the street, avoiding the puddles, turned right, left, right again. She hardly knew where she was going. Her mind had shut off and her legs had taken over — steering her automatically in the direction of the old St Saviour's — the hostel where Hester had had her baby. It had been bombed in the last war, all traces of it razed. A block of cheap and dingy post-war flats had been built in place of it. Last time she had been there, just a month ago, they had all been boarded up, the occupants rehoused. Now she stared in shock. The flats had vanished, too. All that was left was a gaping hole in the ground, a mound of rubble. She glanced around at the broken bricks, the twisted lengths of piping, the rusting sheets of corrugated iron, eerie in the shadows.

Suddenly, she started. She could see a woman standing by the fence — a woman from another age, pale and almost ghostly — long black skirt trailing in the debris, long brown hair scraped severely up and back, young face thin and pinched. She held a baby in her arms, a bald plump baby swaddled in a shawl. The child was crying — a jagged sound which lacerated like barbed wire dragged across the eyes. The woman herself was silent, motionless, head held high and proud, staring towards the North.

Jennifer lurched forward. '*Hester*!' she whispered — sprang towards her, tripped on a length of guttering, lost her balance, fell.

When she got up, the figure had disappeared. There were no footprints in the mud except her own, no sound except the muffled roar of a train on the bridge beyond. Perhaps she had only dreamed it, imagined a woman's shape in the stack of upended planks. Yet the sense of Hester's presence was still almost overwhelming, as if Hester had caught her shadow in the barbed-wire fence and left it flapping there and staring. There was a sense of menace, of foreboding.

Jennifer sank down on a broken crate, tried to stop her legs trembling. Was she really in touch with Hester, or beginning to lose her grip? She glanced around the wasteland. The yawning hole in the ground seemed to have deepened and darkened in the few minutes she had been there, threatening to suck her down. Abandoned water tanks stood on their sides like cages. Shadows dripped from the naked bones of scaffolding on an adjoining building-site. She shivered. She must get out of this place before she imagined something worse. But where could she go, what could she do? Susie was out, might not be back till late or even morning. She had lost touch with her few friends.

There was always Anne and Matthew. She had phoned them only yesterday, but she could phone again, invite herself to dinner. Even with all the lies and Matthew's lecturings, it would still be better than wandering here alone. She suddenly longed to be in a whole big house again, with space and stairs and soaring unbarred windows, to sit down at a proper table with decent food, with children and a family, normal conversation. Putney had seemed a prison when she first decamped to Southwark. Now it seemed a sanctuary. It had light and space and air, generous leafy gardens, old and spreading conifers, horse-chestnut trees, Lyn's precious lumpy conkers.

She had last seen Lyn at Putney, lain in bed beside him, sat at the table opposite. There were still traces of him there, a stray button from his jacket reproaching her on the sideboard, his blue pyjamas crumpled in a drawer, a shirt or two hanging limp and pale in the wardrobe — all she had left of him now.

She eased up from the crate, stared around again. No sign of any woman. The blitzed and ravaged wasteland seemed to stretch for ever, the unscathed streets beyond it collapsing into rubble in the flickering rain and shadow. There was nothing of any permanence — no range of massy

254

Cheviots shouting their defiance to the sky. She longed to return to Hernhope, to Hester's house and centre. Southwark was only exile for them both, shutting them out from field and hill and green. Even the patch of weeds at her feet was sooty and half-trampled. She plucked a dripping fistful. Nothing was weed to Hester. All plants were magical. Even this tattered ragwort and lowly chickweed had featured in her diaries — ragwort for menstrual troubles; chickweed leaves crushed to a paste with cooking lard to make a salve for Matthew's childhood burns. She slipped a sprig of chickweed in her buttonhole. She would go to Matthew's now, salve her-*self*. She needed a change as much as Susie did, a quiet, normal, solid, chatty evening to banish all the spectres.

Her coat was wet and muddy from her fall. She brushed it down, stumbled back to the pavement, walked briskly up the street and round the corner, searching for a call-box. The first one didn't work. The second had been smashed by vandals despite the strong iron bars set round the glass. She trudged towards the third, hair soaked, feet aching.

It was Anne who answered, sounding tired.

'Jennifer here. How are you? I'm . . . er . . . fine.' She switched on the lies again. Yes, she was in London — had come down unexpectedly from Bedfordshire just that morning. Yes, dinner would be *lovely*. Steak, she hoped, or a decent joint of beef. She was sick of the cheaper cuts, the endless economies.

'No, Lyn . . . er . . . won't be with me, Anne. He . . . couldn't come, unfortunately. He's . . . ill again. One of his colds. What? What did you say? *Charles* did? When? He can't have done. Impossible. I mean, why would Lyn . . .?' She tried to keep her voice down, stop herself from shouting. The receiver felt damp and sticky in her hand. She switched it to the other side, tried to breathe more calmly. 'Did Charles say where it was, Anne? Oh, I see. How strange. No, I can't understand it at all. Mind you, I was out last night, so that may explain how . . .'

Steak and beef had faded. She couldn't waste time on dinner — not any more. She tried to make excuses, explain her change of plan. She heard her voice blathering on inanely, talking too fast, too wildly, excitement soaring over worry. The phone hollered for more coins. She stood there, paralysed. Anne's last words had crescendoed to a whine, then spluttered into nothing. Her legs were trembling again. She replaced the receiver, touched the star of chickweed in her buttonhole. Hester was behind this — must have arranged it somehow — come to her aid, brought her husband back. She pushed at the heavy door of the booth, walked dazed into the street. She could see a bus lumbering towards her. 'Waterloo', it said. She raced to the bus stop, put out her hand, jumped on.

'Wait for me, Lyn,' she whispered. 'I'm on my way.'

XIX

The train rattled through the dark and dripping evening, rain stinging on its windows, steel track towed along behind. Jennifer stared at her face reflected in the window, a dark and shivery face which kept fracturing into pieces as streaks and shapes roared past it, then reassembled, weeping tears of rain. She sat on the very edge of the seat, gazing out at factories and warehouses, abandoned depots, empty offices. They were still close to Waterloo. Slowly, the houses took over — people massed together — high and dizzy in tower-blocks, poor and grubby in tenements, streets lurching past the train. Lights lights lights puncturing the darkness, every light a home. She was just a rumble, shaking their floors and ceilings, stopping conversations, griming their net curtains. Or perhaps there were no people. Maybe all the homes were empty, like her cold and empty carriage.

Even Waterloo had been deserted — a chilly Sunday station, bereft of its commuters, the pigeons huddled and drab-feathered. She had found the Cobham train at Platform 9, sat in the dirty compartment with its dim and flickering lights and its reek of stale tobacco, counting the endless seconds until it shuddered away from the buffers and gathered speed past rain-swept sheds and sidings.

She started as a second train flashed past her, a third the other side. Trains tearing through her skull and out again, scorching through the black tunnels of her eyes. Lights, wheels, rain, speed, spinning and distorting, so that inside, outside, backwards, forwards, meant nothing any longer. She closed her eyes. Things quietened. One train speeding in one direction to the one man in the world.

She reached across and wiped her window-face, tried to see beyond it. The houses were thinning now, the horizon opening out. No more strings of lights — glittering constellations of streets, estates and shops — only single lonely homesteads swallowed up in darkness. Lyn was out there somewhere, staring from that darkness, the noise of her train juddering through his world. She had feared him lost, or in some foreign country a thousand miles away, yet Charles had seen him just last night, almost on their doorstep. Charles was a serious boy, steady and reliable. He never lied, never invented things. He had been staying the night with a school friend down in Cobham and had phoned Anne and Matthew to tell them he had spotted a man he was almost sure was Lyn. Lyn in *Cobham*, when she had imagined him a world away! Cobham was only twenty miles or so — half of that now, as the train jolted and swayed towards it, ignoring the pointless stations in between.

Jennifer clenched and unclenched her hands, shifted on the seat. She mustn't be too hopeful. Charles had said '*almost* sure'. How cruel that 'almost' was. And even if it had been Lyn, he might have left by now, could have driven off from Cobham hours ago, and be the other end of England by the time her train pulled in. And why Cobham in the first place? Matthew's little terraced house had long been sold. Lyn had never made any friends there, never declared any fondness for the place.

'Lyn,' she whispered. 'Be there still.'

Her tie with him was holy. When Susie called him a selfish pig or a rotten moody bastard, she was angry with them both — Susie for using words like that, Lyn for giving her grounds for them. Susie ignored his flair and soar of brilliance, his leaf-thin sensitivity which made him moody, but also made him special.

She slumped back in the seat. She loved Susie for a hundred different things — her vulgar cheerful childish bounciness, her wild infectious giggle, her hugs and fads and crazes. And yet Lyn came always first. There were solemn vows which bound her to him, the tie and bond with Hester, her knowledge that she must save him from himself. She had to find him, had to make things right with him.

The train had stopped at Oxshott and was gathering speed again, tearing up the landscape and flinging the pieces in her eyes. Every piece had Lyn on it — the whirling spiral of his thumb-prints, the letters of his name juggled up and spelling loss and love, the dark pupils of his eyes darker than the darkness.

Only one more station. Jennifer jumped to her feet, hand ready on the door handle. No one else got out. She stood alone on the forlorn and tiny platform with its puddled concrete and rusting roof, listening to the last rumbling echo of the train as it drew away. Silence now. Even the rain had stopped. She climbed the steps of the footbridge, paused at the top, stared up at the sky. It arched above the railway track — dark, moody, turbulent — the thin black arms of trees straining up to reach it. The moon was full, but trapped, a swollen yellow eye blindfolded by cloud. It was surely only a fairy-tale that man had ever set foot on the moon. It was too far away, too frail, would crumble if you trod on it.

She shivered, clutched the cold iron rail of the footbridge, descended the steps the other side, towards the ticket barrier. Some crazy irrational part of her almost expected to see Lyn waiting there, come to meet her train. But there was no one at all — not even a porter or a man to take her ticket. The station was like a ghost-place in a dream. No one to smile and say 'good evening', no one to make her real. Just wet and gleaming rails stretching away to nothingness and that vast staring sky.

She turned out of the station, trudged up the road to the small parade of shops where Lyn had sometimes stopped to buy her a Mars bar or a magazine. That was before the book, when they were close and quiet and unpursued, and little things were treats. All the shops were shut now, Cobham a dead land. She had no plan of action, no real strategy. Cobham was only a village, but it was still some task to check every inch of it, especially in the dark. Hopeless, said a mocking voice inside her. She choked the voice, made herself walk on. How could Cobham be dead if Lyn were hiding there? She must find him, resurrect herself.

She quickened her pace, footsteps hammering through the silence. Should she go straight to the river where Charles had said he'd spotted him — search all along its banks — or call first at their old home and make enquiries there? At least the new owners knew of her, were aware of her fame from the book. It wouldn't hurt to knock. Lyn might have had some reason to visit the house, some letter to collect or possession he had left behind. It seemed unlikely after all this time, but she had to start some- where — before she lost her nerve.

She turned left into the main road which led up to the village. The soft light from olde-worlde carriage-lamps gleamed on bow windows and fancy paving-stones, exotic shrubs in stiff formations, pretentious house names engraved on polished plaques. White Mercedes crouched like huge pale moths on pebbled driveways edged with rhododendrons. Yes — Cobham was alive still — very much alive, so long as you were rich and well-connected. It was a mile or two to the poorer, shabbier street where they had lived themselves, its rows of terraced houses squatting behind mangy privet hedges.

She half ran, half walked, scanning every side street, peering into the shadow of every clump of trees. Rain was threatening again, the sky still fretful, swift and swollen clouds caging the moon and stars. She branched right before the village, left, right, left again, and into their tiny street. Number twelve was almost at the end. She hardly recognised it. Their bare-brick workman's cottage had been painted strawberry pink, frilly nets foamed at every window. The knocker was a small brass poodle's head, the 'twelve' spelt out in writing in a fancy gothic script. The house had been prettified in a way which didn't suit it — a simple yokel garbed in fancy dress. She stared at the new glass porch, the ugly carport. It was as if part of her life and self had been detroyed. This was the house where she and Lyn had started life together, and which they had restored and renovated. Now the new owners had done their own restoring, stripped them from the house with brush and blow-lamp, submerged them in pink paint.

She pressed the door-bell, listened to its tinkling chime. No answer. She rang again, looked up and down the road. Some of the houses were in total shuttered darkness, and even where there were lights, the curtains were drawn close, so that she could see no human figure nor welcoming room. She had lived here once, belonged here, but now she was shut out. It was as if the street refused to recognise her; the roofs frowning with their brows drawn down, the windows wearing blank and hostile faces. Up in Mepperton, where the houses were far fewer and the darkness almost solid, unrelieved by street-lamps, she had never felt this lonely and benighted. Your neighbours might be far away in distance, but were always close in spirit. Here, people lived on top of you, but were strangers more or less. Every door seemed bolted, every window barred. And even if they unlocked to her, what was she meant to say? How could she admit that she hadn't seen the man she loved for fifty-two whole days, had no idea whether he was well or ill, north or south, happy or in anguish? It was anguish to admit it to herself.

Instinctively, she turned towards the river, as if she could gather up his traces there, like a fistful of feathers, a handful of weed. Lyn had always loved the River Mole, had followed it once from its source in St Leonard's Forest to where it joined the Thames at Molesey, opposite Hampton Court Palace. He had sketched its reeds, its birds, the broad and stately walnut trees which shaded its bank at the foot of Box Hill. They had picnicked there together, fed the coot, watched them nest, breed, hatch, feed, fly; seen the river bank change from bare brown to tangled green, and back again. Now it was spooky black.

She groped along the path. The grass squelched underfoot, sucking down her thin and silly shoes. Ragged shadows trembled on the water — pointing fingers, fraying faces. There were two moons now, one hanging in the sky, one fallen in the river underneath it, its broken fragments silver on the surface.

She stumbled on, tripping on the tussocky grass, overhanging branches brushing wet against her face. There was no sign of Lyn, no sign of anyone. Charles must have got it wrong. Even with a full moon, the light was too dim to distinguish faces. If he had seen a man at all, it might have been just an angler or a gypsy. She was wasting her time chasing after shadows. But wait — what was that — that hunched shape on the further bank? Just another shadow or a crouching human figure?

She ducked down beside a tree stump, crept a little closer. No, it wasn't man, but bird — a large grey bird fishing in the moonlight — a heron. She had watched them so often up in Mepperton, standing tensed and poised like that, long snaked neck bent back in an S, head cocked to one side and listening. Yet heron were rare on this stretch of river and especially after sunset. She and Lyn had seen them in the daytime, never in the dark. She peered between the reeds. The bird stood so motionless, it could have been carved of stone or painted on a backdrop. The water rippled below it, the clouds retched and heaved above, but neither beak nor plumage stirred. A twig snapped beneath her foot. With a sudden honk, the heron lurched away, wings flapping, legs outstretched.

Jennifer leant against the tree stump. Stupid to feel so dazed. It wasn't a ghost she had seen. Heron did feed after dark, so long as there was moonlight. Lyn had told her that himself. And yet it still seemed like an omen, something else linking her to Hester, drawing her back to Hernhope. She started up at the moon, the same moon which must be prying now through the chinks of Hester's house, showing up the jungled garden, the dusty deserted rooms. She had hoped at first that Lyn might

259

have returned there in a last determined effort to sort out the problem of the missing Will. She had even phoned the Bertrams and asked them to check the place, but all they had found was leaves in the gutters and nettles halfway up the door. Molly had long since stopped her cleaning. What was the point, she asked, of dusting for the spiders, or gardening for the starlings.

Jennifer trailed her hand in the icy water, trying to trap the quick-silver fragments of moonlight shimmering on the top. Hester had written so much about the moon. The sun was a far less frequent visitor to the bleak and shadowed hills of Hernhope than the nightly prowling moon. Hester had sown her seeds when the moon was waxing, predicted the weather by its shape or shadows, studied its different phases. A full moon was always lucky. Hester had made her potions then, exploiting its help in curing illnesses. Did heartache count as illness? Would she cure it by finding Lyn? Hester had recorded the legend that all things lost or wasted on earth were treasured on the moon — misspent time and wealth, broken vows, unanswered prayers, lovers' sighs and yearnings. She stood up, stretched out her hands.

'Help me.' she whispered.

She would follow the river for at least another mile, then return to Cobham centre, search every pub, street and wasteland for her husband. It might be futile, but she owed it to him. She had allowed Susie and her baby to snuff him out too easily, the Women's Group to snub him when they didn't understand.

Her legs ached and the backs of her heels were blistered when she returned, at last, into the allotments. She had trudged four or five miles in all, been recognised by people in pubs, accosted by a stranger, even chatted up. But she was still alone and husband-less. She was almost certain now that Charles had been in error. Lyn was unique, maybe, but there were still a score of lean dark men who could resemble him at a distance in the dark. If he had come to find her, he would have gone direct to Southwark, not to Cobham. There was nothing left at Cobham. Even their allotments would have been re-let to other tenants or reverted back to weeds.

Jennifer shivered in the gloom, wished she had brought her gloves. It was colder now, though the rain was still holding off, some of the cloud dispersing. The moon had slipped its blindfold and looked as plump and solid as a de-rinded Edam. Even so, its light was grudging. She was glad of the near-by street-lamps casting their soft glow on guard-straight leeks and glistening cabbage leaves. It was consoling, almost touching, to see the care lavished on these plots by humble men and women who toiled here every weekend, creating their tiny Hernhopes out of a hundred and twenty-five square metres and a compost-heap. She groped along to plots eleven and fourteen, the two which had been theirs. They were further down towards the fence, past a stretch of weeds and wasteland. She prayed they, too, would not be overgrown. There was tangle enough at

Hernhope, without every place they touched turning into a wilderness.

She stopped by plot eleven, felt ridiculous relief. It was as neat, as ordered as the day that they had left, though everything was taller and more lush now. Humble vegetables looked exotic in the moonlight — silvered spinach, spangled cabbages. She walked up and down between them, bending low so that she could see exactly what was there. The new owner appeared to have kept the plot much as they had planted it — runner-beans towering at the back, lettuce under polythene coddled at the front, cabbage, onions, spinach, sprouts and cauliflower neat-rowed in the centre. Yet, despite the neatness, the lack of weeds and obvious signs of labour, nothing had been harvested. She peered a little closer. The marrows were as large as kit-bags, the runners huge, tough, hard-seeded, curved like scimitars, way past the size for normal picking. All the onion-tops had been neatly folded over, but the onions themselves were bursting out of the soil, as if begging to be lifted. She remembered planting them herself from seed on Boxing Day, cossetting them in seed-trays in the dark, till she could transfer them to the soil in April. It was Hester who had insisted on Boxing Day. She had written in her notebooks that onions received a special blessing and bonus if planted at dawn on the day after Christmas. So she had got up specially early, called down Hester's benediction, and sat in the chilly Cobham kitchen beneath the paper chains, pressing in the tiny blackish seeds. Lyn had come down later and kissed her across the splitting bags of compost, and when all the seeds were carefully tucked to rest, they went back to bed themselves, but not to sleep.

She stared at the onions now. She had chosen Ailsa Craig — a hardy Scottish strain, which Hester had recommended as being proof not only against infection, but against the harsh Northumbrian climate. It appeared to have done just as well in Cobham. But why had nobody lifted the onions, cleared the soil? True there had been no frost yet, but it was already late October and everything would rot or spoil if it were left in the ground much longer.

Yet the new owner was no laggard. He had recently planted a double row of spring cabbage, and lettuce under glass. His winter peas were marked by a line of cloches, a row of little tags. She peered at the name on the labels — Feltham First — a variety they had often chosen themselves. But why did he want more vegetables when he had let these older ones lie wasteful and ungathered? His carrots were quite young still. Jennifer bent closer. Between every third row of carrots was a little clump of sage, its dusty-coloured cushions pale between the feathery carrot tops. Only Lyn plated sage among his carrots to keep carrot fly away. It was a trick they had learned from Hester, an old wives' tale which worked, but which modern gardeners scorned.

The new owner must have copied their idea, replanted both varieties exactly the same way. She smiled at his naiveté. There were no carrot fly till spring, so the sage was quite superfluous for this later, autumn crop.

All the same, she felt absurdly pleased. It provided some tiny continuity in a world where everything else had been destroyed or bulldozed, proved almost a tribute to her and Lyn and Hester and their methods. Some keen allotment holder must have been admiring their plot before they had even left it, then rushed to take it over, and kept it religiously the same. It was almost as if he had saved the harvest for them, tended and weeded their vegetables, but refused to pick or eat them because he was not the one who had sown them in the first place. A crazy thought, but an appealing one. Some part of her and Lyn, their life and work together, still stood like a tiny monument.

She stamped her feet to try and warm them up, blew on her fingers. The silence was less total now. She could hear drippings and ploppings from the trees, the faint screech of a vixen in a distant copse, the soughing of the wind. She glanced around her. Nothing but ghostly rows of vegetables, glistening clumps of nettles. She moved to plot fourteen, the one they had used exclusively for herbs — comfrey and white horehound, feverfew and vervain — names which were almost poetry, herbs which could salve or season, heal or beautify. She stepped on to the soil. This second plot was further from the street-lamps, more closely veiled in darkness. Yet she could just make out the herbs — the more common everyday ones sought out from fields and hedgerows; others, more exotic, purchased with the money which Matthew had first given them for handing over the diaries. That was more than sixteen months ago, just after her miscarriage. She had buried all her grief and disappointment in the soil — coddled her nursling plants like substitute children, feeding them and watering them until they grew tall and strong.

But wait — some of the plants were *tiny* — babies still, only newly sown. And the plot was *full*, whereas she and Lyn had left it half denuded. They had dug up most of the herbs before they moved to Putney, loath to leave them there for a new allotment holder to fling on the rubbish-tip as weeds. She had stripped off all the leaves and flowers and used them for herbal extracts, then replanted the perennials in Matthew's garden. So what were they doing here again, some of them cuttings from his older stock, others newly purchased, the taller ones staked and supported, all meticulously weeded? Even the layout was the same. She had planted the original garden herself, following Hester's plan, and here it was in replica, exactly as before, the bushy cushions of chamomile making an edging in the front, the tall spikes of marshmallow protected by a burdock bush behind.

She threaded her way through the plants, crushing leaves and sniffing them, picking fruits and berries. Yes — there was the figwort in the centre, the hyssop next to it, the musky scent of southenwood, sharper after rain — all the herbs that Hester recommended, in the order she approved. It was strange, uncanny, as if Hester herself had risen from her grave and re-sown this stretch of ground, re-created Hernhope down at Cobham.

No — not Hester — *Lyn*. It was Lyn who must have been here and revived their two allotments, laid out her herb garden exactly as she had done it in the first place, filled in the missing gaps. No one but Lyn would have planted aconite or rue, or known where to purchase skullcap and valerian. Ordinary gardeners stuck to mint and chives, rosemary or thyme. Only Hester's son would have tracked down feverfew or lovage, transplanted them successfully, searched the hedgerows for wood sage and wormwood. Only he would have remembered the exact spacing and siting of all the different varieties, alternating savory with mugwort as Hester recommended, shading peppermint with witch hazel. No new owner, however faithful or admiring, could have recreated a garden which was so distinctly hers and Hester's own.

She turned back to the other plot. Now she could see Lyn's touches everywhere — marigolds sown among the tomato plants to keep the whitefly off; the way he had used the tough outer leaves of his cauliflowers to blanket and swaddle the frail white heads inside: even his home-made cloches constructed on the cheap out of polythene and old wire coat-hangers. He must have returned to Cobham to rescue these two plots — officially re-rent them — but when and why? Their tenancy had been due to expire in early September, but long before September they would have been overgrown and jungled. Had he been creeping back, even in the summer, to do a little secret gardening? But why had he never mentioned it? And why should he sow more vegetables when he had left all the rest ungathered? There were enough on this plot to feed a tribe, and Lyn was on his own — no wife to peel and prepare them, no family to share them, not even a house or larder to store them in.

No, Lyn had come here for an entirely different reason. It was hard to put it into words. It sounded foolish, even crackpot, yet she understood instinctively. This was his gift to her, his offering — this patient dogged labour, this restoring of their plots. He had re-created their life and work together. to prove that it was precious to him, a secret homage to their former way of life, a tribute to their marriage — almost a replacement for their child. He had sown her in vegetables, blazoned her in herbs, written her a message in the soil, telling her he missed her, begging her to come and pluck his harvest before it went to waste. She had arrived only just in time. Another few weeks or even days, and this bounty would be blighted.

She crouched down on the path, grubbed up the smallest of the lettuces, plucked out its heart and ate it leaf by leaf; tugged out a carrot, scraped it clean with her fingernails, cradled it in her hands before biting into it. She picked a tomato, squashed pulp and seeds against her tongue, swallowed . . . savoured . . . found a last late strawberry, spun it out in slow sensual bites. She snapped off a runner-bean, split it with her thumbnail, squeezed out the fat mauve seeds inside, gulped them whole. She must devour his harvest, consume and relish all that he had planted for her, so that she could be one with him and joined to him, swallowing the fruits his hands and breath had touched. She picked a leaf of marigold, already brown and

263

dying; crushed sage between her fingers, sniffed its fragrance. Even humble sage and scraggy marigold were precious. He had sown them between his vegetables as ritual and homage, because she and Hester had done it that way. It revived the old traditions, kept their past unchanged.

She was on her knees now in the centre of the plot. Her hands were stained and muddy, her body tense with cold. Yet she was aware of Hester's presence all around her — in the vast and sequinned night, the gauzy leaves of potent herbs marbled in the moonlight, the raw smell of wet earth. It was Hester who had drawn her here, shown her Lyn's devotion. This was his scrap of country, his substitute for Hernhope, her proof that he belonged with soil and nature. He would never feel at peace in a city or an office. They were both of them refugees, both cut off from their roots.

It was Susie who had trapped her, upset all her values. She couldn't blame the girl — would never break with her — but she must look after her in some less intensive way. Now Sparrow had shown up again, perhaps he could share the room with her, or find another place — and there was always Jo to keep an eye on things. She herself would visit, be present at the birth. She wouldn't break that promise, but in the three long months before it, she must return to Hernhope before it reverted back to wasteland, or their marriage choked in weeds.

She eased up from the ground. The rain had started again — drenching down on her like a slap, a reprimand, punishing her for those selfish, sterile weeks, for allowing Susie to distort her views, so that she had judged her husband unfairly by the standards of cruder and more conventional men. She blundered along the path, blinded by the rain, shoes sinking into the mud. She must shelter before she was completely soaked. She slipped through the allotment gate, followed the track which skirted it. Fifty yards along was a dilapidated barn, abandoned by the farmer who owned the land beyond. She groped towards it, tearing her clothes on brambles, tripping on loose stones.

She stopped at the door, glanced nervously around her. The clouds were hurtling overhead, as if frightened themselves and stampeding away in panic. The drone of the rain mixed with the stealthy tinkle of a dozen home-made bird-scarers, whispering to her over the allotment fence. A white shape in the field beyond changed from spectre to old horse, startling her with its sudden drum of hoof-beats.

Stupid to be scared. Cobham was a law-abiding place, with one of the lowest crime rates in the country. She pushed at the heavy door, heaving her shoulder against it, took a cautious step inside. She could see almost nothing but shadow piled on shadow. She crept between the shadows, groping out her hands in the spidery blackness, trying to find a box or bench or bale of hay where she could sit and rest, remove her sodden shoes. Her foot encountered something heavy lying on the ground. She felt it stir, leapt back in terror. Another body was looming up in front of her, a shadow with real hands.

'No, get off! Get *off*. Don't touch me.'

Screams were scalding from her throat, lending power to her stupid shaking legs. She turned and fled, tripped on a piece of lumber, sprawled her full length on the floor. She was sobbing now with pain and shock. The shadow had solidified to a threatening presence creeping up behind her. She could hear its breathing, smell its sweat. She closed her eyes. No point in screaming any longer. It was all over. She waited for the cosh, the knife.

'*J . . . Jennifer?*'

She jumped, looked up. Her name was as much of a shock as the startle of light now blinding her eyes. She ducked away from the beam, stared at the thin, paint-stained hand holding the flash-lamp. She knew that hand, knew the voice which had spoken her name. She rubbed her eyes. She must be imagining things again, like her fleeting vision of Hester on the site of the old hostel. Except this time, the details were much clearer: the bony wrist, the long tapering fingers — artistic fingers — the broken nails. Her eyes moved from fingers to face, a face which looked older and more haggard than when she had last seen it. She took in the three days' stubble, the dark circles beneath the eyes — eyes which were neither black nor blue nor grey nor . . .

'Lyn,' she whispered. 'Linnet.'

'Jennifer.'

They were both crouching on the damp floor of the barn, only a yard or two from each other. Neither moved, just stared, trembled, until Lyn slowly stretched out a finger, touched her face as if proving it were flesh. His hand burned, yet was as numb and chilled as hers. He kept it there, his breathing rasping and too loud. Neither said a word. The beam of the lamp was directed against the wall now, but even in the shadows, she could see how ill he looked. He was thinner even than usual, his eyes huge and almost feverish in that gaunt and ashen face, his clothes ragged like a tramp's. He seized her hand, gripped it so fiercely it was as if he were trying to solder them together, finger to finger, joint to joint.

'I love you, Lyn,' she whispered. She hardly felt the pain.

'Are you all . . . right?' His voice was hoarse and croaky, as if he hadn't used it for some time. 'You fell.'

She glanced at her knees, touched them with her fingers, felt the hole in her tights, the sticky trail of blood.

'It's . . . nothing.'

'Come over to the bed and I'll clean it up.'

He fumbled for the lamp, shone it in front of her, lighting up the barn. She could see now that he had turned it into primitive living quarters. What he had called the bed was a pile of straw with a piece of sacking spread on top; the kitchen was an enamel mug, a jar of coffee and a battered biscuit tin; the dining-room a camping stool and table made of planks. Dinner had been simple — bread, cheese, fruit. She could see the scrap of rind, the scatter of crumbs, a browning apple core, discarded on an old tin plate. A few

265

rusty nails hammered into the wall did duty as a wardrobe; the laundry-room was two wet and still grubby shirts strung from a piece of rope.

He crouched on the straw, smoothed the sacking out. 'I'm sorry, it's a bit . . . damp.' He sounded embarrassed, as if she were a rich guest who had come by chance to a low-grade dosshouse. 'Here, sit on my . . . jacket.' He took it off, coaxed her down, then turned the lamp on her legs and examined the grazes.

'There's grit in them. I'll get some water.'

'No, really. They . . . hardly hurt at all.' She didn't want him to go away, not even for a second. There were a hundred things she longed to ask — how he was, what he was feeling, how long he had been living here, why he hadn't been in touch. There were seven weeks to fill in, fifty-two whole days to trap and question, yet all his concentration was fixed on two grazed knees — easing out a piece of grit, mopping up the blood.

'Wait there,' he said.

He groped only a few yards away, to a corner of the barn, yet he had taken the lamp with him, and it was dark, suddenly — dark inside her head. She longed to go after him, fling her arms around him, tell him how desperately she had missed him. Yet one wrong move could frighten him, drive him off again. She fidgeted on the straw, glanced at the pile of sketchbooks by the bed, two or three loose drawings scattered on the top. She picked one up, could barely make it out in the fitful light. Wild and broken lines seemed to be hurtling towards each other in a shocked and reeling space. All the fever and suffering in his face was repeated on the paper. She laid it down, blank side uppermost — couldn't bear to look at it. Lyn was back beside her. He had scooped a mugful of water from a bucket in the corner, found two clean handkerchiefs.

'You'd better take your . . . things off.'

She felt nervous now herself. This was her own husband, yet she was bashful like a schoolgirl. She turned away from him as she eased her tights down. Her shadow repeated the movement, gigantic on the wall. Two shadows now, his hovering over hers, dabbing at her knees.

'I've . . . nothing to put on them. No antiseptic or . . .'

'It doesn't . . . matter. They're . . . fine now.'

They were talking like strangers — warily, with pauses. All the things she had ached to say — seven weeks of longing, loving, loss — were dammed up tight inside her. He was still holding the handkerchief cold against her knees, staring down at the grazes, as if he couldn't yet cope with anything beyond them.

He pushed her skirt aside, frowned as he felt it damp. 'Your . . . clothes are wet.'

'Yes, I know.'

'Shouldn't you take them . . . off? You'll get a chill.' That's what she had always said, to him.

'Yes, I . . . suppose I should.' Her fingers fumbled with the buttons of

266

her raincoat, but were too cold and clumsy to undo them. He did it for her, slipped the mac off, unbuttoned the blouse beneath it. She was shivering so much, she could do nothing but just lie there while he undressed her like a baby.

'That raincoat's worse than useless. Even your underclothes are damp.' He sounded angry suddenly — angry with the rain, angry with anything which might do her harm. And yet his hands were gentle, easing off her slip, fumbling for her bra-hooks, and at last his gaze had moved up from her knees. He was staring at her body — breasts, belly, thighs — as if it was the first time he had ever seen it naked.

She was trembling under his scrutiny, shaking like a fool. Even her teeth were chattering. She tried to stop it, but her body was stubborn, out of her control.

'You're cold.'

'N . . . no.'

He stretched up from the straw, still gazing at her, as if he feared she might vanish if he lost her reflection in his eyes; reached out for his duffel coat, spread it over her. He hardly touched her, yet the graze of his coat was almost a caress.

'It's quite . . . warm in here, in fact.' His voice was gruff still, uncertain. He was tucking the coat around her feet.

She nodded, couldn't speak. He had never cossetted her like this before. He was nursing her like an invalid, reversing their roles. Yet, somehow, it made her uneasy, kept them strangers still. He was the one who was ill.

'Look, we'd . . . better save the light.' Total darkness plunged as he switched the flash-lamp off. Now she could no longer see the tiny comforting things which made it home — the mug, the food, the washing-line, the upturned cardboard box he was using as a dressing-table, the unused comb and razor. His body was just a blur now, looming over her, standing guard. She longed for him to join her, lie down on the straw beside her. She wanted a husband, not a sentry. She stared up at the rafters. Part of the roof had fallen in, and a jigsaw piece of sky was peering through the hole, with a swatch of moon inside it. She could hear the rain drumming against the roof, spitting into the bucket which Lyn had placed beneath the hole. She was glad of the noise. It filled and tamed the silence, gave her something to fix on, like a mantra. It was stifling under the duffel coat, yet she couldn't stop her shivering.

Lyn was leaning over her. 'You're still cold.' It was almost an accusation. 'I haven't any blankets, but you can wear my clothes, if you like. At least they're dry. I sleep in them myself most nights.'

'*You*'ll be cold, then.' She remembered his icy fingers on her knees.

'No, I won't.' He was already dragging off his sweater, unbuttoning his shirt. 'Put those on.'

The sweater smelt stale and musty. She slipped it over her head, submerged a moment in dark and blinding wool. When she had struggled free,

Lyn was naked, his body barred with silver like a cage. She slipped her hands through the bars, fractured the moonlight.

And suddenly, he was holding her, pushing up her sweater which she had only just pulled on, covering her with his body instead of with his clothes. She could feel his face pressed close against her breasts, hands quiet and cold, stroking down her back, heartbeat throbbing into hers.

'My *wife*,' he said.

It was very slow, very careful. He didn't rush her, wasn't greedy, didn't make up for lost months or wasted time. There wasn't any time. They had been here all their lives — joined, dovetailed, overlapping — the slow rhythm of his body slowing down all nature, so that the clouds were barely moving now in the scrap of sky above her, and even the rain had stopped again — suddenly — as if holding its breath in awe.

She lay silent, all her senses sharpened, so that she could hear the almost imperceptible sigh and shudder of elm trees on guard outside the barn; could feel every wisp and prickle of straw against her bare legs. Each tiny stir and sound was somehow part of her, part of Lyn, merged with their merging bodies. She could smell rain, straw, damp clothes and tractor oil, all mixed up and overlaid with the musky scent of herbs still fragrant on her fingers. Rue for sorrow, wormwood for bitterness. *Wrong*. She could measure her joy in every thrust of Lyn's body, every throb of her grazed and burning knees as he pressed against them. He was moving faster now, his breathing wild and jagged, his voice broken into snatches.

She shut her eyes. The darkness was brilliant now. Despite his weight and the hard floor underneath her, nudging through the straw, she felt light and free and winged, as if she were soaring above her own slack and grounded limbs.

'Jennifer!' He was triumphing her name, hands scalding down her back. 'My darling. Oh, my darling . . .'

'No, *stop*, Lyn. Stop!'

'What's the matter? What's . . .'

She didn't answer, just lay tense and rigid. She pushed him off, closed her legs against him. He mustn't come. It was the middle of the month — her most fertile dangerous time. She had almost forgotten, almost risked a child. She could see the cellar in Hester's house again, the murky shadows, the cold and musty gloom — not so different from this barn. She had conceived a child there, lost it, lost her husband, lost her peace of mind. It mustn't happen a second time. Nothing must happen between them which could drive him away again, reinstate the fear or the resentment.

Lyn was crouching over her. 'What is it? Did I hurt you?'

'No, no, it's nothing. It's all right.' She had recovered now and was drawing him down again, kneeling between his legs while she coaxed him on to his back. He had already dwindled. She bent over him, cupped him in her hands, moved him towards her mouth.

He tensed. 'No.'

'Yes,' she urged. 'Please yes. I *want* to, and it's safer.'

She wanted him more than she craved a baby, needed a husband before she could add a child. He felt like a child — small and soft and helpless in her mouth. He tasted strange, unwashed. She licked him clean, licked him bigger. He was moving now, responding. She used her lips to rally him, swelled him with her tongue. His cries sounded faint and far away as if they were coming from another world, the smaller colder world beyond her mouth. She couldn't speak herself — there wasn't room. He was filling her whole mouth now, expanding it, moving faster faster faster until he was exploding in it, overflowing, running over. She gulped him down, triumphant, astounded at herself. She had never done that before, always been reluctant. But this time, it was different. She wanted every drop of his seed and self inside her, and if she couldn't have it the usual way, then at least she had swallowed him and saved him, made him part of her body and her bloodstream. They were — as the marriage service said — one flesh.

She could feel him shrinking in her mouth, becoming child again. She kissed his tip, released it, continued the kisses across his belly, up his chest, along his neck to stubbly chin and soft lips.

At last, they rolled apart, lay still, their breathing roaring through the silence. Jennifer turned on her back, the sacking damp against her shoulders, Lyn's jacket soft and crumpled, further down. She was in her husband's bed again, mistress of his house. It didn't matter that the house was poor and simple. It was only a temporary refuge. Hernhope was their true home, and they could return there now, rebuild their life and marriage.

She eased up from the straw, clutched the duffel coat around her, groped to the door of the barn, pushed it open. The sky had cleared and a million stars spelt the tiny glittering letters of infinity. The moon was riding higher now — Hester's full moon which had led them to each other. They would stay together now — never part again. She glanced at her watch, the only thing she was wearing beneath the scratchy coat. The hands pointed to one minute after midnight. Even that was meant — a new day, a new start.

She was shivering again, but only with excitement. The moon was bursting out of the sky, the whole night spinning towards dawn. Only a few hours more, and they could leave. She gazed towards the allotment — dark shapes and shadows beyond a darker fence, the swooning scent of southernwood carried on the wind. They must gather Lyn's harvest, take his produce with them as a symbol of hope and fruitfulness. She turned to fetch him, but he was already there, behind her — silent, staring past her at the stars. She gripped his hand — no need to spell it out.

He and his harvest were ready.

XX

'*Sunday Express*? Give me the literary editor, please. Yes, I'll hold on.'
Matthew shifted the receiver to his left hand and jotted down the list of
other newspapers he could phone, in order of their pulling power or status
— *Sunday Times*, *Observer*, *Daily Express*, *Daily Mail*, *Guardian* . . . He
smiled as he sipped his coffee. He had allowed himself a dash of cream in
it. He felt expansive, celebratory.

'Graham Lord? Ah, hallo! Matthew Winterton here. How are you?
Good, good. Enjoyed your week in Portugal? Wonderful! Look,
Graham, I thought you'd like to be the first to know we've sold half a
million copies of *Born With The Century*. Yes, I did say half a million.'
Matthew was doodling with his pencil on the pad. A figure five, with
five noughts after it. He crossed out the five, changed it to a one, added
another nought. Success like that had always been impossible. Now, he
had London's leading publishers clamouring for contracts, foreign agents
jamming his telephone lines. At the Frankfurt Book Fair, his stand had
been all but mobbed, VIPs begging the honour of a drink with him.

'Yes, of course we're celebrating. We've giving a party here next
month — December 14th. You'll get your invitation in a day or two.
Don't miss this, Graham — it's going to be the party of the year. In fact,
I'll want a word with your gossip columnist later. I think he'll find our
guest list quite impressive!'

Matthew put the phone down, drained his coffee. He had just a month
to make this half-a-million mark celebration the most talked about event
in London. Hartley Davies had suggested the party as a tribute and
congratulation, but had proposed a low-key Christmas luncheon to be
held on their own premises and involving less than a dozen guests.
Matthew accepted both the offer of a party and the cash to pay for it, but
moved the venue to his own offices and upgraded the occasion to a
full-scale jamboree — a secular Te Deum — to be held in the evening and
include London's leading literati and anyone of influence in the media.
That way, the full spotlight of glamour and attention would be directed
on his own firm, instead of on Hartley Davies. The fact of playing host to
such a high-powered gathering would increase his status and attract new
authors to his ever expanding list. It would also help whip up a new surge
of interest in *Born With The Century* — indeed, in all his books — for those
important post-Christmas months when sales were often sluggish.

'Ah, the invitations! Good.' Matthew was fining down his guest list
as Allenby knocked and entered, with Kenneth just behind him. 'I was
hoping they were ready. Let's have a look.'

Jim laid the cards on Matthew's desk. He had grown a little plumper
since the spring and had started wearing hand-made shirts and smoking

Davidoffs. Success had affected all of them, as well as their surroundings. There were new pictures on the office walls, expensive flower arrangements in reception.

'Well, what d'you think?' asked Allenby, glancing at the row of more conventional invitations on Matthew's mantelshelf. Now the firm was thriving, they were invited everywhere.

'Mm . . . Not bad. Not bad at all. Mind you, I think we could have made them more spectacular — something three-dimensional, perhaps or . . .' Matthew stared critically at the drawings of flowers and birds taken from the book. Lyn would have done better; made them more original, added some touch of genius exclusively his own. Except Lyn had been absent now for weeks. In fact, he hadn't seen his half-brother since that disastrous day when he and Anne returned from Tokyo and found the house in chaos. He had had to remove him from the pay-roll, explain to his colleagues that Lyn was convalescing after some new-strain virus infection which had left him debilitated. According to Jennifer, he was genuinely ill. She never brought him with her on her visits — only some excuse. He was sulking, more likely, or deliberately avoiding him, but he didn't press the matter. Lyn's demands for his share of the profits, to be paid immediately and in toto, could prove highly inconvenient. Lyn was a worry altogether, especially now he knew about Hester's bastard baby. He'd been shocked when Jennifer stuttered out that news. *How* did Lyn know, and why had he never mentioned it before? Would he start asking awkward questions, raise fraught and dangerous issues such as copyright? He had tried to buy his silence by paying some of what he owed him directly into his bank account — trifling sums, in fact, but enough he hoped, to keep him compliant. He missed Lyn's work, his unique and quirky talent, but it was safer in the circumstances to employ another artist, a yes-man with no claims on him.

He opened the invitation, checked the printing inside. Even without Lyn's skills, the design was at least unusual — white lettering on a grey and azure ground, and distinctive silver envelopes which would immediately catch the eye in an average morning's mail.

'Yes, they're fine. I'd like to get them off as soon as possible, which means finalising our guest list. Any bright ideas since we last discussed it? Remember, I want as many VIPs as we can coax along. I intend this party to be the talk of London, the sort of occasion that gets turned into publishing myth.'

'It'll be damned expensive,' grumbled Jim.

'That's not our problem. And anyway, it's money to make money. It worked with the book itself and it'll work again. You had your doubts a year ago, and here we are with half a million sales. That's some achievement, Jim, and we want the world to know about it. I think I told you Hartley Davies are going to present us with the half-millionth copy bound in real gold plate. That should make headlines on its own. We'll have it on

271

display, of course — make sure our top celebrities are photographed beside it.' Matthew paused a moment, made a jotting about the catering. Party food was often execrable. He wanted something unusual, even exotic. He must discuss his plans with Anne.

'I think we should also aim for some focal event to be staged halfway through the evening. We don't want formal speeches — they're a killer — but some sparkling or amusing little interlude which works also as a disguised advertisement for the book. I've already arranged for a band of Northumbrian pipers to play Hester's local music, but that will be simply background. So if you've any bright ideas, get them down on paper and perhaps you'd be good enough to see they're on my desk by five o'clock.'

Kenneth opened his mouth to object. He looked tired and drawn.

'All right, make it seven, then. I'll still be here. Now, the next thing I'd like to discuss is the problem of gatecrashers. Once the rumours get round, we may find we're overrun by . . .' Matthew's words were drowned by the shrilling of the phone. He snatched up the receiver.

'Anne, I told you I wanted no interruptions for the next half hour. What? Well, who is he? What d'you mean, won't give his name? I've no intention of . . .' He covered the mouthpiece, gestured to Jim and Kenneth. 'Forgive me, please. My wife's got some . . . nutter in reception.' Back to Anne. 'No, I'm sorry, he *can't* see me — not at the moment. Tell him he'll have to wait.' He tapped his fingers on the blotter. His wife needed stricter handling.

'I'm not arguing about it, Anne. I'm in the middle of a meeting and I instructed you to divert all calls. Don't disturb me again, please.' He pushed the phone away from him, sorted through his lists. 'Yes, do smoke, Jim. We've covered the most important items now, I think. As I was saying, I want this party to be more than just a jolly evening. It's publicity we're after and a clear message to the publishing world that Winterton and Allenby are now . . .'

He frowned as heavy footsteps echoed along the passage outside his office. Jim swung round as the door-knob rattled and a tall but portly man strode into the room. He was dressed neatly in a navy suit which although obviously expensive and well-cut, looked a trifle out of style and was too lightweight for November. His balding head was domed and shining; what hair he had clipped severely short at back and sides and heavily streaked with grey. His suntan looked somehow wrong on him — out of keeping with his rigid, almost military bearing, as he traversed the stretch of carpet from door to desk, then drew himself up in front of the six foot of mahogany.

'Am I addressing Mr Matthew Winterton?'

'You are.' Matthew rose slowly to his feet. The two men were matched for height, but Matthew was overshadowed by the intruder's broad shoulders and heavy build, and looked pale beside his tanned and ruddy face. 'But it is not normal for total strangers to barge in here without a

272

prior appointment or even the courtesy of knocking . . .'

'This is not a normal situation.' The accent was faintly Antipodean, but cultured and low-keyed. 'I have a very urgent matter to discuss with you — one I think you'd prefer to discuss alone. So if you'd like to dismiss your colleagues . . .'

Matthew gestured to Jim and Kenneth to remain where they were. 'I shall dismiss nobody except yourself, Mr . . . er . . .? If you are the same individual who's just been pestering my wife, I understand you refused to give your name.'

'You *know* the name, Mr Winterton, though it may still be a shock to you, since it is one I believe you have endeavoured to suppress.' The stranger's voice was steely. 'It is also the maiden name of the woman who brought you up.'

Jim and Kenneth were staring. Matthew steadied himself against his desk. 'I . . . I beg your pardon?'

'I am Edward Ainsley — Hester Ainsley's first and eldest son.'

Matthew's features registered a fleeting spasm of panic before he forced them into their usual impassive mask. He cleared his throat, as if to find his voice again, turned to Jim and Kenneth. 'I wonder if you'd mind . . . stepping outside. We c . . . can resume our meeting . . . er . . . later on.' He saw them to the door, shut it securely behind them. His hand was shaking as he went to greet his stepmother's bastard child.

'No, I won't shake hands, Mr Winterton. This is not a social call. In fact, I ought to warn you I have come straight from my solicitors.'

'S . . . solicitors?'

'Yes. A leading London firm. I consulted my own lawyer back in Auckland and he recommended . . .'

'Auckland?' Matthew was so disorientated, he could only repeat Edward's words. His head was reeling from the shock of a new-born baby, disposed of more than sixty years ago, resurrecting into this six-foot martinent. How could a housekeeper's obscure and bastard offspring, buried if not in a coffin, at least in secrecy and shame, be now standing in his office threatening him with apparent legal action? And yet he could tell this was Hester's son. The eyes bore witness to it — Hester's eyes and Lyn's, transplanted in that sullen jowly face — eyes of a colour so strange and so distinctive, they trumpeted the Ainsley name. They were narrowed now and frowning.

'Well, Warkworth, to be precise. It's some forty miles from Auckland. I was taken there as a babe-in-arms and have lived there ever since. I can truly call it home in the sense that everybody knows me there, and trusts me — or at least they *did* until these last few weeks. I can only assume that my present . . . er . . . embarrassments are due in some way to your publication of my mother's private diaries — a matter I take the strongest possible exception to.'

Matthew slipped a finger inside the collar of his shirt which seemed

273

suddenly too tight for him. 'Mr Ainsley, please. Your presence here is something of a . . . shock for me. Can't we at least sit down or . . .' He walked over to his elegant Regency chiffonier where he kept the glass decanters. 'Let me offer you a drink — a whisky or a . . .'

'No, thank you,' Edward made a curt dismissive gesture, refusing both seat and drink. 'I find it utterly distasteful that my mother's personal papers should have been hawked around the marketplace until they found the highest bidder, the . . . the . . . intimate details of her life dragged into the public gaze.'

Matthew tensed. That was the line which Lyn himself had taken when he had first mooted publication. Had the two men been in contact — Lyn somehow traced the bastard son and then joined his cause to spite him? Would that explain Lyn's absence, his mysterious illnesses? Surely not. How could anyone have traced that clandestine child, least of all when he had been living half a world away? Who had spirited him to New Zealand in the first place, and why had he come back? Edward was a closed chapter, an infant corpse mouldering in a coffin, a page in Hester's diaries long since burnt and destroyed.

He stared at the corpse, the infant — who seemed to be swelling as he stood there — the huge form bearing down on him, the quiet voice growing shriller.

'I am also extremely upset that my . . . my . . . own existence was totally ignored. I was neither warned nor consulted on a matter which . . .'

Matthew cut in. 'How could I have consulted you when I had no idea that you were still alive? I mean, even now, I'm . . . I'm stunned to see you standing here in front of me — a full-grown man — when I assumed you . . .'

'You knew of my existence, then? That itself is obviously no shock.'

'Well . . . er . . . yes, I . . .' Matthew floundered. Too late to deny it, now. And anyway, if Lyn had already divulged the facts, it would be dangerous to take a different line and be branded as a liar.

'L ... look, Mr Ainsley, all I had to go on was a couple of lines scrawled in Hester's diary — simply a brief and cryptic record of your birth — nothing more at all.'

'Well, that was proof enough that my mother had *two* sons, and not just a single heir. You had a duty to inform your lawyer of that important fact before going ahead with any negotiations. I understand my mother left no Will, or if she did, it has never been found, which means, of course, that I was entitled to be joint administrator with my half-brother, to deal with her affairs. Yet I have just been informed by my solicitor that no one was appointed executor or administrator. Why was that?'

Matthew swallowed. They were on dangerous ground here. He remembered all the agonising, eighteen months ago. Lyn had refused to be administrator, wanted no responsibilities, nothing to do with property or lawyers. At first, he had tried to change his brother's mind. With neither probate nor letters of administration, Lyn's right to deal with the copyright was not officially ratified, and therefore any deal he made with him was not completely watertight and could perhaps be challenged. But then came the bombshell about Hester's bastard child, which had changed the whole affair. How could he perjure himself in front of a lawyer, swear that Lyn was the only son and heir when he knew it to be false? Yet if he admitted his knowledge of the earlier child, the problems and confusion would be greater still. He had also felt instinctively that in these changed and complex circumstances, it was wiser to keep all solicitors at bay. The mysterious bastard baby had most conveniently disappeared and if it wasn't actually dead, it was still best to behave as if it were, suppress its birth and name — simply snuff it out. Yet now this suppressed and stifled child had come to life again and was threatening his private bargain, his brother-to-brother quiet informal pact — dragging in lawyers when he had preferred to bypass them.

'You haven't answered my question, Mr Winterton, which leads me to suspect that your arrangement with my half-brother concerning my mother's assets is open to attack. My lawyers have made every effort to trace my half-brother — as yet with no results. I arrived in England only forty-eight hours ago, and they have acted with admirable speed and efficiency, so they may well have news for me in the next few days . . . Except I cannot *wait* that long. I am being pestered back at home with most unpleasant gossip about my . . . er . . . irregular birth. Which is why I am here now. I can only assume that it was you, or one of your colleagues, who spread these rumours which have finally reached New Zealand and . . .'

'Certainly not,' Matthew interrupted. 'If you've read the Book — which I presume you must have done — you'll see that there is not the slightest reference to Hester's . . . er . . . first pregnancy. I don't mind admitting I was tempted to include it. An item like that — if you'll forgive me, Mr Ainsley — would have a great appeal to readers, but I deliberately omitted the whole incident to spare Hester's name and reputation.'

Matthew paused. He had suppressed it mainly for his own sake. In the most unlikely event of the bastard son having grown to manhood, the last thing he had wanted was to alert the fellow, or anyone who knew of him, so that he could claim his share of everything, disrupt the quiet and careful arrangements which worked largely in his own favour. Yet now, that very thing had happened, despite his care and secrecy. He could no longer suspect Lyn of ganging up with Ainsley, when Edward had just admitted that they had not yet been in touch, and surely Jennifer would never have betrayed him? She was the one who had pressed for total silence. Anyway, how could either of them have known that the infant child was still alive, let alone where to find him? He hadn't time for speculation now. He had to appease this man, disarm him. At least

Edward seemed more concerned with matters of propriety than with actual hard cash. He wished he could sit down. His legs felt shaky and it was difficult to reason when he was standing facing Edward, as if they were both positioned for a duel. He forced a chilly smile.

'You must remember, Mr Ainsley, that Hester was a mother to me as well. She brought me up from babyhood and . . .'

'That is what so shocks me — that you should have made money out of a woman who . . . who mothered you, turned her into a public scandal.'

'I've told you, Mr Ainsley. I did nothing to tarnish her name. My book was a tribute and a thank-offering. Everyone agrees that the diaries show Hester as a wholly admirable figure with . . .'

'And a very *private* one, who hated prying eyes, and shut herself away even from her own village, let alone . . .'

Matthew stifled his retort. They were getting nowhere — only more het up. He must take a different line.

'Mr Ainsley — forgive me — I hadn't noticed the time. It's after one and I'd quite forgotten lunch. I belong to a very pleasant Club just a step or two from here which has a really impressive wine list. We'll be more relaxed with a good claret on the table to help us sort things out.'

'I'm afraid it would be wasted on me, Mr Winterton. I very rarely drink and never when I'm talking business.'

'Well, let's at least eat, then. The chef's young, but very sound, and if you'd like to sample some first-rate English cooking . . .'

'I'm sorry, I'm not hungry, and I rarely stop for lunch, in any case.'

Matthew frowned. He recognised his own line — the abstemiousness, the high-mindedness, the refusal to relax and sip a drink, the refusal even to sit down. He had used all those tricks on his own subordinates, but now they were turned on him, he felt threatened and belittled. Edward was in no way a typical Antipodean. The accent was there — in embryo — the summer suit, the suntan, but in manner and bearing he was more like an old-fashioned British army officer. There was something of himself in Edward — something rigid and uncompromising which made him fear the man still more. His only advantage was that Edward clearly dreaded scandal or disparagement. He appeared to have run away merely to escape a few home truths, and it was obvious that his anger was not so much for Hester, whom he had never even met, but for his own damaged pride. Edward was still speaking in that controlled and civil voice, but the hurt, resentment and bitterness were there, suppressed beneath it. Matthew recognised the signs — the clenched fists, the clamped jaw, the tightly braced shoulders. He tried to relax his own stance. He must impress upon this man that by resorting to solicitors and making a hue and cry, he would only involve himself in greater publicity — not to mention scandal — trumpet the secret of his birth across both their continents, turn whispered rumours into public proclamations.

'May I suggest, Mr Ainsley, that it is in both our interests to keep this matter out of the public eye? I quite understand we need to come to some agreement, but we don't need lawyers to draft it for us, surely? We can talk things over in a quiet and friendly fashion, and then make a private arrangement with far less fuss and upset, not to mention expense.'

'It's a little too late for that.' Edward made an angry impatient gesture. 'And, anyway, my lawyers were not too happy about my calling on you at all, let alone bypassing their services altogether. I must admit I had a certain curiosity about you and . . . er . . . Lyn, since both of you were brought up by my own mother, and Lyn, of course, is my only blood relation. However, since he appears to have gone away — or gone to ground, more likely — I wished at least to meet you. But now I find that you can in no way excuse or explain your . . . your betrayal of my mother, then I suggest we follow my solicitors' advice, and communicate, in future, only through them.' He turned on his heel, raised his voice a fraction. 'You will receive their ultimatum in the morning.'

'U . . . ultimatum?'

'Yes. As they had no address for Lyn, they have written to you instead, which seems appropriate when you are the publisher and appear to have taken all the chief decisions. In the absence of a Will, I am, of course, entitled to half my mother's assets, and since those include the original copyright of the diaries, I also have a legal right to a share of any payments or royalties paid in connection with the published book.'

Matthew strode across to the window, gripped the sill. He had to control himself, think before he shouted. Edward's voice was dangerously civil.

'My solicitors will be asking for a copy of the original agreement you signed with my half-brother and also for full details of all payments made since then, and all contracts and accounts connected with the book, with the figures to be confirmed by your auditors.'

Matthew swung around, clamped his shaking hands behind his back, tried to make his voice sound calm and reasonable. 'Mr Ainsley, please — this is all quite unnecessary. I am more than happy to compromise. Now that I am aware of your existence, of *course* I recognise your claims, and will pay everything I owe you, with an extra sum on top, to compensate for any . . .'

'Money, Mr Winterton, is only secondary. Naturally, I'd like what I'm entitled to, but it's the principle of the thing which almost concerns me, and the personal damage done.'

Matthew winced. Principle — his own word. A word you could never fight against, a word which led to war and bloodshed, set country against country, brother against brother. Edward was still speaking.

'And I cannot understand why you should have any objection to

277

lawyers, when you appear to concede my claims already. It is surely in both our interests to have this matter settled fairly and objectively.'

'Yes, of course, but . . .'

'However, my solicitors take the line that while the dispute is still outstanding, the book should not be published in any country where it has not already appeared, which means that all outstanding foreign contracts will be frozen as from now, and no new ones must be signed.'

Matthew opened his mouth to speak. No sound came out. It was Edward's voice which was roaring through the room and seemed to resound through the entire building, although in fact Edward had hardly raised it above its initial muted pitch.

'I'm sure you will have no objection to these provisions, Mr Winterton, since you've said already you're willing to compromise, but if for any reason you cannot satisfy my solicitors on these points within seven days of hearing from them, then I have instructed them to take the matter to court and to freeze the situation by applying for an injunction. I was a little reluctant, at first, to take a tough line with a man whom in happier circumstances might have been my foster-brother, but since you were insensitive enough to sully not only my own name, but that of the woman who actually brought you up, then . . .'

Edward was already at the door. Matthew blundered after him. 'Mr Ainsley, wait! Another few minutes, please. I can explain everything if only you'll . . .'

'I'd prefer it if you would explain to my solicitors. You'll receive their letter tomorrow, first post, and can contact them directly. Good afternoon.'

Matthew stood trembling at the door, watching Edward's self-righteously upright back glide down the stairs and disappear. He slumped down in his chair, his heart thumping against his ribcage like a piece of machinery which had gone dangerously out of control. His whole future was at risk, his profits slashed, his outstanding contracts challenged, all further ones prohibited, his reputation smirched. He could hardly take it in, hardly believe that this devious dangerous man was the eight-pound baby he had consigned to an infant's grave. Who had dragged him out, who spread those rumours which had brought him thirteen thousand miles to wreak this bitter revenge? A hundred fears and speculations were curdling in his brain, but one overwhelming terror loomed greater than the rest. He dared not face it. *Had* to face it. He stared at his hands, white-knuckled, on the blotter. They felt heavy, leaden, as if all the horrors Edward had just released had seeped like sediment into his fingers, manacling him to his desk.

He could have coped with Edward's threats, even a solicitor's ultimatum, had the matter been as simple as they assumed. All right, he'd lose half of all his profits — more than half, by the time he'd paid the lawyers' bill. It would be a blow, of course, a crushing blow. *Born With*

The Century was subsidising all his other books, keeping his firm solvent, his name respected. But things were infinitely more damaging than that.

He dragged himself up from his desk and over to the window, staring out at the busy street outside. He scarcely saw the buildings, hardly heard the noisy midday traffic. His entire concentration was fixed on one concern — his tax avoidance scheme and whether Edward's action would now haul it screaming into the light. For the last ten years, he had so arranged his finances that he had saved himself almost a hundred thousand pounds in tax. The scheme worked smoothly so long as no one pried or questioned it. But now he had been asked to disclose his contracts, release figures and accounts, he could no longer keep it secret, and therefore safe. Once lawyers were on his track, poking their noses into his private affairs, the Inland Revenue could well be alerted in their turn — awkward questions asked, investigations started. He might be ordered to pay alarming sums of money — sums he couldn't put his hands on, which were tied up in the business, or tied up in . . .

His legs were trembling under him as he walked to his safe with its private combination lock. He stood in front of it, as if ordering Edward and his lawyers to keep their prying hands off. Some of those files were damaging and dangerous. He fiddled with the dial, trying to remember the complex sequence of numbers which released the lock. But his brain was more concerned with other sorts of figures. There was worse to face — if anything could be worse. He had transferred all of Lyn and Jennifer's proceeds from the book into that same secret tax haven, without informing them, and had been enjoying the use of their money ever since. He needed that money to pay off debts and help with cash-flow problems, and anyway, it had been only a temporary measure while he sorted out his finances. True, he had fobbed them off with stories of investment and security, hopes of future profit, but they were genuine hopes and he fully intended to pay them later, with the interest added on. But a court might see it differently, label it theft and fraud. If the facts came out, he would lose all sympathy. The public might excuse him for not having investigated the possibility of Edward Ainsley's continuing existence with more thoroughness and openness, but they would never forgive his deceitful dealings with Lyn and Jennifer — especially Jennifer. The world was still in love with her — using her potions, trying out her recipes, even writing to her for advice or in admiration. He must somehow win her round, bribe her with some cash, present it as the share he had always intended for her and Lyn. She was so naïve about financial matters, she would never know the difference.

But that still wouldn't solve his tax problem. To account for ten years back tax would mean selling everything — house, business, assets — removing his sons from their private schools, crowding into furnished rooms like paupers, and even then he might not raise the sum. He would be branded as a cheat and a swindler, a man who rooked not only the

Revenue, but his own flesh and blood. He had conned a brother who was one of his own employees, married to the girl who had found the diaries in the first place and had helped to make them famous. All the people who had bought and admired his book would now turn on him and tear him to pieces like a pack of hounds. His name would be blackened, swamped in shame and scandal, his new-found fame turn overnight to notoriety.

Was there nothing he could do? His accountant had fled abroad a year ago, to save his own cool million. Could he plead ignorance or wrongful counselling, blame it on his advisers, ignore the ultimatum and brazen it out in court, bribe Edward Ainsley himself? Every course was either impossible or dangerous. Whatever he did, bankruptcy still stared him in the face. He locked the door and returned to the safe, forcing his gibbering brain to recall the numbers, his stiff and clumsy fingers to dial them out. He must sort through all his records, examine royalty payments, contracts, bank statements, tax assessments — destroy some of them, if necessary.

He hardly knew where to start. Every document seemed to have rude accusing words scrawled across it — swindler, liar, cheat. They were wrong, *wrong*. His intentions had been good, even honourable. He had aimed only to secure his children's future, strengthen and consolidate his business, make money out of money so that everyone would be richer in the long run. He picked up a trust deed, put it down again. New, but related fears kept flooding into his head, sapping his concentration. Edward's firm of solicitors were already on Lyn's track, couldn't fail to find him. Christ! His own son, Charles, had seen him down in Cobham just two or three weeks ago, and if he was still living in that flat in Bedfordshire, then he was within reach of *any* London lawyer.

Supposing Lyn let out how reluctant he had been to make any agreement in the first place, how he had been pressurised and persuaded against his will, the deal drawn up in a rushed and arbitrary manner with no outside legal help? If Lyn himself attacked the deal, then Hartley Davies might attack it in their turn, demand what right he had to sign a contract with them, when the original agreement over copyright was possibly defective. He could be sued in court for damages; all his other contracts — foreign contracts — called into question. That would be dynamite, since it was chiefly his foreign monies which he had siphoned into his off-shore trust to avoid paying tax on them.

He slumped against the safe. There must be some way round it. It was vital to keep calm, except his body disagreed and was sweating and shaking like a traitor. The slightest noise alarmed him. A footstep outside was Edward Ainsley returning with new threats, a car-horn in the street was the bray of other publishers laughing at his fall. He jumped like a burglar when the phone rang. Solicitors? A tax inspector? Some sly and sleuthing reporter already on his trail? The *Sunday Express* would be far more interested in a grubby scandal than a glittering celebration.

'Hallo, M . . . Matthew Winterton here.' He tried to keep his voice cool and conversational, ignore the hand trembling on the receiver.

'It's only me — Anne.'

'Wh . . . what do you want? I'm busy.'

'Sorry about the frightful man. He must have been a crackpot. I simply couldn't stop him. He pushed right past me. I didn't even get his name. Anyway, he's gone now. I watched him through the window to make sure he wasn't hanging around. But listen — I've got some really good news! Who d'you think's coming to the party? Yes; definitely. His agent's just confirmed it. Marvellous, isn't it? That's an absolute guarantee of front-page coverage.'

Matthew closed his eyes, transferred the receiver to his other hand.

'Anne,' he said, very slowly, very wearily. 'I'm afraid we've had . . . er . . . a slight change of plan. There's not going to . . . *be* a party.'

XXI

'In, two, three, four. Out, two, three, four, five . . . In, two, three . . .'

Jennifer blew out the last dregs of air, inhaled again, fingers spread across her diaphragm, exhaled more deeply, consulted her breathing-chart. She was practising what the text-book called 'conscious controlled breathing'. If she could master it herself, then it would be easier to help Susie through the birth. It was complicated — four different levels of breathing for the three different stages of labour, with additional techniques such as neuro-muscular disassociation and transition stage drill. It made childbirth sound anything but natural. She wondered how Hester had managed all those years ago. Had she been left on her own to scream and panic through it as best she could? Susie was still terrified; the classes seemed only to make her worse.

Jennifer had just left her at a class, watched her enter the dingy scout-hut with a crowd of pregnant girls, lingered there a moment, envying their self-important bulges, feeling inferior, excluded. She had dawdled back to the bedsit, stared in the mirror at her own flat stomach and barren breasts. Yet she *felt* as if she were pregnant — almost at full term — bloated and lethargic, always tired, although she was doing less and less. She had started ignoring dust and dirty dishes, allowing Susie to talk her into chips and chocolate bars, instead of insisting on the healthy way of life she had learned from Hester and expounded in the book.

She had even given up her job. The harmless little insurance office had become intolerable since the Edward Ainsley drama hit the headlines. She had been promoted from trainee cost clerk to chief butt and cabaret. In the end, she decided to resign — couldn't face the jibes and jokes, the ceaseless questioning from all the gawping staff. Edward's name had first appeared in Jasper Prince's column the morning after he exploded into Matthew's office just two weeks ago — then spread like fireweed to all the other newspapers. She still didn't understand how Edward had been alerted in the first place, how one bastard baby, born more than sixty years ago, and pronounced dead by Matthew within days or weeks of birth, could now be stalking though the newspapers, screaming for his rights. Matthew had explained it only in bursts of outrage, rambling speculations, angry denunciations on the phone. She had done her best to keep away from Matthew. She had too much to hide herself, and was too alarmed that in all the present uproar, the spotlight would fall on *her* again, the press try and hound her out. The book was such Big News that any scandal connected with it would be squeezed for its last drop of sensation, its latest burst of sales.

She slumped back on the scratchy Southwark carpet. She ought to be running through her exercises, practising her breathing. She snatched up the book with its diagrams and detailed explanations. The words were just a jumble. All she could see were those blurred accusing photographs of Edward in the newspapers, a man who never smiled. How could he be the Enemy when he was Hester's son, Lyn's own half-brother, even had their eyes? Lyn was just as much a problem. Every time she thought of him, it was his eyes she saw most clearly — dark, brilliant, feverish — as they had been in the Cobham barn an endless month ago; staring, burning down at her, her own dwarfed self reflected in their pupils. Now they reflected nothing. Their reunion had lasted only five short hours.

She struggled to her feet, paced up and down the gloomy basement room. Susie should be back soon, although every hour lasted twice as long now as it had done in the summer. There was only one date in their strange and snail-paced life — January 23rd — the date of Susie's confinement. She hardly dared look beyond it. She had resolved to postpone the problem of her marriage, the dark and clouded horizon of her future, until after the baby was born. Meanwhile, at least she had a goal, a purpose, something to cling on to, something to fill the void. Susie needed her, depended on her, hadn't rejected her as Lyn had done.

She picked up her sewing where she had left it on the table, forced herself to get on with it. She was making a patchwork pram-rug, a complicated one with a pattern and a border. Patchwork was good therapy, required total concentration. She threaded her needle, jabbed it through the fabric, imagining she was poking it into Jasper Prince's eyes, sewing up the mouth of Rowan Childs. It was they who had caused this trouble, with their snooping and their . . . .

She jumped as footsteps echoed down the passage. Any noise alarmed her now. She was constantly poised for a crisis — some brash reporter bursting in and pinning her down with pen and pad and camera, or even Edward himself, come to repeat his angry scene with Matthew. But it was only Susie shivering into the room, banging the door behind her. She shed jacket, scarf and mittens, made straight for the gas-fire, blowing on her hands. 'God! It's perishing out there. Almost threatening to snow. D'you realise, Jen, it's December 1st tomorrow? Merry Christmas!'

Jennifer retrieved the jacket, hung it up. 'Don't talk about tomorrow! I've got an appointment with Matthew in his office. Ten o'clock sharp, he said. I've tried everything I can to wriggle out of it, but he simply won't listen to any more excuses. This Edward business has really cut him up. He's so suspicious now — about me and Lyn, I mean — what we're doing and where we're living and . . . He's even *expecting* Lyn tomorrow. I keep telling him he's ill, but he said, ill or no ill, if he doesn't show up this time, then . . .'

Susie shrugged. 'I shouldn't worry. You're getting quite a dab hand at the lies. He can't be that suspicious, judging by the cheque he gave you last time. That's the most he's ever parted with. Lies pay off, you see. Just dream up another batch and sit back and wait for your reward.'

'Oh, Susie, *don't*. I loathe all that deceit. Anyway, it's getting quite impossible. How can Lyn be there tomorrow when I haven't heard a word from him for over five weeks?'

'I'd tell Matthew your husband's dead and buried, if I was you. He might as well be for all the . . . I'm sorry, Jen — don't look like that. I didn't mean to hurt you. It just pisses me off the way you let those two men walk all over you.'

Jennifer filled the kettle, switched it on. She had to distract herself. 'Matthew's got a point, Susie. I mean, this Edward thing *has* made things very tricky. The whole of Fleet Street's on Lyn's trail as well now, and it does look odd if Matthew has to say he's no idea where his own brother's disappeared to. They simply don't believe him. He's in a dreadful state about it all. When I last phoned Putney, he sounded close to a breakdown.'

'Serves him right, for treating you all so badly in the first place.'

'It's not that simple, Susie. He told me himself the money side's a nightmare.'

'Oh, yeah? I wouldn't mind a nightmare where I'm coining a cool few grand each week. In fact, I'd hope never to wake up.'

'Yes, but half the money's threatened now, and he never got that much in the first place.'

'Pull the other one!'

'He didn't, Susie — he told me. He had enormous debts to start with, which had to be paid off first, and the firm itself needs vast amounts of capital, just to keep it going. He went on and on about it on the phone. And now with Edward making all these claims, he's really in a spot. The money's tied up, you see. He can't just hand it over when it's working capital. I think that's the phrase he used. I must confess I couldn't follow everything he said. He admitted himself some of it was too technical for him to even begin to explain it.'

Susie snorted. 'You're too damned trusting, Jen. D'you know what the *Daily Mirror* called him?'

'No, I don't. And I'd rather not discuss it any more. I don't think it's fair. Just thank God you're not involved yourself.'

'But I *am*, mate. We all are — now Edward's shown his ugly mug in London. If those nosy-parker reporters sniff you out of your hole and find me here as well, you can bet your life they'll make a steamy story out of it.'

Jennifer ripped the cellophane from a box of cut-price teabags. She no longer bothered with Hester's herbal brews. Susie was right — the parallels between her pregnancy and Hester's would make a very spicy item in the gossip columns — one she had always dreaded.

Susie was grinning now. 'Ah well, I suppose it could be worse. After all, I've always wanted fame. Cheer up, Jen — you've been moping round the place for days. Not that I blame you, mind, cooped up here without a job or a bloke or anything. If only you'd stop fretting over Lyn, you might meet someone else — someone nice and normal.'

Jennifer said nothing. She hated Susie to keep harping back to Lyn. Just his name was enough to start the grief again — pile it on top of the worry over Edward. Even now, all the joy and anguish of that one snatched night in Cobham was re-running in her head like a film in black and white — the black and white of moonlight. An erotic film at first — their bodies clasped and thrusting on the straw, Lyn's gasping cries of pleasure as he poured into her mouth, the slow groping back to earth.

She had stood at the door of the barn, gazing at the stars, Lyn's shadow just behind her, her heart still thumping in elation and excitement. Suddenly, Lyn had grabbed her by the wrists, pulled her back inside, startled her with a flood and frenzy of words, vomited out in bursts, with sudden ragged silences in between them. She had hardly understood him, except he kept returning to some wrong he had committed, and how he had to stay in hiding. She had tried to humour him, suggested they hide together, run away to Hernhope and resume their life up there.

He had exploded then, half in anger, half in a sort of terror, crawling back to the damp and scratchy bed and crouching there like an injured animal. She had followed him, tried to reason with him, made him lie down beside her. When she touched his hand, it felt icy cold. He still couldn't talk coherently, just went up and down the same confused and futile cul-de-sacs, until they finally fell asleep, exhausted, on the straw. It was still dark when she woke. She had clawed at the sacking, groped out her hand for Lyn. He wasn't there.

Jennifer took a gulp of almost scalding tea. Her hands were trembling on the mug. She tried to steady them, drag her thoughts away from late

284

October in that Cobham barn, return to Susie and the bedsit. Susie looked solid enough, squatting in front of the biscuit tin, picking out the chocolate creams and dunking them in her tea, talking with her mouth full about other men and second marriages. Since Sparrow had showed up again, she seemed anxious to forget that she had ever found excitement in a woman's body. Her new crusade was to persuade Jennifer into the arms and bed of what she called a normal healthy bloke.

'You don't understand, Susie . . .' Jennifer broke off. Susie couldn't understand. Susie had never felt for anyone what she felt for Lyn. Susie wanted freedom. Lyn *was* her liberation. She was only free when she was bound and bonded to him, only whole when he completed her. The film was running again — the first erotic part — Lyn's mind and soul and body fused with hers, Hester's moon above, the scratchy kiss of straw, the hosanna of wind and rain outside the barn. Susie called that screwing. She had better words. She picked up her patchwork again, moved over to the light.

Susie drained her tea. 'God! Isn't that thing finished yet? You've been doing it for *weeks*. All that hassle just for a mingy pram-rug, when you could buy one in Mothercare for a couple of quid.'

'Not like this, you couldn't.'

'Yeah, but a baby's not going to know the difference. If you wrapped it in a dish-cloth, it would be just as happy. Anyway, the social worker told me not to bother with clothes and stuff. She said I don't even need to *see* the kid — well, hardly. They can take it away the day I leave the hospital if that's what I want. And I do want. It goes to foster-parents for the first few weeks, or straight to the adopting couple and *they* buy all the gear. You're wasting our precious money, Jen, stocking up on all those baby things.'

'It's still best to be prepared. Something might go wrong. There might be a delay, or the adoptive parents may be poor or badly organised or . . .'

Susie guffawed. 'Hardly! You have to be a bloody saint before you're allowed to adopt at all. That bod at the adoption agency told me there's such a shortage of babies, Dr Spock himself would have to join the queue.'

'You ought to be glad they're so strict. They only do it for the baby's sake.'

'Poor little sod, living with a Super-Mum. It'll probably grow up delinquent just to spite her.'

Jennifer smiled. She, too, felt hostile towards the adoptive parents. They hadn't even been chosen yet, but somewhere they were waiting — that young, fit, kind, reliable couple — ready to snatch the baby the minute it was born. It angered her that even had she been free to adopt the baby herself, it wouldn't have been allowed. She had no proper home, no regular income, no husband living with her, no forms or

285

references, no social worker's stamp. Babies went to conventional couples with the sort of eager loving men who papered walls or pushed the trolley at Safeway's, not tramps and nomads skulking round allotments to escape from imaginary crimes.

She sorted through her box of hexagons. 'Anyway, even a Super-Mum may not have bothered with patchwork. It's special, in a way — a sort of labour of love. So if you go to all the trouble of making it for someone, it's like — well — telling them they're important, or . . .'

Susie turned away.

'What's wrong?'

'Oh . . . nothing.' Susie picked up a handful of pieces, crumpled them in her hands. 'It's just that . . . *I*'d like to be special for a change. You're so batty about this kid, Jen, I sometimes feel *I* don't count at all. I'm just the mug who's having it, the bloody pea-pod. Would you make *me* a piece of patchwork? Just a little thing?'

'Of course I will. I'll make you a whole bedspread, if you like.'

'Would you, Jen? Honest? It'll take you ages though, judging by the pram-rug.'

'I've *got* ages.' Jennifer broke off a length of thread. Once the baby was born and handed over, there might be years and years of emptiness — time to make a patchwork cover for the whole aching universe. How could things have changed so much — the Country Woman shut up in a basement without so much as a potted plant, the skilled and stylish super-cook heating baked beans on a gas-ring or sharing fish and chips with Susie out of a newspaper.

Susie herself wouldn't be there for ever. She only stayed now because she was pregnant and dependent and had nowhere else to go. Even Sparrow was proving difficult. He still hung around, hungry for his perks, but he was nervous of her bulge, angry about the baby, frightened she might change her mind and keep it. There were other men, too, prowling in the background. Even seven months pregnant, Susie attracted attention.

Stupid to be self-pitying. A crush of crass admirers didn't make for happiness. In fact, it was almost worse for Susie — having to endure all the ordeal of childbirth with no joy at the end of it. They needed a change, both of them, a treat to cheer them up. She couldn't hide away for ever, simply because Edward Ainsley was roaring through the newspapers and she was frightened of being recognised. She must take a risk, face the world. It was hardly a risk, in any case. No one would equate her with that simpering painted woman who had once charmed all the media with her quaint old-fashioned clothes and her long hair piled on top. Her hair was shorter now, and straggly; she had put on weight from too much stodgy food, didn't bother with make-up, wore Susie's cast-off jeans. She picked up her sewing, stowed it in a drawer. 'Susie . . .'

'Yeah?'

'Let's go out.'

'What, now? I've only just warmed up.'

'No, Saturday. It's my birthday, then, and I think we ought to celebrate. Let's dress up and go somewhere really fancy.'

'Like dinner at the Ritz, you mean?'

Jennifer grimaced. 'Not the Ritz.' She could see Rowan Childs again, gold propelling pencil boring a secret tunnel to New Zealand. 'Even with Matthew's handouts, we can't afford that. Not dinner, anyway. We could have tea there, I suppose.' Cucumber sandwiches and waiters in black coats. No — she couldn't face those waiters a second time. 'Tell you what — let's have tea at Harrods — a sort of birthday blow-out. They do a special Grand Buffet where you can eat as many cakes as you can cram on to your plate. One of the girls in the office took her mother there and told me all about it. She said it was fantastic. There's even a pianist and . . .'

Susie jumped up. 'Great, Jen! I'd love that. D'you know, I've never been to Harrods, not once in my life. I'll even bung on my maternity dress in honour of the place. Got to wear it once, I s'pose.'

Jennifer was also wearing a dress — in honour of Matthew's office. It was six minutes past ten the following morning and she was still dithering outside his door like a small, scared schoolchild summoned by the headmaster to his study. The whole place made her nervous — the hundreds of glossy books, the impatient braying phones, the feeling of being a stranger and a bumpkin among those chic, clever, sophisticated highbrows, whom she imagined staring after her as she climbed the stairs to Matthew. She smoothed her hair, pulled her skirt straight, knocked.

'Come in.' The voice sounded tired and irritable, changed when Matthew looked up and forced a smile. 'Ah, Jennifer, at last. Where's Lyn?'

'He's . . . er . . . coming.' Why in God's name had she said that? She had meant to explain that Lyn was still unwell — seriously ill, confined to bed, unable to get up. Perhaps he was. She could see his face in front of her — gaunt, haunted, feverish — except it was Matthew's face, and speaking to her.

'What d'you mean, he's coming? I haven't time to waste. I'm up to my eyes this morning.'

'He's . . . er . . . on his way. He'll be here in . . . half an hour.' Jennifer was so shocked by Matthew's appearance, she was talking gibberish. Her rehearsed and polished lies crumbled into dust as she stared across at him. His face was pinched and grey with tiredness, his suit seemed to sag across his chest, his mouth was one thin line.

'Half an hour! What's the matter with him? Why can't you arrive together, for heaven's sake? I warned you on the phone, Jennifer, if we don't sit down and thrash this whole thing out, then . . .' Matthew was pacing up and down, eyes burning in his haggard face. Despite his air of exhaustion, he seemed unable to keep still. Even when he slumped back in his chair again, his fingers were drumming on the desk-top and he kept darting anxious jumpy glances over his shoulder as if he were on the alert for an intruder.

Jennifer was still gibbering. 'He . . . er . . . got delayed. I had to leave before him. He's got quite a long way to come, remember.' From the other end of England, for all she knew, the other side of the Channel. She tried to plan the next lies —.for when he *didn't* come: the car was unreliable; he'd been having blackouts and wasn't meant to drive . . .

Matthew jerked up from his desk again. 'Yes, it *is* a distance from Bedfordshire.' He gave the county a sarcastic, almost mocking emphasis. 'I'm surprised you got here yourself.'

Jennifer froze. Had Matthew somehow guessed that . . .?

He was striding to the door and back. 'Don't you realise Lyn's up to his neck in this? In fact, from a legal point of view, Edward's quarrel is not with me at all, but with Lyn as joint heir. Edward's solicitors have been trying to track him down for two whole weeks now. Surely you can see that if he hangs around much longer . . .'

'But he's coming, Matthew, I told you. There was a slight . . . problem before we left. The . . . er . . . water heater blew up.' Jennifer was trembling. Her own lies frightened her — stupid childish lies which would blow up themselves and scar her.

'There's always some excuse. Lyn's so damned casual. Just because he's got nothing to do himself, he imagines he can . . . Ah, that's him now, I expect.' The phone on his desk was shrilling. Matthew picked it up. 'And if he tries to tell me he's broken down or . . . Hallo? Yes, Matthew Winterton here. Who? Look, I told you not to bother me again. No, I haven't changed my mind. I made it quite clear last time that . . . I'm sorry — the answer's no — and if you're going to take that line, I've no alternative but to close this conversation.'

Matthew's hand was shaking as he banged the receiver down. 'The nerve of these reporters! That was Jasper Prince again. He's phoned me every day for the last ten days. It hurts to be called a liar by a man as . . . base as that.' Matthew picked up his paper-knife, slashed it against the blotter. 'Do you realise, Jennifer, he's trying to make out I was perfectly well aware that Edward was alive still, and that I hushed the matter up to grab all the spoils myself? That's downright libellous nonsense. You know yourself I made every enquiry I could, but there wasn't the slightest shred of evidence that Edward had survived. I mean, a child can't simply disappear. He's either dead or . . . I'm not psychic, am I? Who in God's name would have thought of looking in New Zealand?' Matthew was leaning forward, appealing to Jennifer, pleading with her. 'You believe me, don't you?'

'Yes. Yes, of course I do. It's just that . . .'

'What?' The word was like a gun-shot.

288

'Well . . . I don't quite see how Jasper tracked him down. I mean, if you'd already tried so hard and come up with nothing at all . . .'

Matthew hesitated. 'It was . . . Rowan Childs. She gave him a vital lead. Remember when we met her at the Ritz, she mentioned Hester's sister?'

Jennifer nodded. She had thought about Ellen several times since then, wondered why there were no letters from her among Hester's private papers. Had the two lost contact?

Matthew was still fiddling with his paper-knife. 'Ellen Ainsley was the only person in the world who could have helped any of us. She was the only relative left, you see, and . . .'

Jennifer had a sudden painful image of the bodies of Hester's brothers, bloody in the trenches. All three had been killed before they had a chance to marry, and since both Hester's parents had been only children, there were no descendants at all. 'But I thought you said she was ill and very old and . . .' Was Matthew lying himself — each of them trying to fob the other off — he over Edward, she about Lyn?

'She was. In fact, she's dead now. But she was still alive in the summer. Rowan interviewed her a week before she passed away. That's how she got her lead. Trust Miss Childs to harass a dying woman!'

'B . . . but I thought you said Ellen lived abroad — in Delhi?'

'That's right. She left this country way back in the twenties. I understand she was seeking religion or spiritual enlightenment or something, long before gurus became a Western craze. I suspect myself it was all a substitute for a normal family life. She was very plain, I'm told, and never married.' Matthew grimaced, as if ugliness and spinsterhood were states to be abhorred. 'Anyway, once I knew she was out of the country, I let the matter rest. I didn't intend flogging all the way to India just to question one sick and crazed old woman who would probably tell me nothing anyway. I was far too busy.' Matthew shuffled through the papers on his desk, as if to demonstrate his work-load.

'After we met Rowan at the Ritz, I checked on Ellen again — made a few enquiries via a friend of a friend who had relatives in India and didn't mind a spot of detective work. He came back with the news that Miss Ainsley had suffered a stroke in Delhi and died there, just a month or so before. Unfortunately, the information was wrong — though I didn't discover that till later on. Ellen had had a stroke — yes — but not a fatal one. She was left with one arm slightly paralysed and a problem with her blood pressure. Her doctors advised her to return to England, where she would have a milder climate and better nursing care.' Matthew smiled grimly. 'It appears our English rain does have its benefits.'

Jennifer nodded. So Rowan's rumour was right — though she didn't say so. Matthew hated told-you-so's. She pictured Ellen trying to cope with choppy seas or jet-lag with unsteady legs and a weakened arm. All of Hester's family seemed to have lived harsh or tragic lives.

Matthew was still talking. His voice was calmer now, but his left eyelid was twitching in a continual tiny spasm. He kept rubbing at it, as if he could remove the twitch like a speck of dust. It made her nervous just to watch him. Matthew kept the whole world under his thumb, yet was powerless to control a facial tic. '*I* had no idea, of course, that she had came across to England. She was still dead and buried four or five thousand miles away, as far as I was concerned. But Rowan Childs had been making her own enquiries, and had all the back-up of a wealthy newspaper to help her in the task. An outfit like hers has leads and contacts everywhere — including India. I couldn't compete with that. A few probing phone calls to her Delhi office and she was on the track of a still-living Ellen Ainsley who had just arrived in Bristol . . . Excuse me please.' Matthew's own phone was blaring through his words.

Jennifer tensed. If this were some reporter on the line, trying to track Lyn down, then Matthew would return to the attack. He had been so engrossed in the Ellen story, he seemed to have forgotten Lyn's absence, or at least accepted it. She watched him anxiously. He was jotting down some figures, talking fairly equably. No — it couldn't be a press-man, just a business colleague. He replaced the receiver, stared down at his pad.

'Er . . . what happened then?' she urged. Safer to fill the pause with Ellen than with Lyn.

Matthew added up his figures, scribbled down the total, scratched it out again. 'I'm sorry. Where were we?' He looked confused, disorientated.

'*Ellen*,' Jennifer said. 'Just arrived in Bristol.' Matthew had never needed prompting before. 'Why Bristol?'

'Apparently, she'd lived there before she went to India and it was the only place she still had contacts. Rowan tracked her down in a geriatric hospital and was lucky enough to get an interview — though perhaps "luck" is not the appropriate word. I understand a considerable sum of money changed hands.'

Jennifer stared. 'Surely not? I mean if Ellen was ill and almost senile . . .'

'Not so ill that money didn't rally her. A wad of twenty-pound notes slipped into her handbag and her memory improved dramatically. She not only recalled the baby Edward's birth and all the fuss which followed when her strict and shocked parents more or less disowned Hester and drove her from the house, but also the name of the foster-parents and the fact they were New Zealanders. After that, it was easy. All Rowan had to do was search the passenger lists of any boat sailing to New Zealand in the spring of 1919. In actual fact, she turned the matter over to those odious little people on the gossip column. Rowan likes to keep her hands clean, so when the story showed signs of getting . . . well . . . shall we say a trifle insalubrious, she realised it was more in Jasper's line. So he took over — went to the Public Record Office at Kew, and found a Mr and Mrs Edward Fraser — with infant child — passengers on the *Corinthic* which sailed for New Zealand on

290

March 14th, 1919. I've seen the entry with my own eyes.'

Jennifer was frowning. 'So you did know, Matthew?'

'No, no, certainly not — not then. I only went to Kew a week or so ago, when the story had broken already. Way back in June, I was still completely in the dark. All I *did* discover was that Ellen had left India for England. What happened was that Rowan Childs invited me to lunch and steered the conversation round to Ellen. I still thought she was dead, of course, which is why I hadn't bothered to contact Rowan myself, a second time. But it was pretty obvious at the lunch that Rowan was on to something. She even mentioned Bristol. I realise now it was all a deliberate lead — what the Press call a "carrot", I believe. Rowan hoped I'd bite on it and then spit out my own secrets — give away something she didn't know herself. She was under the illusion that I had a lot more facts on Ellen than I actually did, including, of course, her recent return to this country for her health. Alas — I was a long, long way behind her, though I did my best to catch up — drove straight to Bristol the following morning and scoured every hotel, hospital and old people's home in the area.'

'You didn't tell me, Matthew.'

'I didn't want to worry you. You had enough on your plate as it was, with all the publicity and so on. You were right in the middle of it, then, if you remember, and the last thing you needed was any additional strain. Anyway, my trip proved highly frustrating. I did find out that Ellen hadn't died in Delhi. In fact, she had died in Bristol — just two days before I got there — suffered a second stroke. Rowan Childs had made it just in time. She may even have hastened the death. Strokes are often caused by extra stress and excitement.'

'Ellen was almost *eighty*, Matthew.'

'Yes, all right. But it was still extremely unfortunate. All I managed was to speak to one or two of the staff at the hospital, who told me very little except that Rowan had been there twice and . . .'

'Twice?'

'Oh, yes. Rowan's very thorough. It was on her second visit she left the money.'

'But how did you know all this, Matthew? I mean, if she was dead when you arrived and . . .' Jennifer stopped. Had he used Rowan's methods and offered inducements himself, bribed the nurses at the hospital? She remembered her own cheque, signed in Matthew's hand. 'I wish you'd told me all this, Matthew. I mean, you didn't say a word and . . .'

'You'd only have been distressed. I was trying to spare you.' Matthew eased his back. Both the phones were ringing now, and he was switching between the two of them. Jim Allenby was hovering at the door, waiting to have a word with him, and a secretary had just knocked and entered with a pile of urgent papers for him to sign. She felt a sudden rush of sympathy. Matthew had tried to save her strain and worry — and yet was over-burdened himself. He looked too sick to deal with all that desk-work, on top of everything else. Easy for Susie to criticise when she had never seen him in his office, faced with all the pressures.

She wondered what might have happened if he had managed to talk to Ellen, got in touch with Edward before Rowan tracked him down. She would have welcomed a chance of meeting Ellen herself — come face to face with someone who had actually grown up with Hester, shared her girl-hood, known all her quirks and strengths. She tried to picture Ellen lying in that hospital — old, alone and feeble — betraying her sister's confidence for the sake of a wad of notes she would never have a chance to spend. Perhaps the cash had been used to purchase her coffin and her winding-sheet. She flashbacked seventy years, saw Ellen as an innocent young girl, shocked by her sister's pregnancy, acting as her confidante, torn between sympathy for Hester and loyalty to her parents.

Matthew was off the phone now, though he still had the receiver clenched in his hand, as if he feared to replace it and face yet another call. Allenby and the secretary had gone, leaving their wake of problems and new work. Jennifer stole a glance at her watch. It was already 10.30 and yet he hadn't mentioned Lyn again. He was normally well aware of the time, all too ready to denounce unpunctuality. She had her lies prepared — the faulty clutch, the blackouts — but preferred to postpone them as long as possible. She was bound to make another gaffe. Matthew looked up suddenly, frowned across at her.

'Listen,' she said, jumping in before he could explode again. 'This Ellen thing. I mean, if you didn't see her yourself, when did you first find out that she'd . . . er . . . sold her story to Rowan?'

'I didn't.' Matthew scribbled a note to himself, then pushed the pad away, made an effort to concentrate. 'Well, not until the damage was already done and Edward had come storming into my office. I knew money had changed hands, of course, so I suspected Rowan might have got something for her pains. After that, I read every word she wrote — watched her column like a hawk — and Jasper's. But the subject never came up at all. Weeks passed — still nothing — not even that piece on Fernfield Rowan mentioned. So I assumed she'd *wasted* her time and money and that Ellen had stayed mum.' Matthew reached for his pad again, made another jotting. It was as if the story were reminding him of certain points he could use in his defence. 'What actually happened was that Jasper had passed the matter on to one of his stringers in New Zealand. These Fleet Street types have contacts everywhere. He already knew the Frasers' destination — Warkworth — he'd got that from the records. So he phoned his man in Warkworth, or Auckland, or wherever, and told him to get on with finding baby Edward — though hardly a baby now. That's where the delay began. The New Zealand reporter, who has the unfortunate name of Wilbur Crank, realised that this was the best and biggest exposé he was ever likely to have a finger in, so he decided he'd try and claim the credit for his own exclusive scoop and run the story first in Auckland, under his own by-line. As you know, the book's a bestseller in New Zealand as well as over here. So every time London nudged him over the telephone, Crank simply stalled — said he was digging hard, but had come up with nothing much to speak of. In actual fact, he was doing pretty well, sniffing round anyone and everyone who'd ever seen or heard of Edward — offering bribes to cleaning ladies or greensmen at his golf club, laying on fancy little lunches wherever they'd pay off. Unfortunately for him . . .' Matthew paused a moment, as if the memory were painful for him, also. 'Edward was tipped off just before Crank was ready to confront him and obtain the final clinching interview. Edward was upset enough already. He'd read the book himself, found his mother's maiden name — *his* name — but no record of his birth or existence, nor mention of his father. He'd also heard the rumours which Crank's enquiries had started stirring up, and which had surfaced at the worst possible time for him. You see, he was standing for re-election for the local council. Apparently, Edward's quite a little grandee in his home town — been a councillor for years and JP before that, so his personal reputation is obviously pretty crucial to him.'

Jennifer broke in. 'Surely he didn't tell you all this, Matthew?' From what she had gathered, Edward had stormed in with an ultimatum, not stopped to chat about his career or election prospects. She was confused and bewildered that this whole painful complex story should have been unfolding around her and beyond her, and yet she herself had been in total ignorance.

Matthew was shaking his head. 'Not as such. He mentioned ugly gossip and I could see he was really thrown by it, but he didn't give the details. No — what I did was get on the phone to Colin Bailey — he's the export sales manager at Hartley Davies — a very decent chap. You've met him, actually, at the sales conference last November. Reddish hair and spectacles — remember? He visits New Zealand once a year, at least, and he's always said the country's small enough for him to know a lot of local people there and have a good idea what's going on. Anyway, he did a bit of sleuthing for me and reported back with quite a little saga. Apparently, what happened was that Edward's opponent in the local election — a character called Elkins and quite a nasty piece of work, according to Colin — was one of the people approached by Wilbur Crank. Elkins realised that here was something he could turn to his own advantage. He persuaded Crank to confide in him, made a few enquiries of his own, and then started a sort of . . . smear campaign, based chiefly on rumour at this stage — you know the sort of thing — hints that Edward was an upstart and a fraud who had cashed in on the Fraser name and money when he was nobody and nothing, and had deceived all and sundry by hushing up his background. It appeared to work. Edward lost, in any case, whatever the actual reason. It wasn't just defeat which so upset him, but the danger of publicity and the fact that reporters were involved. As I told you, someone had warned him already that Crank was on his tail, and he was so alarmed by now that he took immediate legal advice and discovered that Crank was under orders from Fleet Street where the probe had originated. He immediately flew to London — in a panic, I suspect — to try and supress the whole damaging issue of his illegitimate birth and so-called shady background before it made the national headlines. But his dramatic dash to London only made things worse. The rest you know.'

Jennifer flushed. She would never forget it — the day that Jasper's story broke — her own guilt and shock as she saw Edward's bewildered face blinking from the gossip columns, the ugly word 'bastard' bandied about by unfeeling journalists. Edward had successfully quashed that word for over sixty years — or so the papers said. He knew he was not the Frasers' son — how could he be when he had a different name from theirs? — knew he was English-born and illegitimate, but he had always hushed the latter up, claimed Ainsley as his true mother's *married* name. If people pressed or probed, he informed them that the young and tragic Mrs Ainsley had been widowed in the Great War before he was even born — and then clammed up, refusing to discuss his background any further. Now, that background was being shouted from the rooftops. There had never been a Mr Ainsley, only a poor, single, shameful pregnant girl. Ellen had given no details of Edward's father, despite Rowan's bribes and pressures, so all the papers resorted to speculation, much of it unpleasant.

Jennifer's nails were digging into her palms. She could see the shocked and sniggering town of Warkworth whispering behind its respectable net curtains, pointing the finger of scorn at baseborn Edward. Susie might shrug off illegitimacy, but Susie was seventeen and easy-going. Edward was in his sixties, living in a small old-fashioned community who regarded bastardy, if not as a crime, then as a stigma and a shame. Edward had been respected and respectable, a pillar of his local church, an elder statesman living a quiet, conservative, almost old-maidish life, untouched by the faintest breath of scandal. Now, all that was changed. Jennifer could hear the racy adjectives resounding in her head, the mocking headlines blistering the newspapers. She herself had helped to bring him down. In urging publication of the diaries, she had overruled his rights as elder son and his claim to copyright, risked his name and reputation. It was no excuse to say she had assumed him dead. Neither she nor Matthew had had any real proof of that, whatever Matthew claimed. Yet, eighteen months ago, Edward had seemed so substanceless — a stifled whisper, two blushing lines on a concealed and secret page.

She glanced across at Matthew. Edward had put that tremor in his eye, aged him ten years in a fortnight. Edward was the enemy, and here she was wasting her pity on him, even though he was attacking Lyn as well, threatening all the profits from the book, wresting Hernhope from them. All her hopes of returning there with some money in her pocket were now totally extinguished. Hester's Will had never turned up, but even in its absence, Edward had a right to half her property. Illegitimacy was no bar to inheritance. She and Lyn could still fight for their half share, but Edward had the edge on them, since he was employing skilled solicitors and was clearly the wronged and innocent party. Lyn wasn't even there to fight, and Matthew was battling chiefly for his own rights, not for a remote and jungled house he had always hoped to sell. True, he had given her money these last few weeks, but what was a cheque or two compared with Hester's home, and his whole financial position was now threatened, anyway. Besides, no amount of cash could be worth this new upheaval, the swoop and jeer of all the journalists as they pounced on Hester's private life and flung it to the goggling bitching world. Some of the papers were fixated on the money side, and had even hinted that Matthew had cheated not only Edward, but her and Lyn as well — exploited them all to make himself a Midas. That was truly libellous. Matthew lived simply, almost frugally. Anyone could see that. He had no time for spending money, no room in his life for luxuries. Work came first and last.

Now, he appeared to have forgotten her existence — even Lyn's as well, although the half hour's grace she'd invented for him had been up some time ago. She was sick with nerves, waiting for Matthew to pounce. And yet he seemed unusually distracted, sorting through his desk, switching from one task to another, one mood to another, apparently unaware of the time. He snatched up one of his letters — began to mutter as he read it, obviously enraged. Suddenly, he ripped the sheet in two, crumpled up the pieces.

Jennifer winced, shifted in her chair, torn between remaining as quiet as possible so that he would forget the reason he had summoned her in the first place, or attempting to return him to the Ellen saga. She decided to stay quiet, stared down at the floor. Edward had been standing on that very patch of carpet just two weeks ago. One of Matthew's staff had leaked the story to the press, who had arrived that afternoon and turned Matthew's tight-lipped 'No comment' into slander and innuendo. She tried to imagine the two men face to face. Impossible. All they had in common was Hester — who had played mother to the wrong one. Had Hester resented Matthew because he wasn't her own son and yet brought back bitter memories, or tried to love him as an Edward, or simply treated him dispassionately as part of the job?

'Jennifer!'

She jumped. Matthew was on his feet, bearing down on her.

'Look here, I don't believe Lyn's on his way at all. I've waited more than forty minutes and there's not a sign of him. He's avoiding me deliberately — has been all along. I'm not so simple that I don't see through your constant excuses and evasions. They're obviously a pack of lies.'

'L . . . lies?' Jennifer ducked, as if warding off a blow. Matthew was looming tall and grey in front of her. He suddenly veered round to the window, stood there gazing out. Jennifer could hear the clock stalking through the silence, feel her own heartbeat painfully loud. The roar of city traffic seemed to have come to a sudden halt, as if Matthew had raised his voice to it.

'Yes, Jennifer, lies.' Matthew swung round to face her. 'I've been up to Bedfordshire — twice, in fact — just in the last few days. I called at the address you gave me — that little flat where you and Lyn have been living for the past three months. Except, of course, you weren't. I found the place. Oh yes — it does exist — I'm sure you did your homework very well. But the Mrs Lane who owns it says she's lived there twenty years and has never heard of a Lyn or Jennifer Winterton in her life.'

Jennifer's cheeks were flaming, her legs twisted round the chair leg. 'Well, you see, I. . .'

Matthew cut her short. 'I've tried to be patient, tried not to pressure you. Oh, I suspected you were lying — I'm not a fool — but I realised there might be . . . problems, so I simply waited, gave you a chance to tell me in your own time. I can't wait any longer, I'm afraid. I've got to speak to Lyn before today's up. It's absolutely essential, with Edward on the warpath. It makes us look guilty if one of the chief parties simply disappears into thin air. It's damaging our case — and, apart from anything else, there's that pack of vile reporters ready to spring. Surely you can see now what an unprincipled lot they are, and how vital it is we present a united front? If we all take a different line, they'll blow our story to bits. They've no respect for truth — and nor have their witless readers. I mean, take this letter here.' Matthew picked up the crumpled pieces, brandished them in her face. 'No — forget the letter.' He tossed it back on the desk. 'Lyn's the one who ought to read it, and I intend to make him do so. What I propose is that we go and confront him now. You can tell me where you're living — the correct address this time, please — and we'll drive there straight away. I've got my car outside. Never mind how far it is — I filled the tank last night and this must be first priority. If Lyn can't get in to see me, then we'll have to visit him.'

Jennifer had groped up from her chair and stood trembling by the bookcase. 'N . . . no, Matthew. We *can't*. It's just not . . . possible. I mean, he isn't . . .'

Matthew ignored her, locked his papers in a drawer. 'It's a waste of my precious day, of course, especially when I'm so pressed for time already, but I can't see any alternative. If Lyn's as ill as you say he is — though bloody-minded is probably nearer the truth — then we'd better make it easy for him, save him all the trouble of a journey. That's fair, isn't it? I've left it long enough, for heaven's sake, tried not to get unpleasant or deliver ultimatums or . . . And what do I get for my trouble — a . . .?'

'I'm gr . . . grateful, Matthew — honestly I am. It's j . . . just that . . .'

'I knew you'd see my point, my dear. All right — I'm sorry if I shouted. Let's both calm down and get our coats on. I'm not a monster — I understand Lyn might feel awkward coming here, having to face old colleagues when he's so much in the news. It's quite a sensible plan, in fact, meeting at your place. He'll be more relaxed on his own ground, and at least there'll be some privacy and a lot less interruption. Right, let's get off then, shall we? I'll have a quick word with Anne on the way out and . . .'

Jennifer had darted to the door and stood in front of it. 'Matthew — listen — we can't visit Lyn. You don't understand. I've tried to get in touch with him myself, but . . .' The stern brown office walls were blurring into dark and shadowy elm trees, the neat brown carpet jungling into an overgrown allotment. She had been back to Cobham several times, searched the place for Lyn, found the barn deserted, his temporary home dismantled. She shut her eyes. She could see the cold sad relics she had picked up from the ground — a mouldy crust, a pencil stub, a handkerchief stained brown with her own blood. Those were all she had of him — those and her still scarred knees. And now he was lost to her completely. No marriage, no address, no shared and cosy home for Matthew to drive to. Nothing but his footprints on a path, the imprint of their bodies on a pile of rotting straw.

She had left two notes for him — one in the barn, one pinned to the door outside. A few days later, both were indecipherable, stained and voided by the rain. She had blundered out of the barn, paced the allotments once more — hopelessly. Lyn's harvest was ruined now — onions split apart and mouldering, runner-beans blown down. No one had eaten his produce except the slugs and pigeons; no one claimed it save the frost. It would be the same at Hernhope — weed and briar in place of sap and shoot — their inheritance snatched away from them, their dowry lost and tarnished. Susie was right. Her life with Lyn was over.

Matthew's office was tipping and trembling as dark Cobham shadows spilt across the no-nonsense City daylight and bulky furniture fractured into a shimmering haze of tears. Matthew came over, steered her gently from the door. His voice was softer now, but still impatient. 'There's no need to cry, my dear. We can sort everything out, if only you'll confide in me. Now come along, just give me that address. You'll feel better once we're on our way. I shan't make Lyn return to work, if that's what you're afraid of. In fact, all I plan to do is . . .'

Jennifer sprang away from him. 'Don't you understand, Matthew?' she shouted suddenly. 'Lyn's not *with* me any more. We've parted — separated.'

'Separated?' Matthew clutched at the edge of the bookcase, sawed the air with his other hand in a helpless, pleading gesture. 'But wh . . . when? Why?'

Jennifer was struggling to control herself. She already regretted her outburst, feared Matthew's interference. 'It's all r . . . right. It's only t . . . temporary.' Her tears denied it. They were falling through her hands now, making damp spots on her dress.

Matthew passed his handkerchief. He looked both angry and embarrassed. 'Why on earth didn't you tell me before? I could have helped you sort it out, talked to Lyn myself. What happened? Was it a quarrel or a . . .?'

'N . . . no. Lyn wants to be . . . alone, to try and . . .'

'Alone? But he's a married man with responsibilities, not a hermit. He's got responsibilities. He can't just walk out and . . .'

'He didn't, Matthew. I . . . agreed. I mean, we thought it . . . better. Just for a little while, until . . .'

'Well, you've had your little while. Now it's time to patch things up. I'm afraid we're all in trouble, Jennifer — very serious trouble. I've tried not to worry you, but the situation is much worse than it appears. This is no time to be indulging in petty little squabbles, when there are really vital issues at stake. We've got to pull together — Lyn as well. What I suggest is that I call on him myself and discuss the whole affair — your marriage as well. He'll soon see sense once he understands exactly what's at risk. He's moved into lodgings, has he?'

'No . . . yes . . . I'm not quite . . .'

'Look, you must co-operate, Jennifer, if you want your husband back. Just tell me where's he's living and leave the rest to me.'

Jennifer sank back in the chair, spoke very slowly and deliberately, as if she were addressing a pre-school child. 'I — don't — know.'

'You mean, he left you no address? I'm sorry, but I can hardly credit that.'

'He . . . er . . . hasn't got an address. He's . . . travelling. Driving round the country.'

'But surely he keeps in touch with you? He must have *your* address.'

'Yes. Well, no . . .' She stopped. As far as Matthew was concerned, she, too, must be a nomad. She had to protect Susie and her baby.

'Where *are* you living, Jennifer? And no more lies, please.'

'I've been . . . er . . . travelling a bit myself — staying with various friends around the country. I'm still not sure about the future, but I . . . thought I'd return to L . . . London, find myself a bedsit, just a temporary place until . . .'

'A bedsit, when we've a whole great house in Putney? That's quite unnecessary. You'll be far better off in a proper family than moping on your own in some squalid little bolt-hole. And why pay rent when there's all that space at home? I'd feel a lot less uneasy with you safely on the premises. I don't want reporters on your trail, distorting what you say. I can ward them off at Putney, keep an eye on things.'

'No, Matthew. I've got to be alone. I need some time and space to think things out, decide what I'm going to do and . . .'

'You can be as private as you like at Putney. We won't intrude at all. You can have Susie's old room, if you prefer, and be all on your own at the top of the house and . . .'

Jennifer swallowed. She could see the rag-dolls and the teddy-bears, Susie's body stretched naked on her bed. Now that room was bare, like the barn was bare, and Hernhope. Soon Susie would be gone as well, the baby handed over. She stared out of the window at an abandoned building opposite, windows boarded, walls black with age and grime. Nothing left but emptiness . . .

The phone was ringing again. Matthew snatched it up, put his hand across the mouthpiece while he spoke to her. 'Forgive these interruptions. After this, I'll get Anne to take my calls. We need some privacy so we can decide on a plan of action. I want you to tell me when you last saw Lyn and exactly what he said to you. We've got to track him down.' He raised his voice, removed the hand. 'Yes, hallo? Matthew Winterton here. Oh, hallo, Mr Phillips. Yes, of course, I've got a moment. Excuse me just a second, please.' He covered the mouthpiece again, gestured Jennifer to the door. 'I'd better take this on my own. It's Edward's solicitor — highly confidential. Wait outside a moment, please, or better still, go down to Anne and ask her to make you a coffee. I won't be long. As soon as I've dealt with this, we'll . . .'

Jennifer blundered out of the room, walked slowly down the stairs. She couldn't face Anne, admit to her and Matthew that Lyn was sick and raving, calling himself a criminal, living like a tramp. Her last memories were precious, despite his fevered state. She didn't want them trampled by Matthew's contempt or Anne's disapproving pity. Already, she had made things worse. By owning up to Matthew, she had confirmed her loss of Lyn and the failure of her marriage. If she spelt it out again, it would become still more inescapable, Matthew's meddling and pontificating stamping it 'official'.

She stumbled down the last few stairs, paused at the ground floor. She could hear a buzz of conversation through half-closed office doors, the grouse of an ancient typewriter. No one had actually seen her — the staircase was deserted — but if she continued down the passage, she would pass Anne's office at the front. Instinctively, she turned the other way, towards the rear of the building. There was a toilet there with a fire exit which led out to the back. The lavatory was empty. She slipped inside, turned the key, stood facing the scarlet letters: PUSH BAR TO RELEASE.

Did she dare escape? Wouldn't it be wiser to behave responsibly, return for Matthew's pep-talk, Anne's interrogation? She slumped down on the toilet seat. She was too dispirited to face anyone at all. She could always write to Matthew, invent the next instalment of lies, fob him off for another week or two.

She stood up, took a step towards the push-bar, pressed against it. Nothing happened. She pushed again — harder. Suddenly, it gave and she lurched out into the open, shocked by the blast of freezing air stinging on her cheeks. She was standing in a backyard with buildings looming tall and dour around her. She glanced up at Matthew's offices, hardly recognisable from the back. The paint was peeling, the brickwork stained and crumbling. All the pomp and polish had been lavished on the front façade — the only one which clients ever saw.

It felt strange to be outside in her flimsy rayon dress. She had left her coat behind — a hostage to Matthew — impounded in his office. She felt vulnerable without it, guilty and exposed, shivering in the searchlight of the raw winter sun. She must hide herself, cloak herself. She darted through an archway, came out into a side street, dodged around the corner to the bus stop.

She waited twenty minutes for the seventy-six. When it came, it had a gold Harrods poster all along one side: HARRODS FOR MORE THAN MONEY CAN BUY. She clambered on, chose a seat at the very front upstairs, so she was sitting over the golden 'H'. In just four days' time, she would be ensconced in Harrods itself, celebrating a birthday whose only claim to commemoration was that it had brought to an end the most ruinous year of her life.

XXII

Just tea for two
And two for tea
Just me for you
And you for me

And . . . something, something . . . Blast! Forgotten the words' Susie broke off, glanced behind her. 'Cor! Look at the queue now. It must stretch right to Hyde Park Corner. Do you realise, Jen, we've heard every song in that wretched pianist's repertoire, and they haven't even let us through the doors yet? That's the second time he's banged out *Tea for Two*. Tea for two thousand, more like it — or tomorrow morning's breakfast.'

Jennifer shifted her bags to the other hand and inched a few paces forward. 'Nearly there now. Only three in front of us.'

'Yeah, look at the sods behind, though. Somebody ought to have warned them to bring camping-stools and Thermoses.'

Jennifer turned to look. The queue snailed right along the corridor and disappeared down the stairs. Although it was only the first week in December, Harrods was already packed with Christmas shoppers — besieging the Toy Department, crowding round the Christmas cards, thronging through the Food Halls, loaded down with parcels or fractious children.

Susie kicked off her shoes, rubbed her aching feet. She had already

300

removed her scarf and coat and cardigan.

'Don't, Susie. It's us now. Quick — put your shoes back on.'

Susie picked them up, limped stocking-footed through the door. The pin-striped restaurant manager was beckoning them in, whisking them across an elegant room, bright with lights and flowers. Floor-length mirrors reflected silver teapots and crystal chandeliers. The walls were panelled, the ceiling a swash of sumptuous decoration. Susie stopped, stared at the centre table, piled with fifty different varieties of cakes and pastries, tarts and gâteaux. The cakes were every bit as fancy as their surroundings. Even the humblest of them wore a tiara of nuts and cherries, or were brightly jewelled with crystallised fruits or coiffed with chocolate curls.

'Cor!' said Susie. 'Is it real?'

She started with éclairs, ignored the bread and butter, went back again for cheesecake and meringues, capsized them in a froth of thick whipped cream.

'Come on, Jen. You're the Birthday Girl and you're hardly eating a thing.'

'Yes, I am.' Jennifer took a small bite of her scone. Up till now, it had been a very low-key birthday — no cards, no presents, except Susie's extravagant pink azalea which she had bought with Jennifer's money and which needed strong light and would only fade and sicken in a basement. She had listened for the postman. Surely there would be a letter from Lyn *today*. He had always been good at birthdays — spent patient fiddly hours making her home-made cards, or constructing three-dimensional cut-outs which opened up to spell 'I Love You'; choosing small but exotic presents.

The postman was late and brought a circular.

When they arrived at Harrods, the birthday changed to Christmas — decorations in every department, the windows full of reindeer and fake snow. Here, in the restaurant, gold foil Christmas trees glittered round the walls, bright with scarlet baubles and swags of tinsel. Even the pianist was weaving the odd Christmas carol into his standard repertoire. Jennifer preferred not to think of Christmas. She and Lyn were always invited to Putney for Christmas Day. Christmas needed families and children, a crowded table, a bright and cheerful house. There would be nothing cheerful about Putney if Matthew remained as tense and agitated as he had been in his office. He would be furious with her now for escaping from his clutches, distraught about her separation from Lyn. She couldn't go there, anyway; couldn't abandon Susie, alone and eight months' pregnant, on Christmas Day. And where might Lyn be, then? Three hundred miles away, grubbing in the hedgerows for his Christmas dinner?

'Cheer up, Jen. My Ma used to say if you're gloomy on your birthday, you're gloomy all year round. What's it like being twenty-six?'

Jennifer forced a smile. 'Just the same as twenty-five.' That was a lie.

301

This time last year, Lyn had still been with her, the book was not yet published, Edward Ainsley just two short lines on a secret torn-out page. Fame had proved as hollow and insubstantial as the meringue which Susie was crunching up to nothing. Even the wealth which she and Lyn had been promised would never now materialise. It would be squandered on solicitors or transferred to Edward's account. Edward didn't need it. According to the papers, he lived comfortably, congenially, with everything he wanted. He had only taken action to try and save his name and reputation, and when he failed in that, he continued to fight his case more from revenge and injured pride than out of any greed for gain.

She couldn't fail to sympathise. Hester, too, had been proud and uncompromising. In fact, in trying to save Hester's name, she had succeeded in blackening Edward's. Yet how could she have known how cunning and persistent those investigative journalists were?

Susie had returned from the centre table with two strawberry tarts piled high with fruit and cream. She placed one on Jennifer's plate. 'Real strawberries in December! Eat up, mate! If we scoff enough today, we won't need to eat tomorrow. That's economy!'

Susie didn't bother with a fork — just bit straight into the tart, cream oozing down her chin, strawberry glaze dripping off her fingers. All her attention was concentrated on what was on her plate. She was like a child — greedy, eager, unselfconscious — licking her lips, relishing each mouthful, trapping the last stray crumbs with a moistened finger.

Jennifer tried a forkful of her own tart. It was just filler in her mouth. The first year of their marriage, Lyn had made her a birthday cake — or *tried*. It had come out wrong, thin and biscuity, with charred bits up the sides. He had covered the burnt with runny yellow icing. They sat in front of the fire, feeding each other morsels. It was one of the best cakes she had eaten in her life.

She wondered if Lyn had remembered her birthday at all — even in his mind. If he were living rough, he might long ago have lost track of days and dates — might be sick still, and disorientated. She tried to blank him out. She ought to be chatting to Susie, not fretting for her husband, but how could she not miss him when everyone else seemed to be in families? At the table next to theirs, a young and doting couple were feeding their baby son with fingers of bread and butter, all three heads bent in towards each other, forming a small closed circle, shutting strangers out. Jennifer put her fork down.

Susie stretched across and stole a strawberry. 'If you don't fancy that, I'll finish it.'

'Go easy, darling. You don't want to be sick.'

'God! I've eaten nothing compared with some of the guzzlers here. See that woman in the corner — the one in all the furs? She's been stuffing non-stop since we got here and she must be fifteen stone at least. Quick — look now — she's just started on her fifth éclair and she's already

302

crammed a couple in her handbag when she thought nobody was watching.'

Jennifer turned round. The woman was sitting on her own, dressed in a matching fox fur hat and jacket, pearls at her throat, diamonds on her fingers, plate piled high with all the richest gâteaux. Jennifer glanced at the podgy hands, the lines of loss and loneliness etched beneath the elaborate make-up. Perhaps she had lost her husband, never had a child. Is that what she herself would do, once the baby had been adopted and Susie disappeared — sit drowning her loneliness in whipped-cream ballast, getting fatter, older, uglier?

She glanced around the other tables. Leftovers littered the plates — lipstick-stained bread and butter, squashed and mangled cheesecakes, bleeding jam doughnuts. Almost everyone had taken more than they could eat. Yet the crowd at the centre table was even bigger now, customers jostling and pushing each other to grab the cakes which would glut and sicken them.

Pack Up Your Troubles, the pianist was playing. She tried to obey. It was only tea, for heaven's sake, and she was turning it into a tragedy, seeing Armageddon in a pile of pastries. She must make an effort for Susie's sake. Susie herself was back at the centre table, hovering over the slabs of Chistmas cake, greedy fingers reaching for the largest.

Suddenly, Jennifer froze. Susie was talking to someone — someone she recognised. She sprang to her feet. 'Oh, no!' she said aloud, stood gripping her chair, trying to decide whether to go across and join them, or make a quick escape.

'Auntie Jennifer!' It was too late now for either. A rush of feet, a swoop of arms, a hug. Oliver was grinning there beside her. 'We thought it was you! We're sitting on the other side behind a sort of pillar thing, but Charles spotted Susie going to get her grub. Isn't it super here? We've only just got in. We waited hours for a table. Why don't you come and join us?'

A thousand reasons! She had written a letter to Oliver's father, excusing her abrupt departure from his office just four days ago, blaming a sudden attack of sickness and diarrhoea, then adding more elaborate lies about accompanying a girlfriend on a motoring tour of Yorkshire, which meant she'd be out of touch. Now the boys would contradict it, report her presence in London, and — worse still — Susie's, too. She was getting careless about the lies, reeling them off almost automatically without thinking out the problems. This was her retribution.

She turned back to Oliver, tried to mumble some excuse. 'We've . . . er . . . finished tea now, darling. We were just about to . . . leave.'

'You can't be. Susie's got her plate full and you haven't drunk your tea. Oh, come on, Auntie Jennifer. Be a sport.'

Susie was walking back towards them, an unmistakably pregnant Susie, looking cornered and embarrassed, Hugh and Robert skipping

303

along beside her, Charles shuffling a little behind. Robert might be still an innocent, but the other three boys knew where babies came from and how long they took to grow, how they were seeded by a husband, sanctioned by a marriage . . .

'Hallo, darlings.' Jennifer's smile felt stiff and unconvincing. She was trapped now and surrounded. 'Fancy seeing *you* here! What a . . . lovely surprise. Isn't Mummy with you?'

Charles stepped forward. 'No, she's not well. She was going to take us, but . . .'

'Mrs Chenies brought us instead,' Hugh broke in. 'You know, the lady who lives opposite. You've met her, haven't you?'

'Y . . . yes.' Jennifer was frantically trying to think, work out some salvage operation. At least Vera Chenies was less hazardous than Anne herself, although she was one of Anne's close friends. Jennifer had met her several times, could see her now, waving from the corner. She couldn't just ignore her, walk out without saying hallo. But she could explain they had to leave, plead another engagement — dinner guests, a party, even a bad headache.

But what was the point of that, when the damage was done? The boys had seen quite enough already to file a full report for Anne and Matthew, undo all her careful lies — she in Yorkshire, Susie in Great Yarmouth. She could see Robert now, casting furtive sideways glances at Susie's stomach.

'You're very fat,' he said, at last. 'D' you come here every day and eat all these cakes?'

Hugh giggled. 'She's having a baby, mutton head.'

'A baby?' Robert's eyes were huge.

Charles blushed. Oliver jabbed his foot against the chair-leg, Robert went on staring. No one said a word. They were all standing like dummies, obstructing the waitresses, blocking access to the centre buffet table.

Jennifer collected up the coats and bags, spoke briefly to their waitress, then shooed the boys in front of her. 'Come on, darlings. I'd . . . er . . . like to say a quick hallo to Mrs Chenies. Shall we go across to your table?'

Oliver whooped. 'Great — you're going to join us! I knew you would. Bags I sit next to Susie.'

The expanse of carpet seemed to stretch for ever. Mrs Chenies had risen to greet them, a fleshy woman with soft wispy hair escaping from its bun, and a plump good-natured face. Her only son, Christopher, was small and fair, with a slight stutter caused by shyness.

'Jennifer! How nice to see you! I was just thinking I could do with a few more females to redress the balance. Five against one is hardly fair! How are you, my dear?'

'I'm . . . er . . . fine. I think you've met Susie, haven't you? She used to look after the boys. Susie Grant.'

'Blenkins,' corrected Susie, who was trying to diminish her bulge by draping her coat in front of it like a shield. 'Jenny always forgets. I've been married several months now, and she still calls me Grant.'

'Married?' Oliver's voice crescendoed to a shout.

'Yeah. I kept it secret. Didn't want you all showering me with confetti or sending me lace tablecloths or something.'

Vera laughed. 'Look, do sit down, all of you. I've had a word with our waitress and she doesn't mind an extra two. Christopher, move your chair a bit, dear, and then we'll all fit in.'

Jennifer was still dithering. 'We shouldn't really stay, you know, we've got another . . .'

'Of course you must stay! I haven't seen you for at least three months. I want to hear all your news. *And* Susie's.' Vera motioned Susie into the seat beside her. 'When did you get married, my dear? Anne told me you had to leave very suddenly, but I understood your mother was unwell.'

'Mmm.' Susie could only mumble as she lit a cigarette. At least she was wearing a wedding ring — a Woolworths one which they had purchased just that morning, partly as a joke, and partly as a concession to what Jennifer called convention and Susie scorned as Harrods' stuffy morals. She exhaled a spiral of smoke, nodded at Vera. 'Yeah — she *was* ill — very. But the doctor gave her some new amazing wonder-drug and she was better in a fortnight. Or perhaps it was my wonder-nursing! I'm quite a little Florence Nightingale, you know. I got my reward and all, because while I was up there doing my bit with the beef tea and the bedpans, I bumped into my old childhood sweetheart, and' — Susie smirked and shrugged — 'things took off from there. I've known him since I was only eight or nine. Love at first sight and all that stuff. It's so damn corny, I didn't want to tell people. There were jokes enough back home.'

Charles was frowning. 'But you only left the first week in September.'

'Yeah. Quick work, wasn't it? I met him the very first day I arrived — went out to get some fags and there he was, hanging around outside the tobacconist's. It was sort of . . . meant, I reckon.'

'What's his name?' Hugh asked.

Susie kicked Jennifer under the table. 'Oz — short for Oswald. Classy, isn't it? Oswald Oscar Blenkins.'

Robert giggled. 'That's a funny name.'

'Nothing wrong with it.'

'Has he got a motorbike?'

'Course. Wouldn't marry a bloke without one. A Harley Davidson 1200. *And* a Lotus Elan.'

'Gosh! You lucky dog. A Lotus!'

'I'd rather have the bike. D'you think he'd let me try it?' Charles was pleading.

' 'Fraid not. He's . . . er . . . left it up at Great Yarmouth. Lent it to his brother. He's only working down here for a month or two. He's a

305

photographer, you see — one of the really top ones — and he gets better jobs in London, working with all the debs and film stars and famous fashion models. We're trying to save all we can at present —' Susie looked convincingly coy — 'Now we're starting a family.'

Vera was pouring tea for eight. 'When's the baby due, Susie?'

'Oh, not till . . . er . . . late spring. Actually, it's . . . twins. That's why I'm so big.'

Vera overflowed a cup. 'Twins? Good gracious me! You will be busy.'

All five boys were staring now. Christopher put his cup down. 'My g . . . guinea pig had twins,' he said. 'But b . . . both of them died and then the m . . . mother ate the c . . . corpses.'

Jennifer swallowed. 'Does . . . er . . . no one want any cakes? You've all get empty plates.'

Susie pushed back her chair. 'I do. I'm ready for my second tea and you lot have hardly started. Race you to the table!'

All the boys stampeded after her. Jennifer slumped back in her chair, stole a glance at Vera. She looked her usual placid self, seemed to have accepted Susie's story without undue suspicion. She probably had her doubts about the date of Susie's confinement, but was too polite to voice them. They would all be relayed to Anne as soon as she got back, of course, but at least the baby was legitimate now, Susie safely married. There would still be the problem of killing off the twins, but she refused to plot that now. She mopped her face with her napkin. She felt as if she had been sitting under searchlights.

'Aren't you eating, Jennifer?'

'I've . . . er . . . had enough already, thanks. How about you?'

'No, I'm trying to lose a bit of weight. I've never had a sweet tooth, anyway. This is the last place I'd ever choose to come, to tell the truth, but Anne had it all arranged and she didn't want to disappoint the boys.'

'What's wrong with her, exactly? She seemed fine when I saw her last.'

'Difficult to say. I suspect it's mainly stress. She's been worrying a great deal over Matthew — he's really in a state — and she works far too hard, in any case. I don't know I'm born, I suppose, with no job and just one child. How she copes with four and all that pressure in the office, I'll never understand.' Vera paused for breath and a gulp of tea. 'I only hope *Susie's* going to manage. I mean, she's not much more than a child herself, and twins are quite a handful. She's *very* big, isn't she? Did Anne not know she was married, by the way? She never mentioned it.'

'No — well — Susie didn't tell anyone, you see. She's been . . . out of touch. I only knew myself a day or two ago. She'd just come down to London with her husband and I bumped into her at . . . er . . . Charing Cross.'

'Is her husband *really* a top photographer? I mean, she used to hang around with very scruffy types, or so Anne was always complaining. Mind you, Susie's quite a stunner, isn't she, and those photographer chappies always go for looks. I'm glad she's done so well for herself.' Vera drained her cup.

'Look, my dear, could I ask you a favour? Would you be an angel and hold the fort here while I dash to the Toy Department? I want to get Christopher's present without him seeing — and just a couple of other tiny things. I tried to do some shopping earlier, but it wasn't easy with all five boys in tow. I won't be long, I promise.'

'No, that's fine. Take your time, please.' Jennifer almost laughed out loud in relief. Far better to be alone with just the boys. They would ask fewer awkward questions and with any luck she could steer them away from the subject of husbands and babies altogether. They were approaching the table now — Susie just behind — giggling and ragging each other, plates piled high with cakes.

Susie put her plate down, then whispered something to Hugh, who repeated it to Robert, who passed it on to Charles.

'Just going for a pee,' mouthed Susie. The boys collapsed in fits.

She was back in just two minutes.

'That was quick,' said Jennifer. 'You can't even have got to the door.'

'Ssshh . . .' said Susie. 'Listen!'

There was a sudden crash of chords from the piano and then the strains of *Happy Birthday To You* tinkled across the room.

Susie grinned. 'They're playing your tune — see?'

'Oh, Susie, you didn't *ask*?'

'Course I did. Why not? Hush up now and enjoy it.'

The pianist had started the tune a second time. All the boys joined in now with the words, Charles waving his knife around as a conductor's baton. Jennifer blushed crimson. Everyone was looking at her. Yet she was touched, despite herself. Her birthday was official now, truly celebrated. Susie had placed a gigantic piece of sticky chocolate gâteau on her plate.

'And that's your birthday cake. Sorry about the candles. You'll have to imagine those.'

Robert screwed up his eyes, drew in his breath and let out a huge puff.'

'All blown out!' he said.

Everybody laughed. Jennifer picked up her fork and started on the gâteau. 'Right,' she said. 'Since it's my birthday, we all get a wish.'

The boys sat silent for a moment with their eyes shut. Jennifer couldn't wish herself. There were too many priorities clashing in her head, too many people clamouring for good fortune — Lyn, Susie, the baby, Edward, Matthew . . . She bit into her cake, smiled around at the five cropped heads. At least she had her family.

Hugh was standing up. 'Can anyone request a tune? Or does it have to be your birthday?'

'Don't see why not. Go and charm the pianist.'

'I don't know what to ask for, though.'

Jennifer was filling cups. 'How about *Baby mine*? For Susie's baby — babies.'

'Never heard of it.'

'It's from *Dumbo*. The mother elephant sings it to her baby.'

'Thanks a lot, Jen! I know I'm big, but . . .'

Hugh made a face. 'I'm not going to ask for that. It sounds worse than wet. *You* go, Robert.'

'I'll go.' Jennifer stood up. The pianist looked lonely — a sad old man, cut off from all the feasting, sequestered at his piano in the corner. No one was taking much notice of him. He was just background music, part of the general ambience, like the Christmas decorations.

She stood behind his shoulder, watched his gnarled fingers race across the keys. 'Thank you for your playing,' she said. 'I've really enjoyed it.'

He smiled, continued the finale to *The Lady Is A Tramp*.

'I wondered if you could play *Baby Mine*? You know, the thing from *Dumbo*. It's for a very special baby.'

'Of course, Madam. What's the baby's name?'

Jennifer paused. 'S . . . Susannah,' she murmured. Why had she said that? The baby wasn't even born, and when it was, the adoptive parents would select the name themselves. They were bound to get it wrong — choose something trivial or commonplace. She wanted the child to have a romantic name. Susannah had been both beautiful and beloved, and somehow connected with them all. She had been Matthew's mother, Hester's predecessor, the boys' long-deceased and never-seen grand-mother, the young and alluring mistress of Hernhope. Even Lyn had had a strange and special tie with her — worshipped her ghost and memory as a boy. Susannah would come to life again if the baby bore her name. And it was close to Susie's own name, so the child would retain something of its mother.

The pianist was easing his cramped fingers before launching into the melody. Jennifer leant against the wall, mouthed the words of the song.

Baby mine, don't you cry;
Baby mine, dry your eye.

She felt close to tears herself, tried to blink them back as the whole bustling restaurant blurred and trembled. The baby *wasn't* hers, would soon be snatched away by some anonymous Super-Mum. The pianist was spoiling the tune, jazzing it up with unfeeling syncopation. The words were sickly, sentimental. Susie would have scoffed at them, the boys described them as 'worse than wet'. But she was crying for some-thing beyond the easy sentiment.

You're so precious to me,
Cute as can be . . .

The child *was* precious, worth waiting for, worth working for, even if she only caught a glimpse of it before it was handed over to a Mr and Mrs X. It was no good her resenting them, when she couldn't rival what they had to offer. The baby's interests must come first. It needed two parents to cherish it, a double dose of security to undo its unlucky birthright, a stable settled home with everything checked and vetted. Maybe she could somehow get to know them, find out where they lived and become a sort of Auntie to the child. Aunts could be important — second only to mothers.

She closed her eyes, shut out everything but the tune's refrain.

Baby of mine,
Baby of . . .

She jumped. Someone was tugging at her arm. It was Charles, face flushed, tie askew, his normally quiet voice rising in panic.

'Auntie Jennifer — quick! It's Susie. Something's *happened* to her. She's having dreadful pains and . . .'

Jennifer dashed across the room and back to their table, hearing the tune swoop and gallop after her in almost mocking irony. Susie was slumped across two chairs, clutching at her stomach. Her face was creased with pain, little drops of sweat beading her forehead. Several waitresses had gathered round, customers interrupting each other, trying to take charge.

'Take her to the rest room . . .'

'Phone a doctor . . .'

'Isn't there a doctor *here* . . .?'

Jennifer pushed through. 'What's wrong, Susie? What happened?' She tried to keep calm, block out the sickening image of her own miscarriage.

'Help, Jen! I've got these awful cramping pains. They came on suddenly and . . .'

'Try and relax, darling. You must stay quiet. Can you manage to do your breathing? In, two, three, four . . . nice and slowly — remember what they told you. Now you stay here while I go and phone an ambulance. I'll only be a moment.'

'No, don't go away! Don't leave me.' Susie was almost sobbing now. Robert burst into tears himself.

'*I'll* go, my dear.' The fat woman in fox furs was one of the crowd of onlookers. 'There's a phone-box on the landing by the picture gallery.'

'It's out of order,' chipped in someone else. 'I've just been trying to use it myself. You can't get any dialling tone. And there's mile-long queues by all the other phones.'

'Hurry!' groaned Susie.

'Look, I'll take her to the hospital.' A younger woman with reddish hair already had her coat on and was fumbling for her car keys. 'My car's parked just two streets away. It'll be quicker than an ambulance by the time we've found a phone and then waited for them to get here.'

'Yes, but maybe an ambulance would be safer — you know, in case she needs . . .' Jennifer's voice trailed off. Mustn't frighten Susie.

309

'The baby's not due yet, is it?' The red-haired woman sounded merci-fully calm.

'No.' Jennifer lowered her voice. She didn't want the boys to hear. 'Still seven weeks to go. But . . .'

'Let me drive her, then. She'll be OK. I've had four myself, you know.'

The boys were looking scared and cowed. More and more people were crowding round their table, offering suggestions and advice.

'Look, please move back. My friend can hardly breathe.' Jennifer picked up a glass of water, held it to Susie's lips. 'Come on, darling, try a little sip. This lady's very kindly offered to drive you to a hospital. D'you think you can walk just as far as the lift?'

'Y . . . yeah, I s'pose so.'

Jennifer turned back to the boys. 'Now you stay here until Mrs Chenies gets back. Tell her not to worry. I'll phone her from the hospital and explain what's happened. All right?' She took Susie's arm. 'Lean on me, Susie, and get up very slowly. That's it. Feel OK?'

Susie nodded, took one faltering step, then let out a sudden piercing yell. 'Oh, Christ! Oh, help! The baby's sort of . . . shifted. I'm going to have it, Jen — I know I am — I'm going to have my baby in bloody H . . . Harrods!'

XXIII

Tiny beads of blood trickled on to the scuffed and dusty lino of the Casualty Department. Jennifer sat and watched them — droplets pooling, darkening, turning from scarlet into stain. The muscly youth beside her was bleeding from the arm and leg, the tall one opposite had two black eyes and was nursing a badly swollen wrist. There had been a fight after a soccer match and the place was full of brawny drunken football fans. The worst cases had been rushed through to the emergency room. Susie was in there with them, the doors firmly shut and insisting NO ADMITTANCE. Jennifer had been told to wait. She had been waiting, waiting, waiting ever since. She had tried to make enquiries, check on Susie's state, but the nurses, rushing to and fro, had only time for patients.

The red-haired woman who had driven them from Harrods had departed long since. It had been a nightmare journey. The first hospital they tried turned out to have no Casualty Department. They were directed to another one, just half a mile away, but a set of broken traffic-lights had jammed up the main road. Susie's screams competed with the honking of impatient horns. In the end, they did a U-turn and sped across the river to Susie's own hospital where she was booked to have the baby. At least it had a Casualty and Jennifer knew the way.

She eased her aching bottom on the uncomfortable wooden bench, inched away from the Millwall supporter's bulk. It was another world from Harrods' velvet chairs and whipped cream opulence. They should never have gone to Harrods in the first place. Susie had been pushed and shoved by crowds of Christmas shoppers, then sat and stuffed herself with an absurdly lavish tea. If anything happened, *she* would be to blame. She had become too lax with Susie, let her live her lazy, feckless way, even begun to follow it herself. She had even allowed Susie to miss her last appointment at the hospital. She hated the check-ups as much as Susie did — the hours and hours of waiting in a stifling basement room, the endless repeated questioning and form-filling, and — at last — the few rushed minutes with a doctor, a different one each time.

But now fate had paid them back, stranded them in the hospital for an even longer time and in far less happy circumstances than their normal routine check-up. At least the antenatal clinic had decent wallpaper — even a few pictures — a scrap of carpet, proper vinyl chairs, whereas here in Casualty, it was public lavatory walls, spartan wooden benches, windows with no curtains to conceal the bleak dark night outside. Antenatal promised new life, new hope; Casualty threatened pain and death. A sick old man with sores was slumped on the bench like a dirty sack, mumbling to himself; a small jaundiced infant whimpered in its mother's arms. At least it had its parents. Susie's baby had nothing — no home, no father, no heritage, no name. *She* was the baby's father. The special bond between them had grown stronger every week. Susie had conceived the child at almost the same date she had conceived her own, just a year before, so the baby was a successor and a substitute.

She jumped to her feet. She had to be with Susie, know what was happening to her, make sure the doctors understood how precious her child was. She strode towards the emergency room. The doors were creaking open, a body on a stretcher-bed being wheeled and jolted through them, trundled along the corridor past the sign which said HOSPITAL WARDS — ADMISSION. Jennifer was shoved aside, pushed into a corner. She glimpsed only a white blanket swaddling the body like a gigantic bandage, long blonde hair tousled on the pillow.

'Susie!' she whispered. She tried to shout, stop the trolley, but fear made her voice as limp and pale as gauze. She rushed up to a nurse, begged her help.

'Sorry, my dear, I know nothing at all about it. I've only just come on. We've had a call from Ambulance Control — an emergency admission. Wait a moment, please, and I'll try and get somebody to help you. It's chaos at the moment.'

Gone. A tannoy message was booming over the loudspeaker, doctors dashing in from other departments. The stretcher-bed had already disappeared. Jennifer tried to fight her way along the passage in the direction it had gone. Where were they taking Susie? Why had she lain so still against the pillow? Susie was never still. All the way in the car from Harrods to the hospital, she had been swearing and moaning, throwing herself about.

Perhaps there wasn't any baby. Just a bloody mess in a slop-bowl like her own unhappy foetus. No — Susie's baby was thirty-three weeks old. A child could live at less than that. It weighed three or four pounds by now, was sixteen inches long. She knew all the facts and figures, had pored over the baby books and handouts which Susie hardly glanced at. There would be hair on its scalp, tiny nails which didn't reach the fingertips, eyelashes and eyebrows.

A group of hospital porters was blocking her way, sweeping her back towards the double doors. The ambulance had just arrived. An overdressed woman in a crêpe de Chine two-piece stumbled out of it, tucking her ranch-mink coat round a small, fair child slumped half-unconscious in a wheelchair. His face was ashen-pale beside her own perfect mask of blusher, shiner, eye-gloss. Only her voice had cracked.

'My s . . . son. Swallowed my sl . . . sleeping pills. Found him on the floor. I thought I'd locked them up, but . . .'

The doors slammed shut behind her. Another child in danger. Once you had borne a child, you could never take life casually again. All the hazards were shouting from the walls: GERMS CAN KILL, FIRE COSTS LIVES, YOUR HOME CAN BE A DEATH-TRAP! No wonder Susie wanted the baby adopted. Nine months was worry enough, without the years and years which followed. The cord was never totally cut. Yet she herself craved the risks and troubles of that tie. She would gladly change places with Susie now, be fighting and suffering for a baby, joined and fused and one with it, rather than separate, unattached.

She marched up to the desk. The queue of new patients was even longer now. A punk boy with a cropped head and an earring was nursing a tattooed arm which had swollen and infected. Pus seeped between the scarlet hearts and flowers. His girlfriend was dragging on a joint, ignoring the 'No Smoking' sign. The receptionist, besieged by forms and phones, shouted above the screeching of a toddler.

Jennifer trailed back to the bench. She couldn't waste the nurses' time by demanding special treatment, when six-year-olds had swallowed sleeping pills. She picked up a tabloid newspaper which had been discarded on the bench. She must distract herself, clamp down any panic. There was blood on the pages, like a real-life illustration to all the horror stories it contained — cars wrecked in smash-ups, girls raped in alleyways, Catholic bombing Orangeman, Arab fighting Jew. On an inside page, was a small excited paragraph on the Edward Ainsley affair. She flushed as she read the details. The entire Casualty Department seemed to be reading over her shoulder, pointing fingers at her. And yet, in reality, nobody had spared her so much as a glance. All were too intent on their private pain and problems. Anyway, even in a decent dress and make-up, no one would now connect her with the Mrs Jennifer Winterton of just six months ago. Fame had broken like a wave, flung her ten feet high, then crashed her down again, leaving a dirty tide-mark of flotsam round her life.

And yet the book itself was still Big News, Edward still floundering in a flurry of speculation and froth of adjectives. She glanced at his photograph — that portly, balding figure who was Lyn's own half-brother, yet, eyes apart, looked so little like him. Secretly, she longed to meet him, had even considered writing to him, trying to heal the breach. Yet she feared him, also — feared that injured pride and outraged sense of justice. He would see her as an adversary — someone who had stifled him as an infant, to cheat him of his rights, then sold his mother's secrets to the world, vulgarised and cheapened Hester, betrayed her love of privacy. Matthew, too, would use the word betrayal if she tried to contact Edward. The two were duellists. Yet, both men had been crippled from the start. Both had lost a mother, one by desertion, one by death; both grown up suspicious and reserved. Susie's offspring mustn't turn out like that, but be cherished and protected. Jennifer's hands were trembling on the newspaper. She tried to read the paragraph, couldn't concentrate. Susie herself kept tangling in the print, her pale scared face superimposed on Edward's scowling one.

Jennifer's head was throbbing, her bottom sore and aching from the bench. The room had been designed to add every additional discomfort to the patient's pain — rigid wooden seating, glaring lights, stifling foetid air. The whole room reeked of Dettol, mingled with the still insistent smell of vomit where one of the Milwall crowd had thrown up his supper and his last six beers. There were no spare seats left now, and people were standing, or leaning against the walls. Some of the patients were simply skint or homeless, and had shambled into Casualty for free heat and light or company, the mother of the overdose whimpering there beside them.

'My baby's dying — dying.'

Jennifer longed to help her, restore her son to her. Yet what could she do or say? Every patient was alone with his own grief, locked into it as if it were a soundless, airless glass cage where you could see other people, but nobody could hear you or stretch out a helping hand.

She groped to her feet, stumbled to the door, slipped across the foyer to the shabby street outside. She needed a breath of air, a moment's respite. The cold black night was like a compress on her face after the sweltering glare inside. She stared up at the sky. The moon was waning, its thin-lipped smile turned towards the west. A waning moon was unlucky —

Hester had written that so many times — unlucky to sow crops, then, unlucky to marry, unlucky to be born. She shivered suddenly. Supposing Susie's baby was . . .

Ridiculous! How could she stand in the shadow of a modern hospital with its panoply of drugs and doctors, its high-powered science and wonder-brained machines, and hark back to superstition? Yet other cultures had. Ancient peoples, wise and civilised, had still prayed to the moon, looked to it for portents. Anyway, science hadn't put an end to suffering. Casualty was proof of that.

A driver hooted and slowed down, trying to chat her up, a motorcycle roared by on the other side, a tom-cat screeched and lusted in an alley. She hardly heard them. She was still numbed by the vastness and the grandeur of the sky, even in this squalid part of London. She could feel again that strange, brooding presence, as if Hester were alive and watching her, reliving her own child's birth in Susie's crisis.

She turned back to the hospital, felt the fug engulf her as she pushed open the door. Fear screamed back like the siren of an ambulance. The queue at the desk was longer still. Jennifer took her place in it, standing behind a small ill-smelling woman who wore a coat above a torn and grubby nightgown. This time, she would take a firmer line, insist on joining Susie wherever they had taken her.

While she waited, she skimmed the newspaper, trying to distract herself with foreign affairs and sporting triumphs. All seemed puny and unreal. Her eye kept shifting to the Edward Ainsley story, which she somehow feared to read in case it beset her with new guilts. Yet it was only about the Frasers and their younger cousin, Wanda, who was still alive in Hamilton and had been dug out by reporters.

'*Over home-made apple wine, Wanda, 78, but looking younger, revealed that the infant Edward had been simply handed over to his foster-parents without any legal papers or formal adoption procedure. Edward left the country — and his mother — without even a birth certificate — so Wanda claimed. Her cousin Alice also told her that . . .*'

Jennifer stopped. Her heart was pounding, her hands clammy on the newspaper. Here was her own solution, and one so obvious and so easy, she was astonished that it had never occurred to her before. All she had to do was to follow the Frasers' example — not adopt the child, but simply take it over — cut out snooping social workers, or fussing forms in triplicate, side-step all those footling rules and checks. Susie would have the baby, but *she* would take it home with her, and no one need even know what they were doing. It would be Susie's child in theory and in law, hers in simple fact.

She shut her eyes, slumped against the wall. She had to think this out. Was it wrong, perhaps, to wriggle through the red tape, unfair to the child itself? She had been insisting just the other day that the baby's interests must come first and last. Yet didn't love count more than any-

314

thing — love and total commitment? No one could love this child as much as she did, identify with it so strongly and so totally, and before it was even born. It was Hester's child, Susannah's child, her own lost, renascent baby.

All she had to do was to dodge the busybodies, evade the bureaucrats and get Susie's co-operation. Susie would play along. She must simply pretend she had changed her mind and now planned to keep the child herself. There was still a host of problems — where to live, what to live on, how to break the news to Lyn while keeping it from Matthew. But she would overcome them. Hester had helped her, pointed out the way.

She wiped the perspiration from her forehead. People were pushing past her in the queue, bumping into her. Her body was on fire, burning with a birth, a genesis, which had not yet reached the bare black world outside. The child might still be at risk, but it was *her* child now, her risk. She was no longer just the father, the provider, but the womb, the source, the home.

'Jennifer Winterton.'

She jumped. She had lost her place in the queue, but the tannoy was crackling out her name. She rushed back to reception.

'Are you the one who brought Susan Grant in?'

'Yes. Yes. I am. How is she?' Jennifer tried to steady herself against the desk. Was the baby all right? Born, thriving, sickly? 'Where is my friend? Can I see her'

'Well, not tonight, I'm afraid. She's been sedated.'

'Sedated?' Jennifer's voice was wilting and fainting itself. 'Wh . . . what happened? What's wr . . . wrong with her?' They wouldn't give a pregnant woman sedatives. Susie must have lost the baby. *She* had been sedated after her own miscarriage. Drugs to drown a death.

'I'm afraid I haven't got the details.' The receptionist was checking someone else's card. 'They just phoned down to tell you not to wait.'

'But I've been waiting hours and hours. And what d'you mean, "phoned down"? Where *is* she?'

'She's been taken to Maternity. You should have gone there in the first place, in fact, instead of coming here. But don't you worry — its all been sorted out now. She's in very good hands up there.'

Maternity? That surely meant Susie was in labour. Maybe even a Caesarian or a stillbirth.

'Now, you just pop off home, my dear, and phone us in the morning. Your friend will be brighter then, and I expect they'll let you . . .'

'But what's wrong with her? No one's told me anything. She could be dead for all I . . .'

'I'm sorry, dear. Maternity's a completely separate department. They have their own procedures, and quite frankly we're far too frantic here to be checking on patients upstairs. Now if you'll excuse me, there's a queue of people waiting . . .'

315

Jennifer turned away, groped to the door, out into the street again, turned the corner to the bus stop. The waning moon — unlucky moon — shone thin and leering in the sky. Cars and buses rumbled past, the roar of Southwark's night-life. She hardly noticed. London had gone suddenly deathly silent, even a ten-torn lorry muffled like a hearse. All she could hear was a muted whimper from the cold glass box which caged her in. 'My baby's dying . . . *dying.*'

XXIV

Jennifer knelt by the tiny perfect coffin — doll's coffin, toy coffin — gleaming brass hinges bright against the elmwood. The flowers around it didn't smell. Stiff, unfeeling lilies, their cold wax noses turned away; wreaths twisted and distorted into staring circles; soft petals pierced with pins. The wreaths were mourning, not the people; tears oozing from the swollen yellow eyes of pale narcissi; roses hot and flushed.

Jennifer trampled over them, snapping stems, crushing stamens. She had to reach the body, hold it, cradle it. She tried to lift the coffin, staggered under its weight. How could a seven-month foetus drag her down like that? She smashed her fist through the casing, ripped wood and brass apart. She was entangled in the winding-sheet, starched white linen choking round her throat. She fought, tussled, nose-dived into consciousness. She was sitting up in bed with the sheet wound round her shoulders and all the blankets tumbled on the floor. 'Susie,' she shouted. '*Susie!*'

No answer. Flowers fading, coffin changing shape into a bedside table, marble chapel blurring into the concrete grime of Southwark. She fumbled for her watch. Ten to eight. How in God's name had she slept so long? Slept at *all*? Last night she had tossed and fretted, added her own darkness to the night's. Now, light had come and morning — clear mocking morning with a spume of frost. She pulled on two sweaters and a pair of Susie's dungarees, pounded to the call-box on the corner of their street. London was just yawning into life — milkmen clattering bottles, tetchy morning traffic beginning to rattle through the streets. The phone-box was empty and unvandalised. She almost kissed the willing working coin-slot as she fed it her ten-pence piece.

'Maternity Department, please.'

Why did they take so long? She had no more coins and if she got cut off before . . .

'Oh, hallo . . . yes.' She started to explain, raised her voice as a lorry

316

thundered past the phone-box . . . No, I'm not her mother. She hasn't any relations — well, not around. You see, she . . .'

Why were they so suspicious? Something must have happened — something serious — and they didn't want to confide it to a mere acquaintance. She tried again.

'I look after Susie. The name's Winterton — Jennifer Winterton. You'll see it on her notes. I'm down as next-of-kin.' The phrase was solemn, binding. She was next-of-kin to Lyn, as well — torn between the two of them — except she had hardly thought of Lyn these last few hours. Her sole concern was Susie and her baby.

'Look, all I want to know is . . .'

She was talking to empty air. The pips had gone, and with no more coins to quiet them, she had been abruptly cut off. Only husbands got the facts, in any case. She would have to go in person and confront Sister or a doctor. She glanced at her watch. Only eight-fifteen, and a Sunday into the bargain. She would probably interrupt an on-the-wards Communion service.

She walked out into the street, turned her steps in the direction of the hospital. At least she could find the ward and sit outside it — wait all day, if necessary, refuse to leave until she had some news of Susie.

'Indigestion?' Jennifer was almost shouting. 'But she had *labour* pains, Sister. I was with her, I brought her in myself.'

'No,' insisted Sister. 'Colic. It's quite easy to confuse them sometimes. Both are cramping, intermittent pains and both roughly in the same area. And remember that Susan's never experienced a real contraction yet, so how was she to know the difference? Also, she was panicking, which made everything seem worse.'

Jennifer relaxed her grip on the chair-arm. The news was miraculous and maddening both at once. Typical of Susie to stuff herself with cream cakes and then kid them all that she was in labour and in danger. She had been buying wreaths and winding-sheets when Susie needed Rennies. And yet it still seemed so . . . unlikely. Perhaps she hadn't understood.

'I'm sorry Sister, but I want to make absolutely certain I've got this right. Susie hasn't had the baby yet?'

'Good gracious, no! It's not due for seven weeks. All she delivered was — if you'll forgive me, dear — the entire contents of her bowel.'

'Oh, gosh — poor love!' Jennifer was grinning with relief. It was comedy, not tragedy, diarrhoea, not death.

'Can I take her home, then?' Call it home, make it sound repectable — a three-bedroomed semi with a steady loving husband warming up Susie's slippers, brewing cups of tea.

'Well, no, I'm afraid you can't. She's still under observation.'

'But I thought you said the pains were . . .'

'It's not the pains we're bothered about — they're all over now. She's got a bit of blood pressure.'

'Blood pressure? You mean toxaemia?' Jennifer possessed more obstetric textbooks than Sister did herself.

'Well, only a very mild form. All she needs is rest and proper care. We'll keep her in a while, so we can check on everything and make sure she doesn't do too much. Now if you'll excuse me, I've got to . . .'

'May I see her, Sister? Please.'

'Well, just for ten minutes and only if she's still awake. She was very difficult this morning, I'm afraid — ranting and roaring and trying to discharge herself. We had to give her something to calm her down, and I'm not inclined to wake her if she has dropped off. Wait here a moment, will you, and I'll go and see.'

Jennifer prayed she'd be awake. She wanted to check on Susie herself. Sister might be hiding something. Toxaemia could be dangerous, as much for the child as for its mother. She remembered one of the books threatening convulsions, premature labour, even foetal death. She sat staring blindly at the strip of floral carpet, seeing foetuses in the flowers, until she heard Sister's footsteps returning along the passage.

She sprang to her feet. 'Is she all right? Can I go through to the ward now?'

'No, I'm sorry, dear. She's fast asleep and it would be foolish to disturb her when she needs the rest. In fact, she could really do with a full day's peace and quiet. Leave it till tomorrow, will you? And try not to look so tragic. She's doing fine.'

Jennifer let herself into the bedsit, stared at the tangled bedclothes, the messy floor and cluttered surfaces. She had hardly realised before what a pigsty she had let the place become. The emergency had brought her to her senses. Things would have to change. She set to work at once with brush and polish, scrubbing and shining with a wild excess of energy as if she had gone into labour, pouring her relief and resolution into squalid chores so that they became something of a sacrament.

By lunchtime, she was finished — except there wasn't any lunch. She shook the stale and dusty dregs of a packet of Frosties into a soup-bowl, ate them dry. She had forgotten to buy milk, and yesterday's was sour. How had she ever had the cheek to stand up and tell the world how to run their kitchens or store their home-made cheeses? She swallowed the last crumbs, rinsed her hands, stared in the mirror above the sink — hated what she saw — the messy hair, the mannish dungarees. She changed into her own skirt, hunted for a clean blouse, paused a moment as she was doing up the buttons. Whatever her appearance, she was still espousing women's lib ideas — having a baby via a surrogate mother, planning to look after it without a husband's help.

318

And yet it was only from necessity. She would have far preferred the baby to be swelling out her own womb, put there by a husband who was still around to see it born and fledged. There was such drama in conception — two people coming together and creating a third out of their passion; three hundred million spermatozoa rushing for a single egg; a tiny cell, smaller than a pinprick, growing into a full-scale human being who might turn out a Messiah or an Einstein, and all within a uterus which started off a mere two and a half inches long. Yet the women at the clinic seemed so stolidly unamazed, slouching there with their legs apart, yawning, snuffling, comparing swollen ankles. Pregnancy for them was a burden, not a miracle. All the excitement and high feeling it might have released in them seemed to have poured into her, instead, seeped even into her dreams — swollen scarlet dreams where she was hugely pregnant and chidbirth was a kind of sacred orgasm, a letting-go, a noisy, messy, heaving, panting climax — part of that same climax which had flung the baby there nine months ago.

In the morning, she folded the dreams away with her pyjamas. But they floated up again and hovered round the bedsit, superimposed themselves on the photos in her textbooks — women in labour, women giving birth. She was haunted by those photographs — the expressions on the faces — wild, rapt and animal. Susie merely scoffed. 'Easy for *you* to go into fucking raptures, mate, when you won't be left with stretch-marks and saggy breasts.' But it was the marks and scars she craved. They were the price of a baby, the proof that you had borne it, gone through that most intense of all experiences.

She squatted down, dragged her suitcase from underneath the bed. It was full of baby clothes. She had ignored what Susie said and prepared the whole layette — just as well, since she was going to need it now. She spread them out on the counterpane, rolled on the bed herself, laid her face against the babygrows, stroked the soft gauzy fabric of the nightdresses against her breasts. Strange to feed a baby, feel a tiny mouth pulling on the . . .

'Balls!' she heard Susie saying. 'Boobs weren't made for babies, but for flagging down the blokes — which is what you *need*, mate — a good hard screw with a hunk of male who doesn't think he's bloody Michelangelo. Then you'd stop slavering over babygrows!'

Jennifer grinned to herself, returned the clothes to the case, swaddling them in tissue, securing the lock as if she were hiding away the evidence of some secret vice. The room seemed strangely quiet without Susie's raucous voice. She would visit her tomorrow, as soon as they allowed it — take her flowers, grapes, even forbidden chocolates. Susie must be spoilt this time. Not only did she deserve some extra cossetting, she had also to be persuaded into accepting Mrs Jennifer Winterton — slut and sham — as official foster-mother.

The doctor's room was half the size of Sister's — more like a generous cubby-hole. The doctor himself was swarthy, with long dark hairs protruding from his nostrils and small restless hands. He had just informed Jennifer that Susie had settled down now, and her blood pressure had stabilised.

'I'm afraid there is a problem, though.' He leaned forward in his chair. 'We've just had the results of her tests and they show she's developed rhesus antibodies in her blood. They won't affect *her*, but they could harm the baby.'

Jennifer swallowed. 'I'm sorry, but I don't quite understand. I thought . . .'

'Well, you know she's rhesus negative . . .?'

'Oh, yes.' She had known that from the start. Susie's blood had been checked on her very first visit to the antenatal clinic, but they had told her quite distinctly that there were rarely any problems with a first child.

'Well, if a rhesus negative mother has a rhesus positive baby, she can develop antibodies against it which filter across the placenta and attack the child's red blood cells — almost as if they were gunning down an invader.'

Jennifer gripped the arm of her chair. 'B . . . but I was told that only happened when . . .'

The doctor cut her short. 'If Susan hadn't missed her last antenatal appointment, we'd have picked it up then. We always try to emphasise how vital those check-ups are. You see . . .' The bleeper in his lapel was emitting a high-pitched whine. 'Excuse me.' He stood up, edged towards the door.

'But, Doctor, I still don't understand how . . .'

'I'm sorry, I'm needed on the ward.' He was already on his way. 'You can see your friend now, but no excitement please.'

Excitement. Jennifer stared out of the window at the blank and sullen sky. London had never looked more dreary. She had visited Susie yesterday, just for half an hour. She had seemed a trifle weak and sleepy, but far more normal than she had even dared expect. She had returned home elated and relieved. The crisis was over, mother and baby fine. But this new complication had set off all the alarms again. She had read up all she could about what was called the rhesus problem when she first knew Susie's blood group. It was an involved and complex business, made still more strange by the fact that Susie was a first-time mother. Only in second or subsequent pregnancies could a rhesus negative mother make these rhesus antibodies — so the textbooks said — or if she had received a blood transfusion. Susie hadn't. So what in God's name had gone wrong? Was Susie some rare exception, some medical enigma which could put her child at risk? Thank God she had decided against adoption. Adoption meant delay. Nothing could be finalised or certain until three months after the birth. A child like Susie's, already sick and threatened, must be swaddled in love and security from the moment it drew breath. She must discuss the matter with Susie right away.

She stepped out into the passage and along to the antenatal ward, stood at the door with a little knot of husbands, grandmas, children. Everyone in families. She walked to the end of the ward — Susie's bed was in the furthest left-hand corner — passing bulge after bulge slumped against their pillows or lumbering up to greet their visitors. Most had expensive flowers on their bedside altars, brought in honour of their motherhood. Hothouse roses and forced carnations looked too exotic for this dingy ward with its speckled lino, shiny walls and huge drab-curtained windows.

Susie saw her, waved a half-eaten banana in greeting. She looked pale and strained, but at least she was sitting up and had regained her appetite — gulping down the banana in famished eager bites.

'How *are* you, darling?'

'Bloody awful! I've had needles stuck in every bit of me. My rear end's like a pin cushion. They've taken so much blood, I'm beginning to think they're all in league with Dracula, and if I see another bedpan, I'll . . .'

'But how's the baby?' Jennifer could see it pushing beneath the bedclothes. Was Susie aware of the latest danger? She laid her shaggy bronze chrysanthemums at the base of Susie's bulge.

'More flowers? You spoilt me rotten *yes*terday,'

'I'm just so glad you're all right.'

'I'm not all right.' Susie turned away.

So she had been told. Jennifer squeezed her hand. 'Look, Susie, I know about this antibody business. The doctor mentioned it just now. Mind you, I still don't understand. He only had a moment and he didn't really . . .'

'Which doctor did you see?'

'Rogers I think his name is — dark and small.'

Susie tossed the banana skin away. 'Oh, he's a pain. Wentworth's the real smasher — tall and blond and handsome. He even held my hand.'

'But, what did he say? I mean, all the books agree you can't make rhesus antibodies, not in a first pregnancy.'

'No . . . you can't. Want a chocolate, Jen? I saved you half the box from yesterday.' Susie was fumbling in her locker.

'No, I want to hear about the antibodies.'

'Don't be boring, Jennifer.' Susie banged the box of Milk Tray down.

Jennifer winced. Susie rarely used her full name or that cutting tone of voice. She glanced along the ward. The other visitors were chattering and laughing, but their voices didn't reach her. It was as if she were in that cold glass cage again, with even Susie dumb and aloof beyond it. The silence seemed to swell.

Susie bit into a hazel whirl, sucked the chocolate from it and removed the hazel. 'Hate nuts. Listen, Jennifer, if I tell you something, you promise not to be shocked?'

'I'm never shocked.'

'You are. You just pretend you're not. That's why I don't always tell you things.'

'What . . . things?'

Susie grabbed the chocolate box, tipped the empty wrappings out and

321

dug into the bottom layer. 'I love those nougat ones. I wish they'd make a box with all nougats.'

'What things, Susie?'

'Can't you guess?'

'No.'

'Don't be thick, Jen. If you can't get rhesus antibodies in a first pregnancy, well, either I haven't got them . . .'

'Which you have . . .'

'Or this isn't my first pregnancy.'

'You mean . . .?' Jennifer was staring.

'Yeah. I'm sorry, love. I know I should have told you, but you seemed upset enough about *this* kid.'

'No, I . . . er . . .' Jennifer stopped. There was sand in her throat, and pebbles. 'Look, when exactly did . . .?'

'Two and three quarter years ago. I was just fifteen. I had an abortion. What else could I do, for God's sake? I was still at school. I've never told a soul until today, not even the antenatal, though, apparently, they've suspected all along. They gave me quite a grilling, but I refused to admit a thing. Anyway, that's why I've got these fucking antibodies. The doctor's just been nagging me. He said I should have had a special injection after the abortion, to prevent any risk if I ever got pregnant again, but it was a backstreet job, you see, and the old hag didn't bother.'

'Old hag? Oh, Susie . . .'

'So you are shocked?'

'No I'm not, just . . .' Yes, shocked, shocked. Sickened by the waste of life. Angry, envious, muddled. How could callous schoolgirls murder babies, when other women longed for them? It was wicked, unforgivable . . .

Susie was pouting. 'You needn't look so prissy. Jen. It was the bloke's fault as much as mine. He promised to marry me if I — you know — did it with him. I *wanted* to get married, then — anything to get out of that rotten house. My Ma had a fancy-man herself and she was always leaving me to look after all the kids, then coming home half-pissed and having punch-ups with my Dad. I'd have married Jack the Ripper, if he'd offered.'

Jennifer's hands were clenched. 'Yes . . . I see.' Of course she didn't see. She had never known a home or life like that. Easy to use words like 'unforgivable' when she herself had been wrapped in tissue paper, fed the Ten Commandments with her cod-liver-oil-and-malt.

'Oh, Susie, I'm . . . *sorry*.'

'It's OK. It's over now. I never liked him anyway.'

Jennifer said nothing, just unpacked her carrier bag, laid books and magazines on Susie's locker. It *wasn't* over. By aborting one unwanted child, Susie had now endangered a second.

'Look, Susie, how dangerous are these antibodies, darling? Did the doctor say? I mean, isn't there anything they can do?'

322

Susie shrugged. 'Not much — well, not at this stage, anyway. They have to wait till the birth. If the kid's affected then, they may do a blood transfusion. Listen, Jen, there's something else. You know Sparrow . . .?'

Jennifer turned away. She could forget the past, bury an embryo which was only cash in an old hag's money-box, but this was a living child at risk. How could Susie lie there, shrugging off blood transfusions, more interested in Sparrow than in her own child's life or death?

'But what about *before* it's born? I mean, surely there's some . . .?'

Susie sniffed. 'Dunno. I wish you'd listen, mate. The doctor asked me who the father was and if I knew his blood group. Apparently, it's important in this rhesus thing. You see, he must be rhesus positive, otherwise I wouldn't have made the antibodies. The doctor's just explained it to me. Well, Sparrow isn't.'

'Isn't what?' She was sick of Sparrow. All he had ever done was to take the best of Susie, then turn his back on her.

'Rhesus positive. In fact, he's O rhesus negative — exactly the same as me. I crept out this afternoon and phoned him, just to check. I was lucky, really. Most people haven't a clue what group they are, but Sparrow knew because he used to be a blood donor.'

'A blood donor?' It sounded totally unlikely. Sparrow had no social conscience, only went to hospitals to be patched up after brawls.

'Oh, not in crummy England. They expect blood for nothing. Sparrow used to sell his blood abroad. It's a way of raising money if you're skint. He sold his sperm, as well. They pay you even more for sperm. Anyway, he knew he was O rhesus negative because it's the blood in greatest demand. You can give it to anyone, you see and . . .'

'Look, Susie, I've had enough of Sparrow. I want to talk about *you*. You've hardly told me anything. I mean what did Sister . . .?'

'This *is* about me, you nut! Just shut up and listen. Me and Sparrow are both O rhesus negative. Don't you see what that means? He's *not* the father! I've told you twice already — I could only have made these rhesus antibodies with a rhesus positive bloke. Which rules out Sparrow.'

'You mean . . .?'

'Yeah. You can stop hating him so much now. Which is just as well because I'm planning to shack up with him. As soon as I've had the kid and handed it over, we're pissing off to Spain. He's got some job lined up — nothing fancy, but at least we'll see the sun and living's cheap.'

'*Spain*? But . . .'

'Torremolinos. They say it's a bit crummy, but a pal of Sparrow's runs some joint out there and he can probably get us both jobs. You're not meant to work without a permit, but he reckons he can fiddle it, if we're not too fussy about what we do.'

Jennifer had retrieved the scattered chocolate wrappings and was screwing up the crinkly golden paper. So, all the time she had been loving and supporting Susie, she and Sparrow had been planning their escape — and not even mentioned a word to her about it. How could gloomy Southwark compete with Mediterranean sunshine, her puny woman's body out-gasp his six-foot male one? Susie had hardly even touched her since Sparrow reappeared.

'Wh . . . why didn't you tell me before?'

'How could I? You're so agin him. Every time I mention Sparrow's name, you change the subject. Anyway, I didn't know I was going until this morning.' Susie was filing her nails now. 'Remember that Sunday he showed up at Southwark? Well, it was then he first suggested it. But to tell the truth, I was a bit pissed off with him. Whatever I said to you, Jen, I was almost certain it *was* his kid, and yet he was no damned help at all, only scared I'd change my mind and keep it. I don't want a child any more than *he* does, but it really got up my nose that he should be so fucking casual when he'd made me pregnant in the first place.' Susie blew a little cloud of nail-filings off the counterpane, attacked the other hand. 'So when I heard he *couldn't* be the father, I felt — well — almost a relief. I can't explain it really, but the whole thing was ruining everything between us, and now I knew I didn't have to blame him, or feel bitter or resentful, everything seemed simpler. Of *course* I could go to Spain — I'd be a bloody mug not to, when he's paying all the bills. And it'll be a new start and a bit of fun and everything — just what I need after nine months of this lark.'

Jennifer said nothing. She had always known that Susie would go her own way. They didn't belong together, not in any permanent sense. Everything divided them — age, background, outlook, values — and yet the actual chilling fact of their separation, now planned and docketed, was like a sudden punch in the face.

'I . . . er . . . hope you'll be happy — both of you,' she murmured, at last. She could see Sparrow naked on some Torremolinos beach, screwing. Susie beneath the palm trees, scattering sperm like sand. 'But for God's sake, do be careful. I mean, you don't want to get pregnant a third time.'

'No fear! I'm going back on the Pill, pronto, pronto. I won't leave here without a prescription grasped firmly in my paw. I should never have come off it.'

'Why *did* you?'

'My periods were up the creek. And then they said I was smoking far too much. They gave me this rotten rubber thing and some jelly stuff that stank. Sparrow loathed it. I wasn't that keen myself.' Susie ripped the cellophane off a carton of cigarettes. 'Got a match?'

'You're not allowed to smoke, Susie. Where did you get those from?'

'God! You sound like some fucking social worker. I'll smoke if I want.'

'No, you won't . . .' Jennifer stopped. She mustn't row with Susie. She was still dependent on her, needed her agreement to remove the baby from the adoption list and become its foster-mother. This child was too precious to risk losing it again.

'Look, I'm sorry, Susie. I'm tired, that's all. I'll get you some matches before I leave. I expect there's a hospital shop.'

'Thanks.' Susie reached out a hand. Jennifer took it, squeezed it, leaned towards the bed. Susie's soft, generous lips were reaching for her own; full breasts straining against the fastenings of her nightgown. She had hardly noticed the breasts this time. Susie had been only a white face and a bulge, an excited indignant voice. There was silence for a moment while she tried to find her own voice.

'Susie . . .'

'Yeah?'

'There's something I want to ask you.'

'What? Well, what? If it's "will I give up Sparrow", the answer's "no". Susie snapped back against the pillows.

'No, it's not that. It's . . .' Jennifer moulded her shreds of paper into a tiny ball, squeezed it tight, tighter, tighter. 'Susie, I . . . I want your baby — to keep. Look after it, I mean. For ever.'

'*What*?' Susie sat up so quickly, chocolate box and magazines cascaded to the floor. Jennifer bent over, laboriously picking them up. It made it easier, somehow, not to look at Susie.

'Oh, I know it sounds ridiculous after all the fuss I've made about proper homes and decent families with money and security . . . But I love your kid, Susie.'

'You can't love a lump. That's all it is at the moment. It may be born a cretin or a criminal.'

'Don't say that. I'd love it anyway.' It hurt to call a precious baby 'it'. 'Look, let's say "her", not it.'

'But supposing it's a boy?'

'No worse than if it's a girl and we've called it "*him*".'

'You're getting as bad as Jo, mate! Anyway, can't we change the subject? I'm sick of babies.'

'Wait a minute, Susie. This isn't just a crazy whim. I've thought about it very carefully, tried to put the baby's interests first. Forgive me, darling, but she hasn't had the best of starts in life. And if you hand her over to the social workers, anything might happen. They could select the wrong parents in the first place or keep her hanging around for weeks and weeks while they fill in all those forms, or even . . .'

'Christ, Jennifer! You were the one who kept pushing the adoption thing. You told me no one was allowed on the list at all unless they were a combination of Jesus Christ and Julie Andrews, with a bit of the Aga Khan thrown in for luck. Anyway, they won't *allow* you to adopt. Sorry to be brutal, but Miss What's-Her-Name would run a mile from Lyn, and as for single parents, well — all they stand a chance of is a coal-black piccaninny with spina bifida or two heads or something.'

'I don't want to adopt. I just want to take the baby over privately, without any fuss or forms or hassle. *You* pretend you're going to keep it, and then hand it over to me instead.'

'How can I?' Susie was jabbing her finger through the holes in the cellular blanket. 'I've told them a million times I want the kid adopted. OK, I haven't actually signed anything, but Miss Whatnot will go spare. What is her name, Jen? Heiffer-something, isn't it? I know I thought it suited the old cow.'

'Hefferingham. She won't mind. She told me herself that mothers often change their minds. She'll be thrilled, in fact She's always saying that even the best adoptive parent isn't a patch on the baby's natural mother.' Jennifer lowered her voice. She was beginning to sound hectoring, had never expected Susie to oppose her plan. 'I admit it's a bit of a fag for you to have to pretend and play the scene and everything. But please do it for me, darling. I know in my heart it's right. It's almost as if . . .'

'*Leave* it, Jen. You can't have the child. You don't understand. It's not that simple.'

Jennifer stood up, tried to stop herself from shouting. Why was Susie being so pigheaded? 'I suppose it's money you're worried about. Look, I will get *some*thing from the . . .' She broke off. A nurse was walking towards them. She stopped at Susie's bed, started pulling the curtains round it.

'Sorry to butt in, dear, but could you wait outside a moment. I want to take Susan's blood pressure.'

Jennifer stumbled out, trailed along the ward. She had almost forgotten Susie was ill at all. She had been tiring her, upsetting her, when she had promised no excitement. And yet how could she stay quiet when this was the most crucial, vital thing she had ever pressed for in her life? She glanced around the ward — children everywhere — unborn ones in the beds, older ones brought in by grandmothers to visit mothers. The chain of procreation. One of the women had a doctor by her bedside, a flurry of nurses in attendance. Another was screaming in a foreign language what sounded like abuse. All the drama of a busy hospital and she had hardly noticed it. Even now, it was Susie who filled the ward. She turned back to her cubicle. The nurse had finished. Susie was lying flat, her face white against the whiter sheet.

'Look, I'm . . . sorry, darling, I didn't mean to upset you, especially when you're ill. I didn't think you'd mind about the . . . In fact, I was stupid enough to imagine you'd be chuffed to have me as a foster-mother.'

'I *am* chuffed.' Susie turned her face to the wall. 'I mean I would be if . . . Oh, bloody hell! Look, it's not . . . me. It's . . .' Susie snatched up a cigarette, hunted for her nonexistent matches. 'Look, I didn't want to tell you, Jen. It'll only upset you and . . .'

'I'm upset already, Susie. If I can't have this baby, then I'll . . .'

'You won't want it when you hear.'

'Hear what?'

'Well, the . . . er . . . thing is . . .' Susie paused. She had unwound the paper from her cigarette and was shredding it to pieces, flicking little strands of tobacco across the counterpane. 'You . . . wouldn't exactly fancy being landed with your own brother-in-law's offspring, would you?' Susie was staring intently at two tiny crumbs of tobacco she had trapped in the fold in the bedspread 'It's . . . er . . . Matthew's kid.'

'Wh . . . What did you say?' Jennifer's voice was flaking and unravelling.

'I'm not much good at maths, Jen, but between January and May, I only slept with three blokes. One didn't come at all, OK, and I had my period, anyway. Sparrow's just been ruled out as father. Which leaves the third.'

'You don't m . . . mean . . .?' Jennifer sank down in the chair.

'Yes, I'm afraid I do. Your precious Matthew screwed me. I suppose you thought he hadn't got a cock?'

'Susie, I . . . I don't believe it. It can't be true, it can't be. Not Matthew, not . . . Anyway, didn't you say the third bloke lived abroad? I remember distinctly. You told me he was foreign and only in London for a month or two. Well, that's not Matthew. Matthew isn't . . .'

'I'm sorry, Jen, I lied to you. I had to. Matthew *was* the third.'

'He . . . he c . . . couldn't be. He's not like that. He's always been so strict and . . .' Jennifer was almost crying with horror and incredulity. 'Anyway he's old enough to be your f . . . father. He wouldn't take advantage of you. I mean, he was your employer, almost your guardian, and . . .'

'Not then, he wasn't. I only pressured him into giving me a job when I knew I'd fallen pregnant. I still thought it was Sparrow's kid. But Sparrow wasn't helping — didn't have a bean, whereas I was well aware that Matthew was loaded, and looking for a girl to help Anne out in the house. It seemed the perfect job to me. No tax, no ties, and an employer in my power.'

Jennifer's tears had turned to steel now — cutting and unshed. How could Susie be so devious? It had always seemed extraordinary that Matthew should have employed a girl like Susie, but she would never have guessed his reason in a hundred thousand years. She snatched up a magazine with a simpering girl on the cover, flung her face downward on the bed. 'H . . . how did you meet Matthew in the first place?'

Susie was dismembering a second cigarette. 'It was at a party — one of those swanky publishing things with pink champagne. I went with another guy I hardly knew. He drank too much of the bubbly and spent most of the evening puking in the toilet. Matthew took me over — you know — filled my glass, fetched me some food, made sure I was OK.'

'Yes, I know.' Jennifer almost spat. She might have guessed the story would be squalid — vomiting in lavatories, Matthew pouncing on other people's girlfriends when he told them all how late he worked at nights. Wonderful work that was — impregnating a teenager, cheating on his wife. She could still hardly believe it. Stern and virtuous Matthew, who wrote letters to the papers about the moral dangers of television, who wouldn't allow so much as a comic in his house, in case it corrupted the boys. She felt corrupted herself, as if all the times she had sat in his study, fed at his table, had left some grimy residue on her skin and hair and hands. And yet it still seemed so improbable. Matthew was a cautious, prudent man. Even if he succumbed to the charms of seventeen-year-olds, surely he wouldn't have risked a pregnancy.

'Didn't Matthew . . . *use* something? Or . . . or . . . check to see if you were on the Pill or . . .?' She couldn't go on. It seemed both sordid and impertinent to be enquiring into Matthew's private life.

'Yeah, he did check, and I told him I had this cap thing, but they're a devil to put in, you know. You have to squeeze jelly stuff all over them, and they slip and slide about, and if anyone tries to kiss you down below, all they get is a mouthful of spermicide. I decided not to use it till . . . well . . . later on. I didn't want to spoil things. I mean, I had every reason to believe Matthew was a stayer. He'd been giving me all this spiel about what an ace lover he was, and how sex wasn't something casual or impulsive, but a sacred act which needed time and preparation. Well, naturally, I reckoned it would be hours before we reached the . . . crunch and I could always excuse myself before that, and put the cap in *then*, when he'd worked through his hundred and fifty spiritual exercises and was still going strong. Actually, it wasn't like that. He came in two seconds flat — just climbed on top of me, shoved his . . . thing in, and . . . that was that.'

Susie flung the bedspread back. Her casual almost jaunty choice of words belied her real emotion. Her cheeks were flaming now, fingers twitching nervously at the sheets. 'That's how I . . . got pregnant. At the time, I refused to believe it possible. I mean, we'd only done it the once and only for half a minute, whereas me and Sparrow had gone on hours and days and . . . Mind you it *was* my dangerous time, and Matthew did stay in. We both sort of lay there. I think we were both shocked he'd come at all. After that night, I just blocked the whole thing out. Pretended it never happened. Even when I realised I was pregnant, I still refused to tie it up with Matthew. Making babies with a guy that old and so uptight really turned me off. I'm sorry love. I know he's your relation, but . . .'

'Hardly a relation.' Jennifer could barely speak for shock. This was the Matthew who fined his sons if they said so much as 'bum', deplored the modern world for its permissiveness, boycotted his local newsagent because it stocked *Penthouse* and *Men Only*. She no longer wanted *any* tie or bond with him. 'Matthew's simply a half brother-in-law. No more. Almost an ex-half brother-in-law, now.'

'Oh, Jenny, don't be bitter.'

'I am bitter. And this time I'm shocked as well. Oh, not with you, with Matthew. It's shameful — when he's married and got four lovely boys already . . . Look d'you *swear* that this is true? I mean if you lied to me before, how do I know you're not lying to me still?'

'But that's the point, Jen — I only lied because I knew the thing would shock you.'

Jennifer fumbled for her jacket. Her coat was still in Matthew's office — had been there a whole week now. She remembered sitting there in front of him, feeling sorry for him, grateful for his hand-outs. Were they simple bribery? A means of buying her silence in case Susie had confided in her, told her the whole story?

'You should have told me before, Susie — way back in the summer — even if I was shocked. It's far worse for me to stumble on it now when . . .'

'I was scared you'd throw me out, Jen, or refuse to help me at all. I hadn't a penny in the world . . .'

Jennifer snatched up her gloves and bag. Susie had used her all along, taken advantage of her naïveté, her foolish gullibility.

'So your're w . . . walking out, are you?' Susie was almost crying now herself. 'I was right, you see. You d . . . don't want Matthew's kid.'

Jennifer didn't answer, just stood trembling by the curtains. Wouldn't it be better to turn her back on Matthew, pack Susie off to Sparrow, and hand the baby over to some quiet, conventional couple not tied to it by guilt, or marriage bonds?

'I . . . I don't know what I want, I'm totally confused. . . I'm going out for a minute — to clear my head. I'll get your matches on the way. All right?'

Susie nodded silently. Her small, scared face looked wrong above the bulge, as if someone had joined a child's head to an older woman's body. Matthew had made that bulge, tried to bridge the thirty years between them by booting Susie from the playroom to the labour ward.

Jennifer stumbled to the door, trailed along the corridor, up some stairs, down some more. She was walking blindly, bumping into people. Matthew had always been the strict and righteous Elder in the family, building up his empire, laying down his laws, leading them all like blind and obedient satellites. Yet, how many lives had he warped and overturned? Susie sick and pregnant, her own precious, precarious marriage blown to pieces by the impact of the book, the book itself impounded by solicitors, Edward shamed and shocked. Yet, without Matthew, she would never have met Susie, never married Lyn. Matthew sowed love and then uprooted it — like the baby she had almost taken over until she knew that it was his. How could she keep a child which he had fathered, a lifelong reminder of his guilt and shame?

She stopped a moment, tried to find her bearings. She had been looking for the exit, but had somehow gone too far and landed in the basement, by the vistors' canteen. At least it was somewhere to sit and rest her brain. She chose a corner table, out of the way. They were almost closing, two girls in orange nylon overalls slooshing disinfectant on the floor. She hardly saw them. The figure looming up in front of her was Thomas Winterton's, stalking huge inside her head. He had died before Lyn was born, left him nothing but his genes. But those genes were Matthew's, too. Both sons had inherited that unique exclusive patterning which made them Wintertons. And since the baby Susie carried was also half a Winterton, then surely there must be some of Lyn in it.

Jennifer picked up a sugar lump from the plastic dish on the table, held it in her mouth. She could feel tiny grains of sweetness seeping into her body, singing through her veins. She knew nothing of genetics, but surely it was possible that this child could duplicate some vital part of Lyn in its blood-stream or its cells, repeat some features of his character or constitution. Because it was Matthew's kid, Susie had concluded that she couldn't or wouldn't want it. But Matthew's kid must be made, at least in part, from the same building bricks as Lyn's would be — the nearest she might ever get to her own husband's child and lineage — a child who belonged to Hernhope, who was half a Winterton, who might even be born with Lyn's eyes or soul or hands. She stared down at the mottled table top. She could see cells in it, branching into lilies, breaking into flowers. This child could well redeem them all, let in some light and sweetness to the frowning Winterton genes. Susie might be slapdash and rebellious, but she was also cheerful and warm-hearted. Even Matthew had his strengths. A child could fuse the best of them, thaw Matthew's frosty gloom with Susie's radiance; temper Susie's sluttishness with Matthew's skill and steel.

But supposing Susie's baby combined the worst of her and Matthew, grew up reckless, hypocritical, promiscuous, neurotic? Environment played a part, of course, but what could she offer to cancel all those threatening genes? She herself was leading a feckless fractured life with no permanency or centre. And as Matthew's sister-in-law (even 'half' or 'ex', the relationship still existed, however she denied it), she was the very worst person to have possession of his child. She was deluding herself if she imagined she could hide from him for ever, especially with a baby he might even suspect was his.

Perhaps she could escape with it abroad, as Alice and Edward Fraser had — but then she would lose touch with Lyn completely. So long as she stayed in London, there was always the chance that he might contact her, even turn up at the bedsit. And yet how could Lyn accept the baby, worst of all one fathered by his half-brother?

She licked the last sweet grains of sugar from her lips.

Lyn might be intrigued, despite himself. The child not only had part of him in it, but also part of Susannah. He had known only Susannah's name and memory, but it was those he cherished, somehow — as an ideal and a romance. Susie was the new Susannah — fair, young and beautiful, and now with child. That child fused them all together — Thomas and his sons, Susannah and her namesake, her and Susie, even her and Lyn. The baby's genes and heritage must always remain a secret, even from her husband, but would carry a hidden charge which Lyn might sense somewhere deep within his soul.

'Mind the floor! It's wet.'

She zig-zagged towards the door across the dry spots. She had to return to Susie before visiting was over. She strode down the corridor, which looked more like a Victorian urinal, with its huge old-fashioned water pipes lumbering across chipped and shiny tiles. It was a relief to enter Maternity and see flowers and windows again.

Susie was lying with her eyes closed, looking peaky and exhausted. Jennifer cut the greetings short. 'Does Matthew know?' she asked.

'Know what?'

'That the baby's his.'

'Well, I've only known myself an hour or two. I could have hardly told him yet. I'm not really allowed to use the phone at all. They caught me ringing Sparrow and went mad because . . .'

'What I meant was did he know *before* — that there was even a chance he could have made you pregnant?'

'I told you, we didn't dicuss it. Couldn't bear to, really. Now the boys have seen me so enormous, it might have . . . entered his head, I s'pose. Mind you, he knew I was having it off with Sparrow, and he was even suspicious of that feller at the party — the one I arrived with.'

'Susie, you didn't sleep with *him*, did you?'

'No, I bloody didn't! I admit I've told a few fibs, but I swear to you on oath — and God strike me dead if I'm lying to you now — that there was only those three blokes and no one else. Don't you see, Jen, it's just as important to me as it is to you? OK, so I'm giving the kid away, but it still makes a hell of a difference who the father is.'

Jennifer turned away. 'Yes,' she murmured. 'It does.'

'Apart from anything else, now we know it's Matthew's, I think we ought to screw him for some cash — maintenance or something.'

'*No.*' Jennifer rapped the word out. Money made for power and ownership, control and interference.

'Why not? You were hard enough on Sparrow.'

Jennifer hesitated. 'Matthew's in enough trouble. There's Edward demanding half of all the profits and . . .'

'So you're his champion now, are you? Half an hour ago, you were saying what a brute he was. Anyway, how about the kid? Matthew could give her every last thing she wanted, and yet you're willing to cut her off without a penny.'

'Don't you see, Susie, it's the child I'm concerned about? I want her to be a love-child — in the proper sense of the word — grow up in love and peace and harmony, not swamped in sordid money hassles or used to pay off scores or stifle guilt or . . .' Jennifer stopped. It sounded fine, but how could she ensure it?

Susie was kicking at her blankets. 'What's it to you, in any case? You don't even want the baby now. That's what you came to tell me, wasn't it? I don't know why we're wasting our bloody breath.'

The bell was pealing at the far end of the ward, nurses bustling in to disperse the visitors. Jennifer leant over, laid her hand a moment on Susie's bulge. 'I do want the baby,' she whispered.

Susie frowned. 'Even though it's . . .'

'Yes.' Somehow she would manage, fob off Matthew, talk Lyn round, scrape a living together.

'You're sure?'

'Yes. But are *you* sure? I mean, you wouldn't prefer adoption with a stranger? Someone less . . . involved?'

Susie grinned. 'Miss Cow-Face would.'

'But would *you*?'

'Out!' said a nurse, sweeping towards them with a thermometer in her hand.

'*Would* you?' repeated Jennifer, almost desperate now that the nurse's bulk divided them.

Susie pushed up on her elbows, ducked her head round the solid blue-striped hips. 'I never agree with social workers on principle. OK, Jen, you're on! And by the way . . .'

'What?'

'Where the hell are my bloody matches?'

XXV

'No! Matthew shouted. 'Get away. Get *off*!'

Edward Ainsley was catching up on him, heavy footsteps hammering through the street, breath hot and clammy on his neck. Matthew tried to put a spurt on, but his legs had turned to cobweb. Edward grabbed him, swung him round, held his face so close to his that the pores of Edward's skin swelled into gaping craters, and his strange Hester-coloured eyes blurred and overflowed.

'You're wrong!' Matthew gasped. 'I didn't do it. I never knew that . . .'

He heard his neck snap off like a flower head, felt his body flop and crumple — a puppet with no strings. He still had arms. He used them — flailing and struggling up between the blankets, fighting off Edward who had now squeezed inside the eiderdown.

He sat up in bed, sweating and shivering at the same time, opened his eyes to darkness. He made a grab at the eiderdown which was entangled round his neck. It felt limp and chilly in his grasp. Edward had escaped. He glanced around the room. Only shadows — the single point of light the red and bloodshot eye of his alarm clock. He couldn't see the hands, but he knew it was three o'clock. It was always three o'clock — that endless nightmare hour when you had neither friend nor hope.

Anne . . .?' he murmured.

She was often sleepless, too, these days, lying there beside him in the second bed, trying to share his troubles when she knew only a fraction of them. At least it was a comfort to have another human being mopping up the silence and the hours. He groped a hand towards her, touched the cold rumpled sheet, the empty pillow.

'Anne?' he said again, fumbling for the light-switch.

She wasn't there. Panic switched on inside him, harsher than a light. Supposing she had left him, somehow found out about his dealings, stormed off in disgust? Everyone was leaving him, rats scuttling from a leaky ship. Lyn was still in hiding, and even Jennifer had given him the slip again, penned him a note with no address on it and packed with new-coined lies. Jim Allenby was suspicious and offhand, his other colleagues openly contemptuous. Had Anne decided to turn her back as well? She had been quiet and brooding recently, probably a cover for suspicion and resentment. Matthew sprang out of bed, darted towards the door. She could have packed her bags and gone while he was off his guard and sleeping. He ran downstairs, bare feet slipping on the stair carpet. He might find her yet, collecting up her things or dashing him off a note — a lying note like Jennifer's, giving no address. He charged into the kitchen — empty — checked the chilly rooms around it. All dark and silent. The light startled him when he swtiched it on in the hall and saw someone staring from the mirror — a haggard man with thinning hair, wearing limp and creased pyjamas. No wonder Anne had left him.

He dragged himself back upstairs. Of course she hadn't left him. She was probably with one of the boys, soothing over a nightmare, fetching a glass of . . . He stopped, steadied himself against the bannister. The boys could be gone, as well. She might have taken all four children with her, arranged a total walk-out. The red whorls on the carpet seemed to be writhing up towards him. He couldn't lose his family. They were part of him, his heritage, his hostage to the future, his bulwark against death or isolation, his ensurance of the Winterton name and line. He had only ever arranged the trust for their sake. He longed for his sons to see him as a generous, princely father, a universal provider who never had to skimp or grudge. He had slaved to give them a decent education, shelter them from over-crowded classrooms or under-trained teachers, or duller, rougher children who might hold them back or teach them farmyard manners. Other men might hoard their money selfishly or squander it on themselves, but all he had ever wanted was a solid standard of living, a decent start in life for those dependent on him.

If he lost those dependents, his strength would leak away. He would be left totally alone to face shame and impending bankruptcy, hounded in the divorce courts, as well as in . . . No — ridiculous to panic. Three o'clock was a wild irrational hour which made problems breed and swarm, tacked huge looming shadows on to trifles. The boys would be safely asleep. He had tucked them in himself, lectured them about wasting time on Westerns when there was homework to be done.

He crept along to Charles's room — his eldest son, conceived when he still paid tax like any other fool, and life was poorer, stricter, and a lot less complicated. He opened the door a crack. The light from the passage shone on to Charles's fine dark head, the outline of his features almost a carbon copy of his own. He steadied himself on the door frame. He mustn't wake the boy, alarm him with a sudden display of emotion. Boys must grow up tough, prepared for a world in which ruin and disgrace could strike at any moment.

He didn't deserve disgrace. Tax avoidance could be regarded almost as a mission. Men like him, working hard and thanklessly, needed some incentive for their labours. It was their commitment which kept the country solvent, subsidised the layabouts who dodged not tax, but work. His scheme was only the rich man's version of moonlighting, and one which cost him highly. There were fees to pay to accountants and advisers, constant vigilance required, a war of nerves to be fought out.

He closed Charles's door, checked the other bedrooms. All the boys were sleeping peacefully. He stood and listened to their breathing, light-headed with relief. Anne wouldn't leave her sons. She was as much a part of this house as the beams and joists were, as firmly embedded in his life as the bricks were in the mortar. He stared through the small uncurtained window on the landing. The cold had breathed on it, leaving a film of spangled frost. Outside, the street lamps threw dark distorted shadows on the pavement. The trees were bare, gaunt. Only his ancient cedar, which blocked all the light and sunshine from the south side of the house, still outsmarted winter, its branches heavy with their prickly foliage.

He suddenly remembered what date it was. He had fallen asleep remembering, and then got swamped in nightmare. If things had worked out differently, he wouldn't have gone to bed at all, but still be deep in champagne corks and congratulation. Last night was the projected date of London's most glittering literary party, fanfare for his half a million sales — except the invitations had never been dispatched, nor the *Moet & Chandon* ordered. Certainly he had made a stir — made the headlines, even — secured his leading position in the gossip columns, but flushed with shame, not triumph.

He shivered suddenly, walked to the foot of the stairs which led up to the attic — Susie's attic, used only as a spare room since the girl had been summoned home. Anne had cleared out piles of Susie rubbish — half-eaten chocolate bars, badges with broken pins, lurid paperbacks and dog-eared magazines. Now the room was empty. Or was it? A thin yellow ribbon of light was trailing from the door. Matthew's hands were clammy as they edged along the bannister. He stopped. Had Susie come back to taunt him, appear to him in nightmare, remind him of things he had tried to lock up like a barred and shuttered room?

Pregnant, his sons had told him, and married to some prick of a photographer who drove a Lotus Elan and knew the Queen. Well, if he was anything like that other chap who had brought Susie to the party, the marriage wouldn't last. Twins, the boys had said — confirmed by Mrs Chenies. Vera Chenies should mind her own damned business. All

334

of them had told him different stories. Hugh had said Susie only married in September and the twins weren't due till May, at least. Robert announced that she was as big as a hippopotamus and had already had the babies in a Harrods ambulance. All the boys agreed she had been carted off from the restaurant, more or less giving birth amongst the cakes. If that were so, then she had conceived the twins well before April and that party, and they were nothing to do with him. Nothing to do with her husband, either, since Charles had reported quite distinctly that she had bumped into her photographer only when she went back to Great Yarmouth. Susie had probably had scores of men, all younger and fitter than he was. He booted them down the staircase, kept only Susie there.

He tried to imagine her pregnant — thick golden hair rippling over a curving, swollen stomach. God! He desired her like that. But she could be dangerous, too — start inventing things, accusing him of . . . Supposing Anne had smelt a rat already? Jennifer might have betrayed him, tipped off his wife about his mistress?

Susie had never been his mistress. You couldn't even use the word 'affair' — just one brief evening, a fraction of an evening, something which almost hadn't happened. But supposing Susie had distorted the whole episode, blown it up to monster proportions and now be claiming him as the father of those twins, without a shred of evidence? A paternity suit on top of everything else . . . The very phrase could disgrace and undermine him. And there were other damaging things which might leak out. He had been paying Susie's wages out of the business, calling her his secretary instead of his wife's home-help. It was only a minor tax dodge, and one which many respectable men resorted to, but added to all the other charges, it could land him in the dock. Wherever he looked, some nightmare figure threatened him — Edward and his cold contemptuous lawyer; Lyn always eluding his grasp; the inspector from the Inland Revenue storming the secret strongroom of his tax affairs, and now Susie and her treacherous accusations.

He crept up the last lap of the staircase, paused on the tiny landing outside Susie's room. The door was half ajar, the light uncertain, coming only from a low-voltage bedside lamp. Someone was sitting on the floor — a woman — bending over with her back to him; a woman in a night-dress, a woman he had seen and touched before, a woman he had lain with. He could see only her silhouette, a shadowy silhouette, but . . .

'Susie . . .' he whispered. He closed his eyes, saw her as he had seen her back in April, spread-eagled naked on his office floor. He had taken her there simply to sober her up. She was too young and innocent to be left at that sordid party, in the clutches of a ruffian high on drink and drugs. All he had planned for her was a cup of coffee washed down with some vocational advice. She had told him she was out of work, and he knew influential people who could fix her up as a receptionist in a smart, high-status office.

He had been launching into the benefits of job security and staff pension schemes, when she yawned full-frontally and started taking off her blouse. He stopped in mid-sentence — stared at the full, high, pushy, blatant breasts. He had never meant to touch them. They simply reached towards him, filled his space and vision, got in the way when he tried to pour the coffee. His hands were trembling as he passed the cup, half its contents slopped into the saucer.

'Ta,' she said. 'I'm boiling.'

'Shall I . . . er . . . open a window?'

'No fear! I loathe fresh air.'

He made every effort to return to luncheon vouchers, BUPA cover, pension funds. She was wriggling out of her skirt, a skimpy thing with a gaping broken zip. He looked away, tried to count the leaves on his astounded rubber plant, glanced back again, made sure. No — he hadn't been mistaken — she wasn't wearing panties.

Nothing might have happened if he hadn't seen her bush. Not fairish, like her scalp hair, but dark and thick and exuberant, tangling between her thighs. Anne's crop was sparse and threadbare, concealed beneath waist-high knickers the colour of blancmange. Anne did it as a *duty*, lying on her back and staring at the ceiling. Susie had flopped on the floor and was lying on her front. Years ago, he had always done it that way. You had to be stiffer, but it was always more exciting. Buttocks over buttocks, crushing breasts against the carpet.

He had grabbed his cup of coffee, burnt his tongue in drinking it. All right, he had touched her once, but only for a second and even then, he had tried to keep on talking, provide her with some guidance, tell her sex was solemn and God-given and must never be debased. He still had all his clothes on. Her hands were reaching through them, unzipping him, refuting him. He forced his scalded mouth to return to matters of employment. 'Always check the perks against the salary, my dear. In fact you should really try and . . .'

She wasn't concentrating. 'You're big,' she murmured. 'I like them big.' Measuring with her hands.

After that, he forgot about her future and invested in the present. He tried to take it slowly, do sound preparatory work. He believed in exacting standards, in the bedroom *and* the boardroom, and this had somehow become both at once. He was still urging her to relax and savour the transcendental dimension, when his body contradicted him and swerved shamefully off schedule — a tiny twitch and dribble instead of thunder and encore. He had lain there, limp and sticky, listening to Susie's sudden switched-off silence. They were still in contact — just. He tried to stiffen again inside her. He could do that in his twenties, when he had first met Anne. But he wasn't in his twenties. He was a greying, leaking, rapidly shrinking bungler, a laughing stock, a write-off.

'I'm . . . er. . . . sorry, Susan.' he stuttered. 'We should never have . . . It was quite unwarranted of me to . . .'

She shrugged him off, snatched up the small portable radio he kept in the office for checking on the Stock Exchange reports, slammed the lavatory door on him, rammed the bolt. He knocked, hovered, kept explaining and apologising, as much to himself as to the deaf unheeding door. His only answer was the wisecracks of some disc jockey on Capital Radio and the blare of punk rock. When she came out, she still had nothing on. He could see her nipples greedy and erect, the bush a dark blaze on her milk-pale body. He should never have kissed her down there. It had made him come too quickly. He took a step towards her. 'It won't happen again, that I promise you. Next time, I'll . . .'

There had never been a next time. In fact, she had blackmailed him for touching her at all. 'If you don't give me that job, I'll tell your wife what happened.'

He shuddered. If she could threaten a thing like that, then she might well pursue him over the pregnancy. The last thing he needed in his life was the faintest breath of any extra scandal. If the newspapers got hold of it, then . . .

He steadied himself a moment against the bannisters. He had been backing down the stairs, away from Susie's room and was now shivering on the lower landing. The December night was freezing. He remembered standing there one Sunday morning in the summer, scorching with heat and lust on that same attic staircase, when everyone else was out, creeping into Susie's room, fingering her tee-shirts, sniffing at her panties, kissing the rumpled hollow in her unmade, teasing bed. When she returned later, giggly and dishevelled with the boys, he had shouted at her for trampling mud into the drawing-room. It was the only way he could cool himself, like throwing a bucket of water over a rutting dog.

Had she sneaked back to make him dog again, trap him and accuse him? He clenched his fists, took one step up. The light was still shining from her room. She had probably gone to sleep with the bedside lamp left on, the heater switched to 'high', wasting money, squandering electricity. It was time he bawled her out again. He heaved back up the stairs, barged into her room. The walls were no longer solid, but billowing and swaying like washing on a line, bed and chair blundering towards him. He tried to fend them off, made a grab for Susie's hair. If she thought she could outwit him, then she'd better damned well realise . . .

'Matthew, what's the matter?'

He froze. The voice was wrong. Susie never spoke like that. Her voice was shriller, gigglier, less polished and controlled. The hair between the fingers was limp and brown and scraggy, not long and thick and gold. It was his wife who was sitting there, dressed in the chaste rebuffing Victorian-style nightdress she always wore in winter. She was surrounded by Christmas wrappings — sheets of coloured paper bright with holly and robins, fancy ribbon, gold and silver bows. On the bed was a pile of presents already wrapped and tagged; at her feet, the toys and toiletries still waiting for their transformation — things she had bought in rushed and hungry lunch-hours and then ticked off her list. She had turned the attic into her private Christmas workshop, so as not to disrupt or untidy the rest of the house. There were stacks of cards waiting on the table, boxes of crackers, rolls of paper-chains. He had taught her himself to treat Christmas as a full-scale operation, almost a military campaign, tackle it with the same efficiency and verve she brought to her job, yet not let it interfere with those vital office tasks. She had taken him at his word, and there she was at three o'clock in the morning, wrapping, sticking, labelling, to save precious working time.

She struggled up to greet him. 'What's wrong, darling? You look awful.'

He forced his mind to focus. What did she mean, 'awful'? Old, feeble, ludicrous? He smoothed his hair, ordered the floor to stop trembling underneath him. He didn't want her pity. 'N . . . Nothing. Couldn't sleep, that's all.'

'Nor could I. Thought I'd get on with this lot. I didn't wake you, did I?'

'No.' It was never she who woke him, only Edward Ainsley tapping on his skull; only Susie shouting obscene erotic words through the bolted lavatory door.

Anne was hiding something under a piece of wrapping-paper — his own present, he suspected — something he wouldn't want or already had. And yet it seemed ridiculously precious, because she had gone out and chosen it, proved she cared. Even now, she was trying to conceal it, so it would still be a surprise for him. She looked older, somehow, slighter; her hair fading from glossy raven to speckled thrush, her neck thin and frail like crumpled tissue paper. If she was old, then *he* must be, as well. His wife was only a reflection of himself. He had grabbed her young and turned her into his duplicate, teaching her his order and his methods, so that she could run the house and family as well and efficiently as he ruled his business and the world. Even when the children were born, she had hardly let out a whimper. She'd had three of them at home, and he had sat downstairs listening to the stoic silence grit and flinch around him.

'Brave,' the midwife had called her. He had shrugged it off at the time. Women were built to have babies and of course they should be brave. Yet, the memory of his own mother had always nudged and scarred him. Women could die in childbirth. Susie could die and he would be called a murderer. Anne could die, or simply disappear. Even tonight, he might have found her gone. He stood at the door, with his back firmly placed in front of it, as if blocking her escape.

I love you, Anne . . . He couldn't get the words out. It had been too long since he had used them. (Had he *ever* used them? If so, they had

338

aborted on his tongue.) Instead, he knelt beside her, picked up the present she was wrapping, a tome on larger British mammals.

'I'll do that.' It was a declaration of support and devotion.

'No, really, Matthew, I'm just filling in time, that's all. Let's go back to bed.'

Matthew smoothed out a piece of gift-wrap. Anything to stop his hands from trembling. If he returned to the bedroom, Edward Ainsley might be lying there in wait for him, huge cavern mouth bawling through the silence.

'I'd like to help. Please.' He stared at the picture of the earth's surface on the cover of an atlas. It was pitted like Edward's face in close-up. He couldn't escape that face. At first, it had kept its distance in the newspapers. Now it thrust into every gap and crack of his existence. He saw it in mirrors, blurred behind his own face, or staring from his plate at mealtimes when he cut, not into veal escalopes, but into Ainsley's tanned and flattened features. And yet the flesh-and-blood face he had seen only once — glowering in his office.

Edward could be anywhere by now, even the other end of England. He might have leapfrogged his lawyers and gone in search of Lyn himself, tracked him down, talked him round, got him on his own side, lured him with a bribe. It wouldn't take much. Lyn didn't need vast sums when he had no responsibilities and had even left his wife. Or had he? Jennifer might well be in the plot herself, her so-called separation from her husband just another lie to put him off the scent. The three of them could ruin him together — plan some new and fatal onslaught on his . . . He snatched up the Sellotape, ripped a piece off in his teeth.

He had no more *time*, for Christ's sake. Things were closing in on him. He had tried to stall, plead illness and overwork, had been to his own solicitor and told him half the story, keeping quiet about his suspect tax affairs. Josef Suzman was bald, fat, Jewish, shamelessly expensive and extremely sound. He had agreed to play for time and told Ainsley's lawyers that his client would co-operate, given a reasonable breathing-space in which to produce the documents. Displaying his usual skills in persuasion and prevarication, Suzman managed to extend the deadline from a week to a month.

But now the month was up — or all but half a night of it. Would there be one of Suzman's letters in the morning, impeccably typed on that heavy cream-laid paper, with the ingratiating phrases now hardening into warnings? *Both* sets of solicitors now threatening ultimatums? If he could beg just another week or so, then Christmas would close the courts for a merciful fortnight. But after that, what then? He would still have to produce the facts and figures, or risk a court appearance which could be still more damaging.

Matthew swore. He had made a mess of the parcel, one end botched and bulky, the other crumpled. He would have to start again. It was

Charles's present and Charles deserved better from a father. He tore the paper off, punched his fist through fatuous robins and damned-fool Father Christmases.

'*Matthew* . . .' Anne was hovering over him.

'What?' He shook her off. 'Well, what?' He hated it when she looked at him like that, a mixture of pity and resentment, even fear.

'Tell me what's wrong. Please.'

'What d'you mean, "What's wrong?" You know perfectly well this Ainsley thing is . . .'

'It's not just that, though, is it?'

He didn't answer. He had tried to conceal how ill and strange he'd felt these last few weeks, the nightmares which besieged him even when awake, as every day ticked nearer and nearer the deadline with the lawyers. He had fobbed her off with facile explanations — he was over-working, wasn't sleeping well. But he could see that she was watching him, silently, alarmedly. He himself had trained her to be observant. He had also taught her to be loyal, discreet, supportive. It would be a relief to have support, share the burden with her. Even now, she was trying to comfort him. She obviously couldn't suspect him over Susie. Thank Christ!

'Look, Matthew, Jim was telling me the Edward business needn't be as bad as it appears. I know your foreign contracts have been hit, but sales over here have really leapt ahead.'

'What's the use of sales without any royalties?' She didn't know half of it.

'You don't lose *all* the royalties, darling, and you'll make up your other losses if the sales go on increasing. Jim said a legal action can actually help a book, whip up so much free publicity, it stays on the bestseller list long beyond its natural span. Even non-readers feel they have to buy it, when it's caused so much furore. So you could still end up on top, even if you have to share the spoils.'

'Anne, you're *not* to talk to Jim. I've told you before, I . . .'

'He talked to me. Anyway, how am I meant to find out what's going on if I don't talk to someone?'

'Jim Allenby knows nothing about it.'

'Well, who does, then? I know you're hiding something. I'm not a fool.'

No, not a fool — an ally — the only one he had, even organising Christmas to his own exacting standards. He dared not think of Christmas. How could he sit through all that sham festivity, thank people for their piddling gifts of wrong-brand after-shave or vulgar ties, when the tax-man hovered like Jack Frost outside the window, ready to strip him bare of everything? Christmas had always been a con. A double celebration — Jesus Christ's and his, yet both black-edged with tragedy. His mother had died in having him, and thus his birthday was also the

340

anniversary of her death. Gloom had shrouded the childhood celebrations, his father's tears quenching the birthday candles, his own guilt turning the cake to sawdust in his mouth. Other children had two days in the year to make whoopee — Christmas itself and then a separate birthday. He had none at all.

Perhaps, this Christmas, he could break the spell, flee somewhere far enough to veto all the miseries, and before the courts re-opened. He could make it appear that he had merely gone on holiday, lure the boys away with the promise of some skiing trip or escapade, and then stay away, escape. Once he left the country, the tax-man couldn't follow him, and even lawyers would find it difficult to trace him, hardly worth the trouble and expense. He would simply go to ground, dodge his creditors. Europe wasn't far enough; it would have to be another continent. South Africa, perhaps, or how about Brazil? Or there was always Singapore or . . .

'Matthew, I really think you ought to go to bed. D'you realise you're perspiring, yet it's freezing cold up here?'

He stared at Anne's pale and anxious face. He would have to confide in his wife. He couldn't sell the house around her, dismantle the business, while she sat amidst the ruins, wrapping *Larger British Mammals*. No, best not to sell at all. That would arouse suspicion, put people on his trail. Just slip away on a little Christmas holiday — the only difference being that it might last for twenty Christmases or more. When things had quietened down a bit, he could always arrange for someone else to sell his assets for him, do it at a distance while he himself laid low.

He reached out to Anne, motioned her to sit on the bed while he positioned himself opposite on the small cane-seat chair. He would have to tell her something to explain their sudden departure, secure her co-operation, make her realise his financial traumas were more than just a matter of losing a few royalties. He hardly knew where to begin. Should he swear her to secrecy, or would that frighten her? Perhaps he should tell her only in instalments, see how she reacted before he confided the whole tangle. He closed his eyes and his wife's white face capsized into Roland Harrap's ruddy one — the schoolfriend turned accountant who had introduced him to the financial underworld.

'Do you remember Roland?' he asked, as if he were recounting just an anecdote. 'Roland Harrap. Little chap with reddish hair.'

'Yes — wait a minute — wasn't he the one who came to dinner once and tried to sell all our guests grand pianos which were really cocktail cabinets and had bottle racks instead of keyboards?'

'That's him. Even at school he had his lucrative little businesses — buying and selling bikes, swapping stamps, insisting on his ten per cent commission. Once we'd sat our exams, I didn't see him for nearly twenty years. Then, nine or ten years ago, I ran into him again. We had a drink — chatted about old times. He was working as an accountant, a highly successful one. One of his specialities was a scheme for

341

minimising tax, a sort of package-deal he offered to his clients — offered to me, in fact.'

'How d'you mean?' Anne was sitting amongst the Christmas packages, still held a toy koala in her hand. Its sad brown eyes stared dumbly up at him. Matthew looked away. They remined him of Charles's eyes. Would his boys accuse him?

'I won't bore you with the details. It was basically a trust — an overseas company set up in a tax haven which has its own bank account and works as a sort of . . . clearing-house where all my foreign monies were transferred, so they weren't liable for tax.'

Anne shifted on the bed. 'Was that *allowed*?' Instantly suspicious. He switched on a casual smile.

'Oh yes. In fact, it was a very sound arrangement until a year or two ago. A lot of highly respectable businessmen were doing much the same. But recently, they've been tightening up the loopholes. There were one or two test-cases where the House of Lords ruled in favour of the Revenue, and started interpreting the law more strictly or looking beyond the mere letter of the law to people's motives and intentions. After that, the taxmen got more aggressive and now schemes like that have become — well — questionable.'

Matthew kicked angrily at the chair leg. He should have wound the thing up straight away. He had only hung on to see which way the wind was blowing; then Jennifer found the diaries, and instantly he had realised their potential. This was the one big book which could really justify his tax arrangement, make the risks worthwhile. Why should the Revenue gulp down all his profits, skim off the cream when he'd done all the work? It was partly Roland Harrap's fault. He had egged him on, shrugged off all the dangers, then coolly disappeared. Matthew dared not hire another tax accountant, who might not only refuse to work with him, but tear the scheme apart. Anyway, the thing was working smoothly. If he had avoided tax for a full eight years or more, it seemed timorous, almost ludicrous to stop.

Anne was picking nervously at the tufts on the candlewick bedspread. 'Well, what then? You dismantled the company?'

'No. I . . . er . . . There were certain . . . complications.'

'Like what?'

Like raising a little matter of a hundred thousand pounds. No — he couldn't admit that. 'It . . . er . . . could be that I owe the Revenue quite a considerable sum. Well, that would be *their* line. It's really a matter of how one looks at it.'

'You've been evading your tax, you mean?' Always direct, always uncompromising — that was Anne. He had taught her himself to quarry for the facts, avoid all euphemisms.

'Avoiding, not evading. There's a world of difference, Anne. One's criminal, the other's common sense, or at least good business sense.'

'So why are you worried, then?'

Matthew hesitated. It wasn't as easy to talk as he'd imagined. They were still seven thousand miles away from Christmas in Singapore. 'It's . . . er . . . just the strain of the Ainsley thing, exploding right on top of it. And it's not a pleasant matter opening one's private files to total strangers, or laying one's whole business on the line when . . .'

'But I still don't understand why it's upsetting you so much. I mean, if you've done nothing *wrong* . . .'

Matthew tried to fill the pause. 'You're . . . you're very undiscerning sometimes, Anne. Can't you see I haven't time to deal with any more problems or distractions? My workload's crushing as it is.'

'You've never complained before, Matthew. You *love* your work. I mean, if I ever try to suggest you slacken off a bit, you always shout me down.'

'Producing books is a completely different matter from producing evidence. How can I run a business when half my energies are being drained away splitting hairs with mealy-mouthed solicitors? My lawyer's phoned me every day this week.'

'But can't you let the tax thing wait a bit, while you deal with all the rest? I mean surely it won't come up immediately? I always thought tax cases took months, or even years. I remember talking to Jim about it once and he said there's a tremendous shortage of tax commissioners and such a backlog in the . . .'

'Anne, if you mention Jim again, I'll . . .' No — mustn't shout, must control himself. He needed his wife as ally and support. But how could he explain things to her when she was so straight and simple-minded? However slow the tax-men were, they had already been alerted. The only way to escape them was to vanish. No one could question a non-existent taxpayer, a missing number on a file. Matthew mopped the back of his neck. He was still perspiring, though his feet and hands were icy. Why did Anne keep harking back to Jim? Had Allenby been grilling her, trying to catch her out? Jim knew about the existence of the scheme — had to really, when they worked so closely together. But it was only a name to him, a paper-plan, a bank account on some shadowy offshore island. Surely he didn't suspect that . . .?

Matthew rubbed his eyes. His back ached, his head throbbed. Once he'd had a cool efficient brain, working as effortlessly as his home computer. Now it was a jumbled mass of wires. Anne had turned away from him, as if he were a dangerous animal which had already nipped her hand. 'I'm sorry,' he said. 'I didn't mean to snap. I'm a little tired, that's all.'

'I can see you are. You look absolutely exhausted.'

He walked over to the window, stood with his back to her. He had hardly explained a thing, yet, let alone confided how he had to flee the country. Better, perhaps, to mention just a joy-trip.

'Look, my dear. . . .' He swallowed. 'Wh . . . why don't we go

343

abroad for Christmas — get a bit of sunshine?'

'Leave the boys, you mean? We couldn't, darling — not at Christmas. They'd never . . .'

'No — the boys as well. All six of us. As soon as they break up.'

'But how can we afford it? I thought things were so much tighter now that . . .'

'We'll manage. We could hire a flat or villa somewhere — something very basic. Rents are often much cheaper out of season. At least it would be a break.' Matthew tried to make his voice sound less despondent. There were a hundred thousand problems — not just where to go, but how to hide his whereabouts, whether to change his name, how to free his capital and set up another business, whom to trust or tell. He edged back towards the bed. The koala bear had fallen on its side, its stern eyes still accusing him.

Anne was looking brighter. 'Well, it would certainly do you good. You need to get away. You haven't let up for months. Even the summer trip was non-stop grind. Whereabouts were you thinking of? Somewhere like the Med?'

Matthew didn't answer. The Mediterranean wasn't far enough, nor deep enough to drown him. He snatched up the bear, muzzled it in gift-wrap, sealed its eyes with Sellotape.

Anne was rattling on. 'I could do with a break myself. I've been ill three times since that summer bug, and I still feel a bit washed out. We might even get some sunshine. Imagine lying in a swimsuit in the middle of December! Mind you, the boys won't be too keen. They'll miss their skating and tobogganing. I suppose we'd take their presents with us, would we?'

Matthew nodded. A few toys and books were safe enough, but nothing else. It could look suspicious if they stripped the house.

'And what about our turkey? I ordered one from Dewhurst's — a twenty-pounder. We'll be driving, I presume? We can take it then — *and* the Christmas puddings. I've made very special ones this year and I wouldn't want to waste them.'

Matthew didn't answer. You couldn't drive to South Africa or Singapore. And a turkey would go bad. Yet how in God's name could he find the cash for six long-distance air fares? He slumped down on the bed. Anne put silver charms in her Christmas puddings. Last year, he had found a tiny silver horseshoe in his portion, glistening among dark and rum-soaked raisins. For luck, the boys had said. He covered his eyes with his hand as if the silver were still dazzling them. It was all a lie. Christmas could only mock.

Anne's sudden surge of cheerfulness had as suddenly capsized, replaced by that anxious haunted look which had arrived with Edward Ainsley. He let her take his hand. It had been months since he had touched anything more intimate. Her hands had aged less harshly than the rest of her and were still smooth and almost girlish. 'Don't worry,' she was murmuring. 'Things will be all right.'

The words were meaningless and magical, the sort of empty soothing words which mothers recited over cut knees or lost football matches or failed exams. He had never failed before. He kissed her for not criticising, let the kiss unite them, bind them together in a world where everything else was fractured and unravelling. They were lying half across the bed now, and somehow his pyjamas were undone. Men looked foolish in pyjamas — even comic. He let her slide them off. He had always longed to lie on Susie's bed. That summer Sunday he had crept into her room, he had perched on the very edge of it, not daring to stretch out, closed his eyes, imagined Susie naked there below him. He had never had a girl as young as that before, as maddeningly attractive. He could feel her nipples stiffening between his fingers, the curve of her buttocks as she humped beneath him on the office floor. Even now, she was taunting him again, running lazy fingers down his chest, working him up too quickly so that he would only let her down a second time.

He swept all the unseasonably cheerful presents off the bed, heard them plunge into the silence. If the wrappings tore, then she could re-do them in the morning. She was a sluggard and a lazybones who didn't earn her wages. He'd summon her to his study, tell her exactly what . . .

No — Susie wasn't there. He'd sacked her, hadn't he? She'd got pregnant by some creep of a photographer, and he had given her her cards. He punched his fist against the pillow. He'd like to smash that lecher's face in, and all the other men she'd . . .'

Anne was hovering over him. He pulled her down towards him, rolled her over, roughly, on her back, dragged her nightie off. Susie never wore a nightdress, slept naked like a slut. He closed his eyes. Now he could see the slut — her full flaunting breasts replacing Anne's more meagre ones. He kissed her, slowly, on the mouth. The lips were thin and clamped. He turned them into Susie's lips, forced them open, grazed his teeth across them, bit her tongue. He knew he was hurting, but it was the only way he could silence her, stop the accusations. He ran his hands along her shoulders. Her long thick golden hair was entangling him, getting in his way. He dragged it up and back behind her head, then lowered himself on top of her, pressed against the shameless pregnant belly. He would ram and ram it until he had crushed the life out of that baby — that dud photographer's child — abort it, smother it, scour all traces of its father off her, make Susie virginal and his. He dug his fingers so tightly into her flesh, he heard a cry escape her. Let her cry. She had diminished him and taunted him, left him for a puny layabout, got pregnant by a stranger. He had trapped her now, though, won her back, and this time he would thrash her. He was stiff already — stiff and hard — a match for all the piddling photographers, the prissy Edward Ainsleys and Roland Harraps, the damn-fool meddling lawyers. He groped his hand down, forced her legs apart. She was trying to pull away.

345

'Gently, Matthew, you're hurting . . .'

Oh, so she was complaining, was she? She had complained the night of the party, not in words, maybe, but in what she hadn't said. He grabbed hold of himself below, used his fingers as a splint, a prop. He was shrinking already — just when he'd got Susie where he wanted. Must fill her up, must fuck her. (Never used the word. Disgusting word, scribbled like graffiti on the white wall of his soul.) She didn't feel like Susie, wasn't tight like Susie, or wet and hot and gripping him as she had done for those few ecstatic seconds on his throbbing office floor. Something was different, wrong. He wasn't making contact. He was buckling on her, slipping sideways, wilting, sliding out. She was castrating him again, slamming the lavatory door on him.

'Look, I . . . leave it,' she was stuttering. 'It'll never work like this.'

What did she mean, 'leave it'? Was she asking him to fail? Taunting him, unmanning him, frigging herself with pansy childhood sweethearts, marrying little runts. And why was she using that martyred plaintive voice? That was a wife's voice — a wife who didn't like it. He felt his hands creeping towards her throat — soft white throat stuffed full of coarse black lies — lies which could ruin him, betray him, accuse him of fathering children, defrauding brothers, cheating on his tax. If he squeezed that throat for long enough, the lies would gag and shrivel — no juice in them, no power.

He squeezed.

She coughed, spluttered, pushed and fought him off. He lay trembling on the bed, staring at the limp and strangled thing between his legs. There was nothing left of him, nothing left in his bank account, nothing left of his name or pride or manhood. Someone's tears were smarting against his cheeks. He slapped them off. Only babies cried. Slowly he sat up, peered around him. The room looked unfamiliar — too small for him, confining. He glanced at his watch — it wasn't there. He wasn't wearing anything. His wife was cowering in a corner, naked too. What was she doing there, surrounded by gaudy Christmas wrappings, but pale and unwrapped herself? He groped towards her, laid a hand gently on her shoulder.

'You're cold, darling,' he said. His voice sounded hoarse and strange. 'What have you done with your nightie?'

She couldn't speak, just pointed to the floor. He fetched it for her, slipped it over her head. Someone had ripped the fabric, left cruel red weals across her throat. He stared at the marks, purpling into bruises. She must have fallen, somehow. He tried to hide them with the collar of her nightdress, fasten the fiddly buttons at the neck, but his hands were trembling too much to manage buttonholes. Perhaps he could kiss them better. She had always done that with the boys — a kiss for every childhood scratch and bump. He edged a little closer. She seemed nervous of him, shrinking.

346

'All better now,' he whispered. He had learnt the words from her when the boys were tiny babies, learnt a lot of things from her. Needed her. He tried to say 'I love you', but the words were still rusted up together and he couldn't pull them free. He stumbled to the window. It was still lumpen dark outside. The curtains were undrawn and he could see the trees like shadowy spies, holding up their arms to block his escape. As he watched, they took a step towards him. He could hear the mutterings in their branches, complaints and accusations, swelling into a roar. He blocked his ears, ducked down beneath the sill. They couldn't get him now. Anne's kind cooling hands were on his forehead. He must save her, save his sons. There wasn't time to waste. He started scrabbling on the floor, gathering up the scattered Christmas packages.

'Quick!' he said. 'Get a suitcase, darling. Wake the boys.'

'Matthew, please — you're not w . . . well. You need to r . . . rest. Let's go back to our room and . . .'

'Don't argue, Anne. We haven't time.' He checked the window again. He could see Edward Ainsley just outside it, leering from the cedar.

'Hurry!' he urged, turning back to Anne and piling the last few parcels into her arms. He hadn't let his boys down. They still had all their presents — expensive toys, educational books. And he was giving them a holiday, the longest in their lives. They would even have their Christmas — traditional home-style Christmas, stiff with silver horseshoes.

'Fetch your puddings,' he whispered. 'Pack them in a hamper. We've got to leave immediately.' He strode back to the window, pulled the curtains close. 'We'll beat them,' he said. 'Don't worry. They can't see us any more and we'll be gone before it's light.' He turned her round to face him, took the heaviest parcels from her. 'I promise you,' he said, kissing her pale face. 'Once we've got away, we'll have the best and luckiest Christmas of our lives.'

XXVI

Christmas morning. Lyn sat slowly up in bed, stared out through the window at the familiar landscape made strange and ghostly by its blanketing of snow. It felt odd to be in a house again, after weeks of living rough; sleeping in a proper bed with a mattress and two pillows instead of crick-necked in his car or damp and aching in a barn. It wasn't that much warmer, though. Long-fingered icicles hung outside the windows, the panes icy even inside. Hernhope had always been a cold house, despite its massive walls — too exposed to expect mercy from the weather.

He had slept in all his clothes. He pulled another sweater on and then his duffel coat, which had doubled as an extra blanket, walked stiffly downstairs to the living-room where he had sat alone last night, gazing into the fire. Leaping flames and crackling logs were now a crumble of dead ashes, as grey and cold as the sky which lay like a clammy hand upon the hills. He must cut more wood, make the place warm and welcoming for his guest. He unlocked the heavy door, stood a moment looking out. It didn't feel like Christmas. Even the snow was not the crisp and glowing Christmas-card variety, but a sullen, treacherous camouflage, concealing paths, blocking roads, threatening the lives of sheep and shepherd. The forest stretched eery, silent, to his right, dark trunks cutting like gallows through the white shroud spread on top of them. The house itself was muffed and cloaked in snow, its harsh grey outlines softened, its roof newly thatched with white.

Lyn tramped a path for himself from door to woodshed. His breath curdled against the shock of the frosty morning air and left a trail of vapour — proof he still existed, was still alive and functioning in a world where everything else was numb. He pinched his arm — felt the pressure on his fingers as bright and sharp as a match struck on a match-box. Pain was life.

The noise of the axe as he split the logs was another, louder pain. At least it helped to fill the silence. Silence was wrong for Christmas. Most of the village would be steaming and thawing in the village church, thundering out *God Rest You Merry, Gentlemen* as the organ wheezed and throbbed. He couldn't hear the church bells — Hernhope was too high and too remote. That was fitting, somehow. If they rang for joy, for triumph, then it was someone else's joy, not his.

He tried to block his thoughts out, fix only on the swing of the axe, the sting of the cold on his cheeks and hands, the hail of icy splinters flying up. He returned inside with his wood, re-laid the fire, swept the floor again. The house had been thick with dust when he arrived. He had startled spiders, removed dead moths, dead leaves, struggled with the kitchen range, scraped mould from weeping walls. Molly Bertram had long ago stopped cleaning or expecting their return. Even now, she had no idea that he was there. Christmas Eve had been the safest time to come. People were cloistered with their friends and families — hadn't time to spy. He had driven past the Bertram farm as quietly as he could. All the curtains had been closed — thank God. He saw no face at the windows, no one pottering outside. The whole family was probably busy with their Christmas preparations.

He, too was entertaining, though the house looked hardly festive. There was no mistletoe or holly, and all the Christmas trees were lowering dark outside, festooned only with snow and frost. Even the food was meagre. He had bought cold and simple fare — couldn't manage a turkey, had never learnt to cook. Hester had always forbidden him to interfere with what she saw as her exclusive role, and once he'd married Jennifer, *she* had taken over. It had been like an embrace, her cooking — not some heavy hotch-potch plonked down in front of him whether he liked it or not, and ordered to eat it up on pain of a ruined day, but all his favourite faddy dishes wooing him and coddling him — the kitchen smelling of Jennifer — spice and scent and warmth. She was coddling *Susie*, now, feeding up that baby.

He stumbled to the window. The snow was falling again in a pointillist landscape of endless whirling dots. The hills seemed to have changed their shape and their position in the blinding, blurring drifts. He could only guess the time. His mother's clock had stopped an hour or so before her death, and neither he nor Jennifer had ever ventured to wind it up again. He had sold his watch and couldn't check with the radio since the batteries had mouldered. There was no electricity. The house had lost its life-supply several months ago when the generator had overheated and seized up. The house was no longer his, so why should he struggle with spark-plugs and cylinders, to light someone else's life? It was enough that he had made it neat and welcoming, remembered to buy plain white candles along with the plain white bread and cheese.

A house could go on functioning without heat or light or family, could still stand strong and solid, while cold and dark inside. He had proved that with himself. He had cut off his wife, his heart, his centre, yet his hands could still lay tables or chop wood, his breath still make smudgy patterns on the pane. All he had to do was not remember, slap his body down if it stirred for Jennifer, forget her mouth around him under that fickle Cobham moon.

He dragged himself upstairs, tidied his clothes, combed his hair, then down again to boil some water to wash and shave. Must keep busy. He banked the fire, set the knives and forks out on the table. He hoped he wouldn't disgrace himself. He had grown too accustomed to eating with his fingers, living like an animal. He washed the few cold supermarket tomatoes, cut them into halves. (Jennifer made radish flowers, tomato roses . . .)

He put the knife down, paced up and down the kitchen. His guest should have arrived by now. Other families would be sitting down to their Christmas lunch, worshipping the dead and risen turkey wrapped in its golden skin like a chasuble, claret-blood poured out to wash it down. He had only plonk, a pale synthetic ham caged in a tin and blushing with chemicals, a loaf, a piece of cheese — simple peasant food for a bastard born in a manger who had ended up as King.

He trailed into the hall, opened the front door a crack. Snow slapped against his face, whirled into the house. Would anyone venture out in such harsh weather? He shut it out, stood at the window instead, watched

349

a plump male blackbird struggling in the snow, its feathers defiant black against the white. The silence was so taut, he could hear his own heart-beat tearing it up around him like a snow-plough.

'Let him come,' he whispered. 'Let him come.'

He spotted the car when it was only a black speck on a white track, swelling slowly into an insect, a bird, a boulder, and then — miraculously — into four wheels and a bonnet, lumbering through the drifts. He gripped the window-frame, stomach churning with fear. Why had he ever suggested this meeting at all? He must have been crazy, raving.

Too late now to hide. The car was drawing nearer, making as much upheaval in the hushed and frozen countryside as if it were a bomb or minor earthquake. Birds were flying up, outraged, snow crumbling under lurching wheels, steam panting from the exhaust, deep scars left all along the track.

The driver stepped out, cursing. Lyn hardly noticed him. He was watching the second man, the taller, more important man who was emerging from the back. He was dressed for a city funeral in a dark suit and heavy black overcoat — too severe for Christmas, too formal for the country. Where was the little angel with his smile, his mop of curls? He had been jealous of that photo when he found it with the Will — that pretty preening child with his lock of golden hair sent by doting Alice Fraser. The curls had disappeared now — and the gold. What hair he had was grey and sparse, the charming infant chubbiness turned to saggy flesh. The smile had gone, as well. The face was grave above its neat silk scarf. Lyn felt suddenly embarrassed by his shabby corduroys, baggy sweaters. He had never thought to change, had no 'best clothes', in any case. He had got too used to living without a wardrobe, wearing the same old garments day and night, like a skin or pelt you couldn't change.

The clotted silence seemed to stretch to the Northern Isles. Lyn could have hugged the driver just for breaking it, for being human and hot-tempered in a world where everything else had turned to ice.

'Bastard of a road, innit? I've risked my bloody neck coming all this way. Gone off the road twice and . . .' He turned back to his passenger. 'If you're planning to return this evening, then you'd better ask some other fool to fetch you. Happy Christmas!'

He grabbed the clutch of banknotes offered him, slammed both his doors and tried to turn the car around on a patch of stony shale which had turned into an ice-rink. Lyn and the stranger used the cover of the noise to mutter greetings. The two sets of eyes stared at each other for a moment, then looked away. Both had seen Hester's eyes imprinted on the other, uniting them — uncanny when everything else about them was so obstinately different. Edward was much the older, with broader shoulders and an imposing frame like a soldier's or an athlete's. Lyn looked brittle in comparison, as if he could be snapped in half like a garden cane. His dark unruly hair, tangling to his collar, contrasted with the thin clipped hedge of grey surrounding Edward's balding pate. Edward's face was tanned and heavy-jowled, Lyn's lean, fleshless, pale.

The car had left a gash in the snow between them, a hole which Edward was struggling to fill in.

'Er . . . Happy Christmas, Mr Winterton. I'm sorry I am late. The roads were very treacherous and we had to take it slowly. In fact, I had no idea how far it was. The house is certainly remote.'

'Yes.' Lyn made no attempt to move. He felt numb — and not with cold. Once this man stepped across his threshold, then everything was over — his house and future lost. The 'Mr Winterton' had thrown him. That was the enemy name. Ainsley versus Winterton, was how the lawyers would see it. He had read about the lawyers in the papers, stumbled on the story almost by accident. He didn't buy newspapers — they were a waste of time and money — filched old discarded ones from litter-bins and benches — not to read, but to use as blankets, cushions, tablecloths, draught-excluders for barn doors, insulation for his car. He had been swaddling his windscreen with a stained and grubby *Daily Express* one raw November evening, when he saw his own name staring at him, just above the windscreen wiper. He ripped the paper off, read the paragraph in horror and astonishment. There had been other accounts since then, but still he didn't know the whole story, or understand exactly what had happened. He had been out of touch since the beginning of September, had moved first to Cobham to be close to Jennifer, find her shadow there. When the shadow turned to solid flesh, he had fled away in turmoil, this time to Northumberland, to be a child again, since now he had lost his marriage and his wife. He had been camping out near Mepperton, as close to Hernhope as he dared, returning where he was born and bred. Maybe it was dangerous, but then everywhere was dangerous, now lawyers were on his trail. After he'd discovered that, he went deeper into hiding, lived like a wolf — nervous, hungry, hunted.

He had read the next instalment of the saga — in the *Daily Mail* this time — which gave the name of the small, secluded, out-of-town hotel, where Edward had fled in a hopeless attempt to dodge cameras and reporters. He had phoned the hotel on a sudden crazy impulse. Didn't believe it existed, really — any more than Edward himself existed. He was still buried in that forest as a tiny helpless baby.

It was a full-grown man who answered the in-room phone — but a softly spoken, apprehensive man, not the ranting bully of the *Mail*. That had thrown him. He had stuttered, mumbled, wasted his precious coins, then suddenly blurted out his idea of a meeting on Christmas Day — a meeting which would be to Mr Ainsley's advantage, but must be held in total secrecy as one of its conditions — no lawyers or reporters, no witnesses at all. Edward sounded as stunned as he felt himself. He was flabbergasted, really, that he had agreed to come at all. It was a hell of a way and Edward had no car and didn't know the country. True, he was probably curious to meet his only relation and view his mother's house, but all the same, he had expected more suspicion and more rancour. Maybe Ainsley was suppressing all his fury until they actually met in person. Which was now.

He glanced at Edward again. He looked cold rather than angry; stamping his feet in the snow, blowing on his fingers. And yet he seemed reluctant to go inside. He was still gazing around at the huge white-mantled hills, the dark gash of the forest. He had retraced his steps towards the road, as if he were looking back the way he'd come, measuring the miles, marvelling at the distance. He stumbled into a snow-drift, almost lost his balance.

'I've never seen snow like this before. It's astonishing. So deep and . . .'

Lyn shrugged. 'This is nothing. Later on, in January or February, you get drifts twenty feet high and more.'

Edward shook his head — 'Incredible' — turned to face the hills again. 'It's so . . . wild up here, so desolate. I can hardly take it in. There's not another house in sight.'

Lyn didn't answer. He walked towards the house, Edward struggling after him, exclaiming at the massive walls and thick oak door.

'I . . . never imagined Hernhope quite like this.'

'No?'

'No.'

'Well, you'd better come in and see it properly. We're getting frozen stiff out here.'

'I'm sorry — you haven't even got a coat on. Forgive me, Mr Winterton, I was so stunned by my surroundings, I didn't notice.'

Lyn tensed. That name again. He had invited Edward as a brother, not an adversary. Yet how could they be brothers when they didn't share the same name? And by inviting him at all, he had betrayed his other brother — Winterton brother — Matthew. He picked up Edward's brief-case which was ominously heavy. Was it stuffed with legal documents; Christmas to be swamped in charge and counter-charge?

Edward followed him into the hall, their footsteps echoing on the cold stone flags. 'It's . . . quite a sizeable house, I see.'

'It used to be much bigger. It had two thousand acres of land attached to it, a thousand sheep and a host of outbuildings — *and* another wing. This is the only part that's left now. Mind you, it's very old — goes back three hundred years.' Why had he said that? Boasting about a property which was no longer his to flaunt, alienating Edward who had got nothing yet at all. He should be making Edward comfortable, offering him a drink.

He ushered him into the living-room, took his coat, tried to make his tongue form welcoming phrases, but it was as if the snow had leaked inside him and frozen up his voice-box. It was Edward who was speaking.

'I brought you a few small . . . trifles.' He rummaged in his briefcase. The legal documents turned into a bottle of Glenfiddich and a vintage port, fresh figs, plump and purple-bellied, a tin of crystallised ginger, boxes of nuts, chocolate, fruits.

Lyn stared at all the bounty. Why should an enemy bring gifts — and on such a scale? He had cheated Edward of his house and was now repaid with a cornucopia. He carried them to the sideboard, arranged them as a still-life. He couldn't open them, couldn't take anything else which belonged to Edward.

'Thanks,' he murmured, fingering the box of *marrons* in its gold and scarlet packaging. They cost six or seven pounds, that size — more than he had spent on the entire Christmas lunch. Edward had put it to shame now, his piddling little picnic. He and Hester had always spent quiet and frugal Christmases. There hadn't been money to spare for *marrons* or liqueurs, nor friends or kin to share them with. Only in Matthew's boyhood had Hernhope rung with carols and groaned with food and wine. He had read about past Christmases in Hester's diaries — the thirty-pound turkeys and twelve-foot-high Christmas trees, the troops of villagers who came for cakes and ale, the Christmas feast for the shepherds. He and Hester had sat alone with a small bony chicken between them and a couple of tangerines — Hester still in black and silence heavy-breathing on the windows.

He ignored the whisky, reached across for his own cheap *vin de pays*.

'A glass of wine?' he asked.

'No, thank you. I very rarely drink. I'd rather have a juice, if that's no trouble?'

Lyn frowned. He hadn't any juice, hadn't bothered with soft drinks, not even a bottle of tonic or orange squash. Money was short and he'd had to shop extremely carefully, buy only the necessities.

'I'm afraid there isn't . . . I mean, I didn't know . . .'

'A glass of . . . water, then. No, really. I'm fond of water, I always think if it wasn't free, then . . .'

Lyn escaped into the kitchen. Water — on Christmas Day! Even the tap was grudging, spluttered when he turned it on, coughed up only a brown and brackish dribble. He poured it into one of Hester's thick and clumsy glasses, stared at the murky liquid. Edward would be used to fresh-pressed juices from exotic fruits, served in cut-glass tumblers on a silver tray. He had read about Edward's luxurious life, his country club, his rich and important friends. He poured the water down the sink, returned to the living-room.

'I'm sorry . . .' He tried to laugh, to cover his embarrassment. 'Even water seems a problem. We have marvellous water, normally — as pure as any in the British Isles, but the pipes must have rusted up or . . .'

'Please don't worry. It doesn't matter at all.'

'Well, have a seat, at least.'

'Thank you.' Edward chose the hardest chair, sat down on the very edge of it.

There was silence for a moment. Lyn strained to fill it. There was too much to say, but nothing safe or neutral.

'The . . . er . . . snow's slackening off a little now.'

'Yes.' Edward wasn't looking. He cleared his throat, leaned forward in his chair. 'I was surprised to hear from you, Mr Winterton — very surprised, in fact. As you know, my lawyers have been . . .'

'Do let's open that wine.' Lyn was still standing, hunting for a corkscrew. 'I need a drink, quite frankly, and I never fancy tippling on my own. It is Christmas, after all.'

'Look, Mr Winterton, I'm most grateful to you for getting in touch with me and inviting me here at all, but I can't pretend that there aren't certain . . . er . . . constraints between us. This isn't purely a . . . social call. Christmas or no, I think we should have a full and frank discussion, to thrash these matters out before we . . .'

'All right, but we can do it over a drink, can't we?'

'Well, just a small one.' Edward took his tumbler grudgingly. 'Perhaps you don't realise, Mr Winterton, but I've been in England over six whole weeks now, and got absolutely nowhere. I'm most relieved you've decided to come into the open and help me get things settled. It's essential that . . .'

Lyn rammed the cork back in the bottle, started pacing up and down. 'I never said I'd . . . What I mean is, there's no point in going over and over grudges or dragging up past history or . . .' He stopped in front of the door. He longed to slam through it, escape from a situation he himself had set up. Bloody fool.

Edward took a cautious sip of his wine. 'We've got to talk, Mr Winterton, we can't avoid it. And we must go back to basics. There are certain things I . . .'

'Well, let's leave it till after lunch. It'll be . . . easier then. We'll be more relaxed and . . .' Lyn was talking to the door. He turned round, tried to sound more welcoming. 'I expect you're hungry, aren't you? People always seem ravenous up here. I suppose it's the air or . . .'

'Thank you, Mr Winterton, but I had a very substantial breakfast at my hotel. What I'd prefer is . . .'

'It's nothing fancy, anyway. If you're expecting proper Christmas dinner, then you're going to be disappointed.' He heard himself sounding peevish, inhospitable. It was a crazy situation. He should have stayed in hiding, fled abroad. Eating would be as difficult as talking. He hadn't managed breakfast, had pushed away his scrappy bit of supper on Christmas Eve.

'I've laid it up in the kitchen. We always eat in there. It's the only room

354

which really fits the table. It's twelve feet long, that table, and two hundred years old. It was made from the decking of a . . .' He was blabbing on, filling in the space with words. At least it stopped Edward talking, postponed that full and frank discussion which meant only loss and void. His guest had eased up from his chair and was standing by the sideboard, rigid and uneasy.

'Yes, bring your glass. The kitchen's just through here. It should be warm. The range is always temperamental, but I cleaned it out thoroughly last night and . . .' Christ! He sounded like some clacking old hen of a woman. If he hadn't been out of his mind, he could have spent his Christmas Day alone.

The table loomed larger even than usual — a mile of wood with a peck of food on it. Jennifer would have made pies, puddings, mincemeat, marzipan, laid the cloth like a work of art — scarlet crackers nestling in snowy napkins, silvered laurel framing gold chrysanthemums.

Edward had followed him and was dithering by the table. He looked wrong in the house, his head too near the ceiling, his frame too large for the narrow wooden chairs.

'No, don't sit there. Sit at the head of the table.' Lyn drew back the larger chair for Edward — the master's chair with arms — Thomas Winterton's chair. *Beloved son.* Since her husband's death, Hester had never used it. It had stood there, empty, joining them at meals, he on its left, Hester on its right. Now, he sat further down the table, on a lower, lesser seat.

Silence again. Lyn wished they could say grace, embark on some soothing formal ritual which would prevent the need for fraught and dangerous topics.

'Er . . . can I give you some ham?' he asked instead. The squat pink oval seemed to have shrunk since he opened the tin. He tried to carve it neatly, but the scrappy slices fell to pieces on the plates. Jennifer's ham was plump and smooth and marbled like her thighs. The knife trembled in his hand, but he went on slicing — cut her off.

'I should have cooked potatoes, I suppose, or Brussels sprouts or something . . . Would you like some bread?'

'Thank you. Just half a slice.'

Lyn hacked him off a doorstep. Hester would never have stood for half slices. His mother had insisted on no-nonsense appetites, cleared and grateful plates, no fads or fuss-potting.

'My mother baked the best bread in Northumberland.' Why had he said that? He remembered it as hard and heavy, scratching down his throat when other kids had light, white, magic bread which God had already sliced in glossy coloured wrappers and which was so soft you could have slept on it. He should have said '*our*' mother, anyway.

'Yes, I . . . er . . . saw her recipes in the book.'

Now they were back on battle-ground again. Edward was right — it

355

was impossible not to talk. Every subject led back to their quarrel or their mother, their future or their past.

'Look, Mr Ainsley,' Lyn suddenly blurted out. 'Don't think I approve of it — that book. I don't. I never did. It's full of lies.'

'So I understand.' Edward hadn't touched his food. 'It's a pity, though, you didn't express that disapproval — eighteen months ago, before it was ever published.'

'I did. At least I tried. I . . .'

'I mean, those were private diaries, and my own existence even more so. The only reason my mother had me . . . er . . . fostered, was surely to prevent any scandal and save her reputation. That was obvious, wasn't it? Yet now what's happened ? The whole world is chewing it over as if Hester was a . . .'

Lyn held a sliver of cold tasteless tomato on his tongue. He forced it down. 'I . . . I . . . realise how you feel. I'd . . . feel the same myself. I told Matthew right from the beginning, we had no business to be . . .'

'So what changed your mind?'

'If you think it was . . . money, it wasn't.' Lyn paused. 'Well . . . not as such.' He could see Jennifer's white and weeping face, the trail of bloody baby from bed to bathroom. Money! He hadn't had enough to buy a Christmas pudding. 'I know you blame me for handing over the diaries in the first place. I blame myself. I'd never have done it if I'd known what . . .' He gripped the edge of the table. He loathed apologising, squirming in embarrassment, making himself a sucker and a fool, yet he had cheated this man, denied him his property, his rights, ignored those rights by signing an agreement with Matthew. 'Look, one of the things I wanted to say today was . . .' He swallowed. 'Well . . . er . . . *sorry* — and I mean that.'

Edward took a gulp of wine and then another. He seemed to be hiding his emotion behind the glass. 'Th . . . thank you, Mr Winterton. That's the first and only apology I've received, and I appreciate it. In fact, I'm sorry myself that all this should have arisen between . . . er . . . family.'

Lyn swallowed a mouthful of ham. It tasted so bland, it could have been chicken, veal, cardboard. 'I don't even approve of the book as a *book*. I worked on it myself and yet it's . . . lies, fantasies. I don't know why. It's based chiefly on Hester's own records, and yet somehow she's . . . not there. They deciphered a hundred thousand of her words and came up with . . . someone else. The Hester they published wasn't the one who lived. The world may know that woman, but *I*'ve never set eyes on her. She simply wasn't like that.'

Edward laid his fork down with the ham still on the prongs. 'What . . . was she like?'

Lyn searched the room for answers. Should he give Edward a loving, noble mother, or a crabbed and bitter one? Had he ever known her, anyway? How much of a mother was desire or dream or myth? The book was no more wrong about her than everybody was, including the son who had shared her life. He tried to find one word to describe her, to trap all the years of love and loss and longing, the parentheses and gaps. He stared at the stout walls, the massive beams holding up the house.

'Strong,' he said, at last.

'The book was right, then — at least in that. She came over as a tower of strength.'

'No.' Lyn frowned. 'It wasn't quite like . . . I can't explain, but . . .'

He could see Edward waiting in the waiting silence. He knew he craved for details — a mother offered to him like a Christmas present, gift-wrapped, tinselled, labelled. That had been done already in the book. He refused to compound the lies. Edward had gifts and heritage enough. He would keep his mother for himself.

'I didn't . . . know her,' he said, almost in a whisper.

'For heaven's sake . . .' Edward sounded snappish, 'You lived with her for thirty years.'

'Thirty-one.'

'Surely you're not saying then . . .?'

'Look, leave it, Mr Ainsley.' His mother's name. Matthew's keeper's name.

'We can't leave everything. It's . . . a little absurd to pretend there's nothing between us — and I don't just mean a lawsuit now. We are, in fact, related. That colours the whole thing. Surely you can see that? I have a natural interest in my mother and her house and . . .'

'Of course. I'm not denying it.'

'In you, as well. I've always wanted a brother, and . . .'

Lyn clenched his fists, concealed them under the table. Brother! Edward's sentiment was more needling than his wrath. Half a glass of Tesco's cut-price red had made him maudlin. He'd be embracing him next, shedding tears of emotion. He was trapped with this 'brother' all damned day now — that peeved officious voice with its clipped affected accent which grated on his nerves. Even the way he held his fork annoyed him. You could kill a man for less than that. He longed for a stronger drink — a slug of that Glenfiddich. At least they could finish the wine. He refilled both their glasses. Edward's careful voice continued.

'I have no other blood relation in the world. That was one of the reasons I agreed to come here. I wanted to meet you — not just to settle the . . . er . . . conflicts . . . though that, of course, remains of prime importance, but also to see my mother's other son. You must realise, Mr Winterton . . .'

'Don't call me that.' Lyn banged the bottle down. The fellow was so damned civil. Mr Winterton this, Mr Winterton that. Winterton was Matthew's name, dragged into the law courts, made a laughing-stock. 'I suppose you find my Christian name ridiculous.'

'I . . . I beg your pardon?'

'You're right, it *is* ridiculous. Stupid, sissy, girlish.'

'Lyn?' Edward looked bewildered, took refuge in his glass again.

'Yes. Lyn, Lyn, Lyn. I used to know a girl called Lyn. She had long golden ringlets and a lisp.'

'It's a boy's name in Wales, a man's name, a very ancient one.'

'So they tell me. But I have no link or tie with Wales at all. I went there once and found myself a foreigner. They were speaking a different language, and I don't just mean the words.'

'I'm half Welsh myself, Mr Winter . . . Lyn. My father was a Welshman.'

'Your father? You . . . didn't know your father.' He saw Hester's eyes again, staring troubled into his own. It wasn't just the eyes they shared. Neither had had a father.

'No, but I know about him. In fact he had your name. Lyn is the shortened form of Llewelyn, one of the oldest, proudest names in Wales. It means leader — and my father was a leader.'

'How do you know that? I mean, I thought . . .'

Edward clasped his hands around his glass, closed his eyes for a moment as if he were struggling with some emotion. He answered slowly, laying down each phrase like a weighty coin or jewel. 'Hester wanted me to know — she must have done. She left me a sort of . . . fairy-tale, written out in her best handwriting in what looks like an old school exercise book. She gave it to my foster-parents along with a few clothes and bits and pieces — oh, and a photo of my father. I didn't see it, actually, until I was a child of six or seven. Then they read the story to me, as a way of . . . well — explaining who I was, I suppose. It was about a girl with golden hair who fell in love with a tall, dark, handsome soldier. The soldier's name was Lyn.'

'Soldiers aren't called Lyn.'

'Yes, they are. My father was.'

'Your father was a soldier?'

'Yes. A Welsh guardsman and an officer. He fought in France and was decorated for bravery, then went back to the Somme and was killed a few months later. Hester told my foster-parents and then wrote it down for me in a way I could understand and would find . . . exciting — you know, knights and crossbows, instead of infantry and guns. The story goes right back to his boyhood — how he grew up in Caernarvonshire in a castle and . . .'

'A castle?' Was Edward mocking him, inventing this whole thing? He was probably so unused to drink, two glasses had unhinged him. Except he sounded sober enough.

'Well, it was originally built as one. But it lost its fortifications and became just a manor-house. Hester and my father came from opposite sides of the country, but they both lived in wild rebellious areas with a history of endless warfare and castles everywhere. The Soldier met the

Princess when she had just turned seventeen and was holidaying with her family in Wales. They fell in love immediately. In fact, the story says the Princess loved her Prince more than woman had loved man before. Wait — I remember the words. I read the story so often, I know it off by heart now.' Edward's voice had suddenly come to life, the slow, careful cadences broken up and blazing. ' *"Their love was as tall as Glyder Fawr, as strong as Llew Llaw Gyffes. Their hearts beat together like two clocks chiming side by side. If one smiled, so did the other — and the sun. If both cried, the whole world cried in rain."* '

Lyn stared at Edward's face. Those thin pedantic lips were speaking poetry. 'H . . . Hester wrote that?' In a schoolbook, as little more than a schoolgirl, when she was lost and panicking in London?

'Yes. I never knew what the words meant, Glyder Fawr and Llew Llaw Gyffes. But I loved the sound of them. I used to repeat them to myself, so they became a sort of . . . magic spell. Later, I found out that Glyder Fawr was a high and mysterious mountain in Snowdonia, and Llew Llaw Gyffes an ancient Celtic god who *did* have magic powers.'

Lyn slumped back in his seat. How could this fussy litigious bachelor believe in ancient gods and magic, or be weaving him fairy-stories rather than drawing up balance sheets or swamping him in barren legal jargon?

'Hester even illustrated the story. There were charming little drawings scattered through the text.'

Lyn reached for his glass, kept it trapped between his hands to stop them trembling. 'Hester couldn't draw.' Hadn't he used that phrase before — to Jennifer? Matthew had ignored it — used Susannah's drawings in the Book and passed them off as Hester's. He had denounced it as a sham. Perhaps it wasn't such a sham. His mother had hidden talents. Had he ever really known her?

Edward was crumbling his bread to pieces. His whole face seemed changed — the impassive mask cracked, the eyes shining. 'She drew almost like a child. But since I was a child, the drawings made more sense to me. Her prince was so tall, his helmet touched the top of the page. He had a silver breastplate and a golden lance. His heart was on the outside and made of scarlet plumes. He loved her so much, he gave her a baby before he died. That was . . . er . . . *me.*' Edward gave a brief and nervous laugh. His cheeks were flushed — with wine, emotion, embarrassment? 'When she drew the baby, it was wrapped in those same scarlet plumes and carried by a stork across the ocean. Storks nest in Europe and then migrate to warmer countries for the winter, so I suppose that was . . . symbolic.'

Lyn stared out of the window. The snow had stopped falling now and the heavy sky was lightening at the edges, the first hint and tremble of sunlight glimmering through the grey. Edward's face was still in shadow, but he himself had thawed. The cold and cautious stranger who had arrived an hour ago, was now opening up, confiding. 'I used to love that

bit in the story. My foster-mother would say ''And the baby's name was
. . .'' and I'd shout ''Edward, Edward!'' — an unfortunate name,
really, in the circumstances, since the Welsh Llewelyns were always
fighting English Edwards. But I don't imagine my foster-parents knew
much about medieval British history. Mind you, I had four of the oldest
English Christian names in . . .'

'Three,' corrected Lyn.

'I beg your pardon?'

'Edward Arthur James.' Lyn could see the names shouting raw and
scarlet from the white void of the Will-form. Edward Arthur James.
Matthew Thomas Charles. Both his half-brothers had three names each,
he three puny letters.

'Edward Arthur James *William*. They added the William later, when I
was confirmed. It was the name of our local Bishop, who performed the
ceremony and was a close friend of my foster-father. But it was all a bit
top-heavy for a child. I was rather a weedy lad and all those formal names
seemed to weigh me down, especially the bishop's. I felt him like a heavy
silver cross hanging round my neck.'

Lyn shifted in his chair. 'Weedy? But you must be more than six feet
tall.'

'I was the smallest boy in my class till I'd turned sixteen. I shot up then,
but I was still so thin, I looked like one of those . . . pines out there — all
trunk and no branch.'

Lyn stared at Edward's broad shoulders, the barrel of his chest. Was
he mocking him again? He tipped the last of the wine into Edward's
tumbler. If a glass or two had loosened him up so much, a third might
encourage still stranger revelations.

'To tell the truth, I felt a . . . bit of a muddle as a child. On top of all
those first names, I also had three surnames — well, not legally, I suppose. But I used to try them out in turn, not just in my head, but in my
writing-books. None of them felt quite . . . *mine*.'

'Why three?'

'Ainsley, Fraser, Powys. Ainsley was the name I always used, of
course. My . . . er . . . mother had apparently insisted. But it made for
complications when I was living with two Frasers. Sometimes I pretended
I was Fraser. That was simpler. Powys was my father's name. I'd been
told it, you see, but I wasn't allowed to use it. I wanted to. Other boys
took their father's name, and I . . . hated being different. If he'd lived, I
suppose he'd have reserved it for his lawful sons who would carry on his
castle and his line. I had nothing of my father — not even his Christian
name. Strange that Hester gave you that, when it really belonged to me.'

Lyn stiffened. Was Edward threatening him? No, his voice was neutral
and reflective. Certain words had fallen on the table and were lying there
like stains. Weedy, distorted, different. This man was tied to him by fears
and frailties, as well as blood and genes. Hester had left them both a

legacy of fear. His mother's eyes were staring at him now — from his father's chair. He and Edward shared not just a mother, but a new stranger-father who had somehow bequeathed to him his name.

'I envy you that name.' Edward was leaning forward, the immaculate necktie trailing in his plate. 'My foster-father's family was old and very respected, and I was given the family Christian names. But they didn't really . . . fit me, since I wasn't his true son. I think I . . . I disappointed him, in fact. I was rather a . . . timid child and he doubtless hoped for better things with my soldier's heritage. Mind you, we never talked about my father. I had only the photo and Hester's . . . fairy-tale. But when I got older, I longed to know the facts — not just magic swords and enchanted castles. I always felt a bit of a . . . blank about my background. I wasn't a Fraser and . . . Anyway, when I was twenty-one, I hired a chap to do some geneological research for me, in Wales. I suppose it was stupid, really, and I always kept it secret. The researcher got quite excited, discovered that the Powys were actually descended from a branch of the family distantly related to Llewelyn ap Iorwerth and going right back to the thirteenth century. They made the Frasers look like . . . new boys.' Edward laughed. 'They had in fact been princes, so the fairy-tale was halfway true.'

Edward paused, took a mouthful of his lunch. He had eaten almost nothing up to now. 'I got so involved and interested, I steeped myself in the whole tangle of Welsh history. Wales is a very impressive place, you know. It has some of the oldest rocks on earth — and one of the oldest languages in the whole Western world — and literatures. And it's always remained — well — independent, however many times it was overrun.'

Lyn put his fork down. How could Edward sprawl there demolishing tomatoes while talking high romance? He had returned to his glass again. For a man who drank but rarely and who had been reluctant to sit down and eat at all, he had certainly relaxed.

'Llewelyn ap Iorwerth became a sort of . . . champion for me. He was the first Prince of Wales and the only Llewelyn to be called "The Great". He and my father became . . . well — fused in my mind, I suppose — the two Llewelyn heroes. That's what so upset me when people back home started . . . speculating about where I'd sprung from and who my real father was — suggesting he might have been a ruffian or even criminal, when in fact he came from such a noble background and proved worthy of it — won a medal, distinguished himself in battle . . .'

Lyn said nothing. He, too, had made those idle suppositions, imagined drunken louts pawing at his mother.

'I never put them right. Why bother? Whatever I'd said, they'd have twisted that, as well.' Edward shrugged and frowned. 'I just kept both Llewelyns to myself.'

Lyn drained his own wine. 'I must admit, I'm no great shakes at history. I've never even heard of Llewelyn the Great.' Edward lived thirteen thousand miles away and yet knew more about the British Isles than he did as a native.

'You ought to read his life, then. He is your namesake, after all. I think you'll find it fascinating. He was a man of many talents with several different sides to him. He was chiefly a warrior, of course, but he patronised the bards and ended his life as a Cistercian monk, so he must have had spiritual leanings, too. In fact, the name Llewelyn seems to have come from a Celtic deity who was god and king at the same time. It's one of the most stirring names I know. I used to keep a book of all the Llewelyns once, and it read like a roll of honour.'

Lyn was silent. His girl's name, his sissy, pansy name had turned into an accolade, a badge of honour. He was first son now, granted the first son's name and privilege. Hester had saved the name for her legitimate son, her best beloved and most important son who was heir in all but empty legal formulae.

Edward had still not touched his hunk of bread. Lyn cut another, thinner slice, divided it in two. Their fingers brushed as Edward took his half slice. Each broke the bread and swallowed. The cheerless meal had become a sacrament.

'Would you like to see that photo of my father?' Edward fumbled for his wallet. 'It's very faded now and almost in shreds. I've carried it around with me for more than . . .'

'No. Thank you, but . . .' Lyn flung his chair back, trembled to the door. 'Excuse me just a moment, will you?' He started up the stairs. There was no need to see a likeness — stolid flesh and blood, something which might jar or disappoint. Hester had already painted her own picture, bright and glowing in that schoolbook. How had his stern and unromantic mother been involved with one of the most fabled families in history, turned her early life into a fairy-tale, loved and lost a prince?

The Hester he had known had been old and crabbed and scorned romance. If she had ever found him reading fancy stories, she'd thrown the book away; she never went to weddings, not even to his own. She blighted love like frost. Yet, all the time, she'd had another, secret side, the gold and scarlet side he had called Susannah and grafted on to her. She had been a Susannah herself, but had hidden the scarlet under widow's black. The marriage to Thomas had been merely convenience — he knew that well enough. His father had needed a permanent and reliable nursemaid, someone who knew his ways and wouldn't leave him for a better job, a companion in his old age — which he never lived to enjoy. Hester, for her part, wanted a home to call her own, the status of a wife rather than the lowly role of housekeeper. Marriage suited both of them, but there had been little love to spare. He had always resented his mother for that — wanted her to love, wished with all the passion of his boyhood that her life had included passion, so that she could pass it on to him, leave it as a legacy.

362

His shame and resentment at her teenage affair had been chiefly that he had seen it as a sordid one, like those gossips back in Warkworth — even rape, perhaps, a brutish assault which had somehow damaged *him*, as well. He had always had high ideals, yearned to believe in love and romance in a grey and grudging world where they seemed so often tarnished. Yet now Edward had brought them back again, made Hester a Susannah and him a Llewelyn. Hester had given him the name of the man she loved more than man had ever been loved before, the hero who was named for heroes, the leader-prince, god-king.

He stopped outside her room, the room she had slept in, died in, and which he had always been forbidden to enter in his childhood, had only ever seen when she was dead. He had sometimes stood outside it as a boy, turned it into Susannah's room — imagined the tumbled underclothes, the glass bottles full of scents and salves — Susannah things, fragrant and forbidden. Now the room was almost nun-like — frowning furniture, simple wood-backed brushes on the battered dressing-table, high and chilly bed. He inched further into the room, touched the pale and faded counterpane. Hester had lain on a bed like that with Lyn, shocked and rumpled it, turned it into a lovers' bower. For a quarter of a century, she had hidden and concealed that love, sent away the fruit of it. Only when he himself was born, had she resurrected it, bestowed on him the honour of being her first son and her second Lyn-Llewelyn.

He walked slowly to the window, gazed out at the hills which had been looking in at his mother for over thirty years. The sun had broken through at last, and was pouring its elation on the snow, every smallest crystal glistening in the golden light, the far ridges touched with pink. He drew the curtain aside. Gold and silver fell across the counterpane as if Hester had embroidered it. He tried to scoop the gold up in his hands. He realised now what riches he possessed compared with Edward. Edward was a bastard and a refugee who had been fobbed off with an alien mother and alien country, sent abroad because he was an expense and an embarrassment; a weedy, muddled boy with no firm name or lineage. Edward might be the elder son, but he was the legitimate one. He had enjoyed his mother's hands and voice and lap, her lifetime and her certainty, when Edward had only a letter and a death. He understood the letter now — it was just a substitute. Edward was bequeathed the house only because he had been deprived of everything else. Hester was simply allaying the guilt she felt towards an infant she had flung across two oceans and several continents and then killed in all the records. A house was only a puff of smoke compared with a mother's presence and thirty years' devotion. It was like a rich child being asked to give up a toy or bauble to an orphan. He might weep to part with it, but the orphan had wept far longer and far earlier.

Lyn ran downstairs, fetched Edward's port and whisky from the sideboard, tore the wrappings from the chocolates. Edward was still sitting in the master's chair, finishing his lunch. Lyn poured port into a clean glass, proffered nuts and figs.

'Happy Christmas!' he said. 'I'm afraid it's your own port, but I do have something for you — a . . . er . . . sort of Christmas present.' Lyn opened the kitchen drawer, drew out a package, not Christmas-wrapped, but stuffed in a plain brown envelope.

Edward smiled. 'For me? You shouldn't have bothered, really. I wasn't expecting . . . presents.' He ripped the envelope, found a second one inside, slit it with his cheese-knife. Was he hoping for a tie, a pure silk handkerchief, a slim carton of cheroots? He drew out a folded piece of parchment.

'What's this?'

'Read it and you'll see.' Lyn was reading it already — in his head. *'I hereby revoke all former Wills heretofore made by me and . . .'*

Edward unfolded the paper, clutched the arms of his chair — Thomas Winterton's chair. 'B . . . but I thought . . .' he swallowed. 'My lawyers said there wasn't a Will. It had either been lost, or never made at all.'

Lyn nodded. 'It *was* lost.' Lies didn't matter any more. 'We searched the place for it. I even came back here on my own and turned all the lofts and attics inside-out. But still no Will. It was only when I came up *this* time that I found it.'

'But how had you missed it before?' Edward still hadn't read the contents. It was as if he were gaining time — crumbling bread, asking questions — before he dared see what it said.

Lyn stared down at the table. Lies were easier told to wood. 'Well, I knew if there had been a Will, my mother would have kept it in her bureau. She kept all her private papers there. We'd searched for it a score of times, emptied the whole thing out, found bills, letters, everything but that. But this time, I was cannier.' The lies came out as smooth as marzipan. He had prepared them carefully. 'I came across a sort of . . . secret drawer, right at the back and concealed behind a panel. I'd seen something similar in an antique shop in Cobham and that gave me a clue. I took the thing apart — and there was the Will.'

It hadn't been quite that easy. He had gone blundering into the forest on a freezing December day, searching for the gigantic Douglas fir which had marked the infant grave. All the firs looked massive. His face was torn by overhanging branches and a cruel stinging sleet began to strafe between the trees. He trudged deeper and deeper in, then round and round in circles, close to panic as the tall trunks hemmed him in. It was only eleven o'clock in the morning, yet as shadowy dark as dusk. After half a numbing hour, he was tempted to give up. Yet he couldn't remain a criminal, for ever on the run.

He tried again, taking it more slowly now, checking every step and landmark until at last, drenched and footsore, he found the spot, started scrabbling like a dog. The ground was frozen hard. Even when he'd loosened it, he had a strange irrational feeling that the package would be gone. It wasn't. Only cold and slimy, streaked with mould and mud. He slipped it under his coat, started to run, ducking under branches, tripping on snaking roots, smashing through the undergrowth, then squeezing through the fence and back to his hidden car. He had flung the package in the boot, not glanced at it again until late last night at Hernhope, when he had swapped the damp and soil-stained plastic bag for that clean brown envelope.

Edward was holding it at a distance, as if it were a trick, a trap. In the absence of a Will, he had been pressing for a half share of all his mother's assets. Did he now suspect that the younger and legitimate son had been named as sole heir, he sent away a second time with nothing? He would look a total fool after all his claims and clamourings, trumpeted round the world. Lyn watched his hands trembling on the still-folded piece of parchment.

'That's really why I got in touch with you,' he added.

'But why? What's wrong? What . . . ?'

'Oh, nothing's wrong. In fact, I think you'll be quite pleasantly surprised. That's the reason I suggested Christmas Day. I felt it was the most suitable occasion to give you your mother's . . . gift.'

'I . . . don't understand.' Edward's voice was wary again, his shoulders tensed. The man who had waxed ecstatic over ancient Wales and Princes had disappeared, leaving only the confused suspicious boy.

Lyn drew a sharp breath in. He was tense enough himself. 'Hester left you this . . . house, Edward, and all its contents. The whole thing — not just half. You're her only heir and . . .'

'I . . . I beg your pardon?'

'Why don't you read it for yourself?' Lyn jerked away from the table. *I bequeath to my first and eldest son . . .* Beloved son. He knew it off by heart now. He walked blindly to the door, laid his head against the cool unfeeling wood, turned round again, tried to calm his voice, act the cool executor, the hard-sell estate agent. 'I . . . I'm afraid it needs some renovation. The roof's leaking, the garden's like a jungle, and if you want electricity, you'll have to start again from scratch. But basically, it's as solid as a fortress. The walls are three foot thick. It was built to last, this house.'

Edward wasn't listening. The Will, the documents, were spread in front of him, but he wasn't reading them. He was staring beyond them to the snow, the hills, the harsh line of the horizon. The sun had disappeared now. For the first time in his life, Edward had his mother in his hands, his past taking shape before him, not in golden fairy-tales, but in stark black ink in formal legal jargon.

'You . . . you didn't know about this?'

Lyn shook his head. He couldn't speak. Despite his elation over Lyn-Llewelyn, it still hurt to be disinherited, to lose a house which had been

365

womb, cradle, bolt-hole, as well as wilderness and prison.

Edward was rubbing his eyes, as if he had just awoken from a dream. 'No, of course you couldn't have known. I'm sorry, it's all a bit of a shock.'

Lyn returned to the table, picked up a walnut, crushed it in the nut-crackers. What was wrong with the man? Edward had been squalling for his rights, yet now he had actually got them, he sounded more alarmed than elated or relieved. He hadn't opened the letters, had hardly glanced at the Will. Was he scared of drawing too close to a mother he had made into a myth, or did he fear that the princess in the fairy-tale would turn into a lonely old woman struggling with guilt and death? Lyn recognised his own fears.

'Look, you'd better read those letters. They may add something to the Will. I'll go out and leave you on your own. It'll be easier, then. While I'm gone, you can look around, view your property.'

'No — please — we ought to talk things over. I . . . I never imagined for a moment . . .'

'We'll talk later. Now I need some air.'

'You'll freeze out there. It's cold enough inside.'

'I'm used to it. I was born up here, remember.' Lyn turned towards the door.

Edward sprang up. 'No, wait — there may be some . . . mistake. This Will may be an old one. We ought to check. Or, if it was hidden so securely, perhaps she never intended . . .'

'No mistake.' Lyn stopped in the doorway. So Edward was scared of becoming Hester's son and heir, of staying alone in the house with her, without him as chaperon. There was something ironical, almost endear-ing, about a man who could jet half-way across the world to save his name and ensure his privacy, thus provoking world-wide public scandal; a plaintiff who thundered for his rights, then panicked when he got them. They were true blood-brothers, shared fears and foolishness. Perhaps *he* was the one who should fall on Edward's neck, shed tears of recognition. He could understand a man who had never dared marry or sire a child, who lived behind a mask, then rushed to lawyers when someone pulled it off, and was hurt and shocked when the hard world mocked his naked-ness. In any other circumstances, he could have made a friend of Edward. But Hernhope had come between them. Because he had lost his house, he had lost his wife. He couldn't forge a bond with a co-respondent, a man who had divorced and disinherited him.

It was that which had ruined the magic night at Cobham, when he'd had Jennifer in his arms again. They had vowed eternity which had lasted for an hour, built a future out of moonlight. But as soon as the moon went out, he'd had to sneak away and leave her, capsize her silver fantasies. It might have been different if she hadn't mentioned Hern-hope, insisted on it, almost, as her bride-price. She couldn't accept him as a man without an inheritance, a husband whose only dowry was him-

366

self, but had imposed a future on him, bracketed him with a house which wasn't his to give. If he had ignored Edward's rights and brought her here to Hernhope, their life would be a lie. Every day, he would hear the hidden Will whimpering in the forest, threatening to betray him. How could they live in a place which Hester had bequeathed to someone else and expect her eye to smile on them? Everything they sowed would be cursed and blighted by her, be it plant or hope or child.

He gripped the door frame so tightly, it hurt his hand. He could see Jennifer's naked body sprawling on the sacking, feel her hot clamping mouth around his prick. Never before had she swallowed him like that, gulped him down with such greed and such abandon. Amazing bloody woman. So demure in public and so wild when he switched her on. He stumbled through the door into the living-room. She was everywhere in this house. He had had her on that hearth-rug, had her in the velvet chair, a hundred times in the double bed which squealed and rocked as she did, once even in the larder, giggling like school-kids among her newly bottled chutneys. Yet, once they left the house, all that had stopped abruptly — the larking and the love. It was as if he had become another man, a colder, crueller lout who always turned away, who couldn't even touch her. He had lost her now, lost her open body, her sheltering arms.

He strode into the hall, dragged on coat and boots. 'I'm going out,' he shouted, heaved the front door open and stepped into a wilderness of white.

*   *   *

Lyn bent his head against the wind, struggled up the sheep-track which was blocked and blind with snow, walked north towards the highest bleakest ground. The cold was like a snowball flung against his face, yet his body burned for Jennifer, still hot and wet at Cobham. He could feel the straw pricking under his shoulders, her nipple stiffening in his mouth. *Her* mouth, sucking and pumping round his . . . Who had taught her that? What was she doing now and who was she . . . ?

He stumbled off the path, tripped on a buried boulder. A frightened group of sheep were shambling in front of him, panicking each other as they blundered out of his way. Only a month or so ago, the strutting swollen rams would have been let loose among the flock — mounting, thrusting — twenty ewes a night. He had watched them as a boy — his horror at the speed of it, the fierce, brutish, indiscriminate coupling — a shake, a snort, a lamb. Rams bred and fed only to sire and screw. Ewes passive, pinioned, violated — made valuable and profitable because a ram had served them. Submissive breeding machines building their lambs while life and leaf shrivelled all around them. Lambs born brute and bloody in the snow. Rams snug in pens while their own offspring bled and tore and whimpered into life.

He quickened his pace and the scatty ewes did likewise. He felt like a

367

ram himself — horned, horny, chasing them, in rut for them — in rut for Jennifer, wanting to mount her from the rear, tup her, serve her, force her.

He fell on his knees, scooped up a handful of snow. He must cool himself, freeze his bloody prick off. Melting snow dripped between his fingers, trickled down his sleeves. He scrabbled for some more, touched something soft and heavy, coffined in the snow. It was the tangled fleece of a sheep, a dead sheep — very dead — stained and yellowed against the whiter snow around it. He tried to kick it free, stared into the empty eye-sockets of the leering skull with its yellow trap of teeth. He shuddered, struggled up. His trousers were sopping, his feet and fingers numb. Jennifer would have fretted, tried to dry his clothes, worried about chills and flu and . . . No one to bother now.

He strode on. He hardly knew where he was going or why he was out at all in such cruel weather. But he had to calm himself, trudge and tramp away that sense of loss. Edward's face and Jennifer's were overlapping in his head, despair and desire fighting in his body. But at least the wind ripped away resentments, the cold numbed shame and guilt. The light was already dwindling, a hushed blue stillness tiptoeing on to the hills. It must be tea-time. Christmas cake and crackers, carols round the fire, families, belonging. He had lost all that, as well, even the chance of it. He could only be a family with Jennifer — husband and son with Jennifer. She let him be a child, gave him the leftovers of marzipan or bowls to lick out or Christmas puddings to stir. Stir and wish. Wish for her to be *there* — hot, wild, willing — back. Oh, Christ, yes! Sweep him from child to lover in a second, her fingers smelling of mincemeat, her bare breasts pressed against his . . .

He broke into a run. Must forget her, trample her down in the snow. He was panting, sweating — sweating in damp clothes and four degrees of frost! He slowed a little, manoeuvred a slippery incline. Despite the fading light, he could still follow the track, even when it foundered in drift and boulder, ridge and rut. If Edward settled here, he would never find the paths, or understand the harsh relentless rigour of the country. He had always thought of himself as alien, but he realised now he knew the land as intimately as he knew the lines and sinews of his own hand. He could tell the time without a watch, predict the weather, eavesdrop on the birds. He understood the moods and markings of the sheep, knew the name of every hill and burn. That was his inheritance from Hester, something which went with the house, was part of it, and which could never be left to Edward, even in a Will. Ainsley lived in the southernmost part of the world — an easy, smiling country with uncapricious weather, where Christmas brought blue skies and tangled flowers. Hernhope would break and baffle him. He would probably try to sell the place and add it to the profits from the book. The house would be bulldozed into a puny row of noughts. He would be shooed from it as he himself had

368

turned out moths and spiders just last night. He stood silent for a moment, watching sky and snow blur into each other, submerging everything.

He had climbed so far and high, he had reached the border with Scotland, marked simply by a narrow wooden fence. Scotland was only another range of hills, a deeper bank of cloud. He brushed snow from a boulder, sat on the bare and pitted stone. For centuries, war had roared across these borders, raids and counter-raids, bloodshed, treachery. The borderers had been split in their allegiance, brother fighting brother; husband wife. He could feel the weight of history's feuds and quarrels pressing down like the black night on the earth.

He had often drawn this landscape, as a boy. It was far enough from Hester to be safe. He had made swift and secret sketches with a pencil stub, or camouflaged his paints as sandwiches and worked on it in watercolour — always muted colour — browns, purples, greens — or endless white. He had lost those skills now. He had tried to go on drawing, prolong that sudden burst of vigour which had so astonished and excited him those few days in the summer. But fear and loneliness had sapped his energy, wrecked his concentration. He needed Jennifer to put her fence around him, keep his talents in. Without her, he was nothing — neither man nor artist. Christ! He couldn't even afford to be an artist. There was no money coming in, and all he had been promised now belonged to Edward. He could no longer rely on Matthew, had never belonged in his office, anyway — churning out those pat designs dictated only by cash and commerce.

He eased up from the stone, ducked underneath the fence. Now he was in Scotland — battle country. He still had his soldier's name. He must fight, endure. He had lost wife, house, art, job, but at least he was coping. He had survived for weeks, for heaven's sake, in harsh and hostile country, without home or larder, wife or wage. Edward couldn't do that. Edward would need his silver trays, his country club, his little clutch of lawyers. Llewelyn ap Whatnot had ended up as a monk. He had better follow suit, cut off his prick with his tonsure and live with no possessions — no ties, no cash, no bloody wives or women. He'd leave tonight, go somewhere wild and far, where no one would ever find him — Wales, perhaps, where Lyns were princes and the land was never conquered.

He slipped through the fence again, started the long trudge back. Although it was downhill now, it was harder going. The dark made snares and booby-traps out of every rock or gully. He had to use his hands, grope like a blind man, sliding and scrambling down the track if he chanced to lose his footing. The cold was more intense, freezing snow to ice, fingers to pain. His ears stung and smarted in the wind. He halted a moment, blew on his hands, stamped his feet, listened to the silence. In nearly two hours' walking, he had seen the lights of only three remote and snow-bound houses — Edward Ainsley's neighbours. Would they accept him as neighbour, or shun him as an alien? You could only truly belong if you were born here, the smell and feel of the country grafted in your childhood.

Hernhope looked almost blind as he approached it. Edward had closed the curtains, drawn the shutters. That was his right as owner. He could even board up the windows if he chose to, tear the place down, dismantle it for firewood. Lyn knocked before he entered. You didn't barge into a house no longer yours. Edward came to the door in his heavy overcoat.

'Where on earth have you been?' Edward sounded edgy, close to panic. 'I've been extremely worried. I thought you'd had an accident or . . .'

'I only went to get a breath of air.'

'Air? There're enough draughts in this house. The fire's gone out, *and* the range. I'm sorry — I couldn't manage them. I got so cold, I had to put my coat on.'

'Better keep it on, then. That range has moods and I've no more fuel, in any case.' Lyn removed his own coat and one of the bulky sweaters. The house felt stifling after the bitter wind outside. It was like a furnace burning off his fingerprints, melting down his childhood, his ownership, the years of Winterton history.

Edward was still fussing. 'You were gone so long, and I wanted to talk to you. This . . . er . . . new development alters everything. I feel quite . . . shaken up, to tell the truth. There are some papers here I'd like you to take a look at, so we can at least discuss . . .'

'Not now. I'm whacked.' Lyn turned away. He refused to play confidant as well as executor. He'd done what his mother had asked him. Why should he scan the other documents, read Hester's private letter and endearments? They were only lies, heaped on Edward in guilty restitution. Why ruin his own inheritance by having to discuss them, count up the 'beloveds'? All he would do was complete his Christmas duties. He picked up the box of fruits. 'I can't offer you tea, I'm afraid. There's no way to boil a kettle. But if you'd like an orange or some grapes . . .' *Edward*'s orange, Edward's grapes. Everything was Edward's now — the chair he sat on, the dark hills closing round them, Susannah's room upstairs.

'No, thank you.' Edward had cupped his hands around a candle, as if its tiny flame were the only light and warmth left in the world. 'I don't think you understand the problems. I mean, take the issue of copyright. That alone is . . .'

'We ought to save those candles. They're already half burned down and we'll need them for later on. Mind you, I don't know what we're going to do for supper. I bought a tin of soup, but we can't eat it cold. There's always bread and cheese, of course, but . . .'

'I'm afraid I won't be . . . er . . . staying for supper. I'd like to talk things over, work out where we stand, but then I must be on my way. The

370

roads are so bad, it'll take two or three hours at least — and I haven't even ordered a taxi yet. I was looking for the phone.'

'Phone?'

'You mean you haven't got a . . . ? But you phoned me yourself, when you . . .'

'Not from here, I didn't. Hernhope's never had a phone. Hester didn't want one. She communicated other ways.'

'Well, how am I going to get back?'

'You can't. You'll have to stay the night.'

'Impossible! I've booked a hotel in Gosforth. I put up there last night, to break my journey. All my things are there, and they're expecting me for dinner and . . .'

'They'll understand, with the roads as bad as this. I can make you fairly comfortable. At least the bedding's thick. It's light I'm more worried about. I've got a torch, but no spare batteries.' Lyn leaned across and blew the candles out — snuffed Edward out, as well. 'Forgive me, but best to save those in case of an emergency.'

'Look, I must get back.' Edward's voice sounded louder in the darkness. I've got urgent business in Newcastle in the morning.'

'Business on Boxing Day?'

'Well, semi-business. I'm lunching with a solicitor. He's a friend of a friend of someone I know in Warkworth. Now the Will's turned up, I ought to take the chance of discussing it with him. My own lawyers are on holiday all week, and there are so many matters to . . . I mean, I'll obviously have problems disposing of this house at all . . .'

'Disposing of it?'

'Well, a sale may be quite tricky, with it being so remote and . . .'

'You can't sell Hernhope! It's Hester's house, an inheritance which goes back centuries and must be kept within the family. She wouldn't want strangers here.'

Edward pushed his chair back. He kept fidgeting and shifting as if he were scared of the dense and clammy darkness which shrouded the whole room. 'Hester's . . . dead,' he said, at last.

The word seemed to sink like a stone into the silence. It was no longer silence. The sharp cry of a dog-fox suddenly tore across the night, a thin and desperate sound distorted by the hills. There were other noises — murmurings and creakings from the house itself — soughing of the wind as it whined down the chimney, fretted at the shutters.

'*No*,' Lyn muttered, groping to his feet. The floor felt no longer level, the room was closing in on him. He had a sudden overwhelming sense of Hester's presence. He could see beyond the shadows, beyond the darkness, to some plane where his own dry throat and burning head hardly mattered any more. He lurched forward, stretched out his hands. His fingers closed on nothing.

'Do you . . . feel something?' he whispered to Edward.

371

He heard Edward catch his breath. 'What d'you mean?'

'Well, a sort of sense of . . .' He broke off. It sounded crackpot. There weren't words for what he meant. 'My . . . er . . . wife used to say that some people had such force or . . . strength in life, that it — well — lived on after them and . . .'

Edward cleared his throat. 'Your wife sounds a little . . . fanciful.'

'Not at all. Jennifer's extremely down to earth.'

'I . . . don't believe in ghosts.' Edward jumped as the ashes in the range stirred and shifted suddenly. Every smallest sound seemed to boom and cannon in the darkness, a sobbing gurgle from the water-pipes, the creaking of the floorboards under his chair.

'Don't you?' Lyn shut his eyes. Hester was still there. He could see her dowdy black dress, her limp and shabby overall with its pattern of tiny purple flowers, her swollen hands with their rough and work-worn skin which she had never bothered to soften with her own salves, her strong determined jaw and firm set mouth. Jennifer was right — had been all along. She had always claimed that Hester was too powerful a character ever to be extinguished, that she lived on at Hernhope, at least in spirit. Hester was at home, watching her two sons together, had maybe brought them together, so that he would understand about the Will, learn about the heritage of his name.

He crept towards the range where his mother had stood so often, stirring, basting, always busy. Sometimes, when he was small, he had laid his face against the overall, smelt grease, yeast, onions, all mixed up. She had pushed him away, roughly, and then relented, offered him a ladleful of stew. He had burnt his tongue in trying to gulp it down to please her, gagged on tiny bones.

'H . . . Hester?' he whispered. He could even smell the stew, bubbling on that cold dead stove, his mouth smarting hot with peppercorns.

Edward started to his feet. 'What? What did you say?' He blundered into something, swore.

Lyn swung round. 'Are you all right?'

'I . . . think so. Bruised my shin a bit. Are you?'

'Y . . . Yes.' Lyn sank back against the range. If Hester were alive still, then he needn't blame himself for having killed her. He felt guilt flake and shred away like meat off bones in Hester's long-cooked stew, resentment boil to nothing.

Edward was still floundering in the darkness. 'It's madness to sit here in the pitch black. Haven't you any paraffin? I found an old oil-lamp while you were out. If we could only light that, we'd . . .'

Lyn shook his head. He hadn't bought paraffin. It was over a pound a gallon, and he'd remembered that there was an old can in the outhouse, dating back to Hester's time. When he went to find it, the rusty punctured can was sitting in a pool of oily black. The scant two inches left had lit half his Christmas Eve. The rest had passed in darkness. 'Just accept

372

the dark,' he said to Edward. 'Like animals do'. He could hear the fox again, sounding fainter and unearthly. He tried to take his own advice, unclench his hands, loosen his hunched shoulders.

Edward slumped back into his chair. Neither man said anything. The darkness seemed to prick and chafe between them, as minute followed minute. A wodge of snow, dislodged by the wind, suddenly slid from the roof and shooshed abruptly past the window, thudding to the ground like a detonation.

'Good God!' Edward was on his feet again. 'What was that?' He started stumbling towards the door. 'Look, I'm going to order that taxi. Surely one of your neighbours has got a phone?'

'Our nearest neighbour is almost four miles away. I'll drive you there, if you like. But I can't guarantee you'll ever get a cab. Not on Christmas Day with roads like these.'

'Thank you. I'll risk it.'

'You'd better wrap up warm, then.' Lyn was still shivering himself. 'There's no heating in my car. Take my second sweater, if you like. I'll just get my keys.' He fumbled into the hall, steadied himself against the carved oak settle. He had always scoffed at Jennifer when she talked about spirits, presences. How had he been so blind? The whole house reeked off Hester. And he was about to turn his back on her, leave her home for ever. He ran his hand along the grainy wood of the settle, envied its solidity. The nomad gypsy moment had arrived too soon. He wasn't ready, hadn't made his plans. Edward was all right — returning to the light and warmth and safety of a city, the shelter of a hotel. He would meet his legal acquaintance in the morning, map his future, tot up all his gains. But what of *him*? Once he handed Edward over to the cab-driver, what road could he take himself?

Edward had followed him into the passage. The two men stood almost touching in the gloom. Lyn cleared his throat.

'There's . . . er . . . no need to bother with a cab. I can drive you to Newcastle. I've n . . . nothing else to do.'

'No, please, that's quite unnecessary. Both the car-hire firms I checked with yesterday assured me they'd be working over Christmas. They charge much more, of course, but that's only to be expected. It's just a question of getting to a phone.'

'You'll find they'll change their minds once they see fresh snow. They're reluctant to come this far out in any weather. And with roads like this, they'll . . .'

'A taxi brought me here.'

'Yes and the driver arrived cussing like a fishwife.' Lyn was tracing the pattern of oak leaves on the settle, his fingers blindly sculpting bumps and hollows. 'I've . . . er . . . got to leave myself, so you may as well come with me.'

'It's very kind, but your car . . . I saw it out in front there.

It's . . . rather ancient, isn't it?'

'Old and strong. Built to battle with these roads. I bought it from a local farmer who lives five miles up a dirt track, so it knows its way around.'

'Well, if you're sure it's no trouble . . .'

'Just give me ten or fifteen minutes, will you? I want to pack some things. Why not sit in the living-room? It's more comfortable there. Take the candles with you — we don't need to save them now. And if you want to open the whisky or . . .' Banalities were soothing, like booze, helped to numb the mind. Lyn dragged himself upstairs. His few possessions were still in his battered bag. He hadn't even bothered to take out his pyjamas, or get his toothbrush wet. All he owned was in this house — raw and living memories. It was those he had to pack.

He fetched his torch, groped along the landing. He could still feel Hester's presence — a younger Hester, now, as the 'eighties concertinaed back into the 'seventies, 'sixties, 'fifties, and he was five years old again, head reaching to her elbow, a thin and restless child with dark unruly hair hacked off by Hester's chicken-jointing scissors. No pretty golden curls or angelic smiles. The only photo he'd seen of himself showed a grubby brat scowling by the hen-house with his socks around his ankles, and even that was out of focus.

He dragged the rickety chair to the high-set landing window, as he had done so often as a five-year-old. It was pitch dark outside, but he wanted to remember how it felt, wobbling there when Hester wasn't looking, gazing down at the steep and winding sheep-track to see if anyone was still alive in his and Hester's world. Visitors were rare at Hernhope. The postman sometimes, with a bill, the paraffin man who called him 'laddie' and had a runny eye, needle-tongued Nan Bertram with some eggs or lambs' tongues or reproof. Most times, there was no one — nothing to see at all, only hills and sky — and sky.

He shut his eyes, watched the seasons change. The mud and flood of spring lapping at his scarlet Wellingtons, new lambs with each new day, green spiking through the brown. Summer and no school and endless evenings when dark played hard-to-get and he lay, long past sleep-time, kicking off the blankets, watching the sun still grinning through his curtains, whilst his mother sang winter hymns downstairs. In autumn, everything ran over on stove and shelf and hedgerow, and Hester filched his conkers for her linen chest to keep the moth away, and his legs prickled in grey school serge again, and there were gaps in trees and leaves in gutters and the first hoarse cough of winter threatening in the wind.

Winter. The longest of the seasons, stretching from scarlet hip to purple crocus and engulfing every colour with its snow. Cold black howling Christmases creeping into besieged and chilblained Februaries with the last handful of flour grimy and weeviled in the sack. Braggart Marches petering out in snow again. Velvet-footed snow camouflaging death's black fist in sly and smiling white. Sheep buried, swept away, lambs dead before they were born. And not just sheep. Dead rooks, dead rabbits; his own heart dead inside.

Lyn slipped down from the chair. It was winter still on the dark and shivering landing. He paced from room to room, watching Hester as she cleaned and dusted, putting her stamp and imprint on the house, tying in her history with the centuries before her. Saw himself, cowering in corners with a forbidden sketchbook, or knees-to-chest in a chimney seat, poring over a catalogue from some long forgotten sale of stock, or hiding under beds with a sickly kitten clawing at his jersey. He stopped in his own room. The torch sent shadows trembling up the walls. He knew those shadows like old friends. There had been no electricity for his first ten years, only paraffin lamps and candles, which turned beds and wardrobes into ghostly ships or monsters, made the whole room heave and flicker. Even with the generator, the house was still plunged in darkness after nine. Hester treated light like grace — something fleeting, insubstantial — which came only in precious flashes and must be hoarded and respected.

He turned his torch off — almost in obedience to her — crept downstairs, continued his tour of the house. He must go into each and every room, say goodbye to it, scoop up his past from every smallest niche. He shivered in the chill of his dead father's long-dead study, shrouded in its dust-sheets and its cobwebs; touched the solemn furniture in the second, smaller sitting-room, remembered the insurance man perching on that sofa in his stiff grey suit, explaining stiff grey things to Hester who refused to bring an ashtray for his drooling cigarette. He stumbled on to pantry, scullery, laundry-room and what Hester called her 'dairy', saw his mother fighting wet and flapping sheets, or straining milk through muslin into an enamel pail, stirring in the rennet, elbow deep in white. He had resented the fact she had always been so busy, but now he realised it was the only way she could have kept them both alive. She'd had resourcefulness and courage. Softly he closed the door, stood motionless outside it. He had been in and out of every part of the house now — well, all except the cellar. Should he venture down there? It was dank and claustrophobic with painful memories, and yet . . .

He swung round suddenly. Edward was calling out.

'Are you nearly ready? It's started to snow again. We really ought to make a start or . . .' The voice petered out in darkness.

Lyn froze. Once they left, he could never return again. Edward could sell, raze, destroy. Even if he kept the house, it would be only for a decade — two at most. Like himself, Edward had no heir. Both were wifeless, childless. And Edward was already in his sixties. In twenty years or less, Hernhope would pass to strangers. He could see the strangers, trespassing up the path, throwing out the furniture, distempering over the past, sanitising, gutting. . . .

'Can you *hear* me?' Edward sounded tetchy. 'Where are you? Up or down?'

375

'D . . . down,' Lyn shouted back. 'Just locking up. I shan't be coming here again, so . . .' He darted down the passage towards the cellar. His own words had panicked him. He couldn't leave — not yet, not empty-handed. He must find some souvenir or treasure, something of Hernhope he could keep for ever, smuggle out with him.

He heaved at the cellar door, locked it behind him, stumbled down the steps, the torch-beam feeble in the plunging black, memories flapping against his face. He started rifling through the chests and trunks, stopped at a box piled high with newspapers, some of them dating from the first decades of the century. Perhaps there was some record there of his mother's soldier-prince — an obituary, or an account of his campaign. He had found a different mother — one he could live at peace with, one who could even draw — had messed about with children's crayons, creating storks and scarlet hearts. He must take that mother with him, find some childish forgotten drawing he could treasure as his own, the equivalent of Edward's fairy-tale.

The newspapers were tattered, damp with mould. He hadn't time to look at them all, but skimmed through one or two, reading snippets from a world already dead. Reza Khan Pahlevi had seized the Persian throne, Roald Amundsen flown by airship to Alaska, Darwin's theory of evolution been banned in Tennessee. He tried to picture Hernhope in the 'twenties — still a large and thriving farm, his father not yet married, but the eldest son and heir, soon to take over, the child Susannah waiting in the wings. The farm had witnessed her marriage, watched her death, then — revived and run by Hester in the 'thirties — had battled on through depression, crash and war. Bereaved herself, Hester had still retained the house. The Forestry tried to buy it with the farm, lease it back to her as a powerless, landless tenant, but Hester had withstood them. The house was hers — and his.

Through all his boyhood he had feared it, found it too grim, too lonely, yet now he saw its courage and tenacity. All those pin-men from the newspapers, those Roald Amundsens and Reza Khans had long since perished. The house had struggled on. Mice had nibbled into Darwin, left droppings on Chamberlain or Churchill, yet Hernhope stood unscathed. He had been part of it, built into it, resenting his own history and strength. Yet, now it was no longer his to flinch from, he felt like a blurred forgotten photo in one of those old journals. You could only avoid oblivion through children or through art, which left something of yourself to outsmart death. And yet he had lost his foetus child, renounced his embryo art . . .

He tore blindly at the papers, as if to bind and staunch his pain with them. His hand struck something hard, the corner of a box. He dragged it out. It was Hester's button-box — not seen for twenty years — the huge square painted biscuit-tin he had played with as a child. He broke his thumb-nail prising off the lid. Yes — there were all the buttons glinting in the light.

He heard a sudden noise, slammed the lid shut again. He ought to get back to Edward. He had left him long enough and Ainsley was fuming to get off. Yet these buttons were his history as much as the house itself, and how strange that he had found them just as he was leaving. Was it Hester's doing again? He could feel her presence even in the cellar — perhaps more in the cellar where she had hidden her diaries and locked up all her past. Wouldn't Edward understand, for heaven's sake? At least he was upstairs in a decent comfy chair, with the embers of the fire to keep him warm. He could light the candles, study all the documents. Damn it — he even had a bottle of Glenfiddich.

He crept with the box towards the second secret cellar, crawled through the tiny door on his hands and knees. It was cold and grimy on the floor, but almost a relief to be hidden so securely, deaf to any shouts. He tipped the buttons all around him, remembered faces, recognised old friends. Hester had always told him where every button came from, attaching each to a name and story, using them as a family-tree or history book.

The two of them had always played with buttons on Christmas Day — making pictures, creating words — starting with their own names which they spelt out in different colours. It had seemed more than just a game. They had shaped the presents they hadn't had, made button flowers, button dreams. He started to make an L. He had a longer name now, which couldn't be scattered so easily by a careless foot. L for leader, love, Llewelyn . . .

He sorted swiftly through the buttons, pushing aside the broken, faded, boring ones, the menials from servants' clothes or overalls, the drab spoil-sports still in mourning. This time, his name must be constructed out of strength. The first L he made of brass buttons, neat and highly polished, fitting for a soldier. The second L was silver for a prince. He had always loved those glinting silver buttons, outshining all the others in the box, the only ones which Hester made mysterious. 'I don't know *where* they come from,' she always said. Were they, in fact, from Llewelyn's uniform, his splendid guardsman's tunic?

The E he made of purple — not a timid colour. Purple for victory and passion, noble birth. He paused on the W. W for Winterton. He must make his father's initial out of all the strongest buttons — bone, horn, ivory, enamel — buttons which could outlast centuries. If he couldn't carry on the name in flesh and heir, then at least he could immortalise it here.

He had cramp in his foot. He rubbed it, then banged his head by sitting up too quickly. It was like a grave, this place, gloomy and restricting, the smell of mould lingering in the shadows, and a cold which froze the bones. He had reached the second E. That he made of Matthew's buttons. Matthew was a Winterton, so he belonged beside the W, lying next to his father. He chose baby buttons only — the mother-of-pearl, the harm-less prep school grey — grinned to himself as he made Matthew small and powerless.

He stared at the half-formed name — LLEWE . . . Just the LYN left now to

377

do — once his own name, now only part of it. He had to get it right. Game or no, it mattered. He sifted through the browns and greys, sullen beiges, sissy pastels, brushed them all aside. He chose red — bold, forbidden red — Susannah's scarlet, which had obsessed and coloured all his childhood; now Hester's scarlet, too, which she had concealed beneath her black. He made the L and Y of the most brilliant reds in the whole box, the red of Llewelyn's plumes.

Only one last letter left, the letter which completed him. That must be Jennifer. There were two N's in her name. It must be blue, the serene blue of her eyes, of sky, water, summer, south. He built the downstroke and the upstroke, the diagonal between them, tipped the letter a little so that it overlapped his Y and they would lie forever touching. Jennifer had always longed to live at Hernhope, so at least she should lie in some smallest secret corner of it, joined to him as she had been joined at Cobham in the moonlight, root to mouth. She and Lyn-Llewelyn would be together there for always, haunting the place like Hester. No one should disturb them, even if the house were sold.

Lyn crawled through the tiny door, locked it, wrenched the handle off, stacked boards and crates in front of it, built a barricade. The torch was failing now, but it would see him through his task. This was Llewelyn's last and strongest castle.

He paused a moment. He could hear muffled shoutings, thumpings on the outer door. Edward had heard him banging things about and had come in search of him, calling out in fear.

'Where *are* you? What are you doing? We must get off. It's snowing really fast now. Can you hear me down there? Are you all right?'

'Yes, yes. I'm coming.' Lyn ripped his thumb on a jagged strip of metal-banding which had worked itself loose on one of the broken crates. He swore, sucked it, mopped the blood off his sweater. His clothes were filthy, anyway.

'Ready now,' he shouted, and as he groped and fumbled back to Edward's house, the last life-blood of his torch dribbled into darkness.

XXVII

Cold bright daring winter sun hung like a golden bauble above the hospital. Jennifer stopped, dazzled. Sun on Christmas morning was an extra present in your stocking. She had already had a stocking — full of crazy things from Susie — cut-outs made from empty cigarette packets, gift-wrapped sherbet dabs and bubble gum purchased from the hospital shop, silver-foiled suppositories wangled from the nurses. Susie was still in hospital. Her few days' rest had dragged into three long weeks, and although they had promised her Christmas Day at home, as soon as she got up and started packing, her blood pressure had risen again. It was only a slight rise and she was otherwise much better, but they had ordered her back to bed, as much for the baby's sake as hers. She was trapped there now, railing against her fate, furious and fretting at the tedium, the timetable, the endless petty rules — what she saw as her ruined shackled Christmas.

Jennifer put her parcels down, rested her arms a moment. Buses seemed extinct on Christmas Day, so she had walked to the hospital, weighted down by a double patchwork bedspread and a clutch of other presents. She had been up all night finishing the bedspread. It took months to make a patchwork of that size, and she had completed Susie's in less than nineteen days. She'd had to use a machine, of course, but somehow that seemed more suitable for Susie, who was a modern machine-age girl, impatient of the slow, pernickety progress of her hand-work. Even so, it had been a gruelling task. 'Labour of love' was more than just a phrase. It meant flayed and fraying fingers, throbbing head, eyes aching from the kaleidoscope of colours. She had sewn love and remembrance into every flowered or striped or spotted hexagon, added a huge entwining double S on the plain blue centre panel.

She humped her parcels up again, trudged the last fifty yards towards the hospital. A tramp in a grimy coat which flapped around his ankles slouched past her, muttering to himself. She longed to wish him Happy Christmas, share existence with him. For the past two weeks, she had felt strangely insubstantial, except when she visited the hospital. The warmth and bustle of the ward, even the rules which Susie kicked against, made things real and purposeful. But once outside again, she felt herself fade and dwindle as the heavy-breathing winter evenings closed around her, and London's seven million people were only empty offices, drawn curtains, deserted streets.

She had never got up alone before on Christmas morning, the empty schmaltz of the chat shows making the silence louder, the uncooked and now superfluous turkey pale and cold with goose-pimples, Lyn's presents piled unopened beside her bed. She had made him a Christmas cake, knitted him a sweater, a scarlet one this time. She hardly knew why scarlet, when her husband always hid in sober colours, but somehow it had seemed right and bright for Christmas. Now it looked merely desperate — bleeding because he couldn't try it on. She had no idea where he was. She hadn't even received a Christmas card. That angered her. He knew her address, knew how much Christmas meant to her, and if he had decided to ignore it, then she would harden her own heart. That ecstatic night at Cobham seemed almost like a dream now. She had been totally committed to him then, and he had repaid her by running off again.

379

Served him right if she switched her concern and allegiance to Susie, put her and the baby first. She had little choice, in any case. Susie was an immediate problem, a vital swelling presence, whereas her husband had made himself a shadow and a stranger.

The hospital had become a sort of refuge. She had got to know the nurses on the ward, helped them when they were short of staff, was always ready to talk to other patients who needed support or company, spent hours by Susie's bed, trying to rally and amuse her. It wasn't virtue or unselfishness. At Southwark, she was no one; on the ward she had a name, a role, a reason for existence. Besides, since Susie was carrying the baby which was going to be her own, then to be with her and concerned for her, was like caring for herself.

She stopped to rest her arms again, glanced around her. Everything was dirty and deserted. Santa Claus had left shiny black dustbin-bags overflowing with rubbish instead of sacks of toys, dumped them in the gutters. A mangy dog was sniffing round them, the only living creature besides herself. The shops were locked and shuttered. There were no Christmas decorations, no holly wreaths on doors. The only seasonal reminder was a torn and flapping poster announcing road accident statistics for last year's Christmas period. Only the sky had bothered to dress up. Ruffs of gold and scarlet were crinolined round the sun, fading into underskirts of pink and pearly grey. Yet, even that was deceptive. It was cold, despite the blaze. The North was deep in snow and sleet, and although the South was spared it, they still had thick frost and zero temperatures.

Jennifer shivered on the pavement, made herself walk on. Susie needed her. Her parents were still hostile, had only relented enough to send her a scribbled 'Merry Xmas' on a Woolworths Christmas card. Sparrow was spending Christmas with his mother and three brothers in Sittingbourne. He hated hospitals. She had to make it up to Susie, be all relations at once — mother, lover, husband, mate. Lyn might be alone somewhere and moping, but at least he wasn't eight months pregnant, lying in a shabby ward with fifteen hugely expectant mothers, coughing, groaning, snoring all around him.

The sun had disappeared now, shut out by the beetling façade of the massive hospital building which was looming up in front of her with its stained and crumbling pillars, its grey forbidding stone. Jennifer faltered up the steps, pushed open the door, moved from frost to fug. Inside, the foyer swung with paper chains. A tall lop-sided Christmas tree stretched balding branches towards the visitors, as if begging for more tinsel. Three patients with paper hats atop their dressing-gowns had trespassed down the stairs and were mingling with the staff, all cheerful and transformed. Jennifer had visted twice a day for eighteen days and had rarely seen a smile before. Now people were chattering and laughing, singing snatches of carols. Christmas had affected everyone, even the normally

380

stern receptionist and the new knife-edged Sister on the antenatal ward. She disapproved of Christmas morning visiting, but it had been introduced by a senior nursing officer who considered herself progressive, so she was doing her best to smile upon her giddy garish ward. Beds were askew with all the extra people, white counterpanes aflame with Christmas paper. Nurses with holly in their caps were munching chocolates, passing round mince pies. Balloons hung in every corner, bottles of Harvey's Bristol Cream had taken over from specimen bottles. Children were screaming, the radio shrilling *Silent Night*. The other patients were surrounded by their families and hardly noticed Jennifer as she picked her way along the ward, dodging toddlers and trolleys. She stopped at Susie's bed — still last one in the corner — stared in shock. It was tidy, made, unrumpled — not a sign nor trace of Susie. No books or papers littered on the coverlet, no fag-ends in the ashtray.

'Ah, Mrs Winterton, we tried to contact you, my dear. That's not so easy when you haven't got a phone. Susan went into labour in the night.'

'Labour? But she's not due for four whole weeks. What happened. What . . . ?'

'Baby got impatient, I presume. Don't worry, she's all right.'

'You mean, she's . . . had the . . . ?'

'Oh, no. Baby changed his mind. We thought he'd be the first Christmas arrival with his photograph in all the newspapers, but obviously he doesn't like publicity.'

'Where is she?' Jennifer cut through all the jokes. It was always jokes in hospitals, tinselling over danger.

'We sent her up to the labour ward. The contractions started again an hour or so ago.'

'Look, I must be with her. I promised her I'd . . . '

'You'll have to ask the Sister there. It's her decision now.'

'But I've been over it all already — with Sister Wilmot — weeks ago. She said as long as . . . '

'Sister Wilmot's off, my dear. She's got four days' leave for Christmas. Gosh! That's a work of art.' The nurse pounced on the patchwork bedspread which Jennifer had unfolded and was arranging on top of the hospital one. 'Did you make it yourself?'

Jennifer nodded. Susie's bed looked bare and deathly pale — she had to brighten it up. She turned the top down, arranged a row of presents along the pillow. Her hands were trembling, her head spinning with a hundred fears and questions.

The nurse was still admiring. 'You are a clever girl! Susan won't be coming back here, though — or not unless the contractions stop again. She'll be moved to postnatal.'

'Wh . . . where is she now? Where *is* the labour ward? I must go up there.'

'Two floors up. If you take the lift, you'll see the sign right in front you.

They may be a bit chaotic, I'm afraid. We're all short-staffed today. But there's a little waiting-room just along the passage. It's for husbands, really, but no one's going to mind. Pop in there and ask the first nurse who comes in.'

Jennifer was too impatient for the lift, took the steps two at a time, collided with a red-haired nurse at the top and started pouring out her story.

'I'm sorry, dear, we've got four in labour at the moment, including an emergency with twins.'

'But they said I could . . . It was all arranged. My friend's on her own, you see, and . . . '

'Well, hold on a moment and I'll try and find Sister. She's already missed both her coffee breaks, but if I'm lucky, I might catch her in her office. Wait in here, would you and I'll see what I can do.'

Wait, wait, wait — that's all she was good for. Even the husbands' room was empty. All decent caring fathers were present at the birth. It was a hideous room with puke-green shiny walls and a scrap of tattered carpet on the floor. The window looked out on a waste of rusting dust-bins, which had vomited half their contents round their feet, and a blank brick wall with SCREW MAGGIE! daubed across it. The only picture showed a storm at sea; the only reading matter was the *Ninth Pan Book of Horror Stories* and a motor magazine already two years out of date.

She picked up the magazine, tried to concentrate on Hot Rod Racing on the Utah Salt Flats, but souped-up Fords kept turning into foetuses. Supposing Susie were panicking, forgetting all her breathing drill, struggling, screaming, haemorrhaging . . . Susannah had had her baby on Christmas Day. It had lived and she had died. She remembered Molly telling her how Susannah's coffin lay beneath the Christmas tree like a gigantic mocking gift, her empty bedroom sick with the scent of lilies. Thomas had eaten nothing for three days, just sat at the table, numb, while goose and turkey were carved and served and sent cold away again. All the Winterton babies had been born in cold and crisis. Lyn arrived in February in a blizzard, Matthew motherless in late-December, Thomas himself in November's sleet and snow.

She slumped in a chair, her own stomach bloated and distended, cramping pains griping like contractions. She turned back to the Hot Rods. Ridiculous to panic. Susie had been doing well, all the nurses happy with her progress, doubly pleased that she had decided to keep her child. The rhesus antibodies had not increased at all and were causing no alarm. Even the minor rise in blood pressure had already stabilised.

So why had labour started four weeks early? Was it labor at all? And why had no one come to fetch her now? Were they hiding something, had bungled something, trying to cover up?

382

She opened the door, peered out. The silence was almost frightening. Everywhere else in the hospital were revels and whoopee; here only a stretch of tense and waiting corridor. The delivery rooms were just a few yards down, beyond hefty double doors labelled NO ADMITTANCE. Five babies struggling to be born, and she shut out like someone uninvited to a solemn and important ceremonial. She longed to be part of it, assisting and involved, instead of powerless in this footling ante-room.

Had they simply forgotten her? Hours must have passed since she had spoken to that nurse. She glanced at her watch. Just six and a quarter minutes. She sat down again, scanned a list of cars for sale. All of them had names — Vauxhall Victor, Morris Marina, Alfa Giulia. The baby was still nameless. Susie was more concerned with the names of Spanish beach resorts. She herself had always favoured Susannah, if the baby were a girl — Susie's namesake and more fitting than she had realised at the Harrods tea — Matthew's child with Matthew's mother's name; a name which he and Lyn and Thomas had all paid tribute to, all woven into dreams.

Yet, now she feared the name. It had been an unlucky omen from the start. Susannah's death had left Matthew motherless, Thomas distraught; made Hester a servant, Christmas Day a tragedy. She erased the name, kicked it out. Susannah had died. This child might, must — please — would live.

The door was opening. She sprang to her feet. It would be the nurse returning with news. Susie's baby was born, safe, thriving, suckling, there.

A tall man in a green gown over shirt-sleeves stumbled through the door. He sank into the only other chair and closed his eyes. Jennifer felt cold unreasoning anger fill the silence like a mushroom cloud between them. Anger because he hadn't come to call her; resentment that here was a father who had been allowed in the delivery room, and who probably had his baby now, a named and breathing child.

'Excuse me . . .' Jennifer frowned at his smug and sprawling legs. 'You haven't seen a nurse, have you?'

He opened his eyes, squinted at the light. 'I've seen about a dozen of them. My wife's just given birth to twins.'

'Congratulations.' Envy doubled.

'Not yet, please. They're only two pounds each and hardly breathing. They've just been rushed to intensive care.'

'Intensive care? For babies?'

'Well, they call it something different, but it's life-support machines, just the same. They're great, those things, unless your own kid's on them. Then every second's a nightmare. I know. We lost our first.'

'Gosh, I'm sorry . . . Is your wife all right? Was it . . . bad?'

'Not as bad as the first. That was murder. Forty-two hours in labour.

Halfway through, they gave her an epidural, but the thing cocked up. She was in agony by the end. And it was all for nothing, anyway.'

Jennifer pressed her cramping stomach with her hands. 'I . . . I'm sorry,' she said again.

'These things happen, don't they?' The man shrugged and rubbed his eyes. 'What are you doing here?'

'Same as you. Waiting for a baby.'

'You don't look much like a husband.' The feeble joke was painful when he sounded so close to tears.

'N . . . no.'

'Your sister's?'

'No, my . . . Look, excuse me a moment, will you? I'd better go and check on her.'

Jennifer stood trembling outside the door. The Special Care Baby Unit was just along the passage. She remembered now she had noticed the sign, but had preferred to blank it out. Babies with rhesus problems could land up there, undergo dangerous procedures like exchange transfusions — horrors she had read about and dreaded, decided to forget. Babies four weeks premature would be even more at risk — too small and weak to rally on their own.

A nurse dashed past, followed by the younger red-haired one she had spoken to before.

'Stop — please stop! How's my friend? What did Sister say? Did you sort it out?'

'Well, no, I'm sorry. She said there's nothing in the notes, so she can't allow you in. We've got a newish doctor on and he won't hear of it unless it's down in writing. He's a bit of a tyrant, I'm afraid. Don't worry though — your friend will be all right.'

Jennifer flounced back down the stairs. They were treating her like a child, a total fool. She would go and drag the Sister out from Susie's previous ward. She might be new, but at least she had the details of Susie's case, was aware of the special circumstances. She would insist she took responsibility, spoke to the labour ward herself and sorted out the muddle.

The reek of turkey fat had taken over from the smell of disinfectant. They were serving Christmas lunch. A long white-clothed table had been set up in the centre of the ward, with most of the pregnant patients sitting round it, one or two in wheelchairs. There was no sign of Sister, though a whole bevy of new nurses was rushing to and fro with plates and glasses, and a moustachioed doctor in pink frilly hat and apron was carving a gigantic turkey.

'Pity I'm not a breast surgeon!' he joked, as he hacked off slices of white breast-meat, nurses giggling and frothing all around him.

No one noticed Jennifer as she dithered at the door. There was too much noise and razzmatazz. Children were pulling crackers, blowing whistles, husbands pouring wine and humping chairs.

'Anyone want stuffing?' bawled the doctor, spooning out sage and onion from the butchered turkey. 'I'm ready if you're willing! Ha ha!' Today was just a joke to him, a caper. If a baby died, a mother died, the Christmas revelry must still burp and bubble on. It was like those Christmas chat shows — all emotions banned except tinselled bonhaomie.

Jennifer turned her back. If she ever prised a nurse away from that stupid sozzled doctor, she would still need Sister's sanction. And Sister was probably dealing with some crisis and would only tell her sharply there were other patients besides Susan Grant. She trudged upstairs again, turned the other way from the labour ward, towards Special Baby Care. For all she knew, Susie's baby might have been born already, rushed down here and shut up in a box. She pushed at the heavy door. She must see those life-and-death machines herself.

'May I help you?'

'Yes. H . . . have you got a baby Grant here?' How could a nurse that young be left in charge? 'Here, let me look myself.'

'I'm sorry. No one's allowed in here except the parents.'

'I've got to check. My friend's gone into labour. I was told I could be with her, but all I've done so far is hang around, and I've no idea if she's even . . .'

'I'm sorry, this isn't the labour ward. You'll have to go and ask up there.'

'I've been up there, for heaven's sake, and no one told me anything. I may as well not exist, for all they care.' Jennifer's voice was rising. She was sick of being treated as a nobody after weeks of centre-stage. Fame was like champagne, frothy and expensive, but exploding into nothing once the cork was drawn, leaving only hangover and headache in the morning. She had been relieved before to escape the whirl and hubbub, retreat on to the sidelines, especially since Edward Ainsley's action had turned fame to notoriety. Several people had recognised her when she visited the ward, asked about the book, steered the conversation in the direction of the lawsuit. She had always tried politely to brush them off, play the whole thing down. But now she *wanted* fame, for the power it brought with it — power to open doors, dispense with rules, override the doctors.

'Look, don't you realise who I *am*?'

The nurse turned away. 'I'm sorry, we're extremely busy. If you'll excuse me, I must . . .'

'No, I won't excuse you.' Jennifer heard herself sounding shrill and vixenish. She never made scenes, never flung her name about or answered back like Susie. 'I've been waiting five fucking months for this baby to be born, and now when she's actually having the kid, I'm not even allowed to . . .'

'Whatever's going on?' An older and more senior nurse had swept through the door and took Jennifer by the arm. 'Who are you, my dear — a patient or a . . . ?

'I'm Jennifer Winterton. That won't mean a thing, I suppose, but . . .'

'Yes, it does. Good gracious me! I recognise you now. You're the one who . . . Yes, I've read your book — I loved it. And I saw you on the television, back in the summer, wasn't it? Fancy seeing you here! How d'you do. I'm Staff-Nurse Catherine Stapleton — Kate, for short. Very pleased to meet you in the flesh.'

Jennifer mumbled greetings, tried to force a smile. At least she'd got recognition and a friendly voice. Perhaps she could exploit them, wangle an entry into Special Baby Care.

Nurse Stapleton was beaming. 'Look, why not come to the office and have a quick glass of sherry? I'd be thrilled to hear about the television — behind the scenes and everything, and perhaps you'd sign my book for me if I bring it in.'

'I'd l . . . love to talk to you — later — and of course I'll sign the book. The problem is I'm a bit . . . distracted at the moment. I've got a friend in labour, you see, and I think her baby may be put in Special Care — or there already. Could you do me a favour — let me have a look?'

'What's your friend's name? I know all the babies in the unit.'

'Grant. Susan Grant.'

'No, we've no baby Grant. I'm certain of that.'

'Oh . . . I see.' Jennifer frowned. Was that good news or bad? Was Susie's baby still struggling to be born, or had it died already, turned out a monster or a mess? 'Could I . . . er . . . see the unit, anyway, have a look at those machines and things?'

'It's not really allowed, my dear. Come and have that sherry. I've got a ten-minute tea-break, and I'd be only too happy to make it something stronger.'

'No. I . . . couldn't drink — honestly. I feel a bit . . . Look, *please* let me in there, just for a few minutes. I won't be any nuisance.'

'Well, just a peep, then. I shouldn't really, but it is Christmas Day, so . . .'

She led the way. Jennifer followed into glaring lights and flashing screens — ten perspex cages wired up to monitors, whole batteries of dials and knobs and levers, letting out a constant hum and whine. She peered through the side of the first germproof incubator. Inside it was not a baby — you couldn't call it a baby — but a bulge-headed, stick-limbed foetus, too tiny to be born. It lay spread-eagled on its back in a pool of liquid faeces, its legs drawn up like the haunches of a skinned and hairless rabbit, eyes bandaged, head shaved. Little strips of sticking plaster were criss-crossed across its head and face, attaching discs and tubes. It was breathing very fast, almost desperately, its stomach pulsing in and out as if it were a hooked fish. Lying beside it were a pink rabbit and a fluffy teddy bear — toys which seemed a mockery since the child could neither see nor touch them. Yet every incubator had its miniature Christmas stocking, filled with toys and sweets. *Sweets* when they couldn't suck so much as a drop of milk!

Jennifer turned away. In the next two cages lay the twins, already separated and strung up like exhibits in a horror-film laboratory — new and bruised arrivals, their stomachs splodged with dried and purple blood, knife-sharp ribs almost cutting through their fleshless skin. Perpex head-boxes cut off their heads from their tiny gasping bodies. A doctor was adjusting the machines, two nurses checking every smallest movement on the screens. The father was there, still in his green gown, nodded wearily at Jennifer, tears streaming down his cheeks. He looked huge against his tiny dying sons. All that powerful apparatus, those miracles of technology, might not be enough to save them.

Jennifer could feel her own tears threatening. She followed Nurse Stapleton to the other side of the room, watched her adjust the nose-tube on a plumper pinker baby who was kicking against her fetters, mouth opening and shutting in what looked like silent fury.

'That's my namesake,' she said. 'Another Kate. She's been with us twenty weeks.'

Jennifer reeled. 'Twenty weeks! Like *that*?'

'She's fine. Warm and snug. No draughts, fed continuously, twenty-four hour nursing.'

'Yes, but . . .' There were more important needs than food. How could anyone know what mental pains those babies might be suffering? The fears, the isolation, the deaf insensible perspex on all sides, their mothers only a shadow blocking out the light. To be twenty weeks with your head clamped at the neck, your body pierced with tubes! A modern miracle. But old-fashioned things like terror, panic, loneliness, could still go on inside. Warning-bells would sound if the chamber overheated or the machine blew a fuse, but nothing could ever register for nightmares or despair. Machines like that could warp a child's whole future. Babies needed arms around them, breasts to suckle, human warmth and contact. Whatever the mechanical marvels, the technological breakthroughs, no machine had been invented which could love and cuddle and commune.

Nurse Stapleton was smiling. 'All right, my dear? There's two other rooms beside this, and a nursery where we keep the bigger babies, but if you'll excuse me, I must get back to work now. Tea-break's over! Pop in and see me about five o'clock if you're still around. I get a longer break, then, and we can talk about your book.'

Jennifer stumbled down to the foyer, stood staring at the notice-board with its endless list of wards — Florence, Wilbur, Goldsmith, Grosvenor — people ill and dying all around her. 'CHAPEL', said another sign. At least it would be quiet there; the Christmas service over, the place a sanctuary. She could smell faint traces of the congregation as she pushed open the door — incense and hot feet.

She stopped in wonder. The chapel was the most handsome room in the hospital. No lavatory tiles or lumbering water-pipes, but blazing mosaics, brilliant glass. Almost automatically, she knelt. It seemed sacrilege to treat a chapel like a hotel lounge and just sit or stand about. There was a Christmas crib to one side of the door, wonky peg-doll shepherds lurching across cardboard rocks and green crêpe-paper grass. The Virgin Mary had just given birth to a papier-mâché baby almost as big as she was, but she still looked strong and smug. The delivery room was a stable, the only incubator hay and ass' breath. No forceps or epidurals, no tubes or mess or fuss. Just 'she brought forth a child'. The Madonna already had done. Hours ago at midnight — when Susie was still struggling and she herself was sick and headachey with patchwork squares — the Christmas miracle had come to pass, the Christ-child born as smoothly as a star. It was so beautiful, so simple, she longed to believe that things like that could happen. Even the lambs, which were normally born so simply and so swiftly, still had their fatalities. She remembered Sooty, the tiny orphan lamb she had bottle-fed in Molly's shed, whose mother had perished from exhaustion after a twenty-two hour labour.

She shuddered, tried to distract herself by gazing round the chapel. There were six lilies on the altar — white Susannah lilies — fusing innocence and death. She had read in Hester's diaries that lilies were favourable in childbirth and should be worn or grown by women who wanted a son. Boy or girl, it hardly mattered any longer. Either would be a miracle, so long as it survived. The lily was also an antidote for sorrow. What had Hester called it? The 'forget-grief herb'. She prayed they wouldn't need it in that context, not for death or sorrow, but for life and resurrection, newborn innocence.

She opened the prayer-book on the bench in front of her. There were no prayers for actual labour — only thanksgiving for a child, or prayers to be said following a still-birth. She dared not glance at either, turned instead to the funeral service, closed her eyes. Lyn was standing in the pew beside her, so pale and strained she feared he would collapse.

'Man born of woman has but a short time to live; like a flower he blossoms and then withers; like a shadow he flees and never stays.'

She preferred the old translation. He cometh up, fleeth, never continueth. Those archaic forms hid the pain behind the words. *'The Lord gives and the Lord takes away.'* Giveth, taketh, it was still the same. He had taken Susannah away, Lyn away, snatched her own baby before it was even born; maybe Susie now and *her* child.

She stared up at the windows. Faith, Hope and Charity glowed radiant in the coloured glass. All were women — sturdy courageous women, holding swords and scripts and palms. *Caritas* had a tumble of children clinging to her skirts, suckling from her breasts; *Fides* looked like Hester, grim and strong, standing alone above the grey and purple hills.

Jennifer stood up. Hester had endured and so must she. If Susie's child was sickly, dying, or still labouring to be born, then Susie needed hope. *Spes* was stern and slender, brandishing a palm in one hand and a sword in the other. She would take that sword and return to the labour ward, and if they still fobbed her off with muddle and excuses, she would search out Staff-Nurse Stapleton again, and beg her help.

She toiled up all the stairs again, feeling drained and exhausted, as if she had given birth herself. Two of the delivery rooms were empty now, the doors standing open, a nurse clearing up inside, humming *Jingle Bells*.

'Excuse me. I'm Susie Grant's friend. I wondered if . . .'

'She's back in the ward.'

'I beg your pardon?'

'Queen Mary Ward, I think it is. One floor up.'

'But has she . . . ?' No, mustn't ask. Supposing the news were bad? She couldn't bear to hear it from that cheerful, humming, heartless, ugly nurse.

'MERRY XMAS' proclaimed the gold and scarlet banner above Queen Mary ward, though Christmas looked paler down below it, appeared to have petered out already in debris and exhaustion. Grounded paper chains were littered on the floor now, leftovers of sweets and sherry abandoned on bedside tables, fractious children wingeing with fatigue, their new-born brothers and sisters howling in their cots.

Jennifer faltered at the door, torn between worry and excitement. There was no sign of Susie, but perhaps she was in the nursery, tending her own child. She must have a child, or they wouldn't shove her in here, in a ward alive with babies.

'May I help you?' The nurse had another wailing infant in her arms. 'Ah, you're Susie Grant's friend, are you? She's been asking for you — beginning to think you'd run away and left her! She's down there on the left. The bed with the curtains drawn.'

'Has she . . . ?' No. Jennifer still couldn't bring herself to ask. Not if the curtains were drawn. That was normally a bad sign. Meant the patient needed extra rest and care. What had Susie been through? Would there be a cot beside her, a baby at her breast?

Jennifer walked between the rows of beds, glancing in at all the other cots. Blue blankets for boys, pink for girls. Big babies, tiny ones, dark, fair, squalling, smiling, crumpled babies. She almost resented them, because they weren't hers or even Susie's. No one smiled at her. She had got to know the patients in the antenatal ward, but these were total strangers. She stopped outside Susie's bed, the only one with curtains drawn. 'Let there be a cot,' she prayed. She fixed her eyes on the tiny blue daisies on the faded cretonne, trying to pluck up courage to go in. The noise behind her — chatter, babies' cries — stuttered into silence as she drew in her breath and stepped forward, wiping her clammy palms dry on her skirt.

'S . . . Susie?' she murmured.

Silence.

'Susie, it's me — Jenny. May I come in?'

No answer. She slipped between the curtains. Susie was lying ominously still, staring straight in front of her. She didn't look up, made no sign of recognition. Her hair was tangled on the pillow, dark with sweat and grease, purple smudges beneath her eyes, her face pale and almost haggard. The covers were thrown off, her blood-stained nightdress rucked up around her knees. She looked tiny without the bulge, like a different person entirely, someone younger and more girlish. And yet her face had aged. There was a fierce and harrowed expression in her eyes, an air of total exhaustion. Her locker was bare — no Christmas food or clutter, no triumphant flowers. Worst of all, no cot.

Jennifer tried to find her voice again. 'H . . . how are you, darling? I've been so worried. I . . .'

Susie turned away. 'You weren't there,' she muttered to the wall. 'You didn't come.'

'I did, Susie. I tried. I've been here *hours*, but they wouldn't let me in. I'm sorry, darling. I'm really truly sorry. I kept asking, but . . . What happened? What . . . ?'

Susie slumped back again to face her, eyes anguished and accusing. Tears were filling them, brimming over, streaming down her cheeks. 'Go away,' she sobbed. 'It's too late, now. I don't want to see you now. I don't want to s . . . see anyone again — ever ever ever. Go away.'

XXVIII

'Right,' Lyn shouted. Now, *push*. PUSH!'

'I am pushing.'

'Harder! The damn thing's still jammed fast. OK, take a breather. I'll count to three and then let's both give all we've got. All right? One, two . . .'

Edward wasn't dressed for snow. His coat stopped just above the knees, his expensive shoes were already stained and water-logged. He tried to get a firmer grip on the back end of the Morris, which had skidded on a patch of ice some twenty miles from Hernhope and was now stuck across the road with its rear nearside wheel in the ditch. He stumbled, clutched at the mudguard.

'Watch out!' Lyn stamped his feet to warm them up. Whirling flakes were stinging against their eyelids, turning to tears on their cheeks. The countryside was choked and gagged with snow, blindfolded in darkness. Strange presences and shadows seemed to stride towards them, then drift away again. There was no other traffic, no comforting lights of human habitation, no sound except the shrill and desperate wind. They might have been on the moon, or in some other darker world or dream, where the only real and solid things were cold and exhaustion.

'Let's start again,' said Lyn, screwing up his eyes against the driving snow. 'Try and lift and push at the same time. Ready? One, two, three . . .' Slowly, inch by inch, the car juddered forward as they heaved from behind, trying to lift it up and out.

'We're winning!' shouted Lyn. 'Keep pushing. Don't slack off.'

Snow whipped them from above, soaked them from below, but at least they had freed the wheel and the car was back on the road in a dip between two hills, nose pointing south again.

'Right, straighten her up a bit. That's fine. I only hope she'll start. Can you push while I drive? That'll help me up the hill, keep me steady.'

Edward nodded dumbly as Lyn climbed in and slammed the door. The car spluttered, coughed, but started. Lyn let the engine crescendo like a hymn of triumph. He was in control now, fighting the road, the elements. Edward was just the garage boy, the slumped and shivering passenger, doing as he was told, getting out, getting in, clearing windows, freeing wheels. They had been driving two long hours already, but had not yet hit the main road, were still stuck north of Elsdon in the wild and rugged moorland west of Harwood Forest. Half an hour from Hernhope, a blizzard had sprung up, howling round the car, bringing new risks to already treacherous roads.

'We must turn back,' Lyn had urged. 'We'll never make it. The roads will be impassable.'

'No.' Edward sat steely and unmoving. 'We're through the worst, surely?'

'The worst roads, maybe, but not the worst weather — not by any means. The climate can be merciless up here. I've known people buried in the snow. Even local folk who know their way around.'

'I'm sorry, but I've got to get to Newcastle. I can't turn back — not now. Can't face that stretch of road again — if you can call it road.'

Lyn knew those can'ts. He used the word himself. Can'ts were close to panic. Edward had been tense and jumpy every inch of the journey, driving from the passenger-seat, braking before *he* did, warning him of hazards he could see all too well himself. Yet insisted on driving on. Lyn knew they ought to stop, but if Edward were so pig-headed, why should he care? He had lost his house, his future, so why not risk his life as well? It was almost a relief to do battle with the roads, take his feelings out on wheel and gear-stick rather than sit passive on his own and stare out at the void.

He had felt a sort of crazed exhilaration at being out at all, when all cautious folk were barricaded safe indoors. He was the only man left in the world — Edward hardly counted, huddled there chewing at the fingers of his gloves. There was some hellbent elation in the skittering wheels, the drunken snowflakes whipping against the windscreen, the sudden bombardments of snow cascading down from overhanging branches as the car lurched and skidded under them. It was damned cold, bloody dangerous, but at least the weather was in sympathy, howling with him for his lost and plundered homeland, paying Edward back by harrassing him with blizzard and black ice. But now it had fucked him up as well, brought him to a standstill.

He wound the window down, shouted back to Edward 'Right — start pushing now. Try and keep the back straight. I'll take it very slowly in second gear, OK?'

'OK.' Edward's voice was shredded by the wind.

The car strained against the hill. The snow was not too deep as yet, but fresh snow had fallen on to old, leaving the roads like ice-rinks. The Morris whined in protest, wheels slithering and spinning. Edward was sliding around himself, suddenly lost his balance and went slap down in the snow. Lyn jammed the handbrake on, stuck his head out of the window.

'Are you all right?'

'I . . . er . . . think so.' Edward floundered up, shaking snow from his coat, checking his hands for grazes.

'You'd better get back in, or you'll break your bloody neck. I think I can manage now.'

Edward hobbled in beside him, panting and out of breath, snow still fringing his trousers.

Lyn pressed his foot on the accelerator. The wheels spun uselessly. 'Blast,' he muttered, tried again.

Edward was fidgeting and fretting, turning round, peering out. 'If you can't go up, why not reverse back and take a run at it?'

'OK, OK. Just be patient, can't you?'

Edward drove a limousine on well-shod city roads where snow would be as miraculous as manna. Even the taxi he'd turned up in had been a bloody great Mercedes. What did he know of ancient fourth-hand cars or force nine gales? He wrenched the gear-stick into reverse, let the car run back a little. The mirror showed him only snow on snow. His head-lights lit up a tiny snow-bound sanctuary around him, then blinded themselves in the darker world beyond.

The car was losing speed now, still creeping backwards, but beginning to jib and shudder as the road curved up behind it in a second hill. The wheels had lost their grip, were sliding out of control again.

'Get out!' Lyn ordered. 'We need some grit for the wheels. Damn — I should have brought a shovel.' He should have brought a lot of things — food, rugs, booze, a proper tool-kit. Edward had suggested taking the whisky with them, packing up a picnic of the bread and cheese, making sure they were well prepared. A proper little Baden-Powell. His own mind had been elsewhere.

'You get in the car,' he had said. 'I'll bring all the gear.' He had turned back to the house, filched one last look at it, found himself fighting off the tears. Bloody fool — blubbing over a pile of stones he had spent thirty years trying to get shot of. He'd been fumbling for a handkerchief instead of searching for a shovel, had forgotten food and drink. Or *was* it just forgetting? It was almost as if he were ill-prepared on purpose, making things as difficult for Edward as they could be — a sort of trial by ordeal in which the alien must fight for his house and win, prove himself against every hitch and hazard.

There was a pile of grit swelling on the roadside, like an abcess frozen hard beneath its bandaging of snow. Lyn kicked at it with his boot, hacked and rammed with the crank-handle, using the whole force of his body. Even so, he dislodged only a few handfuls which he carried like diamonds to the car and scattered round the wheels. He clambered into the driving seat, rivulets of melting snow trickling down his neck from his soaked and straggly hair. His hands were so numb, they felt large and clumsy like the paws of some extinct and cumbersome animal.

He slipped the handbrake off and put the car in gear, made another run at the hill. So long as they moved at all, Lyn felt power. He was Force, Movement, Plan, while Edward was only ballast slumped scared and inert beside him. The last two hours of driving had needed all his skills — blind corners, treacherous surfaces, twisting dipping roads. Edward would have been defeated long ago. He was defeated now himself. The wheels were slipping again, the car sliding out of control. He came to a stop only a few yards past his previous resting-place, trapped between a hill in front and a hill behind. There was nothing he could do now but switch the engine off and wait for daylight or the snow to stop. He could hardly see at all. Snowflakes were slamming at the windows, paralysing the flailing windscreen wipers. He leaned forward, cut the ignition. Silence flooded over them — choking, menacing. Neither man disturbed it. Only the wind made rude and spiteful conversation, whining round the car.

'Surely we ought to go and get some help?' Edward muttered, at last. His voice sounded scared and puny, as if the snow had muffled it.

'Where from, for God's sake?'

'There must be a house nearby. Or a farm, or . . .'

'It's crazy to get out. With snow like this, you can lose all sense of direction. Landmarks simply disappear. Only last year, a shepherd died. He was walking home from Alwinton — knew every inch of the land — but still managed to stray off the road. They found him a week later, buried in a snow-drift.' Lyn switched his lights off. Darkness closed around them, as if in mourning for the buried shepherd. He could feel Edward's fear stretching out towards him like a clammy hand.

'Can't we have a bit of light?'

Lyn switched on just the sidelights, to save the battery. Their beam was so weak, it hardly showed at all. All he could see was blurred and spinning snowflakes whirling into nothingness.

'It's damn hard on the shepherds. Weather like this makes their job a nightmare. I've seen them digging sheep out of ten or twelve feet of snow. The poor crazed creatures are so wild with hunger, sometimes, they tear at their own wool to try and lick the grease from it. When they're rescued, they look as if they're half bald, with bare patches on their sides — if they're still alive at all.'

Edward was still fidgeting. 'We can't just *sit* here. We're stuck in a dip with the wind blowing straight towards us. The car could be covered after several hours. We've nothing to eat or drink, nothing to . . .'

'It's worse outside,' said Lyn. Snow was clinging to the windows, blinding them like shutters. Edward slapped at them with his gloves. Was he claustrophobic, afraid of being coffined in snow? One stranded night was nothing. He and Hester had been snowed up for weeks, no car, no help, no neighbour for five miles. That was claustrophobic. Hemmed in by his mother, her face pale at every window, her shadow black at every door. Winters half a year long, when Edward would be basking in the sunshine, deepening his tan from October through to March.

'You said Elsdon wasn't far off. Couldn't we get out and walk there? Get some help or something? Put up for the night?'

'Out of the question. It's at least three miles away. The only thing I could do is try and reach Eastbrook Farm. That's only half a mile or so. The farmer there's related to the Bertrams and quite a decent chap. I ought to see the house lights if I strike straight across these moors. It's madness to try in these conditions, but . . .' Lyn shrugged. No more crazy than risking his neck on the roads.

'Do you want me to . . . er . . . come with you?'

'No, you stay put.' Edward had property to live for, two houses to tie him down, deeds to sign, repairs to put in hand, lawsuits to fight and win. Edward couldn't perish.

'You won't be . . . too long, then will you?'

Fatuous question. How could he not be long, when every step was a fight against the elements?

'No, I shouldn't think so.'

'Will you be . . . all right?'

'Of course.' He almost welcomed acting irresponsibly, doing something reckless. It stopped him thinking, counting up his losses.

'Well, take my gloves, at least.'

Lyn slipped them on. They were far too large for him, turned his hands into another man's — long-fingered and broad-palmed. He felt a child again, boating about in his father's size eleven Wellingtons, boots cold and dead as Thomas was himself. Edward's gloves were chill against his fingers, the suede clammy from the snow. They wouldn't keep him warm, but they were Edward's talisman, his feeble contribution to their rescue.

'Won't be long,' he fibbed again. Time meant nothing, anyway. He had the rest of his life to waste, or chuck away. He longed to plunge into the snow and be snuffed out like a candle. He realised suddenly that life and death were equal for him now. The boundaries between them had been blurred like those between road and moorland, snow and sky. Edward had no choice. Edward had to survive as householder and heir, whereas he himself had renounced all possessions like the monk Llewelyn, cut all ties.

He stepped into the snowstorm. Cold clawed at his face, the wind rushed for all his weak spots — up wrists and trouser-legs, down neck and into ears. He turned his collar up, used his hands like a blind man, feeling for the hedge, tap-tapping along it until he reached a gate. If it was reckless to get out at all, then it was still more madcap to step off the road and strike across a moorland, when he had neither torch nor compass. Everything looked different in the snow, and this was territory he hardly knew. He turned to look back at the car, its yellow lights still shining faint behind him. It looked absurdly small and stupid, broken-backed and stranded. The next time he looked, even the lights had been swallowed up in darkness. He was alone now with the night.

Every thought, every muscle, was centred on the yard of snow in front of him, feeling for traps beneath it — bog, boulders, sudden mounds or dips. He had to battle against the wind, keep trudging on, however harsh the weather. Cold and Dark were giant figures striding on either side of him, towering over the landscape. He groped towards what he hoped was east. The snow cast a ghostly glow around him, fudging forms and outlines. Black and white had fused in treacherous grey. He stared towards the dead line of the horizon. There were no welcoming lights, no blur of a friendly house. The farm he remembered had perhaps struggled to its feet and lumbered away like a frightened beast at his approach.

The snow was so deep now, he could hardly free his feet. He suddenly realised he was stepping into the hollows of his own earlier footprints, only half concealed by freshly fallen snow. He must have walked in a circle, come back to where he started. It was madness to go on. He had got nowhere at all, so far, and Edward would be panicking. Best that they stayed together this one last night, before they parted for ever in the morning.

He flailed round, struck out for what he remembered as the track back to the road, tried to follow his footprints which were swiftly disappearing. The soft sheen from the snow showed him only wastes of more snow. Supposing he were lost — never found the road? Every time he raised his head, freezing flakes smote against his eyes, fell cold and stinging on his lips. The simplest action such as putting one foot in front of the other, or trying to stand straight against the wind, had become feats of endurance. Little point in shouting out for help. Edward was sitting deaf behind the iced and blinded windows of the car, every human creature safe indoors. It must be long past supper time — cold turkey and hot punch, sherry trifles, jellies. He and Hester had eaten bread and milk on Christmas night. The chicken carcass had to last all week for soups and stew-ups. He would have welcomed bread and milk now, snatched at a dry crust. The mouthful or two of ham he had forced down at lunchtime was only a grumble in his gut.

He groped a few steps forward. The road they had been on ran south and east. He must will himself that way, find the car again. He stumbled into a ditch and out of it. Didn't remember a ditch. He stopped — heard a cry shatter the darkness like a stone thrown in a pool. A rabbit caught by a fox, perhaps. Somewhere there were creatures as cold and hungry as he was — voles, badgers, birds huddled in the bare and shivering trees, all waiting for God's mercy and a thaw

A black shape turned into a bush, tore and scratched his hands. How could he have lost his bearings in so short a time? The countryside looked alien as if he had wandered off the map and strayed into a foreign land.

He tried to walk faster — tripped and fell, spreadeagled on the ground. His body felt damp and heavy like a boulder, a clumsy hulk with neither brain nor feeling. If he left it where it was, it would be buried with the stones and bushes around it. He let himself sink back, closed his eyes. His earlier elation had totally disappeared, swamped in sheer exhaustion. No point struggling any longer. He had learnt long ago you couldn't win against the elements — not up here — couldn't change the climate, switch the seasons. The whole scheme of things was merciless. Foxes pounced on rabbits, crows pecked out the eyes of new-born lambs, man shot roe-deer, God killed man. Everything ground you down — weather, nature, time. Best to submit. If he died, who cared?

He huddled his coat around him, touched the damp wool of his sweater. Jennifer had knitted that — knitted all his jerseys. It was all he had left of her. Her other possessions would be in that squalid Southwark bedsit which he had never dared to visit — the tiny china animals which she had collected since her childhood, her fluffy Angora jumpers which moulted in the wash and left little shreds of her on his darker pants and shirts. His own sweater was baggy now, stained with axle grease. He remembered it growing from her needles like a child, swelling on her lap. She had chosen the wool to match his eyes, scoured twenty shops before she got it right. She had tried it out against her, held it to her chest to measure it. Now it lay against his own chest. He slumped back, closed his eyes.

He had driven her away, lost her through his own fault, rejected her, upset her, made a mess of everything. He was too numb now to battle on, too fagged to force himself. Best simply to give up, accept that he was lost in every sense. He would perish in the cold and his wife wouldn't even know.

He let the snow slam down on his face, cover him like a shroud, heard the tiny cry of the rabbit again, gasping through the night. Other creatures were dying — preyed upon or frozen — sheep plunging into drifts, deer collapsing where they stood. He groped to his feet and listened. Was it just a rabbit? It sounded more like a human cry, muffled and still distant. Yes, there it was again. He *wasn't* lost. Someone was out there, another human being. He lurched towards the voice, dizzy with relief. He suddenly knew he didn't want to die.

'Haloooo. . . . ,' the voice was shouting. 'Where a-aa-*are* you?'

It was Edward's voice, Edward who was approaching him — gloveless, witless Edward, striding out in the snow, risking his neck to come and find his enemy in a completely unknown countryside.

'Over here!' Lyn yelled. Elation made him clumsy. He tripped on a hidden root, measured his length in the snow again, blacked out for a second.

When he opened his eyes, Edward was standing over him, hauling him up, his broad comforting bulk steadying him on his feet. 'L . . . Lyn, you're s . . . safe. Thank God!'

Lyn felt his face crushed against wet cashmere, his chest pinioned in two arms. Edward was embracing him, had used his Christian name for the first time since they'd met.

'God! Lyn, I was frightened. I thought you might b . . . be . . .' The voice stuttered, petered out. Lyn drew away a little. Was Edward frightened for himself, scared to be left alone to starve or perish, or genuinely worried about his only blood relation's life and safety? He sensed the second, longed to thank his rescuer, return his hug.

Instead, he stood rigid and embarrassed. 'It's OK. I was quite all right, in fact. Just . . . er . . . having a bit of a breather.'

'You were gone an hour, you know. I was imagining the worst.' Edward took his arm and started walking very gingerly, feeling every step.

'Yes . . . Well — everything takes longer in this weather.' Lyn stumbled along beside him. 'I couldn't find the farm, in any case. The snow masks all the landmarks. We ought to get back in the car and stay there.' He assumed Edward knew where the road was, let him act as leader. He himself seemed to have lost his strength as well as his sense of direction. His coat was sopping wet, flapping against his trousers. He was astonished to see the car lights shining like a benediction after only a few yards. So it had been that close, after all! He spurted forward, ran towards the hedge.

'Thank God for my old banger! There's nothing we can do now except sit tight until the snow plough comes and digs us out in the morning.'

'But will it come on Boxing Day?' Edward had caught up with him.

'If we're lucky. It depends how bad the weather gets. It'll come in an emergency, even on Bank Holidays. Thank God we got this far, though. It's only the major roads they bother with.'

'You call this major?' Edward smiled for the first time since they had left the house. They stumbled to the gate together. Lyn could see more clearly now. The side-lights blazed a welcome. The car was sanctuary and shelter — if not warm, at least dry and protected from the wind.

Edward fumbled for the door handle. 'Wouldn't it be better if we both got in the back? We can sit closer then and build up a bit of body heat.'

Lyn hesitated. 'Body heat' sounded somehow far too intimate. And yet it was common sense, survival. Animals huddled together for warmth, curled up side by side.

'OK. Let's just push the car on the verge, though. I'd prefer to turn the lights off and we don't want a collision if other cars can't see us.'

'D'you think there will be other cars?'

Lyn could hear the tiny thread of hope in Edward's voice. He was forced to snap it. 'I doubt it — in this weather and on Christmas night. I suppose there might be the odd Land Rover, but anyone with his head screwed on would stay indoors.'

He and Edward heaved the car across the road and up on the verge, the opposite side from the ditch, then clambered wet and panting into the back, Edward's bulky form swamping all the seat space. Lyn tried to squeeze himself into the corner. His coat was not only drenched, but filthy. He had used it as a ground-sheet during weeks of living rough, wiped oil and grease and blood on it, whereas Edward's cashmere was still reasonably clean and elegant. The whole car was dirty, Edward's feet paddling in torn newspapers and oily cleaning rags. It was Jennifer who kept things clean and tidy. Yet Edward was taking charge now, had switched from passenger to boss. 'My coat's drier than yours. Why not take yours off and use mine as a sort of . . . rug for both of us? Come on — otherwise you'll get a chill.'

Lyn grinned — another Jennifer. The two men struggled out of their coats. Lyn slung his on the seat in front, while Edward draped his damp black cashmere over both their laps. Lyn realised suddenly that both of them were wearing sweaters knitted by Jennifer — one slatey-blue, one brown. Edward had taken up his offer back in the house, slipped on his spare jersey underneath his jacket. It made a bond between them. Lyn relaxed a little. It was very cramped — but cosy. Their breath was steaming up the windows, their bodies overlapping. He was reminded of the ox and ass crowding the Bethlehem stable. If Edward was the patient lumbering ox, then he must be the . . .

'I'm sorry Christmas Day turned out like this,' he said.

'Hardly your fault, Lyn. ' It still sounded strange to hear Edward use his name. He gave the Lyn great dignity, as if Llewelyn himself was trumpeting through the letters in a blaze of glory.

'The snow rarely starts this early. White Christmases are rare, in fact, even this far north. January's the worst month. I remember one year we didn't see a blade of grass from New Year to the end of April — and hardly another living soul. It was rather like being besieged.'

'Yes, this is . . . battle country, so I'm told.'

Lyn nodded. 'More castles than any other county in the British Isles.'

'Even Wales?'

'Even Wales.'

They were silent for a moment. Llewelyn Powys seemed to have slipped between them, and Llewelyn ap Iorwerth. Two heroes. Lyn started to hum, almost under his breath, a battle-anthem he remembered from his youth. The tune was catchy, cheerful.

'Shall we sing?' he suggested, suddenly.

'Sing?' Edward sounded shocked.

'Why not? To keep our spirits up.'

'I'm afraid I don't know many songs.'

'You must know *Mary Malone*, or — how about *Cherry Ripe*?'

'Neither, I'm afraid.'

'*Danny Boy*? *The Ashgrove*?'

'No.'

Lyn pulled at the coat to cover their chests. Edward had been more deprived than he had. Hester had sung him songs, taught him verses, even before he could read.

'How about a hymn, then?' Hester had never gone to church, but she had sung hymns about the house, her voice resounding like an organ, making everything too solemn. 'There is a Green Hill Far Away. Everyone knows that.'

'Meaning "even I must"! Yes, I do, in fact.'

Lyn cleared his throat, hummed up and down the scale to find the note, then let his voice leap forward. He rarely sang these days. It felt freeing, jubilant. The words were hot and soaring in his mouth when everything else was cramped and glacial. Edward's powerful baritone was sounding underneath him now, adding harmony and strength. They were perfectly in tune, except the words were wrong for Christmas. It was a hymn for Passiontide, for Easter. Crucifixion, Resurrection. Lyn could feel their voices melting the snow, sweeping away the shivering weeks till April. It had been two cruel Aprils before that, that he and Jennifer had conceived their child — the child he had refused to recognise and which had died because he willed it to.

He stopped suddenly, in the middle of the second verse. Edward's voice went on a moment, the deep, unwavering baritone echoing through the car.

'Forgotten the words?' he asked, breaking off as well.

Lyn frowned. 'No. We're in the wrong season. We need a Christmas hymn.' He stared at the windows, thickly furred with snow. 'Do you know In the Bleak Mid-winter?'

'No. Though it sounds appropriate.'

'It's beautiful. Christina Rossetti wrote it.' Lyn started to recite the words.

'In the bleak mid-winter
Frosty wind made moan.
Earth stood hard as iron
Water like a stone . . .'

Edward shook his head. 'No — never heard of it. Strange, that. I always went to church at Christmas. And most Sundays. My mother was very religious.'

'Hester's your mother. You mean Alice Fraser.'

'Er . . . yes . . .'

Silence.

'Hester liked that hymn. She used to sing it in the middle of summer. When the corn was high and everything green and golden, she'd be booming "Snow had fallen, snow on snow".' Lyn was singing now.

Edward took up the tune. ' "Snow on snow, snow on snow". It's just right for today, isn't it?' He blew on his hands to warm them up. The car was getting fuggy from their breath, but still perishing cold. As the larger

400

man, he was the more uncomfortable — legs cramped, neck and shoulders huddled.

Lyn nodded, finished the verse full-volume, dislodging the coat as he conducted with his hands. It felt strange to be singing at all. His voice was like his sex — something he kept down, mistrusted now. Yet it was somehow right and pleasing to be singing carols on Christmas Day with a relative. He could feel Edward's body shivering into his own. 'I never forget the next verse. It's my favourite.'

Lyn sang just the last four lines, and almost in a whisper. They were too beautiful to shout.

'But only his mother
In her maiden bliss
Worshipped the Beloved
With a kiss.'

All his favourite words were in those four short lines — mother, maiden, worship, beloved. As a boy, he had seen pictures of the Madonna, young yet ripe, maiden and mother both. He had fused Mary with Susannah, the Christ-child with himself, imagined himself beloved, worshipped with a kiss, Susannah's long hair and soft blue veil bending over him in the hay. Blasphemy. Bliss.

Later, Jennifer had been maiden and beloved. But never mother. He had killed her baby, stolen her maidenhead. He glanced across at Edward, blur and bulk in the gloom. No mother had welcomed or worshipped *him*. Only foster-mother, foreign mother. Banished, not beloved.

He cleared his throat. 'Weren't you ever . . . er . . . curious to come to England before this — see your native land?'

Edward hesitated. 'Yes. Yes, I was. I thought about it many times. I was especially keen to visit Wales. I sent for all the brochures, even looked up hotels and worked out routes and . . . But somehow I never made it. Stupid, isn't it? I think I was a bit . . . well . . . worried that it wouldn't quite match up to my expectations. You know how you can build up a place and see it as a sort of fantasy or . . .'

'Fairy-tale.'

'Yes. A country of the mind.'

'And *were* you disappointed?'

'Well, I haven't been to Wales. I've . . .'

'England, then — in general?'

'I haven't seen much of England, either — apart from today, of course — and yesterday. The journey up was most impressive. The train stopped at York and I saw the cathedral from the window. It seemed specially beautiful on Christmas Eve, with the snow falling on that splendid roof and . . . But apart from that' — Edward shrugged — 'I've been in London all the time.'

Lyn was stamping and circling his feet, to try and warm them up. There was no feeling left in them at all. The car was beginning to smell from their fuggy breath and damp clothes. He felt embarrassed by their closeness to each other, the brute animal inadequacies of their two over-lapping bodies. He envied the angels in the hymn — Cherubim and Seraphim — souls and wings instead of stinks and pricks. As a boy he had asked the ranger to show him a Seraphim — imagined it a bird like a curlew or a golden plover. He edged closer into his corner. 'All right — London, then. What d'you think of our capital?'

Edward said nothing for a moment. Lyn tried to imagine London through his eyes. Cold, dirty, inhospitable. No one to welcome him except solicitors. Expensive and impersonal hotels. Streets jammed with Christmas shoppers. Hold-ups on the tube. Strikes. Power-cuts.

'It's . . . er . . . much bigger than I expected — a little overpowering, to tell the truth. People seem in such a hurry all the time. And it's cold, of course — very cold. Back home, I'd be in shirt-sleeves now, admiring the blooms of the red pohutukawa and sipping mango juice before supper on the terrace.'

'Sounds odd for Christmas,' Lyn observed. Surely Christmas should be cold and harsh. Only then could April triumph, limp in pale and convalescent like a Lazarus.

'Snow and ice seem equally odd to me. I've seen pictures of British Christmases, of course, but they always looked so cosy — roaring fires and choirboys, and the sort of fancy stick-on snow that's just a back-ground for a stage-coach. I wasn't quite prepared for . . . well — the harshness of the country.' Edward peered around him, imagining the wilderness which the igloo of the car shut out. It was bad enough inside. He had cramp in his right leg now, a pain across his shoulders made worse by his damp clothes. He tried to ease his body, but it was impossible to do more than shift a fraction.

Lyn was fidgeting beside him. 'This isn't really typical. Remember, we're very far north up here. You probably don't realise, but there's a good-sized chunk of Scotland further south than we are.'

'Is that so? I'd never have guessed, except for the cold, of course. I'm still completely numb, aren't you? Mind you, I'd liked to have seen Scotland — and the Lake District — toured the whole country, in fact. But it wasn't really possible. I was more or less tied to London by my lawyers. They advised me to stay put, so I'd be available if they needed me or in case of new developments or . . . Not that it did me any good. I seem to have got absolutely nowhere.'

Lyn tensed. So they were back to the lawsuit again — had the rest of the night to go in and out of all its complications. He could hardly run away, wedged thigh to thigh with the plaintiff in the back seat of a very minor Morris, with a snow-storm raging round them. Whilst they were singing, he had felt elation, even warmth, now only cold, trapped and hopeless.

Edward had huddled forward again, hugging himself with his arms. 'I mean, now they tell me Matthew's gone away.'

'Gone away?'

'Surely you knew?'

Lyn shook his head irritably, wondered how long it was till light. 'Matthew's never away at Christmas. In fact, we usually spend it with him. It's quite a thing with him — you know, proper family Christmas — presents round the tree and . . .' He felt a sudden sense of loss. He had always grumbled about Christmases at Putney, yet they were like a sacred ritual and he hated rituals broken. 'Where's he gone, for heaven's sake?'

'I wish I knew. I was simply informed that Matthew's solicitor had lost contact with his client, whatever that's suposed to mean. Apparently, he's not answering his phone at home and no one at the office seems to have any idea where he's got to. I suppose it may be just a holiday, but . . .'

'Why didn't you tell me before?' Lyn jabbed his foot against the seat in front. It sounded wrong, alarming. Matthew never went on holiday without piling his subordinates with memos and instructions, emergency addresses.

'I assumed you knew, of course. In fact, if you'll forgive me, I . . . er . . . thought it was all part of some . . . arrangement between you both, to fob me off or gain more time or . . .'

'Of course not. I haven't laid eyes on Matthew now for weeks.'

'You surprise me.'

'You needn't sound sarcastic. It happens to be true. Matthew and I lost . . . touch for a while. There were . . . problems.'

'More problems? That's a pity. I was hoping you could help me in his absence. My lawyers are still waiting for all those facts and figures. Matthew's handed nothing over at all, yet.'

'Well, it's no good asking me. I know very little about his business affairs.'

'But you work for him. You . . .'

'Not any more, I don't. And even when I did, I was very much a junior.'

'But I understood you were the chief artist on the book and . . .'

'I wouldn't even *use* the word artist. I was a commercial hack churning out designs with the sole purpose of jacking up the sales. That's not my idea of art.' Lyn felt disloyal even while he was saying it. He had a sudden vision of Matthew on Christmas Day, doing his best to be jovial and fatherly. He had even once dressed up as Father Christmas, a rigid and embarrassed Father Christmas who handed out the Ten Commandments with the toys.

'Mind you, I suppose I was lucky to get a job at all. Most of my painter friends landed up starving in their non-existent studios, or permanently

403

on the dole. It's never easy to sell a painting, especially ones like mine. You'd hate my stuff. It's . . .'

'I've . . . er . . . seen it, actually. Or some of it, at least.'

Lyn stared at him. 'You can't have done. I've thrown a hell of a lot away and all the rest is hidden or locked up. I never show my work to anyone. I used to, when I was younger, and people said fatuous things like "the sky isn't purple" or . . .'

'Actually, I liked your use of colour.'

'What are you talking about?'

'Look, I . . . hope you don't think I was . . . prying, but while you were out on that walk this afternoon, it got very dark and cold, and I was searching round for something to re-light the fire. I came across this great roll of . . . papers stuffed away right at the back of a cupboard. At first, I didn't realise what it was and was just about to burn it, but when I unrolled the sheets, I found there were ten or twelve paintings, all covered with dust and cobwebs. I'd no idea they were yours, of course, but then I found a . . . letter tucked inside the roll. It was written to you, from Matthew, years and years ago. I suppose I shouldn't have read it, but I must admit, by then I was rather intrigued. Matthew wrote that he was sending back your work and that . . .'

Lyn jerked forward so quickly, the coat fell on the floor. 'God! I remember now. They're donkey's years old, those paintings. I sent a batch of them to Matthew when I was seventeen or so. He was always interested in my work and . . .' Lyn broke off. Matthew had encouraged his art — the only one who had — acted as his counsellor and priest. Maybe he had trained him in the wrong religion, but at least he had kept his skills and gift alight. He had returned those paintings minus one, begged to keep that for himself. He had had it framed (expensively) and hung it on his study wall, just above his desk. Funny how you could forget the things that mattered. 'Yes, Matthew seemed to . . . er . . . like my stuff. I don't know why.'

'*I* liked it.' Edward was kneading his thighs and shoulders to try and restore the feeling to them. 'I have to admit I'm a duffer when it comes to art, but I felt you'd really caught the feeling of this countryside. I know they're not realistic, or naturalistic, or whatever you painters call it, but I recognised those hills immediately. That's exactly how you see them — sort of springing out at you as you come along that road, and then taking over everything, until they fill the whole horizon.'

Lyn nodded, too surprised to speak. He was stunned that Edward had understood — had seen that wild relentless grandeur of the Cheviots, dwarfing man to pygmy, their purple throats gagging on the clouds, the sky pushed back to give them room enough. He remembered doing those paintings as a gawky lad, still in fear of Hester, fighting cold and squall to get them right. Everything was too huge and overpowering — the wind uprooting trunks like twigs, the bare and rugged ridges unfolding back and back and back. Those hills had shaped his art.

404

Edward sneezed, fumbled for his handkerchief. 'Why don't you go on painting? Make it your career? You've obviously got talent, if you were that good as a lad.'

Lyn gave a bitter laugh. 'You need money to paint — almost a private income. It's more or less a luxury to turn out what you want instead of what the market wants or the gallery owners decide is chic or fashionable.' What did Edward know about truth or compromise, integrity or sell-out? Even Matthew had linked art to livelihood, put blinkers on his brush. 'No patron's going to back you if you don't make a profit for them somewhere along the line. The art world's every bit as commercial as Matthew's publishing world.'

There was silence, suddenly. Lyn reached across for his own coat, damp and soggy still, laid it over his feet. Every subject seemed to have reached deadlock — his art cut off in its youth, the lawyers thwarted, Matthew vanished. He was worried about Matthew. Where had he gone and why? He should never have lost touch with him — lost touch with everyone. Wives or brothers could die and he wouldn't know.

He slumped back in his corner. Hours and hours to go yet, and a thousand questions unsettled, even unbroached. The snow was still whirling around them, Edward's watch ticking too slowly on to morning. 'Talent' Matthew had written in his letters 'Undeniable gift'. He had bundled those praises away, let them get as dusty as the drawings.

Edward shifted on the seat, cleared his throat. 'Look Lyn, there's . . . er . . . something I want to ask you.'

'What?' Lyn refused to even look up. If Edward wanted figures, contracts, documents, he wouldn't and couldn't supply them. Wouldn't betray Matthew.

'I'm in a bit of a . . . dilemma. I've been left a house in England — *your* house, Hester's house — and yet I can't stay on here and look after it. It's just not practical. It was only a spur-of-the-moment decision to come to this country at all, and I only intended to stay for two or three weeks at the most. I realise nothing's settled as yet, but my lawyers will have to carry on alone now, consult me at a distance. Otherwise I'll be here till *next* Christmas, the way things are dragging on. I'm glad I've met you, Lyn — very glad — but I've got to get back home soon, and I use that word deliberately. England can't be home for me. Not now. It's too . . . late. I'd be like a fish out of water here. All my friends are back in Warkworth. I belong there — despite the gossip. I thought I could run away from it, but it's followed me even here. Maybe *worse* over here, because it's public in the newspapers instead of private in people's sitting-rooms, and I haven't got my friends to counter it. I've decided to return as soon as . . .'

Lyn cut in, almost rudely. 'So you're trying to tell me you've got to sell Hernhope, are you? I've told you, that house isn't just a pile of stones, or another piddling property like . . . It's Hester's heritage, her gift to you.

405

She left you everything she had, and now you turn round and . . .'

'But I've got a home — already — which is just as much a heritage as Hernhope. My foster-parents bequeathed it to me, to cherish, and it was their parents' home before that. I've lived there all my life, Lyn — which means almost twice as long as you've lived here.'

Lyn said nothing. So Edward was turning tail again, had decided that the malicious buzz and mud-slinging in Warkworth were less threatening than what he had run away to. England had disappointed him — that was obvious from his earlier remarks. The enchanted garden of the fairy-tale had turned into a cold unfriendly metropolis, full of vulgar pouncing journalists, and even Hester's Magic Castle had proved only a grim fortress in a wasteland. *Many* people shied away from Hernhope, feared its harshness, its seclusion. He had warmed to Jennifer because she had fallen instantly in love with it. He heard her voice again, saw her sitting motionless and marvelling, her hand reaching across for his.

He sat on the hand, frowned into the darkness. 'Anyway, it won't be an easy house to sell. Not many people fancy living somewhere so remote. There was another house for sale on that same stretch of hill, about ten years ago. Not a single person came to view it. It's a ruin now, full of nettles and sheep shit.'

Edward rubbed his chin. 'Yes, that's . . . er . . . all part of the problem. Actually, I heard rumours back in New Zealand that Hernhope was abandoned and already becoming derelict, and I must admit it made me very angry. That's one of the reasons I decided to come over. But now I've seen the place, I understand the difficulties. The whole area's so inaccessible and . . .'

'Well, you'd better talk it over with your lawyers. That's what they're there for, aren't they?' Lyn turned away. He refused to play solicitor himself, spend Christmas night chewing over Edward's problems as householder and heir.

'Of course, there is *one* solution.' Edward was almost talking to himself.

'What?'

'Well, I . . . What I'm trying to say is . . . I could get someone to look after the house for me — pay them, of course, for keeping it in good shape and administering it on my behalf — seeing to repairs and so on. Then maybe I could visit here sometimes — make it my base for just a month or two in your summer, when the weather's milder and travelling much easier — a sort of holiday home or . . . The fares would be steep, so I couldn't come too often, but, after all, I've worked hard all my life and had very little time for holidays, so far, and my parents left me money, so . . . The only problem is . . . I'd need someone who knows the area and wouldn't mind the loneliness. What I'm trying to say is, if . . . if *you*, Lyn . . . No — you'd probably be offended, but . . .'

Lyn stared at him. 'You mean . . . ?'

406

'Well, after all, it *is* your house — not legally, but in every other way. You've lived there most of your life and your father's family before you. All your memories are there, your past. Quite honestly, I'd feel a bit of a . . . brute turning you out, in any case. I may have been pressing for my rights, but not at the cost of depriving you of a roof over your head. So why not stay and sort of . . . hold the place on my behalf? It would solve several problems at once. After all, you're going to need a home and . . .'

Lyn could hardly find his voice. 'You mean, you . . . you'd *pay* me, just for . . . living there and . . . ?'

'Well, I'll have to pay someone, so why not the man who's lived there thirty years and knows the problems?'

Problems. Lyn tensed. The old boyhood fears were flooding back again — fears of ties, responsibilities — *new* fears now of being beholden to someone else. Expectations. Obligations.

Edward was speaking more confidently now, as if he were warming to his own idea. '*I*'d keep control, of course. I'd like certain improvements put in hand — decent heating and lighting, for example. I'd pay you a proper annual salary to supervise all that, act as my . . . deputy, agent, manager — call it what you like. We can keep in touch by post and . . .'

Lyn swung abruptly round to face the window. Executor again — that's all it would add up to — running Edward's errands, doing his repairs, while the master sipped mango-juice among the pohutukawas. Deputy, agent, manager, might just as well read servant, stooge and dogsbody. He butted his head against the icy snow-bound window.

'You'd be able to paint, then, Lyn. I'd like to think of you taking up your art again. You should have quite a bit of time free. I wouldn't expect you to do all the repairs yourself, of course. You'd need work-men for the tough jobs. Artists mustn't waste their skills. So long as you were on the spot to see they didn't skimp the work, and took over-all responsibility and . . .'

Lyn winced. That word again. Yet wasn't it money for nothing — jam on his bread, when he had despaired of even the driest smallest crust? Edward was paying him to *paint*, for heaven's sake — the thing he wanted most to do in his life. He would have time and cash enough to struggle with line and form, colour and texture, rather than with bills and boilers, stony ground. He would be salaried, secure — paid simply to keep a house alive. The cost of it, the burden, would now be on Edward's back. A hundred different fears and frets were exploding in his mind. Was he angry, grateful, elated? He hardly knew, could hardly take it in. Hernhope was his again, yet not his. He could live there as Edward's lackey and on his terms. His pride kicked against the contract. Yet some strange shivery dart of sheer relief seemed to be swooping through his body.

He lifted his head from the window, traced a pattern on it. Was it crazy to rejoice? The thing was too damned pat. There was bound to be a catch in it. How did he know he still had skills at all? The paintings Edward had praised had been done twenty years ago. And artist up here meant pansy — he mustn't forget that. He would never be accepted by that hale and simple community of farmers. They might despise him more now that he was under orders to a foreigner. Might despise himself.

Yet wasn't he helping Edward, shoring up his pride, allowing him to run away from cold and fear and loneliness by using fancy terms like deputy? And what about his batch of work this summer — that was *recent* stuff, and good — some of the best he'd ever done, in fact.

He turned back to Edward, fumbled for an adequate reply, 'Look, I . . . I don't know what to say. It's all a bit of a . . . shock. I simply wasn't . . . I mean, Hester mightn't have wanted you to leave, or me to . . . After all, she deliberately left the house to you and . . .' He stopped. Had Hester perhaps arranged this whole affair? Was it simply a continuation of her power and presence in the house, the cellar? She had delayed him there with the buttons, trapped him in her territory until the snow was too treacherous to let him make his getaway. Even now, they were only a few short miles from Hernhope. The house was dragging him back, as it had done as a boy, a youth. Only now, the terms had changed. He was no longer a householder with a sullen demanding property, but an artist with a patron.

Edward was leaning forward, legs apart, hands sawing the air in his enthusiasm. He seemed warmer, more alive. 'I'd like you to make it a real family home — like it used to be in the book. Take your wife there. She likes the house, does she?'

'Mm.' Lyn was grudging. How could Edward refer to his wife as casually as that, as if there were no miles or barriers between them? Edward had enquired about his marriage on the first lap of the journey and he had tried to fob him off by telling him his wife was down in London, nursing a sick friend. What he hadn't said was that the separation was permanent, the friend dangerous and entrenched. Jennifer would never sponge on Edward, anyway. She was tied to Susie and a baby, preferred playing at mothers and fathers to her real and barren marriage. Three months ago, she would have been overjoyed to have Hernhope as her home again. Now, he feared, she had turned her back on it. The offer had come too late.

Edward was squashing his leg, turning towards him in his enthusiasm. 'That's good. If you have children, they can carry on the place. You mustn't think I don't understand the importance of that house, Lyn — its history and tradition. I hated what you said about it falling into ruin, when it's my . . . er . . . mother's house and . . . If that ever were to happen, then part of her would be destroyed, *and* you and . . .'

Lyn closed his eyes and saw Jennifer coming under him — humping, gasping on the cellar floor. 'My wife was . . .' He swallowed, couldn't get the word out — 'Pr . . . pregnant a year or so ago. She . . . lost the child.' It *had* been a child — part of him, a brief unfinished sketch in his portfolio, which he had never claimed before.

'I'm sorry to hear that, Lyn.'

'She . . . wants to try again. I've always been opposed, but now I . . .' Lies, all lies. He was still opposed. And yet, if Jennifer agreed . . . if his wife came back, he would allow her almost anything. Allow himself.

He felt himself stiffen, even in the cold. A ram again, mounting her, twenty times a night. All the ewes round him were in lamb. The tups had done their stuff and every flock would be doubled in the spring. New life, new start. He longed to be a part of it, to career down to Southwark for his mate, scoop her back up here, instal her triumphant in his house. It needn't be too late. She could *still* be overjoyed. Hadn't she told him so often they belonged here, used high-flown words like 'mission'? She was right. Twice he had tried to cut himself off from Hernhope, and twice he had been drawn back to it. It *might* just work, with a wife to help and soothe. It wouldn't be easy, rosy. It was often a struggle to paint at all — to trap truth in two dimensions, cage grandeur in a frame. The problems would still be there — the cold, the desolation. The house was old, difficult to run. There would still be gossip, Philistines, hostile tongues around him. Yet Jennifer could woo them and disarm them, tame the house and land as she had done before.

Edward was restless again, trying to smooth his damp and crumpled trousers. 'Mind you, I don't expect my solicitors will be exactly over-joyed. They're bound to bring up all manner of objections about tenants and probate and . . . Look, perhaps you'd better join me for that lunch tomorrow — if we ever get to Newcastle, that is. You could meet my legal friend, then, and we could draw up a formal contract with no loopholes or loose ends, decide on your salary, work out the priorities.'

Lyn frowned. Edward sounded worse than Matthew. *Two* elder brothers, both making him conform and knuckle under.

'After all, it is a very tricky situation in an already complex case. Though, in fact, I'd prefer to keep the issue of the house quite separate from the book. It's a different matter entirely and what I intend to do on that front is contact Hartley Davies and see if they . . .'

'Edward . . . ?' Lyn cut in, leaned forward. It was the first time he had used Ainsley's Christian name. It sounded strange and almost dangerous on his lips. His shoulders were tensed, hands clutching at each other.

'Well?'

Lyn hesitated, swallowed, then spoke almost in a mumble. 'You wouldn't . . . drop the case, would you?'

Edward drew himself up so swiftly, his head grazed the top of the car. 'You're really going too far, Lyn. I've offered you the house and a salary, but to expect me now to . . .'

Lyn winced. Edward was right — and yet . . . 'I'm not asking for myself, Edward. Let's face it, whatever the legal technicalities, I've hardly received a penny from that book, so no one can come to *me* to ask for cash. It's . . . Matthew.' He broke off. He had felt worried and uneasy over Matthew ever since Edward had mentioned his disappearance. What did it mean, the solicitor had lost contact with his client? Where had Matthew gone? He saw the solemn and bewhiskered Father Christmas handing him a fat expensive volume on Turner's Sketchbooks, reproduced facsimile. There had been precious books before that, posted up to Mepperton. Hester had bridled — waste of money, waste of time. No — those books had helped to train him in his art, had also been a kind of caring, an investment in him, almost.

He grabbed Edward's arm. 'I'm not defending Matthew. God alone knows what he's up to. It's just that . . .' He couldn't find the words, could only see the family harassed and in hiding. What would Anne be doing, silent stoic Anne, fretting in some bolt-hole? And Jennifer's favourite, Charles, who was so painfully shy and conforming, hated change and upheaval?

'Look here.' Edward's voice was shrill. 'Matthew asked for trouble. He simply ignored the fact that I might still exist and have rights and claims of my own. He didn't even show his lawyer that record of my birth. That's irresponsible, if not downright devious.'

'Yes, but your claims are accepted now. Hester acknowledged you as her first and elder son, treated you as her only son, in fact. She left nothing to me at all, and Matthew she didn't even mention, despite the fact she nannied him all those years. *He*'s the one who doesn't exist in her eyes.' Strange to be pleading for Matthew, yet he was still in his debt from years ago — in debt for wife, house, job, as well as art books and critiques. No girl like Jennifer would have looked at him without Matthew as security and marriage-broker. Now he wanted to repay the debt, so his wife would be his, on his own terms, with no one standing over or between them. He yearned to marry her again, free from Matthew, far from London; grab her young and virginal, with Hester rejoicing now, not disapproving. He turned to Edward, still glowering next to him.

'I . . . I know it's a cheek to expect you to . . . withdraw when you're owed a lot of cash and . . . but you don't *need* that money, do you? You admitted that yourself. The Frasers left you everything — not just their house, but . . .'

'That's not the point. It's the principle I'm concerned with.'

'But you've won your case on principle. The whole world's on your side. I've not read a single account which doesn't see you as the injured party.'

'That's the trouble. The whole damned world knows I'm a . . . bastard now.' Edward had never used the word before, spat it out as if it were poison in his mouth.

'OK, but they'll forget it — if only you'd allow them to. Just lie low for a while and they'll turn on some other poor devil and harass him. The worst thing you can do is to keep hollering for your rights. That keeps the thing alive, keeps your name big news. You're playing into their hands — *and* the lawyers'. It must be costing you a bomb, this case, and you admit yourself you've got nowhere yet at all.'

'Matthew will have to pay my costs. That'll all be part of the settlement.'

'What settlement? You're still a hundred years away from it. Why waste all your energy on pointless legal wrangling and make the lawyers rich? OK — so Matthew's wronged you. He's wronged me too, but . . .'

'It's completely different for you, Lyn. I've had my reputation damaged. That's a very serious matter. And I've lost an important council election.'

'Only by a handful of votes — that's what I read in the *Mail*. Anyway, one lost election isn't the end of the world. There'll be another chance, won't there? Why not go back and fight it? Stand up to those scandal-mongers and show them you don't care about the gossip. You said you had friends. Well, true friends don't disown you. Bastardy's not a crime, in any case.' Lyn flushed. How could he be urging Edward to sally forth like some Knight of the Holy Grail, when he himself was a skulker and a coward who ran away from everything? Or was he actually trying to rouse himself, invoking guts and daring because he needed them in his own fight?

Edward hadn't answered. He seemed to be grappling with a score of different emotions. He muttered something, broke off, chewed his lip, heaved back in his seat.

'I lost by exactly seven votes,' he muttered, at last.

'Well, there you are. It was obviously a very close-run thing — not the whole town turning against you.' Edward didn't appear to have heard. He was still slumped back in his seat, withdrawn into himself.

'Edward . . .' Lyn decided to strike, before he lost his chance. 'So what d'you think? Will you let Matthew off, or at least settle privately without . . . ?'

Edward looked up. He no longer sounded petulant. 'I . . . don't know,' he said, slowly, 'It's a . . . very big question and I can't possibly answer it here and now. It depends on a lot of different factors — one of them being your answer to my own question. Will you stay on at Hernhope?'

Lyn drew in his breath. The silence was so deep, the sound seemed to shudder through it. Even the wind had dropped, and was no longer nagging and blustering round the car. Or maybe they could simply no longer hear it. The snow had built up so thickly on the windows, that they were insulated, shuttered. Lyn felt suddenly infinitely weary. He laid his head on the seat in front, tried to think coherently. Was Edward's offer just a trap? Had he thought it out enough, all its implications? He could still refuse, opt to be a no one and a nomad, instead of replacing dependence on one half-brother with dependence on the other.

He glanced across at Edward — blur and shadow still — reproduced his features in his mind. The balding pate, the lined and weathered face, the muscles turned to blubber, the age-spots on his hands. An old man and a bastard, sent away by Hester, disowned as her child. Edward wasn't any threat. Dependence on him was different, hardly counted. Ainsley would soon be thirteen thousand miles away, not breathing down his neck, listening to every murmur through a bedroom wall. He would be free of both his half-brothers, left as only son.

He realised now it was Matthew who was alien, Edward who was foreigner. Both of them lived in towns, spent their days in offices, saw life in terms of cash and contracts; both of them turned their backs on the wild unbridled country of their ancestors. He feared it, but stayed on. He might not have farmed the land or planted forests, but he had captured it on paper and on canvas. You had to draw and paint in order to understand — sense the bones beneath the soil, the spine and sinews holding hills together. His art was born and rooted here, had always shrivelled in London, turned soft and superficial when he caged it up in studios. He would no longer have to grovel to Matthew for his livelihood, sell his talents to a commercial company who wanted only the flashy and the slick. He could show hills devouring hills, God's thumb pressing down on forests, bruising skies. And in the night he could wrap his wife around him, hold her so tight, she could never stray again.

Suddenly, he fumbled for the door-handle, heaved at the door which seemed to have stuck.

Edward grabbed his arm. 'Where are you going?'

'Only for a pee. I'm bursting.'

'Well, don't go too far, this time, for God's sake.'

'Don't worry.' Lyn slammed the door behind him, scrambled up the bank. The snow was no longer falling, but lay deep and white and treacherous, sucking down his shoes. It was easier to see, now. The moon looked pale and peaky, but trailed a grudging light which the snow itself reflected back at it. He turned his back, relieved himself — piss steaming on the snow — then struggled further up the hill, gazing out at the waste of white around him. The whole earth was hard and frozen, the stars too cold to shine, the sky as numb and leaden as the ground. Yet underneath that snow was grass and green, and beyond it whimpered April — milk in the ewes, bread in the furrow, himself in Jennifer. He longed to say 'I will' again, worship her with his body, endow her with all his worldly goods, even if they were Edward's. They had married in the springtime — conventional enough, perhaps — but spring meant more up here. Resurrection after death, light after blindness, hope with soft feet and warm fingers treading down winter and despair.

He trudged a few steps higher, looked towards the South — North-umberland stretching down to Durham, butting into Yorkshire — softer country then, rolling gently into Nottinghamshire, Leicestershire, North-amptonshire (boots and shoes and churches, Robin Hood;) further down to Bedfordshire (wheat and milk and water-meadows); down again to Hertfordshire (motorways, new towns), and on, at last, to London (Jennifer). He longed for ten-league boots to cover nine counties in as many minutes, grab his wife just by stretching out his hand. Even without the snow, he couldn't reach her. She had no phone at Southwark. There was no collection of letters for three whole days and the post offices were closed so he couldn't send a telemessage. He tried to send his own. *'Hernhope is ours. Come back.'*

'Come back!' he shouted suddenly, willing her to hear. Would Hester carry his words for him, waft them down to London? There was a faint shout in reply, coming from behind him. He whipped round. Only Edward floundering in the snow beside the car, flapping his arms and fussing, trying to lure him down.

He squatted on the ground, trailed his hands in the snow, let the cold cauterise his pain. Of course she couldn't hear, wouldn't come. His earlier hopes had been empty dreams, pretty-coloured fantasies. Yet he must still return to Hernhope, manage there without her. It was Hester's wish. His mother had decreed that both her sons should share the house, save it from ruin, bind the three of them together though her heritage.

Slowly, he stood up, clambered to the highest point of the rise, stood between earth and sky. The snow was not just cold and dangerous — choking roads, crippling cars — it was also dangerously beautiful, from every smallest cyrstal and white-gloved twig to this infinite hurl and blaze of black on white, white on black. The world seemed motionless, yet a million million planets were hurtling round their panting suns, new stars scorching into light and life, even the midget earth spinning and astounded in endless space. Somehow, he had to wrench it on to paper, echo it in paint, infuse dead and doltish brush-strokes with this same eternal energy. He might never achieve it — spend a whole lifetime perfecting one small creeping shrub on one small patch of ground, as he had struggled as a boy trying to draw the exact configuration of a pine-cone or the pattern on a leaf on his scrappy bits of paper, but he must still wear out his life in trying, live at Hernhope where the sky was closer to his grasp.

Edward was calling again, louder and more fretfully. Lyn swung round to face him, then started running down the hill towards the car, slipping on icy patches, stumbling over stones.

'Be careful!' Edward shouted.

Lyn grinned to himself, ran faster, slid the last few yards on his bottom down the slope.

Edward fussed towards him. 'You went out without your coat,' he said, passing him his soggy duffel.

Lyn slung it over his shoulders. He was panting, out-of-breath. 'I haven't answered your question, Edward. You asked me if I'd stay at Hernhope.'

'I'm sorry.' Edward looked embarrassed. 'I obviously upset you. I didn't realise . . .' He opened the car door. He had his own coat back on and buttoned up. They were still hours away from daylight, but it was as if he were preparing to part from Lyn already, go his separate way.

'It's all right.' Lyn took one last look at the dark and blinding world, then clambered back in the car, settled down to wait for light and morning.

'The answer's yes,' he said. 'I will.'

XXIX

'Flight number IB 341 to Malaga is now boarding at gate seven. Passengers to Malaga are requested to . . .'

Jennifer blocked her ears against the crackle of the announcement, already repeated twice. Susie and Sparrow were at the very end of the queue, a long impatient queue which had snarled up at the front and was creeping at snail's pace towards boarding-card control, and from there into the departure lounge. She was astonished they had made it in time. One of Sparrow's mates had taken them in his van, driven like a madman, risking amber lights, ignoring pedestrian crossings, and yelling abuse at anyone who dared to hoot him. She still felt sick from nerves and petrol fumes. Susie looked expressionless and haggard. She was still losing blood, hobbling from her stitches. Crazy to leave for Spain on an almost-honeymoon, just six days after a difficult confinement. Sitting down was agony, sex impossible. Other women would be in bed, resting and recuperating. Susie *had* been in bed, still in the postnatal ward, until six o'clock that morning. She had assured the social worker that she was going home to rest.

'I'll rest on the plane,' she promised Jennifer, later, as they slung clothes into suitcases and hurtled from Southwark to Putney and on again to Heathrow in sixty-seven minutes.

Sparrow had cut the farewells short, used his few spare seconds to snatch a double gin. Jennifer felt cheated. There were so many things she hadn't said, hadn't found the words for. Yet she refused to wait in the queue with them. She knew Sparrow didn't want her there, and anyway, it would only prolong the pain of parting — straining to make light bright futile conversation while they shuffled towards a barrier where she must turn back and they go on. She passed a row of kiosks, staring sightlessly at books and magazines, stopped a moment, slumped against the wall. She had hardly slept the last six nights, felt strangely disorientated. The airport seemed oppressive, claustrophobic, with its garish colours, glaring lights and everyone in transit. Her head was reeling from the crush of people round her, the endless tramp of feet, the air of tension, flurry, rush, which seemed to permeate the place.

She could leave now, if she wanted, return to the bracing cold outside, the welcome grey and quiet. In just a few minutes, Susie and Sparrow would have worked their way to the head of the queue, be past that barrier and through to the departure lounge. That was another country, the no-man's-land between them as impassable as a mountain range or ocean. She felt a sudden stab of panic. She might never see Susie again. She swung round, tried to peer back at the queue, but her view was blocked by a gaggle of shrill excited schoolgirls, jostling round their teacher, swapping jokes and sweets. She fought her way through them, broke into a run. She needed one last look at Susie, to imprint it on her mind. The queue was moving faster now, but she could still see Susie's back, Sparrow's brawny arm flung across it as if staking his claim to her. She was wearing a candy-floss fun-fur in shocking pink, a belated Christmas present which he claimed to have picked up for a song. Both of them were smoking, the smoke from their two Marlboroughs mingling in a single spiral.

'Susie!' she shouted, suddenly. She had said goodbye already, *bon voyage*, good luck — all the empty clichés she could cram into sixty seconds and which couldn't express an nth part of the hurt and hope and confusion screaming through her head. How could you find words for love which was forbidden, friendship which was over, pity mixed with jealously, simple aching loss?

Susie turned, took a step towards her. Huge tinted sunglasses hid the purple smudges beneath her eyes. She looked smaller, frailer, overshadowed by Sparrow's hefty physique and weighed down with all her packages. Sparrow had grabbed her by the wrist and she was pulling against his hand like a fractious child, dropping things and swearing, her long untidy hair caught half inside her collar, half streaming down her back. It had lost its bounce and shine, hung limp and thinner now, her face pale against the electric pink of her coat. She was caught between the two of them, handcuffed by Sparrow, yet turning back to gaze at Jennifer, mouthing dumb and frantic goodbyes.

Jennifer stood silent and unmoving. There was nothing more to say, no magic words or reprieves. The few yards of floor between them seemed to be extending like elastic, stretching out and out — further, further,

further — until they were two dwindling pin-head figures on either side of an infinite divide.

Suddenly Susie tugged her wrist free, piled Sparrow with her bags, dumped teddy-bear and chocolates on the floor and darted out of the queue. The elastic floor snapped back with a rush and flurry of feet, a fling of embracing arms, and there wasn't any divide, only fur soft beneath her fingers, hair tickling against her neck, Lily-of-the-Valley drowning out her fainter quieter cologne.

Jennifer couldn't speak, just pressed her face against the coat, stroking it as if it were a precious animal. The noise of the airport was only a faint murmur now, somewhere beyond her and outside her. Her world was bounded by Susie's body, arms clamped so tight around her back, she could hardly breathe.

Susie pulled away at last, wiped her face with her sleeve. 'Oh, J . . . Jennifer . . .' The full name sounded solemn now, not peeved or impatient as it often had. Tears were sliding beneath the plastic sunglasses, running into her mouth. Susie had been in tears several times a day since her confinement, weeping silently into cold porridge or damp fish-cakes, or locking herself in the bathroom and sobbing there until some nurse hammered on the door and forced her out.

She removed the glasses, rubbed fiercely at her eyes. Her make-up had streaked off and she looked a child again, eyes red and puffy with crying, face bare of any art.

'Look, Jen, I just . . . wanted to say . . .' She paused, sniffed, cleared her throat, twisted a strand of hair round and round between her fingers. 'Well, you know . . . thanks — and everything.'

Sparrow had come striding back. 'Buck up, girl. What's the matter with you? We've lost our place in the queue and we'll miss the bloody plane next.' He pushed Susie in front of him, kept her pinioned as they inched towards the desk. She didn't turn round again. Jennifer was waving to her deaf and sightless back, mouthing goodbyes to empty air. Only a few more yards and they would be swallowed up beyond the barrier. She craned forward. The last thing she saw was the gold of Susie's hair trapped beneath Sparrow's arm.

She turned on her heel, stood paralysed a moment. The airport boomed and bustled past her, announcements of other people's departures and arrivals, other people's lives. A troupe of teenagers armed with party streamers and cans of Carlsberg were jostling and ragging each other, already high, although New Year's Eve was only a few hours old. It was still morning — just — five minutes to noon on December 31st, end of a year which had lasted a century, end of a night which had snailed and dragged to dawn. She dodged an Italian bambino escaping from his parents, watched a mob of pilgrims mob their priest. Everyone else seemed to be in groups or families, only she alone. She would have to get used to that.

416

She walked on — past gift-shops, kiosks, information desks — signs and colours clashing in her head, the remorseless loudspeakers cutting conversations into shreds. People were streaming towards the departure lounge, leaving for New Year holidays across the whole of Europe — exotic names flashing on and off the screens. She herself was going to Putney East. She grinned. Better move on. Jo would be wondering where she was.

The journey took well over an hour, by the time she had changed lines and hung about in the fuggy, smelly underground thick with crowds and cigarette smoke, waiting for her train. New Year's Eve was again in evidence, some passengers already drunk and rowdy, young girls in party gear, officer workers flushed. She emerged at East Putney tube station to a cold, dull, sleety afternoon, sharp contrast to the glaring lights and stuffy air below. A smashed champagne bottle lay weeping in the gutter, three men lurched arm-in-arm, singing Auld Lang Syne to the lamp-posts. Jennifer crossed to the other side and walked briskly up the shabby street which led into Jo's cul-de-sac. She had been there only once before, for a consciousness-raising session of the Women's Group. The house was cramped and gardenless — the opposite end of Putney from Anne and Matthew's leafy Victorian grandeur. Jo's work for the Weaker Sex was blazoned across the windows — posters for women's aid, women's rights, women's refuges, even women priests.

Jo came to the door in an Indian peasant dress with a British Home Stores chunky-knit buttoned over it and stained and dingy gym shoes underneath.

'Come in, love. I wasn't expecting you for another hour, at least. Those planes are always late.'

'Theirs wasn't.' Jennifer stepped into the hall which had a battered photocopier as its only furniture, but was littered with brochures and leaflets, strewn in untidy heaps and flurries across the floor. 'In fact, I'm amazed we ever made it. That friend of Sparrow's drives like a maniac. I was terrified we'd all land up back in hospital rather than Heathrow.'

Jo took Jennifer's coat, ushered her into the kitchen. 'How *was* Sparrow?'

Jennifer shrugged. 'OK.' She could see him on the plane, chatting up the air-hostesses, dulling Susie with gins, pawing her . . .

'I doubt if it'll last.' Jo reached across for the biscuit tin. 'Poor Susie. I tried to show her sense, but she wouldn't listen. Ah well — I suppose that's what she wanted, and if she sees a bit of Europe in the process, at least it'll help her education. You must be ready for some lunch, love — if you can call digestive biscuits and peanut butter lunch. I never cook midday.'

'I'm . . . er . . . not very hungry, thanks. Anyway, I ought to see if . . . I mean, is everything all right, Jo?'

'You mean, is *he* all right. Yes, fine. Don't look so worried. I may be anti-men, but babes-in-arms don't count. Actually, I've hardly heard a squeak from the little blighter. Did you sedate him or something before you brought him here?'

'No. Just told him to mind his manners or you'd report him to the Sex Discrimination Board.'

Jo laughed. 'Cup of tea — if you can't face peanut butter?'

'Yes, please. I'm parched. The last one I had was at five o'clock this morning. D'you mind if I take it up there?'

'Course not. You go on and I'll bring it up when it's brewed. I can see you're avid for another peek at your little bundle of joy, or do you just want to make certain he's still breathing? It's OK, I haven't castrated him or anything. Actually, I'm surprised you ever trusted me with him at all.'

Jennifer said nothing. She couldn't admit to Jo that she'd had no alternative. There was no one else to leave a week-old baby with. She had to see Susie off. That was vital. Their last contact — perhaps for ever. And she had to see her off without the child. Susie couldn't relate to her baby, preferred to ignore him altogether, pretend he didn't exist.

She walked slowly up the steep and narrow staircase, paused on the landing, leaned against the bannisters. She still found it hard to believe the baby *did* exist, was real, breathing, perfect, there at all. She opened the spare-room door, felt the now familiar stab of excitement, wonder, awe, as she walked towards the cot.

She would never forget her first miraculous glimpse of him. She had stumbled towards the nursery behind a sturdy Irish nurse who had been rattling on about the weather. There wasn't any weather, just the stifling heat of the nursery and the thunder of her heart which was thumping so wildly she feared it would wake every baby there.

She bent forward, held her breath. All she could see was a fuzz of sparse black hair with a small cross sallow face beneath it. A Winterton baby — dark, male, bad-tempered, anxious-looking, screwing his eyes up against the light. She swallowed, bit her lip. Love hurt.

She had stood there, frozen, for a terrifying second. Once she touched this child, held him in her arms, she would be bonded to him indissolubly, tied to him for twenty years or more, through troubles, sickness, joy.

The nurse was squatting down, fixing a broken shoe-lace. 'Go on — pick him up. He won't fall apart. He's tougher than he looks, that one. In fact, we were all surprised he turned out such a whopper.'

Jennifer opened her eyes. The sterile white-walled nursery was now papered with orange poppies, peeling off in places, the tidy row of cots replaced by Jo's overflow of furniture — a third-hand carry-cot perched on a battered card-table and guarded by a tallboy. Only the baby was the same — dark, solemn, frowning — Matthew's child, with nothing of Susie's pink and golden prettiness nor happy-go-lucky nature. Jennifer scooped him up, held him awkwardly. Susie was right. It wasn't easy to be an instant mother. Her arms felt clumsy, her breasts

418

inadequate. He was nuzzling blindly against them, making little sucking motions with his mouth. She turned him over, frightened for his head. It seemed so vulnerable, not quite fixed or steady on its hinge. She crooked it against her arm, tried to make him more secure. He fixed his eyes directly on her own — strange eyes, huge and slatey-blue — Lyn's and Hester's eyes. Impossible. There was nothing of Hester in this child. All dark-haired babies' eyes were probably that peculiar shade of blue before they changed to brown.

The baby crumpled up his face, put tiny flailing fists up to his eyes as if he couldn't bear to face the world. His mouth trembled on the brink of tears or screams.

'Don't cry,' she whispered. 'You're all right now. We made it.'

*　　*　　*

They very nearly hadn't. From the moment she had slunk between Susie's blue-sprigged curtains and found her pale and weeping, without a cot, she had assumed the worst had happened. The child was dead, had perhaps been born a monster. Susie had seen some slimy stunted thing emerge between her legs and plop into a slop-bowl. There weren't words for horrors like that, so she sat in silence, smoothing Susie's hair, holding both her hands, keeping back her own tears. Gradually Susie quietened.

'D'you want to try and . . . tell me about it', she had stuttered out at last.

Susie shook her head. Ten minutes passed without a word. The noises beyond the curtains seemed to come from another world — other people's babies crying, other women's husbands braying with laughter or talking about strange forgotten things like Christmas food and presents, relatives, the Queen's speech.

Susie sat up slowly, rubbed her eyes. 'It was a b . . . boy,' she whispered. Her voice was so low, Jennifer could barely make the words out. She nodded, didn't trust herself to speak. Susie had said 'was', not 'is'.

Suddenly Susie began to pour out the saga of pain, shock and indignity which had been labelled Christmas Day. Christmas for her had been a collage of shrapnel-sharp contractions, glaring lights, loud confusing voices. Her body had become a broken-down machine, out of her control, man-handled by rough mechanics, wrenched, prodded, forced. Her voice became gradually shriller as she described the great bruiser of a midwife shouting 'Push, mother, *push*,' while she heaved and panted, her feet stuck up in stirrups, tears and sweat streaming down her face.

'And there was this great sort of squelching sound, a terrible wrenching pain and they pulled the baby out and everyone said, "It's a boy . . . it's a lovely little boy" and I could hear it yelling and . . .'

'Y . . . yelling?'

'Yeah. They put it on my tummy all squirming and covered with sort of gunge stuff, and still bawling its head off as if it h . . . hated me already,

419

and I said "Take it away, take it away" and . . .'

'You mean . . . it w . . . was all right — *alive* and . . . ?' Jennifer was saying 'it', like Susie, not daring a 'he' until she was sure beyond all doubt.

'Course it's bloody alive. It wouldn't stop screaming.'

'Why? Was something wr . . . wrong with it?'

'No. Just a damned good pair of lungs — or so the midwife said and . . .'

Jennifer gripped the end of the bed, forced herself to listen to the next instalment — the vomiting, the stitching up, the catheter, the shakes — but all she was really hearing was 'It's a boy — a lovely little boy.' The baby wasn't dead, wasn't a monster or a cretin, offal in a bowl. He was yelling, bawling, triumphantly alive.

Susie stammered on. Every time she mentioned the baby, Jennifer pounced on the tiny jigsaw scrap of information, pieced all the scraps together until she had a whole and healthy child. Her relief and wonder doubled. The baby was not only alive, but normal, perfect, huge — well, five pounds three and three-quarter ounces, which was gigantic compared with those dregs of almost-life in the Special Baby Unit. He appeared completely unaffected by the antibodies, neither jaundiced nor at risk, so they had spared him intensive care. He hadn't needed so much as an incubator, let alone a life-support machine. For all its muddle and shambles, all her own carping and complaints, the hospital still styled itself progressive, and progressive hospitals believed that the bond with a baby's mother was more important than the latest technological hardware. The irony was that Susie had refused that vital bond.

As soon as he was born and weighed, they had laid him naked in her arms, but she had pushed him away, broken down in tears again. Even when they had washed and dressed him, presented him clean and fragrant in his shawl, she had still turned her back, hidden her face in the pillow, refused to have the cot beside her bed.

The next day, no change. Jennifer had tossed and turned throughout that endless night, reliving Susie's labour as if to make it her own, feeling the rude probe of the enema, the jab and gripe of contractions, and finally split apart at dawn by the baby's ramming head. She got up in the pitch dark, fretted through the pointless hours till visiting time, then rushed back to the hospital where she found Sister herself sitting on Susie's bed, trying to talk her round. Susie remained deaf to all persuasion, staring pale and listless at the wall when she wasn't actually weeping. Jennifer felt pity mixed with terror. Susie was meant to be pretending she wanted to keep her child. In fact, she had rejected him out of hand, and in her present state of shock and hostility, might well forget their vital agreement and hand him over for adoption.

It was Sparrow who saved all three of them. On the day after Boxing Day, family duties over, he turned up in the ward in skin-tight jeans and an oil-stained donkey-jacket, waving two airline tickets to Malaga.

'Picked 'em up cheap,' he said to Susie. 'It's time you got off yer arse. If we don't beat it soon, there won't *be* any cushy jobs in Spain. They're dated Thursday — New Year's Eve. I'll call for you here with . . .'

'You can't,' Jennifer interrupted, from the other side of the bed. The baby was still in the nursery, but she was doing her daily stint of trying to calm and rally Susie. 'Susie won't be better by then. She's still very sore and she certainly can't start jetting around on planes just six days after . . .'

'You bet I can!' Susie was sitting up now, trying on the silver lurex boob-tube Sparrow had brought her with the tickets. She seemed to have miraculously rallied already. 'I've had more than enough of this dump and the sooner I get out of it, the . . .'

They argued back and forth for half an hour, Jennifer warning of shock, infection, relapse, Susie pleading the health advantages of rest and convalescence in the sun. Both were dissembling. Susie wanted Sparrow and the quickest possible out, Jennifer wanted the baby. In the end, they compromised. Susie agreed to feign an instant maternal interest in her child, in return for Jennifer's promise to plead with Sister to let mother and baby out first thing Thursday morning.

She was surprised at the opposition, despite her carefully crafted story which avoided all reference to dangerous things like DC 10s and lovers. Sister remained cautious and uneasy, concerned not only about Susie's capabilities, but also about the weather and the risk of an infection.

'If Susie insists on walking out, that's *her* affair,' she frowned. 'We can't actually keep her here by force, but she'll have to sign her discharge. Baby's a different matter. He's still below his birthweight and we're most unhappy about him going home so soon.'

Jennifer sought out Staff-Nurse Stapleton, who had allowed her into Special Baby Care, begged her help again. Although she was on a different ward, she was friendly with the Sister on Postnatal and might be persuaded to use her influence. Kate not only agreed, but even suggested checking on the child herself once he was discharged, since she all but passed their door on her way to the hospital, and it might reassure Sister if she reported directly back to her.

Sister kept her distance, said nothing more at all. By Wednesday evening, the baby was gaining weight, but Jennifer losing hope. In twelve short hours, Sparrow would be marching down the ward again, with suitcases and passports. She had used every possible argument, even turned to Jo, to see if there were some basic law or freedom she could appeal to in the impasse. There wasn't. Jo informed her that the hospital had every right to keep the baby in, if its health or welfare gave reason for concern. She did, however, promise her assistance once it *was* discharged, offering bed, roof, cash and moral support, and pledging total secrecy.

Jennifer sat by Susie's bed in silence, watching another patient pack her case and leave, a conventional married woman with a nine-pound baby and a supportive husband who had brought a couple of bottles of sherry for the staff. When Jennifer left herself, deep in gloom and with nothing yet decided, she could hear the nurses clinking glasses in Sister's office. Sister called her in. Whether it was a sniffter or two of Tio Pepe which tipped the balance in their favour, or Kate Stapleton's assurances, Jennifer never knew, but she got her yes, at last.

It was a reluctant yes, admittedly, hedged about with every possible precaution and instruction, and with the full array of social services alerted and ready to pounce.

'How are we going to dodge them?' Jennifer whispered to the baby, as she sat tense and frowing in Jo's sagging Oxfam chair. She had replaced him in his carry-cot, switched on the one-bar fire. She'd been so relieved to wangle him out at all, she had hardly spared a thought for the problems it had left behind — all those responsible professionals committed to an infant she had spirited away, rushing round to check on it, help and counsel its mother. How could she avoid them, how explain Susie's absence? Jo had offered her a refuge, but could she really cower at Putney while they knocked frantically at the heedless Southwark door? She would have to spin another web of lies. Her head was spinning with all the complications. She still felt weak and weepy from Susie's departure, confused by the whole fraught and hectic morning. She would shut the problems out, let them wait till morning. There were more important things. This was the first instant she had had her baby truly to herself, could claim him as her own. She pulled her chair up closer, gripped his tiny fingers in her own.

'I'm sorry I left you,' she said. 'I won't again.'

It was difficult to talk to him. He seemed so grave and somehow withdrawn. Baby-talk was impossible. He was too dignified for that. He still had the hospital name-tag on his wrist. 'Baby Grant.' Jennifer went to fetch Jo's nail-scissors, snipped it off.

'Baby Winterton now,' she told him. 'I'm afraid you haven't got a first name yet.'

Despite the pressure and suggestions of the nurses, Susie had left the baby nameless. She herself had tried a score of names, but none seemed quite to suit him.

'Graham?' she suggested now. That was her father's name. Her father had died young and unfulfilled. Not Graham. Charles, perhaps — in honour of her favourite nephew. No — that was too close to Matthew and therefore dangerous. Every time she thought of Matthew, she felt a wave of shock that this baby was his flesh and blood — his fifth and youngest son — with the same dark colouring as the other four. Supposing he grew up to look like them (and him) and so aroused everyone's suspicions? She would have to keep away. Yet even that would . . .

'Tea up!' shouted Jo, banging on the door. 'I've brought the little blighter's bottle, too. He didn't seem to want it while you were away, though I shoved it in his direction once or twice. I think I'll leave you to it and grab some lunch in peace. Make yourself at home, love. Sorry things are such a mess, but there's a pouffe thing there you can put your feet up on, and if you want cottonwool and talc and stuff, its all in the bathroom. I'll give the room a clear-up in the morning, make more space.'

'You're an angel, Jo.'

'Angels are males, dear, so I can't accept the compliment.'

Jennifer waited till Jo had gone downstairs again before settling the baby on her lap and offering him the bottle. It was somehow a private moment — a most important one — his first meal out of hospital as her sole responsibility. She let herself sink back, cuddled him against her, watched his screams shudder into silence as he fumbled for the teat. He sucked slowly and in snatches, stopping every few moments and staring round him as if to check there were no dangers, his hands clenching and unclenching against the bottle.

She felt a surge of warmth and strength flood into her bloodstream, as if she were being fed herself. The baby's tininess, his helplessness, made her huge and powerful. She was tower and refuge, shield and anchor. She had a purpose now, as protector and provider, totally committed. Whatever she might choose to do, or want to do, the baby's sheer physical needs would always tug her back. It was almost a relief. She was no longer split three ways, tugged apart by conflicting obligations. Susie had gone; the marriage with Lyn was over. Both hurt. In fact, the loss of Lyn was a pain too huge and cold to measure, yet he couldn't accept a baby, least of all his half-brother's. Why should he? The child was Matthew's responsibility, and Matthew was already in his debt. Even if she passed if off as Sparrow's baby, never breathed a word to Lyn, Matthew himself might guess the truth, start acting strangely, stir up trouble or try to interfere. Better to follow the dictates of the Women's Group and manage on her own.

Money was a problem, but Jo had offered her a job — the sort of menial low-paid work she was always warning women to refuse — as a general help and assistant in all her different feminist activities. But it was only a temporary measure. She would move to another job as soon as she felt more settled — or could find one where a baby would be welcome.

It wasn't safe to be in Putney, anyway, with Matthew living there. Thank God he was away — and for quite some time, so Anne had said in her brief and frantic phonecall before the family left for their holiday abroad. They were taking a longer break than usual, Anne had explained, and had even arranged for the boys to miss some school, on account of Matthew's exhaustion. Both the Winterton men had somehow gone to pieces — Matthew, once a tower of strength, now ill and overwrought; Lyn, feverish and ragged, living on the run. Lyn, too, might be abroad, for all she knew. That would explain his silence, his lack of communication. Less agonising, really, to have him far away — like Susie. Easier, then, to cut them off, start again anew.

She could see it as a challenge, living on her own, finding a place and making it really hers, for once, reflecting her own taste instead of someone else's. She had moved from her mother's chintzy overspill to the junk-shop Edwardiana with which Matthew had furnished Cobham; on again to the gloomy splendour of Matthew's own house in Putney; from there to a shabby bedsit painted Susie-style, and finally to this lumber-room of Jo's. Once she got her own place, it might be bare and poor, but at least she would keep it tidy, make it cheerful. She might even start on Hester's country crafts again, earn a bit of money making patchwork or preserves.

She smiled down at the baby. 'We'll manage,' she told him. 'Somehow.' She had to convince herself as well as him. He had stopped sucking and was gazing anxiously around, his mouth opening and shutting soundlessly, his forehead furrowed still.

He suddenly looked so small — his tiny hands with their diminutive fingernails flailing feebly against her neck, his feet limp and helpless on her giant's arm — rag-doll body, sparrow bones. Had she been irresponsible to remove him from the shelter of the hospital? Supposing something *did* go wrong?

Her hands were not quite steady as she changed his nappy and settled him down to sleep. She had totally forgotten her tea, took a sip of it now, to try and calm herself. It was cold and forming a skin. She went down to make a fresh cup, found Jo still in the kitchen, ironing a long, hairy skirt which looked as if it had been cobbled out of an ancient piece of sacking.

'All fed?' she asked.

Jennifer nodded, sank into a chair.

'You look done in. Why not have a nap and then you'll get your second wind and be fresh enough to come out with us this evening. I've invited a group of girls over. Thought we'd go to our local Chinese restaurant and have a bit of a nosh and a knees-up. You can bring Yours Truly in his carry-cot. The proprietor won't mind. He's got hordes of kids himself. I mean, you can't be all alone on New Year's Eve.'

Jennifer checked her chores — nappies to wash, clothes to iron, suitcase to unpack. She had also promised Sister to keep the child indoors. 'No thanks, Jo. It's sweet of you to offer, but I'm not much good at cat-naps. I'd rather have a really early night. To tell the truth, the best New Year's Eve treat I can think of is to rush through my jobs and be fast asleep in bed by nine o'clock.'

By nine o'clock, she and the baby were still both wide awake. His feeds had got out of phase. He refused to stick to her timetable and took so little milk at a time, she had been warming fresh bottles every two hours or so. She couldn't settle, anyway. The actual fact and presence of the baby

424

after so long and fraught a wait for it, seemed too momentous an event to allow her to sleep at all. She wanted the world to share in her excitement, flock to the cradle and rejoice. Instead, it was busy with other people's parties, fixated on New Year. Ordinary mothers would be showered with flowers, telegrams, cooing visitors, congratulation cards. Perhaps all that razzmatazz helped to soften the shock and startle of another life. *Her* baby had entered the world with hardly a witness or a well-wisher. Up at the Bertrams', she had often felt sorry for the stoic sheep who produced their lambs and then returned to the cold and lonely hillside with no proud father-ram, no admiring grandparents. She remembered one which had refused to mother its lamb. Mick had transferred the tiny shivering bundle to another ewe who had lost her own and was obviously in mourning. Both mother and child had rallied miraculously. She smiled to herself, wondered how Molly was. Nice to have a confidante, someone she could tell 'Today he gained two ounces,' or turn to with a problem. It was hard to be independent, self-sufficient. She had planned a whole lifetime on her own, yet even the first few hours of it were proving lonely and oppressive. It seemed wrong to spend New Year's Eve in her nightie, drinking a toast in baby's Cow and Gate.

She gave up trying to sleep, brought the baby down to Jo's main living-room, decided to sit and read. Jo's early training as a librarian was still in evidence and there were four separate bookcases all overflowing with political manifestos, sociological textbooks, sex and psychology manuals, and every reference book and dictionary from a children's encyclopaedia to a directory of Quaker meeting-houses. Nothing, though, to amuse or entertain. Jo didn't believe in novels, even less in women's magazines.

Jennifer wandered into the kitchen, made herself a cup of coffee. She had already found half a tin of beans and eaten them out of the tin, with Sugar Puffs for pudding — a Susie meal. She had learnt a lot from Susie, felt a sudden wave of loss. If Susie were here, she would be concocting champagne cocktails, cavorting round the room.

She moved the carry-cot closer to the phone, went and sat beside it. It would be comforting to ring a friend, say happy New Year to someone, but she had to be so careful. For Susie's sake and Matthew's, she was forced to lie low, suppress the baby's existence and therefore her own. She had already phoned the hospital, assured them all was well and Susie sleeping. She still hardly dared think about the problems of the morning, the string of lies, or the brazen disappearance, deceiving people who trusted her, dodging the whole gamut of social services. And supposing she needed those professionals — if the baby got ill or refused to feed? If she dashed back to the hospital in some crisis or emergency, but with no Susie at her side, they could wrench the child away from her, put it into care.

She picked up the receiver. There must be someone she could ring, to distract her from such fears. How about Molly herself? Surely she was safe enough, all those miles away in Mepperton? She would certainly be in, presiding at her party in her Sunday Best, which meant a skirt less clogged with dog-hairs than her usual one, and a daring dab of powder to cower her ruddy cheeks. The Bertrams always had a do on New Year's Eve — or Old Year's Night, as they called it in the counties close to Scotland. It was the most important night up there, even more special than Christmas. The date was surrounded with superstition, especially the ceremony of first-footing which had been observed for centuries and was believed to influence the whole succeeding twelve months. If the first person to cross the threshold on New Year's Day (which usually meant a minute after midnight on Old Year's Night) was a young, dark, male stranger bringing gifts of bread and fire, then the house would have good luck for the coming year. There weren't many strangers in Mepperton, so they usually chose a local dark-haired man who would do the rounds of the village, calling on as many houses as he could, to bring them good fortune and prosperity. Molly had explained the custom to her, how it wasn't just an empty ritual, but something almost as serious and solid as an insurance policy. This year, she was particularly excited, as her husband, Mick, had been chosen as first-foot. They had invited almost a hundred people to come and eat and drink with them before Mick set out on his rounds at the stroke of midnight. It would be a good time to ring them now, before the party got too riotous. She dialled the number, relaxed back in her chair.

'Ah, hallo, Molly? Is that you?' It was a woman's voice, but difficult to know which one, with all the background noise.

'No, it's her daughter here. Shall I fetch her for you?'

'Please.' There was so much she had to tell, so much news to catch up with, but it would have to wait. Jo had said 'Use the phone. Make yourself at home,' but it wasn't fair to abuse her generosity, indulge in rambling long-distance calls. All she would do was wish the Bertrams a successful party and a happy New Year. She could confide about the baby later, when she had found a room, coax Molly down for a visit, swear her to secrecy.

'Hi, Molly. It's Jennifer here. Jenny Winterton.'

'Jenny! How nice. Look, you'd better shout, my dear. I've got hordes of people milling about and I can hardly hear for all the noise. Where are you?'

'Er . . . Putney, at the moment.'

'With Anne and Matthew?'

'No, with . . . oh, never mind. Look, I just wanted to say happy New Year.'

'Same to you. When are you coming up?'

'I beg your pardon?'

'Well, now that Lyn's back, I hoped you'd be planning to join him.'

426

'L . . . Lyn?' Jennifer tried to repeat the name, but her voice had skidded away from her. She clutched at the edge of the chair. It, too, felt unsteady, insubstantial. The whole room had started trembling. 'Wh . . . what did you say?'

'Lyn's sort of camping out at Hernhope. Didn't you know, love? I'm sorry, I assumed you . . .' There was a sudden crackling noise and Molly's voice stuttered into silence.

Jennifer shook the phone, shouted down it. 'Molly? Are you still there? What happened? Hallo? *Hallo*?'

Nothing.

Should she dial again? She had to re-establish contact, find out what Lyn was doing. It was extraordinary, miraculous, that he was back at Hernhope when she had assumed him in some alien land, or at least on the run and footloose. Her heart was thumping, a crazy excitement surging through her body. She had to find out more, but the phone was silent still and dead. Supposing the lines had just come down with all the snow, and they were cut off now for several days? It happened often up at Mepperton.

There was a sudden click and Molly's voice returned, loud and reassuring. 'Ah, that's better. There was some sort of interference on the line, but I think it's cleared now. Mind you, it's bedlam here with all these people. We've got forty guests already. Hold on a sec and I'll take it on the phone upstairs. OK?'

Jennifer waited in a fever of impatience. How could just her husband's name set up such a turmoil? There was anger mixed with the excitement and relief. What was he doing, sneaking back to Hernhope when he had assured her so vehemently he could never return there again? And if he were safe and well and not abroad, then why hadn't he been in contact, sent her at least a card?

'Ah, hallo, Jen? I've shut the noise out now. Mind you, this is nothing. We'll be more or less overrun by midnight. I only hope the food lasts out. I've made enough for a regiment, but you know what they're like up here. They've already gone through three dozen sausage rolls and a whole two pounds of . . .'

'You said . . . Lyn . . .'

'Yes. He's back at Hernhope. Perhaps I shouldn't have mentioned it? I'm sorry, love, I'd no idea the two of you were so completely out of touch. I realised things were bad, of course, but I hoped you might have patched it up by now. Mind you, I said to Mick it was odd you hadn't phoned for such a time, and then Lyn just turning up like that, without . . .'

'Look, what's he . . . ? I mean, have you . . . ? How is he?'

'I haven't actually seen him, I'm afraid. I've had three of the children down with flu, and we were so frantic over Christmas, I didn't have time to turn round until the Monday, and the snow was so thick by then, I dared not risk his road. I reckon he must be more or less snowed up. The weather's been quite shocking. I expect you've heard it on the radio. One of our farmhands fell on the ice and . . .'

'So how d'you know he's there, then?' Molly could be wrong, might have mistaken him for someone else, could have . . .

'Young Tim saw him driving up on Christmas Eve. We were all inside with the curtains closed and up to our neck in chores, but *he* was in his tree-house, getting it ready for Christmas, or so he said. I told him he'd break his neck, out there in the dark and cold, but he's a real desperado, that one. I mean, only last week, he . . .'

Jennifer shut her eyes, tried to steady her breathing. Molly rambled so. There were more of Tim's exploits before she returned to Lyn.

'There was another car on Christmas Day. That's unusual. It's like a morgue up here, once everyone's returned from church. I didn't see it myself. I was basting the turkey and by the time I'd manoeuvred it back into the oven, the car had turned the corner. But Helen saw it — a dirty great Mercedes, she said . It *must* have been going to Hernhope. I mean, we're the last two houses on the road.'

Jennifer's legs were twisted round each other, her hand clenched painfully tight on the receiver. Lyn didn't have friends with Mercedes, hardly had friends at all. What was going on? Had he only returned to Hernhope to share it with someone else? It must be a close friendship if he had invited them for Christmas.

'I meant to call, Jen — see if I could help or invite him round or something. But Ruth came over queer right in the middle of Christmas dinner and by Boxing Day, I had three of them in bed with streaming colds and temperatures. Then Mick's great-aunt came to stay. She's quite a handful on her own. She's still here, actually. You ought to see her — over eighty and all dressed up like . . .'

Jennifer wasn't listening. Only Lyn existed, not the brimming Bertram household. Why had he taken someone else to Hernhope when he refused to take his wife? Except she wasn't his wife — not in fact or spirit. Hadn't she just decided to go it alone, devote herself to the child? So why should it concern her that Lyn was back at Hernhope? The marriage was over. Lyn had annulled it by his actions, by withdrawing his body and his presence.

'Jen, are you still there, love? I can't hear a dicky bird. This line's impossible. I suppose it's all the snow. Actually, we've only just got the phone back on. All the lines have been down the last few days. Damn! there's another ring at the door. I'd better go. Mick'll be wondering where on earth I've got to. Look, try and come up and see us soon. We'd love that, and maybe Lyn will feel different . . . now he's back in the house. I mean, he'll need a woman there. There's not even any electricity. The generator broke down weeks ago. It must be pretty grim for him. I'd liked to have helped, you know that — but I wasn't too sure he'd welcome any overture. I mean, after what you told me about him wanting to be on his own and everything. Help! Another invasion by the sound of it. Must dash now. Mick's hollering for me. Happy New Year!'

'Happy New . . .' Jennifer rose slowly from her chair, paced up and down the room, dodging chairs and chests of drawers, every conflicting emotion battling in her head. Should she dash straight up to Mepperton, have it out with Lyn, rage at him, rebuke him? Or dash straight up to Mepperton and fall into his arms? But what about the baby? Lyn wanted nothing to do with babies. Anyway, she had promised to keep the child in in the warm. If she couldn't risk three hundred yards to Jo's local Chinese restaurant, then she could hardly embark on an odyssey to the other end of England. She must stay down south and simply shrug Lyn off. The baby needed her, had no existence at all outside her own, whereas Lyn had proved he could live without her, maybe even preferred being alone and independent.

Alone? She shut her eyes, saw a tall, rich, glamorous woman who drove her men as wildly as her Mercedes, lunging towards him in the lightless house, using the darkness as a cover for her passion. No. Lyn hated woman like that. Perhaps it was a different type of girl — artistic, deep, someone who shared his interests, spoke his language, and who had no ties, no dependents. Was she still up there, or had departed after Christmas? It was unheard of for her husband to have company on New Year's Eve. He and Hester had always crouched in the house unvisited, shut out from the celebration of Old Year's Night. Not only was their house the furthest and least accessible, but Hester had disapproved of all the flushed and boozy revels, the whisky-sozzled night.

Molly had told her how, after Thomas's death, the Wintertons were never again included in first-footing. Six months after the funeral, the tall dark shepherd who was first-foot for that year, had struggled up to Hernhope in ice and snow. Hester had refused to open the door. Next year, the visits finished at the Bertrams' house. Not once, during Lyn's whole boyhood, had he ever received the first-foot with his gifts of food and fire. He and Hester had gone to bed at nine, like any other night, with the fire damped down, the larder locked. Some rumoured in the village that was the reason Hester had always had bad luck. The locals took their superstitions seriously. Molly herself believed in them, was always telling tales of first-foots in the past who had been the cause of sudden illness or bumper crops of lambs.

They weren't all idle stories. There was just the possibility of some ancient truth embedded in those superstitions. Old Year's Night had always been a magic night, even centuries ago, marking not just a change in calendar, but a vital and mysterious transition from one state to another for nature, man and universe. That was so true of herself, this year. Everything was changed — new role, new start, new home, new job, new baby. So why turn back to the old, the problematical, which had proved itself a failure? She must keep her gaze fixed only on the future, live chiefly for the child. He was her new life.

And yet . . . She stumbled across to the window, pulled the curtain aside, stared beyond the tidy roofs to the astoundment of the stars. Wasn't Lyn the one who understood best about rituals and mysteries? He had always seen the terror in the world, but also its immensity. He knew the importance of Christmas, New Year, Easter — the victories over cold and dark, the vital switch from one state to another, fear surmounted, life continuing. He understood the ceremonies, became part of them himself — not in obvious ways like eating, drinking, partying. It went deeper than that with Lyn. He died with winter, rose again with spring, was in tune with earth and nature. It sounded phoney and pretentious put like that, but it was only now she realised how she missed it.

Susie lived on a different plane entirely. The world for her was just a supermarket — a familiar, even boring place, where you grabbed what you wanted at the cheapest price, and which was bounded by the check-outs and the polystyrene ceiling. There were no stars for Susie, only the strobe lights of the disco; trees were simply things in parks which shaded you from freckles, or which you could nick an apple from, whereas Lyn saw grandeur in a single leaf. She suddenly realised now why resentment had dulled her pity on Christmas Day. It wasn't just Susie's rejection of the baby, but her whole attitude to birth itself. Its astonishment, its awe, its extraordinary alchemy of wonder and trauma mixed, had totally eluded her. Susie had fixated only on the pain. Easy for her to criticise when she had sat on the sidelines, shut out from all the blood and sweat and tears, but she knew that even doubled up with labour pains, she would still have realised she was taking part in something humbling and momentous, some vital act of creation, which joined her to all nature, however agonising and messy it might be.

Lyn would understand. He was frightened of birth and babies, but only because he saw that power, acknowledged it. He was aware of all the vastnesses — the gaps in the sky which let God's finger through, the creak of the earth as it shuddered on its axis. It was only rarely and haltingly that he put such things into words, but they were such raw and urgent words, they excited and inspired her. He had transformed the world for her, made it stranger and more startling than it would ever have been without him. It was as if she were standing on his shoulders, seeing things shut off to her when her feet were on the ground, breathing thinner air.

She jerked back from the window. She needed Lyn — his depths, his soul, his poetry — even his strangenesses and moods which were only their dark underside — missed him so fiercely it was like a real and stabbing pain. And yet she was bonded and committed to a child. Both ties seemed equally essential, both loves precious and compelling, yet the two were tugging her in opposite directions. The child would have to win. She hadn't been entrusted with a frail and precious infant so she could risk its life and happiness in fulfilling her own needs. Lyn didn't want her, anyway. He had made that all too obvious — returning to Hernhope without inviting her, letting Christmas come and go without a word. She hit out in rage and disappointment, punching empty air, then sagged back on the sofa. She was overreacting, exhausted from her six-days'-long ordeal. A good night's sleep and she would see things in perspective, leave Lyn in the past, get on with washing nappies rather than trying to share his vision and see eternity in pebbles or kaleidoscopes in stars. And if she couldn't sleep, at least she could relax. Best to blank out the phone-call altogether, forget it was New Year's Eve and settle down for a normal cosy evening.

She turned on the television, an ancient set which shuddered into focus. A Scot in kilt and cummerbund was singing sentimental ballads. She switched to another channel — a line of sequinned can-can girls kicking up their frills. Old Year's Night in the South — plastic song and dance, hollow lyrics, tat. It would get worse as the night wore on — gloating chat-shows, garish cabarets, popping balloons, tangled stream-ers — until the final frenetic hiccupping of Auld Lang Syne. How could she forget the date, when every entertainer was determined to impress it on her? She switched the sequins off, went to check on the baby. He was sleeping now, though even in his sleep, one tiny hand still twitched and clutched, making frantic grabs at nothing as if he were trying to save himself from drowning. Was he struggling in a nightmare, fighting some Lyn-like terror?

She swung back to the bookcase. There must be something she could read, to take her mind off Lyn. She leafed through a casebook on violence in the home, skimmed the chapter headings in a volume entitled *Non-Orgasmic Women*, dug out a dictionary of folklore. Almost without think-ing, she turned to the 'Fs' — Fig Sunday, Fingal's Cave, Fionnuala, First-footing. *First-footing*. She leant against the shelves, pored over the small print, the even smaller footnotes.

'. . . *ancient ceremony confined not just to Scotland and the North of England, but known to peoples as far apart as Peking and Connemara*'. She turned the page, surprised to see how long the entry was. More and more details appeared to have been added over the years, as to the best and luckiest attributes of a first-foot. Not only must he be a young dark healthy male, but he must be neither flat-footed nor cross-eyed. The book suggested the reason for this was that both these disabilities would be obstacles to early man, the hunter. Jennifer was intrigued, took the book to the sofa and settled down with it. '*The first-foot*', she read, '*must not have bushy eyebrows which meet across the nose, as that was considered a common sign of an early death or misfortune in love*'.

She only hoped the Bertrams hadn't heard of that. Bushy-browed Mick was an odd choice altogether. Although his eyes were brown, his hair was light in colour and his complexion fair beneath the wind-burn. Neither was he young. The only thing in his favour was his sex. Female first-foots were considered disastrously unlucky. Jo would have fumed about such crude discrimination, lodged a formal complaint to the Equal

431

Opportunities Commission. Jennifer grinned, stroked a finger across the baby's fuzz of hair. He was dark — truly dark — hair almost black, skin sallow and dark-toned. Even his eyes looked slatey in the half-light, and would soon change to Matthew's uncompromising brown. They were in no way crossed, nor did his eyebrows meet in the middle, but were so faint and fine as to be hardly there at all. *He* would be a stranger up in Mepperton — a total stranger, never seen before by anyone, and born three hundred miles away. She drew the blanket back, slipped off his bootees. Supposing he were flat-footed? She cupped one tiny foot in each of her hands, felt the high curve of the arch.

'You're lucky', she whispered. 'Do you know that? You could be a first-foot if you wanted. Though I'm not sure babies count.'

They should. If the first-foot must be young, to symbolise the fresh uncorrupted innocence of the New Year, then why not very young — a newborn like the year itself? If only she were up at Molly's, she could drive the few miles further on to Hernhope, and carry the baby over the threshold, making sure he entered first. That way, she could bring good fortune and prosperity to Hernhope for a twelvemonth.

She sprang up from the floor. Miraculous thought! A first-foot at Hernhope after more than thirty years without one — new start, new luck, new year. The baby was far more suited to the job than mouse-haired Mick. It was as if he had been tailor-made to fit the role. If only he weren't so fragile, she could travel up with him, leave immediately, arrive in the nick of time. She wouldn't make it by midnight, of course, but so long as the stranger was the first to cross the threshold on New Year's Day, even if it were six o'clock in the morning, then the luck still held. It wasn't impossible. There were heated high-speed trains and she had money for the fare — not much, admittedly, but enough to get to Newcastle.

She rushed and fetched her handbag, counted out the notes — more than she had thought. Susie had handed over all that she could wangle out of Sparrow, Jo had given her what she grandly called an advance on salary, and there was still a little remaining from Matthew's handouts. All the same, it wouldn't last her long, and she ought to save it for more important things — like keeping herself and the child alive. And what about the journey on from Newcastle? She would have to take a taxi and that would cost a fortune, if she could even find one in the early hours who would be willing to drive so far. He would be bound to charge her double, and that on top of the train fare would completely clean her out. It would have to be a coach, then. They were three or four times cheaper than British Rail. They also took double the time.

Was she mad, for heaven's sake — planning an all-night journey on bumpy snowy roads with the tiniest of babies who should be moved no further than from cot to lap, treated like cut-glass? If she waited just another month or so, the child would be stronger, and Mick or Molly would meet her at the station, drive her up from Newcastle. She would

432

save precious money, cut down any risk. She would also destroy her overriding reason for going there at all — to bring luck and joy to Hernhope through a first-foot. Only this one night counted. If she left it just a day, let alone a month, the magic disappeared. The house needed a new chance. She could see it standing desolate and blinded, dust and nettles choking it, damp seeping through its seams, gasping for its dark and lucky stranger. She and Lyn and the child — they, too, were in desperate need of luck, a change in fortunes.

The baby was crying now, as if he sensed her agitation. She carried him to the bathroom — he was wet and needed changing — sponged his tiny penis. She was suddenly wildly glad he was a boy. Only males could bring good luck as first-foots, carry on the line. Hernhope craved both luck and heir, and this child was truly heir, grandson of Thomas Winterton himself. Lyn didn't want an heir, yet could he really object to one so tiny and so vulnerable, more or less an orphan?

Yes, he could and would. The whole idea was preposterous, totally absurd. What kind of luck would it be if the first-foot died of pneumonia, the symbol of new life perishing itself? And if the journey didn't harm him, her problems still weren't over. She might drag all that way up North, only to find that Lyn had left already, run away again. Even if he *were* there, he wouldn't admit a bastard child, agree to share his life with it. She buttoned the baby back into his stretch-suit, returned him to his cot. There probably weren't any coaches, anyway, not this late on New Year's Eve. That would end the matter, and she could settle down and stop wasting her time on pipe-dreams.

She picked up the S to Z directory, turned to the Vs. V for Victoria Coach Station. All the main coach lines went from there. It wouldn't hurt just to make enquiries. She might need the coach times later, when she planned a visit to Molly. She dialled the number, let it ring some time. No one seemed in any hurry to answer. Perhaps they had gone off duty, or the service was suspended on New Year's Eve. Better really to forget the whole idea, fix herself a drink and try and . . .

'Oh, hallo. I wondered if there was still a coach to Newcastle tonight? What? 10.15? Hold on a second, will you.'

She peered at her watch. It was already a quarter to ten. More or less impossible to catch a coach which left in half an hour, when she wasn't even dressed. On the other hand, she could always hitch her nightie up, fling a coat on top, order a taxi and offer it double if it broke the speed-limit. Victoria wasn't far.

'Look, do I need to book, or shall I just turn up? Oh, *no!*' She slumped back in her chair. The coach was fully booked. She could simply go along, the girl had said, in the hope of a last-minute cancellation, but there wasn't much of a chance. The 10.15 was the last coach leaving for the North and was usually packed out. Why risk the cold, only to be unlucky, trail home again with a chilled and whimpering baby? Yet if she did get on, their luck might last a twelvemonth, even longer. The right first-foot could change a family's whole fortune, set it on a different path. She drummed her fingers on the table in a fret of indecision. There wasn't time to dither. Every second wasted was one less to get there at all. She checked her watch again. 10.47 now. The thing was quite ridiculous. She would need bottles for the baby, Thermoses of boiling water, all his clothes and gear. By the time she had collected those together, phoned a taxi and waited for it to come, the coach would be pulling out of Victoria as she opened the front door.

The girl at the coach station was still miraculously holding on. Jennifer could hear her chatting to someone the other end of the phone.

'Excuse, me please. Are there any other coaches, different lines, perhaps, which might leave later, or go from somewhere else, or . . . ?'

'Well, there are the independent companies, but I don't know much about them, I'm afraid. I doubt if they'd run this late, in any case. There's nothing else from *here* tonight. I'm sorry.'

Jennifer thanked her, replaced the receiver. If only she had spoken to Molly earlier . . . No — it was just as well she hadn't, and that the last coach was fully booked. It had brought her to her senses, stopped her racing off on some madcap escapade she would later regret. She must settle down, forget the whole idea. She pushed away the phone-book, relaxed back with the dictionary of folklore which was lying on the table, still open at First-footing.

'*In Scotland and the Borders, the first person to enter the house on New Year's Day receives a kiss, in silence, from whomever opens the door.*'

Lyn would open the door. He wouldn't kiss a baby, but he might kiss her. She remembered his mouth — soft lips and sharp stubble and the graze of his teeth beyond that restless probing tongue which fused with hers until she hardly knew which was which or where his lips and hers began or ended. On their wedding night, he had used only his mouth, kissed her everywhere — fiercely, famishedly, as if he wanted to devour her. Only in the morning had he actually entered her, his mouth still joining in, his dark embarrassed eyes shut against the light while she opened everything towards him.

. . . *A man shall leave his father and mother and shall be joined unto his wife and they shall be one flesh.* They had been one flesh, that morning — joined, clinched, coupled, breathing in time with one another, hands clasped, tongues entwined. And Lyn had left mother and father — his mother literally. Risked Hester's jealousy and anger in taking a wife at all. She remembered his frantic attempts at recompense, the never-acknowledged presents, the letters penned in guilt and ruined sleep. He'd been torn between wife and mother — and wife had won. So how could she allow him to lose in her own similar tussle between husband and child, hack herself away from her own flesh?

She returned to the book, to try and calm herself. Memories were dangerous — kindled desires, then confused them with regrets. The tiny print was trembling on the page. '*A kiss under the mistletoe is particularly propitious since it is a pledge of peace and goodwill, and symbolises reconciliation where people have been estranged.*'

Reconciliation. The very word produced a stab of longing. To heal things with a kiss, to start again . . . Jo had a bunch of mistletoe hanging in her hall, a withered bunch already gathering dust. If only she could put it to some use. Hester had written in her diaries about the power of mistletoe, how country people called the plant 'All-Heal', how it was the symbol of new life and hope because it was sappy green when its host was brown and dead. On an impulse, she darted out to the hall, broke off a tiny sprig, stuck it in her dressing-gown. If she couldn't go up to Hernhope, then at least . . .

What did she mean, couldn't? There were still trains, weren't there? If she blued her last penny on train and taxi fares, it was money well spent. Trains were safer, anyway, and faster. Only three hours to Newcastle and a toilet on board where she could sponge and change the baby. She darted back to the phone, grabbed the A-D directory this time, opened it at the Bs for British Rail, ran her finger down the list of regions. North-East England — that was the one for Newcastle.

She dialled the number wrong, re-dialled, sat waiting in a fever of impatience. The last train might be leaving as she sat grounded in Jo's house, listening to that mocking ringing-tone.

'Answer,' she muttered. '*Answer.*' The man at the other end was probably drunk or dozing off. She would count to ten, and if no one had answered by then, she'd order a taxi and go directly to King's Cross, chance her luck.

'Eight, nine, *nine* . . .' The number was still ringing, though she was counting slower and slower. She would make it twenty, then. 'Eleven, twelve, thirteen . . .' She'd better take a waterproof sheet, a flannel in a sponge-bag. 'Fourteen, fifteen . . .' Bottles, nappies, Thermos. 'Sixteen, sev . . . Oh, hallo. Thank God! I thought nobody was there. Look, can you tell me . . . ?' She tried to calm her voice. She sounded choked, hysterical.

'I beg your pardon? Seven o'clock? It's *gone*, you mean? It can't have! Surely there's something later than that? Yes. I know, but . . .'

The man had rung off. The last train on New Year's Eve to anywhere in the North left at nineteen hundred hours. That was gospel.

She walked slowly to the window, sick with disappointment. Well, that was retribution for refusing to stick to her original decision to go nowhere and do nothing. She would have to content herself with memories of Lyn, his stars, his winter skies. She tweaked the curtain back, stared in shock. There were no stars, only snow — swift soft-footed flakes tearing tiny holes in the strobed and whirling darkness. When had it started and why had it not been forecast? They had promised milder weather for the

435

South. She closed her eyes. The snow went on falling, falling, underneath them, until it lay deep and silent on the Cheviots. April back in Hernhope twenty months ago. Sun raw and radiant on the snow, and that mysterious voice beyond it. '*It is well that we are here.*' Hadn't she known at that moment that she and Lyn belonged at Hernhope? Had Hester sent this snow to nudge her memory?

She rushed back to the cot. The baby was still awake, eyes huge and staring in the darkness. There was something strange about this child who slept so little, watched so anxiously — what had Sister said about him — old before his time? She took him back to the window, still swaddled in his blankets, lifted up the curtain. He must share this moment with her, witness his first snow. She shut her eyes, swapped London's streets for the white and watching hills. Again, she felt Hester's presence, Hester's strength. She had been fretting about cold, risks, pneumonia, other women, when perhaps she was protected — Hester's power around her, as before.

She must dare, for once, have faith, courage, scorn and surmount the risks. It wouldn't be easy — she didn't kid herself. Lyn might refuse to listen, might even shut the door on them as Hester had done to first-foots in the past. The weather was at its cruellest. That April had been the last lame dregs of winter before the softer, gentler spring. Now they had three long months of brutal cold before them. She pressed her face to the window, watched the snow slam on to the rooftops, the wind rip gashes through it. It wasn't meant to be easy. Hester's life had always been a struggle and if she was heir to it, then struggle was her dowry.

'*Be not afraid . . .*' She jumped. Who had spoken? Was she merely kidding herself along, inventing voices because she feared the silence? The Bible was full of 'Fear nots'. There had been one in the passage she had just recalled, when the dazzling cloud enveloped the disciples and they were 'sore afraid'. Transfigurations could happen even now, thirty years of darkness slink away in the blaze of one new candle. It would come again — the glory, the shining, blinding spendour on the mountain top.

She let the curtain fall, tucked the child in his blankets. She couldn't reach the moutains without some means of transport. She had to get to Hernhope now. Hester was waiting, had offered her protection. Lyn needed her up there. Hernhope had no light, no eyes, cried out for a ministering wife.

She stood tense and hunched, trying desperately to think up some solution. Whichever way she travelled, it would take hours to reach the house. If she didn't leave immediately, it would be too late altogether. Someone else might call there in the morning, cross the threshold before she had even got as far as Newcastle — someone fair, unlucky, unchosen — a tradesman or a forester, Molly Bertram herself. She sank down on the sofa, almost crying with frustration, sprang up again, seized the Yellow Pages. The independent coaches — she had quite forgotten them. They didn't sound too hopeful, but she must clutch at any straw.

She turned to the Cs, then back to the Bs — swore. Coach services came under B for Buses. Even when she found it, the list was disappointingly short. The first number didn't answer, the second was engaged. The third was friendly but operated only in the South. The fourth had stopped its service to Newcastle just six months ago, but could recommend another larger company which still served the North. The baby was screaming now and she could hardly hear at all. She took him on her lap, tried to calm him while she scribbled down the number. The screams continued through the call.

'I'm sorry, I can't hear you. No, Newcastle, I said. You *do*? What time? Oh wonderful! Tonight, though — New Year's Eve? You're sure? It's not full, is it? You're absolutely certain? Can I book, or do I . . . ?'

She slammed the receiver down, hand shaking with relief. Was it just good luck, or had Hester somehow . . . ? There wasn't time for speculation. She had to get to Pancras Road, where that miraculous coach departed. She picked up the phone again, dialled the first of a list of taxi firms which Jo had tacked above it.

The baby was still screaming. She rushed upstairs with him, wrapped him in a second layer of woollies, with a shawl on top of those. Her own clothes were still in the suitcase she had packed to come to Putney, Lyn's new red Christmas sweater lying on the top. She tugged it out, tucked it round the baby. Red not for danger, but for daring, love. She whipped off her nightdress, exchanged it for her warmest skirt and jersey, emptied all the useless clutter from her bag and filled it up with baby clothes and nappies. Then pounded down to the kitchen, switched on the kettle, found a Thermos flask, collected powdered milk and bottles. She scribbled a note to Jo, added an IOU for the long-distance call to Molly and her advance on salary, left her Lyn's Christmas cake as a New Year offering. She could bake him a hundred other cakes once she and he . . .

Only fifty minutes before the coach set off. If only it wasn't so far to Pancras Road. She pulled on her coat, switched off lights and fire, lugged bags and carry-cot into the hall. She was ready to go now — but the taxi wasn't.

'Hurry,' she prayed. '*Hurry.*'

She opened the door a crack, to see if it was pulling up outside. The dark angry night rushed in through the gap, wind rasping, snowflakes clawing at her hair. She heard the cackle of a New Year's party spill from the house opposite, throb of a stereo, whoop of a trombone. A tinselled laurel swag, festooned above the window, sent strange spiky shadows across the path.

Laurel! She closed the door, dashed back to the kitchen. She had forgotten something vital. The first-foot was only lucky if he bore important gifts — she had just read that in the book — a sprig of evergreen for continuing life and fertility; bread as an ancient token of welcome and to ensure an ample supply of food for the coming year; salt to symbolise wealth; coal to promise year-long warmth and heat. She hacked a slice from Jo's staling wholemeal loaf, tipped a shake of salt into a paper bag. Coal? There wasn't any. But what did they say — 'coals to Newcastle'? Well, that shouldn't be a problem, then. She grinned to herself, felt crazily elated. Only evergreen now. There was nothing green in Jo's brick-and-concrete back yard, and she could hardly steal that neighbour's laurel wreath. But Putney was full of gardens. They must stop on the way and break off a piece of fir or yew or holly — perhaps from Matthew's house — his one offering to his child. The Winterton garden was dark with yews and laurels. When she had first visited, she had shied away from them — felt they were gloomy, poisonous, blocking out the sun. But after Hester died, the old crone up at Mepperton who had acted as both midwife and embalmer in her time, had told her that the yew tree lived to such an immense old age, it had become a symbol of immortality. All evergreens were powerful, could never fade or brown, and therefore triumphed over death and dissolution. She had followed the woman's suggestion, placed a branch of yew in Hester's coffin, laid it between her hands. She would repeat the ritual, pick a sprig from Matthew's oldest tree and take it up to Hernhope, so that Matthew's seed, his child, should bring the house new and vigorous life.

If she ever got there. She glanced at her watch. Only forty-three minutes to go now, and still no sign of the taxi. All her preparations would be pointless unless it arrived in the next few seconds. She fretted up and down the hall, disturbing flurries of brochures, dodging the bunch of mistletoe swinging from.its shaggy loop of string.

Mistletoe! She had almost forgotten it — an evergreen which promised peace as well as immortality, and was also an emblem of fertility because it flourished all year without a ground root. Hester had made potions of it for women trying to conceive. She reached up, snapped off a second sprig, a larger one this time and thick with berries.

The baby's screams were echoing through the hall. Was he hungry, wet, soiled? There wasn't time to check. She would have to feed and change him on the coach — except she would probably miss it now. She dared not look at her watch again, see those cruel hands pouncing on the seconds, stranding her in London, cutting off her luck. The baby seemed to be howling out her own frustration. She tried to soothe him, stuck the sprig of mistletoe in the hood of his carry-cot.

His screams quietened, and suddenly there were loud crunching footsteps up the path, the shadow of a man darkening the glass panel in the door. She flung it open before he had time to ring, scooped up the cot in one hand, the bags in another. The driver had already grabbed the suitcase.

'Emergency, they told me. Is everything all right, Miss?'

'It may be,' she panted. 'If you can do Pancras Road in thirty-seven minutes, with one brief stop on the way.'

438

The baby whimpered as the first blast of freezing air shocked against his face.

'Courage,' she whispered, as the driver helped her in and slammed the doors. 'We're going back where we belong, so you'll have to get used to the cold.'

XXX

Hernhope shivered in the cold, the embers of a small wood fire the only dying point of light inside its blinded windows. Slowly thawing snow fell with a ghostly thud from roof and sill. Inside, a man slept fitfully, alone. Old Year's Night was over now, midnight fraying into slumped and grey-eyed morning, but no one had crossed the threshold yet.

The house waited, listened. Far away on the road from Newcastle, it could hear the muffled wheels of a taxi labouring in the clogged and treacherous slush. In the back was a new-born baby — a dark-haired boy-child, stranger to these parts — who neither slept nor cried. He was cold, frightened, bumped and winded, his nappy soiled, his stomach queasy, but he simply stared into the darkness, waiting for his time. The woman with him, tired and pale, rocked and soothed and sung him lullabies. She was hungry and nibbled at a slice of bread, sprinkled with salt from a crumpled paper bag. She had a branch of yew beside her, roughly broken off, a lump of coal wrapped in a nappy liner. A sprig of mistletoe drooped above the cot, wilting but still green.

The house waited. It would be an hour or more before the car arrived, the darkness lifted, but at least the snow was melting, the wind veering to the kinder, calmer south. The house was cold itself, and old — roof leaking, walls crumbling, damp seeping through its flagstones, its agues and ills too long neglected. It needed youth, new blood. Hester had found them, sent them here, would still watch over them. With any luck, things would be mended now, amended.

In the New Year.